The 1920 HOLIDAY ANNUAL

ETON — LORETTO — HARROW — REPTON — FETTES — WINCHESTER — RUGBY — ST PAULS

To introduce this new edition of THE HOLIDAY ANNUAL OF 1920 we can do no better than quote the late William Gander, editor and publisher of the STORY PAPER COLLECTOR (Canada):

"This is a collector's item of rare price for many reasons. Not only did Warwick Reynolds illustrate the cover, and many stories inside, but Charles Hamilton (Frank Richards, Martin Clifford, Owen Conquest) wrote three long tales especially for this issue . . . plus an eighteen-chapter Rookwood story."

And to quote Donald Webster:

"With cartoons of our favourite characters, the Who's Who, maps of the schools, the Greyfriars Gallery . . . every taste is catered for."

"Today, original editions of this work sell (when available) at £10 per copy and more. This is the rarest of all GHA collector's items."

W. O. Lofts
President, OBBC (Cambridge)

The first~ever Holiday Annual

PUBLISHERS' PREFACE

One of the major events in the popular 'annual' field between the wars was the publication of the now legendary Greyfriars Holiday Annual. Today, old copies change hands at many times the original prices.

The steady increase in the number of Collectors in recent years has endowed yellowing, frayed copies still in existance with a value undreamed-of by their initial purchasers.

In 1969 Howard Baker embarked on a programme of producing iconographs, facsimile editions, and part-works of the most well-beloved of these pre-war publications, on durable paper, and case-bound.

The Greyfriars Holiday Annual 1920 ranks highest amongst these much-sought-after rare collectors' items and it is with pleasure that we present this new volume of the 1920 edition as a worthwhile accompaniment to our series of Magnet and Gem reproductions.

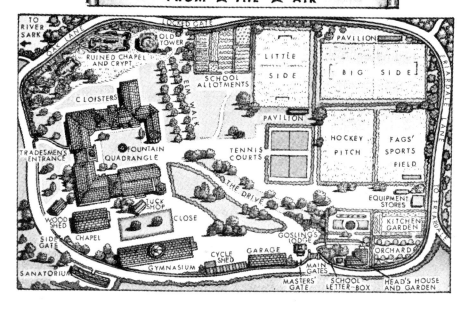

GREYFRIARS SCHOOL
FROM ★ THE ★ AIR

THE (GREYFRIARS) HOLIDAY

1920 ANNUAL 1920

Anniversary Edition

HOWARD BAKER

LONDON

THE GREYFRIARS HOLIDAY ANNUAL 1920

© Copyright: The Amalgamated Press Ltd., 1920, 1975
© Copyright: Howard Baker Edition 1975

ISBN: 0 7030 0062 4

Published by Howard Baker Press Ltd. (The Greyfriars Press)
27a Arterberry Road, Wimbledon, London, S.W.20, England.

Printed in Great Britain by Per Fas Printers Ltd.,
Croydon, Surrey.

Frank Richards

The writing phenomenon known to the world as Frank Richards (real name Charles Hamilton) died at his home at Kingsgate in Kent on Christmas Eve 1961 at the age of eighty-six.

By then it is estimated that he had written the equivalent of one thousand full-length novels.

His work appeared continuously for over thirty years in those famous Fleetway House magazines *The Magnet* and *The Gem*. Most famous of all was his immortal creation Billy Bunter, the Fat Owl of the Greyfriars Remove, whose exploits together with those of the other boyhood heroes Harry Wharton and Co., delighted generations of readers from 1908 to 1940.

The war unhappily saw the end of *The Magnet* but though the post-war years brought the return of Greyfriars stories in other formats nothing ever quite recaptured the evergreen magic of the original much-loved boys' paper. It was for this reason that, four years ago, W. Howard Baker presented the first of his now world-renowned faithful facsimiles.

The brilliant character studies of boys and masters created by Frank Richards ensured his own immortality. Apart from the boys of Greyfriars, not forgetting Horace Coker, the duffer of the Fifth, there was the unforgettable Mr. Quelch, the Remove form-master ("a beast, but a just beast"), the Rev. Dr. Locke, venerable Headmaster of the School, William Gosling, the crusty, elbow-bending school porter who firmly believed that "all boys should be drownded at birth", Paul Pontifex-Prout, the pompous form-master of the Fifth, the excitable but kind-hearted "Mossoo" (M'sieu Charpentier, French master), the odious Cecil Ponsonby, involved in murky goings-on at The Three Fishers, and peppery Sir Hilton Popper, irascible School Governor. All these characters and many, many more are to be found in the pages of these volumes.

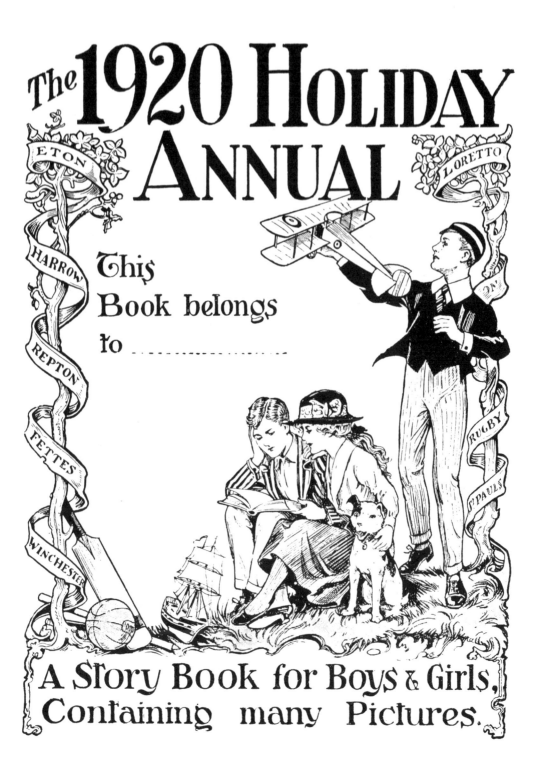

The 1920 HOLIDAY ANNUAL

ETON

LORETTO

HARROW

REPTON

FETTES

WINCHESTER

RUGBY

S'PAULS

This Book belongs to ....

A Story Book for Boys & Girls, Containing many Pictures.

Introduction by the Editor.

THE HOLIDAY ANNUAL has been expressly designed to meet the wishes of thousands of boys and girls throughout the British Empire. The favourite characters in the "MAGNET" and "GEM" Libraries and the "BOYS' FRIEND" have been brought together in one volume; and this permanent record of their schooldays should make an irresistible appeal, not only to readers of the journals aforementioned, but to every boy and girl who revels in clean, wholesome fiction.

Greyfriars, St. Jim's, and Rookwood rank among the most famous schools in modern fiction. To nearly every British boy the names of Harry Wharton, Tom Merry, and Jimmy Silver are familiar as household words. These great rivals and equally great sportsmen, whose exploits have for years been an unfailing source of delight, are indeed fitting companions for the Christmas fireside.

The object of THE HOLIDAY ANNUAL is primarily to give amusement and entertainment, by means of cheerful, healthy fiction and verse, to the boys and girls of Britain.

Many world-famous authors and artists have had a share in the compilation of this Annual; whilst the Editor and his staff have worked hard and unremittingly to make it one of the landmarks in boys' literature. It has been a labour of love. And if it prove successful—if this bumper production should be the means of bringing sunshine and happiness into the lives of our young friends at home and beyond the seas—then we shall indeed be well repaid for our labour.

THE EDITOR.

The Fleetway House,
    Farringdon Street, London.

Ructions at Greyfriars!

A Complete Story of School Life and Adventure

By FRANK RICHARDS

THE FIRST CHAPTER.

Bribing Bunter!

" ONE pound of sugar——"

"Hallo, hallo, hallo!"

"Half-pound of butter——"

"Bunter——"

".Quarter-pound of syrup——"

"Look here——"

"Pinch of salt——"

"Bunter!" roared Bob Cherry. "Billy Bunter!"

Bunter of the Remove, did not heed. He was blinking through his big glasses at a fragment of crumpled and not over-clean paper, held in his fat fingers. And he went on:

"Add a little water——"

"BUNTER!"

"Two tablespoonfuls of vinegar, just before the toffee is done——"

"You fat duffer——"

"Pour into a clean, buttered pan——"

Bob Cherry strode into No. 7 Study, and grasped Bunter by the shoulder. He gave the Owl of the Remove a vigorous shake.

"Bunter!" he roared.

"Yarooooh!"

"Look here, Bunter——"

"Leggo, you silly ass!" howled Bunter. "I'm busy! Can't you see I'm busy? Leggo!"

"I want you——"

Billy Bunter jerked himself away.

"Never mind what you want, Cherry," he said, "I'm busy just now. By the way, though, can you lend me a pound of sugar?"

"No!" growled Bob.

"Well, can you lend me half a pound of butter?"

"I'll lend you a thick ear, if you like."

"You see, I've got a jolly good recipe for making butter toffee," explained Bunter, blinking at him. "It's a good recipe—a really good one; but the trouble is, I haven't any of the materials—excepting a little water. I can get that all right. I can manage the pinch of salt, too. But the sugar and butter, and syrup——"

"I want you——"

"Are you coming, Bob?" came Harry Wharton's voice from along the Remove passage. "Isn't Bunter there?"

"Yes, he's here!" growled Bob Cherry.

"He's burbling about toffee. Look here, Bunter, I want you——"

"It's simply rotten!" said Bunter, following his own train of thought. "Here I am with a jolly good recipe, and it's a half-holiday and I've got lots of time, but there's a shortage of materials. I can manage everything except the sugar, the butter, and the syrup."

Harry Wharton and Co. came along the passage, and looked into No. 7. Wharton and Nugent, Johnny Bull and Hurree Singh were in Norfolks, and Bob Cherry was similarly clad. The Famous Five were evidently going for a spin that fine, sunny afternoon.

"Look here, Bunter——" began Wharton.

"Oh, don't worry," said Bunter. "I can get the syrup from the housekeeper, I think. But what about the sugar?"

"We're going for a spin."

"I can't come, Wharton. I'm busy."

"Fathead! It isn't that. Mr. Prout has asked Bob to go down to the post-office for him——"

"Well, let him go, and leave off worrying a fellow who's trying to think out a problem," exclaimed Bunter warmly. "The chief question is, the sugar——"

"Bob can't go," explained Frank Nugent. "He's booked to come with us. We're going riding with the Cliff House girls. We want you——"

Bunter paid some attention at last.

"Oh, if it's Marjorie and Co., I'll come," he said. "I shouldn't like to disappoint Marjorie. I know she won't enjoy it if I'm not there."

"You fat chump!" roared Bob.

"Oh, really, Cherry——"

"We want you!" howled Johnny Bull.

"Well, I'll come, only one of you will have to lend me a bike, mine's out of order. Bob can lend me his, if he's going on an errand for old Prout. Of course, it's understood that Marjorie will ride with me—none of you fellows shoving in, you know, and spoiling sport."

Bob Cherry made a movement towards Billy Bunter, but Wharton pushed him back in time. The chums of the Remove had come there to demand a service from Bunter;

and to begin by bumping him on the study carpet was certainly not judicious.

"Hold on, Bob!"

"Look here——"

"Shurrup! Bunter, we want you——"

"That's all right. I'll come!"

"We want you to go to the post-office instead of Bob——"

"Eh?"

"You see, Bob's booked to come with us, only he can't refuse Prout. Form-masters have to be humoured. We want you to go down to Friardale instead of Bob. Everybody else has gone out——"

"Well, of all the cheek!" exclaimed Bunter.

"It isn't much trouble," said Harry. "You've got nothing to do this afternoon"

"I'm making toffee——"

"Oh, bother your toffee!"

"I don't mind putting it off to look after Marjorie, if I can have Bob's bike," said Bunter. "If you choose to spoil Marjorie's outing, by leaving me out, that's your bizney. I'd just as soon get on with the toffee, as a matter of fact. Shut the door after you!"

"We want—you——"

"Good-bye!" said Bunter.

"There's nobody else to go!" roared Bob Cherry. "I can't refuse to go for Prout, but I can tell him another chap's going. See?"

"Well, find another chap, and tell him. Ta-ta!"

"We want you——"

"One pound of sugar!" said Billy Bunter, blinking at the recipe again. "I simply must have the sugar. The question is, whose sugar can I——"

"Look here, Bunter——"

"I say, you fellows, I wish you wouldn't keep on interrupting me," said Billy Bunter peevishly. "Where the sugar is to come from, is a mystery. Of course, I can't do without it. If you fellows were decent, you'd try to help a chap, when he's hung up for a pound of sugar."

"Look here——"

"And then there's the butter——"

"Will you go to the post-office for Prout?" roared Bob Cherry. "This blessed packet has got to be registered. You can take it.

(4)

"Come out at once, Bunter!" thundered the Fifth-form master. "Your well-merited chastisement, sir, awaits you!" (See page 21.)

We're late already, owing to old Prout stopping me. Will you go?"

"I think I can manage about the syrup——"

"Bunter——"

"But the sugar," said Bunter, blinking seriously at the exasperated juniors. "There's the rub! What about the sugar?"

"My esteemed chums," murmured Hurree Jamset Ram Singh, "I have a wheezy good idea. Let us clubfully together collect our sugar, and bribe the excellent and disgusting Bunter——"

"Good!" exclaimed Wharton. "Bunter, you fat bounder, if you'll take that packet down to Friardale and register it for Prout, you can collect what you want in our studies."

"Oh!" said Bunter.

The fat junior seemed amendable to reason at last.

"Sure you've got as much as a pound of sugar?" he asked cautiously.

"Yes, among the lot of us," grunted Bob Cherry. "Take the lot—if you'll take the packet. Is it a go?"

Bunter nodded.

"It's a go," he said. "I'll oblige you. Mind, I'm doing you a favour. I want that distinctly understood."

"Br-r-r-r!"

"The favourfulness is terrific, my worthy and ludicrous Bunter." said Hurree Singh.

"Here's the key of my study cupboard," said Wharton. "Now, get off to Friardale at once, Bunter."

THE
GREYFRIARS GALLERY IN VERSE

By Dick Penfold

No. I: Bob Cherry

Who routs us out at half-past five,
And grimly bids us look alive,
Lest boots upon our shins arrive ?
>   BOB CHERRY !

Who's had a cheerful grin since birth,
And always overflows with mirth ?
Who plays the funniest japes on earth ?
>   BOB CHERRY !

Who shines in many a footer scrum,
And leaves the goalie dazed and dumb
By hurling him to kingdom come ?
>   BOB CHERRY !

Who stands before the stumps and hits
Till every window's smashed to bits,
And Quelchy has ten thousand fits ?
>   BOB CHERRY !

Who boasts a punch like Billy Wells,
And many a blustering bully quells,
Whilst all the gym. resounds with yells ?
>   BOB CHERRY !

Who stands supreme in school and sport—
A really right-down ripping sort ?
All Greyfriars makes the swift retort :
>   BOB CHERRY !

"All right."

"Come on, you fellows—we shall have to hustle now. You can cut in and tell Prouty that Bunter is taking his packet, Bob—he may see us jazzing off, and think it's forgotten."

"Right-ho !" said Bob.

The Famous Five, relieved in their minds now, hurried away. Billy Bunter blinked at the sealed packet on the table, and at the key—and it was the latter he picked up.

Harry Wharton and Co. sped downstairs—by way of the banisters ; which was against the rules, but quicker. Four of them ran out for the bicycles, while Bob Cherry dashed away to Mr. Prout's study.

Mr. Prout was in his quarters, in conversation with Mr. Quelch, the Remove master. Mr. Prout, who was a great sportsman, was cleaning a rifle while he talked. Bob Cherry caught the words " grizzly bear," as he came breathlessly up to the door. The master of the Fifth was relating one of his ancient exploits, probably for the fiftieth time, and Mr. Quelch was bearing it with exemplary politeness and patience.

"Excuse me, sir———."

"He was within six feet of me," said Mr. Prout, blinking over his rifle at the Remove master. "Figure the position to yourself, sir—a grizzly bear within six feet, and my gun———."

"Excuse me, sir———"

"Really, Cherry———"

"Bunter is taking the packet to the post-office, sir, if you don't mind. He will bring you the receipt."

And without waiting for Mr. Prout to state whether he minded or not, Bob Cherry scudded away. A minute later, five merry juniors were cycling at a great speed for Cliff house school.

THE SECOND CHAPTER.

Bunter's Way!

"BOIL very slowly," murmured Billy Bunter.

The Owl of the Remove was busy.

No. 7 Study, in the Remove passage, was warm—very warm. It was not a cold day, by any means; and there was a good fire going. Billy Bunter was warm, too; his fat face was almost crimson in hue, and there were beads of perspiration on his plump brow.

But he did not flinch.

Had his task been a less important one, Billy Bunter would have rolled out into the quadrangle for a breath of fresh air under the shady old trees. But he was making toffee—with a view to eating it. It was not a time for slacking.

"Boil very slowly, and stir all the time," murmured the fat junior. "Groogh! It's warm! But it's going all right."

Bunter was warm; but Bunter was very happy.

He had obtained the supplies he needed from the studies of the Famous Five. He had obtained other supplies, too, that were not included in the bargain. A cake here, a bag of biscuits there, and a pot of jam somewhere else—all was grist that came to Billy Bunter's mill. He did not believe in wasting opportunities.

There was a glorious spread waiting for him at tea-time—an early tea-time. His study mates, Todd and Dutton, were out, and Bunter was not sorry for it; he hoped they wouldn't come in before tea. The Famous Five were going to have tea with Marjorie & Co., at Cliff House, so they were safely out of the way. Bunter was looking forward to an extra-special spread—with the home-made toffee to wind up with—to fill any crevice, as it were, that was left in his plump inside after he had disposed of the cake, and the biscuits, and the jam, and his other plunder.

No wonder a happy smile suffused his fat face, as he bent over the simmering toffee, and kept it stirred.

"And pour out into a flat, buttered dish!" murmured Bunter, blinking at his famous recipe through his big glasses. "That's all right! Lucky I was able to borrow that tin pan from Russell's study—lucky Russell was out. It was just what I wanted."

The tin pan, ready buttered, lay in the armchair, all ready for the toffee to be poured into it.

Billy Bunter blinked at the clock.

"Jolly nearly done!" he murmured.

He continued to stir while the toffee boiled slowly, according to instructions.

The delicate operation was completed at last.

Bunter lifted the frying-pan from the fire with great care, and poured the contents into the flat tin pan on the armchair.

The frying-pan was then shoved into the bottom of the cupboard. It would have been judicious to clean it at once; but Bunter was not thinking of that. Perhaps he thought that his study mates might as well clean it when they wanted to use it next time; or perhaps he did not think at all.

He blinked at the toffee in the tin pan with great satisfaction.

"Now it's got to cool," he murmured. "My hat! It's warm."

He crossed to the study window and opened it, and put his fat crimson face out into the fresh air.

Then he gave a start.

Far below, in the quadrangle, a portly figure was pacing to and fro; the figure of Mr. Prout, the master of the Fifth, with his hands clasped behind his back as he paced majestically.

Mr. Prout was apparently in a thoughtful mood.

"Oh, crumbs!" ejaculated Bunter.

The sight of the Fifth-Form master brought back the packet to his memory. It still lay on the study table.

Bunter had been too busy making up his materials into toffee to remember the compact by which he had obtained the materials.

Mr. Prout's packet, which was to be registered, was not registered yet—it lay on the table where Bob Cherry had placed it. Bunter jumped back from the window, fearful of catching Mr. Prout's eye. By that time he certainly ought to have posted the packet, and taken the receipt to the Fifth-Form master—and he had forgotten all about it!

"Blessed lot of trouble about nothing," growled Bunter discontentedly. "What does he want his blessed packets registered for? Only some of his rot—I know that. I'd slip it into the letter-box, only he would make a fuss about the receipt—it would be like him. I suppose I've got to go down to the post-office, and if the beast sees me going he'll ask me why I haven't been before. B-r-r-r-r!"

The fat junior peevishly picked up the packet, and slipped it into his pocket, along with the sixpence Bob Cherry had left to pay the postage.

He took another look at the toffee before he quitted the study.

It was beginning to set, and Bunter was satisfied. After all, he had to wait for the toffee to cool, and a walk down to Friardale would give him an appetite for tea—not that his appetite needed much improving.

He quitted the study at last, and went cautiously downstairs.

He did not want to meet Mr. Prout.

That gentleman attached much more importance to his registered packet than William George Bunter did; and it was very probable that he would cut up rusty if he found that it was not posted yet. That packet contained the design of something new in breech-blocks which the sporting Form-master had invented, and which he was submitting to an expert in London. If Mr. Prout had discovered that the packet had been left lying about Bunter's study for hours, a volcanic explosion would certainly have followed.

Billy Bunter blinked cautiously out of the doorway, and jumped back as he saw Mr. Prout pacing only a dozen yards away.

"Beast!" he murmured.

And the fat junior scuttled away through the house, and escaped by a back door. He quitted Greyfriars by the tradesman's gate, and hurried away to Friardale as fast as his fat little legs could carry him.

He was half-way to the village, when there was a whirr of bicycles behind him, and a bunch of cyclists came sweeping out of Westwood Lane into the road. Billy Bunter blinked round, and recognised Harry Wharton and Co., and Marjorie, Clara, Babs, and Mabs of Cliff House School.

"Hallo, hallo, hallo! Bunter!" exclaimed Bob.

"I say, you fellows——"

"You've been to the post-office?" asked Bob, slackening down.

"Just going!"

"Just going!" roared Bob wrathfully.

"Why, it's two or three hours since I gave you the packet. You fat slacker——"

"Oh, really, Cherry——"

"Lazybones!" growled Johnny Bull.

"The lazybonefulness is terrific," said Hurree Singh.

"I say, you fellows, one of you can give me a lift on a bike to Friardale——"

"We're going by Redclyffe Lane to Cliff House," answered Harry Wharton. "Come on, you fellows."

"Look here, Bob, you can give me a lift——"

"How can I, when I'm going to Cliff House?" demanded Bob. "We've had our spin, and you've had time to go to the post-office half a dozen times."

"I've been making toffee and resting a bit, and I had to have a snack, and——"

"Oh, rats!"

The cyclists were pedalling on, and Bunter set his fat little legs into motion to keep pace.

"Look here, Bob Cherry," he howled. "You can give me a lift on your foot-rests to the village. I'm tired."

"Bosh!"

"I think you're an ungrateful beast, Bob Cherry—after my taking all this trouble for you. Look here, you go to the post-office, and I'll have your bike. Marjorie would like my company better than yours—wouldn't you, Marjorie?"

"Not at all," answered Marjorie.

"Oh, really, you know——"

"Good-bye, Bunter!"

"I say, you fellows——"

"Ta-ta!"

"Look here, I'm not going any further!" roared Bunter, in great indignation. "There's your blessed packet, Bob Cherry, and you can take it or leave it. I'm disgusted at you."

And Bunter tossed the packet at Bob Cherry. It just missed Bob's head, and dropped into the road.

"My only hat!" ejaculated Bob.

Billy Bunter turned, and started back to Greyfriars. He felt that he had done enough—especially as he received such ingratitude in return.

Bob Cherry jumped off his machine, and picked up the packet.

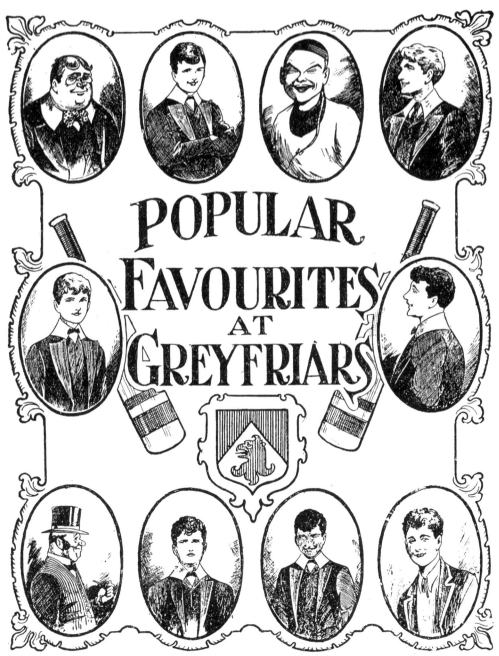

POPULAR FAVOURITES AT GREYFRIARS

Reading from left to right: Billy Bunter, Mark Linley, Wun Lung, Bob Cherry, Frank Nugent
John Bull, Mr. Gosling (porter), Harry Wharton, Hurree Singh, Robert Ogilvy.

"Bunter!" he roared.

The fat junior rolled on without answering.

"Bunter!"

Billy Bunter turned a corner, and vanished.

Bob Cherry was left with Mr. Prout's packet in his hand, and an extraordinary expression on his face.

"Well!" he ejaculated. "Of all the——"

"Come on, Bob!" called back Nugent.

"That fat villain has planted this rotten packet on me——"

"Ha, ha, ha!"

"Blessed if I see anything to cackle at. I shall have to go to the post-office now; I can't leave it stranded."

"It's too bad!" said Marjorie. "We'll ride slowly, Bob, and you can overtake us."

"That's right; get a move on," said Harry.

"I'll catch you up at Cliff House, then," said Bob.

He rode on to Friardale, packet in hand, while the rest of the party turned into the lane to Cliff House. And as he rode, he mentally promised William George Bunter all sorts of things when he returned to Greyfriars.

THE THIRD CHAPTER.

Right Behind!

Mr. Prout knocked at the door of No. 7 Study in the Remove, and threw it open, with a frowning brow.

Mr. Prout was annoyed.

It was five o'clock—quite three hours since

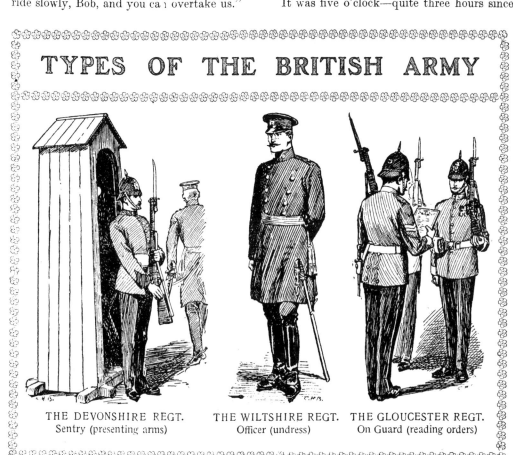

TYPES OF THE BRITISH ARMY

THE DEVONSHIRE REGT.
Sentry (presenting arms)

THE WILTSHIRE REGT.
Officer (undress)

THE GLOUCESTER REGT.
On Guard (reading orders)

"Look here, I'm not going any further," cried Billy Bunter, in great indignation. "There's your packet, Bob Cherry, and you can take it or leave it!" (See page 8).

he had handed his precious packet to Bob Cherry for the post. Bob had informed him that Bunter was taking it to the post-office; and naturally Mr. Prout expected Bunter to turn up with the receipt.

But Bunter hadn't.

Mr. Prout had thought of his packet several times, and he was getting anxious about it. As Bunter did not come to his study, he decided at last to go to Bunter's study. It was a case of Mahomet going to the mountain, the mountain would not come to Mahomet.

Naturally Mr. Prout was annoyed, as he climbed the Remove staircase, and rustled along to No. 7. He was still more annoyed to find No. 7 Study empty.

"Bless my soul!" murmured Mr. Prout. "This is really too bad! I shall speak very severely to Bunter and to Cherry. If my packet should be lost——"

The bare thought was dismaying to the inventive gentleman.

He looked angrily round the study. The table was laid for tea, which looked as if Bunter did not intend to be long absent. Mr. Prout decided to wait there till he came in.

He crossed the study to the armchair, and sat down.

The back of the big armchair was turned towards the window; and Mr. Prout was no longer blessed with the keen sight he had enjoyed in those great days when he had hunted the festive grizzly in the Rocky Mountains. He did not observe the large, shallow pan in the armchair, and naturally, as he sank into the chair, he sat in the pan. Fortunately the toffee was getting cool by that time, though it had not hardened—and fortunately Mr. Prout's coat and gown interposed between him and the toffee-pan. Quite unaware of the disaster he had brought upon the fruit of Billy Bunter's labours, the portly gentleman settled down, and stretched out his toes to the fender.

Mr. Prout would have been booked for a long wait in No. 7 Study, if Bunter had not met the cyclists in the lane. As it was, however, the Owl of the Remove was hurrying back to Greyfriars, and he was not far away.

Billy Bunter came breathlessly up the stairs, and headed for his study, by the time Mr. Prout had reposed in his armchair for a quarter of an hour. Billy Bunter hoped to find his pan of toffee nicely set. It was nicely set by that time—quite firmly set, and attached to Mr. Prout's gown as if it were glued there.

The fat junior came rolling into the study, certainly not expecting to find Mr. Prout there. He jumped at the sight of the form-master in the armchair.

Mr. Prout gave him a stern look.

" Oh ! You have returned, Bunter ? "

" Oh ! " gasped Bunter.

He blinked at Mr. Prout as if mesmerised.

He was thinking of the toffee.

Seeing Mr. Prout in the chair, he naturally expected to see the pan of toffee somewhere else—but he didn't. And the dreadful conviction forced itself upon him that Mr. Prout was sitting on the toffee!

Bunter stood rooted to the floor.

The Owl of the Remove was not a particular fellow ; but even he did not quite care for toffee that had been sat on. And he was smitten with horrid misgivings as to what Mr. Prout might say—and do—when he discovered the toffee.

" I have waited for you," Mr. Prout was saying, " sixteen minutes by this clock, Bunter."

" Oh ! "

" I understand, from Robert Cherry, that you had been entrusted with the packet for the post-office," said the Fifth-Form master.

" Oh ! Yes ! Oh ! " gasped Bunter.

" Very good. Did you post it immediately to catch the five o'clock collection from Friardale ? "

" Nunno ! I—I——"

" You have been very remiss, Bunter ! Pray, why are you staring at me in that peculiar way, Bunter ? "

" Was—was—was I, sir ? "

" You were, Bunter—and you are ! " snapped Mr. Prout. " Is anything the matter ? "

" Nunno, sir ! Oh, no, sir ! Certainly not ! The toffee——"

" What ? "

" Nothing, sir ! There—there isn't any toffee, sir, of course. Nothing of the kind in the study ! " gasped Bunter. " I—I haven't been making toffee this afternoon, sir. It—it was some other fellow."

" I fail to understand you, Bunter. You really seem to me to be wandering in your mind ! "

" Oh, sir ! "

" Kindly give me the receipt for the packet, if it is posted at last ! " snapped Mr. Prout.

" Bub—bub—bub——"

" Eh ? "

" Bub—Bub—Bob Cherry's taken it, sir I—I met him, sir, and—and he insisted upon taking it. He—he thought it would be safer, sir."

Mr. Prout uttered an impatient exclamation.

" Pah ! And where is Cherry now ? "

" I—I think he's still out, sir."

" I shall speak very severely to Cherry. That packet was very particular—most particular. Its value is very great. Pah ! "

Mr. Prout rose irritably from the armchair, and whisked to the door. Billy Bunter blinked into the vacant chair.

He anticipated seeing the toffee squashed over the pan and the chair. But it wasn't. The chair was quite vacant ! Bunter gave a gasp. The toffee had " set " to the form-master's gown, and the pan had risen with him. Behind Mr. Prout, as he whisked to the door, went toffee and pan.

" What is the matter, Bunter ? " Mr. Prout glanced back at the door, as Bunter stood with horrified gaze fixed on the empty chair. "Eh? Oh!" stuttered Bunter.

"Have I left anything in the chair?" asked Mr. Prout, thinking that he had dropped a pocket-book or some such article, from Bunter's looks.

"Oh, no, sir! I—I wish you had—I—I mean, you haven't, sir—certainly not!"

"You are a very stupid boy, Bunter!"

"Oh, yes, sir—thank you, sir!" stammered Bunter, hardly conscious of what he was saying in his confusion.

Mr. Prout gave a sniff, and whisked out of No. 7. Billy Bunter rolled to the door after him, and blinked at the retreating figure of the form-master in horror and dismay.

Behind Mr. Prout shone a very bright surface—the outside of the toffee pan. It caught the sunlight from the windows of the Remove passage, and glinted cheerfully.

"Oh, my hat!" gasped Bunter.

Clang!

The toffee-pan, on the trailing gown, caught the banisters as Mr. Prout whisked down the Remove staircase.

Clang!

The Fifth-Form master stopped in great astonishment, and looked round him.

"Bless my soul! What is that?"

He whisked right round in his surprise.

Clang!

Mr. Prout jumped.

Click! Clank! Clang!

"What—what—what——"

THE FOURTH CHAPTER.

Trouble for Bunter.

MR. PROUT stood transfixed on the Remove staircase, two steps from the landing. He was too astounded to move.

That weird metallic clinking and clanging followed his movements; and what was the cause of it was quite beyond the Fifth-Form master's comprehension.

Billy Bunter blinked at him from the doorway of No. 7 Study, in horror; wondering dazedly what was going to happen next.

"Bless my soul!" exclaimed Mr. Prout. "This—this is most extraordinary! I heard—I distinctly heard—a sound as of the impact of metal upon some solid substance. It is most extraordinary."

The astonished form-master blinked round on the staircase, revolving upon his axis, so to speak, so as not to leave a spot unscanned. But nothing of a metallic nature met his inquiring eye—which was natural enough, as the toffee-pan turned with him, adhering to his gown behind.

"Extraordinary!" repeated Mr. Prout.

"Ha, ha, ha!"

It was a sudden outburst of laughter on the lower stairs. Vernon-Smith, Redwing, and Squiff, of the Remove, were coming in to tea—and they sighted Mr. Prout above, with the glistening toffee-pan following him round as he revolved.

It was not very respectful to chortle; but the Removites couldn't help it. They chortled before they thought.

Mr. Prout glared down the staircase.

"Vernon-Smith!"

"Yes! Yes, sir!" murmured the Bounder.

"What are you laughing at?"

"Oh, sir!"

"Are you playing some trick, Vernon-Smith?"

"I, sir?"

"Yes, you!" thundered Mr. Prout.

"Oh, no, sir! Certainly not."

"A trick of some kind is being played," exclaimed Mr. Prout. "A peculiar clanging sound——"

"Ha, ha——"

"Vernon-Smith! You are laughing again!"

"W-w-was I, sir?"

"I shall report this impertinence to your form-master, Vernon-Smith."

"Oh, sir!"

Mr. Prout whisked down the staircase in great wrath. The juniors stood respectfully aside on the next landing to let him pass. Mr. Prout whisked round the turn of the stairs, and there was a loud clang as his gown brushed the banisters.

"Bless my soul!"

The Fifth-form master spun round and caught Vernon-Smith by the shoulder.

"It was you!" he exclaimed.

"Eh! what—which——" stuttered Vernon-Smith.

"Undoubtedly it is you, playing a disrespectful trick," exclaimed Mr. Prout, " I shall take you to Mr. Quelch at once——"

"But I—I—I—what have I done?" gasped Vernon-Smith. "It's the pan sticking on your gown, sir——"

"What?"

"There's a pan sticking to you, sir," said Redwing.

"Impossible!"

Mr. Prout whisked round, and the three juniors suppressed a chortle as he did so. The portly form-master looked remarkably like a cat chasing its tail at that moment.

"I can see nothing of the kind, Redwing——"

"It goes round when you go round, sir," gasped Vernon-Smith. "Here it is, sir. It's stuck to you somehow."

He caught the whisking toffee-pan, and dragged it round to Mr. Prout. The Fifth-Form master gathered up his gown, and the toffee-pan—and gazed at the latter in bewilderment.

"What—what—what?" he stuttered. "How—how—how can that—that cooking utensil—have become attached to my—my gown?"

"You must have sat in it, sir," stuttered Redwing. "I think it's toffee in the pan, sir."

"Oh!" gasped Mr. Prout, "Bunter—disrespectful young rascal—wicked, impertinence—outrageous, practical joke—upon my word—Bunter——"

With those incoherent ejaculations, the Fifth-Form master rushed up the staircase again.

He remembered sitting in the armchair in Bunter's study—and that was evidently the only place where he could have gathered up the toffee-pan.

He had not the slightest doubt that he had been the victim of a practical joke. It certainly was very careless of Bunter to have left the pan of cooling toffee in the study armchair; but Mr. Prout was not disposed to attribute the action to mere carelessness. He was more inclined—at that moment of exasperation—to suspect that Bunter had deliberately delayed posting his packet in order to inveigle him into the study—to sit in the toffee!

Billy Bunter saw the Fifth-Form master coming back along the passage at express speed. He did not wait for him to arrive. Bunter was not a very bright youth; but he was too bright to wait for Mr. Prout just then.

He gave the form-master one startled blink and fled.

"Bunter!" shouted Mr. Prout.

"Ow!" gasped Bunter; and he scuttled on up the passage.

"Stop!" roared the Fifth-Form master.

Wild horses would hardly have stopped Bunter at that moment.

He rushed on and scudded up the stairs to the top box-room. It was the only way of escape open to him.

Mr. Prout halted at the bottom of the little stair.

"Bunter!" he shrieked.

It was too undignified for Mr. Prout, wrathful as he was, to chase Bunter up and down staircase, and among the garrets. He stopped in the Remove passage, breathing stertorously.

"Bunter! Come back at once."

Bunter did not heed.

"Do you hear me, Bunter?"

No answer.

"Bunter! You young rascal! Do you hear me?" thundered Mr. Prout.

Like the celebrated Dying Gladiator, Bunter heard, but he heeded not!

Mr. Prout fumed in the passage; Billy Bunter had vanished, gone from his gaze like a beautiful dream.

A chuckle in the Remove passage recalled Mr. Prout to himself. Six or seven Remove fellows had come in to tea from the fields or the river; and they seemed greatly interested in Mr. Prout, and the semi-detached toffee-pan that swung behind him.

Breathing hard, Mr. Prout hurried away—toffee-pan and all. That article had to be removed from his gown at the cost of considerable trouble—in the privacy of his study.

It was half an hour later that Bunter emerged from the dusty recesses above, and blinked cautiously into the Remove passage. Mr. Prout was not to be seen. Bolsover major

" Have I left anything in the chair ? " asked Mr. Prout, supposing that he had dropped a pocket-book or some such article, from Bunter's look. Billy Bunter gave a gasp. The toffee had set to the Form-master's gown, and the pan had risen with him. (See page 13.)

and Ogilvy were lounging in the passage, and the fat junior called to them :

" I say, you fellows ! Has he gone ? "

" Er—who ? " asked Ogilvy.

" Old Prout ! "

" Haven't seen him for a dog's age," grinned Ogilvy. " You'd better not let him see you, either. I think he's wrathy."

" I—I say, he's spoiled my toffee, you know," said Bunter pathetically.

" Go and ask him for it," suggested Bolsover major, with a chuckle.

" No jolly fear ! "

" Are you going to let him keep your toffee-pan ? " asked Russell, looking out of his study.

" Oh, I don't mind. 'Tain't mine," answered Bunter. " It's the toffee I'm thinking of. I suppose it's spoiled ; and I took no end of trouble with that toffee. There was a pound of sugar, and half a pound of butter, and a quarter of a pound of syrup——"

" And Prouty's bagged the lot ! " roared Bolsover major. " Ha, ha, ha ! "

" Blessed if I can see anything to cackle at—I think it's an awful waste. I shouldn't care to eat it now," said Bunter dolorously. " I'm going to let Prout keep it if he likes."

" And the pan, too ? " grinned Ogilvy.

" Oh, that doesn't matter, as it isn't mine !

THE
GREYFRIARS GALLERY IN VERSE

By Dick Penfold

No. 2: Billy Bunter

❀✿❀✿❀✿❀

Who's always cadging for a loan ?
Who says he's merely skin and bone,
Yet turns the scale at fourteen stone ?
　　　　　Why, BUNTER !

Who scoffed a dozen plates of ham,
Six doughnuts, and a jar of jam ?
Then said, " How very thin I am ! "
　　　　　Why, BUNTER !

Who snores enough to shake the dorm.
Till heavy boots begin to swarm
Upon his frail and fragile form ?
　　　　　Why, BUNTER !

Who rolls out fibs so smooth and sweet
That Ananias can't compete,
And even Kaiser Bill is beat ?
　　　　　Why, BUNTER !

Who calls himself, with oily grace,
The scion of a noble race
(Which everyone has failed to trace) ?
　　　　　Why, BUNTER !

Who, when he's buried (Reader, sob !)
Will leave the man who does the job
A postal-order for a bob ?
　　　　　Why, BUNTER !

Lucky I only borrowed that, in case it don't turn up again."

" Nice for the owner," grinned Russell.

" Well, I can't help his troubles, can I ? " argued Bunter. " You don't mind, I suppose, Russell ? "

Russell stared.

" Not at all. Why should I ? "

" Well, it was your toffee-pan, you know."

" What ? "

" Still, if you don't mind, Russell, I'm sure I don't, so it's all right—— Here, I say, wharrer you at ? Yaroooop ! "

And Bunter fled for his life again.

THE FIFTH CHAPTER.

No Volunteers.

HARRY WHARTON AND CO. came in cheerily as dusk was falling on Greyfriars.

The Famous Five had enjoyed their bike ride that fine afternoon. They had spun through green lanes, over hill and dale ; and they had had a first-rate tea at Cliff House School—with a cake of Marjorie's own making, which was tip-top, as Bob Cherry emphatically declared. If it had resembled plaster of paris Bob would probably have considered it tip-top all the same—as Marjorie Hazeldene had made it with her own fair hands. But all the Co. agreed that it really was tip-top ; and if the proof of the pudding is in the eating, the quality of that cake could be considered as indubitably proved, for they had not left a crumb of it.

The chums of the Remove rode home from Cliff House in great spirits, and arrived at Greyfriars in a merry mood.

" You've got to see Prouty, Bob," said Harry Wharton, as they dismounted. " I'll take your bike to the shed—you cut off and deliver the goods. I shouldn't wonder if he wants his receipt by this time."

" My hat ! I'd forgotten that," said Bob. " I suppose he won't mind my not having come straight back with it."

" Bit late to wonder whether he'll mind or not," grinned Nugent. " Take it in, and chance it."

Bob Cherry headed for the Fifth-Form master's study.

He was rather doubtful as to the reception he would get.

Of course, he was not to blame in any way. Bunter had agreed to take the packet to the post-office; and certainly he ought to have taken it. When it had been "planted" on Bob again in the lane, he had duly posted it—but then he was due at Cliff House for tea, and biking back to Greyfriars with the post-office receipt was not to be thought of. And Bob certainly didn't think of it. Besides, the receipt was safe enough in Bob's pocket; so what did it matter, anyway?"

Bob tapped at the Fifth-Form master's door; and a voice that seemed to have a knife-edge to it bade him enter.

Bob opened the door in a rather gingerly manner. Mr. Prout's tone was a sufficient indication that Mr. Prout was cross.

The Fifth-Form master was seated at his table, with a heightened colour and a frowning brow, at tea—a rather late tea. He had been rather busy with a gown and a toffee-pan for some time.

"Oh, it is you, Cherry!" he ejaculated, his eyes glinting at Bob over his glasses.

"Yes, sir. I—I've brought your receipt, sir," murmured the junior meekly.

"You may place it on the table."

Bob placed it on the table.

"Cherry!"

"Ye-es, sir."

"I requested you to take that packet for me to the post-office."

"I—I've done it, sir."

"After first leaving it to another boy——"

"Ahem! I—I—you see, sir——"

"You were perhaps not aware, Cherry, that that packet was of the greatest importance!" snapped Mr. Prout.

"Nun-no, sir!"

"Why, then, did you suppose that I wished it to be registered?" demanded Mr. Prout.

"I—I——" stammered Bob. As a matter of absolute fact, Bob hadn't supposed anything about it. But he did not like to tell Mr. Prout so.

"You have been careless, Cherry!"

"Oh, sir!"

"And wanting in proper consideration."

"I—I hope not, sir."

"It is useless to hope not, Cherry, when such is the fact. I have been anxious for the safety of that packet, the contents of which were of inestimable value."

"Were they really, sir?" stammered Bob.

"Nothing less, Cherry, than the design of an invention of my own——"

"Oh!"

"And you did not bring me the receipt for that packet till"—Mr. Prout glanced at the clock—"till after six o'clock."

"I'm—I'm sorry, sir——"

"That is all very well, Cherry, but it does not alter the fact of the matter. If you were in my Form, Cherry, I should punish you."

Bob Cherry was glad that he was not in Mr. Prout's Form.

"I trust," continued Mr. Prout, with a gleaming eye, "I trust, Cherry, that you were no party to the reprehensible trick Bunter played on me."

Bob jumped.

"Has Bunter—— Oh, sir—certainly not. I didn't even know——"

"Owing to this packet changing hands, Cherry, I was inveigled into Bunter's study, where the young rascal had placed a pan of toffee for me to sit upon——"

"Oh, crumbs!"

"I sat in the toffee, Cherry, and ruined my gown! I desire to know, sir, whether you were a party to that outrage?"

"Oh, no, sir. I never knew——" gasped Bob.

"Huh!" snorted Mr. Prout.

"But—but perhaps Bunter didn't mean you to sit in the toffee, sir!" Bob ventured.

"I have already told you, Cherry, that he did!"

"Yes, sir, b-b-but perhaps it was an accident—Bunter isn't likely to waste toffee if he could help it!" murmured Bob. That fact was self-evident to Bob Cherry, if not to Mr. Prout; and the junior felt bound to put in a word for the unfortunate Owl of the Remove.

"Have you come here to argue with me, Cherry?" thundered Mr. Prout, apparently not disposed to listen to reason.

"Oh, no, sir! Certainly not!"

"Then kindly do not do so. You may

leave my study. Find Bunter at once, and tell him to come to me."

"Very well, sir."

Bob Cherry quitted the study, glad to escape. He did not envy Billy Bunter his coming interview with the Fifth-Form master.

As Bunter was in the Lower Fourth, Mr. Prout was not properly entitled to administer punishment to him; but it was pretty clear that Mr. Prout was going to stretch a point in his own favour, in this instance.

Bob Cherry hurried up to the Remove passage, where he found his chums in No. 1 Study.

"Seen Bunter?" he asked.

"No—but we've heard about him," said Harry Wharton, laughing. Squiff was in the study, and he had evidently been relating the adventure of the toffee. "He's been in hot water."

"And Prouty's been in toffee," said Johnny Bull.

"Prout wants him," said Bob. "It seems that he's sat in Bunter's toffee, and he thinks Bunty put it there on purpose. He don't know Bunter if he thinks that fat bounder would waste toffee on a form-master."

"Ha, ha, ha!"

"I say, you fellows——"

"Hallo, hallo, hallo! Here he is!"

A fat face and a pair of glimmering glasses blinked into the study. Billy Bunter gave the Famous Five a dolorous look.

"I say, you fellows, that toffee's been spoiled!" he said. "Under the circumstances, I think you ought to let me have a fresh lot of stuff. What do you think?"

"I think you'd better go and see Prouty!" grinned Bob Cherry. "He's just told me to find you and send you to him."

"Oh, dear! I—I say, does he look waxy?"

"Yes, rather."

"Blessed old Hun!" said Bunter. "He might be satisfied with spoiling my toffee, without wanting to lick a chap as well."

"He says you've ruined his gown."

"Bother his gown," said Bunter peevishly. "I know he's ruined my toffee. It won't be fit to eat now; and I shouldn't care to ask Prouty for it, anyway; under the circumstances."

"You'd better go to him," said Harry.

Bunter shook his head decidedly.

"I'm jolly well not going! He wants to lick me."

"'Tain't polite to keep a form-master waiting when he wants to lick you!" grinned Johnny Bull. "Buzz off."

"No fear!"

"You'd better go," said Bob seriously. "Prout will get waxier and waxier if he has to wait for you, Bunter."

"I—I say, you fellows, couldn't one of you go?" suggested Bunter. "As—as captain of the Remove, Wharton, it's really up to you, you know. Don't you think so?"

Wharton stared.

"What's the good of my going?" he asked. "Prouty doesn't want to see me."

"He wouldn't mind—he only wants to lick somebody because he's waxy," urged Bunter.

"You fat duffer! I had nothing to do with putting the toffee in the chair for him, had I?"

"Well, you could say you had."

"What?"

"You—you could confess, you know, in—in a straightforward and—and manly way, and he might let you off, you know."

"Well, my hat!" ejaculated Wharton blankly.

"I think it's up to you," said Bunter, blinking at him. "After all I've done for you, too——!"

"You fat owl, what have you done for me?"

"Oh, really, Wharton—if you're going to be ungrateful——!"

"Suffocate him, somebody," said Wharton.

"Perhaps you'd care to go, Nugent—you're a good-natured chap, not a selfish beast like Wharton!"

"My dear man, I'm exactly just such another selfish beast, in this case," chuckled Nugent. "I'm not going to Prouty to tell lies and get a licking, to please you, you owl."

"Oh, really, Nugent! Perhaps you, Inky——"

"The perhapfulness is terrific," chortled the dusky nabob of Bhanipur. "The declinefulness is also great."

"I might have known that you'd be a selfish

The **chums of** the Remove-form could not help grinning, as they looked at one another. "What a set of pictures!" murmured Bob Cherry. (See page 31.)

rotter, Inky. What about you, Bull? You've got more pluck than these funky duffers---you're not afraid to face old Prout, are you?"

"Can you lend me a cricket stump for five minutes, Wharton?" asked Johnny Bull.

"Certainly; here you are."

"I—I say, Bull, wha-a-at are you going to do with that stump?"

"I'm going to lay it round a fat, cheeky owl," answered Johnny Bull.

"Oh, really, Bull—oh, my hat—gerroff, you beast—oh, crikey!"

Billy Bunter dodged out of No. 1 Study. He departed hurriedly—but not in the direction of Mr. Prout's quarters. The inevitable meeting with Mr. Prout was to be postponed to the latest possible moment.

THE SIXTH CHAPTER.

Mr. Prout Looks In.

"OH, crikey!"

No. 7 Study was at prep. when a hasty footstep sounded in the passage outside. To speak more correctly, Peter Todd and Tom Dutton were at prep.—and Billy Bunter was toying with his work—slacking even more than he usually did.

Bunter simply couldn't put his mind to prep. that evening. He was thinking of the catastrophe of the afternoon. It was not simply the loss of the toffee—though that was serious enough. But the angry face of Mr. Prout loomed before Bunter's imagination. He had not heeded Mr. Prout's invitation to his study—too much of the spider-and-the-fly bizney about that, he had told Toddy. But as he did not go to Mr. Prout, he expected that Mr. Prout would come to him—Mahomet and the mountain over again! He was not likely to give much thought to prep. under such harrowing circumstances.

And the heavy tread in the passage drew a dismayed ejaculation from him. He knew Mr. Prout's tread! Mahomet was coming to the mountain at last!

Billy Bunter jumped up.

"I—I say, Toddy, he's coming!"

Peter Todd looked up from his work and nodded.

"Looks like it," he agreed. "He was bound to corner you sooner or later, Bunter you can't dodge a form-master for ever. Grin and bear it!"

"You silly ass!" gasped Bunter.

"Better go through with it, and get it over," advised Peter Todd sagely. "After all, a licking's only a licking. My only hat! Wharrer you up to?"

Billy Bunter dived under the table.

It was true, as Peter remarked, that a licking was only a licking; but possibly Peter was enabled to take that calm and detached view by the circumstance that he wasn't the fellow who was booked for the licking. Bunter appeared to take quite a different view.

A fat, dismayed face blinked up at Peter imploringly from under the edge of the table-cover.

"Don't let him know I'm here, Peter!"

"Oh, crumbs!"

There was a hand on the door. The table-cover dropped into its place, and the Owl of the Remove was hidden from view. Tom Dutton stared at it blankly. Tom Dutton was the only fellow in the Remove who hadn't heard the story of the toffee—and that was because he was deaf. Peter Todd was going to tell him, because it was quite a good story; but he hadn't told him yet—there was considerable physical exercise in telling Dutton a story.

"What's Bunter at?" asked Dutton.

"Shush!"

"Eh?"

Peter placed his fingers on his lips as the door opened and revealed the portly form and frowning features of Mr. Prout. Tom Dutton understood the sign, and was silent.

Mr. Prout came majestically in.

"Is Bunter here?" he demanded.

"Bunter?" repeated Peter Todd, to gain time. "D-d-do you mean Billy Bunter, sir?"

"I mean Bunter of the Remove!" snapped Mr. Prout. "Whom else should I mean, Todd? Don't be foolish!"

"Oh! You—you might have meant Sammy Bunter, of the Second Form, sir."

"I did not mean Bunter of the Second Form, Todd. I referred to Bunter of the Remove—your study-mate. I repeat, is he here?" thundered Mr. Prout.

Peter looked round the study, as if in search of Bunter.

"I don't see him here, sir," he answered.

Peter was greatly inclined to kick under

the table to reward the Owl for placing him in such an awkward position. But he was loyal to his study-mate, and he did not mean to betray the fat junior.

"Have you seen him lately, Todd?"

"I—I saw him at lessons, sir."

"Pah! I am not referring to this morning. Have you not seen him since lessons?"

Peter reflected.

"Yes, sir, I saw him about two hours ago——"

"Nonsense! Dutton, have you seen Bunter?"

"Eh? Did you speak to me, sir?"

"I certainly spoke to you, Dutton. I am looking for Bunter. I believe that the disrespectful young rascal is deliberately keeping out of my way," exclaimed Mr. Prout.

"Eh?"

"Bunter played a most disrespectful trick upon me this afternoon, and I am going to punish him with the greatest severity. Where is he, Dutton?"

"None at all, sir."

"What?"

"We haven't any."

"You haven't any what?"

"Mutton, sir."

"Mutton!" repeatedly Mr. Prout dazedly. "Mutton! I was not speaking to you about mutton, boy!"

"I'm sorry, sir," said the deaf junior. "But we never have mutton in the study, sir. We couldn't very well cook it here."

"Bless my soul! If this is impertinence——"

"Dutton is rather deaf, sir," hinted Peter Todd.

"Oh! Ah, yes, I recall that fact! Dutton!" shouted Mr. Prout, "have you seen Bunter lately?"

"Are you speaking of Bunter, sir?"

"Certainly."

"Well, sir, you do surprise me," said Dutton innocently. "Fat, if you like—but stately! My word! I've never heard anybody call Bunter stately before."

"Bless my soul! I did not say stately; I said lately!" shrieked Mr. Prout.

"Eh?"

"Have you seen Bunter? Do you know where he is at present?"

Tom Dutton looked still more surprised.

"I'm sure you're very kind, sir," he said. "I shall accept it with very great pleasure, sir."

"What—you will accept what?" shrieked Mr. Prout.

"Your present, sir."

"Mum-mum-my present?"

"Yes, sir, and thank you very much indeed!"

Mr. Prout blinked at Dutton, and Dutton looked cheerfully at Mr. Prout, apparently waiting for him to produce the present.

"Bless my soul!" said the Fifth-Form master.

He gave Dutton up, and turned to Peter Todd again.

"Todd, I am very desirous of finding Bunter. I supposed that he was in this study? Has he not done his preparation?"

"I think not, sir."

"Has he been here at all?" demanded the Fifth-Form master suspiciously.

"Ahem. I—I'll think, sir——"

"I should not be surprised if the young rascal is concealed somewhere in the room at this very moment," exclaimed Mr. Prout.

There was a gasp from under the table.

"Ow! I—I'm not, sir!"

"What?" Mr. Prout stooped to jerk up the table-cover. "You are there, Bunter."

"No, sir—not at all. I'm not here—oh, crumbs!"

"Come out at once, Bunter!" thundered the Fifth-Form master. "Your well-merited chastisement, sir, awaits you!"

"Yaroooh!"

"If you do not emerge immediately, Bunter, I shall thrust my cane under the table——"

"Yow!"

Billy Bunter rolled out from under the table. Mr. Prout made a grab at him—but the fat junior squirmed desperately and eluded him. He made a flying jump for the door.

"Bunter—stop—will——"

Whack!

Bunter did not stop; and Mr. Prout's cane caught him across his fat shoulders as he fled. There was a wild yell from Bunter as he vanished.

A PAGE OF PICTURE PUZZLES

For Boys and Girls who are clever with their eyes

" Boy ! Come back ! "

Mr. Prout rustled wrathfully into the passage. Peter Todd closed the door after him, and gasped.

" Poor old Bunter ! I'm sorry for him, if Prouty catches him now ! "

" What's the matter with Prout, Toddy ? " inquired Tom Dutton.

" Off his onion," answered Peter.

" Onion ! He said mutton at first," said Dutton in surprise. " I don't see why he should come to a Remove study for either. Do you, Toddy ? "

" Ha, ha, ha ! "

" And he said he was going to give me a present—and he didn't," said Dutton in perplexity. " I'm blessed if I quite understand Mr. Prout coming to a junior study for onions and mutton, and talking about a present. I shouldn't like to think he had been drinking, but really—really——"

And Dutton shook his head very seriously as he settled down to his prep. again ; and Peter Todd chuckled and followed his example.

THE SEVENTH CHAPTER.

Something Like a Stunt!

" I SAY, you fellows ! "

Prep. was over in No. 1 Study, and Bob Cherry, Johnny Bull, and Hurree Jamset Ram Singh had dropped in for a chat with Wharton and Nugent. The Famous Five were discussing baked chestnuts, when the door opened suddenly, and Billy Bunter entered, closing the door quickly behind him.

" Amazing ! " ejaculated Bob Cherry.

" Eh ! what's amazing ? " asked Bunter.

" How did you know we had chestnuts ? "

" I—I didn't——"

" Gammon ! "

" Still, I'll have some, as you're so pressing," said Bunter. " I'll help myself, if you don't mind. Thanks ! "

Without giving the Removites time to state whether they minded, the Owl helped himself.

" I say, you fellows——" he recommenced, with his mouth full, " I say, I'm in an awful scrape, you know."

" Seen Prouty yet ? " chuckled Johnny Bull.

" Well, I've seen him," admitted Bunter ; I—I didn't stop to speak——"

" Ha, ha, ha ! "

" It's all very well for you to cackle," said Bunter, pathetically ; " but I'm in an awful scrape. Prouty's hunting me like a wild tiger. He came to my study for me, and routed me out from under the table——"

" Ha, ha, ha ! " yelled the Co.

" Oh, don't cackle ! " howled Bunter. " It ain't funny—there's nothing whatever funny in this, that I can see. You fellows wouldn't like to have a fat old form-master after you with a cane, like a wild tiger in the jungle. I just dodged him, by the skin of my teeth, you know—and dodged into Wibley's study in time. Wib hid me inside one of his blessed costumes—his theatrical rot, you know ; and there was I stuck in a cupboard as stuffy as anything—nearly suffocated——"

" Ha, ha, ha ! "

" Funny to be nearly suffocated, ain't it ? " hooted Bunter. " I had to stick there while old Prout was rooting up and down the passage looking for me. He's just like a Hun—a wild Prussian Hun ! He actually thinks I stuck the toffee there for him to sit in—as if I'd waste good toffee on a silly old form-master——"

" Why not explain to him ? " asked Harry Wharton, wiping his eyes.

" He wouldn't listen—he started in with the cane the moment he saw me," said Bunter. " He gave me a terrific lick, before I got clear. I'd rather try explaining to a wild Hun. Besides, he wouldn't believe me. People often don't believe what I say——"

" Go hon ! "

" It's a fact," said Bunter, sorrowfully. " A truthful chap like me, you know—a fellow who couldn't tell a lie, like that chap who had a little hatchet——"

" Oh, my hat ! "

" Well, you've dodged him so far," said Bob Cherry. " Keep it up, Bunter ! It's quite entertaining. You can keep it up till bed-time, anyhow. I don't quite see what you'll do if Prouty comes to the dorm. for you."

" I say, you fellows—you might sympathise with a chap who's down on his luck," said Bunter. "It's all your fault, Bob Cherry."

"Hallo, hallo, hallo! How is it my fault?"

"If you'd posted old Prout's packet as he asked you, it wouldn't have happened at all."

"Well, perhaps it wouldn't," agreed Bob. "But if you'd gone to the post-office at once, as you agreed, it wouldn't have happened either. Prouty only came to your study because he hadn't got his precious receipt, I suppose. So it was your own fault my fat pippin."

"After landing me in this awful scrape, you fellows, you might help a chap," said Bunter reproachfully.

"It seems to me that you landed yourself in it," said Harry Wharton. "But what can we do? We'll help you out if we can."

"The helpfulness will be terrific, my esteemed and disgusting Bunter, if there is anything doing," remarked Hurree Singh.

"Well, I made a suggestion—if one of you owned up to Prout——"

"Kick him out!" said Johnny Bull.

"I—I don't mean that—I—I've got another idea, and Wibley's agreed to help, if you fellows will play up!" exclaimed Bunter hastily.

"Give it a name!" said Bob. "If we can do anything, we'll do it—though you deserve a licking, you fat bounder. I've missed a cake and a pot of jam from my study, since I came in."

"If you think I'd touch your cake, Bob——"

"I jolly well do."

"Of course, I never even knew you had a cake, any more than I knew that Bull had a bag of biscuits," said Bunter. "I never touched either of them. Besides, it was only a measly small cake, with hardly any sultanas in it—not at all like the cakes I get from home."

"Well, my word!" said Bob.

"Not that I touched it—I wouldn't!" said Bunter. "I hope I'm a fellow to be trusted with the key of a chap's cupboard. But to come back to business, you fellows, I think it's up to you to help me out, after landing me in this fearful scrape—and Wib's willing to help. He said so."

"Well, if Wib's willing to help, I suppose we can help," said Harry Wharton. "You don't deserve it, but we'll try. What do you want us to do?"

"Good!" said Bunter with great satisfaction. "It's a splendid idea I've got, really splendid—I thought it out for myself, you know."

"That doesn't argue much for it," remarked Bob. "But let's hear it. Blessed if I can see anything that we can do."

"Old Prout's in the quad now," said Bunter.

"Well?"

"He always takes his evening trot at this time," went on Bunter. "It's pretty dark in the quad—especially on the path under the elms where Prouty does his evening canter."

"Do you want us to waylay him and kidnap him?" inquired Johnny Bull sarcastically.

"Nunno! Not exactly that——"

"Oh, good!"

"But it's a splendid stunt—really splendid! Wibley's going to help with the disguises."

"Disguises!" ejaculated Wharton.

"Yes. I asked him, and he said he would. Wib's always ready for anything in the theatrical line, you know. He's coming here with the things."

"What on earth are you driving at?" demanded Wharton, in great mystification. "What do we want disguises for?"

"So that Prout won't know you, of course. You see, when you rush on him——"

"Rush on him!" yelled Bob Cherry.

"Yes, when you rush on him."

"Rush on a form-master?"

"That's it—when you rush on him and seize him."

"S-s-sis-sis-seize him?"

"When you rush on him and seize him, he will take you for Bolsheviks."

"Bolsheviks!" howled Bob.

"That's the idea. You rush on him and seize him, and brandish a knife over his chivvy."

"D-d-do we?" gasped Wharton.

"I don't think!"

"And then I rush to the rescue," went on Bunter brightly.

"You—you—you rush to the rescue?"

"Yes—happening to be strolling in the quad, thinking of—of my lessons, I hear the

GREYFRIARS SCHOOL, KENT

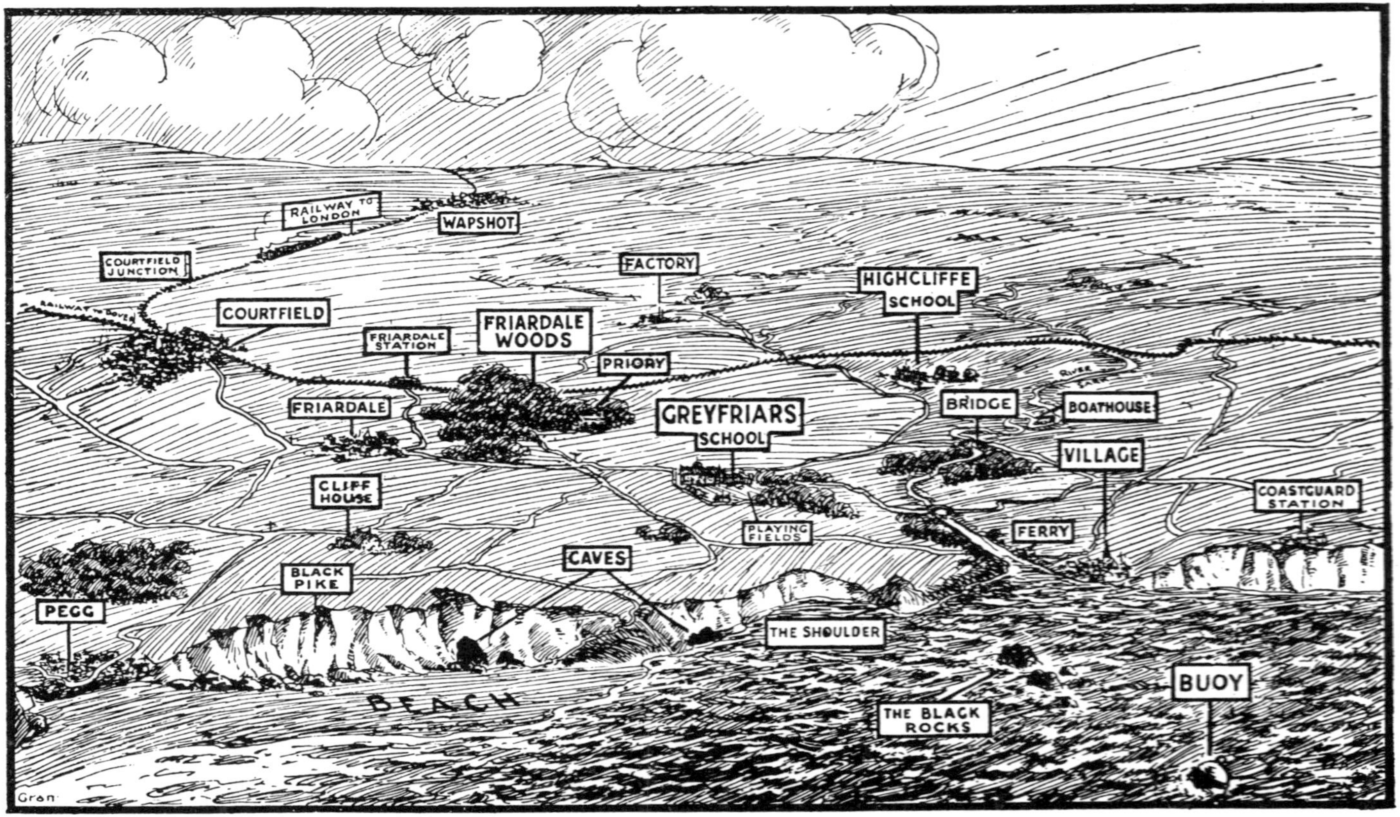
RAILWAY TO LONDON
WAPSHOT
COURTFIELD JUNCTION
FACTORY
HIGHCLIFFE SCHOOL
RAILWAY TO DOVER
COURTFIELD
FRIARDALE STATION
FRIARDALE WOODS
PRIORY
RIVER SARK
BRIDGE
BOATHOUSE
FRIARDALE
GREYFRIARS SCHOOL
VILLAGE
CLIFF HOUSE
COASTGUARD STATION
PLAYING FIELDS
FERRY
CAVES
BLACK PIKE
PEGG
THE SHOULDER
BUOY
BEACH
THE BLACK ROCKS
Gran

A GENERAL PLAN OF SURROUNDING DISTRICT

row, and rush to the rescue. Scattering you fellows with blows right and left, I——"

" I'd like to see you do it ! " roared Bob Cherry.

" Well, you will see me do it. That's all right."

" Scattering us ! " growled Johnny Bull. " Why, you—you frabjous jabberwock, you couldn't scatter a hutch of bunny rabbits."

" Of course, you fellows will agree to be scattered," said Bunter. " That's in the programme. Seriously, of course, I couldn't thrash the lot of you at once."

" Not all at once ? " ejaculated Wharton.

" Not more than two at a time, I think," answered Bunter calmly. " I'm not a Hercules, you know."

" He—he—he couldn't thrash us more than two at a time he thinks ! " babbled Bob Cherry. " Oh, my Uncle Christopher ! Oh, my Aunt Belinda ! Wake me up presently ! "

" Of course, I sha'n't really hurt you," said Bunter reassuringly. " I shall simply knock you right and left."

" I can see you doing it, I don't think ! " grinned Nugent.

" Of course, you're to let me do it—that's the programme," said Bunter peevishly. " Hurled right and left by my gallant attack."

" Ye gods ! "

" You bolt for your lives, leaving me victorious. I raise Prout from the ground——"

" Are you going to take a steam-crane in your pocket ? "

" Well, I help him up, you know, and he thanks me, with tears of gratitude in his eyes. See ? "

" Oh, crikey ! "

" That's the stunt—to appeal to his gratitude," explained Bunter, evidently quite satisfied with his marvellous scheme. " After I've rescued him from a gang of Bolsheviks, he can't very well pitch into me, can he ? "

" Bolsheviks ! " repeated Bob Cherry dazedly. " And how are you going to account for Bolsheviks being at Greyfriars ? Lenin and Trotsky don't live here."

" Oh, there are Bolsheviks in England, lots of them. Old Prout was at the meeting in Courtfield the other day, denouncing the Bolsheviks," said Bunter. " Suppose some of

them heard him—well, they might come along one evening to give him a hiding. Besides, it won't be necessary to account for them. You fellows will get your rig off, long before Prouty has got his second wind, if you bump him rather hard."

" Oh ! "

" It will remain a mystery where the ruffians came from, and where they disappeared to," said Bunter triumphantly. " See ? What do you fellows think of the stunt ? "

Harry Wharton and Co. didn't tell Bunter what they thought of his remarkable stunt. They couldn't. They could only gasp.

The study door opened, and Wibley of the Remove came in with a big bag in his hand, and a business-like expression in his face.

" Here I am ! " he announced cheerfully. " You fellows ready ? "

THE EIGHTH CHAPTER.

Reluctant Recruits.

HARRY WHARTON AND Co. blinked at William Wibley. That cheery youth was ready for business, though the Co. certainly were not. Anything was welcome to Wib if it gave him a chance of performing in his favourite line, and where anything in the nature of theatricals was concerned, Wib did not stop to think of the consequences. But the Famous Five did. The consequences of attacking a Form-master, even in the character of Bolsheviks, seemed likely to be a little too serious.

Wibley set his big bag on a chair, and opened it. He drew out a handful of false beards to begin with.

Billy Bunter blinked on with approval.

" Good ! " he said.

" Look here, Wib——" began Wharton.

" I've got a pretty good assortment of things here," said Wibley, " I can rig you up in great style. You needn't be afraid that anybody will know you when I've finished. Your own paters and maters wouldn't know you when I've done. Rely on me."

" But——"

" Something hairy and dingy and wild—that's Bolshevik style," explained Wibley. " I'll knock you off to a T."

" We're not going to be made up ! " roared Bob Cherry.

" Eh ? "

" You can take that rubbish away."

" Rubbish ! " exclaimed Wibley warmly. " What are you calling rubbish ? "

Bob Cherry pointed to the bag.

" Ass ! " said Wibley. " Fathead ! Duffer ! Chump ! Why, these are some of the best props of the Remove Dramatic Society. You howling, frabjous chump——"

" I say, you fellows ! "

" Look here," exclaimed Harry Wharton, in exasperation, " it's all rot ! We're not going to do anything of the kind."

" Oh, really, Wharton——"

" Then what the thump was I brought here for ? " demanded Wibley wrathfully. " Here I've sorted out suitable props for Bolshies, and arranged the whole bizney, and now you tell me you haven't nerve enough to go through with the game. Look here——"

" 'Tain't a question of nerve, fathead. But——"

" Cold feet, what ? " snorted Wibley.

" No ! " roared Johnny Bull, " Bless your cheek ! It's nothing of the sort."

" Then what is it ? "

" We're not going to play the goat, and get a flogging all round from the Head for it, you silly ass."

" What did you arrange it for, then ? "

" We haven't arranged it——"

" Bunter said——"

" I—I—I say, you fellows," stammered Bunter.

" Bunter said it was all arranged," snapped Wibley, " I've come here to fix you up. Now you tell me there's nothing doing. Br-r-r-r."

" Bunter, you cheeky clam——"

" I—I meant it was going to be arranged, you know," stammered Bunter, " and—and it is arranged now. Wharton's promised."

" Promised ! " howled Wharton.

" Yes, certainly."

" I haven't promised anything of the kind. I——"

" You have ! " roared Bunter, indignantly. " You said you'd do anything you could, didn't you ? "

" Yes ; but——"

" Well, you can do this."

" You fat duffer ! " exclaimed Frank Nugent warmly. " We weren't thinking of committing assault and battery on a form-master, when we said we'd do anything we could."

" We never thought——" began Bob.

Bunter sniffed scornfully.

" Well, you should think, before you make promises," he answered. " You've promised now."

" We haven't ! " shouted Johnny Bull.

" You jolly well have ; and I hold you to it," said Bunter.

" I- -I—I'll jolly well——"

" Here, you keep off ! " howled Bunter. " I'm not going to lick you now, Bull. You've got to play up. You can't back out now. Don't be a funk."

" A—a—a funk ! Why, I'll—I'll——"

Billy Bunter dodged round Wibley. Johnny Bull was looking quite dangerous.

" I say, you fellows, keep him off ! I—I say, Wharton, you promised to help me out of my scrape, you know—and it was Bob landed me in it, wasn't it ? It's up to you, and you know it is."

" But this stunt is all rot," exclaimed Wharton. " It's all bosh ! How can we handle Prout—a form-master——"

" Easy enough," said Wibley, who evidently did not want to be disappointed. " I can make you up so that Prout won't know you from Lenin or Trotsky. You lie low under the elms, and jump on him suddenly. You mop him up, in the wink of an eye. It's easy enough."

" You crass ass," said Johnny Bull, " you're as big an idiot as Bunter ! Suppose Prouty spots us ? "

" He won't, if I make you up."

" But suppose he does ? " hooted Johnny.

" What's the good of supposing the impossible ? If I make you up, you can't be spotted," said Wibley confidently. " The fact is, I rather like the idea—it will be experience for me. Any experience of this sort is useful to a chap who goes in for private theatricals. I don't think you fellows ought to back out."

" Are you going to help ? " asked Bob.

" I'm going to make you up."

" But in handling Prout——."

" That's not in my line. I simply come in as dresser," explained Wibley, " I can promise you a really artistic make-up, that would take in Lenin himself. If Trotsky met you, after I've done, he'd take you for his long-lost brothers."

" Oh, you ass ! " gasped Bob.

" It's really too bad of you fellows to get funky, after all the trouble I've taken, and Wib's taken," said Bunter, plaintively. " I really thought you fellows had more nerve."

" You've got plenty of nerve, anyway, to ask us to play the goat in such a fatheaded way," said Harry, angrily.

" Well, you said you'd do what you could——"

" We can't do it ! Handling a form-master is too serious. Why, it would mean a flogging all round, if it came out."

" And it would be bound to come out," said Nugent.

Wibley shook his head.

" Not unless you give yourselves away on purpose," he said, " I tell you, with my make-up, you could take in anybody. Lenin himself——"

" Oh, hang Lenin ! "

" Or Trotsky——"

" Hang Trotsky ! "

" Well, I dare say they'll both be hanged some day," assented Wibley, " but that's neither here nor there. The question is, are you fellows game enough to carry out the scheme ? "

" We're game enough, but——"

" The butfulness is terrific," said Hurree Singh, with a shake of his dusky head.

" I say, you fellows, it's as easy as falling off a form," urged Bunter. " You clear off as soon as I've rescued Prout, and you get your rig off in a jiffy and vanish. Nobody would think of connecting you with the Bolshevik ruffians who had attacked Prouty."

" Bolshevik rats ! It's too idiotic."

" Prout would be no end grateful to me, and he would shake hands with me instead of giving me a thundering hiding," said Bunter. " Think of that ! "

" I don't see that it matters if you get a thundering hiding."

" Oh, really, Cherry——"

" Besides, how do you know he would be grateful ? " demanded Wharton restively. " I haven't noticed anything specially grateful about old Prout. More likely he would be in a fearful wax, and he might take it out of you."

" Well, he would be bound to be grateful to a fellow who rescued him at the risk of his life," said Bunter. " Even form-masters have feelings, just like human beings. I'll chance that, if you'll play up. And you've as good as promised, too. I'm really relying on you fellows."

" Oh, rot ! " said Harry uneasily.

" It would be rather a lark ! " remarked Bob Cherry doubtfully. " If—if we got away without being spotted——"

" No end of a lark ! " urged Wibley.

" Well, if it's such a lark, you can take a hand in it yourself," grunted Johnny Bull, " you can take the lead, Wib, and ask your study-mates to play Bolshevik. Rake and Morgan and Desmond will jump at the chance —I don't think."

" Oh, be reasonable ! " said Wibley.

" Isn't that reasonable ? " hooted Johnny Bull.

" The question is, are you fellows game ? " snapped Wibley. " If you're not, say so, and I'll clear."

" The gamefulness is terrific, but——"

" Rot ! " said Johnny Bull. " Suppose we agree——"

" That's right," said Bunter. " I'm glad you agree. Now——"

" I said, suppose we agree——"

" All right ; and suppose we get on with it, instead of talking so much," said Bunter briskly. " There's an awful lot of jaw goes on in this study, I must say. You chaps talk too much."

" I say, suppose we agree," roared Johnny Bull ; " then how are we going out of the house got up as Bolsheviks ? Suppose we meet Quelchy, or the Head ! Suppose we meet Wingate or Loder ? Suppose——"

" You're supposing a thumping lot——"

" Well, there's something in that," admitted Wibley. " Better not make up here. We'd better get round to the wood-shed, and I'll

Five shadowy, shaggy-bearded, slouch-hatted figures rushed on Mr. Prout from under the trees. The rush was so sudden that Mr. Prout was taken utterly by surprise. (See page 34.)

make you up there. That's quite a valuable suggestion, Bull. Come on."

"Come on! Where?"

"To the wood-shed, of course, if I'm going to make you up there."

"But we haven't agreed——

"Oh, I thought you had. I wish you'd make up your minds—life's short, you know," said Wibley sarcastically.

"I think it's all dashed rot!" growled Johnny Bull. "What does it matter if Prouty thrashes Bunter? It will do him good."

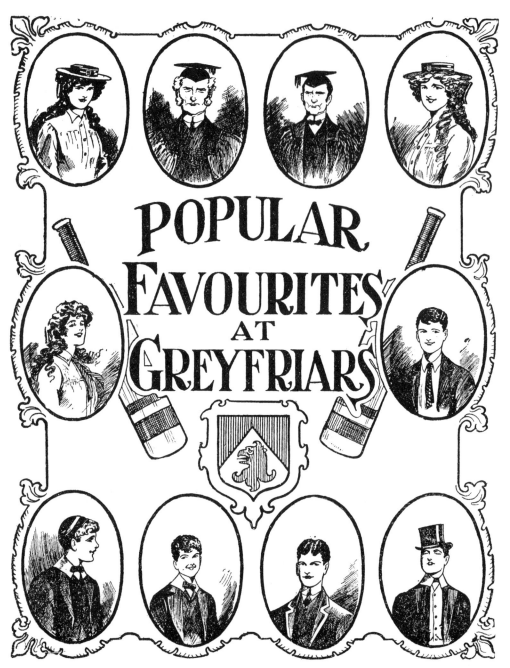

POPULAR FAVOURITES AT GREYFRIARS

Reading from left to right: Marjorie Hazeldene, Dr. H. H. Locke (Headmaster): Mr. Henry Quelch, Clara Trevelyan, Phyllis Howell, Frank Courtenay, Dick Penfold, Dick Nugent, Peter Hazeldene, Lord Mauleverer.

" And he's asked for it," said Nugent.

" The askfulness was great."

" I say, you fellows, I'm relying on you, you know. I thought my old pals would stand by me," said Bunter reproachfully. " Have a little pluck, you know."

" You fat idiot ! "

" And you've as good as promised—in fact, quite promised."

Harry Wharton made an impatient gesture.

" I think it's all rot," he said. " But I dare say we could pull it off. We have sort of half-promised that fat rotter——"

" Oh, really, you know——"

" We're game if it comes to that," continued the captain of the Remove. " Look here, I'm willing to put it to the vote. I'll play up if you fellows care to."

" That's right ! " said Bunter. " Come on, then——"

" Oh, anything for a quiet life," said Bob Cherry. " Besides it will really be rather a lark."

There was a grunt from Johnny Bull, but he assented at last ; and Hurree Jamset Ram Singh and Frank Nugent gave in their assent also. And the decision having been reached, the Famous Five followed Bunter and Wibley from the study—to make their preparations for carrying out Bunter's amazing " stunt."

THE NINTH CHAPTER.

The Amateur Bolsheviks.

A BIKE lantern and a candle glimmered in the wood-shed, while William Wibley unpacked his bag.

Wibley was quite enthusiastic.

He was looking forward to turning out five really artistic Bolsheviks, true to type ; worthy followers of Lenin and Trotsky. It was an opportunity for exercising his peculiar gifts. Wibley thought of that and of little else. The fellows who were to play Bolsheviks naturally thought a little more. But they had consented now.

The Famous Five looked very restive, but they raised no further objections—having agreed.

As for Billy Bunter, he was purring with contentment.

He was going to escape a terrific licking, and he was also going to shine in the rôle of heroic rescuer. Bunter was picturing, in his fat mind, quite a dramatic scene, when Mr. Prout would shake him by the hand and thank him, in a voice full of emotion, for his devoted courage. Bunter had reason to be pleased with the prospect—which the schoolboy Bolsheviks hadn't.

Wibley was quickly at work.

There was no time to waste if Mr. Prout was to be caught before he finished his evening stroll in the quadrangle.

Mr. Prout's regular evening canter, as Bunter called it, generally occupied half an hour, or so, and he had already started.

Harry Wharton and Co. meekly followed Wib's directions. Over their own clothes they donned the garments Wibley had selected for them, as suitable for amateur Bolsheviks.

The additional garments gave them quite a bulky appearance, and they certainly looked a large size for schoolboys.

Wibley, with charcoal and grease paints, started work on their faces, and the difference he made in their looks was startling.

Five fresh young faces were changed into five swarthy, wrinkled visages that looked at least fifty years old.

The addition of shaggy beards and whiskers and moustaches completed the transformation.

The chums of the Remove could not help grinning as they looked at one another.

" What a set of pictures ! " murmured Bob Cherry.

" I don't think Major Cherry would know you now—what ? " remarked Wibley complacently.

" My hat ! I think not."

" I say, you fellows, you do look a set of guys ! " chortled Billy Bunter. " He, he, he ! I should like to meet you lot on a dark night ! "

" Kick him ! " growled Johnny Bull.

" Here's your hats," said Wibley.

Five slouched hats were added to five shaggy heads, and Wibley rubbed his hands with deep satisfaction.

Whether the Famous Five looked like Bolsheviks, was a little difficult to decide, as none of those cheery gentry had ever been seen at Greyfriars. But they certainly looked like a particularly reckless and ferocious set of ruffianly Anarchists.

" I think that will do," said Wibley. " Mind, you're not to speak while you're tackling Prouty. That would give it away. Unless you could speak a few words in Russian. That would add to the effect, of course. Any of you know any Russian ? "

" No, ass ! "

" I think I could manage a few words," said Bob Cherry. " Such as caskowiski, buzzoff, gotsuchakoffski——"

" Ha, ha, ha ! "

" I say, you fellows, you'll do splendidly ! " said Bunter. " You look an awful lot of ruffians—much more so than usual——"

" What ? "

" I—I mean, you'll do first rate. Now I'll get off, and keep an eye on Prout, ready to rush in when you handle him. Make a row when you tackle him, because I mustn't get too near him—he mustn't spot me before I rush to the rescue, or he might pile in with the licking at the wrong moment. Are you fellows ready ? "

" Oh, we're ready."

" I'll get off, then."

Billy Bunter rolled out of the wood-shed, with a soft chuckle. Everything in the garden, so to speak, was lovely, from Bunter's point of view.

Wibley gave a few finishing touches to his artistic handiwork.

" Oh, that'll do," said Johnny Bull. " Let's get out."

" You'll scoot back here afterwards," said Wibley. " I'll help you off with the things. You can change, and wash your chivvies here, and then we'll all join in the crowd—there'll be a crowd, you know, as soon as it gets out that there's Bolshies in the quad——"

" I should say so ! " grinned Nugent.

" We crowd round with the rest, and nobody's the wiser," said Wibley. " Easy as winking, you know. I'll wait here for you, and I'll have the soap and water all ready. Now you can get going."

The Famous Five got going.

They left the wood-shed, and disappeared into the shadows, and Wibley watched them from the doorway till they vanished.

He turned back into the wood-shed, with a chuckle, greatly pleased. There was a tap in the shed, and Wibley proceeded to prepare for the ablutions of the Bolsheviks—which would have to be conducted rather hurriedly when the time came. He drew a basin of water, and placed soap and towels and scrubbing brushes and sponges in readiness.

He had just finished when there was a step in the wood-shed, and he spun round from the sink.

" Hullo, you back already ! Oh, my hat ! "

It was Gosling, the porter.

Gosling stared at Wibley, with grim suspicion.

William Wibley blinked at him.

Wibley had thought of a good many things ——of nearly everything, in fact—but he had not thought of Gosling.

The light in the wood-shed had drawn Gosling's attention, as he was making his evening round, and he had naturally come there to investigate.

" Well, Master Wibley ? " said Gosling grimly.

" Well ? " stammered Wibley.

" P'r'aps you'll explain what you're hup to 'ere, at this time o' night," suggested Gosling, with sarcastic politeness.

" I—I—no reason why I shouldn't be in the wood-shed, if I want to," said Wibley, feeling deeply thankful that Gosling had not happened to come along there ten minutes earlier.

" P'r'aps—and p'r'aps not," said Gosling sourly. " Wot I says is this 'ere, you're up to some game 'ere, Master Wibley. I knows you. Wot are you droring that there water for ? "

" Why shouldn't I ? "

" Going to wash 'ere, p'raps ? " suggested Gosling, in the same vein of sarcasm.

" Perhaps ! "

" And wot's all this 'ere ? " continued Gosling, with a nod towards the grease-paints that were still in view on the bench close at hand.

" Ahem ! "

Bump! bump! bump! The Famous **Five** did not explain what they were at; it was **a** time for deeds, not words. William Wibley sat on the dormitory floor, and gasped, when they had finished with him. (See page 50.)

"P'raps you'd rather not explain, Master Wibley, what you're up to 'ere."

"Well, it isn't your bizney, is it?" remarked Wibley.

"P'raps, and p'raps not. It's my business to report yer," answered Gosling sourly. "I knows that! You can explain to Mr. Quelch, Master Wibley, and if there ain't any 'arm in it, why, you're all right, ain't you?"

"Oh, my hat!" murmured Wibley.

"P'raps you'll be so kind as to come to Mr. Quelch with me now," went on Gosling, with grim humour.

Wibley drew a deep breath.

" The—the fact is, I— I've been doing some —some practice at make-up, Gossy," he said. " No harm done, you know. By the way, I believe this half-crown is yours, Gossy."

Gosling's horny hand closed on the half-crown, and he grinned faintly. He hesitated, but no doubt he argued it out in his mind that a half-crown was a half-a-crown, for he turned to leave the wood-shed. Wibley almost gasped with relief to see him go.

But as Gosling passed through the doorway, there came a sudden, terrific uproar from the direction of the quadrangle—and Gosling halted, rooted to the ground.

THE TENTH CHAPTER.

A Bolshevik Atrocity!

M R. PROUT ambled gently along the path under the elms, his hands folded behind his back, and a thoughtful expression on his face.

Probably he was thinking of those exciting old days when he had hunted the festive grizzly in his native lair—glorious old days upon which Mr. Prout loved to dwell, in thought and in conversation.

Indeed, those old days were more glorious now than they had been at the time, for Mr. Prout's memory was enriched by the passing years, and his ancient exploits grew more and more heroic and startling seen through the mists of time.

He was not thinking of Bunter. He had not forgiven Bunter, by any means ; but he had given up looking for the elusive fat junior. He intended to drop in at the Remove dormitory at bed-time, when he was sure of finding Bunter. Meanwhile, the owl of the Remove was dismissed from his mind.

Mr. Prout, as he paced majestically up and down the shadowy path between rows of dark trees, was fighting ancient battles over again. From the Rocky Mountains his active mind wandered to the Russian steppes, where he had also played Nimrod in those old days when the centuries numbered only nineteen. Russian steppes brought Bolshevism to his mind—and Mr. Prout frowned. Mr. Prout stood very sturdily for law and order, and he was down on Bolsheviks with

a tremendous down. He had attended meetings, and addressed meetings, in denunciation of Trotsky and Co.

Anyone observing Mr. Prout's plump face just then might have been very much entertained. The frown was succeeded by a smile—a tender smile—and Mr. Prout glanced up at the stars. Certainly Mr. Quelch, if he had been on the spot, could have guessed the Fifth-form master's thoughts at that moment, for Mr. Quelch had been the recipient of Mr. Prout's confidences on the subject of a certain lovely Russian countess, into whose dark eyes, as Mr. Prout expressed it poetically, he had gazed, and found them all too beautiful —or as the Removites would have described it, to whom Mr. Prout had given the glad eye !

Mr. Prout had reached that poetical stage in his reflections, when there was a sudden stir under the dark trees.

The next moment, lovely Russian countesses and everything else were jolted out of Mr. Prout's mind, as five shadowy, shaggy-bearded, slouch-hatted figures rushed on him from under the trees.

The rush was so sudden that Mr. Prout was taken utterly by surprise.

Before he knew what was happening, he was grasped on all sides, and rushed off his feet.

Bump !

" Oh ! Ah ! Yooop ! Whoooop ! "

The Fifth-form master plumped on the ground and spluttered.

Over him loomed shaggy-bearded ruffians.

Hands grasped him on all sides as the astounded form-master floundered and spluttered and gasped.

" Good heavens ! What—what—— "

" Seize him ! " came a deep, bass voice.

" Help ! "

" Chop off his headski ! "

" Bless my soul ! Release me ! Who—what —yarooooh ! "

" Where's the knifovich ? Bolsheviki biski wiski ! "

" Help ! "

Mr. Prout hardly knew whether he was on his head or his heels.

He rolled on the ground, in the grasp of

"The gallant lad is wounded!" exclaimed Mr. Prout. "Lean on my arm, Bunter—let me support you, my boy! Bless my soul! Only to think that a few hours since, I was about to inflict corporal chastisement upon this noble boy!" (See page 38.)

many hands, bumped and rumpled and flustered and breathless.

The hoarse ejaculations of the ruffians who had seized him struck terror to his soul.

Among those remarkable ejaculations the word "Bolsheviki" struck him, and it made him realise into what terrible hands he had fallen.

"Help!" shrieked Mr. Prout. "Police! Help! Yaroooooh!"

"Bolsheviki booshki wooshki!"

"Cut his head offski!"

"Gimme the dynamitavich."

"Help! Yarooooh! Help!" roared the Fifth-form master. "Police! Help! Leggo! Yarooooop!"

A fat form loomed up in the shadows.

A pair of big spectacles glimmered through the gloom.

It was Bunter rushing to the rescue.

"Look outski! Here comes somebodyovich."

"Help!"

"I'm coming, sir!" shouted Billy Bunter valorously.

And he came.

Considering that the Bolsheviks were five to one their retreat was rather inglorious.

But they did retreat.

As Bunter rushed into the fray the shaggy ruffians rushed out of it.

Bunter—no doubt with the idea of making the scene more realistic—hit out at them with his fat fists, and there was a fiendish yell as one of his drives caught a Bolshevik under the ear.

A drive with Bunter's weight behind it was no joke.

The hapless Bolshevik reeled over Mr. Prout, and fell on him, just as the Fifth-form master was seeking to rise, and flattened him to the earth again.

A gasp of anguish escaped from Mr. Prout as he was flattened.

"Groogh! Help! Ooooop!"

"Yow!" roared the Bolshevik. "Oh, my hat!"

Four Bolsheviks were running under the trees, and the fifth scrambled off Mr. Prout in a hurry.

The Fifth-form master made a clutch at him—the fighting instinct of the old huntsman was roused now—and grabbed the Bolshevik by the beard.

Mr. Prout would certainly have secured a prisoner, but fortunately the beard and the Bolshevik parted company.

The beard remained in Mr. Prout's hand, and the Bolshevik jumped at Bunter.

"Yarooh!" howled Bunter as the shaggy ruffian—not quite so shaggy now that Mr.

Prout had shaved him, as it were—grasped him hard. "Leggo! You silly ass! Yoooop."

Pommel, pommel, pommel!

"You fat idiot!" hissed the voice of Johnny Bull. "Wharrer you punch me for? Take that, and that!"

Mr. Prout scrambled breathlessly up.

"Help!" he roared. "Is—is that you, Bunter? Hold him. I am coming to your aid."

The Bolshevik released Billy Bunter as if the owl of the Remove had suddenly become red-hot.

As Mr. Prout clutched at him he darted among the trees and disappeared.

"Yow-ow-ow!" came from Bunter.

"Oh, dear! Bless my soul!" gasped Mr. Prout. "Help! Bolsheviks—actually, Bolshevik ruffians! Help!"

There was not much need for Mr. Prout to shout now. The uproar had been heard all over Greyfriars.

Doors and windows opened on all sides, and lights flashed and gleamed into the dusky quadrangle. Inquiring voices shouted from all directions.

"What's the row?"

"What the thunder ——"

"Help!"

"Ow, ow!"

Mr. Prout continued to roar, and Bunter to howl. Amid the shadows of the quadrangle five Bolsheviks were fleeing for their lives.

The drama had been enacted, the gallant rescue had been performed, and it only remained for the Bolsheviks to vanish from the face of the earth and for the Famous Five of the Remove to return to existence.

There was no time to lose, and Harry Wharton & Co. ran hard to get quite clear before the gathering crowd arrived on the scene of the Bolshevik outrage. They swept round the corner of the schoolhouse at a distance from the building, and headed for the wood-shed.

"Hold on, we're not all here!" gasped Bob Cherry. "Who's missing?"

"I'm coming!" came a voice from behind, the voice of Johnny Bull. "I only stopped to punch Bunter."

"You ass!"

"Well, he punched me!"

"Where's your beard?"

"Blessed if I know, unless Prout's got it! He grabbed me. That fat idiot Bunter fairly planted me on him."

"Oh, my hat!"

"Buck up!" panted Wharton. "We've got to get clear—quick! There'll be a search. Buck up! Into the wood-shed—quick!"

The breathless five rushed on to the wood-shed.

There was a sudden collision in the gloom and a howl.

"Ow! Who's that? Oh, my eye!"

"Gosling!" stuttered Nugent.

"Oh, crikey! Bunk for it!"

The juniors, in utter dismay, scattered and fled. The wood-shed was barred as they had run into Gosling almost in the doorway. It was cruel luck just as they had been so successful.

They ran for the darkness, but they reckoned without their host, in the shape of Gosling. Gosling, startled by the uproar, and terrified by the sudden appearance of five shaggy ruffians, was backing away; but as the ruffians ran Gosling gave chase. It was Gosling's duty to deal with those ruffianly invaders of the school precincts, and, as they were running, Gosling felt himself as brave as a lion.

"Stop, you raskils!" yelled Gosling valiantly.

"Put it on!" gasped Wharton.

"You bet! Oh, my hat!"

Hurree Jamset Ram Singh stumbled in the dark and fell on his knees. He jumped up, and, as he did so, Gosling ran into him from behind. The nabob of Bhanipur sprawled forward on his face, with a gasping yell, and Gosling sprawled over him.

"Got one of 'em, anyhow," gasped Gosling. "'Elp! 'Elp! 'Elp!"

THE ELEVENTH CHAPTER.

Heroic Bunter!

"BUNTER! My brave lad——"

"Oh, sir!"

"Are you hurt, my gallant fellow?"

"I—I think I've been shot, sir——"

"What?"

"I—I mean stabbed——"

"Bless my soul! Help!"

Wingate of the Sixth rushed up, with a bike lantern gleaming in his hand. The alarm was general now; juniors, seniors, and masters were turning out on all sides. The Head himself was in the doorway of the school-house, looking out into the dusky quad with startled eyes.

"What is it?" gasped Wingate.

"Help!"

"But what—what——" exclaimed Mr. Quelch, the Remove master, coming up breathlessly.

"They are gone!" gasped Mr. Prout, blinking round ferociously. "The ruffians have made off. It is well for them—had they remained, I would have——"

"The—the what?"

"The Bolshevik ruffians——"

"Bub-bub-bolshevik ruffians!" stuttered Mr. Quelch.

"Yes, sir; I have been attacked by savage Bolsheviks——"

"Mr. Prout!"

"By savage Bolsheviks, sir—irreclaimable ruffians, sir—here in the quadrangle of Greyfriars——"

"Impossible!"

"Sir!"

"Really, Mr. Prout—what you say is—is—is——" Mr. Quelch paused and blinked at the Fifth-Form master's flushed and excited face. He knew that Mr. Prout was a temperate man, as a rule, but he could not help wondering whether the form-master had not, for once, been indulging in the cup that cheers and also inebriates.

"I repeat, sir, that I have been attacked by Bolsheviks, and that the ruffians are still at large, within the walls of Greyfriars," exclaimed Mr. Prout, warmly. "Bunter, who gallantly came to my help, has been stabbed——"

"Good heavens! Bunter——"

Billy Bunter gave a deep groan. He was a little hurt; Johnny Bull was a hard hitter. But there really was no occasion for that deep groan, save for dramatic effect.

However, it produced its effect.

THE
GREYFRIARS GALLERY IN VERSE

By Dick Penfold

No. 3: Horace Coker

Who seeks to take the world by storm,
And thinks he's ruler of his Form
In class, and playing-field, and dorm?
　　　　　　Why, COKER!

Who grinds out poems by the yard,
And really is a comic card?
Who'd benefit by "six months' hard"?
　　　　　　Why, COKER!

Who once played footer in his pride,
And caused amusement far and wide
By netting for the other side?
　　　　　　Why, COKER!

When Aunty's "tips" come on the scene,
Who sits before a spread serene
With one who's Potty, one who's Greene?
　　　　　　Why, COKER!

Who keeps his schoolmates bright and gay
By spelling "captain" with a "k"?
Who gave the "Koker Kup" away?
　　　　　　Why, COKER!

Who really is a mighty man?
Who japes Removites (when he can!)?
Who leaves George Robey "also ran"?
　　　　　　Why, COKER!

"The gallant lad is wounded," exclaimed Mr. Prout. "Lean on my arm, Bunter—let me support you, my boy! Bless my soul! Only to think that, a few hours since, I was about to inflict corporal chastisement upon this noble boy——"

"Bunter! Bring your light here, Wingate, please! Where are you wounded, Bunter?" exclaimed Mr. Quelch.

"I—I—I——"

"I see no trace of blood," said the Remove master drily, as he examined the heroic youth in the lantern-light. "Kindly tell me precisely where the wound is situated, Bunter."

"I—I think the knife must have missed me, after all, sir," said Bunter. "I—I struck the villain a fearful blow at the same moment, sir, and—and the knife must have passed between my arm and my body, sir."

"Oh!"

"I—I felt it pass, sir—a gleaming, flashing blade——"

"What a terribly narrow escape," exclaimed Mr. Prout. "I am thankful it is no worse. Bunter—my brave lad——"

"Oh, not at all, sir," said Bunter modestly. "Any fellow would have done it, sir."

"Possibly!" said Mr. Quelch, who was not nearly so romantic an old gentleman as Mr. Prout. "But what exactly did you do, Bunter?"

"I rushed to the rescue, sir——"

"What?"

"Seeing Mr. Prout attacked by Bolsheviks, sir——"

"Nonsense."

"Not at all nonsense, Mr. Quelch," exclaimed the Fifth-Form master, hotly. "Bunter's statement is exactly correct. I was attacked by Bolsheviks, and they are still at large. At any moment they may fire upon us, if they are armed with automatic pistols, as these miscreants generally are. We are wasting time, sir——"

"But——"

"They must be sought for at once, sir, and seized!" exclaimed Mr. Prout. "But we must be armed—armed! I will fetch my rifle——"

"Mr. Prout——"

"What ever is the matter?" demanded Dr. Locke. "Bolsheviks, sir!" howled Billy Bunter. Mr. Quelch was about to speak, when from the distance beyond the school-buildings came a husky yell. (See page 40.)

"There is not a moment to be lost, sir!" thundered Mr. Prout. "Do you wish to see Greyfriars the scene of massacre and bloodshed, sir?"

And Mr. Prout rushed off to the school-house for his famous rifle. Mr. Quelch devoutly hoped that he would not be able to find his cartridges. If he did, it was only too possible that there might be bloodshed and massacre at Greyfriars.

"Shall we—ahem!—hunt for the Bolsheviks, sir?" asked Wingate, with a cough.

"Not just yet, Wingate—Bunter had better tell us precisely what has occurred," said the Remove master drily. "I really fail to see how Bolsheviks could be in the school quadrangle, or why they should be here. Bunter, you say you saw Mr. Prout attacked——"

"By a gang of blood-thirsty Bolsheviks, sir," said Bunter.

Billy Bunter was swelling with importance now. There was a crowd round him, and all eyes were on Bunter. The Owl's original idea had been to earn Mr. Prout's gratitude, and thereby escape a licking; but he realised now that there was the chance of a lifetime for reaping glory.

Bunter had always been a hero in his own eyes; and he was quite willing to be a hero in the eyes of all Greyfriars.

"How did you know they were Bolsheviks?" inquired Mr. Quelch.

"Oh! I—I——"

"Well, Bunter?"

"They—they—they were talking in Russian, sir," stammered Bunter.

" Are you acquainted with the Russian language, Bunter ? "

" Nunno, sir."

" Then how do you know they were speaking in Russian ? "

" It—it—it sounded like Russian, sir—like—like a cat sneezing, sir."

" Oh ! And you came to help Mr. Prout——"

" I rushed on them like a lion, sir."

" Indeed ! That was not what I should have expected—from my knowledge of you, Bunter."

" W-w-wouldn't you, sir ? "

" I should not, Bunter. How many were there of these ruffians ? "

" Five, sir."

" And what happened when you rushed upon them ? "

" They—they ran, sir."

" Very extraordinary. I fail to see why five desperate ruffians should run away from you, Bunter."

Some of the onlookers were grinning now. It was pretty clear that Mr. Quelch did not take a dramatic view of the affair at all.

" They—they were frightened, I—I suppose, sir," said Bunter. " I—I'm rather a dangerous fellow, sir, when my blood's up."

" Ha, ha, ha ! "

" Silence, please. I really fail to see—what is it, Temple ? "

Temple of the Fourth was holding up something he had picked from the ground. Mr. Quelch blinked at it in the light.

" It's a false beard, sir," said Temple.

" Bless my soul ! "

It was Johnny Bull's beard which Mr. Prout had grabbed off and dropped. Mr. Quelch gazed at it blankly. This was an indubitable proof that someone—Bolshevik or not—had been there, and that the whole affair was not a hallucination of Mr. Prout's.

" Oh, crumbs ! " murmured Bunter. " The silly ass——"

" Bunter, what did you say ? "

" N-n-nothing, sir."

" It is certainly an artificial beard, such as is used in private theatricals, I believe," said Mr. Quelch, inspecting Temple's trophy.

" The—the ruffians may have been in dis-

guise, sir," ventured Bunter. " If—if they were Lenin and Trotsky——"

" Don't be foolish, Bunter."

" Oh, sir ! "

There was a rustle, and the crowd made way for the Head.

" Whatever is the matter ? " demanded Dr. Locke. " Mr. Prout has just rushed past me. He called out something, but did not stop."

" Bolsheviks, sir," said Bunter.

" What ? "

Mr. Quelch was about to speak when from the dark distance beyond the buildings came a husky yell.

" 'Elp ! 'Elp ! 'Elp ! "

The Remove master started.

" That's Gosling ! " exclaimed Wingate.

" Perhaps he's got them," exclaimed Coker of the Fifth.

" Oh, crikey ! " stuttered Bunter.

" 'Elp ! "

Wingate was already dashing off, and after him went Coker and Temple, and a crowd. Mr. Quelch stood nonplussed, wondering whether Mr. Prout's amazing tale was well founded after all.

" Bless my soul ! " said the Head. " This is—is—is——"

There was a rapid clatter of footsteps, and Mr. Prout rushed up, rifle in hand, with a bloodthirsty gleam behind his spectacles.

" Now I am ready for them ! " thundered Mr. Prout. " What—what—what is the matter, Quelch ? "

" Kindly turn that rifle in another direction, Mr. Prout."

" 'Elp ! " came a husky roar from the distance.

" Ha ! Gosling, they are attacking him. To the rescue ! " shouted Mr. Prout.

And he sped away with his rifle ready.

" I—I—I hope there will not be an accident ! " gasped the Head.

" It is most extraordinary ! I do not understand."

" 'Elp ! 'Elp ! "

The Head and Mr. Quelch hurried after the rescuers. They were almost wondering whether it was a dream, or whether Lenin, Trotsky, and Co. had really descended upon Greyfriars in force.

FATTY WYNN IS LEFT BEHIND!

(See "THE WANDERING SCHOOLBOY")

PRESS DAY IN THE OFFICE OF "THE GREYFRIARS HERALD."

" Well, Master Wibley ? " said Gosling grimly.   " Well ? " stammered Wibley.   " P'r'raps you'll explain what you're hup to 'ere, at this time of night ? " suggested Gosling, with sarcastic politeness.   (See page 32.)

THE TWELFTH CHAPTER.

The Prisoner!

" HERE they are ! "
        " 'Elp ! "
" We're coming ! "
" Stick to him, Gosling ! "
" Play up ! "

The rush of the rescuers surrounded Gosling and his prisoner, who were struggling on the ground.

Had the captured Bolshevik produced a knife or an automatic pistol, as a captured Bolshevik might have been expected to do,

Gosling would certainly have let him drop like a hot potato. But the Bolshevik didn't. He struggled to escape, and in the struggle Gosling made the discovery that he was a good deal bigger and stronger than his prisoner. So Gosling held on to him valiantly, and yelled for help as he held on.

Help came very quickly, which was unlucky for the helpless Bolshevik. Four fleeing juniors had discovered that one of the party was missing, and were turning back, and from another direction William Wibley was about to cut in to the rescue. But rescue was impossible, as Wingate, Coker, Temple, and two score more fellows rushed up with bike lanterns gleaming, and surrounded the struggling pair.

Wibley dodged into the wood-shed again in blank dismay. And Harry Wharton and Co. backed out of the circle of light equally dismayed.

"Who's missing?" gasped Wharton.

"Inky, I think."

"Inky!"

"It's poor old Inky!" stuttered Bob Cherry. "Gosling's got him. What awful luck! And now——"

"Oh, my hat!"

"Keep out of sight!"

That was all the unhappy Bolsheviks could do now. They could not charge through fifty fellows and rescue the unfortunate nabob of Bhanipur. But what was going to happen now was an appalling thought.

Round about Gosling and his prisoner the crowd surged in wild excitement. There was no doubt as to the truth of Mr. Prout's amazing tale now. For here was the Bolshevik—a shaggy, dingy, frowsy-looking ruffian, struggling in the grasp of Gosling the porter.

His struggles ceased quickly enough as Wingate and Coker grasped him, and then so many hands were laid upon him that there was hardly room for another finger.

"All right now, Gosling."

"Ow! I've got him!" gasped Gosling, pumping in breath. "He give me a 'ard fight. But I've got him!"

"Hurray!"

"There was others—a dozen or more!" spluttered Gosling. "A whole crowd of 'em—savage-looking brutes, too—jest like this one."

"Hold him!"

"Better knock him on the head!" exclaimed Coker of the Fifth. "Anybody got a club? Better stun him. Safer."

"Yaroooooh!"

"Hallo, he's found his voice!" said Temple.

"Better knock him clean on the head——"

"Let him alone, you ass," said Wingate, "we've got him safe enough. Put him on his feet."

The Bolshevik was dragged up.

"Hallo! Here comes Prout!"

"Look out! He's got his gun!"

"Oh, my hat!"

Mr. Prout came dashing up. The Fifth-Form master was his old self again now—once more the valiant Paul Prout of early years, who had tracked the grizzly in his lair, and whose gun had been so great a terror to the wolf and the bear as it was now to the Greyfriars' fellows.

"Is that one of them?" thundered Mr. Prout.

"We've got him, sir——"

"Surrender, ruffian — yield, Bolshevik scoundrel!" roared Mr. Prout. "One movement, and I will blow out your brains!"

"Mind that gun!"

"I say, keep that gun away!"

"I hope to goodness it's not loaded!"

"Where are the others?" demanded Mr. Prout. "There were four others—as rascally and hangdog as this ruffian!"

"They seem to have got away!"

"I will search for them—I will hunt them down, like vermin! Give me your lantern, Wingate! Follow me!"

Holding the lantern aloft in his left hand, and with the rifle in his right, Mr. Prout started. Some of the fellows followed him—but they kept well behind. The Bolshevik peril was not the greatest peril there.

Wingate and Coker, grasping the prisoner by the arms, marched him off to the school-house, with a dozen fellows round them. In the light from the big doorway they met Mr. Quelch and the Head—and Billy Bunter! Bunter's jaw dropped at the sight of the prisoner.

"What—what—who is this?" exclaimed the Head.

"One of them, sir," said Coker of the Fifth. "Shall I knock him on the head, sir?"

"Certainly not, Coker. Bless my soul! What a dreadful looking character," said the Head.

"A most abandoned looking ruffian!" exclaimed Mr. Quelch.

"I got him, sir!" said Gosling. "They was rushing at the wood-shed, the 'ole gang of 'em, sir!"

"Dear me! What could they have wanted in the wood-shed?" ejaculated the Head, in surprise. "Surely they could not have intended to steal the faggots ? "

"Why, he's larfing ! " exclaimed Gosling. The prisoner had certainly grinned for a moment.

"We'll give him something to laugh for, soon," said Coker, tightening his grip on the captured Bolshevik.

"They bunged right into me sir," went on the porter.

"They—they what, Gosling ? "

"Bunked into me, sir—biffed into me, I mean. I collared this cove, and the others 'ooked it," said Gosling.

"Bring him into the house, Wingate."

"Certainly, sir."

"He must be well guarded till the police can be called in."

"Why, he's larfing agin ! " exclaimed Gosling, in angry astonishment.

"Come on, you cheeky villain ! " said Coker.

The Bolshevik was marched into the house. The Greyfriars fellows, in a buzz of excitement, followed him in. Mr. Prout loomed up from the quadrangle, with a look of bitter disappointment on his face. He was not carrying the lantern now—he had a peculiar hairy bunch in his hand, and his rifle under his arm. He held up the bunch before the Head's astonished eyes.

"What—what—what is that ? " ejaculated Dr. Locke.

"False beards and whiskers, sir," said Mr. Prout. " The scoundrels were in disguise."

"Oh, crikey ! " murmured Bunter.

"They must have discarded their disguises, and fled from the precincts of the school," said Mr. Prout. " I am sorry they got away. I found these by the wall—in a heap. Had I sighted them I should certainly have shot them dead ! "

"Ow ! "

"Pray be silent, Bunter," said Mr. Quelch, frowning.

"I should have regarded it as justifiable homicide, under the circumstances," said Mr. Prout, ferociously. " I should have winged them, sir, with as little compunction as if——"

"Yes, yes, certainly. But——"

"This ruffian will doubtless reveal where his associates may be found, when he is in the hands of the police," said Mr. Prout, glaring at the captured Bolshevik, who was still helpless in the prasp of Wingate and Coker. " He will be charged with attempted murder—they were attempting my life when Bunter so gallantly rushed to my aid ! Bunter —where is Bunter ? You need not go away. Bunter."

"Oh ! Oh, really, sir ! "

"This gallant lad, Dr. Locke, dashed to my rescue, while I was struggling in the grasp of these lawless ruffians ! "

"Bless my soul ! "

"Bravo, Bunter ! " chirruped Squiff of the Remove.

Billy Bunter was not swelling now. He was waiting in anguish for the real identity of the captured Bolshevik to be revealed. Bunter's " stunt " did not seem now quite so ripping to its hapless originator.

"As the other ruffians were in disguise," continued Mr. Prout, " doubtless this rascal is also disguised. Perhaps you will ascertain, Mr. Quelch, while I keep my rifle ready, in case he should resist."

"Oh ! Certainly ! "

Mr. Quelch stepped towards the prisoner, whose shaggy face betrayed the most lively apprehension at his approach. The prisoner had not uttered a single word so far. The Greyfriars' fellows wondered whether he could speak English. As a matter of fact, they would have recognised his variety of English at once if he had spoken.

The Remove master was stretching his hand towards the prisoner's shaggy beard, when he stopped and uttered an ejaculation.

"Dear me ! What is that—what is that poking in my back ? "

"Merely the muzzle of my rifle, Mr. Quelch."

"Wha-a-at ! "

"My dear sir, there is no danger—my finger is very sure on the trigger. I should not be likely to press it by accident."

Mr. Quelch was spinning round like a spinning-top while Mr. Prout was speaking. He did not wait for him to finish.

"Mr. Prout, I insist upon that dangerous

THE REMOVE FOOTBALL TEAM

BY ONE WHO IS IN IT!

Our footer team's a perfect dream,
  Applaud it, heart and soul!
Away with "blues"! We'll never lose
  While Bulstrode keeps the goal!

The backs are Brown, of great renown,
  And Bull, a ripping sport;
And side by side, when sorely tried,
  They hold the giddy fort.

The half-back line is really fine,
  There's Peter Todd and Cherry,
And Linley, too; a noble crew
  That's always making merry.

The forwards shoot with fearless boot,
  What splendid chaps they are!
When Wharton plays, in awed amaze
  We watch that brilliant star.

Another strain of this refrain
  Might make you look quite blue, gents.
But mind you prize, and don't despise
  These ardent lines of Nugent's!

BY ONE WHO IS LEFT OUT!

Our crackpot team's a perfect scream,
  It makes you roar with mirth.
Such hopeless freaks cause endless shrieks.
  Oh, wipe them off the earth!

The backs are Brown, a stupid clown,
  And burly, blustering Bull;
Try how I may, I cannot say
  Which is the bigger fool!

The half-back line no words of mine
  Could faithfully describe:
With Peter Todd, so quaint and odd,
  The funniest of the tribe!

The forwards play in such a way
  To make the angels weep:
And Wharton's game is simply tame.
  Oh, send me off to sleep!

This ghastly crew, so sour to view,
  Will never come out winners.
So learn the truth, oh, Greyfriars youth,
  Of these remarks of Skinner's!

firearm being removed!" he exclaimed, in great excitement.

" Really, Mr. Quelch!"

" I refuse, sir—I distinctly refuse to be at the risk of being, sir, shot through the body! I refuse most emphatically!"

" Pooh—my dear sir! Pooh!"

" Is your rifle loaded, Mr. Prout?" asked the Head, mildly.

Mr. Prout gave a start.

" Why—bless my soul! I—I fear not. I—I remember now—in my haste, I forgot to load it—most unfortunate!"

There was a chortle from somewhere.

" I do not regard it as unfortunate—not at all," said Mr. Quelch, tartly. " I greatly prefer your rifle unloaded, Mr. Prout—very greatly."

And reassured now, the Remove master turned to the prisoner again. That unhappy Bolshevik blinked at him with apprehensive dark eyes—and outside the big open doorway four juniors with smudgy faces looked in, also apprehensive. The Remove master grasped the Bolshevik's shaggy beard, and it came off in his grasp.

A smooth and youthful chin was revealed—and to the astonishment of all beholders, it was of a darkish bronze colour.

" An Asiatic!" exclaimed Mr. Prout, " a Russian Asiatic, of course—the miserable doctrines of Bolshevism have spread among the Asiatic races. Doubtless he is a Georgian—or a Circassian—bless my soul, the ruffian is actually grinning at me!"

Another jerk from Mr. Quelch, and the whiskers and moustache came off. And then, in spite of the grease-paint, it could be seen that the face was a boyish one, and that there was something decidedly familiar in it.

" What—what—who are you?" gasped Mr. Quelch. " It is a boy—an Indian boy! I have seen your face before—why—it is—is—is—is it possible that you are Hurree Singh, of my Form?"

" What!" roared Mr. Prout.

There was a howl of amazement.

" Hurree Singh!" ejaculated the Head.

" Boy!"

" And then the prisoner spoke—not in Russian.

" Esteemed sahibs——"

" Ha, ha! It's Inky!"

" Inky! Oh, my hat!"

" Silence!"

" Esteemed sahibs, the sorrowfulness is terrific. It is my excellent and ludicrous self, and from the bottom of my heart I offer profound and inestimable apologises!"

THE THIRTEENTH CHAPTER.

All Up!

" HA, ha, ha!"

It was an irresistible roar of laughter. The Greyfriar's fellows roared, and yelled, and howled. The discovery that the terrible Bolshevik was Hurree Jamset Ram Singh, of the Remove, was too much for them. They shrieked.

Mr. Quelch did not laugh—nor the Head. Neither did Mr. Prout. But they were the only ones who didn't. Everybody else seemed to be in a state verging on hysterics.

" Hurree Singh!" repeated the Head dazedly. " What—what—what does this masquerade mean, boy?"

" Boy!" gasped Mr. Quelch. " You—— you——!"

" Wretched trickster!" thundered Mr. Prout. " You—you—you—it—it—it is a—a —a practical joke! A—a—a practical joke —on—on—on me!" Mr. Prout was volcanic at that moment. He stuttered and he stammered, breathless and furious. " Boy! Rascal! How dare you?"

" Esteemed and ridiculous sir," began the nabob meekly.

" And the others!" stuttered Mr. Prout. " The other Bolsheviks—I mean the other ruffians—that is to say, the other persons— they were also juniors, I presume—bless my soul!"

" Ha, ha, ha!"

" Silence!" rapped out Mr. Quelch.

" Ha, ha, ha!"

Mr. Prout looked at the prisoner—he looked at the hysterical crowd—and he looked at his rifle. His plump face became crimson. He rustled away hastily, trying to keep the rifle out of sight as much as possible. That rifle really seemed rather out of the picture now.

" Silence ! " repeated Mr. Quelch. " How dare you laugh ? Wingate, I am surprised at you ! Coker, if you cannot behave your-self——"

" Sorry, sir. Ha, ha——"

" Ha, ha, ha ! "

" Silence ! As for you, Hurree Singh ! " Mr. Quelch grasped the dusky junior by the shoulder, and shook him. " Boy ! What does this mean ? "

" The sorrowfulness is terrific, esteemed sahib. It is simply a small stuntfulness."

" Wha-a-at ? "

" My heye ! " murmured Gosling. " My heye ! 'Urree Singh ! Then it's heasy to guess who was the others, Mr. Quelch, sir."

" Ah ! Very probably," said the Remove master. " Wharton and the rest, I have no doubt. Hurree Singh, is that the case ? "

The nabob did not answer.

" Dr. Locke, the boy will doubtless answer you."

The Head had been gazing as if spellbound at the revealed nabob. He found his voice at last.

" Hurree Singh ! Who were your as-sociates in this rascally trickery ? "

" The namefulness of the esteemed persons is not the proper caper, most respected and ludicrous sahib," said the nabob, firmly.

" I command you——"

But there was no need for the Head to command. Four smudgy-faced juniors pushed through the crowd. The hapless Bolsheviks had removed their Bolshevik attire in the quad, tossing it away, and they had left their beards and whiskers where Mr. Prout had found them. They had made an attempt to wash their complexions off in the fountain— not with complete success. Now that the game was up, the Co. were prepared to take their share of the gruel. William Wibley, no doubt, would have shown up alongside them—but just them Wibley was excitedly hunting under the trees for his theatrical props.

Wibley was breathing fire, flame, and fury as he hunted for trousers and coats and slouched hats, and beards and whiskers. And he was not thinking of anything else. If Lenin, Trotsky and Co. had actually appeared at Greyfriars, Wibley would probably have gone on collecting up his theatrical properties.

But Wibley was not wanted. Harry Wharton and Co. pushed their way through the grinning crowd, and joined Hurree Jamset Ram Singh.

The nabob gave them a dolorous look.

" I am sorrowful, my esteemed chums," he murmured. " The excellent and rotten Gosling caught me bendfully, and I could not get awayfully."

" Can't be helped," grunted Johnny Bull.

" It's all the fault of that fat idiot," growled Bob Cherry, with a glare at Bunter.

Billy Bunter was standing rooted to the floor. His fat brain was undergoing unaccus-tomed exercise. He was trying to think out how he was to get clear of this, somehow. He was not so much distressed by the exposure of the Bolsheviks, as by the awful probability that he would have to share their punishment, as well as the punishment due from Mr. Prout. For it was clear, even to Bunter, that it would not be any use making an appeal to Mr. Prout's gratitude now.

Mr. Quelch's eyes had often been compared, by his boys, to gimlets ; but they had never looked so much like gimlets as they did now, as they were fixed on the Famous Five.

They almost seemed to bore holes into the hapless juniors.

" So you were Hurree Singh's associates in this outrage—Wharton, Nugent, Cherry, and Bull," said Mr. Quelch.

" Ye-e-es, sir," murmured Wharton.

" You attacked Mr. Prout—a Form-master——" exclaimed the Head.

" Not exactly attacked, sir," stammered Wharton. " We—we—we——"

" We—we——" stammered Nugent.

" It—it was only a stunt, sir," groaned Bob Cherry. " We didn't hurt Mr. Prout, sir. We wouldn't have hurt him for worlds ! "

" A stunt ! What do you mean ? What is a stunt ? " said the Head testily. The reverend Head of Greyfriars was not well posted as to the latest American imports.

" A—a—a wheeze, sir," gasped Bob. " We —we did it to—to save Bunter, sir——"

" What ! What had Bunter to do with it ? "

" Nothing, sir ! " chimed in Billy Bunter.

"What—what—who are you?" gasped Mr. Quelch. "It is a boy—an Indian boy! I have seen your face before—why—it is—is—is—is it possible that you are Hurree Singh, of my form?" (See page 45.)

"Nothing at all, sir. I never knew anything about it. Wharton will bear me out in that."

"Why, you—you——" stuttered Wharton.

"I hadn't the faintest idea of it!" howled Bunter. "The fact is, sir, I was in the dormitory at the time."

"In the dormitory?" repeated the Head.

"Yes, sir. Having a bit of a headache I went up to the dorm to lie down——"

"I understood that you were on the spot, Bunter, and that you went to the help of Mr. Prout when he was assailed——"

Bunter jumped.

"I—I—I mean, sir——"

"Well, what do you mean?" exclaimed the Head.

"I—I mean——" Bunter gasped. "I—I mean I—I rushed to the rescue, sir, like a—a —a lion——"

"You have just stated that you were in the dormitory at the time. Is it known where Bunter was, Mr. Quelch?"

"Bunter was certainly on the spot," said the Remove master.

"Then what do you mean, Bunter, by stating that you were in the dormitory at the time?"

"I—I—I meant that I wasn't in the dormitory at the time, sir," gasped Bunter.

"What?"

"That—that's what I really meant to say, sir. I—I hope it's quite clear now, sir," stammered the Owl of the Remove.

"Bless my soul! The boy seems to be as obtuse as he is untruthful," said the Head. "Wharton, explain this extraordinary affair to me at once. You may be silent, Bunter."

"Oh, really, sir——"

"Silence!"

Billy Bunter quavered into silence, and Harry Wharton proceeded dismally to explain.

THE FOURTEENTH CHAPTER.

A Very Happy Ending.

DR. LOCKE listened with a stern brow to Wharton's recital.

But the sternness of his brow relaxed a little as the captain of the Remove proceeded.

Even Mr. Quelch looked a little less severe.

As for the crowd of fellows in the hall, they grinned, and suppressed their merriment with very great difficulty.

The extraordinary "stunt" was almost too much even for the gravity of the headmaster.

"Upon my word!" said Dr. Locke, at last. "This is—is—is—— Well, upon my word! You made a disrespectful assault upon a Form-master, Wharton. I am willing to believe that you did not intend to hurt Mr. Prout, and that you did not mean to be disrespectful—but that is what it amounts to."

"We—we—we're awfully sorry, sir," murmured Wharton.

"I have no doubt that you are sorry, Wharton, especially in view of the punishment it will be my duty to inflict——"

"Oh!"

"But—but—how could you be so utterly absurd as to adopt so very ridiculous a disguise? You are surely aware that there are no Bolsheviks in this country! I have never, never heard of such an utterly hare-brained trick. The only possible extenuation of your conduct," added the Head severely, "is that you appear to have acted in this unheard-of-manner to save a schoolfellow from punishment."

"Yes, sir!" gasped Wharton.

"Bunter——"

"It wasn't me, sir."

"What?"

"It wasn't, sir, I assure you! Wharton's making a mistake. I didn't know anything about the matter at all. They'll all tell you so, sir, if you ask them," gasped Bunter.

The Head glanced at the Famous Five. They were grimly silent. If Bunter chose to dodge his share of the licking, they would not give him away; but certainly they were not going to speak untruthfully to shield him. That was asking rather too much.

"You knew nothing of it, Bunter?" said the Head sternly.

"Nothing at all, sir! Not a word! I—I —I'm shocked at them—surprised at them, sir."

"They appear to have acted as they did on your account, Bunter."

"That's their look-out, sir! I wasn't there —I never suggested the idea, and I never said that Wibley would make them up as Bolsheviks. I wasn't in the wood-shed while they were making up. Was I, Wharton?"

"Ha, ha, ha!"

"Indeed! How do you know these boys were making up in the wood-shed, Bunter, if you were not there?"

"Oh, I—I didn't, sir! I didn't know! That's what I meant, sir—I never knew anything about it. As for downing old Prout——"

"What?"

"I—I mean Mr. Prout! As for downing old—Mr. Prout on my account, that's all bunkum, sir—I—I mean, it's all my eye! Prouty—I mean Mr. Prout, wasn't going to

Billy Bunter—no doubt with the idea of making the scene more realistic—hit out at the shaggy ruffians with his fat fists, and there was a fiendish yell as one of his drives caught a Bolshevik under the ear.
(See page 36.)

pitch into me—he never sat in the toffee at all——"

"Sat in the toffee!" repeated the Head blankly.

"No, sir. He never sat in the toffee, and he never suspected that I put it in the chair on purpose, and he hasn't been chasing me up and down all the evening, looking for me with a cane——"

"Bless my soul!"

"And—and I never thought of appealing to his gratitude for rescuing him from the Bolsheviks, sir—really, you know. Never thought of such a thing! Besides, I wasn't there!"

"Ha, ha, ha!"

"Bunter! You are a most untruthful boy——"

"Oh, sir! Me, sir?"

"These foolish lads seem to have acted in a thoughtless and reckless manner for your sake, and the suggestion appears to have come from you—a suggestion worthy of your stupidity!" exclaimed the Head. "You will follow me to my study—all of you!"

Harry Wharton and Co. moved dismally after the Head as he rustled away. Dr. Locke glanced back.

"You also, Bunter!"

"Me, sir!" gasped Bunter. "Wha-at for, sir? C-c-c-can't I go now, sir?"

"Follow me!" thundered the Head.

"Oh!" gasped Bunter.

And he followed.

We will draw a veil, as a novelist would say, over the painful scene that followed. It was a very painful scene. The Head felt that it was his duty to administer a severe lesson—and he did his duty well. The unhappy schoolboy Bolsheviks thought he did it rather too well. Especially Bunter. The Owl of the Remove was looking as if he did not find life worth living, as he crawled from the Head's study, after Dr. Locke had so well done his duty.

In the corridor, six gasping juniors met Mr. Prout. Five of them passed him unheeded—the sixth dodged in vain. Loud yells from Billy Bunter followed the Famous Five—falling upon unsympathetic ears. The Head had considered that Bunter had enough, but Mr. Prout did not seem to think he had had enough—and he gave him some more. It was only too evident that Bunter had made a mistake in counting upon Mr. Prout's gratitude.

" Yow-ow-ow-ow-wow ! "

Thus William George Bunter, as he rolled into the Remove dormitory. The Removites were there—grinning, with five exceptions. The Famous Five did not feel like grinning just then. They groaned.

" Yow-ow-ow-wow ! I say, you fellows ! I'm suffering awful pain ! " groaned Bunter. " Ow, ow ! First the Head, and then Prout. Fancy Prout, you know, after the way I rushed to rescue him ! Ow-wow-wow ! "

" Ha, ha, ha ! "

" Ow, ow, ow ! "

" You fat rotter ! " exclaimed Bob Cherry wrathfully. " I think you've had enough, or I'd mop up the dorm with you for your blessed stunt ! As for that idiot Wibley——— Hallo, hallo, hallo——— "

Wibley came into the dormitory—late and wrathy. He rushed up to the Famous Five.

" You silly chumps——— "

" What ? "

" I can't find half the things—my props—my theatrical props—lost—can't find half of them, you silly chumps ! Yarooh ! Wharrer you at ? Leggo ! Oh, my hat ! "

" Bump ! Bump ! Bump !

The Famous Five did not explain what they were at ; it was a time for deeds, not words. William Wibley sat on the floor and gasped when they had finished with him. That was his reward for his share in the ructions of Greyfriars.

HOW I RUN
The Greyfriars Herald
By HARRY WHARTON

"THE GREYFRIARS HERALD" is, as everyone knows, the mouthpiece of the Remove Form. In it we chronicle all our adventures and escapades, and publish contributions, in prose and verse, from various fellows at Greyfriars, and occasionally from other schools in the locality.

Our object in launching "The Herald," several terms ago, was to produce a weekly paper on brighter and more entertaining lines than the usual type of school magazine.

The Editorial Staff of "The Greyfriars Herald" is comprised as under:

HARRY WHARTON .. Editor.
FRANK NUGENT .. Art Editor.
H. VERNON-SMITH .. Sports Editor.
ROBERT CHERRY .. Fighting Editor.

JOHNNY BULL 〔 Members of
HURREE SINGH Staff.
DICK PENFOLD

"We are seven," as the poet has it; and, although ours is a labour of love, and we derive no financial profit from it, we enjoy the job immensely.

You ought to see us on press day!

However, in spite of all the petty irritations, I would not relinquish my post of Editor for worlds. The merry little "Greyfriars Herald" has won a permanent place in the affections of British girls and boys; and the following extracts from it will, I hope, provide cheer and amusement for all readers of THE HOLIDAY ANNUAL.

HARRY WHARTON.

HOW I RUN
Tom Merry's Weekly
By TOM MERRY

ONE unkind person recently referred to my little paper as "TOM MERRY'S WEAKLY."

I don't think it is quite so bad as all that. Indeed, though I say it, I think our little journal can claim equality with most other school publications.

Running a paper is not a joke.

Imagine a long stream of contributors, extending the whole length of the Shell passage at St. Jim's, with manuscripts and poems clutched feverishly in their hands, and making a noise like the Tower of Babel and the destruction of Sennacherib rolled into one! Then you'll get a faint idea of what it's like.

The undermentioned fellows form the Staff of "Tom Merry's Weekly." (There are dozens more who claim to be on the Staff, but their claims are like their contributions—worthless!)

TOM MERRY .. .. Editor.
JACK BLAKE .. .. Art Editor.
REGINALD TALBOT .. Sports Editor.
HARRY MANNERS 〔 Members
MONTAGUE LOWTHER of
ARTHUR AUGUSTUS D'ARCY Staff.

Of course, we receive contributions, in verse and prose, from all sorts and conditions of people, and a number of extracts have been handed to the Editor of THE HOLIDAY ANNUAL for publication therein.

If—as I sincerely hope—they will be the means of bringing sunshine into hundreds of homes, then I shall rest well content.

TOM MERRY.

"WHO'S WHO!"

A brief summary of information concerning the Principal Characters of Greyfriars, St. Jim's and, Rookwood.

GREYFRIARS SCHOOL

WINGATE, GEORGE BERNARD.—Captain of Greyfriars.

BLUNDELL, GEORGE.—Captain of the Fifth.

COKER, HORACE JAMES.—A Fifth-former. Imagines himself good at everything, and inclined to be heavy-handed, but in the main a real good fellow.

TEMPLE, CECIL REGINALD.—Captain of the Upper Fourth.

WHARTON, HARRY.—The central figure of the stories. Captain of the Remove and leader of the Famous Five. Has real qualities of leadership, and is a fellow in a thousand. A fine all-round athlete.

BOLSOVER, PERCY.—The oldest and biggest fellow in the Remove. Inclined towards bullying.

BULL, JOHNNY.—A sound and sturdy member of the Famous Five. A keen cartoonist.

BUNTER, WILLIAM GEORGE.—The most amusing character ever created. Plump and greedy, and living in daily expectation of a postal order which will never come.

CHERRY, ROBERT.—The sunniest-tempered and most lovable fellow at Greyfriars. Good at all games, and the champion fighting man of the Form.

FISH, FISHER TARLETON.—An enterprising junior from New York.

FIELD, SAMPSON QUINCY IFFLEY.—Commonly known as "Squiff." A rattling good fellow. Hails from New South Wales.

GOSLING, MR.—The school porter. He loves the boys, but has a curious way of showing it. Very fond of tips.

LINLEY, MARK.—One of the noblest fellows at Greyfriars. A scholarship boy who previously worked in a Lancashire factory. Bob Cherry's best chum.

KIPPS, H.—Of the Remove Form. Fond of practical jokes, and a keen conjurer.

MAULEVERER, THE EARL.—The slacker and dandy of the Remove, but plucky and popular.

NUGENT FRANK.—Harry Wharton's closest chum. A straight, clean fellow, proud and plucky, and one of the leading lights of the Remove.

OGILVY, ROBERT.—In the Remove Form. Very gallant, and a true Scots boy.

PENFOLD, DICK.—In the Remove Form. Very pleasant disposition, and a keen photographer.

RUSSELL, RICHARD.—Best known as a boxer of brilliance and skill.

SINGH, HURREE JAMSET RAM.—Nabob of Bhanipur. A deadly bowler and a speedy forward. Also a member of the Famous Five.

SKINNER, HAROLD.—The worst fellow in the Remove.

TODD, ALONZO.—The "Duffer of Greyfriars." Transparently honest, and, although soft-hearted and soft-headed, a fellow of really high principles.

TODD, PETER.—Alonzo's cousin, but not nearly so guileless. One of the cleverest fellows in the Form. Good value at games.

VERNON-SMITH, HERBERT.—Perhaps the most interesting fellow at Greyfriars. His cool resolution and fearless spirit make him an admirable character. Once a bounder, but now a sound sportsman and a real good fellow.

WIBLEY, WILLIAM.—An amateur actor of outstanding ability.

WUN LUNG.—A Chinese junior. A very clever juggler.

BUNTER, SAMUEL TUCKLESS.—Bunter minor, and a smaller edition of his brother. In the Second Form.

WUN LUNG

JACK BLAKE

ALONZO TODD

BOB CHERRY

H. KIPPS

JOHNNY BULL

BILLY BUNTER

PERCY BOLSOVER

NUGENT, DICKY.—Frank Nugent's minor. Mischievous and spoiled and wrong-headed, but with good stuff in him. One of the leading lights of the Second.

FRANK NUGENT

DICK PENFOLD

DICKY NUGENT

ARTHUR AUGUSTUS D'ARCY

ROBERT OGILVY

ST. JAMES'S SCHOOL

KILDARE, ERIC.—Captain of the school, and one of the best.

KNOX, GERALD.—The black sheep of the Sixth.

MONTEITH, JAMES GARSTON.—Head of the New House.

MERRY, TOM.—Junior captain of St. Jim's, the leading character in the stories. A fine specimen of the very best type of British schoolboy. Plucky, straightforward, and athletic.

GRUNDY, GEORGE ALFRED.—A big, burly fellow in the Shell, with an exalted idea of his capabilities.

LOWTHER, MONTAGUE.—One of the Terrible Three. A loyal chum, a good sportsman, and a witty humorist.

MANNERS, HARRY.—Also a member of the Terrible Three. A quiet and studious fellow with a heart of gold.

RACKE, AUBREY.—The purse-proud son of a war profiteer.

SKIMPOLE, HERBERT.—A brainy, weedy eccentric type of fellow.

TALBOT, REGINALD.—Ranks with Tom Merry himself as a sportsman and in the esteem of his Form. Came to St. Jim's as a cracksman, but his new environment wrought a complete reformation.

BLAKE, JACK.—Leader of the Fourth Form. A first-rate fellow.

HERRIES, GEORGE.—Jack Blake's chum, and in the same study. He loves bulldogs.

CARDEW, RALPH RECKNESS.—A comparatively late-comer to the school. A spoiled boy, and a very queer mixture. Very much of a dandy, with a turn for sarcasm, but straight and plucky.

CLIVE, SIDNEY.—From South Africa. Cardew's chief chum.

D'ARCY, THE HON. ARTHUR AUGUSTUS.—The great Gussy. Lives up to the high traditions of a noble name. Rather a Beau Brummel, but possesses a heart of gold.

FIGGINS, GEORGE.—The acknowledged leader of the New House juniors. Quite a good sort.

KERR, GEORGE FRANCIS.—A Scot, long-headed and crafty. One of the best at all sports.

LEVISON, ERNEST.—Once a black sheep, but now thoroughly straight.

MELLISH, PERCY.—A dog with a bad name.

REDFERN, RICHARD HENRY.—One of the best fellows at St. Jim's. A fellow of character and marked ability, who should go far. Boxer, swimmer, and journalist.

TRIMBLE, BAGLEY.—The Bunter of St. Jim's. Braggart, sneak, and glutton, but always amusing.

WYNN, DAVID LLEWELLYN.—One of the very best. A big eater, and fond of tuck, but not to be classed with Bunter and Trimble. A tiptop goalkeeper and a splendid bowler.

D'ARCY, THE HON. WALTER ADOLPHUS.—The leading light of the Third, and Gussy's younger brother. Fun-loving and plucky.

LEVISON, FRANK.—Levison minor. In every way a splendid little fellow.

MANNERS, REGINALD.—Another Third-former, spoilt and wayward but with little real vice in him.

ROOKWOOD

BULKELEY, GEORGE.—Captain of Rookwood, and a splendid fellow.

CARTHEW, MARK.—The black sheep of the Sixth. A detestable fellow.

SILVER, JAMES.—Leader of the Classical juniors. A sterling fellow of the Wharton and Tom Merry quality.

DODD, TOMMY.—Jimmy Silver's great rival. Leads the Modern juniors in all sorts of japes.

MORNINGTON, VAL.—The Vernon-Smith of Rookwood. An admirable fellow in every way.

SMYTHE, ADOLPHUS.—The dandy of Rookwood.

HERBERT SKIMPOLE

MR. GOSLING

GEORGE HERRIES

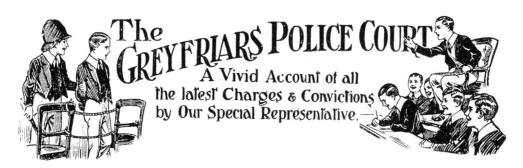

The GREYFRIARS POLICE COURT

A Vivid Account of all the latest Charges & Convictions by Our Special Representative.

AN OLD OFFENDER.

WILLIAM GEORGE BUNTER (fifteen), of no fixed abode, appeared before Mr. Justice Wharton on a charge of loitering and soliciting alms.

Mr. R. Cherry, K.C., for the prosecution, said it was a very shocking thing.

Magistrate : "If you are referring to your face, I heartily agree with you!" (Laughter.)

Mr. Cherry, proceeding, said that the accused bore a very bad reputation. He had been an ardent cadger from birth, and all efforts to reform him had proved futile.

Magistrate : "He is incorrigible—what ? "

Mr. Cherry : "That's a good word, your worship. I'll back it both ways." (Laughter.)

Magistrate : "Cut the cackle, and produce the first witness ! "

Mr. H. Vernon-Smith, a gentleman of independent means, on being called, said that the accused had approached him in the Close and mumbled something about a postal-order.

Magistrate : "I seem to have heard of that postal-order before." (Laughter, accompanied by cries of "Tell me the old, old story.")

Mr. Vernon-Smith : "The postal-order in question has been due to arrive ever since the Flood. It has grown side-whiskers and a flowing beard. This is not the first time I have been molested by the accused, your worship."

Mr. H. Skinner, K.C., C.A.D., for the defence, urged that Bunter was collecting sums of money on behalf of a local charity.

Magistrate : "This is the first time I've heard Bunter's tummy referred to as a local charity." (Loud and prolonged laughter.)

Mr. Skinner : "Bunter is a very generous, open-handed fellow, your worship——"

Magistrate : "So am I. Take that ! "

(Exit counsel for the defence.)

His Worship, summing up, said that this was undoubtedly a very bad case. The accused had for years been imposing on the Greyfriars public, and his previous record showed that he had already served a term of penal servitude for housebreaking. He would be sentenced to three hundred and ninety-nine strokes with the fives-bat, to be administered on the instalment system by all present.

Prisoner (wildly) : "Ow ! Yah ! Yaropski ! "

Magistrate : "He appears to be of foreign extraction. I shall recommend him for deportation."

NO CHANGE FOR BOLSOVER.

PERCY BOLSOVER, pugilist and weight-lifter, was booted into the dock on a charge of committing assault and battery upon George Tubb, who did not appear.

Magistrate : "At it again, are you ? Do you admit striking a fellow half your size, you hulking lout ? "

Prisoner : "The answer is in the infirmary, your worship."

Magistrate : "Then you will shortly join him there ! "

Prisoner was sentenced to be hanged, drawn and quartered, a fag of the Second being detailed to clear up the mess.

THE FOLLY OF A FAG.

SOBBING in terrible spasms, a small child named Percival Spencer Paget was summoned for driving a hoop without showing a rear light, in contravention of the Defence of the Elms Regulations.

P.-C. Wibley deposed to being on duty in the Close at the time of the offence. He said he was the victim of a fearful collision with prisoner's vehicle.

Magistrate: "So you went through the hoop?"

P.-C. Wibley: "No, your worship. The hoop jolly nearly went through me!"

(Laughter)

Magistrate (sternly): "If these cackling asses don't shut up, I shall clear the court!"

Prisoner: "That would be a jolly good wheeze, your worship!"

Magistrate: "Silence, sir! I cannot allow the lives of the public to be endangered in this way. The hoop will be handed over to the next itinerant vendor of old iron who comes along. As for you, you will be flayed alive forthwith!"

The sentence was duly carried out, and likewise the prisoner.

THE FALL OF FISHY.

FISHER TARLETON FISH, an enterprising business man from Noo York, was charged with embezzling the funds of the Greyfriars Pork-Pie and Pawned Pickle-Jar Corporation, of which he was the president.

Mr. H. J. R. Singh, for the prosecution, said that the trickfulness and rascality of the ludicrous Fish were terrific. He had fraudfully converted the funds of the esteemed Corporation to his own use.

Magistrate: "What was the amount, my dusky and learned friend?"

Mr. Singh: "The nimble and elusive tanner, honoured sahib."

Magistrate: "And I suppose he's rigged himself out with motor-cars and fur-lined coats—what?"

Prisoner (excitedly): "I guess you're all wrong! I didn't go within a mile of the beastly greenbacks. I didn't touch a single red cent. You're a slabsided jay, and——"

Magistrate: "Take a term's hard labour for contempt of court!"

Prisoner: "I guess——"

Magistrate: "I kinder sorter guess and calculate you can vamoose to the cells. You will be sentenced to receive the Order of the Boot—and may the Head have mercy on your sole!"

ASTOUNDING SCENE IN COURT.

MAGISTRATE MAULED BY A WITNESS.

PETER TODD, who was remanded at the last Tuckshop Sessions, was brought up again before Mr Justice Wharton on a charge of high treason.

Mr. R. Cherry, K.C., for the prosecution, said that prisoner had uttered seditious phrases, calculated to cause unrest in the Remove. He had inferred that the Captain of the Form was a chopheaded chump, and that he—Todd—ought to boss the show.

Magistrate: "Gimme the black cap! I must pronounce sentence right away. Can't stand this sort of thing!"

Mr. M. Linley, Counsel for the defence: "Hold on, your worship. Fair play's a jewel!"

Magistrate: "All serene. Call the first witness."

(At this juncture a loud clamour arose in Court, and voices were heard bawling, "Dutton! Tom Dutton!");

Magistrate: "Go ahead with the merry chorus. Never mind me!"

P.-C. Wibley: "Shall we fetch the witness in question, your worship?"

Magistrate: "Yes—on an ambulance, if necessary." (Laughter.)

(Enter Dutton, after an interval of ten minutes.)

Magistrate (addressing witness): "Todd, here, has been charged with high treason——"

Witness: "Eh! You be careful what you're saying!"

(55)

Magistrate : " W-w-what ! "

Witness : " Lost my reason, have I ? My hat ! I—I'll slaughter you ! "

Magistrate : " I said ' treason,' not ' reason,' you silly duffer ! "

Witness : " Yes, and so will you if I get near you ! If you think I've lost my reason, and you're going to make me suffer, you're quite offside ! "

Magistrate : " A megaphone—a megaphone—my kingdom for a megaphone ! " (*Laughter.*) " Now look here, Dutton, old chap——"

Witness : " You're right. I *am* a glutton for a scrap ! Take that—and that—and that ! "

(*Hereupon witness leapt from the box, and proceeded to chastise his worship with his magisterial wig.*)

Magistrate : " Keep off the grass ! "

Witness : " Silly ass, am I ? I'll jolly soon show you ! "

Biff ! Bang ! ! Thud ! ! !

Magistrate : " Yow-ow-ow ! Clear the Court ! Bring the stretcher-bearers ! Sound the fire-alarm ! Yah ! Gro ! Gerroff me chest ! I'll give you all the money in the poor box, Dutton, if you'll let me alone ! "

Witness : " So I've lost my reason, I'm a silly ass, and I'm going to suffer—what ? Well, I rather think the boot's on the other foot. Just let me roll my sleeves back. Then you'll see some fireworks ! "

SENSATIONAL FAG SUIT.

GERALD Loder, a hulking lout of seventeen, strode into the Court and demanded a divorce from his fag, Richard Nugent, on the grounds of desertion and neglect.

Loder conducted his own case, and there was no defence.

Magistrate : " Why can't you live in harmony together ? "

Loder : " The young rascal burnt my toast, scoffed my cake, used my sporting papers to light the fire, refused to go down to the Cross Keys for me, and when I had arranged for a big supper party he went off to play marbles."

Voice from the Gallery : " Bow-wow ! "

Magistrate : " Put that puppy outside ! "

When the subsequent scuffle had died away, the following letter was produced and handed round the Court :

" Dear Loder,—I feel I kannot stand you any longer. I'm fedd-up ! You can go and eat koke ! You are a beastly booly ! I hate you with a never-lasting hatred. Yah ! Cook your own moldy bloters in fewcher ! I hope they choke you ! — Yours in sollum kontempt,

" R. NUGENT."

Magistrate : " The number of divorces just lately is most alarming. This case is particularly touching and moving, so much so that I think Loder ought to be touched and moved too. Out with him ! "

(*Loder, owing to circumstances over which he had no control, hurriedly left the Court. There was the sound of a distant bump, accompanied by a yell of anguish.*)

Magistrate : " Have you removed the nuisance ? "

P.-C. Wibley : " Yes, your worship. It was hot work, and I think I deserve some slight recognition——"

Magistrate : Yes, yes. Take a penny out of the poor box ! "

THE SOAP-STEALER.

A DIMINUTIVE, grubby-looking youth, giving the name of George Tubb, appeared in the dock, charged by Police-constable Johnny Bull with stealing a piece of soap.

Magistrate : " Impossible ! "

P.-C. Bull : " I saw him with my own eyes, your worship."

Magistrate : " I am amazed and gratified at such evidence of reform on the part of the prisoner. He evidently stole the piece of soap with a view of cleansing his neck for the first time in history." (Laughter.)

Prisoner was bound over to keep the piece for six months.

The Court then adjourned.

GRUNDY'S DREAM!

Written in George Alfred Grundy's Best Style

THE sun came down in torrents
  From a cleer and clowdless
    sky ;
The First Elevven were batting,
  And I was standing by.

Kildare was at the wickit,
  He smote with mite and mane ;
Till his middel stump went spin-
    ning,
  Then he toddled back again !

Monteith took up the running,
  And he gave a sudden rore
As the ball removed his nee-cap.
  Said the umpyre, "Leg be-
    fore !"

Then Darrel, Gray, and Baker
  Went in to try their luck ;
But they all came back defeeted,
  And each won got a duck !

Kildare broke down with sobbing,
  And he turned to me and cride,
"Arise, George Alfred Grundy,
  The last hope of his side !"

I rose up like Napoleon,
  And grasped my trusty blade ;
When the feeldsmen saw me com-
    ing
  They staggered back, dismade !

Two hundred runs were wanted
  To give St. Jim's the match.
"The skool shall win !" I mut-
    tered,
  "I sware by Colney Hatch !"

I flogged the pewtrid bowling
  North, south, and east, and
    west ;
And the feeldsmen sank exhawsted
  For they had to give me best.

"O stay, George Alfred Grundy !
  O stay thy mighty hand !
Your batting terns us giddy,
  It farely beets the band !"

I still kontinewed slogging
  That week and feeble stuff.
"Declare !" the feeldsmen
    showted.
  "Oh, crumms ! We've had
    enuff !"

I rattled up a hundred,
  And then a hundred more.
The Head came out to see me,
  He marveled at my score !

"Well played, George Alfred
    Grundy,
  By all St. Jim's adored !
Your wunderful performance
  Doth merrit a reward !"

The Head advanced to meat me.
  "You're simply grate !" he
    said.
I blinked, I gasped, I shivvered,
  And then sat up in bed !

"You silly ass ! You're snor-
    ing !"
  Said Lowther, in disgust.
Then he skweezed the spunge with
    vigger,
  And my merry dreem went
    bust !

Figgins DWynn H Skimpole Tom Merry G.Herries A.A.Darcy M.Lowther J.Blake

HINTS ON DRESS

WRITTEN IN THE NATIVE TONGUE OF ARTHUR AUGUSTUS D'ARCY.

Tom Mewwy has wequested me
  (He says its vewy pwessin'),
To give in choicest poetwy,
  Some useful tips on dwessin'.

Few fellahs in the Fourth an'
    Shell
  Take pwide in their appeawance;
They don't agwee it would be well
  To pwactise persevewance.

They cwease their coats, an' seldom
    twy
  To pwess their wumpled twou-
    sahs :
My own are somewhat damaged
    by
  A savage twick of Towsah's !

Howevah, I will now wemark
  That no young lad is sillay
To emulate the gay young spark
  Who stwuts in Piccadillay !

You may forgive the bold, bad
    blade.
  But who can take compassion
On one who all his life has stwayed
  Fwom the pwevailin' fashion ?

To start with, you should be
    possessed
  Of twenty suits of clobbah ;
An' lock 'em in the old oak chest
  Away fwom any wobbah.

You must have gwey, an' blue,
    an' bwown,
  An' yellow is permitted ;
An' don't forget, when you're in
    town,
  To have them twied an' fitted.

Of neckties you must keep a stock,
  With colours fairly hummin' ;
An' guawanteed to give a shock
  To all who see you comin' !

Your spats must be in perfect
    taste,
  Your shoes of patent leathah ;
An' always sport a slendah waist
  In any sort of weathah !

Your Sunday toppah must not be
  Atwocious, old, an' mossy,
But spick an' span, like mine, you
    see—
  Delightful, smooth, an' glossy !

Your silver cane, held in posish,
  Will make you look most
    dashin' ;
And will be useful when you wish
  To give some cad a thwashin' !

So, weadah, wise an' do your duty,
  With wesolute endeavah ;
An' make yourself a thing of
    beauty,
  Likewise a joy for evah !

GRUNDY'S CHRISTMAS PRESENT!

Being the Correspondence between George Alfred Grundy, of the Shell Form at St. Jim's, and his Devoted Uncle.

I.

" My deer Uncle.—I must appolergise for writing to you so soon on the subjick of a Krissmus pressent, but I want to give you plenty of time to look round the shopps. I don't beleeve in uncles being rushed at the last minnit.

" Last year, you will remember, you bought me a hansom silver watch. Allthough it's been in the wars a good deel since that time, it still tix. The dile is busted, and the two hands have been ampewtated just below the elboe ; but apart from these drawbax the watch is in topping condishun.

" This year I want a motor-skooter. They are all the rage just now, and you can kable to Amerrika for won. It will be grate fun to wizz round the passidges at St. Jim's, and bole people over.

" Pleese despatch the skooter as soon as you like to

" Your affeckshunate Nephew,
" GEORGE ALFRED GRUNDY."

II.

" My dear Nephew,—Thank you for your letter.

" You do not tell me how you are progressing with your lessons, but I suppose your natural modesty keeps you from mentioning that you are at the top of your class.

" With regard to the motor-scooter, I shall be happy to do as you desire, and am already getting in touch with the American agents. These scooters cost a great deal of money, and I am afraid your allowance of pocket-money will have to be cut down a little to admit of your having such an expensive toy.

" With all good wishes, believe me,
" Your affectionate uncle.
" ROBERT GRUNDY."

III.

" My deer Uncle,—It is so nice of you to go to all this trubble ; but I have desided not to have a motor-skooter after all. The beestly things use up so much pettrol.

" I have been diskussing the matter with Wilkins and Gunn, my studdy mates, and we have come to the konclusion that the best present you could send would be a big fat tuck-hamper, krammed with good things from top to bottom.

" Don't forget the terkey, and as much ice-kake as three helthy fellows could eat in a fortnite.

" Your affeckshunate nephew,
" GEORGE ALFRED GRUNDY."

IV.

" My dear Nephew,—I note with approval that you no longer wish to possess a motor-scooter. I am very glad. I was afraid you would do yourself an injury.

" I do not altogether approve of the animal appetites of you and your study mates. However, Christmas comes but once a year, and I will endeavour to send you a tremendous hamper as you request.

" Your affectionate uncle,
" ROBERT GRUNDY."

V.

" My deer Uncle,—Your are a brikk ! I new you would come up to the skratch.

" I have arranjed for a duzzen fellows to come down to the station with me, and help me to bring the tuck-hamper up to St. Jim's.

" We are all very eksited. Wilkins says he is not going to have any more grub in hall, so that he can pave the way for the mity feed.

" Of course, I am a very poppular chap here, and I have invited heeps of fellows to help me dispose of the good things ; so don't forget to make the hamper a rekord sighs.

"With watering lipps, I remane,

"Your affeckshunate nephew,

"GEORGE ALFRED GRUNDY."

VI.

"My dear Nephew,—A very Happy Christmas to you!

"I have been pondering over the question of a suitable present for you, and have come to the conclusion that it would be unwise to send you a tuck-hamper.

"I therefore enclose something which is far more appropriate to your needs—namely, a spelling-book. I trust your education will be greatly improved by a diligent perusal of thi little manual.

"Ever your affectionate uncle,

"ROBERT GRUNDY."

VII.

"Deer Uncle,—I despise you with the uttmost despishun! Yah!

"GEORGE ALFRED GRUNDY."

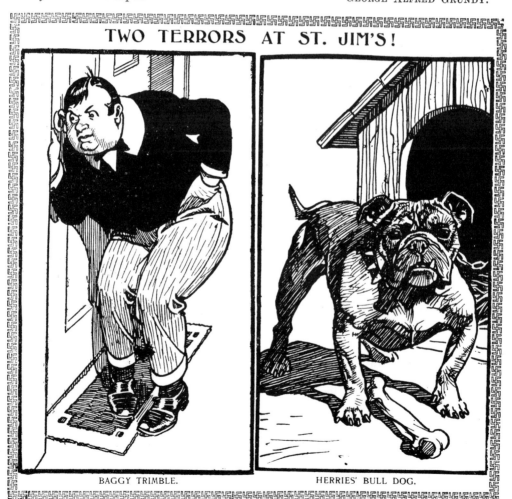

TWO TERRORS AT ST. JIM'S!

BAGGY TRIMBLE.

HERRIES' BULL DOG.

OUR HEART TO HEART CHATS
CONDUCTED BY MONTY LOWTHER

" Trot your troubles out, you fellows !
Get them off your little chests !
I will ease your cares and sorrows,
I will drive away the pests ! "

" SORROWFUL SKIMMY."—I was overjoyed, brother, to receive your three-hundred-and-ninety-eight-page letter. Do not despair, my dear Dictionary. You are the salvation of St. Jim's. The good work which you are doing in reforming the weak, wayward, and wilful will never be cast upon the scrap-heap of failure. Go on, and prosper ! Point out to your erring playmates the folly of their ways. Lead them back gently to the fold. Although you may receive a couple of black eyes and a damaged nasal organ in the process, the labour and the wounds will not be in vain. Your good deeds will glimmer like tapers in a naughty world. Lift us in your mighty arms, and plank us upon the straight path. Save us from the pangs of Pentonville —from the horrors of Holloway !

" Take courage, brother ! Do your best,
    And serve your fellow man well ;
Till you at last are called to rest
    Within the shades of Hanwell ! "

" CAREWORN CUTTS."—Yes, brother, you are indeed in a bad way. Shun the paths of evil, my dear cutlet, and tread not the thorny road that leads to the Green Man. What ? You have been mixed up with card-playing ? Naughty, naughty ! But then, you always were a queer " card," you know. You seem to me to be suffering from " too much fag." Pull yourself together, my dear brother. All will come right in the end. There's a silver lining to every cloud, and you may even yet be able to dodge the horrors of Dartmoor.

" Beware of billiard balls, old sport,
    And never try to poke 'em ;
For picking pleasures of this sort
    May lead to picking oakum ! "

" GENTLE GRUNDY."—It was very noble of you, my wayward and boot-faced brother, to confess to me that you have been indulging in fisticuffs with your brethren. Alas, my poor Grundy ! You must not let the sun go down upon your wrath. Learn to turn the other cheek. If a schoolfellow smites you, ask him to do it again. Healthy exercise for the young is always to be commended. Let me recommend to you that tender and touching story, " Docile Dick : The Boy Who Failed to Get His Blow in Fust." They buried him in Wayland cemetery.

" Dear children, you should never let
    Your angry passions rise ;
Your hands weren't fashioned, don't forget,
    To tear each other's eyes ! "

" A JILTED ARISTOCRAT " (No. 6 Study).—Alas, my poor brother ! What can I say to comfort you in your great anguish of mind ? Have you told the young lady at Wayland all that is in your heart—and bank ? Have you girded yourself in fine raiment and cast yourself in blind devotion at her feet (size nine) ? Have you whispered sweet nothings to her in the threepenny seats at the Wayland Cinema ? Have you poured out her charms in piffling poetry ? If you have left any stone unturned, my brother, turn it at once ! You always were good at giving turns, you know. I gather from your letter that you are contemplating committing suicide by locking yourself in No. 6 Study with Herries and his cornet. Take no such rash step, dear brother. The sun will turn, and the tide will shine. Take another trip into Wayland, and see if those yellow-and-pale-pink socks won't work the oracle.

" A damsel's love may always prove
    A source of care and sorrow ;
But smite her with your dazzling socks,
    And she'll ' come round ' to-morrow ! "

" FED-UP FATTY."—It is with real regret, my plump and barrel-like brother, that I learn of your terrible collapse, due to the consumption, at one sitting, of ninety whipped cream walnuts. (The walnuts aren't the only things that deserve to be whipped.) Pull up in time, my heavy-laden brother. Let me tell you a little story. A small boy bought a toy balloon, once upon a time, and started to blow it up. (His father blew *him* up afterwards, but that's another story.) The balloon grew bigger and bigger, until at length, to the lifelong regret of the purple-faced child, it went bust ! Beware, O my brother, lest you share a similar fate !

" Man wants but little here below,
    Nor wants that little long ;
And ninety walnuts at one go
    Is just a bit *too* strong ! "

FAG WANTED ! Must produce certificate to show that he has washed once since Armistice Day. Must also be able to make tea which doesn't taste like pea-soup. Good opening for a smart, lively kid. Salary, 2d. per week, with free use of fireplace. Apply, GEORGE WINGATE, Captain of Greyfriars.—[ADVT.]

YOUNG, hustling American desires a partner, with 500 dollars capital, to finance a great new stunt. Nothing " fishy " about this offer. No, sir ! Apply (with the dollars) to FISHER T. FISH, Study No. 9, Remove Passage.

*   *   *

LOVELORN SCHOOLBOY, aged fifteen, is eager to make the acquaintance of a nice girl living within a twelve yards radius of Greyfriars. (Too much fag to go further afield). Applicant must have auburn hair, blue eyes, and dainty feet. No one with false teeth or cross-eyes need apply. Write, giving full particulars, to LORD MAULEVERER, " Slackersdale," Remove Passage.

*   *   *

NOTISS !—The Brittish Troops on the Rine are grately in need of chokkerlate, jamm-puffs, and doe-nutts. All kontribewshuns should be sent to W. G. BUNTER, who will be pleesed to foreward them to the proper kwarter. Adress all hampers to me at Studdy No. 7, Remove Passidge.

*   *   *

SCHOOLBOYS ! WHY NOT GROW A BEARD ? With the aid of my marvellous preparation, you will be able to possess, within twenty-four hours, a flowing beard, also side-whiskers. Be manly ! No more smooth chivvies ! Try my marvellous preparation to-day !—HAROLD SKINNER, Box 13, " Greyfriars Herald " Office.

*   *   *

FUNDS URGENTLY NEEDED to save the shipwrecked souls of the South Sea Islanders ! Can you refrain, my dear fellows, from contributing to so charitable a purpose ? TOOTHPICKS FOR TIMBUCTOO also form one of the crying needs of the hour. Pause, gentle reader, and reflect——

(We regret there is insufficient space for the remaining chapters of this advertisement. Further information can be obtained from ALONZO TODD, Study No. 7, Remove Passage.)

BILLY BUNTER'S "BIKE!"

By BOB CHERRY.

THE FIRST CHAPTER.

First prize — a magnificent bicycle, complete with three-speed gear and latest accessories. Guaranteed to last twenty years!"

Billy Bunter fairly rolled the words on his tongue, as if they were strawberry ices.

We were in the junior common-room—generally known as the Rag—when Bunter read that announcement.

The fat junior had either begged, borrowed, or stolen—probably the latter—a copy of "The Weekly Joker," which contained details of what it was pleased to call an absorbing and fascinating competition.

" I say, you fellows!" said Bunter, blinking at us, " I'm going to bag that bike!"

" Go hon!"

" There are twelve pictures here," continued Bunter, flourishing the paper, " and they represent the names of railway-stations in Great Britain. Of course, no ordinary fellow could be expected to solve even half of them. You want brains for that sort of thing."

" Then why're you competing?" asked Frank Nugent. And there was a general laugh.

" You can dry up, Nugent!" said Billy Bunter, with dignity. " I don't want any insults from a fellow of your low order of intelligence!"

" My hat!"

Bunter spread the paper out on one of the desks, and we glanced over his shoulder.

" Take the first picture," said Bunter. " It shows a castle, with an elephant in the foreground. That's Cowes, of course!"

" Elephant and Castle, you ass!" said Johnny Bull.

Bunter sniffed.

" If you had studied your geography, Johnny Bull," Bunter said, " you'd have know there was no such place as Elephant and Castle."

" My only aunt!" said Peter Todd. " You'll be saying there's no such place as London next!"

" Well, there may be something in what Johnny Bull says," said Bunter, on reflection. " All the same, I shall stick to Cowes."

" Thereby losing any faint chance you might have had of bagging the bike," said Wharton.

" Oh, rot! The second picture's dead easy; it's a black pool of water. Even a fellow of dull intelligence, like Johnny Bull, can see that it's Waterloo!"

" Blackpool, you fat chump!" said Vernon-Smith."

" You're wandering in your mind, Smithy. Who ever heard of a place with a name like that?"

" You won't find a seaside resort in England to beat it!" said Mark Linley, loyal to Lancashire.

Bunter said he was convinced that the solution was Waterloo. However, he was careful to scribble the word " Blackpool" in his notebook.

" The third picture's a queer sort of archway," said Bunter. " Of course, you're all agreed that it's Whitechapel?"

" Trust you to make a hash of things, Bob Cherry!" said Bunter. " The next picture shows a pen, a ton weight, and a small house. How's that for Swiss Cottage ? "

" Right off the wicket ! " said Nugent. " It's where you'll end your days, Bunty—Pentonville ! "

" Ha, ha, ha ! "

Bunter continued to make entries in his notebook, until—thanks to our timely aid—he had completed the list of solutions. His fat face was beaming as he stowed the notebook in his pocket.

" I'm the winner all the way ! " he said. " A magnificent bike, you fellows ! Just think of it ! Of course, it would have been more considerate of the editor to make the first prize a tuck hamper. Still, I shall be able to sell the bike, I expect, and have no end of fine feeds at the tuckshop. Mrs. Mimble will jolly soon play up to me when she sees the colour of my money."

" When ? " grinned Wharton.

And we all joined in the chorus :

" When I get some money,
    I'll be in the Upper Ten ;
When I get some money,
    When, when, when, when, when ! "

" It'll be sooner than you fellows think ! "

" Anybody got a stamp ? "

" Better try Friardale Post-office," said Peter Todd.

" What ! You think I'm going to fag all that distance for a mouldy stamp ! Surely one of you fellows can oblige an old pal ? Hi, Dutton ! Have you got a stamp about you ? "

" Certainly ! " said Tom Dutton, the deaf junior.

And, stepping forward, he gave Bunter a box on the ears which sent him staggering.

The fat junior roared with anguish.

" Wharrer you up to ? " he demanded, wrathfully.

" You told me to clout you," said Dutton in surprise.

" I didn't ! I asked you if you had a stamp.'

Dutton looked mystified.

" What on earth do you want a lamp for ? " he said. " 'Tain't dark yet."

" Oh, help ! " moaned Bunter. " Have you got a stamp—a thing that you stick on letters ? "

" So you think that I ought to know better, do you ? " roared Dutton. " I'll jolly soon show you ! "

And he boxed Bunter's ears again—harder this time.

We simply yelled.

" Ow ! Pulverise him, somebody ! groaned Bunter. " Look here, how can I send in my entry for the competition unless I have a stamp ? "

" I should let the Editor pay tuppence on the letter," said Skinner. " Editors are very generous sort of chaps, you know."

" Or you mark the envelope ' O.H.M.S.,' " said Nugent thoughtfully.

" ' O.H.M.S.' ! " said Bunter. " What does that silly rot mean ? "

" Oh, Help Me Somebody ! "

" Ha, ha, ha ! "

" I think you are a set of beasts ! " said Bunter, blinking at us through his big window-panes. " You're all rolling in filthy lucre, yet you're too mean to dish up a stamp ! I sha'n't let any of you ride my bike—when it comes ! "

And Bunter rolled out of the Rag in high dudgeon.

He devoted the next hour or so to stamp-collecting.

Nugent minor came to the rescue with a halfpenny stamp, which he extricated with difficulty from a mass of toffee, crayons, and chewing-gum. Bunter took his word for it that it really was a half-penny stamp. It looked more like a paper pellet that had lost its way.

Another weather-beaten stamp—a penny one this time—turned up from the pockets of Sammy Bunter, who, as a return for handing it over, insisted upon being allowed to use his major's bicycle whenever the spirit moved.

That evening Billy Bunter posted his entry form.

A black cat was crossing the Close at the time, and Bunter hailed it as a symbol of good luck.

When the fat junior dropped off to sleep that

night in the dorm., we could hear him murmur, in between his snores :

"Magnificent bicycle . . . three-speed gear . . . latest accessories. . . . Winner——W. G. Bunter, of Greyfriars!"

THE SECOND CHAPTER.

MR. QUELCH did not find Bunter a very attentive pupil next morning.

Bunter never was, as a matter of fact. He considered that a little learning was a dangerous thing; therefore, he acquired as little as possible. But on this particular morning he was the limit. When Mr. Quelch asked him where King Charles the First was beheaded, Bunter replied, in an abstracted tone, "Clapham Junction, sir!" and received a hundred lines for his pains. When he went on to tell Mr. Quelch that the Magna Charta was signed in Piccadilly Circus, the imposition was doubled.

The fat junior swerved to one side, in the hope of avoiding Mr. Prout ; but the latter swerved at the same time, and there was a grinding collision.

Finally, when Bunter gave the startling information that William the Conqueror came over to England on a magnificent bicycle, with three-speed gear and latest accessories, he received a couple of stinging cuts on each hand, and came back to earth with a jerk ; and his great expectations were forgotten.

But not for long.

Bunter had that bike on the brain. He bored us stiff by gloating over the good times he intended to have as soon as the machine arrived.

"Of course, I shall ride it for a bit," he said, "and when something goes wrong with the works I shall sell it for twelve quid or so. It will be simply great! I shall be able to buy Mrs. Mimble out of house and home! A fellow can get a good many jam-puffs for twelve quid"

"You've got to get the twelve quid first!" growled Johnny Bull.

"To say nothing of the bike!" I interjected.

"Don't talk rot! I've sent in twelve correct solutions, and, therefore, the bike's a cert. I believe you fellows are eaten up with jealousy because you know I'm going to win."

"You—you think we're jealous of a conceited bladder of lard like you!" stuttered Wharton.

"I don't think—I know! It's this personal jealousy on your part that has kept me out of the cricket and footer teams. Why don't I kick runs and hit goals for the Remove? Jealousy, of course! Why haven't I been elected skipper of the Form? Jealousy again! You fellows know, in your hearts, that I'm a born leader, but you deliberately keep me under! Sheer bad sportsmanship, I call it."

"Oh, slay him, somebody!" ejaculated Nugent.

We were fed-up with Bunter. As the days advanced, we became still more so. He strutted about with his nose in the air, as if he owned the earth and all that therein is. In fact, you simply couldn't hold the fat beast.

He was soundly bumped on several occassion; but all the bumping in the world wouldn't stop him from swanking.

After a while we put our heads together, and decided to teach Bunter a lesson.

It was Sampson Quincey Iffley Field—commonly called Squiff—who suggested the most novel wheeze.

"Bunter thinks he deserves a bike," said Squiff, "and he sha'n't be disappointed! It would be too awful if all his castles in the air came tumbling down. He's thought and dreamed of a bike so much that he's genuinely convinced he'll get one. And so he shall."

"What!" yelled Peter Todd. "You're going to present Bunter with a bike?"

"Certainly!"

"Then you must be potty!"

"The pottyfulness of the esteemed Squiff," murmured Hurree Singh, "is terrific!"

"Wait!" said Squiff. "I haven't told you what sort of a bike. During my wanderings in Courtfield, I've discovered the whereabouts of an old-iron shop."

We began to see what Squiff was driving at.

"In the yard at the back of the shop," he went on, "there's a very ancient bike, thick with cobwebs, and rusty as old Quelchy when he's on the warpath! The bike was invented over a hundred years ago, and it's about the most weird-looking thing you ever struck. The front wheel stands higher than I do, and the handle-bars are the last word."

"Then it is a thing of booty and a toy for ever, as your English proverb has it?" said Hurree Singh.

"Exactly. And it'll suit Bunter——"

"Down to the ground," chuckled Nugent.

"Ha, ha, ha!"

"I propose that we collar the ancient 'bus," said Squiff, "and leave it at Friardale Station,

addressed to W. G. Bunter, Esq., 'to be called for.'"

"Ripping!" said Wharton.

"And we'll concoct a letter, presumably from the editor of the 'Weekly Joker,' stating that Bunter has been awarded the first prize. How's that?"

"Top-hole!" said Peter Todd. "There's just one point, though. This bike will cost money, and we're all on the verge of being stony."

"Set your little mind at rest, Teddy," said Squiff. "Instead of our having to pay the proprietor of the shop, he'll pay us—for removing a dangerous obstruction from his premises."

"Ha, ha, ha!"

We fell in with Squiff's idea at once.

When afternoon lessons were finished we biked over to Courtfield, and rescued the ancient contrivance from the scrapheap.

The proprietor was only too glad to see the back of it. He told us it had been a positive eyesore to the place, and had lost him a lot of custom.

Then we piloted the prehistoric bike to the railway-station at Friardale, and left instructions with the porter.

Two mornings later there was a letter in the rack for Bunter.

Letters for the fat junior were not as plentiful as blackberries, in spite of all his high talk about titled relations and fat remittances.

Bunter pounced on the letter at once.

Quite a crowd of fellows drifted up to see the fun.

"Hallo!" said Bolsover major. "Letter from Lord Bunter de Bunter?"

"It's not from one of my titled relations this time," said Bunter. "There's no crest on the back."

"Perhaps it's from the uncle who keeps the Bunter Arms?" I suggested. "Trot out the joyful tidings, Billy."

Bunter inserted a fat forefinger in the fold of the letter, and ripped it open.

The next moment his little round eyes were positively gleaming with delight.

"It's come!" he exclaimed.

"Not the postal order, surely?" said Skinner, in surprise.

"No, it's the letter announcing that I've won the first prize in the picture-puzzle competition."

"Gammon!"

"Read it yourself, then," said Bunter.

And we all crowded round to see the letter. It ran as follows:

"Editorial Office,

THE WEEKLY JOKER,

London.

"W. B. Bunter, Esq.,

Greyfriars School,

Friardale, Kent.

"Dear Sir,— I have much pleasure in informing you that you have been awarded the first prize in our recent picture puzzle contest.

"The magnificent bicycle, complete with three-speed gear and latest accessories, awaits you at Friardale Station.

"I congratulate you most cordially upon your success, which I sincerely trust may be the forerunner of many more in this respect.

"I am,

dear sir,

"Yours faithfully, "THE EDITOR."

Tom Dutton stepped forward and gave Bunter a box on the ears which sent him staggering. The fat junior roared with anguish.

Squiff had compiled that letter, and he had sent it to a pal in London to post on. Most of us knew it was a fake, of course; but Bolsover major and Skinner, who weren't in the know, were frankly astonished.

"Congratulations, Bunty!" said Skinner, when he had recovered from the shock. "You're a much cleverer fellow than I imagined."

"Yes, rather," said Bolsover. "This does you credit, I must say. You're a giddy genius!"

"I always said Bunter had some brains stowed away somewhere," said Russell.

"Ha, ha, ha!"

"You fellows needn't toady up to me now that you know I've won," said Bunter. "I don't mind telling you in advance that only two people are going to use my bike—and they're me and Sammy."

"Can I ride on the step if I'm very good?" asked Nugent.

"No, you can't. You've often refused me the loan of your bike Nugent, and this is where I get my own back. You fellows are jealous of me more than ever now, I can see. It sticks in your gills to know that I've won the first prize. Why don't you go and cultivate some brains?"

"You'll cultivate a thick ear, if you're not careful," said Bolsover major.

And then the bell rang for morning lessons.

THE THIRD CHAPTER.

JUST as we were going strong with Roman History, Billy Bunter rose in his place.

"If you please, sir——"

"Sit down!" snapped Mr. Quelch.

"Oh, really, sir! I——"

"If you have any request to make, Bunter, kindly defer it until afterwards."

"But it's important, sir."

"It cannot be more important than your Form-work, Bunter."

"You really must listen to me, sir."

"Sit down!"

Mr. Quelch's voice resembled the booming of breakers on the beach.

"If you utter another word, Bunter, I shall cane you!"

Billy Bunter dropped into his seat with a groan.

He was restless and uneasy as lessons proceeded; and presently, when Mr. Quelch had his back to the class, and was writing on the blackboard, Bunter slipped from his seat and moved towards the door.

We stared at him with fascination—almost with awe.

It was unheard-of for a fellow to walk out of the Form-room in the middle of morning lessons.

Bunter was half-way to the door, and Mr. Quelch was still engaged at the blackboard.

We held our breath, wondering if Bunter would succeed in getting clear in time.

But the luck was against him.

As he moved forward on tiptoe, his eyes were fixed upon Mr. Quelch. Consequently, he failed to notice an obstruction in his path, in the shape of Bolsover major's boot, which protruded from the end of the desk.

Bunter cannoned into it, and pitched forward into space.

Crash!

The fat junior landed in a heap at the door of the Form-room.

"Yarooooop!"

Mr. Quelch spun round from the blackboard.

For a full minute he stood petrified, unable to move or speak.

When he did find his voice, it resembled the rumble of thunder.

"Bunter!"

"Ow! Yessir!"

"How dare you grovel on the floor in that ridiculous manner?"

"Yow! Some silly ass stuck his feet in the way, sir——"

"Get up at once! How came you to be near the door?"

"Ahem! I—I was on the point of opening it, sir. We want some fresh air in the room. 'Tain't healthy, sir."

"You are prevaricating, Bunter!"

"Nunno, sir! Certainly not, sir! I wouldn't dream of telling an untruth, sir."

"Good old Georgie Washington!" murmured Squiff.

Mr. Quelch picked up a cane.

"Tell me the truth at once, Bunter!" he rapped out.

"I—I—well, you wouldn't listen to me in the first place, sir!" said Bunter wildly. "I wanted to go and get my bike, and you wouldn't let me explain. So I thought I wouldn't worry you again, sir, and I was just—ahem!—slipping out of the room."

Mr. Quelch could scarcely believe his ears.

"You were in the act of leaving the Form-room without permission, for the purpose of getting your bike, as you call it?" he thundered.

"Ow! I—I didn't think you'd mind, sir."

"You are a perverse and wicked boy, Bunter! I shall flog you most severely!"

Mr. Quelch strode towards Bunter, and the cane came into play. It rose and fell with deadly accuracy, and Bunter's yells fairly awoke the echoes.

"There!" panted Mr. Quelch, when he had finished. "Let that be a lesson to you, Bunter."

"Yow-ow-ow! M-m-may I go and fetch my bike now, sir?"

"No, you may not!" roared Mr. Quelch. "Go to your place at once, or I will administer a further castigation."

Billy Bunter limped back to his seat, and the lesson proceeded. There was no further attempt on the part of the fat junior to sneak out of the Form-room.

Directly lessons were over, however, Billy Bunter rushed away like a whirlwind.

There was no stopping him. He was hot on the track of that magnificent bicycle, complete with three-speed gear and latest accessories.

"I should like to see Bunter's face when he gets to the station," said Nugent. "It will be worth a guinea a box."

"Let's go along and meet him," said Wharton. "We'll give him a rousing reception as the winner of the first prize."

Mr. Prout resumed his attack upon Bunter. "As soon as you have removed those evil-smelling components from your person," he bawled, "you will wait upon me in my study!"

"Hear, hear!"

Quite a crowd of us started off for the railway station. Some had brought mouth-organs, and others, for want of better instruments, had armed themselves with combs and tissue-paper.

"When I give the order," said Wharton, "we'll strike up 'See the Conquering Hero Comes.'"

"Ha, ha, ha!"

We got to the station just in time to see Billy Bunter pushing the ancient bike out into the roadway. His fat face was a picture.

He had certainly got his bike—but what a bike! Instead of a smoothly-running modern cycle, it was a dreadful-looking monster. Only a skilled acrobat could have climbed up on to the seat; and as for steering it—well, very few of us would have cared to run the risk.

"I say, you fellows, I've been spoofed!"

"Ha, ha, ha!"

"This ain't a bike at all—it's a beastly gridiron!"

We roared.

" I shall write and tell the editor of the ' Weekly Joker ' what I think of him ! " snorted Bunter. " How the dickens does he suppose I'm going to ride this old crock ? "

" We'll give you a hand, Bunty," said Bolsover major, obligingly.

" Here, hold on ! I—I mean, leggo ! " yelled Bunter, in alarm.

Skinner held the bike, while Bolsover and several others, grunting and groaning under Bunter's weight, lifted the fat runior up on to the seat.

" Now," said Bolsover. " One to be ready —two to be steady—three to be——"

" Off ! " chuckled Skinner.

Bunter lurched forward. He was clutching the handle-bars as if his life depended upon it —as, indeed, it did. For if Bunter relinquished his hold there was no telling what might happen.

" Strike up, you fellows ! " gasped Wharton, in between his sobs of merriment.

And then the band started, " See the Conquering Hero Comes."

" Goes would be more correct," gurgled Nugent. " Good-bye, Bluebell ! "

Bunter had reached the brow of a hill by this time ; and he disappeared over the top.

We raced along in the rear to see the fun.

Bunter careered down that hill at a most alarming pace. He gathered impetus as he went, and he hung on like grim death.

Labouring up the hill, at that moment, came Mr. Prout, the master of the Fifth.

Mr. Prout was taking a constitutional ; and when Bunter loomed on his horizon he stopped short, wondering if he had suddenly been transplanted into the eighteenth century.

Billy Bunter lifted up his voice.

" Stand clear ! " he yelled.

Mr. Prout declined to stand clear. In the days of the Great War he had faithfully served his country as a special constable, and it had been part of his duty to stop cyclists—and others—who were riding in a manner dangerous to the public.

Accordingly, Mr. Prout stepped into the middle of the road, with a fierce frown on his florid face.

Boy ! Bunter ! How dare you imperil the lives of pedestrians in this reckless manner? Stop ! Stand clear ! I command you ! "

Billy Bunter saw that Mr. Prout was a fixture—that wild horses would not drag him away from what he conceived to be his duty.

The fat junior swerved to one side, in the hope of avoiding Mr. Prout ; but the latter swerved at the same time, and there was a grinding collision.

" Oh, my aunt ! " sobbed Squiff. " I—I'm sure I shall bust a boiler in a minute ! "

Mr. Prout lay on his back in the roadway, blinking up at the heavens, and wondering why the stars should suddenly appear at midday.

We rushed up to render first-aid ; but beyond a few bruises the Form-master was unhurt. But he was consumed with a wrath which equalled that of Jove of old.

" That young villain ! That depraved hooligan ! " spluttered Mr. Prout. " Stop him ! "

" Afraid he's gone too far now, sir," said Nugent solemnly.

Bunter had.

By a miraculous stroke of good fortune, he had survived the collision with Mr. Prout ; but it seemed that he had merely passed out of the frying-pan into the fire.

He continued his headlong flight down the hill, at the foot of which lay a green and slimy duckpond.

Bunter's nerves were in such a state by this time that he had lost all control of his machine.

He headed straight as a die for the pond, pitched over the handlebars like a fat fowl in flight, and turned a complete somersault into the water.

" A fitting climax to such harebrained tomfoolery ! " snapped Mr. Prout.

A moment later, a fat and slimy porpoise rose up from the bottom of the pond. Reeds and mud clung lovingly to his face and neck, and he bore a distinct resemblance to the Wild Man of Borneo.

" Groooogh ! " spluttered Bunter, gouging frantically at his eyes and mouth. " Ow ! Yah ! I'm dying ! I've busted both arms, and fractured my spinal column ! "

" Ha, ha, ha ! "

Mr. Prout hurried to the spot, and we followed.

"You have only yourself to blame for this, you errant and foolish young rascal!" stormed Mr. Prout. "How dare you attempt to defile the King's Highway by riding such an absurd and clumsy contrivance as that?"

And Mr. Prout pointed to ye ancient grid-iron, which lay half-submerged in the slimy ooze.

Bunter staggered out of the pond. His clothes were full of water, and he was blown out like a balloon.

"Anybody got a pin?" inquired Peter Todd.

"Ha, ha, ha!"

Mr. Prout resumed his attack upon Bunter.

"As soon as you have removed those evil-smelling components from your person," he barked, "you will wait upon me in my study. I will endeavour to teach you that practical jokes of this sort are not in good taste!"

"How could I help it?" roared Bunter, squelching mud all over the place. "I wasn't riding the beastly thing for fun!"

"That's so, sir," said Bolsover major. "It was I who suggested Bunter should ride the bike, sir."

"Then you will take five hundred lines, Bolsover," snapped Mr. Prout. "And I will acquaint your Form-master with what has occurred."

"Thank you, sir!"

A general move was made in the direction of Greyfriars.

The cane rose and fell with deadly accuracy, and Billy Bunter's yells fairly awoke the echoes!

"Not going to leave your bike behind, Bunter, surely?" exclaimed Wharton.

"Especially when you can get twelve quid for it," chuckled Johnny Bull.

Billy Bunter turned, and flourished a fat fist in our faces.

"Beasts!" he muttered. "I don't believe that letter came from the "Weekly Joker" at all. This is a jape, at my expense."

"Go hon!"

"Pride goeth before a fall," said Nugent. "You shouldn't have swanked so much about your blessed bike, then this wouldn't have happened."

Bunter said no more.

When we reached the school he made hurried tracks for the nearest bath-room, and for quite an hour afterwards came a sound as of much rubbing and scrubbing.

Billy Bunter hated soap and water; but he realised that a liberal application of both was necessary on this occasion, unless he wished to smell like a duckpond for the rest of the term.

"Poor old Bunter!" I remarked. "He'll dry up about his precious bike after this."

But I was wrong.

THE FOURTH CHAPTER.

NEXT day, Billy Bunter was crowing again as loudly as ever.

He had left the bike of yesterday to rust in the duckpond. Bunter was finished with it; and it had nearly finished Bunter.

But the bike of to-morrow—the bike he yet hoped to obtain from the "Weekly Joker"—formed his main topic of conversation. He chattered about it in his sleep, and he never let us hear the end of it by day.

A few mornings later Bunter received a letter—a genuine one this time—from the Editor of the "Weekly Joker." The name and address of that periodical were printed on the top of the notepaper, so there was clearly no hoax this time.

The letter ran thus :

"Weekly Joker" Office,
Fleet Street, London.

W. G. Bunter, Esq.,
Greyfriars School,
Friardale, Kent.

Dear Sir,—It is my pleasure and privilege to inform you that you were successful in solving the whole of our picture puzzles correctly.

" A further communication on this subject will be sent you in due course.

" Meanwhile, with hearty congratulations on your good fortune,—I am, yours faithfully,
" The Editor."

"There you are ! " said Bunter triumphantly. " I told you merit would tell ! I've won the bike, after all, and I think some of you fellows ought to go down on your knees and apologise."

We were certainly very much taken aback.

Was it possible that Bunter had really won the magnificent bicycle awarded by the " Weekly Joker " ?

If so, our practical joke would have fallen flat, and Bunter would have the laugh of us at the finish.

We all waited, in a state of great suspense, for the " further communication " to arrive from the Editor.

Bunter always made it a point to waylay Bogg, the postman, on his way to the school. The fat junior was almost bursting with impatience and excitement.

At last the letter came. The fellows swarmed round Bunter like bees as he opened it.

" Read it out, Billy."

" Have you won the bike ? "

" Is it waiting for you at the station ? "

Bunter pulled out the letter, and read it aloud to us.

" Dear Sir,—I am writing you again, as promised, on the subject of the picture puzzle competition.

" You will be glad to learn that you, in company with seven hundred and ninety-nine other competitors, have qualified for the first prize, namely, a magnificent bicycle, complete with three-speed gear and latest accessories.

" As it is hardly feasible to divide the bicycle into eight hundred parts, and send you a pedal or a brake-block, it has been decided that the sum of £20 shall be divided equally among the successful competitors. This being so, I have pleasure in enclosing herewith postal order for 6d. (sixpence).

" Yours faithfully,
" The Editor."

Bunter went purple.

" It's a swindle ! " he yelled. " A swindle from beginning to end ! "

" Ha, ha, ha ! "

" Instead of a bike they've sent me a mouldy postal order—for sixpence ! "

" And it's made payable to W. G. Bunter at Courtfield Post Office," chuckled Nugent. " That means you've got to tramp all the way to Courtfield to cash it."

Bunter's face worked convulsively.

He was not a fighting man, but if the Editor of the " Weekly Joker " had put in an appearance at that moment, Billy Bunter would have scalped him.

" Sixpence ! " gasped Bunter.

After all his boasting, all his puffed-up vanity, all his great expectations, he had received, not a magnificent bicycle, but the princely sum of sixpence !

" Competitions," said Billy Bunter, " are a snare and a delusion. I shall never go in for 'em again—never ! "

" Hadn't you better get your postal order cashed, Bunter ? " said Wharton.

" I suppose so," grunted the fat junior. " It means some tarts and a ginger-pop at Uncle Clegg's, anyway."

And he started off on the long, long trail to Courtfield.

THE END.

THE SPIRIT THAT WINS!

(Suggested by Rudyard Kipling's Grand Poem, "IF.")

BY THE HEADMASTER.

If you can play the game as heroes play it,
   Nor from the path of duty turn aside ;
  And worship not the world, but He Who made it.
   Though cynics sneer, and scoffing tongues deride.
If you can fight for all that's worth the winning,
   And give no heed to slander or to spite,
And find yourself more sinned against than sinning,
   And ever keep your face towards the light.

If you can work with energy and vigour,
   If you can play with equal zeal and zest ;
If, though you cut a sad and sorry figure,
   You still strive manfully to do your best.
If you can lose—and lose again hereafter,
   And bear no malice for each bitter rout ;
And meet reverses with good-humoured laughter,
   Yes, even though **you**'re feeling down and out.

If you do well in class, and others slight you,
   Declaiming you a hopeless sort of swot ;
If boys of bigger bulk desire to fight you,
   And blustering bullies give it to you hot.
If you can summon up the grit that's in you,
   And square your shoulders gamely in the fray ;
If you, through thick and thin, can yet continue
   To keep the even tenor of your way.

If you hold fast to all the fine traditions
   Which others do not scruple to disgrace ;
If other fellows win the high positions,
   And leave you stranded early in the race.
If you can bear these blows, and still keep smiling,
   Nor yield to disappointment and despair,
When life seems out of tune, and Fate is riling,
   And your ambitious hopes are crossed with care.

If cruel thorns beset your paths of pleasure,
   And demons of unrest before you flit ;
If, though deprived of luxury and leisure,
   You hide from all the world how hard you're hit.
If you can hold your head erect when needed,
   And keep your honour like a torch in flame ;
Then, spite of all your failures, you've succeeded !
   All honour to you, lad—*you've won the game !*

Figgins D.Wynn H.Shimpole TomMerry G.Herries A.A.Darcy M.Lowther J.Blake

(73)

OUT OF BOUNDS!

A Story of St. Jim's in 1950.

By Bernard Glyn.

THE FIRST CHAPTER.

SMITH MINOR was grousing. He was dissatisfied. It was Wednesday afternoon? a half-holiday at St. Jim's, and it was raining. Cricket was out of the question. But Smith minor would not have cared for the rain if he could have carried out the little scheme he had planned for that afternoon. It was raining on earth, but the stellagraph had reported fine weather nearly all round the Zodiac, and, once mounted on his air-bike, Smith minor would soon have been far above the rain.

His ripping new air-bike, a present from his Uncle George, had arrived at St. Jim's, and Smith minor had made one or two trial trips on it after lessons, as far as the Pyrenees one evening, and as far as the Hebrides another. Now he was simply burning for a really long ride on it, and he had fixed that afternoon for a run to the moon.

It was easy enough. Leaving St. Jim's at half-past two on his air-bike, he could catch the great ether-plane which started from Cape Town at 3.30. He would have a couple of hours on the moon—long enough to see most of the sights—catching the return plane in time to land at Cape Town by eight. Then a rapid run home on his air-bike, and at the worst he would be late for evening call-over.

But it was not to be.

The Head had placed the moon out of bounds. It was all the fault of Perkins minimus, of the Third. That young ass had tumbled into a crater on the moon while on a trip there with a gang of fags, and there had been no end of trouble fishing him out. And so the Head had come down heavy, and placed the moon out of bounds for all fellows below the Sixth Form.

It was a bitter disappointment to Smith minor, who had been looking forward for weeks to his trip to the moon. He was the only fellow in the Fourth Form who had not been there, and it made him feel wild to hear the other fellows talking in the studies about their rambles over the interesting planet, and the manners and customs of the inhabitants.

But the fiat had gone forth: and Smith minor groused. His major in the Sixth spotted him mooching about with his hands in his pockets, and a face as long as a fiddle, and kindly tried to comfort him.

" 'Tain't much of a catch, that tripping to the moon!" Smith major said. "It's only the novelty of the thing. Why not have a run over the Himalayas on your bike, kid?"

"Blow the Himalayas!" grunted Smith minor. "A chap can air-bike over to the Himalayas any day after lessons. This is a half-holiday."

"Well, what about a run across the pampas in South America?"

"I did that last week. Snooks, of the Shell, gave me a lift on the carrier of his bike."

"The moon's no great catch—and they cheat you awfully in the tea-shops there," said Smith major. "Cheer up, kid, and I'll tell you what—I'll take you with me to Mars in the vac."

But Smith of the Fourth wasn't comforted.

A run to Mars in the vac was all very well; but the vac was a long way off.

"Dash it all," said the Sixth-Former. "When I was a kid in the Fourth, we were jolly glad to get a run across India or South America on a half-holiday. You fags want too much."

"Every other chap in the Fourth has been," said Smith minor sulkily. "It wasn't my fault young Perkins tumbled into a crater. He's an ass, anyway. I've a jolly good mind to go."

"Out of bounds, you know." said Smith major severely; and he walked on.

Smith minor grunted.

Of course, it was rather a serious thing to break bounds; but after all, there was no harm in a run to the moon, and all the other fellows had done it.

Smith minor thought it over as he looked out of a window into the rain dropping in the quad.

He made up his mind at last.

He was going.

Even if he missed call-over that evening, and was called over the coals by his form-master, there was no reason why that gentleman should guess that he had been to the moon. He would come whizzing home on his air-bike, just as if he had merely been to the North Pole or New Zealand for the afternoon.

Having made up his mind, Smith minor lost no more time. He had none too much to spare now, if he was to catch the ether-plane at Cape Town.

He hurried to the bike shed.

In five minutes the handsome new air-bike was ready, and Smith minor's face was bright as he jumped into the saddle.

"Hallo! Whither bound?" called out Snooks, of the Shell, as he started.

"Moon!" answered Smith minor briefly.

"Out of bounds, you know."

"I'm chancing it."

"Look out for the asteroids!" called out Snooks. "The up 'plane yesterday had quite a narrow shave, according to the paper this morning."

Smith minor laughed.

"Bow-wow!" was his answer.

And off he went.

The air-bike was in splendid fettle, and it simply whizzed. Smith minor was a good rider, but he had only had short runs before, within the limits of Europe. His heart beat a little as Spain vanished behind him, and he found himself over the Mediterranean. Like a silver streak, the Mediterranean vanished in the distance, and Africa lay below.

He smiled a little as he thought of the ancient days when men had built a railway from the Cape to Cairo. He was quite excited by his first view of the Congo, and rather sorry that he had no time to stop to take a second glance at the Zambesi. There were quite a lot of interesting things to see on the Zambesi, and he determined to run along again on Saturday and have a look at them.

He glanced at his watch as he buzzed along over the Transvaal; it was 3.25 when he passed the Orange River. He had only Cape Colony to pass now, but only five minutes left to catch the ether-plane at Cape Town. Would he do it?

Smith minor knitted his brows as the air-bike rushed on, fairly humming with its speed. It would be too cruel if he came all that way, and missed the ether-plane after all.

Cape Town was in sight at last. But it was turned half-past three, and Smith minor's heart sank.

If the ether-plane had started to time, he was too late! He had delayed too long thinking it out at St. Jim's.

" Oh, rotten ! " groaned Smith minor.

Then his face brightened up.

Rising above Cape Town. was the huge, sprawling form of a mighty ether-plane.

He was five minutes late---but apparently the 'plane was late, too, by a glorious chance Smith minor headed for the 'plane instead of for the landing-place. It was not uncommon for belated passengers to catch the 'plane after it had started, in a swift air-bike ; so long, of course, as the 'plane was within the limits of the atmosphere. When once it had passed beyond that an air-bike could not follow.

The ether-plane was rising fast ; but Smith minor calculated well. He buzzed alongside, and hooked on, at a height of four miles. A 'planeman rushed forward to help him aboard.

" Just in time, sir ! " he said cheerily. " Buck up and get on your ether-mask—we shall be outside the atmosphere in one minute now."

" Righto ! " gasped Smith minor.

He lost no time. He jumped into the electrically warmed ether-suit provided for all passengers, and buckled on the ether-mask. He had scarcely fastened the last buckle when the ether-plane was outside the earth's atmosphere, and cleaving its way through air-less space.

Smith minor could have danced with elation. He had caught the 'plane after all, and his trip was coming off. With a light and airy tread he went into the ticket-office amidships.

He laid down ten shillings, and the booking-clerk looked at him. With a tired expression, he connected up the speaking-tube from his ether-mask to Smith minor's.

" Thirty shillings, sir ! "

" What ? "

" Thirty bob ! "

" Oh, draw it mild ! " exclaimed Smith minor warmly. " It's ten shillings return to the moon."

" Who's talking about the moon ? " grunted the booking-clerk testily. " It's thirty bob single to Mars."

" Mars ! " stuttered Smith minor.

" Yes."

The St. Jim's junior blinked at him.

" Is—is—isn't this the 'plane for the moon ? " he asked faintly.

" Of course it isn't. The moon 'plane left five minutes earlier."

Smith minor almost tottered.

He understood now.

The 'plane for the moon had left at scheduled time. Five minutes later the 'plane for Mars had started ; and it was the Mars 'plane he had caught.

For a moment he was almost overcome as he thought of call-over at St. Jim's, and the grim brow of the Head.

" You wanted the moon 'plane ? " asked the man in the office, with a grin.

" Yes," gasped Smith.

" Well, you're booked for Mars now. Don't worry—it's only a two-day trip."

" Two days ! " gasped Smith minor. " It's bed-time at St. Jim's at half-past nine. I shall get into no end of a row if I miss dorm."

The clerk shrugged his shoulders.

" Can't be helped now. Passengers shouldn't make mistakes." he grunted. " Thirty bob, please."

Smith minor suppressed a groan, and paid over the thirty shillings. It was all he had, and it was intended to see him through his afternoon's expenses on the moon.

" I---I say, they'll be anxious about me at St. Jim's if I don't turn up for dorm," he stammered. " C-c-can I send a stella-graph ? "

" Next window for stellagraphs."

And the man turned to another passenger.

Smith minor moved along to the next window, and connected up with the stella-graph clerk.

" How much for a stellagraph to the earth? " he asked timidly.

" One-and-six."

" I—I—I've only got twopence——"

The stellagraphist gave a shrug.

Smith minor moved away from the window in a worried mood. Away on the lee of the ether-plane he caught sight of the moon, looming large and bright, but it did not interest him now. He was thinking of the painful interview with the Head when he returned to St. Jim's after two days' absence without leave.

THE SECOND CHAPTER.

"SMITH MINOR!"

The Head was taking the roll-call in Big Hall at St. Jim's.

Smith major looked round from the ranks of the Sixth. His minor did not answer to his name.

The Head frowned, and marked the Fourth-Former down as absent.

But it was not till bedtime that they were anxious about Smith minor. He did not turn up for dormitory, and the Fourth-Formers went to bed wondering where he was.

It came out that he had been seen starting on his air-bike, and the Head, fearing an accident, rang up a dozen quarters of the earth on his wireless telephone. But there was no news of Smith minor from any of the five continents.

It was nearly ten o'clock when Smith major presented himself in the Head's study, with a troubled brow.

" Has the boy returned ? " asked the Head.

" No, sir. I—I'm afraid he's gone out of bounds," answered the prefect. " If you think proper, sir, I will catch the night 'plane for the moon, and look for him."

" Do so, by all means," said the Head.

It was morning when Smith major returned to St. Jim's, only to report that the missing junior had not been heard of on the moon. It was certain that he had not caught the moon 'plane the day before at Cape Town, and that was all.

There was excitement at St. Jim's that day. Where was Smith minor ?

" The young ass ! " said Snooks, of the Shell. " I know he started for Cape Town. Tumbled into the Congo or the Zambesi, as like as not."

For two whole days there was no news of Smith minor.

The wireless telephone was going frequently,

and several times the Head rang up the moon on the lunaphone.

But no news came through.

But at last—just before dorm the second night—there came the buzz of an air-bike in the quadrangle, and the fellows rushed out—and there was Smith minor !

" Where have you been ? " shouted a dozen voices.

But Smith minor only answered with another question :

" Is the Head waxy ? "

" Just a few ! " grinned Snooks.

A Sixth-Form prefect took Smith minor by the collar, and marched him into the Head's study. From that dreaded apartment there came the sound of steady swishing, accompanied by loud yells from Smith minor.

Smith minor was looking quite doubled up when he came out. He wore a worried look in the Form-room the next morning. But as the effects of the licking wore off, Smith minor brightened up. He hadn't been to the moon—but he was the only fellow in the Lower School who had been to Mars !

He was the centre of a crowd in the common-room after lessons that morning.

" Oh, ripping—tip-top ! " he said. " The moon—oh, bother the moon ! Hardly worth a fellow's while goin' there, you know. Rather small beer, what ? But Mars—Mars is the real goods ! Yes, the Head laid it on rather hard, but I don't mind—it was worth it ! I palled on with a Martian chap while I was there—quite a sportsman, and he's coming down to see me next Wednesday. Of course, this ether-planin' bizney is only in its infancy—it's simply rot to spend two days goin' to Mars and back. I shall be jolly glad when they start the six-hour service they're talking about. My idea is, we ought to fix up a match with a Martian school—we could meet them on the moon, to save a bit of the journey on both sides, see ? "

On Wednesday afternoon Smith minor was the cynosure of all eyes as he swanked about the quad showing the sights to the chap from Mars ; and as the licking had worn off he wasn't at all sorry that he had gone Out of Bounds.

THE END.

MY BIGGEST FIGHT.

BY PERCY BOLSOVER

(Bully of the Remove).

Now I'll set forth in black
and white
Full details of that grap-
ple,
That fearful and historic fight
I had behind the Chapel.

My foeman was a hefty lout,
His name, I think, was Tubb,
And when the words came,
"Seconds Out!"
The brute began to blub!

Although not more than twice his
size
I smote my foe with vigour.
He often paused to wipe his eyes,
And cut a sorry figure!

I landed out with left and right,
And very rarely missed.
My victim backed away in fright
And urged me to desist.

"Lie down, you dog!" I made
reply,
Then shattered all his hopes,
By slogging him, till with a cry
He reeled against the ropes!

He landed with a fearful thump
Upon the frosty ground;
And then they biffed the silly
chump
Until they brought him round.

A storm of cheering rent the air:
A burst of frenzied yells!
"My hat! He's great beyond
compare!
He'd knock out Billy Wells!"

They swept me off my hefty feet,
They swung me shoulder-high.
The thrilling news of Tubb's
defeat
Attracted passers-by.

My keen admirers round me
swarmed.
I volunteered to lick
All cripples, feeble and deformed,
Who hobbled on a stick!

That challenge still holds good
to-day:
Come forth, ye halt and blind!
Advance (on crutches) to the fray,
And don't be left behind!

My fame will spread from shore to
shore
In record time, I wager;
And may new honours ever pour
On me—Bolsover major!

THE LAST WILL & TESTAMENT OF

WILLIAM GEORGE BUNTER

(Of the Greyfriars Remove.)

EDITOR'S NOTE.—We understand on good authority that Alonzo Todd has threatened to have Bunter's Blood. This being so, we have saved our fat friend a good deal of trouble by making out his Will for him in advance.

WHEREAS ME, WILLIAM GEORGE BUNTER, haveing been so savidgely attacked by Alonzo Todd that my koller-bone, spine, and back are broken; and being konvinced that I am walking in the shaddo of death—(Surely you mean " debt " ?—ED.)— I hearby make my last Will and Testameant, as under.

(1) I give and bequeeth to my studdy-mate, Peter Todd, the bike which I borowed from him last weak.

(2) To Alonzo Todd, kousin of the afoursaid Peter, I bestowe my pen-nife, which I fownd in Wharton's desk. This will show that I freely forgive him for his krime.

(3) To my other studdy-mate, Tom Dutton, I leeve a strong rekwest that he provides himself with an ear-trumpett as soon as possible.

(4) I give and bequeeth to my affeck-shunate brother Sammy the sum of tuppence-halfpenny (2½d.) which has been lodged with my solliciters, for Sammy to inherrit when he comes of age.

(5) To Harry Wharton, kaptin of the Remove, I leave my valluable book, " How To Play Krickit," By One Who Nose.

(6) My pare of trowsers (garanteed to hold three persons) I leeve to Lord Mauleverer, as a return for menny acts of kindness. Whatever Mauly may say about the kwallity of the trowsers, he won't be able to complane of the kwontity !

(7) To Fisher T. Fish, my partner in menny a wunderfull wheeze, I leeve all my pawn-ticketts.

(8) To Harold Skinner, of the Remove, I leeve my glasses, hopeing he will see things a bit differently than he does now.

(9) To Bolsover major I bestowe as menny jam-puffs as Mrs. Mimble will allow him, in the hope that they will choke him.

(10) To my deer old pal Bob Cherry, I sollumly give and bequeeth my famus postal-order (compleat with beerd and side-whiskers) —when it comes !

GIVVEN UNDER MY HAND AND SEEL THIS FIRST DAY OF APRIL, IN THE YEAR OF GRACE ONE THOUSAND NINE HUNDRED AND NINETEEN,

WILLIAM GEORGE BUNTER.

RALLY ROUND!

A Song for Readers of "The Holiday Annual."

Words by G. R. SAMWAYS.

Music by FRANK WITTY.

With a marching rhythm.

Ral - ly round the Ban-ner, Boys! Keep it flutt'ring high! Rend the air with a mer-ry noise, For-ward! nev-er say die! Loy-al young Brit-ons, heart and soul, Swing-ing a-long to-wards the goal!

CHORUS:

Tramp to - geth-er! Tramp to - geth-er! Bear-ing all be - fore us!

THE SWORDS CROSSED AND THE CLANG OF THEM RANG THROUGH THE HALL!

(See "IN MONMOUTH'S CAUSE!")

THE SIX NEW HOUSE FELLOWS HAD NO SUSPICION OF THE FOE AT HAND.

(See page 102.)

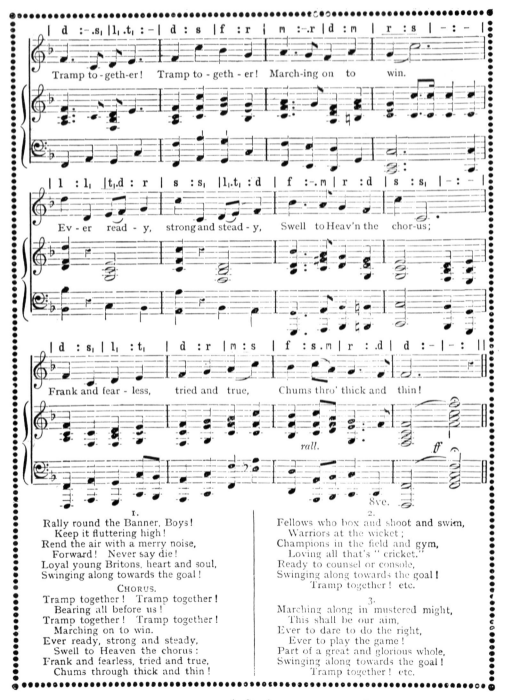

|d :-.s₁|l₁.t₁ :-|d :s |f :r |m :-r d :m |r :s |- :-|

Tramp to-geth-er! Tramp to-geth-er! March-ing on to win.

|l :l₁ |t₁.d :r |s :s₁ |l₁.t₁ :d |f :-.m |r :d |s :s₁ |- :-|

Ev-er read-y, strong and stead-y, Swell to Heav'n the chor-us;

|d :s₁ |l₁ :t₁ |d :r |m :s |f :s.m |r :d |d :-|- :||

Frank and fear-less, tried and true, Chums thro' thick and thin!

rall.

ff

8ve.

1.

Rally round the Banner, Boys!
Keep it fluttering high!
Rend the air with a merry noise,
Forward! Never say die!
Loyal young Britons, heart and soul,
Swinging along towards the goal!

CHORUS.

Tramp together! Tramp together!
Bearing all before us!
Tramp together! Tramp together!
Marching on to win.
Ever ready, strong and steady,
Swell to Heaven the chorus:
Frank and fearless, tried and true,
Chums through thick and thin!

2.

Fellows who box and shoot and swim,
Warriors at the wicket;
Champions in the field and gym,
Loving all that's " cricket."
Ready to counsel or console,
Swinging along towards the goal!
Tramp together! etc.

3.

Marching along in mustered might,
This shall be our aim,
Ever to dare to do the right,
Ever to play the game!
Part of a great and glorious whole,
Swinging along towards the goal!
Tramp together! etc.

A Cliff House Comedy

A Clever Complete Story, Written in Three Parts, by Miss Phyllis Howell, Bob Cherry, and Hurree Singh.

THE FIRST CHAPTER.

By Phyllis Howell.

WHEN I saw myself addressed on the envelope as " Fillis," I knew the letter had come from Coker of Greyfriars.

Among the many things that Coker can't do, his best achievement is spelling.

I must confess I felt rather annoyed when Marjorie Hazeldene brought Coker's letter along.

It isn't nice to be addressed as " Miss Fillis Howl." No wonder Marjorie was smiling.

" Oh, dear ! " I exclaimed. " That boy Coker will be the death of me ! He seems to devote all his spare time to writing me letters. Why doesn't he give me a rest, and start on you or Clara ? "

" Because," said Marjorie, " he knows we wouldn't be soft enough to reply."

I fired up at this.

" Do you suggest that I'm soft ? " I demanded heatedly.

" Oh, no ! Not at all ! But you seem to give Coker a trifle too much rope, Phyllis, dear."

" Coker's a nuisance ! " I said.

(I might not have said the same of Bob Cherry, had he written. But then, Bob's a far too sensible fellow to keep pestering a girl with letters.)

As it happened, however, this wasn't a letter. It was something a thousand times worse—a poem.

Now, there are poets—and poets. Coker comes under the latter heading. His prose is awful enough ; his poetry is a sight for gods and men and little fishes.

" Read it out," said Marjorie, laughing.

" I can't."

" Why not ? "

" Because I shall have to get it translated first."

Marjorie chuckled, and looked over my shoulder. This is what we saw :

" O Fillis, you are charming,
    O Fillis, you are IT ;
  Your bewty is alarming,
    It gives a chap a fit."

" Why, the fellow is being quite rude ! " I said indignantly.

" Nonsense ! " said Marjorie. " He means well."

" But he says that my beauty gives him a fit——"

" That's Coker's way of being complimentary. He had to say ' fit,' because it was the only rhyme he could think of for ' IT.' "

We continued to read :

" The freshness of a daisy
    Your lovely chivvy has !
  It sends a fello crazy,
    It makes him dance the Jazz ! "

Marjorie began to sob—with laughter.

" Don't ! " I implored. " Don't hit me when I'm down ! "

" Oh, dear ! I really can't help it ! That boy is too funny for words ! How does it go on ? "

" Fare Fillis, I am yerning
  To see you wunce agane ;
My manly cheeks are burning
  As if with sudden pane."

" Oh ! " gasped Marjorie, pressing her hands to her sides. " It's I who have got the sudden pain ! "

And she rocked with laughter.

I rocked, too—with anger.

I would have destroyed Coker's silly piffle there and then, but Marjorie shot out a restraining hand.

" It would be such a pity to miss the rest of this masterpiece," she said.

So we read on.

" I've raised a teem to meat you
  In a big crikit match ;
We'll guarantee to beat you
  If you'll come up to skratch."

" What awful nerve ! " murmured Marjorie.

" Just tell the girls to dress up
  In their best toggs, you see,
To gaze at G. L. Jessop—
  In other words—at ME ! "

" We'll meat you and defeat you,
  But if perchance you win,
We'll take you out and treet you
  To a divine tuck-in ! "

" A very sporting offer ! " I said.

Marjorie stared.

" You're surely not going to accept it ? " she exclaimed.

" Indeed I am ! "

" Phyllis ! "

" I don't know a mighty lot about cricket," I said. " But I've seen Coker play, and I'm convinced that we could easily beat a team of Cokers."

" Hear, hear ! " said Clara Trevlyn, coming into the room. " I don't know whether you are talking about cricket or hopscotch, but we could beat a team of Cokers at either ! "

Marjorie looked doubtful.

" Coker is a big boy——"

" And a very silly one ! " I cut in. " It's

like his cheek to want to play a girls' school at cricket. The sooner he's put in his place the better."

" That's the stuff to give 'em ! " said Clara approvingly.

" I shall write to Coker," I said, " and accept his challenge."

" I don't think——" began Marjorie.

" No," said Clara crushingly, " you never do ! That's why Cliff House marks time instead of doing big things."

" Really——" said Marjorie, flushing.

I hastened to pour oil on the troubled waters. And then, taking up a pen, I wrote a brief but emphatic reply to Coker's challenge. It ran as follows :

" Dear Coker,—Your poem (?) has been duly translated, and, on behalf of the Cliff House girls I accept your challenge to a cricket match.

" We shall be pleased to meet your eleven in our playing field on Saturday afternoon at two.---Yours sincerely,

" PHYLLIS HOWELL."

Marjorie insisted that I was impulsive and hot-headed. To which Clara, in her slangy way, replied " Rats ! " And Flap Derwent, when she heard of my letter to Coker, heartily backed it up. So Marjorie was in the minority.

For two days after the despatch of the letter nothing happened.

Then, whilst we were chatting in the gateway of Cliff House, in the cool of the evening, a cyclist rode up.

It was Harry Wharton, of Greyfriars.

I couldn't help feeling a certain amount of resentment towards him for not bringing Bob Cherry along.

" Wherefore this late call ? " I asked.

Wharton was looking serious. He usually is.

" It's about that letter you sent to Coker," he said.

" Well ? "

" I—I thought I'd bike over and warn you not to play his eleven at cricket."

" Sorry ! " I said, " but it's all cut and dried."

" You're going to play Coker's lot ? "

" Yes ! "

" Every time ! " chimed in Clara.

Wharton flushed.

" You'll be whacked to the wide ! " he declared. " Coker will show you up in front of everybody ! "

" That remains to be seen," I said warmly. " I suppose you've got the stupid idea into your noddle that girls are no good at anything —bar needlework. You think we can't play cricket ? "

" Ahem ! Not exactly."

" We shall make rings round Coker's prize comedians," said Clara.

Wharton shook his head.

" Sorry to disagree," he said, " but Coker's not quite such an ass as you think. He can't play cricket for toffee—but the other fellows in his team can ! You ought to see the eleven he's getting up. He's persuaded Blundell and Bland and Hilton and Fitzgerald, of the Fifth, to turn out—and they're all good men. They're joining in mainly for the fun of the thing ; but they mean to give you a fearful licking ! "

" We'll chance that ! " I said stiffly.

" Look here, Phyllis, I don't want to see you whacked——"

" You won't ! " I said confidently.

" But there's Blundell and Bland and Hilton——"

" Don't let us have that chorus all over again ! " said Clara. " What do those fellows know about cricket, anyway ? "

" They know enough to give the Remove a close game."

" The Remove ? Why, we could lick the Remove gagged and bound and blindfolded ! "

Wharton burst into a laugh.

" I can see it's no use arguing with you ! " he said.

" Not a scrap ! " said Clara. " Good-evening ! "

" I really think Harry is right," said Marjorie.

" Rats ! "

" Well, I've warned you," said Wharton, mounting his machine. " I hope you'll think the matter over, and decide to withdraw. Cheeroh ! "

And the Greyfriars fellow rode away in the gathering dusk.

THE SECOND CHAPTER.

By Bob Cherry.

" WHEREFORE that worried brow ? " Johnny Bull put the question to Wharton, who came into No. 1 Study with a frown.

" It's no good," said Harry, throwing his cap into the corner and himself into the arm-chair.

" Do you mean to say the girls won't withdraw ? " said Nugent.

" Right on the wicket ! "

" My hat ! " I exclaimed. " They'll by booked for a fearful licking."

And Inky remarked that the lickfulness would be terrific.

Wharton grunted.

" I warned them that Coker was raising a strong team," he said, " but they didn't seem to care a rap—except Marjorie. And now they'll be licked."

" And Coker will crow for the rest of the term ! " groaned Nugent. " It's nothing to crow about really—licking a team of girls. But you know what Coker is."

" Can't we do something to help the girls ? " said Johnny Bull, desperately.

" We've done everything possible," said Wharton. " They've had a fair warning."

At that moment Peter Todd looked in.

" Well, you're a bright lot ! " said Peter, glancing round at us. " You look about as cheerful as a set of boiled owls ! What's wrong ? "

Wharton explained the situation.

" The girls will be beaten all ends up," he concluded dolefully. " I'd do anything to prevent it—but there's no way out."

" Isn't there, though ? "

Toddy's eyes were sparkling, and we could see that a wheeze was working in his mighty brain.

" Can you suggest anything, old scout ? " asked Wharton, at once.

Peter nodded.

" There's only one thing for it," he said.

" You're thinking of kidnapping Coker's team ? " I hazarded.

" Wrong, as usual ! " grinned Peter. " I know a dodge worth two of that."

" Out with it ! " we exclaimed.

Peter chuckled.

" I propose that seven of us—Smithy, Tom Redwing, myself, and everybody here barring Inky—whose dusky complexion would give the show away—turn ourselves into members of the fair sex—for one afternoon only ! "

" What ! "

We stared blankly at Toddy.

" It's been done before," said that cheerful youth, " and it can be done again. The girls, of course, would not stand an earthly against fellows of Blundell's weight. But if we are on the spot, and join forces with Marjorie, Clara, Phyllis, and Flap Derwent, we shall succeed in trouncing Coker's gang."

" My hat ! "

" Can't be done ! " said Nugent, after a pause.

" Why not?"

" Coker & Co. would know we weren't Cliff House girls."

"Dear me ! " murmured Mr. Prout. " Thank goodness that was merely a trial ball !"

" Rats ! Phyllis could introduce us as new girls. We shall be rather a crowd, but that can't be helped. It's not impossible for seven new girls to be at Cliff House."

" No," agreed Wharton. " But what about the clobber ? "

" Moses, in Courtfield, can do the needful.

We shall want plenty of grease-paint, and all the rest of it, of course. But, as I say, it won't be the first time we've togged up as girls."

" It's risky," said Johnny Bull.

" What of that ? You don't funk taking a few risks, surely ? "

" Toddy's right," said Wharton at length. " We must persuade the girls to let us join in. I think they will. The jape will appeal to them."

" Bed-time, you kids ! " came the cheery voice of Wingate of the Sixth.

We trooped up to the dormitory, and discussed Toddy's scheme in detail.

Next day I biked over to Cliff House myself, and told the girls what was in the wind.

They were awfully bucked, and were quite willing to own us as schoolmates for the space of an afternoon.

We became quite excited as the time drew near.

So did Coker.

The great Horace had drawn up a very strong eleven—with two exceptions.

The exceptions were Coker himself and **Mr.** Prout.

We couldn't believe our ears at first when Coker told us that Prout had volunteered to play in his team. But it was so.

It happened that Prout had nothing to do on Saturday afternoon. Quelchy had broken off a golfing appointment, and left him stranded.

Prout fancies himself as being a bit of a cricketer—he played umpteen years ago at college—and when he heard of the fixture he requested that he might play. The request amounted to a command.

We revelled at the prospect of playing against Prout.

This would not be the first occasion on which Prout would give a comic turn in public. Once upon a time he skippered an eleven to play against the Old Boys—and a very pretty mess he made of it. He wasn't likely to fare much better this time.

Coker didn't want to play Prout, of course. But he could hardly say no to a form-master. And, even with such an obstruction as Prout in the team, Coker thought that they would lick the girls to a frazzle.

Needless to say, we thought differently.

THE THIRD CHAPTER.

By Hurree Singh.

SATURDAY turned up arrivefully. The sun blazefully streamed down upon the esteemed playful field of Cliff House.

The other members of the Famous Five, together with the worthy Todd, and Smithy and Redwing, had disguisefully attired themselves in the girlful garb. They asked me to come over and performfully undertake the umpireful duties.

We had not been longfully waiting on the ground when the ludicrous Coker appeared with his teamfulness.

The sahib Prout was there, dressed up killfully.

The charming Phyllis introducefully presented her eleven to Coker, who did not smell the ratfulness.

Then the game commencefully started.

Phyllis Howell won the tossfulness, and she and the fair Marjorie opened the innings.

Girls cannot play the cricketful game;

and Phyllis and Marjorie would have been bowlfully got out but for one reason.

Coker insisted on bowling at one end, and the sahib Prout at the other.

Phyllis and Marjorie made the esteemed fur fly.

The score rose with the boundful leapfulness.

Prout mopped his learned brow.

" Oh, dear ! " said he gaspfully. " Really, this is too bad ! I had no idea that girls knew how to make runs."

" They wouldn't do it if I were bowling, sir ! " said Blundell, throwing out the esteemed hint, as it were.

" Nonsense, Blundell ! Do you dare to suggest that you are a better bowler than your Form-master ? "

" Nunno, sir ! "

" When I get into my stride," said Prout, " the wickets will fall like ninepins—like chaff before the reaper, Blundell ! "

" Rats ! "

" Did you speak, Blundell ? "

" I—I was just muttering to myself, sir ! "

" That is an extremely bad habit, Blundell. Are you quite right in the head ? "

" Eh ? "

" Is the sun too warm for you ? "

" My hat ! I—I'm quite all right, sir."

" Then do not behave like a demented creature ! "

So saying, the worthy Prout proceedfully continued to bowl.

The girls smote hitfully. The score rose mountfully. The spectators chuckled grinfully.

The bowlfulness of Prout was awful ; the bowlfulness of Coker was more so.

Presentfully Blundell took a hand, and it was a change betterfully.

Phyllis was bowled, and Marjorie shared the same fatefulness.

Then Clara and Flap Derwent came in to perform batfully. They knocked the Proutful stuff all over the shopfulness. But Blundell settled their esteemed hash.

But the score had reached bigful proportions, and it got bigger when Harry Wharton, in the disguise of a fair maiden, came to the wicket.

Prout was whackfully exhausted. He threw himself down in the grassfulness and groaned.

"Bless my soul! Who ever would have thought these girls had the strength to hit like this? You had better take my place at this end, Bland."

Bland obeyed with promptfulness.

He and Blundell performed manfully; but they could not shiftfully get rid of Wharton.

Coker's jaw fell dropfully.

He had expectfully anticipated to win; but the girls had already scorefully knocked up 150.

Wharton was catchfully disposed of at last. But our Cherryful chum took up the esteemed running, and the fieldsmen perspired pantfully.

Runs came fast and thickfully.

After an hour's smitefulness, the girls' team declared, with the scorefulness at 270.

Prout gave the gaspfulness.

"It is a tremendous score," he said. "I should feel very dubious about our chances of beating it, but for the fact that I am in great form. There is no wielder of the willow who can hold a candle to me—Paul Prout!"

"And there's me, too!" said Coker. "Between us, sir, we ought to knock off the necessary number of runs. I've put you down first on the batting list, sir."

"Under the arrangement we made," said Phyllis, "you're to treat us to a tip-top tea." Coker was in a tight corner, but he was a fellow of his word.

"That was a very right and proper thing to do, Coker!"

They put on the padfulness and walked strollfully to the wicket.

Harry Wharton was bowling, and his first ball swervefully curled round Prout's bat, and crashfully shattered his wicket.

"Dear me!" murmured Prout. "Thank goodness that was merely a trial ball!"

"A—a what, sir?" gasped Wharton.

"A trial ball. The first ball, of course, does not count!"

"Oh!"

"We live and learn!" murmured Nugent.

I told Prout he was out, but he glared at me fiercefully.

"Do not be absurd, Hurree Singh! You know as well as I do that the first ball is merely a preliminary. It does not matter whether one hits or misses it. I shall certainly not dream of going out!"

"As you rule it, my honoured sahib," I said resignedly.

Prout ran out at the next ball, with the purposeful object of smiting it to the esteemed horizon.

But the ball glidefully whizzed between his legs, and again wreckfully damaged his wicket.

"How's that?"

"Out!" I said, with distinctful emphasis.

Prout swung round upon me sharpfully.

" You appear to gloat over my downfall—which was purely accidental ! " he barkfully rapped out. " I happened to be looking somewhere else when the ball came. However, I will retire. I have no doubt that Coker will be able to get the necessary runs."

But Coker was despatchfully sent back to the pavilion shortly afterwards. Vernon-Smith, although his skirts got in the way, managefully contrived to send Coker packing.

" Fluke ! " said Coker growlfully.

" Strikes me there will be a few more flukes by the time we've finished," murmured our Cheeryful chum.

Blundell came in, and he played with the esteemed desperation.

But the goodfulness of the bowling was terrific.

Wharton and Vernon-Smith were at the topful height of their form.

Blundell went back, and Bland and Hilton and Fitzgerald did the trotful caper. They could not defendfully keep up their wickets for long.

Coker's face worked with the convulsiveness. He had imagined it would be easy to lickfully defeat a team of girls.

He could not understandfully make it out. Neither could Prout. Coker tore the hairfulness, and Prout would have done likewise, but for the baldfulness of his pate.

" We've made six runs ! " growled Coker. " A mouldy six ! "

" And there are five wickets down ! " said Prout snapfully. " Really, Coker, I wish you had taken more care in the selection of your team ! "

" Mum-mum-my hat ! "

" I should certainly not have played, had I known you were fielding a set of incompetent boobies ! " said Prout.

" But—but you didn't do any scoring yourself, sir ! "

" Ahem ! I allowed myself to be bowled out, in order to give the girls some encouragement."

" Oh ! "

" There goes another wicket ! " said Blundell " It's awful ! "

" Faith, an' it's too bad, entirely ! " groaned Fitzgerald.

Wharton and Vernon-Smith bagfully took the remainder of the wickets, and Coker's eleven were all out for 14 !

In the ranks of Coker there was weeping and grinding of teeth gnashfully.

Phyllis Howell came up to Coker with a sweetful smile.

" I rather fancy we've won ! " she said.

Coker grunted.

" Under the arrangement we made," said Phyllis, " you're to take us out and treat us."

" Oh, my hat ! "

Coker was in a tightful corner, but he was a fellow of his esteemed word. He had expressfully promised to stand treat to the girls if they won ; and he did not attemptfully try to back out. His Judyful aunt had sent him a remittance, and he was able to foot the billfulness.

" All serene," he said. " Come along to the bunshop in Friardale."

So Marjorie and Clara, Phyllis and Flap Derwent followed in the wakefulness of Coker. And Mary Wharton and the others, whose identity Coker did not suspectfully· guess, followed.

Coker stood the handsome spreadfulness. And he never knew how it was that the lickfulness had been imparted to his team by the girls.

As for Prout, he tramped back to Greyfriars with a scowlful brow. And he vowed that he would never again enlist under the Cokerful banner in the esteemed cricketful game.

THE END

Against all Comers
By Dick Russell

ooo꧁oꞛooo

THE FIRST CHAPTER.

"WHERE's Smithy ? "

There was a note of concern in Harry Wharton's voice as he asked the question.

The Famous Five were gathered together in the Close with their bikes.

It was a half-holiday, and the weather was too cool for cricket and too warm for footer.

A cycle-spin had been agreed upon ; and to this end Harry Wharton and Co. sought Vernon Smith's company.

Time was when none of us would have cared to ask Vernon-Smith to take part in an excursion of any sort. But since the days when he sowed his wild oats Smithy has changed considerably for the better. He was not exactly a close chum of Wharton's, but the captain of the Remove felt that he would be a useful companion for the afternoon's outing.

But on this occasion, just when he was most in demand, Smithy was missing.

The Famous Five mounted guard over their bikes with an air of impatience.

"Wonder where the silly duffer's hidden himself ? " said Bob Cherry.

"Here comes Bunter," said Nugent. " Per-

haps he can tell us. He knows all the latest movements of the nobility and gentry."

" Ha, ha, ha ! "

Billy Bunter rolled up, bubbling with excitement. He intercepted the question that Harry Wharton and Co. were about to ask him.

" You're waiting for Smithy ? "

" Yes ! " grunted Johnny Bull.

" Then you'll have to wait a jolly long time. Smithy's miles away."

" What ? "

" It's a fact. I was outside his study just after dinner, and I happened to hear him talking to Tom Redwing———"

" You happen to hear a good many things that don't concern you," said Wharton contemptuously. " I only wish I'd caught you with your ear glued to the keyhole. I'd have rolled you along the passage and down the stairs, like the barrel you are ! "

" Oh, really, you know ! I couldn't help hearing what they were saying. Smithy's got such a penetrating voice, you see. I heard him suggest to Redwing that the pair of them went over to Wapshot this afternoon, to run in the Marathon Race."

" My hat ! "

The Famous Five were astonished.

They knew Vernon-Smith for an adventurous sort of chap, rather inclined to recklessness, but his latest enterprise fairly took their breath away.

" He's potty ! " said Bob Cherry. " Why, the Marathon Race is open to all the crack runners in the county. What chance has a school kid got, I should like to know ? Even Wingate of the Sixth wouldn't stand an earthly."

" It's just the sort of thing Smithy would do," said Wharton thoughtfully. " And Tom

Redwing, too. Those two are never happy unless they're up against long odds."

"Is it too late to stop them?" asked Nugent.

"Yes, rather!" chimed in Billy Bunter. "The race was due to start at two o'clock, and it's past that already."

Harry Wharton glanced at his watch.

"The race finishes at Courtfield," he said. "If we buzz over on our bikes, we shall be in time to see the finish."

"Good!"

"I—I say," said Bunter. "Before you run away what about giving me a—a little tip, you know? I gave you the information about Smithy, and it's up to you to do the decent thing."

Bob Cherry spun round upon the fat junior.

"You really think you're entitled to a tip?" he asked.

"Certainly!"

"Well, here goes!"

And before Bunter could faintly realise how it all happened, he found himself lying on his back in the Close.

"There's your little tip," grinned Bob Cherry.

"Ha, ha, ha!"

The Owl of the Remove sat up, breathing threatenings and slaughter against the Famous Five.

But those cheerful youths were already cycling at top speed out of the gates; and Billy Bunter's outpourings were wasted on the desert air.

Courtfield, usually a sleepy, old-world place, was stirred to excitement as Harry Wharton and Co. rode through the straggling High Street.

The pavements were thronged with people, all waiting to see the finish of the Marathon Race.

There had been other sports earlier in the day; but the Marathon Race put everything else in the shade. It was far and away the biggest event of all. And the entrance to the recreation-ground, where the race would actually finish, was besieged with people. They were all intently scanning the distant stretch of roadway.

"No one in sight yet," said Johnny Bull.

"We'll make ourselves comfy here, and carry that precious pair of idiots back to Greyfriars when they turn up. They'll both be fagged out, I reckon."

"And they'll come in last if they come in at all," said Harry Wharton.

But that was where Harry, for all his customary shrewdness, made a mistake.

THE SECOND CHAPTER.

IT was to Tom Redwing that Smithy first confided his idea.

Although he had not been a great while at Greyfriars, Tom Redwing had won for himself a very creditable position in the ranks of the Remove, and he was seldom in the background when there was anything doing.

"I wish to bring two facts plainly before your notice," said Smithy. "Firstly, there's a Marathon Race being run this afternoon; and secondly, I'm going to be the winner of that race."

"But, my dear ass," protested Tom Redwing, "it's an open event. There will be champions competing from all over the county. You will absolutely get left!"

"I'm pretty swift on my pins."

"Yes, I know. I'd back you against anybody in the Remove—or in the Upper Fourth, come to that. But there's a big gulf between schoolboys and crack runners. Look here, Smithy. Don't fool away a perfectly good half-holiday on that stunt. Why, we could go and enjoy ourselves——"

"And so we will, my son! We'll have the time of our little lives!"

"But where do I come in?"

"You'll make the pace for me. I've sized you up, and I know what a topping runner you are. With you and me in partnership we shall be a match for all comers."

"You—you're not joking?" stammered Redwing.

"I was never more serious in my life."

"Then it's a go!" said Tom.

He admired Smithy for his venturesome spirit, and determined to back him up loyally in this undertaking; though he was very dubious as to the result.

The two juniors changed into their

running togs, and proceeded by train to Wapshot.

On their arrival, they told the officials governing the sports that they were anxious to enter for the Marathon—a statement which evoked roars of laughter.

"Hadn't you better go away and grow up first?" suggested one of the men. "The race is for adults—not children."

Smithy's lips set in a firm line.

"Never mind that just now," he said. "If I come in last, I shall deserve all the uncomplimentary remarks you care to fling at me. Meanwhile, kindly shove down our names—Herbert Vernon-Smith and Tom Redwing. Thanks!"

It transpired that there were forty runners altogether.

About half of these were country yokels; and Smithy, as his keen eye swept over their clumsy figures, knew he had nothing to fear from them. But there were other runners—men whose names were not unknown to the sporting press—men who had done a great deal of hard running in their time, and were ready to do a good deal more.

Sharp at two o'clock the runners got off the mark.

Tom Redwing went ahead at a rattling pace. He meant to play his part to the very best of his ability. He would run until he dropped.

As he raced along through the country lanes, past wood and copse, green meadow and sunny orchard, Tom Redwing glanced from time to time at the fellow who ran side by side with him, and noted with admiration how fit and confident Vernon-Smith appeared, and the ease and length of his stride. Redwing knew him for a good runner; but even he had underestimated his chum's capabilities.

The country yokels were out of the picture at an early stage of the race. Most of them had failed to realise that a Marathon Race is not a joke, but calls for pluck and endurance, and iron resolution.

"How do you feel, old man?" panted Tom Redwing, after two villages had been left behind.

"Fit as a fiddle!" responded Smithy. "Do you think we can pass that tall beggar in front?"

"I've not the slightest doubt of it, if we hustle."

"Right!"

Tom Redwing set a strenuous pace, and shortly after their brief conversation the two juniors were leading, save for a small, wiry man who seemed to skim over the ground like a swallow.

Smithy paused when he came to the fallen runner. "Rough luck!" he jerked out sympathetically. Newman looked up with a faint smile.

This wiry gentleman, had the juniors but known it, was a man who had made running his profession. Harry Newman was his name; and as a long-distance runner he could hold his own against any man in the county.

What chance, then, was there for Vernon-Smith, a mere schoolboy, and a junior at that?

But these thoughts did not trouble the two juniors.

They sped on in the wake of the wiry man; but though they ran with all the strength that was in them, they could not gain an inch. Newman was still skimming over the ground at top speed.

And then, a mile from home, Tom Redwing collapsed. His hand went to his head, and he rolled over in the long grass by the roadside.

"I'm done!" he muttered.

But he had played his part well. He was not out for honour and glory. It had been his simple duty to set the pace for Smithy; and he had done so, with courage and fortitude which had never wavered.

"You've got all your work cut out!" he said to Smithy. "Don't stop for me. Go right ahead—and jolly good luck to you!"

A curious lump rose in Smithy's throat as he went ahead with his swinging stride. He was touched by his chum's loyalty. Tom

Redwing was a brick, he told himself—a fellow in a thousand.

These reflections, however, soon had to be swept aside.

Smithy had to devote all his energies to overtaking the man in front. And for the life of him he could not quite see how he was going to do it.

Courtfield was in sight now. The tower of its old Norman church stood in bold relief against the sky.

Smithy was fagged.

He was running his hardest, yet he failed to gain on Newman, whose energy seemed inexhaustible.

Despair began to seize him in its grip. His strength was failing him. He was exhausted, played out, finished.

"If only I could overtake that beggar in front!" he murmured, over and over again.

And then, just as he was about to abandon the struggle—for his head was throbbing painfully, and his legs felt like leaden weights—a startling thing happened.

Harry Newman, tripping up on a stone, which lay in his path, fell prone in the roadway with a sprained ankle.

It was indeed a stroke of good fortune for Smithy. He could never have hoped to overtake the champion in the ordinary way. Good runner as he was, he had his limits.

"It was a jolly fine performance!" said the chairman heartily. And then, raising his glass of ginger-pop aloft, he gave the toast, in tones which rang through the study: "The Winner of the Marathon!"

Smithy paused when he came to the fallen runner.

"Rough luck!" he jerked out sympathetically.

Newman looked up with a faint smile.

"Jove, kid, you've got some grit in you!" he said. "Never mind about me. Just you run on. There's another chap coming on behind."

And so there was.

The tall fellow whom Smithy and Redwing had passed at one stage of the race was now gaining ground rapidly.

Smithy set his teeth, and continued the struggle.

He lurched forward painfully, his breath coming and going in great gasps.

He wondered, as the green hedges slowly receded on each side of him, whether he would be able to last out.

And now he rounded a corner: and behold! the end was at hand.

He could see a crowd of people thronging the entrance to the recreation ground. And in the foreground were Harry Wharton & Co., waving their caps in the air, and shouting wildly.

"Smithy! Smithy! Good old Smithy!"

And now came the swift patter of feet behind him, and Smithy realised that he must put forward one supreme effort, or be vanquished.

Gamely he struggled towards the outstretched tape.

The other runner was almost level with him—almost, but not quite.

It was a near thing, but Smithy reached the tape first.

For one dizzy second he reeled; and then, flinging up his hands, pitched forward on his face. But the afternoon's adventure had not been in vain. Smithy had won the Marathon!

. . . . .

Three hours later, rested and refreshed, Smithy was the guest of honour in No. 1 Study, where a stunning spread had been prepared.

When the feast was in full swing, Tom Redwing came in. He had taken longer to recover from his exertions than Smithy, who was hard as nails.

No reference was made to the Marathon Race until the last chocolate macaroon had disappeared from the dish. Then Harry Wharton rose to his feet.

"We were very bucked to see you pull off the Marathon, Smithy," he said. "Nobody here thought you could do it—nobody except Tom Redwing, that is. We called you a madman and a fool. It seemed such a big thing to undertake. We expected to see you come in last, if you came in at all. And instead of that, you ran like a giddy Spartan, and won! We all congratulate you, and there is no doubt about it being one up to Greyfriars and two up to the Remove!

"Six up to the Remove!" cried Bob Cherry.

"Remove a good first; Fifth-form and all others nowhere!"

"Spare my blushes," murmured Smithy.

"It was a jolly fine performance!" said Harry Wharton heartily.

And then, raising his glass of ginger-pop aloft, he gave the toast, in tones which rang through the study:

"The winner of the Marathon!"

THE END

SIMPLE BOXING FOR THE BEGINNER

By
STANLEY HOOPER
(Fly-weight Champion of Essex)

Late Instructor
to the
Royal Air Force

Boxing is undoubtedly the most popular sport of the present day. Taking into consideration the possibility of the manly art of self-defence becoming compulsory in all schools in the near future, and also the splendid qualities derived from participating in this great sport, the following article for beginners will be found most instructive and useful.

The Correct Position

This is attained by placing the left foot anywhere from twelve to twenty inches in advance of the right, just according to the length of the leg.

It is important at all times to maintain a perfect balance, equally dividing the weight of the body on both feet.

The left foot should be placed flat on the floor, pointing straight to your front, and the right foot with the toes pointing at an angle of about forty-five degrees, with the heel slightly raised.

The left hand should be extended about twelve inches from the shoulder, and should be held in a direct line towards the adversary's chin.

The right arm is best placed across the body so that the glove is nearly on a level with the left shoulder. Keep the right arm about two inches from the body and hold both arms loosely and easily. Slightly incline

THE AUTHOR,
who has boxed in mimic and actual contests with most of the leading men of the day.

the body forward, and you are ready for attack and defence.

Judgment of Distance

Having thoroughly mastered the correct position, the next thing to learn is to judge your distance. This requires special and careful attention.

A simple way to practise is to make a mark upon the wall so that it is level with your chin. Spar up to the mark just as you would to an opponent, and lead off with the left, slowly at first, so that when your arm is fully extended your gloved hand just touches the mark. Then try your right hand, bringing the right foot forward simultaneously. This, in time, will give you an excellent idea of judging your distance, so that in boxing none, or very few, of your intending blows will go astray. When hitting with either hand you will notice that if you turn your hips (so that when your glove reaches your opponent's face you will be facing almost sideways) you are utilising the width of your shoulder, greatly increasing your reach (a wonderful advantage in boxing), and you are able to put the whole weight of your body behind the blow. This latter is the real secret of punching power.

Footwork

Footwork is one of the A B C's of boxing,

and without sufficient knowledge of this important branch of the art, nothing can be accomplished in orthodox boxing. The position of the feet controls every kind of offensive and defensive movement. It is absolutely necessary that you should get about easily and

Getting out of a clinch.

quickly on the feet, and the following simple movements will enable you to master the preliminaries of footwork.

Stand in proper boxing attitude, then step forward with the left foot and follow with the right. Take three paces like this forward, then retreat in the same manner, only using the right foot first, following back with the left. The same thing applies in stepping sideways to the left or to the right. If stepping to the left side, use the left foot first ; if to the right, then the right foot first. Do these movements slowly at the beginning, gradually increasing in speed until you find that you are easily able to avoid a blow without losing your balance.

The forward movement will be found useful for attacking purposes, whilst the backward movement will quickly take you out of reach of a threatened rush or onslaught on the part of your antagonist.

A golden rule to remember at all times, no matter in what position your opponent may have forced you, is TO KEEP YOUR RIGHT FOOT IN A DIRECT LINE BEHIND YOUR

LEFT. Do not on any account stand facing your opponent with legs wide apart. The slightest tap from him will send you over backwards, with nothing to prevent you from falling heavily to the boards.

You will understand from this how essential it is for the purpose of both offence and defence to maintain your equilibrium.

The Use of the Left Hand

I cannot impress too strongly on the beginner the importance of having a good left hand. When you have thoroughly mastered the use of the left you have overcome one of the greatest difficulties in acquiring the art of scientific boxing.

As I have said before, when sparring up to an opponent your left hand should be pointing direct to his chin, so that you are able to stop any rush or forward movement on his part by merely shooting your left out.

This method, or blow, if applied in the proper manner, will very soon stop your

The Author takes a left lead to the head and sends a blow to the ribs of his opponent with the right.

opponent's tactics and cause him to act entirely on the defensive.

Now for leading off with the left. Stand in boxing attitude, then slowly push your left out and just as slowly draw it back. While doing this take care that your elbow is pointing downwards and not out.

After a short practice like this, try shooting the left out quickly, at the same time bringing the left foot forward smartly a few inches, but take great care that you do not step in first and then deliver your blow. These movements must be done at one and the same time. As soon as your blow has landed, get out of distance at once, unless, of course, opportunity presents itself for another dose. Do not lead off in half-hearted fashion, but step in boldly with springing movement. Never lead off until you have properly gauged your distance and are in a position to do so. Don't draw your hand back first, as this "telegraphs" to your opponent your intention to hit.

And the Right

While giving great attention to your left hand you must not forsake entirely the right. This hand is used principally for guarding, but also for what is termed "finishing off purposes." That is to say, when you have either drawn your opponents' guard, or sent in a blow with the left hand, it should be followed up with the right, at the same time bringing the right foot forward a trifle to enable you to get some weight behind the blow.

You must not forsake the right

It is not wise to continually guard blows with your right forearm, as I will explain. This mode of defence is purely an old-time custom. Modern boxing, blended with experience, teaches us to evade unnecessary exertion, and the continual warding off of blows with the forearm will be found a most painful and tiring process.

Defence

Defence, of course, plays a prominent part in boxing, and should be given special attention. A man without a good defence completely crumples up before a determined attack.

The use of arms and hands in defence is generally considered to be the chief means of protection. But there are other ways, such as the use of the head in ducking, and the judgment of distance in stepping back just far enough to allow a blow to either pass you harmlessly (a swinging blow or hook) or fall short by a matter of two or three inches (a straight blow), which will enable you to get back in time to land your counter.

It is imperative to learn the use of the head in jerking same to the side (slipping a blow), ducking the head under (to avoid a left or right swing to the face), or drawing the head and body back out of reach, for, as I have stated before, the incessant guarding of blows with the left or right forearm is very tiring, and will be found by the beginner to have a weakening effect.

Slipping, ducking, etc., will only come to you by experience and constant practice with an opponent as near your weight and size as possible.

Now for slipping a left lead to the head. Get your opponent whom you are practising with to slowly push out his left hand to your face. When his hand has travelled, say, half the distance, just incline your head slightly to the right, so that his blow passes harmlessly over your left shoulder.

You are now in a position to send the left to the face and the right to the body.

Ducking a left swing to the face.—Let your opponent swing his left very slowly round to your face, and, as you see the blow coming, duck under it to your right. His effort will have been wasted, and if he has placed any appreciable force behind his blow he will have swung himself completely off his balance.

You will find yourself presented with an excellent opportunity with either left or right —or both. Take care you don't let a chance like this slip by. Ducking a right-hand swing is performed in exactly the same manner, but, of course, you duck your head under his right, taking a circular downward movement to your left.

It is always advisable, when ducking, to keep the right or left arm across the face as a protection against a possible uppercut. Never, however, get yourself mixed up or flurried! If you have made up your mind to duck a blow, don't lose your head at the very moment and attempt to guard as well. Your mind must be made up quickly, and if you are going to duck, put your confidence in your head, as it were, and do the movement cleanly.

Sidestepping is another valuable asset to the boxer's make-up. It is usually brought into use to evade a rush or in getting out of a corner after you have feinted and drawn a lead and is generally executed in the following manner :

Step back with the right foot first, drawing back the left, placing the right toe directly behind and in a straight line with the left heel. Now turn sharply, facing your right, and take a quick, long step with the right. Follow up with the left and turn, facing your adversary in boxing atti-

An Ideal Pose

tude. Guarding the body is a valuable feature of boxing that is not always done entire justice to by writers of the sport. A left lead to the body is avoided by either knocking his left down and outwards with your right—never try to guard a body blow upwards—or by drawing the body in quickly, at the same time letting fly with your left to the face.

Of course, there are times when it is essential for you to use the hands and arms for guarding purposes, and you will find that if you keep your right arm slanting (so that the glove is nearly on a level with the left shoulder) in parrying an opponent's left lead to the head, the blow will glide off your arm, which you will find a much less painful process than the old-time square forearm guard.

A Few Blows

The Left Arm Parry and the Right to the Ribs.—This blow is very effective and, if used in the proper manner, will send a fellow clean off his feet nine times out of ten. Wait for your opponent to lead off with his left, knock his blow up with your left arm, at the same time pushing him toward your left (see illustration). You will find that in the process you have made an excellent opening for your right hand, which should be sent without hesitation to his ribs (side), thus catching him off his balance.

Another good move is to swing your left round for your opponent's jaw, intentionally miss by a few inches, keep your hand in same position, and wait for the inevitable rush. Then, as he comes for you, bring your hand back in the same direction, catching your man fair and square on the side of the face with the knuckle part of your glove.

A counter I have found extremely useful is performed in the following manner : Wait for your opponent to lead off with his left, knock the blow sideways to your left with your right hand, and then shoot your left to the face like clockwork.

A useful feint is to drop your eyes to your opponent's body and shoot your left to the same spot. When your hand is within, say, six inches of the body, alter its course and jerk it upwards to the face. You will find that your opponent will be completely deceived by this very valuable feint, and, before he has recovered, you will probably be able to get over your right to either head or body, providing you are quick enough.

The Right Cross Counter for the Jaw.—Draw a left lead from your opponent, slip it in the manner already described, and then send your right over his extended left arm to the jaw, or " point." This is the punch that most frequently causes " the knockout."

A Few Hints in General

The training of a boxer plays a great part in his success, or otherwise. Stamina, wind, and perfect condition are everything to one who has ambitions in the fistic world. Dieting has a deal to do with condition. Plain, wholesome meals only are required. Have nothing to do with patent foods of any description. Exercise frequently out in the open air and get in as much boxing practice as possible. It does infinitely more good to the beginner to practise and spar with an opponent who has superior knowledge of the noble art. Skipping is a fine exercise for loosening the muscles, whilst for stamina, plenty of road-walking should be indulged in. Regulate your breathing whilst walking, filling your lungs to their utmost capacity with each breath you take until you feel that they are going to burst ; then you know for sure that the exercise is doing you good.

The importance of breathing for health's sake seems to be very little understood by the average boy. The blood demands oxygen in quantities that is controlled by the occupation, habits, and temperament of the individual. Thus the strenuous pastime of various sports, especially boxing, calls for the fullest amount of oxygen possible for the requirement of the blood.

Keep the limbs nice and supple when walking, and head erect. Inhale through the nostrils and exhale through the mouth.

The above hints will prove of utmost value to the boxing enthusiast, and will go a long way to clear his path to success. Just one last word of advice to beginners. Go in for the sport with zeal, and stick to your purpose with rugged determination. The value of being able to take a knock or two in a sporting manner will not be lost upon you, and will help you in all your acts in after life.

⑨⑨⑨

THE KNOCK-OUT!

⑨⑨⑨

⑨⑨⑨

THE END.

⑨⑨⑨

The Wandering Schoolboy

by Martin Clifford.

A Splendid Complete Story of
School Life and Adventure.

—✳✳✳✳✳✳✳✳—

THE FIRST CHAPTER.

Looking for Gussy.

"D'ARCY!"
    "Gussy!"
"Where's that duffer?"

Half a dozen fellows or more were asking that question up and down the School House at St. Jim's.

They were asking it in wrathful tones, and no answer was forthcoming.

Arthur Augustus D'Arcy, the ornament of the Fourth Form, was wanted, but Arthur Augustus was not to be found.

"Where's that duffer?"

"Where's that ass?"

Tom Merry and Manners and Lowther, the Terrible Three of the Shell, were seeking him in the studies. Blake and Herries and Digby, of the Fourth, hunted for him in the passages and the Form-rooms.

Cardew and Clive and Levison sought for him in the quad.

"Anybody seen D'Arcy?"

"Where has that howling duffer got to?"

"Just as we're going to start!" exclaimed Jack Blake wrathfully. "Isn't it just like him? Gone to see his tailor, very likely."

"Or trying on a new silk topper!" growled Herries.

"Or a necktie!" snorted Dig.

"Anybody seen Gussy?"

Three search-parties met at last, in the big doorway of the School House, to compare notes.

"Found him?"

"No!"

"The ass!"

"We haven't looked in the dormitories," remarked Tom Merry.

Blake snorted.

"He can't have gone to bed, can he?"

"Ha, ha! No. But we've looked everywhere else. Let's try the dorm, and if he's there we'll bump him for giving us all this trouble.

"Why not start without him?" suggested Manners. "After all, he won't be much use in a scrap with the New House bounders."

"Good idea!" assented Lowther.

But Blake and Co. did not seem to think it a good idea. They glared at the Shell fellows.

"Rot!" said Blake, with great decision. "We're not going without Gussy. As for being of use in a scrap, any chap in Study No. 6 is more use than any Shell bounder I've ever seen."

"Hear, hear!" said Herries and Dig.

"Bosh!"

"Look here, Lowther——"

"Peace, my infants!" said Tom Merry soothingly. "Peace! Let's look in the dorm, and if Gussy's there we'll bump him; and if he isn't there we'll give him up, and start. Hallo, Talbot, have you seen Gussy?"

Talbot of the Shell came in from the quad. He shook his head.

"Not since classes," he answered.

"Oh, let's look in the dorm!" exclaimed Levison. "We can't spend what's left of the afternoon hanging around for Gussy. Come on!"

A crowd of juniors marched for the stairs, most of them in a rather exasperated frame of mind. It was really exasperating of Arthur Augustus D'Arcy to vanish in this way when a very important expedition was about to start.

Blake and Co. were wrathy; but they declined to entertain for a moment the idea of starting without Arthur Augustus. Study No. 6 in the Fourth were inseparable.

Tom Merry hurled open the door of the Forth-Form dormitory. And then there was a general exclamation.

"There he is!"

There, undoubtedly, he was!

Arthur Augustus D'Arcy was there, and he was busy. On his bed five or six very handsome waistcoats were spread out, with a number of ties that were things of beauty and joys for ever. Arthur Augustus was in his shirt-sleeves. He was trying on a waistcoat before the glass, and his noble brow was very serious

—as was natural when the matter in hand was of so serious a nature. With his celebrated eyeglass screwed into his eye, Arthur Augustus surveyed the reflection of his noble person, and turned slowly to right and left to catch the effect of the waistcoat from every possible angle.

"Gussy!" roared Blake.

Arthur Augustus started, and glanced round.

"Bai Jove, what do you fellows want?" he asked.

"Ass!"

"Weally, Blake——"

"Fathead!"

"Weally, Tom Mewwy——"

"We're waiting for you!" shouted Monty Lowther.

"I have no objection to your waiting for me, Lowthah, deah boy. What do you think of this waistcoat, Blake?"

"You—you—you——" gasped Blake.

"I weally think it is wathah nobbay!" remarked Arthur Augustus, with a satisfied glance into the glass. "I wathah think I shall wear this waistcoat to-mowwow. The colour scheme is wathah suitable for wearin' with a toppah—wathah an important point for a well-dwessed fellow to considah. I have seen fellows wearin' waistcoats with a toppah that were only suitable for wearin' with a stwaw hat. I know it sounds howwid, but it's twue."

And the swell of St. Jim's shook his head seriously.

"You—you—you——" stuttered Tom Merry. "We've been hunting you high and low, and you've been up here playing the goat all the time!"

"I have not been playin' the goat, Tom Mewwy. I have been selectin' the clobbah to wear to-mowwow aftahnoon. As we are goin' to meet our fwiends fwom Gweyfwiahs, and they are goin' to bwing ladies with them, I wegard it as bein' up to me to be decently dwessed. One well-dwessed fellow at least is wequired to keep up the cwedit of the school."

"Oh, bump him!" exclaimed Cardew.

"Weally, Cardew——"

"Have you forgotten that we're going on the war-path?" demanded Tom Merry.

"Don't you know we've got to catch Figgins and Co. on the island?"

Arthur Augustus started.

"Bai Jove," he ejaculated. "I feah the mat̶ah entiahly slipped my memowy, deah boy. I was thinkin' about meetin' Miss Marjowie to-mowwow——"

"Ass!"

"I wefuse to be chawactewised as an ass, Tom Mewwy. Pewwaps you had bettah wait anothah half-hour or so. I have not twied all the waistcoats yet!"

"Let's go without the silly chump!" growled Levison.

"I feah, Levison, that I could not consent to your goin' without me. You fellows would be bound to make a mess of the affaih if I were not with you."

"Why, you—you——"

"Bump him!" howled Blake.

"Weally, you know—oh—ah—welease me!" yelled Arthur Augustus, in great wrath.

But Tom Merry and Co. did not heed. They collared the ornament of the Fourth Form, and bumped him forcibly on the dormitory floor. It was a welcome relief to their exasperated feelings. As he smote the hard, unsympathetic floor, the repose which stamps the caste of Vere de Vere was quite lost by the swell of the Fourth, and he struggled and roared.

"Yawooh! Welease me, you wottahs! Oh, cwikey! Ow!"

THE SECOND CHAPTER.

On the War-path.

BUMP! Bump!

"Yawoooh!" wailed Arthur Augustus. "You feahful wuffians, you are wuinin' my twousahs! You are wumplin' my waistcoat! Ow!"

"There!" gasped Jack Blake. "Now are you ready to start?"

"Ow! Certainly not! I——"

Bump!

"Are you ready now?"

"Oh, cwumbs! Yaas! Yaas, wathah!" gasped Arthur Augustus. "Oh, yaas! Quite!"

"Ha, ha, ha!"

"Then come on!" growled Blake.

Arthur Augustus D'Arcy scrambled to his feet. His noble face was pink with wrath.

"You uttah wuffians!" he gasped.

"Are you coming?"

"I wegard you——"

"Give him another!" grinned Monty Lowther.

Arthur Augustus jumped back.

"Keep your distance, you howwid boundahs. I will come as soon as I get this waistcoat off——"

"You'll come as you are," said Herries. "Yank him along!"

"I must put a jacket on!" shrieked Arthur Augustus. "I cannot appeah in public in my shirt-sleeves, you uttah asses!"

"I'll bring your jacket," grinned Tom Merry. "You can put it on going down."

"I wefuse——"

"Then come without it!" chuckled Blake.

Arthur Augustus was marched out of the dormitory, the captain of the Shell following with his jacket. Arthur Augustus discovered that he could put on his jacket on going downstairs. The dreadful alternative was appearing in public in his shirt-sleeves, so there was really no choice in the matter.

"I wegard you——" he began, as they reached the bottom of the staircase.

"Ring off, old chap," said Blake. "No time to waste while you exercise your chin. We may be late already!"

Tom Merry and Co. started for the gates. There were ten juniors in the party, and Talbot and Kangaroo joined them in the quad, and Julian and Reilly and Kerruish at the gates. So the party numbered fifteen when the school was left behind.

It was a very important expedition from the point of view of the School House juniors. Figgins and Co., of the New House, were picnicking on the island in the river. Warfare was perennial between the juniors of the rival Houses at St. Jim's, and such an opportunity of scoring over their old rivals was not to be lost by the heroes of the School House. While the New House fellows peacefully picnicked, their rivals of the School House were called to arms, so to speak, for a raid. The raid was a little late, owing to the exasperating proceedings of D'Arcy of the Fourth.

" Buck up with the boat ! " said Tom Merry, as they came out on the bank of the Ryll.

" I suppose Figgins and Co. have started ? " asked Dig.

" Yes ; D'Arcy minor saw them start. They've been gone half an hour or more."

" Bai Jove," said Arthur Augustus, " we ought to have been aftah them befoah this, you know. If Fatty Wynn has had half an hour at the gwub, there won't be much plundah left."

" Whose fault is that ? " grunted the captain of the Shell.

" Yours, pwobably, as you are leadah, deah boy."

" Why, you silly ass, we've been——"

" Pway excuse my intewwuptin' you, Tom Mewwy, but hadn't we bettah start ? You can continue your wemarks in the boat, you know."

Tom Merry suppressed his feelings. The biggest boat available was run out from the raft, and the juniors crowded into it. It was pretty well filled when they were all aboard.

Six oars plunged into the water, and the School House fellows pulled up the stream. Arthur Augustus sat in the stern, and occupied himself with putting his tie straight. There was a rather worried frown on his brow. He was thinking of the elegant " clobber " that remained spread out on his bed in the Fourth Form dormitory. He wondered whether it was quite safe from damage.

" They're there ! " remarked Talbot, pointing to a thin column of smoke that rose among the trees on the island ahead.

" Quiet ! " said Tom Merry, as the boat bumped into the rushes on the island. " We are going to take the bounders by surprise ! "

" Yaas, wathah ! Pewwaps I had bettah take the lead, Tom Mewwy——"

" Ring off ! "

" My only desiah is to make a success of the mattah," said Arthur Augustus with dignity.

" Bow-wow ! "

" Weally, Tom Mewwy——"

" Dry up, Gussy ! "

Arthur Augustus gave utterance to a sound suspiciously resembling a sniff, and dried up.

But he shook his head doubtfully. His offer of leadership had been declined, and he had his doubts about the success of the expedition now.

There was a smaller boat already secured to a stump on the bank of the island—evidently the craft belonging to the New House party. Tom Merry tied on to the same stump, and the School House crowd poured ashore. Thick trees and bushes hid the picnickers from their sight ; but they were not far away, and a murmur of voices reached the ears of the raiders.

" Mum ! " murmured Tom Merry, as he led the way cautiously through the trees.

" Yaas, wathah ! Don't talk, you fellows."

" Shurrup ! " whispered Tom ferociously.

" I am only warnin' the chaps not to talk, Tom Mewwy——"

" Will you dry up ? " hissed Blake.

" Weally, Blake——"

" Brain him, somebody ! " murmured Lowther.

" Wats ! "

The School House raiders pushed on with great caution. They came through the trees to the border of the little glade where the enemy were camped. And a fat, satisfied voice reached their ears—the voice of David Llewellyn Wynn, of the New House.

" The spuds are done ! "

There was a camp-fire in the glade ; and Fatty Wynn, with a crimson face, was busy with a frying-pan. George Figgins was stoking the fire. Kerr was opening a tin of milk. Redfern, Owen, and Lawrence were looking on, their services not being required.

The six New House fellows had all their attention fixed on the cooking, and they had no suspicion of the foe at hand. Tom Merry and Co. grinned at them, unseen, from the thickets.

" Done to a turn ! " continued Fatty Wynn, with a beatific smile of satisfaction upon his plump, good-humoured face. " Sosses and spuds—done to a turn. You can make the coffee, Reddy."

" Right-ho ! " said Redfern cheerily.

" Ripping idea to have a feed out here. instead of tea in the study," remarked Kerr " Quite a bright idea of yours, Figgy."

"Ready?" he whispered.

"Yaas, wathah!"

"Charge!"

And the School House charged.

THE THIRD CHAPTER.

A House "Rag."

"Go it, School House!"

"Give 'em socks!"

"Pile in, deah boys!"

"Hurray!"

There was a shout from Figgins and Co. of surprise and wrath. The attack took the New House quite by surprise.

Fatty Wynn sat down, and Figgins rolled over. Kerr put up his hands, and was hotly engaged. Redfern, Owen, and

"What-ho!" assented Figgins. "Topping, I call it."

"You've brought the plates?" asked Fatty Wynn.

"They're in the basket."

"Trot 'em out! Ready for serving now."

"Good!"

Tom Merry, under the trees, glanced back at his followers.

"You've run away from school!" said Billy Bunter, pointing a fat forefinger accusingly at the swell of St. Jim's. "You've hooked it!" (See p. 129.)

Lawrence were swept back by the rush, across the glade. But they rallied there and resisted.

Tom Merry, like a good general, had gathered sufficient forces to make resistance hopeless on the part of the enemy. But, though resistance was hopeless, the New House crowd resisted all the same.

"Back up !" roared Figgins, scrambling to his feet.

"Yah ! School House rotters !"

"Stand up to them !"

"Down with the New House !"

"Surrender !" roared Tom Merry. "You're done, Figgy. Give in."

"Rats !" was George Figgins's answer to that.

And the battle raged.

It was six against fifteen, and Figgins and Co. had not the ghost of a chance. But they put up a gallant fight. For several minutes there was scrapping in the glade on the island, at a great rate. There were yells, and howls, and gasps ; and there was bloodshed—though only from the nose.

Tom Merry and Co. showed signs of severe damage by the time the resistance of the enemy was overcome. The offensive had been successful, but there had been casualties.

Six gasping and furious New House juniors lay on their backs at last in the grass, with six School House fellows sitting on them to keep them there.

"Victory !" chuckled Tom Merry, as he mopped his nose.

"Yaas, wathah ! Where's my eyeglass ?"

"Hurrah for us !"

"Yah ! Let us up, you rotters !" roared Fatty Wynn. "Gerroff my neck, Cardew, you silly beast ! Ow !"

"I'm quite comfy, thanks," answered Cardew.

"Yow-ow !"

Fatty Wynn, apparently, was not "comfy." But it was impossible for everybody to be satisfied, in the circumstances.

"I think this is our picnic," remarked Tom Merry.

"It's ours !" shrieked Fatty Wynn.

"But we've raided it, and that makes it ours, according to the laws of war," grinned Blake.

"Yaas, wathah !"

"Still, we'll grant terms of peace in the proper way," said Tom Merry. "Having beaten the Huns——"

"Ha, ha, ha !"

"We'll give 'em a peace treaty. We annex this picnic——"

"We do—we does."

"Not annex it," said Cardew, with a shake of the head. "Annexation is not the thing. Annexation belongs to the old barbarous times. We don't annex it. We give ourselves a mandate to administer it."

"Oh, my hat !"

"That sounds better, and it comes to the same thing."

"Ha, ha, ha !"

"Are you willing, Figgins, for us to administer this picnic ?"

"No !" roared Figgins.

"You don't recognise our mandate ?"

"No, you ass !"

"Then we'll bump you till you do."

"Ha, ha, ha !"

"Bump ! Bump ! Bump !"

"Is this our picnic now, Figgy ?"

"Yow-ow-ow ! Grooogh ! Ooooch !" spluttered the hapless Figgins.

"Speak in English, Figgy. German is barred."

"Ha, ha, ha !"

"Ow-wow-ow ! Yes, it's yours, you beasts !" gasped Figgins. "Anything you like ! Oh, my hat ! Grooogh !"

"Good ! Now the picnic's ours, we'll turn those Huns out. Pitch 'em into their boat."

"Yaas, wathah ! Ha, ha, ha !"

"Bring 'em along."

The New House crowd attempted another struggle as they were yanked to their feet. But the odds were too great. Two or three of the victors grasped each of the vanquished, and they were bundled down through the thickets to the New House boat.

Bump !

Figgins landed first in the boat—and it rocked.

Then his hapless comrades bumped in after him, one after another, till six breathless and dishevelled juniors sprawled in the rocking craft.

"Cast off !" said Tom Merry.

Talbot gave the New House boat a shove, and it rocked away on the water. Figgins scrambled up and took an oar to steady it.

Tom Merry and Co. waved their hands in farewell.

" Good-bye, deah boys ! "

" Good-by-ee ! "

" Ha, ha, ha ! "

The School House boat was dragged up on the bank into safety, and then the victorious raiders returned to the picnic. Most of them bore signs of damage, but they were smiling in great good-humour. They counted another victory in the unending warfare between the rival Houses of St. Jim's, and that was enough to discount any damages sustained in conflict.

" Bai Jove—the gwub has been upset ! " remarked Arthur Augustus. " Those sosses look wathah dustay."

" Rub them clean on your jacket," suggested Monty Lowther.

" Bai Jove, I wefuse to do anythin' of the sort, Lowthah. I wegard the suggestion as howwid."

" Ha, ha, ha ! "

While Figgins's boat drifted away downstream, Tom Merry and Co. set to work with the picnic. The New House party had laid in plenty of supplies—Fatty Wynn had seen to that. There was not more than enough for fifteen fellows, certainly ; but there was enough, and enough, as Blake sapiently remarked, was as good as a feast.

Tom Merry and Co. enjoyed their picnic.

THE FOURTH CHAPTER.

Mr. Ratcliff Disapproves.

" FIGGINS ! What—what——"

" Oh, my hat ! " murmured Figgins, in dismay.

Six dusty and untidy juniors had entered the school gates, not in great spirits. It was the return of the New House picnickers. Figgins and Co. were wrathy, but they had accepted their reverse in a philosophical spirit ; it was only the swing of the pendulum, as Kerr observed. They had defeated the School House often enough, and they would defeat them again. But they were rather anxious to slip quietly into the New House, and make themselves a little more tidy before they were noticed by masters or prefects.

They passed Monteith and Baker of the Sixth, two New House prefects, near the gates, but the two Sixth-Formers looked another way, much to the relief of the dishevelled juniors. But as they came into the quadrangle, Mr. Ratcliff, the house-master of the New House, loomed up before them, and his sharp voice called on them to stop.

Mr. Ratcliff had been speaking to Mr. Railton, the house-master of the School House, in the quad., but at the sight of the dusty six he quitted his colleague and came towards them. Mr. Railton glanced at them, perhaps with a little sympathy ; he knew the sharp temper and sharp methods of the New House master. However, it was no business of his, and he walked away to the School House.

Mr. Ratcliff's sharp eyes glittered at the woeful half-dozen. Certainly, they did not look a credit to any school just then. They had put up a great fight on the island—in fact, they had fought not wisely but too well.

Figgins had a crimson and swollen nose ; Kerr's nose was still oozing red ; Owen and Redfern had dark shades round their eyes. And all of them were dusty, and a little torn, and decidedly untidy.

It was no wonder that the house-master's glance was disapproving.

" Figgins ! Redfern ! Stop, all of you ! "

The juniors stopped.

There was despondency in their looks. Mr. Ratcliff was the very last person they had wished to meet just then.

" What does this mean ? " exclaimed the New House master harshly. " How dare you appear in public in this disgraceful state ? "

" Ahem ! "

" You have been fighting ? "

" Ye-e-es."

" With whom ? "

" Some—some School House chaps, sir ! " stammered Figgins.

" Where have you been ? "

" On the island, sir ! "

" You went there to quarrel with the School House boys ? "

" Oh, no, sir ; we went there to picnic."

" And you found them there ? "

" Nun-no—they—they came after—— "

" Who began the quarrel ? "

Figgins set his lips.

"There wasn't any quarrel, sir," he answered. "It was simply a House rag. We—we don't mind——"

"Not at all, sir," said Kerr.

"You may not mind," said Mr. Ratcliff acidly, "but I mind very much seeing boys of my House in this disgraceful state. I very strongly disapprove of these incessant bickerings——"

"We don't bicker, sir."

"Nothing of the sort, sir," said Redfern. "It's really only fun."

"Incessant bickerings!" repeated Mr. Ratcliff harshly. "Don't contradict me, Figgins. I disapprove strongly of them. Did you commence the dispute with the School House boys?"

"Nun-no! We—we——"

"Then they commenced it?"

Figgins did not answer. He did not intend to be drawn into making an accusation against the School House fellows.

"Do you hear me, Figgins?"

"I hear you, sir."

"I take it that the School House boys were the assailants. Very well! Kindly give me their names."

There was no answer to that; but all the juniors looked very dogged. Mr. Ratcliff might seek to turn a House rag into a serious quarrel, if he liked, but Figgins and Co. did not intend to help him. The New House master's ill-humoured glance rested on them angrily.

"I shall inquire into this," he said, after a pause. "You may go to your House now, and make yourselves tidy. I shall certainly not allow this disgraceful affair to pass; and I shall see that justice is done."

Figgins and Co., with feelings too deep for words, tramped on to their house.

Mr. Ratcliff glanced after them with great disfavour, and then resumed his walk in the quadrangle.

But he did not go far from the gates.

He guessed, probably, the identity of most of the School House juniors with whom Figgins and Co. had "scrapped"; he was aware that Tom Merry and his chums were the leaders in such affrays on the School House side. But

he wanted to make sure. Mr. Railton would have passed over the affair unnoticed, as a harmless ebullition of youthful spirits; but that was not Mr. Ratcliff's way. Mr. Ratcliff did not approve of youthful spirits; indeed, he did not quite approve of youth at all.

He kept a sharp eye on the gates.

It was close on locking-up when a cheery crowd came along and turned in at the gates of St. Jim's. Tom Merry and Co. had arrived; and as Mr. Ratcliff's sharp eyes scanned them, he noticed swollen noses and other signs of damage among the party.

He stopped in their path to the School House and held up his hand.

"Kindly stop!" he said acidly.

The School House party halted, in surprise.

"Yes, sir!" said Tom Merry.

"You have been on the island in the river?"

"Yes, sir."

"You made an attack there on certain boys of my house."

"Oh!" ejaculated Tom.

The juniors exchanged glances. They guessed that Mr. Ratcliff had seen the return of the New House six; and that, in his usual way of making a mountain out of a molehill, he was going to make a fuss.

"Answer me, Merry!"

"We had a bit of a scrap, sir," said the captain of the Shell. "No harm done on either side. Only a rag."

"Merely a wag, sir!" said Arthur Augustus D'Arcy, cheerily. "I assuah you, sir, that it is all wight."

"Silence, D'Arcy."

"Certainly, sir, but there is nothin' whatevah——"

"Silence!"

"Oh, vewy well!"

"I am determined that this kind of thing shall cease," said Mr. Ratcliff. "The New House boys do not seem to blame in the matter. If, however, you accuse them of——"

"We certainly don't accuse them of anything," said Tom Merry coldly. "and I know perfectly well that they haven't accused us, or made any complaint."

"Yaas, wathah."

"Hear, hear!" murmured Blake.

(106)

"We've been hunting you high and low, and you've been up here playing the goat all the time!" cried Tom Merry. "I have not been playin' the goat, Tom Mewwy," replied D'Arcy. "I have been selectin' the clobbah to wear tomowwow aftahnoon." (See page 100.)

"Do not speak to me in that tone, Merry. It is impertinent. This matter will be dealt with——"

"We are ready to go before our house-

master, if you choose, sir," answered Tom Merry.

"Quite weady, Mr. Watcliff."

Mr. Ratcliff's thin lip curled. He had more

than a suspicion that Mr. Railton would pooh-pooh the whole affair; and he did not want the whole affair pooh-poohed. He wanted punishment administered.

"I shall take you before the Head!" he snapped. "Follow me!"

"Bai Jove!"

Mr. Ratcliff whisked away towards the School House, and the juniors followed him, rather dismayed. The matter became serious if the Head was brought into it. But there was no help for it now.

"Perhaps—perhaps it was rather too much of a rag!" murmured Monty Lowther. "But——"

"Oh, Ratty's always looking for trouble!" growled Tom Merry, "Let him rip! I don't suppose the Head will bother much about it."

"I twust not, deah boy."

Mr. Ratcliff whisked into the School House, and the juniors followed him more slowly. They were looking very restive, as they marched in the wake of the house-master to the Head's study.

THE FIFTH CHAPTER.

Gated!

DR. HOLMES glanced inquiringly at Mr. Ratcliff, and the procession of discomfited juniors that followed him in. He laid down Sophocles with a sigh. The Head had been spending the interval before dinner in company with that ancient and interesting gentleman; but Sophocles had to give place to Mr. Ratcliff.

"Well, Mr. Ratcliff?" murmured the Head.

"Dr. Holmes, I have brought these juniors to you!" said Mr. Ratcliff, "A very serious affair has occurred—an assault upon boys of my house by this crowd of School House boys."

"Bless my soul!" said the Head.

"Judging by the appearance of my boys, they have been attacked in the most ruffianly manner," said Mr. Ratcliff, who was evidently in his happiest vein. "My boys went to the island in the river for a picnic. Merry and his companions followed them there and assailed them. Considerable injuries were done to some of the boys of my House."

"Dear me!"

Tom Merry and Co. blinked at one another. Listening to Mr. Ratcliff, they wondered whether they really were the heroes of the exploit he referred to. It was really remarkable how an affair could be misrepresented, without any actual untruth being told.

Dr. Holmes regarded the juniors severely.

"Have you anything to say, Merry?" he asked.

"Certainly, sir."

"Yaas, wathah, sir."

"Merry may speak——"

"Weally, sir——"

"Kindly be silent, D'Arcy. Merry can explain," said the Head. "It appears, Merry, that you and your friends followed the New House boys to the island?"

"Yes, sir; but——"

"And assailed them?"

"We rushed them, sir—but——"

"And there was fighting?" asked the Head, his glance lingering upon certain damages visible on the various countenances before him.

"Lots, sir—I mean——"

"Your words bear out Mr. Ratcliff's statement entirely."

"Quite so, sir, but there was no harm done—I mean—it—it was—what we call a rag!" stammered Tom Merry.

"Simply a wag, sir."

Dr. Holmes nodded.

"I daresay, Merry, it seemed to you what you call a rag, as you say; but, Mr Ratcliff, whose boys have been injured, takes a more serious view of the matter. I shall not cane you——"

The juniors brightened up, and Mr. Ratcliff frowned. Mr. Ratcliff had come there to witness a perfect orgy of caning.

"I shall punish you by detention," said the Head mildly. "As you probably did not realise that your actions were very blame-worthy, I should be sorry to administer severe punishment. You will all be detained within gates to-morrow afternoon. Now you may go."

The Head made a gesture of dismissal.

It was not really a severe punishment. Being "gated" allowed the juniors the run of the school and the playing fields; it only cut off any outside excursions during the half-holiday. The Head undoubtedly intended to be lenient, while acceding to a certain extent to Mr. Ratcliff's desire to see punishment inflicted.

The juniors were very much relieved, and all the more pleased because they noted the darkening of the New House master's brow. But Arthur Augustus D'Arcy did not turn to the door with the rest.

"Pway excuse me, Doctah Holmes," he began.

"You may go, D'Arcy."

"Thank you, sir. But if I may be allowed to make a wemark——"

"Come on, Gussy," came a stage whisper from Herries.

"Pway do not intewwupt me, Hewwies, when I am speaking to Dr. Holmes. The fact is, sir——"

"I have told you, D'Arcy, that you may go," said Dr. Holmes.

"You are vewy kind, sir. But it happens that to-morrow aftahnoon I particulahly desiah to——"

"Do you wish me to cane you, D'Arcy?"

"Bai Jove! No, sir."

"Then leave my study at once!" rapped out the Head.

"Yaas; but—leggo my arm, Blake."

Instead of letting go Gussy's arm, Jack Blake fairly yanked him out of the study. Mr. Ratcliff followed them out, and with a rather bitter look at the juniors, passed on. Ratty was far from satisfied with the extremely mild punishment inflicted upon the delinquents, but he could not venture to attempt to gainsay the Head.

Arthur Augustus turned a rather excited face upon his comrades in the corridor.

"Welease me, Blake!" he gasped.

"Rats! Get a move on."

"I had bettah speak to the Head—"

"Take his other arm, Dig."

"You fellows seem to forget that we have an important engagement for to-mowwow aftahnoon," exclaimed Arthur Augustus. "Wharton and his fwiends and the girls are coming to Abbotsford."

"Can't be helped."

"We were goin' ovah to see them there."

"That's off now, fathead."

"Wats! I considah that if I explain fully to the Head——"

"You howling ass!" roared Blake. "Do you want a caning as well as detention? That's what you'll get."

"I shall wefuse to be detained undah the circs, Blake."

"Oh, my hat!"

"And I insist upon explainin' to the Head."

"Yank him along," said Cardew.

"I pwotest—I—I—oh, dear, you feahful wuffians! Oh, cwumbs!"

In the grasp of many hands, Arthur Augustus D'Arcy marched along to the end of the corridor. There, as the grasp of his friends relaxed, the swell of St. Jim's jerked himself away, turned, and ran back towards the Head's door.

"Gussy!" roared Tom Merry.

"Stop, you ass!"

"Stop, you duffer!"

"After him!"

Tom Merry and Co. rushed in pursuit. Arthur Augustus put on speed, quite determined to explain to the Head about that very important engagement for Wednesday afternoon.

Whether the Head was likely to listen, or to regard the engagement as so very important if he did, were questions Arthur Augustus did not pause to consider at the moment.

He ran hard, and his pursuers ran hard. But Arthur Augustus had the start, and he was an easy winner. He came up to the Head's study with a breathless rush, just as the door of that sacred apartment opened, and the doctor stepped forth majestically.

Arthur Augustus had not counted on that.

As he said afterwards, how was a fellow to know that the Head was coming out of his study at that particular moment? It was simply an unfortunate accident.

But it was very unfortunate—very unfortunate—there was no mistake about that; no mistake whatever.

Crash!

Full upon the majestic, portly figure of the Head-master of St. Jim's came Arthur Augustus in dreadful collision.

Reading from left to right: Koumi Rao, Dick Redfern, Ralph Cardew, Clifton Dane, Mulvaney (minor), Wally D'Arcy, Dick Julian, Tom Merry, Cousin Ethel, Levison (minor).

Tom Merry and Co. halted—frozen to the floor with horror.

Dr. Holmes staggered.

"Oh!" gasped Arthur.

There was a rushing of feet. For one moment Tom Merry and Co. had stood rooted. Then they fled. Before the Head had gasped twice, fourteen juniors vanished round various corners like ghosts at cock-crow.

But Arthur Augustus did not flee. He could not. Dr. Holmes's hand dropped on his shoulder as he stood gasping.

"Boy!" The Head's voice was almost inarticulate. "D'Arcy! Boy!"

"Oh, sir!"

"BOY!"

"I—I am sowwy—weally sowwy—quite an accident, sir—a feahful accident!" stuttered Arthur Augustus. "I—I was simply comin' back, sir, to—to mention——"

"Go into my study, D'Arcy!" said the Head, in a voice of thunder.

"Yaas, sir."

Arthur Augustus went in. The Head, gasping, followed him in. He picked up a cane from his desk.

"Hold out your hand, D'Arcy."

"Weally, sir——"

"Obey me!"

The Head's tone did not admit of argument; Arthur Augustus held out his hand.

Swish, swish, swish, swish!

Dr. Holmes pointed to the door with his cane. Arthur Augustus D'Arcy limped from the study—no longer thinking of attempting an explanation of the very important engagement fixed for the morrow afternoon. He limped away down the passage, squeezing his hands under his arms, and looking as if he were trying to fold himself up like a pocket-knife.

"Had it bad?" asked Tom Merry, as he met him—at a safe distance from the Head's study.

"Ow! wow! Yaas."

"Well, you asked for it, old scout," said Tom comfortingly.

"Yow-wow-ow!"

And Arthur Augustus limped on, feeling—for the next quarter of an hour—that life on this troublesome planet was hardly worth living.

THE SIXTH CHAPTER.

Up to Gussy.

THAT evening there were shades of thought upon the aristocratic brow of Arthur Augustus D'Arcy, of the Fourth Form.

The licking had worn off; but more serious matters occupied the noble mind of the Honourable Arthur Augustus.

All the School-House fellows who had been on the island that day were gated for the morrow. Most of them took it quite cheerfully. It was, as Tom Merry said, all in the day's work, and it couldn't be helped—and he added his usual philosophic reflection:

"Why grouse?"

Arthur Augustus was not exactly grousing. But he was very thoughtful, and very serious.

On the morrow afternoon, Harry Wharton and some of his friends of Greyfriars School were to be at Abbotsford. Marjorie Hazeldene, Clara, and Barbara, of Cliff House School, were to be with them. It was a little excursion to see Abbotsford Castle, and to pass a pleasant half-holiday. As Abbotsford was within reach of St. Jim's, Wharton had mentioned the matter in writing to Tom Merry a few days before; he would have been glad to see some of the St. Jim's fellows there, if they cared to join the party.

Naturally, some of the juniors had decided to go. They liked the Greyfriars fellows, and they liked Marjorie. Five or six of the juniors had decided to spend the half-holiday at Abbotsford.

Among them, of course, was Arthur Augustus D'Arcy.

Now they were detained for the afternoon, and couldn't go. They were sorry, but did not allow it to dash their spirits. There were plenty of other ways of spending the half-holiday—in fact, Tom Merry was already arranging an extra match with the New House juniors. The little scrap on the island did not prevent him from meeting Figgins and Co. on the cheeriest terms the same evening.

But Arthur Augustus wasn't satisfied.

Arthur Augustus was punctilious.

The Greyfriars fellows having been told that some of the St. Jim's chaps would be there, would expect to see them. To fail to turn up was not in accordance with the Chesterfieldian code of politeness to which Arthur Augustus was accustomed.

It was in vain that Blake assured him that it would make no difference to the Greyfriars party whether they turned up or not. D'Arcy's reply to that assurance was simply "Wats!"

"You see, deah boys," said Arthur Augustus seriously, "there are ladies in the case."

"Marjorie won't expect to see us if we're detained," said Tom Merry.

"But she will not know we are detained."

"Oh, she'll guess," yawned Tom. "I don't suppose she'll care twopence either way."

"You do not appeah to wegard the mattah as sewious, Tom Mewwy," said Arthur Augustus, with severity.

"Well, is it?" asked Tom.

"Yaas, wathah."

"Bow-wow! I don't see it."

"I do, however. Without bein' a conceited chap, I think I may wemark that in a case of doubt, you can wely on me to tell you the wight and pwopah thing to do, deah boy."

"Will you be playing to-morrow, old scout?"

"I shall not be playin' to-mowwow, Tom Mewwy. Havin' weflected on the mattah, I feel that I am bound to turn up at Abbotsford, accordin' to awwangement."

"What about detention?" howled Blake.

"Undah the circs, I feel bound to diswegard detention."

"Oh, you ass!"

"I have wemarked befoah, Blake, that I wefuse to be called an ass," said Arthur Augustus with dignity.

"Fathead, then!"

"Ow, wats!"

Kildare of the Sixth looked into the common-room to shepherd the juniors off to their dormitory, and the discussion ceased. Arthur Augustus's chums hoped that he would have thought better of it by the morning.

By the morning, however, Arthur Augustus had not thought better of it. Having reflected on the matter, he decided that it was up to him as the pink of politeness to keep the appointment at Abbotsford. Gussy had made up his mind; and when Gussy had made up his mind, there was an end of it.

On such occasions he was wont to display the firmness of a rock; though his chums preferred to describe it as the obstinacy of a mule.

Whether Arthur Augustus was as firm as a rock, or as obstinate as a mule, it came to the same thing—he was going to Abbotsford that afternoon.

Breaking detention meant a caning; but in the cause of Chesterfieldian courtesy, Arthur Augustus was fully prepared to risk a caning.

It was, as he expressed it, the weally wight and pwopah thing to do.

He wore the same thoughtful expression during morning lessons; though, as Mr. Lathom discovered, his thoughtfulness was not all bestowed upon form work.

At dinner there was a reflective wrinkle in his noble brow, as some of the juniors observed with a grin.

After dinner Blake joined his noble chum.

"Still thinking of playing the goat?" he inquired.

"I am not thinkin' of playin' the goat, Blake."

"Are you going out of bounds?"

"Yaas."

"Now, look here, Gussy——"

"I wegard it as bein' up to me, Blake; besides, I do not like the ideah of old Watty scorin' ovah us," said Arthur Augustus seriously. "Upon weflection, I do not think it would be diswespectful to the Head, as Watty miswepresented the mattah to him, and he does not weally know how the mattah stands. Aftah the unfortunate incident in his doorway yestahday, I do not feel that it is any use goin' to him to explain furthah——"

"Ha, ha! I should say not."

"Gussy, old man——" began Tom Merry.

"Pway do not argue, Tom Mewwy; my mind is made up," said Arthur Augustus, and he retired to the dormitory for the extremely necessary preliminary of selecting the "clobbah" for the great occasion.

When Arthur Augustus reappeared in public it was evident that the time spent in selecting his clobber had not been spent in vain.

From the crown of his head to the toes of his elegant boots, Arthur Augustus was a picture.

ST. JAMES' COLLEGE, SUSSEX.

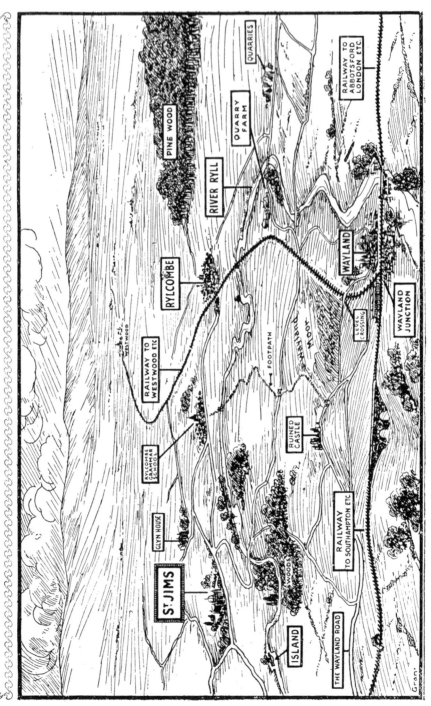

A GENERAL PLAN OF SURROUNDING DISTRICT.

As Monty Lowther remarked in great admiration, Solomon in all his glory was simply not in the same street with him.

Any other fellows going out of bounds for the afternoon would have dropped quietly over the wall in some secluded spot. But that was not possible in the case of Arthur Augustus. His spotless clobber would not have stood a climb over the school wall.

He walked down to the gates.

His friends, having argued with him in vain, did the next best thing—they formed a crowd round him to screen him from general view, and blocked the gateway when he departed, so that his departure should not be observed, especially by old Taggles, the porter.

Having seen Arthur Augustus off in that friendly way, Tom Merry and Co. returned into the quadrangle to attend to their own occupations for the afternoon.

Arthur Augustus walked down the lane briskly.

It was no time for a reposeful saunter; he had to get out of sight of the school as quickly as possible.

" Hullo, Gussy ! "

At the first turning in the lane, Fatty Wynn hailed him. David Llewellyn Wynn had a book under his arm, and an apple in his fat hand. He grinned cheerily at the swell of the School House. His bike was standing against the hedge.

" Hullo, deah boy ! "

" Ain't you detained ? "

" Yaas."

" Hooking it ? " asked Fatty with interest.

" Yaas, wathah. I am bound to go to Abbotsford this aftahnoon."

" My hat ! Look out, then," said Fatty Wynn. " Old Ratty's out of gates——"

" Bai Jove ! "

" Phew ! There he is ! "

As Fatty Wynn spoke, the angular figure of Mr. Ratcliff came round the turning into the lane.

Arthur Augustus breathed hard.

He was not a hundred yards from the gates of St. Jim's—and he was face to face with Mr. Ratcliff ! It was not a happy beginning !

THE SEVENTH CHAPTER.

A Reckless Resolve.

" D'ARCY ! "

Arthur Augustus raised his shining topper to Mr. Ratcliff. He was dismayed by the meeting ; but no amount of dismay could have robbed Arthur Augustus of his good manners.

" Good-aftahnoon, sir ! " he faltered.

Fatty Wynn, with a commiserating glance at the swell of the School House, wheeled his bike towards Rylcombe. He had been " scrapping " with Arthur Augustus the day before ; but that was nothing. He was so concerned for the elegant Gussy now that he even forgot to bite his apple.

Gladly enough would the swell of St. Jim's have followed him. But Mr. Ratcliff stood before him, a lion in the path, frowning darkly.

" D'Arcy ! You are detained this afternoon by the Head," he snapped. " Yet I find you out of gates."

" I have a wathah important appointment, sir——"

" What ? "

" A vewy important appointment——"

Mr. Ratcliff raised his hand.

" Return to the school at once ! " he exclaimed harshly.

Arthur Augustus did not move. His eye gleamed behind his eyeglass. Either the firmness of a rock, or the obstinacy of a mule upheld him, and he remained where he was.

" I shall take you to the Head," snapped Mr. Ratcliff. " As you cannot be trusted to obey Dr. Holmes's injunctions, I shall see that you are confined in the punishment-room, D'Arcy. Come with me."

Mr. Ratcliff dropped his hand on D'Arcy's shoulder—and then, his bitter temper gaining the upper hand, he changed that for the junior's ear. Arthur Augustus gave a little surprised squeak as a sharp finger and thumb closed on his ear. His face was flooded with crimson.

" Mr. Watcliff ! " he gasped.

" Come with me."

" Welease my yah, sir ! " said Arthur Augustus, in a voice trembling with wrath and indignation.

Mr. Ratcliff compressed his grip, and pulled the junior round towards the school.

Arthur Augustus breathed hard.

To be marched into the school, across the quad, under a hundred pairs of eyes, with a finger and thumb compressing his ear, was too great an indignity for the swell of St. Jim's to endure. A fag of the Third Form would have been indignant; Gussy's feelings were simply indescribable.

"I wepeat, sir," he gasped, "welease my yah."

A sharp jerk at his noble ear was the only answer.

"I wefuse, Mr. Watcliff," said Arthur Augustus; "I wefuse absolutely to be led along in this undignified mannah."

"Silence!"

"I wepeat—yawooooooh!"

Mr. Ratcliff jerked at his ear again.

Two Sixth-formers of the School House, Kildare and Darrel, were coming along from the gates, and they stopped, in surprise, at the peculiar scene. Kildare frowned angrily. He was head prefect of the School House and had a hearty dislike for the New House master's interfering ways. But a house-master was, after all, a house-master, and he hesitated to intervene.

"Come with me at once, D'Arcy!" snapped Mr. Ratcliff.

"I wefuse!"

"Boy!"

"If you do not welease my yah at once, sir, I shall stwike your hand away!" gasped Arthur Augustus.

"You impertinent young rascal! I—oh!" Smack!

The noble blood of Arthur Augustus was at boiling point now. He raised his walking-cane, and struck Mr. Ratcliff's wrist a smart rap.

There was a howl from Mr. Ratcliff of surprise and pain, and he let go D'Arcy's ear fast enough then.

The moment he was released, Arthur Augustus scudded away.

"Come back!" shrieked Mr. Ratcliff.

Arthur Augustus did not heed. The house-master stood in the road, clasping his wrist with the other hand, gasping with pain and wrath; and Arthur Augustus vanished round the bend in the lane. He almost ran into Fatty Wynn, who was watching the scene from the corner.

"Oh, Gussy!" gasped the New House junior.

Arthur Augustus pulled up.

"Will you give me a lift on your bike, deah boy?"

"Yes, but——"

"Before Watty can spot you, old chap—quick!"

"All right."

Fatty Wynn mounted his machine, and D'Arcy jumped on the foot-rests behind. The fat Fourth-former bent over the handle-bars and scorched.

The bicycle whizzed down the leafy lane.

A couple of minutes later Mr. Ratcliff came trotting furiously round the bend, but the double-loaded machine was out of sight. The New House master, with bitter wrath in his acid face, stalked away towards the school to lay his complaint before the Head. He passed—with a frown—Kildare and Darrel, and whisked on furiously.

Fatty Wynn drove at the pedals, not knowing whether the house-master was behind or not. He was more than willing to help Arthur Augustus, but he naturally did not want his house-master to see him so engaged; it would have meant trouble to come.

Arthur Augustus stood on the foot-rests, with his left hand holding on to Wynn's shoulder, and his right hand clutching his handsome silk topper, to save it from being blown off. With a rush, the bike came into the narrow old High Street of Rylcombe, and there Fatty Wynn slacked down, and Gussy jumped off.

"Thank you vewy much, deah boy," said Arthur Augustus breathlessly.

"I say, there'll be an awful row, old chap," said Fatty Wynn. "Old Ratty will go to the Head with a yarn that you struck him."

"I stwuck his w'ist, deah boy."

"Well, Ratty's wrist is part of Ratty, isn't it?"

Arthur Augustus smiled faintly.

"Yaas," he assented. "I felt that under the circs, that exceedingly unpleasant person left me no othah wesource. But I hardly think that the Head will agwee with me."

"I'm afraid it means a flogging," said Fatty, dismally. "I'm awfully sorry, old fellow."

Arthur Augustus knitted his brows.

"I shall wefuse to be flogged for havin' acted within my wights," he said quietly.

"You can't refuse the Head."

"I should be vewy sowwy, Wynn, to appeah diswespectful to the Head, but I certainly cannot submit to be flogged for havin' acted within my wights. I feah there is only one wesource."

Fatty Wynn eyed the swell of St. Jim's anxiously. Arthur Augustus's ideas were rather what the more prosaic fellows regarded as "high-faluting," and there was really no telling what Gussy might do next.

"What are you going to do, old boy?" murmured Fatty uneasily. There was an expression of resolution on D'Arcy's face that alarmed him.

"Undah the circs, Wynn, I shall not weturn to St. Jim's."

"Wh-a-a-at?"

"I feel that that is the only wesource," said Arthur Augustus. "A floggin' is out of the question, and the Head would not wegard my statement that Watty is a bullyin' and disagweeable old boundah. I wefuse to submit to a disgwaceful punishment, and the only alternative is to wemain away fwom the school, at least for the pwesent."

"But—but if you go home——"

Arthur Augustus shook his head.

"I cannot vewy well go home, Wynn; my governah would most likely be waxy."

"I should jolly well think he would!" murmured Fatty Wynn.

"I shall have to considah," said Arthur Augustus. "Meanwhile, I have my appointment to keep at Abbotsford. Pewwaps the Gweyfriars fellows may offah me their hospitality for a time——"

"What!" gasped Fatty.

"Pway excuse me, deah boy; I have only time to catch my twain."

"But—but——"

"Au wevoir. You might tell Blake I will w'ite."

Arthur Augustus scudded into the station, leaving the fat Fourth-former rooted to the ground. Like one in a dream, Fatty Wynn stared after him. He could scarcely believe his ears. But as he realised that the reckless junior was actually thinking of running away from school, Fatty Wynn woke to life, as it were, and rushed into the station after the swell of St. Jim's.

He was in time to see a carriage door slam after the elegant figure of Arthur Augustus. Before he could reach the platform, the train was steaming out of the station. Fatty Wynn went back to his bike, with a worried brow. He leaned on his machine, and munched his apple, in deep thought.

After long cogitation, Fatty Wynn mounted his bicycle and rode away; but he did not ride towards St. Jim's. His bike was turned in the direction of Abbotsford.

It was a long, long way to Abbotsford, but Fatty had made up his mind to it, in the hope of catching Arthur Augustus before he carried out his reckless resolve, and persuading him to return to St. Jim's. And with red cheeks and perspiration streaming down his fat face, the Falstaff of the New House bent over his handle-bars and drove at the pedals.

THE EIGHTH CHAPTER.

Fatty Wynn is Too Late.

"HALLO, hallo, hallo!"

It was Bob Cherry, of the Greyfriars Remove, who uttered that exclamation.

The red sunset glowed on the old country town of Abbotsford, and on the old castle outside the town. On the ancient grass-grown ramparts a merry party of picnickers were finishing tea.

Harry Wharton, Bob Cherry, Frank Nugent, Johnny Bull, and Hurree Jamset Ram Singh —the Famous Five of Greyfriars—looked remarkably cheery. And their fair companions —Marjorie and Co. of Cliff House School— were smiling sweetly.

The chums of Greyfriars had enjoyed their half-holiday.

It was a long run from Greyfriars, but the chums agreed that a half-holiday couldn't be better spent than in taking a long run, and

Marjorie, Clara, and Barbara agreed. They had arrived early at Abbotsford, and looked out at the station for St. Jim's fellows—half expecting to meet Tom Merry or some of his friends there; as certainly they would have done, but for Mr. Ratcliff's fussy interference.

But not one was there, and the Greyfriars party rambled over the town and the historic old castle, and finally camped for tea on the ramparts. Tea was nearly over when an elegant figure dawned upon them.

Bob Cherry waved a welcoming hand.

" This way, D'Arcy ! "

" Trot along ! " called out Harry Wharton.

Arthur Augustus came up, raising his shining topper with his own inimitable grace to the ladies, who smiled a welcome.

" I am vewy glad I have found you," he said.

" The gladfulness of our esteemed selves is also terrific," remarked Hurree Jamset Ram Singh politely.

Fatty Wynn was busy. His book lay upon the table—and before him was a large cake, upon which the fat Fourth-former was beginning operations. (See page 120.)

" Simply terrific ! " grinned Bob Cherry.

" I was goin' to meet you at the station, when you awwived," explained Arthur Augustus. " In fact, quite a cwowd of us were comin' ovah, but the othah fellows are detained. Leavin' in wathah a huwwy, I omitted to ask Tom Mewwy the twain you were comin' by."

" Too bad ! " said Harry, with a smile.

" Yaas, wathah ! Howevah, I was suah I should find you all wight," said Arthur Augustus, " I looked in at the station, and then started lookin' for you. And heah I am."

" Just in time for tea," said Miss Clara, with a smile. " Pile in."

" Thank you vewy much."

" Make D'Arcy some fresh tea, Babs."

" Just going to," said Barbara.

" Here's a camp-stool for you, D'Arcy," said Johnny Bull. " Don't mind me—I prefer these old stones."

" Bai Jove ! You are vewy good."

SPORTSMEN THREE AND SPORTSMEN TRUE!

Tom Merry

George Figgins

Eric Kildare

Arthur Augustus sat down in great contentment.

Having missed the Greyfriars party at the station, and having found them again, all was serene—for the present. Circumstances at St. Jim's might be troublesome; but his present surroundings were delightful; and Arthur Augustus determined to think of the present and allow the future to take care of itself.

He was quite ready for tea—and there was quite a handsome spread. And the three girls smilingly looked after his wants.

In the presence of so much good-humour and hospitality, it was scarcely possible to be otherwise than cheerful; and Arthur Augustus was very cheerful indeed.

Not a word passed his lips as to the trouble he was booked for at his school. He knew the Greyfriars fellows would have been concerned about him; and he would not dash the merry spirits of the excursionists.

"What twain are you fellows catchin'?" he asked, as he finished his third cup of tea.

"Five," said Wharton. "It's a long run home, you know—we've come rather far afield."

Arthur Augustus paused a moment and coughed.

"Some time ago, you fellows asked me to visit you at Gweyfwiahs," he remarked.

"Always glad to see you there, old scout."

"Yes, rather," said the whole party heartily.

Another pause.

"I am goin' to ask you wathah a favah, deah boys. Pway do not mind speakin' quite candidly in weply——"

"Go ahead," said Harry Wharton, in some surprise.

"The fact is, I am goin' to be away from school for—for a time—pewwaps a few days—pewwaps longah——"

"Lucky bargee!" said Johnny Bull. "I'd like a few days away from school. I wonder what Quelchy would say if I asked him!"

"The snapfulness would be terrific."

"Would it be poss. for you fellows to obtain permish for me to wemain at Gweyfwiahs for a time——"

"Quite easy!" said Harry Wharton at once.

"Bunter had his cousin staying with him for days on end and he came into class with us. There wouldn't be any difficulty at all, if you liked."

"I feel that I am wathaw makin' a vewy extwaordinawy wequest——"

"Not at all; we'd be delighted," said Harry Wharton, cordial though puzzled. "I could arrange it quite easily. You could have a bed in our dormitory. That's been done before."

"If you are suah——"

"Quite sure."

"You see, though I am stayin' away fwom St. Jim's for a time, I do not want to slack,' explained Arthur Augustus. "I should be vewy glad to attend lessons with you fellows, for a time, if your form-mastah had no objection."

Harry Wharton laughed.

"That would make Mr. Quelch love you like a long-lost grandson!" he answered. "He was quite taken with Bunter's cousin because the chap wanted to come in to lessons. We can fix it quite easily; though I must say that attending classes is rather a new way of spending a holiday."

"I'd rather go to the seaside," remarked Miss Clara.

"Well, Greyfriars is at the seaside," said Marjorie with a smile.

"Hallo, hallo, hallo! Time we got a move on," said Bob Cherry, looking at his watch. "If we lose our train——"

"Oh, my hat!" ejaculated Miss Clara.

There was activity at once. The teathings were packed, and the excursion party came down from the grassy ramparts—Arthur Augustus D'Arcy walking between Marjorie and Clara, falling, as it were, into his natural place.

The party headed for the railway station.

Outside that building, when they reached it, stood a dusty bicycle, leaning against the wall.

Arthur Augustus started as he saw it.

The bike had evidently come a long way; and it seemed to Arthur Augustus that he recognised the machine. He had seen it before—that afternoon. He paused to turn his eyeglass carefully upon it, and murmured:

"Fatty Wynn, bai Jove!"

It was Fatty Wynn's "jigger." Arthur Augustus gave a quick look round, but the fat Fourth-former of St. Jim's was not in sight. His brow was thoughtful as he accompanied the Greyfriars' party into the station.

He could guess what had happened. Fatty Wynn had followed him to Abbotsford, to dissuade him from his reckless intention. Arthur Augustus had not the slightest intention of being dissuaded; the matter was settled. But he did not want the peculiar circumstances to come out before the merry party—especially the girls. Afterwards, he intended to explain quietly to Wharton—but the present moment was not propitious.

He could guess that Fatty Wynn had stopped at the station to wait for him there; and he looked round anxiously as the party entered the platform for the Courtfield train. Fatty Wynn would know, of course, that the Greyfriars fellows would leave by that train, though he would not know the time; and it was easy to divine that he would station himself on that platform to keep watch for Gussy.

But he was not visible on the platform.

Arthur Augustus glanced towards a doorway over which was a large sign bearing the magic word "BUFFET"!

He could guess where Fatty Wynn was.

Fatty had probably been some time at the station; and he was not likely to remain long outside the buffet, if he had to wait there.

Arthur Augustus stole a glance into the buffet as the party walked along the platform.

He caught a glimpse of a plump figure, seated at a little table.

Fatty Wynn was busy.

His book lay on the table, and before him was a large cake, upon which the fat Fourth-former was beginning operations.

Arthur Augustus walked on hastily.

"Lots of time," remarked Bob Cherry cheerily. "Five minutes to wait yet."

Those five minutes seemed long ones to Arthur Augustus D'Arcy.

He wondered whether Fatty, engrossed by the cake, would think of looking out on the platform. Probably he had seen more than one Courtfield train leave already during his wait.

"Train!" said Johnny Bull.

It came rolling in, and stopped. Arthur Augustus's heart beat. As the party rushed for their seats, he fully expected to hear the voice of Fatty Wynn behind. But he did not hear it.

Slam!

The doors were closing.

"Hallo, hallo, hallo!" ejaculated Bob Cherry suddenly. "There's a St. Jim's chap."

"Bai Jove!"

Arthur Augustus backed away from the carriage window.

In the doorway of the buffet stood a fat form. Fatty Wynn had been awakened at last by the rustle on the platform. His book was under his arm, and the cake was in his hand, as he looked out.

"Is that a Courtfield train?" he called to a porter.

"Yessir."

"Oh, my hat!"

Fatty Wynn ran out of the buffet.

"Hallo, hallo, hallo!" hailed Bob Cherry.

Fatty Wynn looked at the train, and at the familiar faces in the carriage windows. The last door had been slammed.

"Stop!" yelled Fatty Wynn.

"Stand back there!"

"D'Arcy——"

"All serene—D'Arcy's with us!" shouted back Bob Cherry as the train moved.

"Oh, crikey! D'Arcy—Gussy——"

Fatty Wynn rushed on. He was prepared to take the train too, and get out at the next station—with Gussy! But he was too late.

The train was gathering speed now.

"Stand back!"

"Stop—oh, my hat—oh, dear——"

Harry Wharton and Co. looked in astonishment from the carriage windows. The last they saw of Fatty Wynn was the plump junior wriggling in the grasp of an alarmed porter. Then Fatty, and the porter, and the platform vanished from their sight, as the train rushed on.

THE NINTH CHAPTER.

At Greyfriars.

"I SAY, you fellows!"

Billy Bunter was adorning the gateway

Full upon the majestic, portly figure of the Headmaster of St. Jim's came Arthur Augustus, in dreadful collision. Tom Merry and Co. halted—frozen to the floor with horror. (See page 109.)

at Greyfriars with his podgy person, when the excursionists returned in the dusk of the evening. It was close on locking-up at Greyfriars. Harry Wharton and Co. had seen their fair companions as far as Cliff House, and then hurried on to Greyfriars—with D'Arcy of St. Jim's in their company. And they found the Owl of the Remove waiting for them.

Billy Bunter blinked at the Famous Five reproachfully through his big spectacles. Evidently he had a grievance.

"Hallo, hallo, my bright-eyed old Owl!" exclaimed Bob Cherry cheerily, giving Bunter a slap on the shoulder that made him jump.

" Yarooooh ! " roared Bunter.

" Why, what's the matter ? "

" You silly ass ! " roared Bunter, " you've jolly nearly broken my shoulder ! Ow ! ow ! wow ! "

" Pain in one shoulder ? " asked Bob.

" You-wow ! Yes."

" Never mind—I'll make the other match it. Stand steady."

Bob Cherry raised his hand ; but William George Bunter did not stand steady. He backed away in haste.

" Oh, really, Cherry——-"

" Come along," said Wharton, " we're only just in time for last roll-call."

" I say, you fellows, you left me behind, you know," said Billy Bunter reproachfully. " I was waiting at the gate to join you when you started——"

" That's why we went out the other way, old top."

" Oh, really, Wharton——"

" The esteemed Marjorie would not have enjoyed the company of the excellent and disgusting Bunter," explained Hurree Jamset Ram Singh. " In fact, the fair and elegant damsels would have been infuriated."

" Oh, really, Inky—I—I say, who's this ! Why, my old pal Gussy ! " exclaimed the short-sighted Owl of the Remove, perceiving Arthur Augustus D'Arcy for the first time.

" How do you do, Buntah ? " said Arthur Augustus politely.

" My dear old chap ! " exclaimed Bunter. " Put it there ! "

He held out a fat hand.

Bunter's hand was not exactly the hand Arthur Augustus was eager to shake ; for it was not only podgy and warm, but it was rather jammy, and rather ginger-poppy, and rather grubby. Moreover, Arthur Augustus was blissfully ignorant of the fact that he was Bunter's old pal at all. But the fat junior was so full of enthusiasm at seeing his old pal that it was impossible to rebuff him. Once more Gussy's Chesterfieldian politeness came out strong. He shook the podgy, sticky hand, and manfully repulsed a shiver at the contact.

" How jolly glad I am to see you, Gussy ! " said Bunter.

" You are vewy kind, deah boy."

" Fancy seeing you here ! " continued Bunter. " What a surprise."

" Wharton has kindly asked me to stay a few days, Buntah."

" My dear man, consider yourself my guest," said Bunter. " I can arrange it with the Head —I've got rather a lot of influence with the Head."

" Bai Jove ! Have you weally ? "

" Yes, rather. You leave it to me. I'll see you through," said Bunter confidentially.

The Owl of the Remove linked arms with Arthur Augustus as they walked towards the school-house. As Arthur Augustus was a good deal taller than the fat Removite, it was not very easy for them to walk with linked arms—but Bunter did not mind, whatever might have been Gussy's feelings on the subject. He hooked on, and hung on.

" My hat ! " exclaimed Bob Cherry, glancing round, " you can't carry Bunter in, D'Arcy. He's not a featherweight, you know."

" He's not carrying me, you ass ! " roared Bunter.

" If you're tired, Bunter, I'll lend a hand," said Bob, unheeding. " D'Arcy simply couldn't negotiate your weight on his own.

" I tell you—leggo ! "

" Here you are, my fat tulip."

Bob Cherry grasped Bunter's other arm. The fat junior was propelled forward at a good rate, gasping.

He was jerked away from Arthur Augustus, as Bob probably intended. The swell of St. Jim's smiled slightly.

" You silly ass, Bob Cherry ! " gasped Bunter as he arrived breathless in the house. " You—you—you crass idiot."

" Is that how you thank a chap for helping you home, Bunter ? "

" You—you—you silly fathead ! Ow ! "

Billy Bunter blinked round for D'Arcy, through his big spectacles. The swell of St. Jim's came in with the Co.—a good many fellows glancing at him rather curiously. Arthur Augustus was well enough known at Greyfriars ; but it was rather surprising to see him there at so late an hour in the day. But he received cordial greetings on all sides.

Harry Wharton went to Mr. Quelch's study

Mr. Ratcliff was the very last person the despondent juniors wished to meet just then. "What does this mean?" exclaimed the New House master harshly. "How dare you appear in public in this disgraceful state?" (See page 105.)

at once to obtain the Remove master's permission for Arthur Augustus to remain as a guest of the Remove. Mr. Quelch was a little surprised, but he assented, taking it for granted that Arthur Augustus was on leave from his school — as indeed Harry Wharton was taking it for granted.

The captain of the Remove rejoined Arthur Augustus to inform him that it was "all serene."

"Thank you very much, deah boy," said Arthur Augustus gratefully. "I weally feel that I am wathah plantin' myself on you, you know——"

"Not a bit of it," said Harry cheerily. "We're jolly glad to see you here."

"The gladfulness is terrific, my esteemed and ludricous D'Arcy."

"I say, Gussy, old fellow——"

"Buzz off, Bunter," grunted Johnny Bull.

"Oh, really, Bull!" exclaimed Billy Bunter warmly. If you think you're going to shove in between me and my old pal——"

"Roll away!" growled Johnny Bull; and at that point he introduced a large-sized boot into the conversation. William George Bunter rolled away in haste.

When the chums of the Remove marched into Hall for roll-call, Arthur Augustus accompanied them—receiving a good many glances. Then he was walked off to No. 1 Study in the Remove for supper. There was no doubt about the hearty hospitality of the Greyfriars fellows, and Arthur Augustus was soon feeling quite at home.

As he had arrived at Greyfriars without baggage of any kind, it was necessary for the Famous Five to provide for his wants in some respects—which was easily and hospitably done. Bob Cherry borrowed a beautiful set of silk pyjamas from Lord Mauleverer—without bothering about consulting Mauly on the subject. And at bedtime, a bed was ready for Arthur Augustus in the Remove dormitory; and he turned in there, tired but contented, and slept the sleep of the just.

THE TENTH CHAPTER.

D'Arcy of the Remove.

CLANG! Clang! The familiar sound of the rising-bell awakened Arthur Augustus D'Arcy, as the early sunshine glimmered in at the dormitory windows.

He opened his eyes and looked about him.

For a moment he expected to find himself in the familiar surroundings of the Fourth-form dormitory, in the School House at St. Jim's. He gave a start as he realised where he was.

Clang! clang!

"Bai Jove!" murmured Arthur Augustus, as he sat up and rubbed his eyes.

Billy Bunter sat up in bed and bestowed a friendly blink upon the swell of St. Jim's.

"Good morning, Gussy!" he chortled.

"Good mornin', deah boy."

"I hope you've slept well, old chap," said Bunter, with great solicitude.

"Yaas, wathah! Like a top."

"Good! We'll have a run in the quad before breaker," said Bunter.

"Oh, yaas."

The effusive friendliness of Billy Bunter was not to be gainsaid. It was evident that Arthur Augustus was going to be Bunter's old pal, whether he liked it or not.

Billy Bunter, for once in his life, was one of the first out of bed. Arthur Augustus bathed and dressed, in a thoughtful mood. His departure from St. Jim's had been so hurried that he had brought nothing with him but what he stood in—and one of the first necessities, therefore, was shopping. That matter was so important that it had the effect of putting less pressing matters into the background, and Gussy did not think very much about the state of affairs at St. Jim's.

He went down from the dormitory with the Famous Five—Bunter rolling after him. It was bright and sunny in the quadrangle, and Arthur Augustus was in good spirits.

"Would it be poss. for me to use the telephone heah, deah boys?" he asked, as he walked into the quad.

"Oh, yes," said Wharton. "Anything special?"

"I should like to let them know at St. Jim's that I am—am all wight. Pewwaps I could wun down to the post-office befoah bwekker——"

"There's a telephone in the prefect's room," said Harry. "I'll ask Wingate, and he's sure to let you use it, under the circs."

"If it won't be a feahful twouble——"

"Not at all."

Wingate of the Sixth gave the required permission, cheerily enough; and Arthur Augustus rang up the exchange and asked for a trunk call to St. Jim's. Arthur Augustus was considerate, as he always was, and he did not want Dr. Holmes to be alarmed about him. Fatty Wynn was certain to tell his friends where he was, but, of course, he would not give him away to the school authorities; his friends would not be alarmed, but it was possible that the Head might be.

He went cheerily in to breakfast with the Removites ; and, after brekker, Trotter the page brought him the news that he was " through " to St. Jim's. He returned to the prefect's room, which was empty at that hour in the morning—much to his satisfaction. He did not want his talk on the telephone to be heard.

" Hallo ! Is that St. Jim's ? " he inquired of the transmitter.

" Yes."

" Bai Jove ! Is that Mr. Wailton's voice?"

" It is Mr. Railton speaking. Is that D'Arcy ? I think I recognise your voice," came the severe tones of the School House master at St. Jim's.

" Yass, sir ! "

" D'Arcy ! You have stayed away for the night, without leave——"

" Undah the circs, sir, I had no choice in the mattah. It is not my intention to weturn to St. Jim's for the pwesent."

" What ! "

" I twust, sir, that you were not alarmed by my wathah huwwied departure."

" Your unexplained absence caused very much uneasiness, D'Arcy."

" Bai Jove ! I am sowwy for that, sir ! I am weally vewy much distwessed."

" D'Arcy ! What does this extraordinary conduct mean ? " demanded Mr. Railton. " Are you out of your senses ? "

" Not at all, sir. I had no wesource but to wemain away fwom school, as I could not possibly submit to a floggin' on Watty's account—I mean Mr. Watcliff."

" What ? "

" I was tweated, sir, with uttah indignity," said Arthur Augustus, his voice thrilling with indignation. " Mr. Watcliff seized me my the yah, sir. It was quite imposs for me to submit to be led into the school by the yah, sir."

" Bless my soul ! "

" Undah the circs, sir, I had no wesource but to make Mr. Watcliff welease my yah, sir, by stwikin' his w'ist."

" D'Arcy ! "

" I am awah, sir, that the Head will wegard

it as a vewy sewious mattah ; and undah the circs, I decided to wemain away fwom school. Howevah, sir, I assuah you that I am not wastin' my time or slackin'. I have not yet quite decided what I am goin' to do finally, as I am in wathah a difficult posish, but I am goin' to attend lessons as usual."

" Are you at some other school, D'Arcy ? "

" I twust you will excuse me, sir, if I do not weply to that question. I do not wish to weveal my whereabouts."

" D'Arcy ! I command you——"

" Pway do not do anythin' of the sort, sir, as I am wesolved not to weveal my whereabouts. I assuah you, howevah, that I am not goin' to slack ; and you may inform my governah so, sir, if you communicate with him. I am goin' in to lessons as usual this mornin'."

" Then you are at a school ? "

" I would wathah not answah that, sir."

" Bless my soul ! "

" I wish you, sir, and the Head, to wealise that my action was not intended to be in any way diswespectful. I should be vewy distwessed if the Head supposed that I was wantin' in wespect. But a floggin'——"

" D'Arcy, you must return to the school at once. Kindly tell me, immediately, where you are at this moment."

" Imposs, sir. I am with some vewy good fwiends. But my whereabouts must wemain a secwet, sir.'

" Upon my word ! "

" Do you wish to take another call ? " came an inquiry in feminine tones from the exchange.

" Thank you, no, miss."

Arthur Augustus put up the receiver. As he turned away from the telephone, a fat face and a pair of large spectacles glimmered in at the doorway.

" He, he, he ! " came from Billy Bunter.

" Bai Jove ! Buntah ! "

" You've hooked it ! " grinned Bunter.

" Weally, Buntah——"

The Owl of the Remove gave him a fat wink.

" Rely on me, old fellow," he said re-assuringly. " I'll keep it dark."

" I twust, Buntah, that you will not wepeat

anythin' you may have heard me say on the telephone," said Arthur Augustus coldly.

"Certainly not, old chap. I'm your pal, ain't I?"

"Oh!" said Arthur Augustus.

"Come along with me, old sport," said Bunter, and he hooked on to the slim St. Jim's junior again, and walked him out of the prefects' room. "I've been waiting for a chance to speak to you, Gussy, without those beasts chipping in."

"If you are alludin' to my fwiends, Bun-tah——"

"In fact, it's jolly lucky you're happening along like this," remarked Bunter affectionately. "You haven't forgotten how rippingly we got on when I was at St. Jim's, Gussy——"

"Bai Jove! Did we?"

"Yes, rather! Don't you remember?"

"I'm wathah afwaid I don't, Buntah."

"Ahem! By the way, Gussy, I'm in a bit of a fix."

"I am sowwy to hear it."

"I'll tell you how the matter stands," said Bunter, blinking at him. "I'm expecting a postal order——"

"Oh!"

"It's coming this afternoon," explained Bunter. "It's from a titled relation of mine. I expect it will be for a pound. My titled relations shell out rather liberally, you know."

"That is wathah nice of them."

"Yes, isn't it? But the fact is, Gussy, I'm rather short of tin at the present moment. I suppose you could cash that postal order for me?"

"Yaa-a-s, I suppose so."

"It would be all the same to you, I suppose, if you cashed it now, and I handed you the postal order when it came?"

"Ya-a-s, I pwesume so," said Arthur Augustus, rather doubtfully.

It was a long time since he had seen Billy Bunter; but he had a rather distinct recollection of Bunter's postal-order. He had an idea that that postal-order did not arrive quite so often as it was expected.

"Done, then," said Bunter briskly, holding out a fat hand. "Remind me when the post comes in this afternoon, won't you? I might forget. It's rather a bore for a wealthy fellow to remember these small sums."

"Oh!"

"A pound, I said," hinted Bunter, as Arthur Augustus seemed to hesitate.

There was a pause; and then Arthur Augustus placed a currency note in the fat paw. It disappeared like magic into Bunter's pocket.

"Thanks, old chap," he said carelessly. "This afternoon, you know. If there should be any delay in the post, I suppose you wouldn't mind waiting for this till to-morrow morning?"

"Weally, Buntah——"

"Or to-morrow afternoon at the latest—the very latest. Ta-ta for the present, old bean. I shall have to hurry. Lessons, soon."

Billy Bunter scuttled off, his fat little legs going like clockwork. He headed for the school shop. Arthur Augustus gazed after him, with a very thoughtful expression on his noble brow. Fortunately, he was in funds; but it was pretty certain that he would not long remain in funds if there were more postal-orders to cash for William George Bunter. Arthur Augustus was an easy-going fellow; but he decided, on the spot, that the first postal-order should also be the last.

THE ELEVENTH CHAPTER.

Bunter Means Business.

BILLY BUNTER had a happy smile and a smear of jam on his fat face when he came into the form-room with the Remove that morning. Whether he had expended the whole pound on tuck, Arthur Augustus did not know; but certainly the fat junior looked as if he had been enjoying life, in his own way, and he was breathing very hard.

Mr. Quelch spoke a few words of kindly greeting to Arthur Augustus in the form-room. The Remove master was a little puzzled by D'Arcy's visit to the school, but it did not occur to his mind for a moment that the St. Jim's junior was absent without leave. Arthur Augustus's desire to attend classes while he was staying with his Grey-

Six oars plunged into the water, and the School House fellows pulled up-stream. (See page 102.)

friars friends was a desire of which the Remove master cordially approved.

As he worked with the Remove that morning Arthur Augustus could not help thinking about St. Jim's, and Tom Merry and Co. there.

His trunk call had relieved any possible anxiety on his account, and he felt that he had done all he could.

As for returning, that was out of the question.

His future plans were vague; there was only one point upon which he was determined, and that was that he would not return to St. Jim's and undergo a flogging for having, as he regarded it, checked the fearful impertinence of the New House master.

It was really impossible to decide about

(127)

the future ; but so long as no one was caused anxiety on his account, Arthur Augustus felt that he could safely leave the future to take care of itself.

Meanwhile, he was quite comfortable at Greyfriars.

After morning lessons he came out of the form-room with the Removites in very cheery spirits. Billy Bunter kindly gave him a rest till dinner, but at dinner he grinned effusively at Gussy, and after dinner he joined him coming out. As the Owl was about to hook on, however, Bob Cherry chipped in, having a pretty clear idea as to how much Arthur Augustus enjoyed Bunter's society.

" Coming for a trot in the quad, Bunter ? " asked Bob.

" Not just now."

" Wouldn't you like a little walk with me ? " asked Bob, in a pained tone.

" No, I wouldn't," snapped Bunter. " Leggo my arm, you beast ! "

" My dear fat tulip, it's your own fault for being such a fascinating chap," said Bob, as he tightened his grasp and marched the unwilling Owl into the quad. " I'm going to enjoy your society."

" Look here, you rotter——" howled Bunter.

" I'm going to revel in it."

" Beast ! "

" This way, old tulip."

William George Bunter was marched on, willy-nilly, with a fat furious face. He had to let Bob enjoy his society for a good ten minutes, much against his will.

Arthur Augustus, with a smile, sauntered into the quad. He sat down on one of the benches under the elms, having a little problem to think out. After lessons, shopping in Courtfield was to be the order of the day, and Arthur Augustus desired to know what were his exact financial resources. With his handsome little Russia-leather purse on his knee, the swell of St. Jim's made a calculation.

" Bai Jove, that's wathah good ! " he murmured. " It was vewy fortunate that the governah stood me a fivah this week, and that Aunt Adelinah turned up twumps at the same time. Now let me see—there's the fivah, and thwee cuwwency notes—that's

eight pounds. Two ten bobbahs—that's nine. And some silvah—quite a lot of silvah, by Jove—not countin' the coppahs ! That boundah Buntah has annexed a pound, but it doesn't mattah—this will see me thwough."

" Gussy, old chap ! "

" Oh, deah ? "

It was Bunter again.

Arthur Agustus hastily slipped the purse into his inside pocket. But Billy Bunter had seen the cash, and his little round eyes were glistening behind his spectacles. Never had he felt so friendly—in fact, affectionate—towards any fellow, as he did towards Arthur Augustus D'Arcy at that moment.

He sat down beside the swell of St. Jim's, beaming.

" I say, Gussy, I'm sorry to say that my postal order hasn't come," he remarked. " Delay in the post, you know."

" It doesn't mattah, Buntah."

" Well, really, it's a matter of very little consequence, as it happens," said Bunter. " I'm getting a rather large remittance to-day—a cheque, in fact."

" I'm glad to heah it, Buntah."

" My pater, you know," said Bunter carelessly. " He frequently sends me a cheque for a tenner. In fact, I get tenners from my pater as often as I get handsome postal orders from my titled relations."

" I have no doubt you do, Buntah."

" Exactly," said Bunter, with a rather suspicious blink at D'Arcy. " Now, I'm expecting that cheque this evening, Gussy."

" I twust you will weceive it, Buntah."

" No doubt about that—none whatever. If it didn't come," said Bunter, loftily, " I should ring up my pater at Bunter Court, and ask him what the thump he meant by it. But it will come all right. Now, what I was going to say is this—don't go away yet, Gussy."

" I am goin' to speak to Wharton."

" I've not finished yet. What I was going to say is this : it's a bit difficult to cash a cheque here. Could you cash it for me ? "

" I will see whether I can, Buntah, when it comes."

" Ahem ! It's coming by the evening post, you know ; but as the matter stands, I'm rather short of tin till it does come. I suppose it would make no difference to you if you lent me, say, five pounds, to be returned out of the cheque this evening ? "

Arthur Augustus breathed hard.

" It would make a vewy considewable diffewence, Buntah."

" Oh, really, Gussy——"

" I feah, Buntah, that I shall be unable to lend you any more money, as I wequiah all I have."

Arthur Augustus rose again.

" Hold on, old chap," said Bunter. " Perhaps I could do with a pound till my postal order—I mean my cheque—comes."

" I am sowwy I cannot oblige you, Buntah."

The friendly grin faded from Billy Bunter's fat face. His little round eyes were gleaming through his spectacles now.

" That won't do, D'Arcy ! " he said.

Arthur Augustus turned his eyeglass upon the fat junior.

" What ? " he ejaculated.

" When I am doing a fellow a favour," said Bunter warmly, " I expect him to treat me as a pal."

" I was not awah, Buntah, that you were doin' me anythin' in the nature of a favah. I should certainly be vewy sowwy to accept a favah at your hands," said Arthur Augustus.

" I'm keeping your secrets for you, ain't I ? " demanded the Owl of the Remove indignantly.

Arthur Augustus started.

" You've run away from school ! " said Billy Bunter, pointing a fat forefinger accusingly at the swell of St. Jim's. " You've hooked it ! "

" That is my biznai, Buntah."

" You can't deny it—you've hooked it from school, and I know all about it," grinned Bunter. " I think I'm doing you a jolly big favour by keeping it dark."

" You have become awah of the circs, Buntah, in a vewy suwweptious mannah, and it is up to you not to wepeat what you learned by eavesdwoppin' ! " exclaimed Arthur Augustus warmly.

" I happened to hear you at the telephone—quite by chance, of course——"

" Wats ! "

" Now, look here, Gussy, if you're not going to be friendly——"

" I am certainly not goin' to be fwiendly with you, Buntah. I wegard you——" Arthur Augustus paused, remembering that he was a guest at Greyfriars.

" Oh, very well," said Bunter loftily. " I was willing to treat you as a pal. You refuse ? "

" I certainly wefuse."

" In that case you can't expect me to keep your shady secrets, D'Arcy."

" My secwets are not shady, you fat wottah ! " exclaimed Arthur Augustus, in wrath. " If I were not a guest heah, Buntah, I should give you a feahful thwashin'."

Billy Bunter dodged away hastily.

" Keep your wool on ! " he gasped. " Look here, I could do with a pound till my cheque comes——"

" I do not believe you are expectin' a cheque, Buntah, or a postal-ordah eithah, and I wefuse to hand you any money."

" Why, you—you——" spluttered Bunter, indignantly. " You—you cheeky rotter ! Do you think I want your blessed money ? I refuse to accept a loan from you, D'Arcy—no you can ring off, it's no good offering it now——"

" I was not goin' to offah it."

" I refuse to accept it. As for your shady secrets——"

" Bai Jove ! I——"

" I sha'n't give you away," said Bunter, blinking at him wrathfully. " I hope I'm not a sneak. But I'm not satisfied with allowing you to remain here in this syrupstitious manner——"

" This—this what ? "

" Syrupstitious manner," said Bunter scornfully.

" Bai Jove ! If you mean suwweptious, you fat boundah——"

" I despise syrupstitious proceedings. Being frank and manly myself, and open as the day, I expect the same in others. I'm not satisfied with this—in fact, I'm shocked at you, D'Arcy. I can't help despising you. Under the circumstances, I feel that I'm bound to consult my form-master, and ask his advice on the matter."

"If you intend to betway me, Buntah——"

"Nothing of the kind. I'm not a sneak, I hope. But I feel it my duty to ask Mr. Quelch's advice on the subject."

"You uttah wottah——"

"Hallo, hallo, hallo!"

The Famous Five came along through the elms, and Bob Cherry's grasp closed on the back of Billy Bunter's collar; and there was a howl from the fat Removite.

"Yarooooh!"

THE TWELFTH CHAPTER.

A Sudden Exit.

SHAKE! shake! shake!

"Yow-ow-ow-wow!"

Shake!

"Yooop!"

"You fat bounder!" exclaimed Bob Cherry wrathfully. "What game are you up to now?"

"Yow-ow! Leggo!" hooted Bunter.

"Are you sticking D'Arcy for cash, you owl?" demanded Harry Wharton angrily. "I hope you haven't lent him any, old scout. You'll never see it again if you have."

"It's all wight, deah boy."

"He's run away from school!" howled Bunter. "Yah! I'm going to tell Quelchy—yow-ow—leggo; s-s-stop shaking me, you beast——"

"Run away from school!" ejaculated Harry Wharton blankly.

"My only hat!"

"D'Arcy——"

"My esteemed and ludicrous friend——"

Arthur Augustus stood with a crimson face. It was out now, with a vengeance. The Famous Five stared at him, as if transfixed. They had been surprised by D'Arcy's sudden visit, certainly; but that he had run away from school had not even occurred to their minds.

Billy Bunter's furious yell had been heard by other ears, too. Bolsover major and Ogilvy, Squiff and Fisher T. Fish, Lord Mauleverer and Wibley, and several more of the Remove looked round, and came up. Temple, Dabney and Co., of the Fourth, who were sauntering under the elms, paused to look on in wonder. The St. Jim's junior was the centre of quite a crowd.

His crimson face showed that Bunter's statement, startling as it was, was well-founded.

"I—I—I——" stammered Arthur Augustus.

"Run away from school, by gad!" said Temple of the Fourth. "What next? Hold on to Bunter, Cherry——"

"I'm holding on," grunted Bob.

"Yarooh! Leggo! I'm going to tell—yoop! I mean I'm not going to tell anybody!" wailed Bunter. "I wouldn't, you know."

"D'Arcy!" exclaimed Harry Wharton. "Surely——"

"Pway allow me to explain, deah boys," said Arthur Augustus, with quiet dignity, though his cheeks were red, "I intended to acquaint you with the facts, Wharton, in confidence, but I have not had an opportunity yet. Buntah listened to me speakin' on the telephone this mornin', but he has not got the facts quite wight. I have not exactly wun away from school."

"He has!" shrieked Bunter. "He's hooked it—he—yarooooh! Leave off shaking me, you beast!"

"Keep that fat rotter quiet. Go on, D'Arcy."

"I have not wun away fwom school—I should wegard such a pwoceedin' as wantin' in dignity. I have wetired fwom St. Jim's for a time."

"Oh!" ejaculated Wharton.

Some of the juniors grinned. Evidently there was a distinction in Gussy's noble mind between running away from school and retiring for a time without leave.

"It was a vewy unfortunate concuwwence of circumstances. I was tweated with gross diswespect by a house-mastah——"

"Oh, my hat!"

"I was compelled to use wathah wuff measures towards that house-mastah——"

"Rather rough measures towards a housemaster!" murmured Frank Nugent. "Oh, dear!"

"As the Head was not likely to see the mattah fwom my point of view, it was pwetty

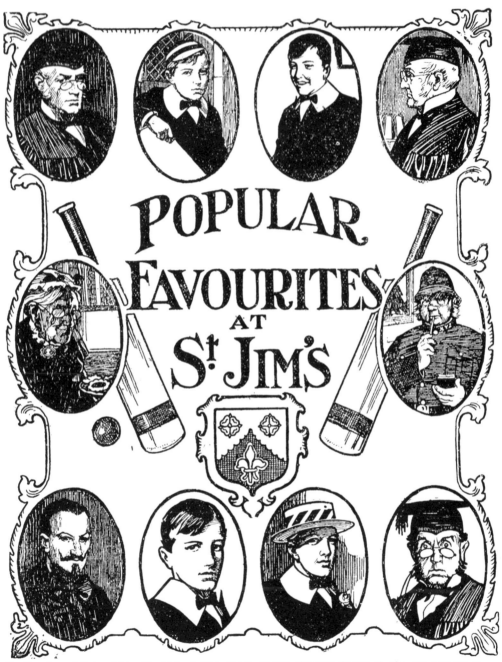

POPULAR FAVOURITES AT St JIM'S

Reading from left to right: Dr. Holmes (the Head), Reggie Manners, George Herries, Mr. Lathom, Dame Taggles (the old lady of the tuck shop), P.C. Crump, Mossoo, Levison (major), Bernard Glyn, Mr. Selby.

certain that he would have administahed a floggin' to me for hittin' a house-mastah——"

" Great Scott ! "

" So I felt that I had no wesource but to wetiah fwom the school—for a time, at least. As you had been so kind as to ask me heah, Wharton, I decided to avail myself of your hospitality for a few days."

" My dear chap, you're as welcome as the flowers in May, now or any other time," said Harry. " But if the Head knew—or Mr. Quelch——"

" I am awah that they could hardly allow me to wemain, without the permish of my own head-mastah," assented Arthur Augustus. " Now that the mattah is made public, I shall leave at once."

" If—if your head-master knew you were here——" stammered Johnny Bull.

" He would send a mastah or a pwefect to fetch me, of course," said Arthur Augustus. " I should nevah submit to being taken back to St. Jim's in disgwace. My personal dig would not allow it."

" Oh ! "

" But—but—if Quelchy hears this, he's bound to telephone to your school at once," said Harry.

Arthur Augustus nodded

" Yaas, wathah ! Now that the mattah is out, I shall leave Gweyfwiahs immediately. I sincerely twust that you will not be blamed in any way for my comin' heah——"

" Not at all. I didn't know you'd taken French leave," said Harry, laughing. " If I'd known it—ahem !—I should get into a row ; but I should have asked you here all the same, old chap, and chanced it."

" Stay here now," said Temple of the Fourth. " It's all right—all these fellows will keep it dark ; and we'll bottle up Bunter somehow."

" Yow-ow-ow ! Leggo my neck, Bob Cherry, you beast ! "

" Stick to us, D'Arcy ! " exclaimed several voices.

Arthur Augustus smiled slightly.

There were more than a dozen fellows within hearing, and others were coming along, attracted by the gathering of the crowd. It was pretty certain that in a quarter of an hour all the Lower School of Greyfriars would be buzzing with the startling news—and that it would spread further. Even if Billy Bunter was " bottled up," as Temple suggested; it was quite clear that Gussy's escapade could not possibly be kept a secret.

" Stay here and chance it," said Bob Cherry. " As for Bunter, we'll slaughter him if he says one word."

" Yaroooh ! "

The swell of St. Jim's shook his head. He would gladly have stayed ; but he realised very clearly that it would not do.

" Thank you vewy much, deah boys," he answered. " You are vewy kind. But now the mattah is known, I shall have to twavel. If Mr. Quelch knew he would detain me here till I was fetched back to St. Jim's."

" I—I suppose he would. But——"

" I am vewy gwateful for your kind hospitality, deah boys. But I shall have to go I think——"

" Hallo, hallo, hallo ! There's the bell for classes ! "

" Leggo, Bob Cherry ! I won't tell Quelchy —I won't tell anybody ! " wailed Bunter. " I was only jug-jug-joking—yow-ow-ow ! "

" I had bettah not come into classes, deah boys," said Arthur Augustus quietly, as some of the juniors moved off towards the school-house. " Pewwaps you will be kind enough, Wharton, to make my excuses to Mr. Quelch."

" Certainly, old chap. But——"

" Good-bye, deah boys ! "

Arthur Augustus shook hands with the Famous Five. He was in a hurry to get out of the gates of Greyfriars—there was danger of detention any moment now. Billy Bunter had spoiled his sojourn at Greyfriars ; and the wandering schoolboy had to look for fresh quarters—and the sooner the better, that was clear.

" We'll see you to the gates, anyhow," said Harry. " I—I wish——"

" It's all wight, old scout."

Arthur Augustus was seen to the gates by the Famous Five—and Billy Bunter. Bunter went because Bob Cherry's iron grasp was on his fat neck, and he couldn't help it.

" Good-bye, Gussy ; and good luck ! "

" Good-bye, deah boys ! "

Arthur Augustus started for Courtfield.

He glanced back and waved his hand. His last view of Greyfriars was the old grey stone gateway—and the Famous Five in the gateway, bumping Billy Bunter.

Bump! Bump! Bump!

Faintly from the distance floated the howl of the fat junior.

"Yarooh! Yow-wowooop! Beasts! Oh, yah, yah! Yooop!"

The anguished tones of the Owl of the Remove died away behind, as Arthur Augustus walked on—with the world before him once more.

THE THIRTEENTH CHAPTER.

Adolphus Smythe is too Funny.

"COOMBE!"

"Bai Jove! That's my station!"

Arthur Augustus D'Arcy detached himself from a comfortable seat in the corner of a first-class carriage, as the train stopped. He jammed his celebrated monocle into his eye, and took down his silk topper from the rack above, and disposed it carefully upon his noble head.

Then he stepped down to the platform.

The little rural station of Coombe looked very sleepy and very rural in the light of the setting sun. There were banks of flowers past the platform, scarlet geraniums predominating. An old porter trundled a trolley along in a leisurely manner. Three passengers alighted—one of them being the wandering junior from St. Jim's. Coombe was not a busy station.

Arthur Augustus glanced about him; and the porter spotted him, and woke up to something like life. He abandoned the trolley, and came along, touching his cap.

"For Rookwood, sir?" he asked.

"Yaas."

"Noo young gentleman, sir?" asked the porter, wary for tips.

"Bai Jove! No. Simply a visitah!"

"Oh!" said the porter.

His interest evaporated at once, and he returned to his trolley, and resumed propelling it up the platform, at the rate of about a mile in a couple of years.

Arthur Augustus walked slowly to the exit,

and gave up his ticket, and strolled out into the ancient High Street of Coombe.

There he looked about him. Having had to leave Greyfriars in a hurry, and being as resolved as ever not to return to St. Jim's while the question of a flogging was in doubt, Arthur Augustus had made up his mind to look in on his old friends, Jimmy Silver and Co., at Rookwood School.

More than once, when Jimmy Silver had been at St. Jim's for a match, he had impressed upon Arthur Augustus that he would be glad to see him at Rookwood, if he ever found himself in that quarter. Jimmy Silver's kind invitation was useful to remember now.

Arthur Augustus glanced about the old High Street, thinking that possibly he might see some of his Rookwood friends in the village. It was past the hour when the Fourth Form was dismissed at Rookwood.

Jimmy Silver and Co. were not to be seen in Coombe, however, and Arthur Augustus walked down the street from the station. He paused as he was passing Mrs. Wicks's little shop. He remembered having had refreshment at that establishment on a previous visit, and he was in need of refreshment now—it was past tea-time.

As it happened, there were several Rookwood fellows in the tuck-shop. Smythe, of the Shell at Rookwood, was entertaining several of his friends there—Tracy and Howard and Gilbey of the Shell, and Townsend and Topham of the Fourth. Smythe and Co. were the "nuts" of Rookwood, and it was the firm persuasion of Adolphus Smythe that he was the last word in elegance. Expensive Adolphus certainly was, but he looked more loud than elegant when Arthur Augustus D'Arcy stood near him.

Smythe and Co. stared at the St. Jim's junior as he came up to the little counter. It was not elegant to stare, certainly, but the manners of the Rookwood nuts sometimes left a little to be desired.

Arthur Augustus raised his shining topper politely to Mrs. Wicks and gave his modest order. Adolphus Smythe extracted an eyeglass from his waistcoat pocket and screwed it into his eye, and surveyed the St. Jim's junior at his leisure.

"By gad, I've seen that fellah before," Adolphus remarked to his companions in a voice that reached D'Arcy's ears.

"I remember him," yawned Tracy. "He came over with the St. Jim's cricketers, I believe."

"Oh, yaas," said Howard.

Arthur Augustus sat on a stool at the counter, unheeding. He remembered Smythe and Co., and that nutty crowd remembered him perfectly well. For, on one occasion of a match at Rookwood, Adolphus had generously invited Lord Eastwood's son up to his study for a game at banker, and had been very much offended by Gussy's curt refusal.

Adolphus remembered that circumstance very keenly.

He came along the counter towards Arthur Augustus, and his friends watched him with suppressed grins. They could see that Adolphus was going to have a little fun with the newcomer.

"D'Arcy, I believe?" drawled Smythe.

"Yaas," said Arthur Augustus. "Thank you, madam." He took his plate of cake and began to dissect it elegantly.

"Goin' to Rookwood, what?"

"Yaas."

"Visitin' us, hey?"

"I am visitin' Silvah of the Fourth," said Arthur Augustus. "Pewwaps you can tell me whethah Silvah or Lovell is in Coombe this aftahnoon."

"I'm afraid I don't know much about the movements of Fourth Form fags!" yawned Adolphus. "Sorry, you know."

"It does not mattah."

"Would you mind reachin' me a bottle of ginger-pop, yonder?" asked Smythe, with great civility. "I can't quite reach without pushin' past you——"

"Certainly."

Arthur Augustus's feet were on the rail of the high stool he was sitting on. He rose, and extended his hand across the counter to the ginger-beer bottle. As he did so, Adolphus Smythe's hand came from behind him, and he laid a fat and juicy jam tart on the seat of the stool. That action being performed behind D'Arcy's back, the swell of St. Jim's was quite unaware of it.

There was a suppressed chortle from the Rookwood nuts. They waited, in breathless expectation, for the St. Jim's junior to sit down.

"There is the bottle, Smythe."

"Thanks so much!" murmured Adolphus.

"Not at all."

Arthur Augustus sat down.

Squelch!

"Ha, ha, ha!" yelled the Rookwood nuts in chorus.

"Goodness gracious!" exclaimed Mrs. Wicks. "What—what——"

"Gweat Scott!"

For a dreadful second, Arthur Augustus sat as if glued to the stool. In point of fact, he was very nearly glued to it.

Then he jumped off.

On the seat remained the squashed fragments of the jam tart. Most of the jam was adhering to Arthur Augustus's beautiful trousers.

"Deah me!" gasped Arthur Augustus, in horror.

"Ha, ha, ha!" shrieked Smythe.

"You uttah wottah!" shouted Arthur Augustus. "You feahful cad! You placed that howwid tart for me to sit in——"

"Ha, ha, ha!"

"Bai Jove, my bags are all jammy——"

"Ha, ha, ha!"

The Rookwood nuts shrieked with merriment. Adolphus Smythe almost doubled up in an excess of mirth.

But his mirth was short-lived.

Arthur Augustus was a good-tempered fellow. He could forgive most injuries—he could have forgiven even Mr. Ratcliff if that unpleasant individual had apologised as one gentleman to another. But there were limits. Wilful damage to his elegant clobber was past the limit—far beyond it.

Wrath gleamed behind Gussy's eyeglass.

As Smythe doubled up, gasping with merriment, Arthur Augustus rushed upon him.

The next moment Adolphus was in his grasp, and the Shell fellow's head was in chancery.

Thump, thump, thump!

"You uttah wottah! Take that—and that—and that——"

Smythe and Co. were ingloriously driven·into a corner of the tuck shop, where they yelled for quarter.
(See page 137.)

"Yoooop!"

Adolphus Smythe was still yelling, but it was not with merriment now. His yells were the yells of anguish as he spun round the wrathful swell of St. Jim's, struggling frantically, his head in chancery, and Arthur Augustus's fist beating time on his nose.

THE FOURTEENTH CHAPTER.

Washed Out.

"YAH! Oh! Ow! Rescue! Help!" shrieked Smythe.

"You uttah wuffian——"

"Help!"

"Back up, dear boys!" called out Townsend.

The Rookwood nuts had stood staring for a minute or more, taken quite by surprise. Perhaps Smythe might have been expected to help himself, as he was considerably bigger than the Fourth-former of St. Jim's. But it was pretty clear that he couldn't.

The nuts rushed to the rescue at last.

Hands were laid on Arthur Augustus D'Arcy on all sides.

"Welease me, you wottahs!" shouted Arthur Augustus. "Faih play! I am goin' to give this wuffian a feahful thwashin'!"

"Collar him!"

"Rag him!"

"Bump him!"

The nuts of Rookwood crowded to the attack, strong in numbers. Arthur Augustus was dragged off Adolphus, who staggered away, roaring.

"Yow-ow-ow-ow! Oh, my nose! Oh, dear! Oh, gad! Ow, ow, ow!"

"Down him!" yelled Tracy.

Arthur Augustus fought furiously. His noble blood was at boiling-point now, and though the enemy were six to one, he gave a good account of himself.

Tracy went down before a drive from the shoulder, and Gilbey rolled over him with a howl.

But the odds were too great. Arthur Augustus was borne to the floor, and five or six angry fellows scrambled over him.

"Gentlemen—gentlemen!" exclaimed Mrs. Wicks, in horror.

But the gentlemen did not heed.

"Smash him!" howled Adolphus Smythe. "Spiflicate him! Look at my nose! Ow, wow! Jump on him!"

"You uttah wottahs!" panted Arthur Augustus. "I will thwash any two of you! Oh, deah! Gerroff!"

Tracy snatched a syphon of soda-water from the counter.

"Stand clear while I bathe him!" he shouted.

"Good egg!"

"Bai Jove, you feahful wottahs!"

"Pulverise him!" howled Smythe.

There was a tramping of feet in the doorway, and four juniors of Rookwood came on the scene.

"Hallo, what's the rumpus!" exclaimed the cheery voice of Jimmy Silver, the captain of the Fourth.

"Smythe and Co. on the war-path!" grinned Arthur Edward Lovell.

"Wescue!"

"D'Arcy!" shouted Jimmy Silver, in amazement.

"Stand back, you rotters!" exclaimed Tracy. "You're not going to chip in here!"

"Ain't we just!" retorted Jimmy Silver. "Six to one isn't Rookwood style. Give 'em socks!"

Jimmy Silver, Lovell, Raby, and Newcome rushed into the fray.

The Fistical Four of the Fourth were probably not sorry for a "row" with the nuts of Rookwood; indeed, Arthur Edward Lovell had often confessed that he never saw Adolphus Smythe's nose without wanting to punch it.

And there was good reason for chipping in now, that was clear.

Jimmy Silver jerked the soda-syphon away from Tracy in time, and as he seized it with his right, he let Tracy have his left.

Tracy sat down with a jar.

"Mop 'em up!" roared Lovell. "This is for your nose, Smythey."

"Oh, gad! Yooop!"

"Oh, dear, dear, dear, young gentlemen!" wailed Mrs. Wicks.

But Mrs. Wicks was not heeded. The Fistical Four were warming to their work, and the fact that the enemy numbered six against four did not worry them in the least. Besides, as soon as Arthur Augustus was released by the nuts—under the necessity of defending themselves—he scrambled up and joined in the fray at once.

And the swell of St. Jim's was certainly equal to any two of the nuts.

Smythe and Co. were ingloriously driven into a corner, where they yelled for quarter.

"Stoppit!" shrieked Tracy. "We give you best, don't we? Stop it, you villains! Oh, my eye!"

"Chuck it! We give in!"

"Hands off!"

"Help!"

"Kick 'em out!" roared Lovell.

"Gentlemen—gentlemen!" beseeched Mrs. Wicks.

"It's all right, ma'am; we're only going to kick these hooligans out of your shop."

"Ha, ha, ha!"

"But Master Smythe hasn't paid."

"Oh! Ha, ha! I see. Pay up, Smythey."

"Oh, gad! Ow! By dose! Oooooch!" Leggo!" howled Adolphus as Arthur Edward Lovell grasped him by the neck and marched him up to the counter.

"Pay up, my pippin, and smile."

"Ha, ha, ha!"

Adolphus Smythe paid up, gasping, though he certainly did not smile. He was feeling more like weeping and wailing and gnashing his teeth than smiling. But he paid up, and Lovell released his hapless neck.

Jimmy Silver stood by the doorway, the soda-syphon in his hand.

"Out you go!" he said.

"Look here," began Tracy, with an uneasy eye on the syphon.

"Kick them out!"

"This isn't a kick-out—it's a wash-out," said Jimmy Silver. "All serene, Mrs. Wicks. I'm going to pay for the soda. I'm standing these chaps a soda. Are you going, Smythey?"

"You—you—if you dare!" gasped Adolphus.

"Start him with your boot, Lovell."

"What-ho!"

"Yah! Oh!" roared Adolphus, as Lovell started him with his boot. He did not wait to be restarted. He bolted for the door.

"Sizzz! squish!"

Adolphus caught the stream, fair and square, as he fled. He rolled out of the doorway, drenched and gasping and spluttering.

"Bai Jove!" grinned Arthur Augustus D'Arcy. "Go it, Silvah, deah boy. I wegard that as bein' the weally wight and pwopah thing to do."

"Start those fellows—one at a time."

But Tracy and Co. did not want to be started one at a time. They preferred to try their luck with a rush, and they sped for the door in a crowd. The doorway was not built for a crowd. There was a jamb in it, and on the jambed juniors the soda-water played merrily.

Squish! Sizzz! Sloooosh! Splash!

"Ha, ha, ha!"

The jamb in the doorway broke, and the nuts rolled out helplessly, gasping and spluttering. There was a squeaky fizz as the last remnant of the soda-water followed them.

"Wait while I get another syphon!" shouted Jimmy Silver.

"Ha, ha, ha!"

But Smythe and Co. did not wait. They ran for their lives.

THE FIFTEENTH CHAPTER.

Arthur Augustus Arrives at Rookwood.

ARTHUR AUGUSTUS D'ARCY smiled genially at Jimmy Silver and Co. Those cheery youths had arrived in the nick of time, and Arthur Augustus was duly grateful.

"Thank you so much for chippin' in, deah boys," he said, as the howls of Smythe and Co. died away.

"Not at all, old scout—it's a pleasure to handle Adolphus at any time," answered Jimmy, laughing, "What are you doing in this part of the planet?"

"I was comin' to see you, Silvah."

"Good man!"

"Jolly glad to see you," said Arthur Edward Lovell, with great cordiality, though he was perplexed. Rookwood was a good distance from St. Jim's, and it was rather curious for a St. Jim's fellow to arrive on a visit so very late in the afternoon. Certainly he had no time to return before locking-up. Lovell did not yet know that Gussy was not returning.

"You're looking a bit dusty, old chap," said Raby, "Mrs. Wicks will let us use her kitchen for a wash and brush up, if you like."

"I should be vewy gwateful. That howwid boundah Smythe put a jam tart on my stool."

"Ha, ha!"

"Bai Jove! I do not wegard his action as funnay. My twousahs are all jammay."

"Too bad!" said Jimmy Silver, sympathetically. "Come along and we'll get the jam off."

In Mrs. Wicks' kitchen, there was washing and brushing—which all the juniors needed after the "scrap" with Smythe and Co. Then they came back into the shop for the interrupted spread.

"We came in for ginger-pop, after a trot, but we'll have tea here, as you're here, D'Arcy," said Jimmy Silver. "Our spread, you know. You must be hungry after your journey."

"Yaas, wathah!"

Jimmy Silver gave liberal orders, and there was quite a spread on a little table in a corner of the tuck-shop. Arthur Augustus did full justice to it, much to the satisfaction of his hospitable entertainers.

He beamed with smiles across the little table, as the spread was disposed of, much relieved by the hearty welcome the Fistical Four had given him.

But his aristocratic visage became grave as the spread was finished.

"I feah I am goin' to make wathah a peculiah wequest, you fellows," he began, colouring.

"Any old thing," said Jimmy.

"Could you put me up at Wookwood to-night?"

"I was thinking you'd be pretty late back," remarked Lovell. "We can put you up easily enough, old scout."

"Certainly," said Jimmy. "Mr. Bootles knows you, and he will consent like a shot."

"I am goin' to be quite fwank with you, deah boys," said Arthur Augustus. "I have left St. Jim's——"

"Left St. Jim's!" ejaculated Jimmy Silver.

"For a time," explained Arthur Augustus hastily. "I twust the mattah will blow ovah, and I may be able to weturn. But, for the pwesent, I am not goin' back to school."

"Oh, my hat!" murmured Newcome.

"Pway do not think that I have done anythin' wong," said Arthur Augustus. "I was tweated with gwoss diswespect by a housemastah——"

"Eh?"

"And I wefused to stand it. It was imposs for me to allow old Watty to take me by the yah."

"Oh!"

"For that weason, I have wetired from St. Jim's for a time, and I do not think it would be judicious to go home. The governah would pwobably fail to undahstand. Owin' to Buntah's vewy disagreeable conduct, I have had to cleah out of Gweyfwiahs."

"Oh!"

"But I have a very stwong objection to slackin' while I am away fwom St. Jim's. I should not like to be suspected of clearin' off to dodge lessons, you know."

"My hat!" murmured Lovell.

"Now, as you fellows were kind enough to ask me to visit you, I should be vewy glad to do so now, if it would not place you in an awkward posish. In that case, pway do not wefwain fwom tellin' me, deah boys."

Jimmy Silver and Co. blinked at the swell of St. Jim's.

They did not reply for some moments. Arthur Augustus had almost taken their breath away.

Arthur Augustus regarded them anxiously.

He was very anxious not to impose upon the hospitality of his friends. At the same time, he would have been very glad to find a temporary refuge at Rookwood.

"Well!" said Jimmy Silver, at last, "I needn't ask you if you've cleared off without leave—you have, of course. What will happen if you go back?"

"A floggin', I feah."

"Don't go back, then," said Arthur Edward

"I hear, Kildare," said Mr. Railton kindly, "that you and Darrell were witnesses of the serious occurrence yesterday between D'Arcy of the Fourth and Mr. Ratcliff. (See page 142.)

Lovell, at once. "Look here, we can manage it. You come to Rookwood as our guest, and we'll fix it up with Bootles somehow for you to stay—for a time, anyhow."

"What a lark!" said Raby, with a grin.

Arthur Augustus was relieved.

"Thank you vewy much!" he said gratefully.

Lovell chuckled.

"It's no end of a lark," he said. "We'll jolly well keep you at Rookwood, safe and sound. Won't we, Jimmy?"

"We'll jolly well do our best, anyway," said Jimmy Silver, heartily. "I suppose your friends know you're safe, D'Arcy?"

"That's all wight—I telephoned to Mr. Wailton fwom Gweyfwiahs this mornin'."

Jimmy Silver rose.

"Then we'll try it on at Rookwood," he said. "Come on."

Jimmy Silver settled the bill at the counter, and the five juniors left the tuck-shop, and started for Rookwood. Lovell and Raby and Newcome were grinning, greatly tickled by D'Arcy's escapade. Jimmy Silver was a little more serious. He was all hospitality and good-nature; but he wondered what was to come of the queer affair. He did not think it likely that Arthur Augustus would be able to remain in his new refuge for long.

"Hallo! Is that D'Arcy?"

Mornington and Erroll met the juniors at the gates of the school. They greeted Arthur Augustus cheerily, though naturally surprised to see him there at that hour.

doesn't much matter, either, you inquisitive duffer."

"Well, it's queer, you know," said Tubby Muffin. "The Head has been on the telephone, I heard the bell buzzing. I say, Jimmy ——"

But Jimmy Silver was going on with Arthur Augustus, and Tubby was left to con-

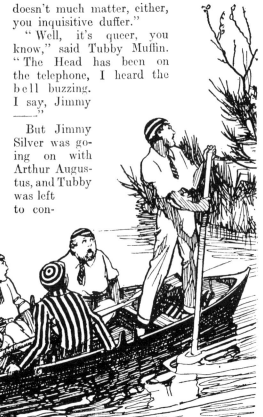

"Yes, he's come to stay with us for a bit," said Jimmy Silver.

"Oh, good!" said Morny.

Arthur Augustus walked across towards the School House with the Fistical Four. Tubby Muffin met them in the doorway, and gave the St. Jim's junior a fat and friendly grin.

"Is Bootles in, Tubby?" asked Jimmy Silver.

"Yes, and there's something up," said Muffin. "Bootles has been to see the Head, and he came back looking quite bottled. I was taking in my lines, you know, and old Bootles was saying 'Absurd!' 'Extraordinary!' What do you think is up, Jimmy?"

"Blessed if I know," said Jimmy. "It

tinue his remarks to the Co. Jimmy led his guest to Mr. Bootles' door.

"I think it will be all right," he said. "Mr. Bootles knows you, and there's no reason why he should guess that you've taken French leave. Put on your nicest smile, old chap."

"Yaas, wathah!"

Jimmy tapped at the door.

"Come in!" came Mr. Bootles' voice.

Jimmy marched into the study with Arthur Augustus. Mr. Bootles was seated at his table, and he blinked at Jimmy over his glasses. Then his eyes fixed upon the swell of St. Jim's. What happened next was amazing.

Mr. Bootles jumped to his feet, blinking at Arthur Augustus as if the latter had been a spectre.

Talbot gave the New House boat a shove, and it rocked away on the water.
Tom Merry and Co. waved their hands in farewell. "Good-bye, dear
boys! Good-bye-ee!" (See page 105.)

"D'Arcy!" he gasped.

"Yaas, sir," said Arthur Augustus, in amazement.

"Bless my soul! D'Arcy! Upon my word!"

"D'Arcy's come to see us, sir," began Jimmy Silver.

"Goodness gracious! The—the boy has—has actually come to Rookwood!" stuttered Mr. Bootles. "Bless my soul! Close the door, Silver. D'Arcy, remain here! You will be detained here——"

"Bai Jove!"

"Silver, see that D'Arcy does not leave this study while I speak to the Head."

Mr. Bootles, in great excitement, whisked out of the room. He left Jimmy Silver and Arthur Augustus D'Arcy rooted to the floor, staring at one another in blank astonishment.

THE SIXTEENTH CHAPTER.

Mr. Ratcliff Climbs Down.

"Merry!"

"Yes, Kildare!"

"Mr. Railton wishes to speak to you. Go to his study."

"Oh! Right-ho."

Lessons were over for the day at St. Jim's. The Terrible Three were sauntering in the quadrangle, discussing the escapade of Arthur Augustus D'Arcy of the Fourth.

D'Arcy's chums were not anxious about him, so far as his personal safety was concerned. Fatty Wynn had imparted the information that Gussy had gone home to Greyfriars with Harry Wharton and Co. But they were very anxious about what was to happen to him as a result of the escapade.

However Arthur Augustus might look at the matter himself, the fact actually was that he had run away from school, and that was a very serious matter indeed.

"Railton wants to know if you know anything, Tommy," remarked Monty Lowther, as Kildare turned away. "Keep it dark, of course."

Tom Merry nodded.

"Mum's the word," agreed Manners. "Gussy has played the ox, but it's up to us to stand by him. I—I suppose it would be better for him to be fetched home."

"No doubt about that. But we can't give him away," said Tom. "And old Ratty has made it pretty bad for him when he does come back."

Tom Merry went into the School House to his house-master's study. He found Mr. Railton with a grave brow.

"I have sent for you, Merry," said Mr. Railton very seriously, "to ask you whether you can enlighten me as to D'Arcy's present whereabouts."

Tom coloured.

"From a telephone message I received from him this morning, I am aware that he is at some other school," continued the house-master. "I have questioned Blake, and I believe Blake is aware of D'Arcy's hiding-place. He has not revealed it to me, however."

"Oh!" murmured Tom.

"I quite understand the sense of loyalty you boys feel in this matter," said Mr. Railton kindly. "But the case is very serious. D'Arcy must be found and brought home, or his parents must be communicated with, causing them unnecessary alarm. As head boy in the Lower School, Merry, you have some responsibility, and you must help me."

"I—I——" stammered Tom. "You—you see, sir——"

"Well?"

"I—I suppose D'Arcy is going to be punished, sir?"

"That is unavoidable, Merry. Mr. Ratcliff has laid a very serious complaint against him."

"Mr. Ratcliff was to blame, sir," exclaimed Tom. "Wynn says that both Kildare and Darrell saw what happened, and they could tell you——"

"The matter will be fully inquired into, Merry. But D'Arcy must return at once. He is at some school now—apparently with the idea of continuing his lessons, although he is absent from here. It can only be some school where he is known and has friends. Doubtless you know the place."

Tom was silent.

"I have already telephoned to Rylcombe Grammar School," said Mr. Railton. "He is not there. I have also inquired at Abbotsford School, but nothing has been heard of him. He has apparently gone further afield. I believe, Merry, that you and your friends are on specially friendly terms with some boys at Greyfriars School, in Kent, and at Rookwood School."

"Ye-es, sir!" stammered Tom.

"Are you aware whether D'Arcy has gone to either place?"

Tom Merry did not answer.

"Very well, Merry; you may go," said Mr. Railton, after a pause.

Tom Merry was glad to get out of the study.

He was glad, too, that he had had to deal with Mr. Railton, and not with Mr. Ratcliff, of the New House. "Ratty" would certainly not have been so lenient.

Mr. Railton remained for some minutes in thought, and then he left the study, and looked in at Kildare's room. The captain of St. Jim's was sitting down to tea with his chum, Darrell. The two Sixth-formers rose respectfully as the house-master looked in.

"Don't let me disturb you," said Mr. Railton kindly. "I hear, Kildare, that you and Darrell were witnesses of the serious occurrence yesterday between D'Arcy, of the Fourth, and Mr. Ratcliff."

"That is so, sir," said Kildare.

"Will you kindly tell me exactly what happened?"

"Certainly, sir."

Kildare described the scene in the lane, Darrell putting in a corroborating word or two. Mr. Railton listened very attentively, and then took his leave. He left the School House, with a grave brow, and walked across the quad to the New House.

"Come in!" rasped the acid voice of Mr. Ratcliff, as a tap came at his study door.

Mr. Ratcliff looked up surprised, as the School House master entered.

He grunted out an ungracious request to Mr. Railton to be seated. Mr. Railton sat down.

"There is news of D'Arcy?" asked Mr. Ratcliff, peering at him. "The young rascal has been found?"

"D'Arcy has not yet been found," said the School House master, quietly. "I think, however, that I have an idea where he may be found."

"That is good."

Mr. Ratcliff rubbed his thin hands. He was evidently looking forward to Arthur Augustus's return, and the flogging that was to follow.

"That is why I have come to speak to you, Mr. Ratcliff," pursued the School House master, in the same quiet tone. "You have laid a very serious complaint before the Head in regard to D'Arcy—that he struck you——"

"Precisely."

"I have now heard a somewhat different account of the matter."

"Indeed!"

"It appears from two witnesses, that you seized this boy, belonging to my house, and over whom you have no authority, sir, by the ear—to drag him into the school in a most ignominious manner," exclaimed Mr. Railton, his voice rising a little.

"I certainly intended to compel the boy to come into the school as he was out of gates without permission."

"You have informed the Head that he struck you. I learn that what he actually did was to rap your wrist to make you let go his ear."

"Do you justify such an action on the part of a junior?" asked Mr. Ratcliff, with a sneer.

"Certainly not. But the matter is very much less serious than the Head has been led to suppose."

"Mr. Railton!"

"I am speaking plainly, sir; it seems to be necessary. This is not the first time that trouble has been caused by your interference with boys of my house."

Mr. Ratcliff bit his thin lip hard.

"D'Arcy was out of bounds——" he began.

"That was a matter you could have reported to me, as his house-master. You had no right whatever to lay hands upon the boy, especially in such a humiliating manner."

"Sir!"

"The result was that the boy acted recklessly in a moment of excitement; and then becoming alarmed, he has run away from school. All this might have been avoided, Mr. Ratcliff, if you had cared to remember that your authority does not extend over the boys of my house."

"I decline to hear more of this, Mr. Railton."

"You may decline, if you wish, sir—but Dr. Holmes will not decline to hear my statement of the affair, and my resolve that this interference in my province shall cease," said the School House master, quietly. He rose to his feet. "I shall now place the matter before the Head, Mr. Ratcliff, and request him very seriously to see that your activities, in future, are confined to your own house."

"Stay!" muttered the New House master, as Mr. Railton turned to the door.

"Well, sir?"

"I— I have no desire for an—an unseemly dispute to be taken before the Head!" gasped Mr. Ratcliff. "It—it is true that I—I omitted certain details in—in my description of the occurrence, owing to—to excitement at the moment. On—on calmer reflection, I am prepared to admit that D'Arcy's action was not—not quite so serious as it appeared at first. I—I shall not insist upon the boy being flogged."

Mr. Railton paused.

"I certainly have no desire for anything like an unseemly dispute," he said at last. "But I cannot allow injustice to be done to a boy in my house. D'Arcy acted recklessly, but he was very much provoked. If you care to explain to the Head in such a way that——"

Mr. Ratcliff forced a laugh, though he was feeling more like grinding his teeth. It was not the first time that the interfering house-master had been brought up sharply.

"The fact is, Mr. Railton, that I was very much exasperated, and—and perhaps the matter was unduly stressed," he said. "I trust I am not a vindictive man. I am willing to let the matter pass. I can say no more than that, I suppose."

"That, certainly, is quite satisfactory—you will doubtless inform the Head that on reflection the matter appears trifling, and that you desire to let it drop."

Mr. Ratcliff snapped his teeth.

"Certainly!" he gasped.

"Thank you very much, Mr. Ratcliff."

The two house masters walked across to the School House together. Mr. Ratcliff went to the Head's study—where his halting explanation was listened to by Dr. Holmes with some surprise, but much relief. Mr. Railton went to his own study, where he was busy on the telephone for a considerable time.

He had two trunk calls to make. The first that came through was Greyfriars; and from Mr. Quelch, at Greyfriars, he learned that Arthur Augustus D'Arcy had certainly been there, and had attended classes with the Remove that morning—but had suddenly left after dinner.

A little later he was "through" to Rookwood School. But from Rookwood there was no news. Dr. Chisholm, at Rookwood, was surprised at his inquiry, and assured him that no St. Jim's boy had been at Rookwood that day—but promised to inform him if anything was heard there of the runaway. And with that, the School House master had to be content for the present.

THE SEVENTEENTH CHAPTER.

On Parole!

"EXTWAORDINAWY!"

Arthur Augustus D'Arcy made that remark in tones of the greatest astonishment.

He blinked at Jimmy Silver; and Jimmy Silver blinked at him.

"My only hat!" was all Jimmy could say.

"Mr. Bootles appeahs wathah excited."

"He do—he does!" gasped Jimmy.

"If your form-mastah was not such an extwemely wespectable old gentleman, Silvah, I should weally suspect that he had been dwinkin'. He has told you not to let me leave this studay."

"He has!"

"But why, deah boy?"

"Blessed if I know!" said Jimmy Silver. "It beats me—hollow."

Arthur Augustus D'Arcy rubbed his noble nose, in deep thought. Mr. Bootles' conduct seemed quite inexplicable.

"Bai Jove!" ejaculated D'Arcy suddenly. "Is it poss that Mr. Bootles suspects that I have wun away fwom school, Silvah?"

"I don't see how he could."

"No; but—weally—it is very extwaordinawy."

The study door opened, and Bulkeley, of the Sixth Form, looked in. He smiled a little as he saw D'Arcy.

"Come along, young shaver!" he said.

"Are you addwessin' me?" inquired Arthur Augustus.

"Yes."

"Then you must allow me to wemark, deah boy, that I object to bein' addwessed as a young shavah."

Bulkeley laughed.

"You're wanted in the Head's study," he explained. "I'm to take you there, and see that you don't bolt. See?"

"Bai Jove!"

"Get a move on," said the captain of Rookwood impatiently.

Arthur Augustus hesitated.

"Does the Head know?" he began.

"He knows you've bolted from your school, you young ass! He's heard from St. Jim's on the telephone. Come on."

"Oh! I—I—I see."

All was clear now.

"The game's up!" murmured Jimmy Silver, in dismay.

"Bai Jove, the game does appeah to be up, so fah as Wookwood is concerned. Bulkeley, deah boy, I am sowwy I cannot come with you."

"What?" ejaculated Bulkeley.

"Undah the circs, I think I had bettah cleah off without delay. You see——"

"I see that I'm going to take you to the Head," answered Bulkeley, with a grin. "Sharp's the word—I'm waiting."

"Pway expwess my wegwets to Dr. Chisholm," said Arthur Augustus calmly. "I wish him to undahstand that my wathah sudden departure does not imply anythin'

Six gasping and furious New House juniors lay on their backs, at last, in the grass, with six School House fellows sitting on them to keep them there. " Victory ! " chuckled Tom Merry. " Hurrah for us ! "

(*See page* 104)

THE St. JIM'S JUNIOR FOOTBALL XI.

Reading from left to right (standing): H. Manners, D. Wynn, P. Reilly. (Seated): R. Talbot, H. Noble J. Blake, Tom Merry (Captain), M. Lowther, R. H. Redfern. (In foreground): G. Figgins, G. Kerr.

like diswespect to him personally. Now kindly allow me to pass."

Bulkeley chuckled.

Instead of kindly allowing Arthur Augustus D'Arcy to pass, he kindly took him by the shoulder.

"This way!" he remarked.

"Weally, Bulkeley——"

"Move on."

"Oh, deah!"

Bulkeley was smiling and good-natured; but his grip on the junior's shoulder was like iron. Arthur Augustus wished to head for the big doorway, where Lovell and Co. stood looking on in dismayed surprise. But he did head for Dr. Chisholm's study—constrained by that iron grasp on his shoulder.

"Look heah!" he gasped.

"Come on, you young ass!"

"I wefuse to be called an ass. And I desiah my fweedom——."

"Bosh!"

"Weally, Bulkeley——"

"Dry up, you young ass," said the captain of Rookwood, impatiently.

"I desiah to point out——"

"Cheese it!"

"That you are wumplin' my jacket!" said Arthur Augustus with dignity.

Bulkeley laughed, and marched the swell of St. Jim's onward, with a reckless disregard for his rumpled jacket. He tapped at the door of Dr. Chisholm's study, and marched the delinquent into that awe-inspiring apartment.

Mr. Bootles was there, in a state of

fluttering excitement. Dr. Chisholm, calm and grave, peered at Arthur Augustus over his spectacles.

" This is the boy ? " he asked.

" That is D'Arcy, sir ! " gasped Mr. Bootles.

" Dear me ! D'Arcy, it appears that you have run away from school——"

" Not at all, sir. I should wegard such a pwoceedin' as undignified."

" Wha—at ? "

" I have wetired fwom St. Jim's for a time, sir, owin' to havin' been tweated with gwoss diswespect by a house-mastah."

" Bless my soul ! "

Mr. Bootles blinked, and Bulkeley suppressed a grin. But Arthur Augustus was as grave and serious as the Head of Rookwood himself. He did not see anything to grin at, personally.

" And now, sir, I should be obliged if you would instwuct this wathah wuff person to welease me," said Arthur Augustus, with dignity.

" Bless my soul ! " said Dr. Chisholm. " This is a—a—a rather extraordinary boy. D'Arcy, I have been requested by your housemaster to detain you, if you should come here. You will be detained at Rookwood until you are sent for."

" Oh, deah ! "

" I shall telephone to Mr. Railton, informing him that you are here," said the Head of Rookwood. " You will stay the night and be taken away in the morning, I presume. Mr. Bootles, you will see that this boy does not leave the precincts of the school."

" Certainly, sir."

Dr. Chisholm turned to the telephone. Arthur Augustus was led from the study with Bulkeley's hand on his shoulder. He was very palpably looking out for a chance of escape.

The hapless wanderer was taken back to Mr. Bootles' study, where Jimmy Silver was still waiting, wondering in dismay how the affair was going to end. There Bulkeley left him with the form-master, and walked away smiling. Arthur Augustus smoothed his rumpled jacket.

" D'Arcy ! " said Mr. Bootles, blinking at him. " You appear to be a—a—a somewhat extraordinary boy."

THE GREYFRIARS GALLERY IN VERSE

By Dick Penfold

No. 4 : Gerald Loder.

Who makes us sh-sh-shake with fright,
Whene'er he c-c-comes in sight ?
(Or thinks he does, the silly kite !)
        Why, LODER !

Who wields an ashplant might and main,
And makes us cry, in tones of pain :
" Pup-please I'll never do it again " ?
        Why, LODER !

Who, when the stars begin to peep,
And nice young boys are all asleep,
Towards the village starts to creep ?
        Why, LODER !

Who plays the game with skill and zest,
(He fancies nap and poker best),
Who finds us in bed—fully dressed ?
        Why, LODER !

Who built a mansion in the sun ?
Who thought the captaincy he'd won ?
And then was diddled, dished, and done ?
        Why, LODER !

Who, when he reads this gentle verse,
Will give a none too gentle curse ?
Who'll never change—except for worse ?
        Why, LODER !

"Weally, Mr. Bootles——"

"I have no desire to use rough measures," said the mild little gentleman. "Silver, you are well acquainted with D'Arcy, I believe——"

"Oh, yes, sir!" said Jimmy.

"Can you answer for it that if the boy gives his word not to leave Rookwood, he can be relied upon to keep it?"

"Certainly, sir!" said Jimmy Silver at once.

"Very good; I certainly have that impression of him. D'Arcy, will you give me your word to remain in the school until you are sent for?"

"I am sowwy, sir, that I feel bound to wefuse."

"Otherwise, it will be necessary to lock you in a room by yourself——"

"Bai Jove!"

"I should be very sorry indeed, D'Arcy, to have to take such measures," said Mr. Bootles kindly.

Arthur Augustus was silent for a few moments. But he rose to the occasion with all the dignity that was natural to the swell of St. Jim's.

"Undah the circs, sir, I will give my pawole," he said.

"Your—your what?"

"I will give my word not to leave Wookwood, wathah than be detained in a humiliatin' mannah, sir."

"Very good; I accept your word, D'Arcy. A bed shall be prepared for you in the Fourth-form dormitory to-night. Silver, you will doubtless see that your friend has anything he requires this evening——"

"Oh, certainly, sir!"

"Very well; you may go."

And Jimmy Silver left the study with Arthur Augustus D'Arcy—landed at last after his wanderings. Stone walls do not a prison make; but Arthur Augustus's word was his bond.

But, dismayed as he was, the swell of St. Jim's slept soundly enough that night in the dormitory of the classical Fourth—leaving the morrow to take care of itself; which was really all he could do, under the peculiar circumstances.

THE EIGHTEENTH CHAPTER.

All's Well That Ends Well.

"THEY'RE coming!"

There was keen excitement at St. Jim's.

Morning lessons were over at the old school, and it was known that Kildare had not appeared in the Sixth-form room that morning. Trimble of the Fourth, who knew everything, declared that the prefect had gone to fetch D'Arcy from somewhere—and Tom Merry ventured to inquire of his house-master.

Then all St. Jim's knew.

Arthur Augustus D'Arcy had been located at Rookwood School, and Kildare was gone for him by an early train; and was expected back to dinner. Tom Merry and Co. did not give much thought to dinner. Even Fatty Wynn, for once in his career, forgot a meal-time. A crowd of juniors gathered round the gates to see Arthur Augustus when he arrived.

There was a buzz as Figgins, out in the road, announced that they were coming!

"There he is—with Kildare!" said Blake.

"Poor old Gussy!"

"Poor old Gus!" said D'Arcy minor, of the Third. "Always looking for trouble, and always finding it. Just like Gussy!"

"Is that what you call brotherly sympathy in the Third?" inquired Blake.

Wally grinned.

"Oh, Gussy's all right!" he answered. "Gussy rolls out of a scrape as fast as he rolls into one. Besides, Ratty's let the matter drop—Kildare said so——"

"Here they come!"

Kildare of the Sixth came striding up to the gates, with Arthur Augustus walking by his side. There was a calm and lofty repose in the manner of Arthur Augustus. If he was alarmed, he was certainly not allowing any signs of it to appear upon his aristocratic countenance.

"Welcome home, Gussy!" sang out Wally of the Third.

"Thank you, deah boy."

"Feeling a bit funky, what?" inquired Grundy of the Shell.

"Weally, Gwunday——"

"Where did they catch you?" asked Dig.

"That is hardly the way to descwibe it,

(148)

Adolphus caught the stream, fair and square, as he fled.   He rolled out of the tuck-shop doorway, drenched and gasping and spluttering.   (See page 137.)

Dig. Kildare called for me at Wookwood this mornin', and wequested me to accompany him. As I have a vewy gweat respect for Kildare, I felt that I could not vewy well wefuse his wequest."

" Oh, my hat ! "

Kildare grinned. He had certainly requested Arthur Augustus to accompany him back to St. Jim's, being prepared to take him by the collar if he refused. Fortunately, Arthur Augustus had not refused.

" Come on, kid," said the captain of St. Jim's.

" Certainly, deah boy."

" Best of luck, old chap," said Kerr.

" Thank you vewy much, Kerr," Arthur Augustus paused. " Wynn, I twust you did not ovah-exert yourself the othah day at Abbotsford. You looked wathah wed and bweathless when I saw you last, deah boy."

Fatty Wynn chuckled.

" It's all right," he said. " I jolly nearly dropped my cake, and if that ass of a porter had trodden on it——"

" Ha, ha, ha ! "

" But I just saved it," said Fatty Wynn. " So it was all right."

Tom Merry and Co. walked on to the School House with the returned wanderer. Mr. Ratcliff glanced at the procession from his study window, in the New House, and frowned. Mr. Railton glanced at it from his window, and smiled. Quite an army marched into the School House with the swell of St. Jim's, as far as the corridor of the Head's study. There they had to stop ; while Kildare conducted the delinquent into the presence of Dr. Holmes.

" D'Arcy, sir ! " said Kildare.

And he retired, leaving the ornament of the Fourth Form to face the music. At the nearer corner in the passage without, Tom Merry and Co. waited in an anxious crowd.

" Did the Head look waxy, Kildare ? " Tom Merry ventured to ask, as the captain of St. Jim's came back.

" Not very ! " said Kildare, with a smile.

" Good ! "

And the juniors waited—a good deal more anxious for Arthur Augustus than that placid youth was for himself. Dr. Holmes had fixed a severe glance upon the returned wanderer, which Arthur Augustus met firmly but respectfully. As Arthur Augustus could not see that he was to blame in any way, he naturally had the support of a good conscience.

" Well ! " said the Head at last. " So you have returned, D'Arcy."

" Yaas, sir."

" You do not seem aware, D'Arcy, that you have committed a very serious fault in running away from school ! " exclaimed the Head sternly.

" I did not wun away, sir ! " said Arthur Augustus firmly. " I should wegard wunnin' away fwom school, sir, as undignified, and also as wantin' in wespect to you, sir, as headmastah. I wetired fwom St. Jim's for a time. I wegard that as quite a different mattah."

" I do not quite see the difference," said the Head. " You have been absent from school without leave——"

" I assuah you, sir, that I have not been slackin'. I attended classes at Gweyfwiahs, and should have continued to do so, but for that vewy unpleasant person Buntah——"

" Really, D'Arcy——"

" I was goin' to ask permish to attend classes at Wookwood, sir, if I had wemained there. I weally twust, sir, that you will not wegard me as havin' any desiah to slack."

" I accept your assurance on that point, D'Arcy, but——"

" As for my weason for clearin' off, sir, I wegarded myself as havin' no othah wesource. Watty——"

" What ? "

" I—I mean Mr. Watcliff, sir, tweated me with gwoss diswespect——"

" It was my intention, D'Arcy, to administer a flogging for your conduct towards Mr. Ratcliff——"

" That is why I decided to wetire fwom the school for a time, sir," said Arthur Augustus with dignity. " I twusted that you would be appwised, in the long wun, of the actual facts, and then it would be poss for me to weturn in honah, sir."

" Bless my soul ! " said Dr. Holmes, regarding the swell of the Fourth very curiously over his glasses. " As it happens, D'Arcy,

POLICE-COURT NEWS AT GREYFRIARS

With Profuse Apologies to the Daily Papers.

By Our Special Representative.

A SENSATIONAL SCENE !

The Court was in a turmoil when Percy Bolsover, prize bully, was brought into the dock by twenty constables. He was formally charged with ill-treating Percival Spencer Paget on the 14th instant by laying into him with a cricket-stump.

Magistrate: " Words cannot express my contempt for your conduct, you hulking lout !"

At this juncture, prisoner caught up an ebony ruler, and hurled it with all his might at the magistrate. His worship ducked, and the missile merely struck Mr. Skinner, K.C., on the nose.

Magistrate: "I will call no witnesses. It would be a superfluous proceeding. Prisoner will be made to run the gauntlet six times over !"

The barristers formed up in two rows, took off their wigs, and severely lashed prisoner with them. Bolsover was conveyed to the sanatorium in a critical condition.

A FOOTBALLER'S FAILURE.

Hurree Jamset Ram Singh, a dusky youth of Oriental extraction, was charged with deliberately muffing an open goal in the recent match with Highcliffe, thereby causing the Greyfriars Remove to lose.

The magistrate, in tones vibrant with emotion, said it cut him to the heart to see such an old pal in the dock. Prisoner had borne a good character for many hours, and now it was to be forfeited as the result of a moment's folly.

Mr. H. Vernon-Smith, giving evidence, said that in the last five minutes of the fatal game he lobbed the leather across to Hurree Singh, but the latter, left with an open goal at his mercy, simply sat down on the ball, and stayed there until an opposing back cleared.

Prisoner: " It was done accidentally, your esteemed worship. I tripfully skidded on a ludicrous puddle, and sat down bumpfully !"

The magistrate, after consulting several eminent lawyers, dismissed the case, stating that unless prisoner performed the hat-trick in the next match, he would be subjected to a severe bumping.

Mr. Ratcliff has withdrawn his complaint against you, and requested me to allow the matter to pass. I have acceded to his request."

" Oh, bai Jove ! "

" As that matter is now at an end, it is unnecessary to inquire into it further. But your action in running away from school——"

" Weally, sir——"

" In absenting yourself without leave, at least, is very serious, and I shall punish you accordingly, D'Arcy."

Dr. Holmes picked up his cane.

" Vewy well, sir," said Arthur Augustus, with dignity. " If you considah that I am deservin' of punishment, I am bound to accept your judgment, as my head-mastah, sir."

" You must be aware, D'Arcy, that you have been guilty of disrespect to me, in acting as you have done."

Arthur Augustus looked distressed.

" Bai Jove ! I certainly nevah looked at the mattah in that light, sir. I should be vewy sowwy if you thought me lackin' in wespect to my head-mastah. I should wegard that as vewy bad form."

Dr. Holmes coughed,

" Really——! " he said.

" I do not mind a lickin', sir," said Arthur Augustus. " I am quite weady. But I weally twust, sir, that you will not continue to wegard me as havin' acted in a diswespectful mannah. That is vewy distwessin' indeed to me."

Dr. Holmes looked at Arthur Augustus long and hard. He laid down the cane at last.

" If you assure me, D'Arcy, that you will not act again in this foolish and reckless mannet ——" he said.

" Certainly, sir, if you wish."

" Then, as you assure me that you did not intend to act disrespectfully——"

" I assuah you, sir, as one gentleman to anothah !" said Arthur Augustus, with dignity.

" You may go, D'Arcy !" said the Head hastily.

" Thank you, sir."

And Arthur Augustus left the study. As he closed the door, he heard a faint sound from within, and started—but it was impossible to suspect the Head of laughing, and he dismissed the idea from his mind.

He walked down the passage with his noble head held high. At the corner, twenty fellows surrounded him.

" Well, you duffer ? "

" Well, you ass ? "

" Licked ? "

" Flogged ? "

" What's happened ? "

" Bai Jove ! " Arthur Augustus arranged his eyeglass carefully in his eye, and surveyed Tom Merry and Co. calmly. " Pway don't all speak at once, deah boys. I am happay to inform you that I have not been licked. There was nothin' for me to be licked for. I explained the mattah to the Head."

" Oh ! "

" I was wathah distwessed to find that he wegarded me as havin' acted diswespectfully, but I have fortunately wemoved that unfounded ideah fwom his mind. The Head is wathah an old sport, deah boys."

" And you're not licked ! " ejaculated Tom Merry.

" Not at all."

" Well, my hat ! "

" It's duffer's luck ! " said Blake.

" Weally, Blake——"

" Duffer's luck, and no mistake," agreed Tom Merry.

" Weally, Tom Mewwy——! "

" As the Head hasn't licked him, I think we ought to lick him for worrying his old pals and turning their hair grey," said Blake.

" Hear, hear ! "

" Wats ! " said Arthur Augustus cheerily. " Gentlemen, I am vewy pleased to be back again. The Head is a bwick. I wequest you all to accompany me to the tuck-shop, and dwink the Head's health in gingah-pop."

" Bravo ! "

" Ha, ha, ha ! "

" I twust that all my fwiends will come," said Arthur Augustus.

And they did ! And there was quite a cram in Dame Taggles' little shop when Arthur Augustus arrived there, accompanied by all his friends, who were only to happy to celebrate the safe return of " The Wandering Schoolboy ! "

THE   END

TYPES OF THE BRITISH ARMY.

THE ROYAL SCOTS.   THE BLACK WATCH.   THE ROYAL IRISH RIFLES.

PIPER—THE GORDON HIGHLANDERS.   THE ROYAL IRISH REGT. (DRUMMER).   THE SEVENTEENTH LANCERS.

THE FUNNY ADVENTURES OF BUBBLE AND SQUEAK, THE TERRIBLE TWINS

"Look here, Master Squeak, you've the kindest of hearts,
So chop up this wood, and I'll give you some tarts."
"What-ho !" chuckled Squeak. "I am on like a shot !
It won't take me long to chop this little lot ! "

So Squeak began chopping the firewood in stacks,
Doing great execution with his mighty axe ;
While Bubble was hatching a plot round the corner —
A plot to get grub, just like Little Jack Horner.

Then he dragged out the barrel, and buried poor Squeak,
Who descended to earth with a bump and a shriek.
"I've got you !" cried Bubble. "I'm sorry it hurts ;
But I think you'll admit that you've got your deserts."

Poor Squeak disappeared, in a dozen blue fits ;
He thought that an earthquake had blown him to bits.
"Hurrah !" exclaimed Bubble. "I'll pick up the wood,
And say to the housekeeper, 'Ain't I been good ? ' "

Then Bubble went up to the lady of charms,
And firewood in plenty reposed in his arms.
"Well done !" said the housekeeper. "Good little boy !
These apples and tarts I feel sure you'll enjoy."

Then Squeak staggered up with a cry of despair.
"The tuck's gone to Bubble ! " he yelled. "It's not fair !
It was me who chopped up all the firewood, not Bubble ! "
But his well-laden twin disappeared at the double.

STAMP COLLECTING
FOR BOYS AND GIRLS

Lettland

THE KING OF HOBBIES AND THE HOBBY OF KINGS
By
FREDERICK J. MELVILLE
Director of the Philatelic Institute

Esthonia

Ukraine

Stamp-collecting is one of the finest hobbies boys and girls can take up, for it provides an ever-ready means of occupying spare time indoors and developes a taste for orderly methods, and stimulates the mind along a great variety of lines of interesting and fascinating study. It is a wonderful help in throwing light and interest upon your school studies, and most headmasters recognise nowadays that stamp-collecting is a great factor in education. It makes dull studies become interesting and attractive.

It is not just a "kiddish" hobby; it is enjoyed by grown-ups as well as by boys and girls. His Majesty King George has been a collector since his midshipman days, and his collection to-day is one of the finest in existence. His son, H.R.H. the Prince of Wales, is also a collector and is President of the Royal Philatelic Society So, you see, stamp-collecting is not only the king of hobbies, it is also the hobby of kings.

If you are not already a collector, let me give you a few hints as to the best way to start.

How to Start a Collection

The first necessity in forming a collection is stamps. Some of us are fortunate in having relations and friends abroad who can send us stamps for our collections, but for the most part stamps have to be bought and paid for. The best thing we can do at the start is to buy a large packet of varieties, that is to say, a packet of stamps that are all different. The larger that first packet the better the start. Packets of this sort, containing nice clean stamps, cost :

	s.	d.
250 different	5	0
500 ,,	7	6
1000 ,,	15	0

Suppose you have bought a packet of 500 different, you will then

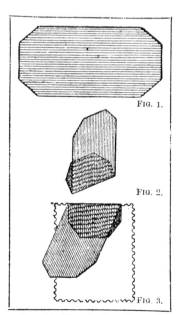

FIG. 1.

FIG. 2.

FIG. 3.

How To Mount Your Stamps

start to reap the pleasures of your hobby by examining them, and trying to classify them according to the countries from which they have been issued. This will be rendered easier by the aid of one of the stamp dealer's catalogues, and by the illustrations in your album.

The Album

That brings us to the consideration of the album. A beginner does not need a large album to hold a small collection, and it is better to start with quite a modest one. Money is better spent on stamps than on costly albums. From 3s. to 5s. is quite enough to spend on an album, and all the cash you have available for your hobby should be reserved for the acquisition of more stamps.

Don't "Handle" Stamps

A pair of tweezers, of almost any pattern, provided the points are not too sharp, will be necessary also, for it does not do to finger stamps. They are delicate things and won't stand a lot of handling. Get into the habit of using the tweezers for handling stamps so as to preserve your specimens in good condition.

PERFORATION GAUGE

How to Mount Stamps

Stamp mounts or hinges will also be required, and you should get the right kind as supplied by the stamp dealers. These mounts are little strips of thin, gummed paper which you fold with the gummed side outwards to form a hinge, one part of which is lightly affixed to the stamp, and the other part to the album. The little diagram shown on page 155 will explain exactly how the mount should be folded. Fig. 1 shows the mount as it is sold in packets of 1000 for 6d. Fold it as shown in Fig. 2, with the gummed surface outwards ; this forms a hinge, one arm of which is about one-third of the length of the mount. This short arm is lightly moistened and fixed to the back of the stamp, as in Fig. 3. Then you moisten the long arm of the hinge, turn the stamp over and place it in its proper square in your album.

It is a false economy to use stamp edging or ordinary common gummed paper, as such paper will not readily separate from the stamp afterwards if you wish to re-mount your stamps.

Measuring Perforations

One other necessity for the collector is a perforation gauge. It will not be necessary to buy one at present, as I am printing one herewith which you can always keep handy in your HOLIDAY ANNUAL. To use the gauge you pass the stamp up the column of dots and note when the perforations of the stamp coincide with the dots on the gauge. The figures at the side of the row of dots which fits the perforations of your stamp tell you what the perforation of your stamp measures. The measure of the perforation is reckoned by the number of holes made in a standard length of 20 millimetres, so that when we say a stamp is " perf 14 " we do not mean there are 14 perforations on the stamp, but that there are 14 perforations to the space of 20 millimetres.

New Issues Since the Armistice

Never has there been so interesting a period of new stamp issues as during the few months since the end of the war. These new stamps are the expression of the new birth of the hitherto oppressed nations of Europe, which have now gained their freedom and self-government.

The new countries created out of the dismemberment of Russia, and which have issued stamps, are Esthonia, Lettonia, Lithuania, Finland, Poland, and the Ukraine. Finland gained a measure of independence early in the war, and has had its republican stamps since 1917. Esthonia, the independent republic of the Esths, was proclaimed at Reval, the capital, on November 11, 1918, and almost immediately the new government set about overprinting captured German military stamps (as used by the German Eastern Command) with the inscription "EESTI" (Esthonia). These served as the first stamps of Esthonia, and they were followed by stamps of special design inscribed "Eesti Post."

Lettonia, the republic of the Letts, established since the Armistice, was suffering from a paper famine, and to print her first stamps she used the backs of German military maps. The stamps printed on the backs of maps are already somewhat scarce.

The Ukrainers have used Russian stamps with an overprint of a triform device which is an emblem of the Ukraine Republic.

THE
GREYFRIARS GALLERY IN VERSE

By Dick Penfold

No. 5 : Fisher T. Fish

WHO hustles round with might and main,
And concentrates his mighty brain
On getting rich (then gets a pain) ?
                            Why, Fishy !

Who votes this sleepy island slow,
And sadly lacking push and go ?
Who'd dearly love to boss the show ?
                            Why, Fishy !

Who kinder sorter calculates
That in the great Yew-nited States
A man makes fortunes while he waits ?
                            Why, Fishy !

Who tried his hand at many tricks
For raising heaps of spondulics,
And then received, not pence, but kicks ?
                            Why, Fishy !

Who murdered Wharton's magazine
By spelling which, when it was seen,
Made even Coker turn quite green ?
                            Why, Fishy !

Who thinks that fortune-hunting pays,
But who, on one of these fine days,
Will vanish by mysterious ways ?
                            Why, Fishy !

WHIMSICAL TRIFLES

Little Tricks and Toys Which Cause Endless Amusement.

THE GROWING BOY.

The first thing you have to do is to fold back the line B until it reaches the dotted line A. Then fold back the dotted line A^1 until it reaches the line B, which is now at the boy's waist. Your figure will then appear as sketched in Fig. 1.

Now, if you catch hold of the feet with one hand, and hold the folds carefully with the other, by pulling the feet down it appears as if the boy has grown. When you let go of the second fold, the boy still grows.

STRING HANDCUFFS.

Take two pieces of string, and tie one piece to your friend's wrists, as shown in the diagram. Tie one end of the other piece on to another friend's wrists, pass the other end over the string of the first piece, and then tie the end to your friend's other wrist.

To free them without untying the knots at the wrists, take the piece marked C, and pass it under the loop round the top wrist marked B. This will pull A's right wrist

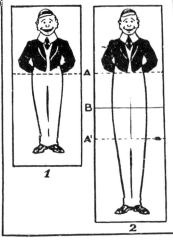

The Growing Boy.
MAKE A LARGE SCALE COPY OF THIS ON PAPER.

String Handcuffs.

nearer to B's. When you have pulled the string through the loop B, pass it over B's right hand, and you will find, on A straightening his string, that he is free.

THE MAGIC POKER.

This little trick can be performed better in the " half-light "—when it is getting dusk.

First of all tie a piece of black thread to either leg, as shown in the diagram, and marked A. Then you want to tell your friends you will make the poker stand by itself, not straight, but at an angle.

Secure the poker, and place it behind the black thread, as indicated by B in the sketch, and then, taking the top of the poker between the palms of your hands—see C— moving it about until you can feel the thread.

This gives the impression that you are trying to balance the poker on the floor. When you feel that the poker will rest against the thread, remove your hands.

Take care that your friends do not see you tying the thread to your

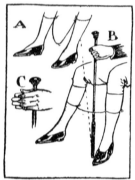

The Magic Poker.

legs—do it outside the room, and it will not show when you walk in, because it is black.

DISSOLVING THE PENNY.

This is a trick which requires a good deal of practice to make perfect.

Before you are ready for your trick, you must first of all get a tumbler of water and a piece of glass that will fit in the inside bottom.

Borrow a penny and a handkerchief from one of your audience, and tell them you are going to dissolve the penny in the water.

Talk to them while you palm the piece of glass as shown by A, then hold the penny as shown by B keeping the back of the hand towards your audience. Cover the penny with the handkerchief, and as quickly as you can, change the positions of the penny and the piece of glass. Cover the glass right over with the handkerchief, drop the piece of glass in the water, and the tinkling noise it will make will appear to be caused by the penny falling in the glass. Remove the handkerchief slowly and the penny has apparently become dissolved, because the glass cannot be seen.

Remember →

Dissolving the Penny.

practice makes perfect !

HOME-MADE THUNDER.

Do you know how to give your friends an idea as to what thunder sounds like ? You can show them at any time, or in any weather.

Home-made Thunder.

Take a piece of thread about four feet long and place it round your friend's head in the manner illustrated by the accompanying diagram, and marked A.

Ask your friend to push the thread well into his ears, as marked B in the sketch. Then, taking the thread between your finger and thumb, as shown by the mark C, run it through until you get the ends of the thread.

The firmer the pressure on the thread while it is passing through your finger and thumb, the louder will be the sound—or the thunder.

THE EGG AND HOOP TRICK.

This is a little trick you can perform by yourself, and is very simple.

Ask your friends if they can put an egg on the floor so that they cannot smash it with a hoop. They will probably try all kinds of positions for the egg; but, as a matter of fact the way in

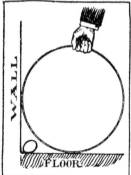

The Egg and Hoop Trick.

which the egg is placed on the floor has nothing to do with the trick at all.

All you have to do is to put the egg in one of the corners of the room, as indicated by the diagram, and in that position it is absolutely impossible to touch the egg with a hoop from any position. Strictly speaking, this is not a trick, but a "catch."

FREEING THE BEADS.

First, get hold of a piece of thin leather, or thin cardboard, or thick brownpaper, and cut two parallel lines, as shown in the sketch. Directly underneath the end of the cuts, make a hole which is the exact width of the two parallel lines. Take a piece of string, pass it through one of the cut lines, and through the other, and drop the two ends through the hole. On to the two ends tie two beads. The trick is to get the beads away without cutting the paper—we will say you have chosen the stiff brownpaper —or the string.

The way this can be done is shown in the right-hand portion of the sketch. Bend your paper right over, and pull the strip—you made this strip by cutting the parallel lines—through the hole, taking the string with it, of course. You will then find that the beads can be freed.

HOW TO CLIMB THROUGH A SHEET OF NOTEPAPER.

To say one can climb through a sheet of notepaper sounds impossible, but it can be done. Follow the direc-

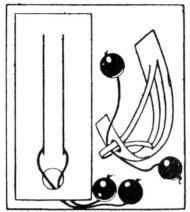

Freeing the Beads.

tions, and you will see. Take a sheet of notepaper, and fold it neatly in half. With a pair of scissors, cut the paper as shown in the top part of the sketch. You must first cut up one side of the paper at intervals of three-quarters of an inch, or less, thus making slips. Turn the paper round, and from the other side cut in between the first lot of cuts.

Then, taking the paper where it is folded, cut up from the second slip to the last but one. This is shown by the thick, black line in the bottom part of the sketch.

You will then be able to open out your paper into one huge circle, through which you will have no difficulty in passing.

THE ANIMATED SAWMEN.

This is a little toy which will amuse you not only in the making, but in its peculiar effect.

The first thing you have to do is to make a large sketch on the same lines as that reproduced. Then cut out your sketch, and you are ready for a little gum and a pencil. Look closely at the diagram, and across the two black figures you will notice two white lines.

Take a piece of fairly thin paper, and, placing your pencil between the two white lines, paste the remaining part of the sketch to the back of your paper. This raises a kind of hump on the backs of your paper figures. The mark A on the diagram shows

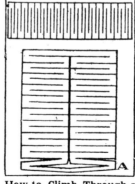

How to Climb Through a Sheet of Notepaper.

The Animated Sawmen.

what the back of your paper should look like when you have finished.

Then, by placing a candle about six inches away from the paper, and moving it backwards and forwards, the men appear to be sawing a block of wood.

THE WATER-MAIN PUZZLE.

Make a copy on a large scale of the top part of the diagram marked 1. A, B, and C are houses within a wall enclosure, and D, E, and F are water-main connections.

What you have to do is to bring the water from D to C, and from E to B, and from F to A without one of your lines crossing, or without passing outside the wall.

To get any amusement out of this puzzle you must not look at the solution until you are forced to admit that you cannot do it. The solution is given in the portion marked 2 of the sketch.

But before you even look at it, try and puzzle the way out by yourself.

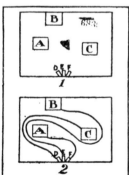

The Water-Main Puzzle.

A NEAT CATCH.

Place four pennies on the table, and ask a friend if he can make a cross with them. He is almost certain to make it as shown in the sketch marked A.

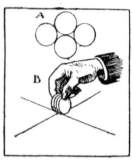

A Neat Catch.

You agree that he is right, then you take one of the pennies away, and ask him to make another cross with three. Remembering how he made the cross with the four pennies, he will try all manner of ways to make another in the same way.

He will give it up at last ; then you hold the three pennies in your hand, as shown by B in the sketch, and mark a cross on the table by moving the pennies first crossways, then downwards !

A SIMPLE STRING TRICK.

Take a piece of string, about eighteen inches long, and knot the two ends together in as small a knot as possible. Then push one of the double ends through one of your buttonholes, as shown in the diagram marked A. Taking the loops by your thumbs, take hold of the lower string, held by your left thumb, with the little finger of your right hand. Then with your left little finger take the top string held by the right hand.

Let the string go with your right thumb and your left little finger, and jerk the string with your left thumb and right little finger, and the string will come out of the buttonhole. Look at diagram and see how it is done.

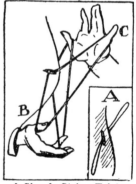

A Simple String Trick.

THE KING'S ROYAL
RIFLE CORPS

CRESTS
of
Famous
British
Regiments

THE ROYAL IRISH

THE SEVENTEENTH
LANCERS

THE EAST KENT
REGIMENT
(The Buffs.)

THE LANCASHIRE
FUSILIERS

THE ROYAL REGIMENT OF
ARTILLERY

THE DEVONSHIRE
REGIMENT

In Monmouth's Cause!

A Stirring Tale of Monmouth's Invasion of the West Country

By
DUDLEY FROBISHER

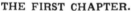

THE FIRST CHAPTER.

"I BID thee, under pain of my Royal displeasure, to muster such force that is within thy means to strike a blow for thy rightful ruler.—MONMOUTH."

Old Sir Stephen Athelney looked round hastily as he read this last sentence. It was part of a letter which had been left at the castle, on the previous night, by a horseman, who had not stopped to rest or sup, but spurred on his tired steed as if the whole of the Royal dragoons were at his heels.

"Monmouth knows his friends," Sir Stephen muttered, his eyes flashing, his usually pallid face flushed with excitement. "But these old limbs are too weak to bear war's harness. Odds life, 'tis well I have a son. Ralph shall go, and, whate'er comes o' this rebellion, Monmouth shall have no cause to say that the house of Athelney did not take its part."

Sir Stephen glanced round the great hall once more, then he crossed over to where a fire of logs burnt on the hearth, and thrust the letter amongst the glowing embers. Truly it was indeed a time when a man had reason to be cautious, for suspicion, nothing more, was near enough to bring a sentence of death upon the suspected.

"I thank thee!" Monmouth cried, in a high, clear voice, "and I thank ye all, citizens, for the welcome!" (*See page* 176.)

As the last fragment of the paper flared up the sound of fast-beating hoofs reached Sir Stephen's ears. The old man glanced hastily to where a sword hung upon the wall, but before he could reach it the door was flung open, and a tall, handsome young man, about twenty-one years of age, dashed into the room. His dress was that of a Cavalier, without being gaudy, and he wore his own hair upon his shoulders, despite the fact that wigs were the fashion at court.

"Ralph!" Sir Stephen cried, "I am glad it is thee. In these troublous times enemies may come as oft as friends. What news hast thou?"

"Of the best, father," Ralph answered eagerly; "Monmouth lands at Lyme to-night!"

"To-night!" Sir Stephen ejaculated.

"Ay!"

"Then there is no time to be lost, Ralph. Methinks 'twould take but little to make my old frame don back and breast plates again; but there, Ralph, the honour of Athelney lies with you!"

"You mean, father?"

"I mean that already I have heard from Monmouth, the man who should sit upon the throne of England, calling upon me to raise my men in arms to help his cause."

"And the letter—where is it?" Ralph asked eagerly.

"Where such things are safest—in the fire. Remember, lad, Monmouth is not yet king, and Kirke's dragoons scour the country, ready to arrest on the smallest evidence any man believed to favour any but King James II."

"I am ready to ride when thou wilt, father," Ralph said quietly.

Sir Stephen nodded.

"Ralph," he said, "by evening ye must take the road. I had thought to keep thee with me a few days more, but now ye will be safer in Monmouth's camp. I can fit ye out befitting our house, and by to-morrow at daybreak ye should be in Lyme."

"I am ready, father," Ralph answered quietly.

Just after dusk that evening Ralph rode through the park and out on to the road.

He was fully equipped in back and breast plates, and every other piece of armour of use to a Cavalier. His good sword hung by his side, and a brace of reliable pistols were in his saddle-holsters. He bore a letter from his father to Monmouth, and carried funds enough to serve him in case of need.

The night was dark, and Ralph jogged along easily, not wishing to tire his horse, for there was a long ride before them. His blood tingled with excitement as he thought of the mission upon which he was bound, and that he was to strike a blow for Monmouth and against the king, whom all decent subjects had learnt to loathe.

At midnight Ralph halted beside a small brook to breathe his horse. He loosed the girths, and rubbed the brute down as well as he could with a piece of stick. Suddenly a pistol-shot rang out, and he caught the sound of galloping hoofs.

Seizing the bridle of his horse, Ralph drew him behind a line of trees, waiting to see what would happen. The galloping drew nearer; a solitary horseman flashed by, bending low on his steed's neck, then three, in the uniform of the dragoons, came charging after him.

With the steadiness of a man whose nerve is not easily shaken, Ralph tightened the girth, swung himself into the saddle, and galloped after the men who had charged past him. The sight of the uniforms had given him some inkling of the truth. The solitary horseman was probably a man bound for Monmouth's camp, and somehow he had fallen into the hands of the enemy.

Ralph loosened his sword in his scabbard as he galloped along, and listened for the beat of the hoofs to guide him. He drew nearer to the sound, then it stopped abruptly. Away to the left a shot rang out, followed quickly by another. Without the slightest hesitation Ralph put his horse at the hedge, and galloped across the field on the other side.

He had not far to go. Through the darkness showed a still darker shape—a barn. A man stood with his back to this, keeping at bay the three dragoons, who had dismounted.

Ralph plucked out a pistol, dropped his bridle, and fired. One of the dragoons fell.

He thrust the empty weapon back into its holster, and with drawn sword charged down upon the remaining men. Only once he struck, catching his man a nasty blow on the arm; then, leaving their wounded comrade to his fate, the other two dragoons darted to their horses, clambered hastily into the saddle, and spurred away into the night.

Hardly had they gone than the man who had been defending himself single-handed against them sank to the ground. Ralph dismounted, and knelt beside him.

" Ye are hurt," he said quietly. " Where ? "

" It doth not matter," the man answered in a weak voice, " nothing can save me. I thank thee for thy aid, though it came too late."

Ralph saw that the man spoke the truth, and that in a few minutes he would be dead.

" It's naught I can do for ye ? " he asked.

The dying man raised himself slightly, peering up into Ralph's face.

" Your name ? " he asked eagerly.

" Ralph Athelney."

" The luck favoureth," the man muttered. Then, raising his voice, he added : " Ye can prove that ? "

Ralph drew the letter from his pocket that his father had given him for Monmouth, and pointed to the words, " By the hand of my son Ralph."

The dying man raised himself still more, his eyes straining until they could make out the words.

" Good ! " he said weakly. " Ye will find a packet of papers beneath my breastplate. They must be placed in Monmouth's hands. It was to save these I rode. It is a list of those faithful to Monmouth. Had it fallen into the hands of those dragoons many a good man would not have lived to draw sword for the right king. Take them to—Monmouth."

Ralph found the packet and placed it safely beneath his own plate.

" I shall not fail ye," he said quietly. " Is there naught that I can do to ease thy pain ? "

" Death alone can do that," the man answered weakly. " Ride—that will ease it, mayhap. I shall know they—are safe ! "

Realising that he could do nothing more, Ralph mounted his horse, called good-bye

to the dying man, and galloped away, making a slant for the road. Already he was working for the cause for which he had sworn to give his life, should it be asked of him.

THE SECOND CHAPTER.

At daybreak the next morning Ralph, weary and travel-stained, jogged into Lyme. The place was decorated with banners and arches of evergreens, with here and there great scrolls bearing the words, " Hail to Monmouth, our King ! " The streets were full of rough-looking men, some armed with swords or guns, but most carrying sickles and scythe-blades ; a few had nothing but stout staves. On the face of every man was set determination, for they were of the breed that dies hard when once roused to fight. In all there were a matter of six thousand men in the town, drawn from all parts of the country and from all classes.

Ralph dismounted at the door of an inn, and gave his horse in charge of a groom. Then, tired though he was, he washed, and was ready to see Monmouth.

" He has come ? " he asked of the landlord.

" Late last night," the man answered, " he be at Master Stern's house, back there. Ye have business wi' him ? "

" Ay, and it will not keep, my friend."

" Then my boy shall take ye there, sir."

Guided by the small boy, who was sufficiently aware of the importance of his mission not to wish to stop and eye every group of strange men, Ralph reached the house of Master Stern. Before the door of this two men, dressed as Cavaliers, stood on guard. They drew their swords as Ralph approached the door.

" I have urgent business with his Majesty," Ralph said quietly.

" Which must needs wait, sir," one of the Cavaliers answered. " He is closeted with Master Wade and Doctor Ferguson, and must not be disturbed."

" Send that in to his Majesty," Ralph said, drawing his father's letter from his pocket ; " I ask no more of ye."

" Stap me," the Cavalier remarked with a smile. " But alack, there may be poison within such a missive."

THE FUNNY ADVENTURES OF BUBBLE AND SQUEAK, THE TERRIBLE TWINS

"Will you give me a chocolate?" said Bubble to Squeak.
"You've got enough there to last you a week!"
But Squeak waved him off, and replied with a grin:
"Just keep off the grass while I have a tuck-in!"

So Bubble strolled off to the orchard near by,
And on many fine apples he feasted his eye.
"They're nicer than chocolates!" he chuckled, with glee.
"If I pick a good lot I sha'n't need any tea!"

Then the farmer bobbed over the brow of the hill.
"Oh, crumbs!" faltered Bubble. "He'll catch me, he will!
I'd better buzz off while I've still got a chance,
Or that merry old farmer will lead me a dance!"

Squeak had finished his chocolates when Bubble appeared.
"I've brought you some apples," he said, and Squeak cheered.
He held out his hat with a confident grin.
"That's nice of you, Bubble, you thoughtful old twin!"

But alas! for the farmer then came on the scene,
And Squeak's boyish face turned an art shade in green.
"I've caught you red-handed!" the farmer declared.
"You've stolen my apples! You shall not be spared!"

Then the farmer conducted poor Squeak to the Head.
"This boy has been raiding my orchard," he said.
Squeak's knees knocked together; he stood there aghast.
"Ha, ha!" chuckled Bubble. "I've floored him at last!"

"Nay, sir," Ralph answered, "but do me the favour to send it in."

Five minutes later Ralph was ushered into the house, and shown into a small room in which three men were seated. He had no difficulty in recognising Monmouth, whose handsome, beautifully cut face wore an expression of worry. He dropped on his knee.

"Nay, Master Athelney," Monmouth said, with a pleasant smile, "only my enemies shall do that."

"Ay, they shall be bowed down," Dr. Ferguson cried, with a strong Scotch accent, a light almost of madness on his fanatical face—"they shall be bowed down like the corn before the wind."

Ralph could not refrain from glancing at this man, of whom he had often heard as half a madman and wholly a fanatic. The other man, Wade, had been a lawyer, and it had been said that he was practically entirely responsible for this attempt to place Monmouth on the throne.

"Let us trust so," Monmouth answered; "but in the meantime there are other matters to attend to. Sir Stephen saith that he hath two hundred men willing to follow me, Master Athelney?"

"That, or more, sir," Ralph answered; "two for certain, but mayhap three. Fire soon spreads, your Majesty."

"Ah!" Monmouth ejaculated, with a pleased look, "I like that saying, 'Fire soon spreads.'"

"But I have other news for you, sire."

"Speak freely, Master Athelney."

In as few words as possible Ralph told his adventure of the previous night, and at the conclusion handed over the papers which the dying man had entrusted to him. Monmouth took them eagerly, broke the seal, and scanned the contents hurriedly.

"Ye have done well," he said earnestly. "Had this been lost many good men, leaders, too, would have passed into the hands of the usurper."

He paced up and down the room, his brows knit. When he stopped, he placed a hand quietly on Ralph's shoulder.

"Ye have done well," he repeated; "will ye do more?"

"My life is yours, sire," Ralph answered quietly.

"Then rest ye till to-night. Then to horse, and ride for Taunton. Call on your father, the loyal Sir Stephen, tell him that the trysting-place is Taunton; tell all the faithful ye meet, and await me in that town, where I shall unfold my standard."

"It shall be done, your Majesty."

"Good! Would that I had ten thousand men like ye!" Monmouth said.

"The right is better than ten thousand," Dr. Ferguson said, with a roll of his eyes.

"Granted. But the men are useful, doctor."

Ralph, dismissed from the royal presence, hurried back to the inn, ate a hurried meal, then sought the rest which he so much needed. It was evening when he awoke, refreshed and ready for anything. His first care was to see that his horse had been properly tended during the day; secondly came a substantial meal.

As the clock of the parish church struck eight Ralph rode out of Lyme, threading his way among the encampments in streets. Great fires were burning, over which oxen were roasting whole. At some of the corners ministers were preaching fervently, and there was not one of them but had a good audience.

Athelney Castle lay not more than ten miles from Taunton, and Ralph reckoned to make his home by the next morning, and reach Taunton on the following evening. Earlier than that he did not expect to reach his destination, for he knew that he would most probably have to make a circuitous route to avoid the king's troops. He rode steadily on once he had left Lyme, keeping as much as possible off the main road, knowing that most of the danger lay there. That the dragoons were scattered about the neighbourhood he had reason to be aware, as the reader knows. Nothing happened until he had covered a clear ten miles of his journey, then, to his annoyance, his mare cast one of her hind shoes, and he was forced to dismount or risk laming her.

Away to the left, not more than a mile distant, a light or two shone out, and Ralph guessed that the village of Little Hillham

THE
GREYFRIARS GALLERY
IN VERSE

By Dick Penfold

No. 6: Lord Mauleverer

Who dreams away the golden hours
On sofas and in shady bowers,
While we display our batting powers?
                    Why, Mauly!

Who votes school life a beastly drag,
And seldom joins in jape or rag,
Because he finds it too much fag?
                    Why, Mauly!

Who flirted with the fair Miss Bunn,
And made us call him, just for fun,
The hare-brained offspring of a gun?
                    Why, Mauly!

Who, on one famous trip to town,
Unearthed a fact which made him frown—
Miss Bunn belonged to Private Brown!
                    Why, Mauly!

Who drives his schoolmates to despair,
And fairly makes them tear their hair
By leaving banknotes everywhere?
                    Why, Mauly!

But who, in spite of many a fad,
Is really quite a charming lad—
A real good fellow? Yaas, begad—
                    It's Mauly!

lay there. Leading his horse by the bridle, he cut across the fields, and in less than a quarter of an hour entered the main and only street of the village. The clink of a heavy hammer reached his ears, and as he looked in the direction of the sound he caught sight of a broad beam of light issuing from an open door. The smith, despite the lateness of the hour, was still at work.

Ralph approached the open door cautiously, for there might be dragoons within. To his relief, his fears were not confirmed; only the smith and another man, evidently of the yeoman class, were in the forge. It was the latter's horse that was being shod—a fine, heavy brute, well fitted to be a charger.

"Evenin', sir," the yeoman said, touching his hat respectfully.

"Good-evening," Ralph answered; and, having tethered his horse to a ring in the wall, he waited quietly.

No more was said, for at such times, when no man knew who his enemy might be, it was unsafe to indulge in even the most ordinary conversation.

The smith humped the horse's hoof on to his knee, a burning smell filled the smithy, and his hammer tapped sharply. In five minutes the shoe was fixed. The yeoman took the horse's bridle, paid the smith, and passed out of the forge.

"Be sharp, my friend," Ralph said, as he handed over his horse. "I have little time this night."

"And many others tell that tale, sir," the smith answered, as he prepared to get to work; "mayhap some'n won't be havin' time tew live soon."

From outside came a sharp cry, followed by the clash of steel. Ralph's hand leapt to his sword, and he sprang towards the door. The smith gripped him by the arm, holding him back.

"It were best for ye not to look," he whispered hoarsely; "strange things is coom tew us."

Ralph shook himself free and sprang through the doorway. In a moment he saw what had happened. Two dragoons, their horses standing close by in charge of a third man, were fiercely attacking the yeoman, who had nothing with which to defend himself but a stout cudgel.

"Surrender, you dog!" one of the dragoons cried to the yeoman as Ralph emerged. "Spit

"Split his pate, Jack!" the man holding the horses cried.

Hardly had the man spoken before the yeoman's cudgel was cleft in half by a sword-cut, and he stood unarmed, at the mercy of the savage troopers.

"Will ye give up the horse?" one of them cried, brandishing his weapon.

"I surprise ye," the man said, with a slight smile, observing Ralph's amazed expression. "Permit me to do the honours, and present myself. Sir Lawrence Lamore, banneret, your most humble servant." (*See page* 173.)

me, but d'ye take us for horse-thieves?"

"Mighty like it," the yeoman answered, still stoutly defending himself with his stick.

"No!" the yeoman answered fiercely.

The swords whirled above the man's head, but before they could descend Ralph had gripped one of the men round the waist from behind, whirled him above his head, and flung him at his comrade. Both fell heavily, and the yeoman, seeing his chance, snatched up the sword that one of them had let fall.

The dragoons struggled to their feet, but drew back hastily before the ready swords of Ralph and the yeoman.

"Ye shall pay for this!" one of them yelled. "Ye crop-eared rebel! I'll spit ye with——"

"Try," Ralph broke in sternly, "or go."

With a torrent of abuse the dragoons retreated to their horses, and, digging their spurs in savagely, dashed away down the street. Ralph turned and went quietly into the forge, but the yeoman followed him.

"I owe ye the horse, sir," he said gratefully, "an', methinks, my life. Ye ride for Monmouth?"

Ralph looked at the man sharply, his hand on his sword.

"A dangerous question at such a time," he said. "What side claims ye?"

"None did," the man answered boldly, "but now it's Monmouth. I'm against these horse-thieves and their master. Monmouth, say I."

"Then the trysting-place is Taunton," Ralph whispered, having no wish that the smith, who was busy with the mare, should overhear him.

"Ye ride there, sir?"

"Yes."

"Then let me ride with ye. The roads are full of the vermin we have just met; two swords are better'n one. Let me ride with ye."

"Let him, sir," the smith said shortly, glancing up from his work; "a better man nor Master Jack Truman ne'er owned a horse."

Ralph hesitated a minute, then he held out his hand to the yeoman.

"We ride together," he said heartily, "and strike together for the right."

THE THIRD CHAPTER.

As soon as Ralph's horse had been shod he mounted and rode out of the village with Truman, who had in the meantime fetched a sword from his house, which was close by, and was now ready to throw in his lot with Monmouth. Ralph found him a distinct addition, for he was full of chatter, most of it idle, yet helping to pass away the long hours of the night.

At daybreak Athelney Castle was reached, and Ralph saw his father once more for a few minutes to give him Monmouth's instructions. Little did he think how many months were to pass before he would see him again.

No real halt was made here, and by eight o'clock the two men rode into the little village of Liddlecoomb. At this early hour the main street was practically deserted, and the man who took the horses at the inn door was fully three parts asleep. Ralph led the way into the inn, but before he had taken more than half a dozen steps a red-faced, jolly-looking man stepped quickly out of a side room.

"Gentlemen," he said quickly, with a sharp glance behind him, "don't ye coom——"

Before he could finish speaking another door opened, and a long face, crowned by a steel cap, was thrust out. A moment later a tall, thin man, garbed as an officer of dragoons, clanked out into the passage.

"Marry," he said, with a grin, "but ye come at a good time, gentlemen. My brother officers and myself—I am Colonel Spiller—are tired of winning guineas from each other, and would have fresh sport. What say ye?"

Ralph glanced over his shoulder at Truman, whose hand was ready on his sword-hilt.

"Have we time?" he queried.

Before Truman could answer the dragoon had approached, and was staring keenly at the two friends.

"Nay, but ye must have," he said, with a sinister look. "There can be no hurry. Those that ride for Monmouth needs must be quick, or we'll kill their king before they see him. But ye—why need ye rattle off like witches on a stick?"

"We accept your offer, sir," Ralph answered boldly, seeing that nothing else could be done.

Ralph and Truman followed the soldier into a large room at the back of the building, the window of which opened on to a garden. Ralph noticed that stout iron bars were across it. In the room were four men, all in the uniform of the Royal dragoons. Wine and dice-boxes were before them ; they were using the former eagerly but the latter listlessly, and already they were all more or less affected by the wine they had consumed.

"Comrades," Spiller cried, "I make a wager. Who will back my stroke against this gentleman's ? "

" I will, colonel, an' easy won," a man in the uniform of a cornet cried drunkenly. " The test ? "

" The steel cap there," Spiller answered, taking it from the wall as he spoke and placing it upon the table. " He who makes the deepest cut to be the winner."

All the other officers had stopped their gaming now to watch their superior officer.

" Wilt take me, sir ? " Spiller asked, with a touch of insolence, turning to Ralph.

" Yes. And the stakes ? "

" A hundred of your guineas against another hundred which, on the honour of an officer and a gentleman, I swear to pay ye as soon as convenient, should I lose."

This test did not please Ralph. He had little fear that this man would beat him, and he guessed that the effect of defeat upon the officer would not be pleasant. Spiller had already drawn his sword, and was cutting at the air, his face already wearing a triumphant expression, as if he felt that his victory was as good as won.

" We will throw for first cut," he suggested.

" Nay," Ralph answered, with a shake of the head ; " your seniority, both in the matter of experience and years, gives ye the right."

Without further ado Colonel Spiller approached the table, and took a firm stand, his feet apart, measuring the distance with his eyes. His cavalry sabre flashed up, then descended upon the helmet with a crash, making the table creak.

" Something like a stroke, colonel," the cornet said admiringly, eyeing the line cut into the steel. " Canst beat that, sir ? "

" I can try," Ralph answered coolly. " I have seen greater dents cut than that."

" Dent, ye call it ! " Spiller cried savagely. " Out on thee for a poor loser ! Try thy stroke, then speak ! "

Ralph had meant to lose, if only to conciliate the officer, but the insulting tone of the other angered him, and he meant now to win if he could. He swung his heavy sword over his head, and brought it down full upon the helmet. There was a clank and a crash, and both helmet and table lay in halves upon the floor. The dragoon officers looked at them in amazement, hardly as yet able to believe the evidence of their eyes.

" He has ye there ! " the cornet yelled, roaring with laughter.

" It is nothing, gentlemen," Ralph said hastily. " Let us have some more sack."

The sack was brought, and the officers were soon engaged in disposing of it to their satisfaction. Ralph, his example followed by Truman, emptied the contents of his mug from time to time on the floor. He grew as hilarious as any of them, but it was only feigned. One other man, too, was not drinking, although he seemed to be. That was Colonel Spiller. An angry light was in his eyes, and he watched Ralph as a cat watches a mouse, waiting for his chance to spring.

Before long the wine, added to that which they had already drunk, began to have its effect upon the officers, and one after another lay back in his chair and slept. The first, apparently, to succumb, was Colonel Spiller himself.

" Time to act," Ralph whispered, rising to his feet. " Quietly to the door, Truman, then a bolt for the horses."

" Ah, I have ye ! " Spiller cried, springing to his feet. " Rebels, are ye ? "

Remembering something the landlord had told him, Ralph rushed to the chair on which the arms of one of the soldiers lay, snatched up a pistol, and discharged its contents into the ceiling.

" Get that trap-door free," he said sharply to Truman, " and drop ye through."

As Ralph finished speaking, Spiller, sword in hand, leapt at him, and their blades crossed. The other officers, roused by the din, opened their eyes and looked stupidly round. Truman had already dropped beneath the table.

Acting entirely on the defensive, and keeping as near the table as possible, Ralph kept the infuriated officer at bay.

"Help, comrades!" Spiller cried fiercely, as he saw that alone he was no match for his opponent. "Kill this rebel!"

"Ready, sir?" rang out in Truman's voice.

With a quick movement of his wrist, Ralph disarmed Spiller just as the latter's comrades, roused from their stupor, were snatching up their swords. Then he dropped on his knees, darted beneath the table, and dropped through the open trap-door to the room below.

"There's a bolt, sir," the voice of the landlord said, close to his ear.

Ralph looked up at the opening, and as he did so the infuriated face of Spiller appeared. He drove his fist hard at it, and it was quickly withdrawn. The next moment he had slammed the trap-door to and pushed home the bolt.

"The horses are ready!" the landlord cried.

He spoke the truth, and a few seconds later Ralph and Truman were in the saddle.

"They'll be avenged upon ye for this, my good fellow," Ralph said hurriedly to the landlord; "we cannot leave ye to face it alone."

"Ride!" the man cried quickly.

At the same time he drew a knife from his belt, and before either of the men could stop him, had drawn it across his forehead, inflicting an ugly cut. He went white with pain, but a smile was on his lips.

"See, I tried to stop ye," he said. "Ride!"

Seeing that there was nothing for it but to obey, Ralph and Truman shook their bridles and galloped away over the cobbles. They had little fear that they would be pursued, for beyond the village were many parties of peasants marching towards Taunton, all armed in some fashion or another.

Taunton! The word had passed rapidly through the country, as Ralph knew, for the parties he and his companion had passed previously had all been on the road for the appointed trysting-place.

THE FOURTH CHAPTER.

"An' who'd have thought to see John Truman ridin' to the wars this day!" Ralph's companion remarked, as they eased their steeds up a sharp incline. They had not been pursued by the dragoon officers, and now, as evening was falling, they were within five miles of Taunton, the lights of which they could see glinting in the distance.

"It is a wise man who knows what the morrow will bring," Ralph answered. "And methinks ye are as well here as ye would be in the village."

"Ay; think not that I have grumbled," Truman said quickly, and with evident sincerity; "my hands itch to be at the knaves—the hired murderers of James II."

"And so do mine," Ralph agreed; "but ye need not fret that there will be no fighting for thee. I am too young to have seen civil war, but my father, Sir Stephen Athelney, hath seen it. Blood floweth in rivers, he hath told me; no man knoweth his enemy, or what the chance of a minute will bring."

They rode on slowly, for their horses were none too fresh, and they had no wish to enter Taunton with steeds needing a week's rest to make them fit for anything. They passed no bands of rebels pressing on to Taunton now, for those who had not already gained the city had camped by the roadside for the night. Looking back, Ralph could see their fires, and hear their voices as they lustily sang.

"What was that?" Truman said suddenly, peering into the hedge on his bridle-arm.

"Naught; what should there be?" Ralph answered carelessly. "Another couple of miles an' we shall be in Taunton."

A hundred yards ahead the road branched off into three directions, the centre path leading to Taunton, the others to small villages.

As the two horsemen approached this spot the dark form of a man and horse emerged from the shadow of a line of trees.

"A happy meeting, gentlemen," he said, in a quiet voice. "A most enchanting spot—sink me if it is not—for a little passage of arms."

Ralph handed his horse to Truman, advancing to within three yards of the man. He expected to see the usual highwayman, the reckless common type, but to his surprise this fellow bore none of the outward attributes

The galloping drew nearer, a solitary horseman flashed by, bending low on his steed's neck, then three, in the uniform of the dragoons, came charging after him. (*See page* 164.)

generally supposed to be possessed by the gentlemen of his profession. He was a man of medium height, slim in build, but with a grace of carriage seeming to indicate a sinewy strength. He was dressed in the Court fashion of the times, a long riding cloak edged with lace reaching to his heels. His boots, narrow in the foot and high of heel, showed signs of wear, but they were of good make. The hilt of his sword was of gold.

"I surprise ye," the man said, with a slight smile, observing Ralph's expression. "Permit me to do the honours and present myself. Sir Lawrence Lamore, banneret, your most humble servant."

"Sir Lawrence Lamore!" Ralph cried, in amazement. "Ye jest!"

"'Twould be a sorry jest," the other answered coolly; "but I marvel not that ye are surprised. Hard times, my good sir, hath brought me to this. I had thought to reap something of a harvest from the rebels bound for Taunton, but, split me, ten paltry guineas yesterday—now no more. Faith, but had I known how ill-paid the business was I should have tried something else."

"Put up thy sword, Sir Lawrence," Ralph answered, unable to suppress a smile, and sheathing his own weapon.

"Nay, nay," the other said indignantly, "I had thought to kill or be killed—the issue would be mighty indifferent to me—a gentleman of the road doth deserve better treatment than this."

"Ye seem to seek danger," Ralph answered, in surprise.

"Why not?" Lamore said bitterly. "What have I left, that I need fear to lose me life. Faith, 'tis all they have left me."

Ralph turned to Truman and drew him aside. An idea had occurred to him, but he felt bound to ask his comrade's permission before putting it into execution.

"Why not take this gentleman on with us, Truman?" he said. "He hath pluck, and Monmouth hath sore need of such men."

"Why not?" the yeoman answered readily. "This man hath but done what others of his rank have done. A brave man is a brave man, whatever else he may be."

"Sir," Ralph said quietly, turning once more to the amateur highwayman, "why should ye not ride with us ? I can promise ye use for that sword, and a life fit for a man."

Sir Lawrence Lamore displayed more energy than he had so far shown, and drew away from the tree.

" Ye ride to join Duke Monmouth ? " he asked eagerly.

" Yes," Ralph answered boldly ; " we shall await him at Taunton, the lights of which ye see two miles distant."

" Then, stap my vital breath, but I am with ye ! " Lamore cried. " I had not thought of that. I have been considered mighty neat at sword-play. Gentlemen, may I know your names, that I may swear allegiance to ye ? "

Ralph mentioned them, and the Cavalier bowed low.

" Your most humble servant, sirs," he said. " And now for Taunton. My horse'll just manage the two miles, poor brute ! " He drew a small flask from one of his pistol-holsters and handed it to his new friends.

" A little drop of cordial, the last remnant of my property. Drink, gentlemen, and let the toast be—' In Monmouth's Cause ! ' "

Half an hour later Taunton was reached, and the three men rode slowly down the main street, threading their way through crowds of drilling men, despite the lateness of the hour. Orders, sharp and warlike, broke the stillness of the night, but above even the orders rang the harsh voices of ministers, or the roared refrain of a hymn.

" They will fight," Ralph whispered to Lamore.

" Ay, and they will," the other agreed, with a smile ; " and so shall we, too. I have no cause to love our present king. A new one, say I, and may he mount the throne soon ! "

THE FIFTH CHAPTER

JUNE the eighteenth had arrived, and with it the news that Monmouth and his army, numbering some eight thousand men, would enter Taunton early that morning. Within the city all was excitement ; great preparations had been made.

Ralph, Truman, and Lamore, mounted on their horses, took up a position by the gate

Four Splendid

Find the boy's father.

Find the two Redskins.

Puzzle Pictures

Find the two men.

Find the hunter.

through which Monmouth and his men would enter, for they were anxious to see the type and number of men that he had with him. Ralph had, of course, already seen Monmouth, but the others had not.

Near to where the three men sat on their horses a fanatical preacher, mounted on a tub, his eyes blazing with a light not far short of madness, was preaching in a loud, harsh voice. One sentence reached Ralph, and he started and stared at the man.

"What want ye with kings?" the man cried.

"Mighty near treason that," Lamore remarked carelessly, flicking a speck or two of dust from his cloak. "Think ye we should stop his ranting tongue?"

"Nay," Ralph answered hastily. "The men will fight for Monmouth none the less staunchly despite that fanatic's words."

"Look!" Truman cried, touching Ralph on the arm—"Monmouth!"

As Truman spoke. a burst of cheering broke from the men and women crowding the windows above. The army was in sight. The head of it was descending the hill a mile from the city gates, and it was quite possible to discern Monmouth, surrounded by a smiling body of horsemen, riding ahead of the army, the men of which were marching six abreast, their banners waving right bravely.

"There must be a great number, think ye?" Ralph said eagerly.

"Not more than eight to ten thousand, my friend," Lamore answered coolly. "Numbers are deceptive at a distance."

When the army had advanced to within half a mile of the gate it halted, and Monmouth and his party, the former bareheaded, came galloping on alone.

"A right royal figure," Truman said enthusiastically.

"May he fight well; I ask no more!" Lamore growled between his teeth. "There are various tales o' this man's nature. Some hath seen him brave as a lion, others hath known him play the coward to perfection."

So far as Monmouth's appearance was

concerned there was little lacking. He was in his thirty-sixth year, and he sat his horse with all the grace of an accomplished horseman. His face was white and thin—naturally, not through ill-health—and his great curled wig accentuated the pallor. He was dressed sumptuously, as befitted his kingly rank, his back and breast plates being of silver and inlaid with gold, while his sword-hilt was crowned by a great gem.

Cheer after cheer rang out as this gallant person rode towards the gate with his escort close behind him, and reined up in the opening. The Mayor of Taunton, an old man of the name of Master Lucas Fairgood, approached and sank on one knee, offering an address as he did so.

" I thank thee ! " Monmouth cried in a high, clear voice, " and I thank ye all, citizens, for this welcome." He motioned Master Fairgood to rise. " I see ye have some more brave men for me, good Master Mayor."

" Nigh upon four thousand, your Majesty," the old man answered, with a glow of pride ; " many trained to the use of arms."

" Ye have done well," Monmouth said, with a smile. " We shall not forget our friends when we are safe upon the throne."

" His family were always main ready with promises," Lamore whispered to Ralph, " but not so apt to keep them."

Monmouth had now drawn aside. A man amongst his escort raised his sword, and the army advanced towards the gate, swinging along six abreast, with some little show of order. First came the horse, very few in number, some of the men in armour, others ready to meet the foe with nothing but their good swords to protect them. Nevertheless, their appearance raised a hearty cheer from the citizens of Taunton. Next came the foot, and a strange mixture of men they were.

Last of all came the waggons and carts, some holding ammunition and food, others bearing the personal belongings of the soldiers. It was impossible for all these to enter the city, and they took up a position before its half-ruined walls.

All had passed, and Monmouth, his Cavaliers behind him, rode through the gate of the city. Ralph and his comrades raised their swords to the salute as he passed, and were favoured with a slight bow and an approving glance.

A sharp grip on his arm caused Ralph to face round upon Truman.

" Look," the latter whispered—" the fanatical preacher ! "

Ralph turned his eyes in the man's direction, and as he did so he saw him spring from his tub with the agility of a monkey and land clean behind Monmouth, bestraddling the horse with his long legs. He held a bludgeon in his hand, and raised it high above his head.

" Kings shall perish ! " he shrieked, " and the righteous rule the righteous in this chosen land ! "

Saying this, he aimed a blow at Monmouth's head which would certainly have killed him, had he not just at that moment leaned forward in his saddle, and the bludgeon fell harmlessly on to his back-plate. Again it was raised, but before it could be used again, this time probably with more effect, Ralph had urged his horse forward, his sword flashed from its scabbard, and the madman fell back from the horse.

Monmouth turned his head sharply and saw what had happened. The whole affair had taken place so quickly that it was difficult to realise that the attempt had been made at all.

" Ah, 'tis you, Master Athelney," Monmouth said, with a smile. " This is the second time ye have served us. We thank thee. Ride with the escort ; ye must join my officers."

" And my friends, your Majesty ? " Ralph asked boldly.

" Thy friends are my friends," Monmouth answered, with a bow. " Let them join our person, too. We go to hold counsel in the church, and shall be glad of thy advice."

Ralph and his comrades obeyed the order, and rode down the street behind Monmouth. They halted before the square old church of Taunton, and the whole party dismounted. There were men of many nationalities among the escort, but French outnumbered the rest. Dr. Ferguson and Wade kept close to the king as they entered the church.

The interior of the building had been cleared of the benches used by the worshippers, and a series of tables ran down the centre, forms placed by them. At the head of the farthest table a raised chair had been placed, and in this Monmouth took his seat, Dr. Ferguson on his right and Wade on his left.

"My friends," Monmouth said, in a clear voice, "I am glad to see ye here, ready to uphold me in this just cause. There are documents for me, good Master Mayor."

The mayor produced a bundle of letters and placed them before Monmouth, who tore them open and glanced quickly at their contents. As he read the last his pale face flushed with pleasure.

"Gentlemen," he cried, "we have good news for ye. Sir James Strangeways, whose castle lies ten miles from here, hath five hundred arms at our disposal—petronels, fowling-pieces, and others. We have but to fetch them away! Ay, and we must make all good speed. There is much work to be done. Time taketh wings against us, and the enemy is massing his forces on the plain of Sedgemoor. Let the arms be fetched from yonder castle, and we will hasten on our way."

THE SIXTH CHAPTER.

BRIDGWATER was reached, and Monmouth and his troops were received with open arms, all that the town held being at their disposal. But little time was wasted, and all through the day Monmouth and his council sat, discussing plans for the future. Only a few miles away, encamped upon the plain of Sedgemoor, lay King James's troops, considerably outnumbering their opponents, and, moreover, all well armed and accustomed to war by long training.

By ten that night the men had fallen in, their officers at their head, and all was ready for the attack. Ralph and his regiment, and two more regiments of cavalry, were to advance in the van, so that at the given moment they might charge into the enemy's camp.

At eleven to the minute Monmouth, mounted on a powerful horse, galloped down the line, and a buzz of welcome broke from the rough soldiers. His face was hard and set, which could hardly be wondered at, for on the night depended all. By the morrow he would be on a fair way to mounting

the throne of England or he would be no better than a hunted fugitive.

Orders were issued in low tones, and the army left Bridgwater, striking across the Parrat and on to the bare plains on the other side. Ralph, leading the way with his cavalry, advanced very slowly, for here and there the plain was cut by great ditches, used for draining the ground, and the bridges spanning them were inconveniently narrow. At last, however, they had all been crossed, and a mile ahead the lights of the enemy's fires shone dimly through the misty night. Ralph glanced back at the great line of men stretching out on either side. The ground was soft, and the shuffling of the thousands of feet sounded only faintly.

So far all had gone well, and there seemed every reason to believe that the surprise would be effected. Ralph spurred his horse and cantered to where Lamore and Truman rode at the head of their men.

"When the order comes," he said, in a low voice, "charge. And mark this, both of ye. Should the fight go against us we stick together, die together if need be, or escape together."

"We'll win, Ralph," Lamore answered, in a whisper, "but I shall remember."

Ralph cantered back to his men, and they drew nearer and nearer to the enemy's fires, until they sparkled not four hundred yards ahead. From time to time Ralph turned his head towards the spot where Monmouth rode, waiting impatiently for the order that was to convert the slow advance into a reckless charge.

At last! A bugle rang out shrilly, others answering it.

"Charge!" Ralph cried, and set spurs to his horse.

Over the uneven ground the cavalry charged, making straight for the line of fire, across which dark forms were moving hurriedly. Cries of alarm rose from the enemy's camp. The surprise was complete. Before the soldiers would be fully aroused many of them would have fallen, and the rest, alarmed by the fate of their comrades, would——

Of a sudden, with a force that nearly brought him to the ground, Ralph reined in his horse, throwing him back upon his haunches. His men followed his example—all save two, who, charging on, fell with a loud splash into the ditch which stretched right across the path of the advancing troops.

"On, on!" officers, who could not guess why the troops in front of them had halted, yelled. "On! It is our chance!"

Ralph thrust his horse right to the edge of the ditch, and peered across it. It was fully fifteen yards wide; too great a jump to be expected of the horses. The bugles were ringing out in the camp of the enemy, and already Ralph and his men could see dark forms on the opposite bank.

"Have ye such a thing as a bridge about ye?" Lamore cried coolly, not the least moved by the unexpected check the advance had received, and addressing a tall figure which showed dimly on the other side of the ditch. "Split me, but this is most infernally annoying; I had quite thought to have the killing o' ye by now."

The only answer to this was a pistol-bullet, which, luckily, did no more harm than to graze Lamore's left wrist.

"Just ye wait till I come over," he cried, "and ye shall receive greater interest than any rascally money-lender would ask."

"Down on your faces, lads!" Ralph cried, as a line of men appeared on the opposite bank.

Hardly had he spoken before a volley screamed out; the night was lit by bright flashes of light, and the battle had begun in deadly earnest.

An officer galloped wildly up to Ralph, his face pale with excitement.

"Hath the surprise failed?" he asked sharply.

"Ay," Ralph answered between his teeth; "this ditch hath thrown aside our plans."

"Then take your men to the left flank; only the foot are of use here. Be ready to stop the enemy's cavalry if they charge. Monmouth doth think they will ford this place higher up, then charge down upon us."

The officer galloped away. Ralph gave the order to his men to mount, and they forced their way along on the flank. This was no easy matter, for the foot soldiers had reached the edge of the ditch, and now packed it closely. At last, however, clear ground was reached, and there Ralph halted with his cavalry, unable to do anything but watch the progress of the fight. Soon, nevertheless, he was to have his fill of fighting, with a vengeance.

"They're at it in right good earnest now!" Lamore cried, waving his sword towards the ditch. "Look! The enemy are massed on yonder bank, firing volley after volley."

"Ay, and our brave fellows return it just as steadily," Truman answered sharply. "The surprise hath failed; but they mean to fight for Monmouth none the less stoutly."

"May it avail them aught," Ralph said between his teeth.

"What mean ye?" Lamore asked quickly, turning towards him.

"Just this. We are here, a matter of close upon a thousand mounted men; but how many, think ye, have the enemy?"

"How should I know?"

"Five thousand! In all probability they will be down upon us ere the dawn, and then——"

"Glorious!" Lamore cried. "It will be glorious—even to die!"

The air was now full of the smell of powder. The discharge of the guns was so continuous that it had become one deafening roar, and the flashes of light darted everywhere like shooting stars.

Ralph, unable to restrain his anxiety, left his troop under the command of Lamore and Truman, and galloped down to the fighting line. He found the men who were armed with any kind of firearm lining the edge of the ditch, two deep, spitting bullets into their guns, and firing with the steadiness of the finest soldiers in the world. Behind them lay a line of wounded, attended to by pikemen. All were as cool as ice, and there could be little doubt that they would hold their own against the enemy, unless—that was the one weak point—unless the cavalry charged on the flank. Ralph wheeled his horse and galloped back to his men. Truman and Lamore waited him anxiously.

"Methought I heard the jingle of harness yonder," he cried, pointing to the left. "Surely the cavalry cannot have got across yet?"

With straining ears Ralph bent sideways in the saddle, trying to hear something more than the deafening report of the guns. As he did so a bugle rang out sharply, sounding the charge. He turned sharply to the officer of the nearest foot regiment.

"Form your men into squares, sir!" he cried sharply. "The cavalry are upon us!"

He turned back to his men, spurring his horse until he was at their head.

"Charge!" he cried. "Let us meet them half-way!"

The men needed no further bidding. Spurs were thrust home, faces shone with fierce excitement; never did men ride so willingly to their death. It was five hundred against at least four times that number; yet the smaller troop rode as if certain of victory.

With a crash the two forces met, and the shock was so great that a score of horses went down. No man thought of guarding; it was slash and thrust, thrust and slash, with one object on both sides.

Ralph, the light of battle in his eyes, wielded his great sword with deadly effect, and so fierce was his onslaught that he positively hewed his way through the enemy. Close behind him rode Truman and Lamore, both doing their share of the fighting right well. Not a man of the inexperienced cavalry flinched. Though they fell fast before the overpowering numbers of the enemy, yet not one of them died before leaving his mark upon his foe.

For ten minutes the fight raged with terrible fury; but at the end of that time the enemy had cut their way through, and were charging down upon the foot. Ralph shouted fierce orders.

"Keep the men together!" he cried to

Ralph looked up at the opening, and, as he did so, the infuriated face of Spiller appeared. He drove his fist hard at it, and it was quickly withdrawn. The next moment the trap-door was slammed to, and the bolt pushed home. (*See page 172.*)

(179)

Lamore and Truman; "we must charge back to the help of the foot!"

Orders rang out, and the cavalry formed up as well as it might. It was a terrible sight; five hundred men had ridden in the charge, but now little more than one hundred remained, and practically every man amongst these was wounded, some so severely that only will-power kept them in the saddle.

"Back!" Ralph shouted. "Another blow for Monmouth!"

A cheer answered Ralph, and the men swept along behind him, ready for the worst. The foot, each man fighting like ten, had been broken up by the cavalry, and were now fighting in little groups, a pile of dead and dying before them. Ralph's men split up now, every one singling out his man and fighting him.

Ralph, Lamore, and Truman kept well together, riding here and there, imploring, helping, ordering, although they saw plainly enough that the fight was lost. The firing of their men had grown less continuous, and they guessed rightly that the ammunition was giving out.

Daybreak!

As the light of day grew stronger it revealed a spectacle warranted to shake the strongest nerves. All about the plain lay heaps of dead, while along the ditch they seemed to lie in one long line that had no end. Here and there small knots of haggard men were still fighting, surrounded by cavalry.

Ralph looked round sharply, seeking Monmouth. It was not long before he found him, the centre of a small knot of horse and foot, warding off the attack of a score of the enemy's cavalry.

"To the rescue!" Ralph cried, his one idea being to save Monmouth, and charged with his two friends towards the spot. The three horsemen, mainly by the fury of their onslaught, managed to turn the tide of war in their favour for a moment.

"Get thee gone, friends!" Monmouth cried hoarsely, as he recognised Ralph and the others; "save your lives while there is yet time."

"Not unless we save thine, sir," Ralph answered boldly.

THE SEVENTH CHAPTER.

MONMOUTH looked round sadly, saw the small groups of men who still fought, and realised the terrible truth—the day was lost.

"I shall die with these brave fellows," he said fiercely. "Let me but slay one more of these paid murderers!"

"Nay, your Majesty," an old officer broke in, "escape. While ye live ye may come into thine own. Dead—what is left but the grave?"

"Ye are right!" Monmouth answered, his pale face flushing for a moment. "I am with ye, Athelney; lead the way."

Ralph spurred his horse, and galloped across the field of battle, Monmouth and his two friends close behind him. He hoped that in the excitement the enemy would not be able to distinguish them from their own friends, and so give them a chance to get away. He turned in the saddle and addressed Monmouth and the others.

"Loose your breast and back plates as ye ride," he commanded. "Once we have left this place we must have no look of the soldier about us."

At midday Ralph called a halt, which was much needed by both horses and men, at the side of a small stream.

Monmouth, to make his disguise more complete, ripped most of the gold lace from his garments, and so robbed them of their royally rich appearance. For three hours did the four men rest beside the stream, the pangs of hunger reminding them that it was many hours since they had eaten. At the end of that time Ralph gave the order to mount, and once more they proceeded on their way. Night fell, and they entered a small village, but dared not halt. Bread was bought, and they ate it as they jogged on through the village. Many a curious eye was turned upon them, but they did not notice it.

"By to-morrow night, sire," Ralph said, as they jogged along a road bordered on both sides by trees, "we shall be at my father's castle. Ye will be safe there."

"As ye will," Monmouth answered sadly. "Truth, but I have little wish to live."

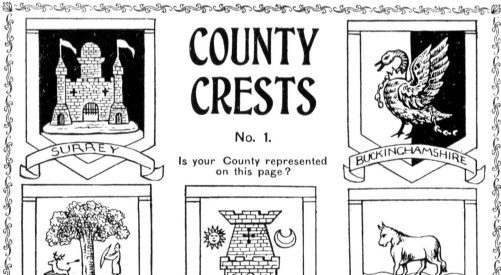

COUNTY CRESTS

No. 1.

Is your County represented on this page?

SURREY

BUCKINGHAMSHIRE

HUNTINGDONSHIRE

WARWICKSHIRE

OXFORDSHIRE

SHROPSHIRE

SOMERSETSHIRE

MONMOUTHSHIRE

CORNWALL

KENT

DURHAM

Suddenly, without the slightest warning, Ralph pulled up his horse.

"Hist!" he whispered.

The others followed his example, and sat perfectly still, listening. From some distance away came the rapid beat of hoofs and the jangle of harness.

"Cavalry," Ralph said shortly. "Can they be on our track?"

"Like as not," Lamore answered carelessly. "How many, think ye, are they in number?"

"Six or eight," Ralph said, after listening intently for a minute or so; "we had best push on. See to it that your pistols are loaded. If it comes to a fight we must be ready. They may have put them upon our track back at the village."

"Fight it will be," Truman said hoarsely. "Our poor nags could scarce gallop, whatever the danger might be."

The four men jogged on again in silence, listening to the beat of the hoofs, which every moment was drawing nearer. It was a moonlight night, but on this tree-shaded road the light shone only in patches. Ralph rode with his ears on the alert, waiting impatiently for the moment when the horsemen would come into view. There was just the chance that they might be fugitives from Monmouth's army, but it was unlikely.

Seven horsemen, riding in a close body, swept into view, and Ralph recognised, as they passed a patch of light, the uniform of the dragoons.

"Halt!" The order rang out sharply, and was accompanied by a pistol bullet, which passed unpleasantly near to Truman. The latter pulled a pistol from his holster, and was about to answer the shot, when Ralph gripped his wrist.

"Not yet," he commanded sternly. "We must get a gallop from our nags until we reach a likelier spot for a fight. Do not spare your horses now. Our lives depend on't."

Urged on by spur and voice, the horses quickened their pace to a gallop, and, for a short time at least, drew away from the pursuers. But that it could not last long every one of the four men knew, for their horses were near foundered.

As he rode on Ralph looked eagerly to right and left. Round a bend in the road they swept, the lines of trees ceased, and on either side stretched level grass land.

"Halt!" Ralph cried sharply. "Do ye, sire, and ye, Lamore, take your stand on the left side, back from the road, that ye may not be observed; Truman and myself will take the right. Have your pistols ready, and do not fire until I give the word. We cannot spare these men. Our own safety depends upon it."

Monmouth and Lamore urged their horses to the left, Ralph and Truman went to the right. The whole of the four held their pistols ready, cocking them over their left elbows to make more certain of their aim.

Nearer and nearer drew the clatter of the cavalry, and the waiting men set their teeth. The soldiers were riding boldly forward, little thinking of the surprise in store for them. With a rush they passed the fringe of trees.

"Fire!" Ralph shouted.

Four pistols flashed out together, and four of the soldiers fell from their horses. Every ball had accounted for his man.

"The others must not escape!" Ralph cried. "At them!"

Urging their horses to one more effort, Monmouth and his three staunch supporters charged at the remaining soldiers, who had wheeled their horses round.

"Surrender, rebels!" their leader cried savagely, "or your lives shall pay the forfeit!"

"Remain behind, sire," Ralph said coolly, turning to Monmouth; "they shall have fair play."

Ralph, singling out the officer, charged at him, his sword raised. The weapons of the two men met, and a fierce fight followed. The officer, maddened by the fall of his men, fought with the ferocity of a tiger, and it was all that Ralph could do at first to guard the rapid cuts and thrusts. But the officer's fury very soon commenced to tell its tale, and Ralph assumed the offensive, driving the man hard. His chance came, his sword thrust sharply forward, and the man reeled from his horse, a gaping wound in his neck.

Now that his adversary was done with Ralph turned to see how his companions were faring, and as he did so he saw Truman reel from his horse, wounded in the shoulder. The dragoon who had administered the wound bent from his saddle to finish off his fallen foe, but before he could do so Ralph had charged to the rescue. To strike the man dead from behind was not Ralph's nature. He passed his sword to his bridal hand, and his right, clenched hard, struck the man behind the ear, sending him stunned and senseless to the ground. At the same moment Lamore dropped his man.

"We must ride on, sire," Ralph said, riding up to Monmouth. "The country swarms with such men as these. We shall not be safe until my father's castle is reached."

"And even then?" Monmouth queried, with a bitter smile.

"It shall be no fault of mine if ye do not escape the country," Ralph answered shortly.

Till daybreak the little party rode on, then they were forced to halt to rest their horses. During the day they pressed on again at a little faster than a walk, keeping as much as possible off the roads, and by evening Athelney Castle was in sight. Until night had fallen the four men loitered in the park, deeming it wiser to make their entrance under cover of the night.

THE EIGHTH CHAPTER.

SIR STEPHEN ATHELNEY sat alone in the great hall, his head bowed in his hands, his arms resting on the table. From time to time his lips moved.

"Defeat," he muttered bitterly, "and after we have waited so long. Ah, Ralph, Ralph, shall I ever see thee again?"

An old servant entered the room with quiet step and touched his master on the shoulder.

"What want ye, Simon?" Sir Stephen demanded, almost angrily. "Canst not see I am in no mood to be disturbed?"

"There are those who would see ye, Sir Stephen," the man answered, a smile on his face.

"Tell them I will not," the old man answered quickly. "Treat them well, Simon, but do not disturb me."

"Ye had better see them, sir," the servant persisted.

Sir Stephen looked into the man's face, and something there brought the blood tingling to his hollow cheeks.

"Not Ralph?" he gasped. "The lad is safe? Tell me, quick!"

Before the servant could answer, Ralph himself, followed by his three companions, stepped into the hall. The old man embraced his son eagerly, with tears in his eyes, then bowed courteously to the others.

"These gentlemen?" he queried.

"Sir Lawrence Lamore," Ralph answered readily, "and Master Truman—both stout soldiers of the fallen cause."

"And the other, Ralph?"

"King Monmouth!"

With a cry of joy Sir Stephen sank on his knee before Monmouth.

"Welcome to Athelney Castle, sire!" he said, in a shaking voice. "Little had I thought to see my king once more."

"A king?" Monmouth answered bitterly, at the same time raising Sir Stephen. "A king without a throne, without a country, without an army, and without a guinea—a hunted fugitive, holding to his life fraily by the aid of his trusty friends. Yes, if a king can be in such straits, then am I still a king."

"Enough, sire!" Ralph interrupted sharply. "None must know, not even the servants, who ye really are. Father, remember, this is Sir George Fairwell. Now, canst order dinner, for we are nigh famished?"

Within ten minutes a bountiful meal had been spread, and Monmouth and his comrades were very soon doing full justice to it. When the latter had somewhat appeased his appetite he turned to Ralph.

"What, think ye, must be our next move, friend?" he asked.

"That ye may leave to me, sir—Sir George," Sir Stephen answered quickly. "I have known for some time that if this effort to place ye on the throne failed I should be compelled to flee the country. I have a lugger waiting a day's ride from here. To-morrow we can set out to join it, and I shall go with ye."

"Good!"

The clatter of horses' hoofs on cobbles caused the men to spring to their feet, their

THE BALLAD
OF THE
POSTAL ORDER

By JOHNNY BULL

Billy Bunter was a citizen
  Of " credit " and renown ;
He called on me one sunny day
  And borrowed half-a-crown.

He promised me right faithfully
  That he would play the game,
And pay it back most promptly, when
  His postal-order came !

I waited for a week or so,
  And then my anger grew ;
Quoth Bunter : " It's delayed, you know.
  The postman's down with 'flu ! "

I waited till the end of term ;
  Said Bunter : " It's no catch !
The titled cove who's sending it
  Is now in Colney Hatch ! "

When holidays were past and gone,
  I called for my half-crown ;
But Bunter said : " I'm sorry, John,
  I've left my quids in town ! "

I waited on for many moons,
  And so fed-up was I
That each time Bunter came in sight
  He got a damaged eye !

That postal-order grew a beard,
  It grew side-whiskers, too !
And to my long-lost half-a-crown
  I sadly bade adieu !

Then dawned a day of dire alarms,
  Deep in my mind it sticks.
The chap who kept the Bunter Arms
  Sent Billy two-and-six !

" 'Tis mine ! 'Tis mine ! " I fondly cried.
  " Deliver up the loot !
Just hand that half-a-crown to me,
  Old barrel-face, and scoot ! "

So Bunter, weeping tears of blood,
  Gave up the half-a-crown ;
I placed it in my study, and
  Walked off with Rake and Brown.

We went to Mrs. Mimble's shop,
  And planned a stunning spread ;
We ordered cakes and ginger-pop :
  " My treat ! " I proudly said.

But in the study, that same night,
  I gave a sudden yell ;
For that p.o. had vanished, quite,
  And Bunter had, as well !

hands on their swords. A terrified servant rushed into the room.

" The soldiers ! " he cried, in a trembling voice.

" We have been followed ! " Monmouth ejaculated, whipping out his sword.

" Nay ; 'tis probably but chance," Sir Stephen answered quickly, speaking in Monmouth's ear. " There are many such parties in the neighbourhood, and more than one hath been quartered here before. Sit ye down, sire, and sheathe thy sword."

As Monmouth and his friends seated themselves a big, burly man, dressed as an officer, clanked into the room and stared round sharply. He singled out Sir Stephen, and advanced to him, a paper in his hand.

" Sir Stephen Athelney ? " he demanded, in a harsh, commanding voice.

" At your service."

" Good ; 'tis as well. I have his most gracious Majesty's order here to quarter my men upon ye so long as they remain in this neighbourhood."

" How many men are with ye ? " Sir Stephen asked coldly.

" A matter of a score."

" They shall be attended to. Meanwhile, ye see food and drink upon the table ; it is at thy service."

From time to time, between his intervals of eating and drinking, the officer looked, with insolent carelessness, at Monmouth and his two companions.

" A strange time for Sir Stephen to entertain his friends," he said, a sneering note in his voice, as he tilted back his chair.

" His house is his own," Ralph answered, with difficulty suppressing his anger.

" There ye are wrong, my young friend, and ye may take the word of Colonel Peter Norfell for it," the soldier answered insolently ; " it is his Majesty's, more especially when its owner's loyalty hath been doubted. His son, it is said, did join the traitor Monmouth."

He looked keenly at the men before him, noticing the swords at their sides, and the signs of travel upon their boots and dress.

" Ye have seen naught of the war ? "

" What war ? " Truman answered shortly.

" Faith, but ye have hit it ! " Norfell cried,

laughing boisterously. "War, did I call it. Truth, but the breaking of a rabble from its camping-ground. What could such crop-eared knaves do against his Majesty's soldiers? As much use as that slim sword ye carry, sir, would be against my blade."

Monmouth, who had been drumming his fingers upon the table, fixed his calm eyes upon the soldier.

"Mayhap it could do as good service," he answered coolly; "'tis the skill that tells."

"Ye insult me!" Colonel Norfell roared, leaping to his feet. "The sword of a soldier hath its skill. Mark ye there, or I'll teach ye the truth of it in some stronger way!"

"Nay, I did but say that skill won the day."

"Wouldst dare to pit thy skill against mine?" Norfell cried, his face aflame with anger.

"Why not?" Monmouth answered coolly, rising in his turn. "Ye could want no better place than this in which to show your skill."

"And ye shall see it," Norfell answered, whipping out his sword. "Push back the table."

While Truman obeyed, Ralph rose and whispered in Monmouth's ear.

Two men, dressed as Cavaliers, stood on guard before the door. They drew their swords as Ralph approached. "I have urgent business with his Majesty," Ralph said quietly. (*See page* 165.)

"Ye must not do this, sire," he said.

"Nay, but I must," Monmouth answered, with determination. "This braggart shall learn his lesson at my hands."

The table had by this time been pulled back to the wall, and the floor of the hall lay bare. Monmouth drew his thin sword and calmly walked into the centre.

"We need no seconds, sir," he said haughtily, "in an affair in which 'tis but an exhibition of skill."

"He who draws first blood to be the winner?" Colonel Norfell queried, as he took his stand facing Monmouth.

"As ye will, sir."

At that moment Sir Stephen returned, and a look of horror crossed his face as he saw what was about to happen.

"This must stop, gentlemen," he said quickly.

"Hold thy tongue!" Norfell commanded instantly.

"Let it proceed, Sir Stephen," Monmouth added quietly.

The swords crossed, and the clang of them rang through the hall. Norfell attacked furiously, obviously with the intention of beating down the other's guard or snapping his slender blade. But Monmouth caught all the strokes close to the hilt of his weapon with the greatest of ease, and the soldier's face darkened with fury. His strokes fell faster than ever, but in his anger he paid little heed to his defence. Monmouth's sword darted forward, and pierced the man's sword-arm, slitting it from wrist to the elbow.

Faint from the shock of the wound, Norfell dropped to the ground, his sword falling from his hand. Monmouth knelt beside him, and examined the wounded arm.

"A scratch," he said quietly, "no more."

With hate in his eyes Norfell looked up at Monmouth's quiet face, then down until his gaze rested on the slender hands, on one of the fingers of which a ring sparkled. Monmouth saw the glance, and withdrew his hand hastily, but too late.

"Monmouth!" Norfell cried hoarsely, his face wild with triumph, and leapt to his feet.

His lips opened to give the alarm; but at the same moment Ralph gripped him by the throat and forced him back against the panelled wall.

"Bind him," he said quickly, glancing over his shoulder at Truman, "and gag him."

A handkerchief was thrust into the officer's mouth, and made secure by another fastened at the back of his head. A belt was passed round his body, pinning his arms to his side, and his ankles were bound with a scarf. The man lay helpless in the presence of the man whom he would have given so much to capture.

Leaving Norfell on the floor, Monmouth and the others drew away to the farther end of the room.

"What can we do now?" Ralph queried.

"It has but hastened things, my son," Sir Stephen replied quietly. "We must ride at once for the coast. I can trust old Simon; wait ye here while I get the horses saddled. Guard the door, and let no man enter."

"That I should bring ye to this, good friends," Monmouth said bitterly. "Fate hath played me a scurvy trick; but why should ye suffer?"

"Because ye are our king," Sir Stephen answered quietly, then hurried from the hall.

Monmouth seated himself moodily at the table, and Ralph and Truman stationed themselves one on either side of the door, their drawn swords in their hands, ready to act at a moment's notice. A day's ride and they might all be safe, and life is not so mean a thing that either Ralph or Truman meant to part with it easily. Lamore leant idly against the wall, yet with a watchful eye upon Colonel Norfell.

A step in the passage made Ralph advance to the doorway. It was only Sir Stephen, now garbed ready for his ride.

"All is ready," he said quietly. "Simon hath taken the horses to the park, and I have money enough to see us safe out of this country. Follow me closely, and make not a sound as ye value your lives."

The little band of men passed out of the hall, leaving Norfell to glare helplessly at their retreating forms, and struggle vainly to free himself of his bonds.

THE NINTH CHAPTER.

THE castle was left in safety, and the horses reached. Monmouth leapt lightly into the saddle, and the others quickly followed his example.

"It'll be a stiff ride, sire," Sir Stephen said earnestly, "for soon the officer will be discovered, and ye will have the whole pack in pursuit."

"Nay, we shall be safe by then, my friend," Monmouth answered lightly.

Sir Stephen, born and bred in the neighbourhood, led the way at a swinging canter. All the party had been supplied with fresh horses, and they had little fear that they would not reach the coast by early the next morning. At an hour after midnight they clattered over the cobbles of the village of Penhurst, and by then half their journey had been accomplished.

Monmouth, who had been riding moodily along, suddenly turned his head upon his shoulder.

"They pursue already," he said sharply.

"I think not, sire," Lamore, who had also caught the sound, answered; "it is but one man."

"We had best wait, then," Ralph suggested; "he may be from the castle with news."

The horsemen reined up, their horses stretching across the road, so that none could pass. The beat of the hoofs drew rapidly nearer, and a solitary horseman came into sight, bending low on his horse's neck. So hard did he ride that he only caught sight of the obstacle in his path when about twenty yards distant. He reined in hastily, throwing his powerful horse back on its haunches.

"Let me pass, sirs," he cried quickly; "I ride on a mission of life and death."

"And ye do not recognise your master, Simon?" Sir Stephen answered.

"Heaven be praised!" the man ejaculated; "I rode to tell ye the dragoons are on your track. I got off while they were saddling their horses."

"What of that?" Ralph said. "How can they tell the road we have taken?"

"They have a bloodhound with them, sir," Simon answered hoarsely.

"A bloodhound!" Monmouth cried fiercely. "Am I not more than a slave, that they hunt me down with dogs? Faith, but civilisation is a tricky word, and hath many meanings."

"Ye must ride on," Simon said quickly. "Hark! Hear ye not the clatter of the hoofs already?"

Yes, faint and distant, but still quite distinct, came the clatter of many hoofs. The dragoons were in hot pursuit. Sir Stephen set spurs to his horse and swept on, with his companions close behind him. Simon set his horse at the hedge that bordered the road, for he had no wish to meet the soldiers on his homeward journey.

"We need have no fear on such horses as these," Truman said coolly; "we'll be well at sea before they reach the coast."

For an hour the horsemen galloped on, and the sounds of pursuit drew no nearer. Another two hours at the most, and they reckoned to be at the spot where the lugger was waiting.

Of a sudden a hare darted across the road, right in front of the horses. Monmouth's steed reared, plunged forward, and came heavily to his knees, shooting his rider over his head. The horse scrambled up again, and Truman snatched at the bridle before he could bolt, but Monmouth lay quite still.

Ralph slipped from the saddle, threw his bridle over his left arm, and knelt beside Monmouth. The fallen duke had sustained a nasty cut on the head, and was stunned. What was to be done? Every second the dragoons were drawing nearer, led by the unerring instinct of the bloodhound, and here was the most important man of all rendered senseless, while his horse was so lamed that it was more than likely that he would go down again if hard pressed.

Lamore, too, had dismounted, and now stood over Monmouth, peering down quietly at his ghastly face.

"He must be moved," he said quietly. "Help me to put him on my horse."

Not as yet understanding Lamore's motive, Ralph helped to place the senseless man on the former's horse, Truman and Sir Stephen holding him there. Lamore quietly took the bridle of the injured horse and turned to Ralph.

"Monmouth's signet," he said quietly, "give it to me."

"And why?" Ralph asked, in surprise.

"Because I am now Monmouth."

The answer was given in a calm, level voice, which had not the slightest tremor of excitement in it.

"You mean that——" Ralph started sharply.

"I mean that Monmouth must be saved. It hath been said that I favour him. Give me the ring; then ride ye on, I shall follow."

"But ye cannot escape on that lame brute?"

"But Monmouth can on mine." Lamore quietly drew the ring from Monmouth's finger and slipped it on to one of his own. The sound of the pursuing soldiers was drawing very near, and it was obvious to all that there was not a moment to be lost.

"Let me stay instead," Ralph said eagerly.

"Or I," Truman added. "I am but a plain yeoman—none would miss me."

"Nay," Lamore answered calmly. "I thank ye; but I stay. Neither of you favour Monmouth. Ride, or else ye make my sacrifice of no value—ride!"

For a moment Ralph hesitated. Then he realised that Lamore spoke the truth, and that there was no other way of saving Monmouth. He bent down and shook his friend's hand warmly.

"As ye will, Lamore," he said hoarsely. "But, mark me, I shall come back for ye."

"Save Monmouth; then do as ye will."

Ralph, his father, and Truman, supporting the unconscious Monmouth between them, galloped away, leaving Lamore standing by the side of his lame horse. He listened to the sounds of pursuit, now very near indeed, and swung into the saddle.

"Faith, but they must not take me too easily," he muttered, "or they might suspect the trick!"

He swung into the saddle, and, at the risk of a bad fall, spurred the lame horse into a canter. Not more than a mile ahead a dim light or two indicated the position of a village. As Lamore noticed this an idea occurred to him. He would reach this place, demand admission at some inn door, leave his horse tethered outside—to act as a bait—then await the coming of the soldiers. He had no fear of death; but he had every intention of robbing King James of a soldier or two more before he himself went under.

Chancing the fall, Lamore spurred the horse on, and the sounds of pursuit only drew slowly nearer. He reached the village, which was in total darkness, save for a dim light or two in some of the upper windows, probably rooms where nervous children slept. At one point a beam of wood stretched clean across the road, and from the centre of it hung a creaking board, bearing the words "Royal Inn."

Lamore slipped from his horse, fastened the bridle to a ring let into one of the doorposts of the inn, and knocked loudly on the door. In five minutes the soldiers would arrive.

There was no answer to the summons, and Lamore beat upon the door a second time, using boot and sword with great effect. A window right above the door swung open with a complaining squeak, and a nightcapped head was thrust out.

"What want ye?" the owner of the nightcap quavered. "We are closed for the night!"

"Then ye must open again!" Lamore answered fiercely. He could hear the pursuers coming rapidly nearer. In the street he would be ridden down before he could strike a blow; but in the inn passage he knew that he would be able to render a better account of himself.

"Are ye opening, or must I break the door down? Split me, but I am in no mood for trifling."

"One moment, good gentleman, one moment!" the landlord answered hastily. "I will come down. Ye shall have no cause for complaint. But in these times of blood and——"

"Enough!" Lamore interrupted. "Come down!"

In another couple of minutes the soldiers would be there. Already Lamore could hear the faint baying of the bloodhound, and as he did so he drew one of his pistols from the saddle-holster.

"The brute shall not live to carry on the pursuit," he muttered.

The door of the inn opened, and Lamore stepped quickly in.

"Ye may leave the door open,"' he said coolly. "Hark ye, my friends draw near!"

"But ye will come through to the room, sir," the landlord said; "a fire hath but half died there."

"Nay; get ye gone," Lamore answered sternly, "if ye would save thy fat body!"

With a howl of terror the landlord bolted for the stairs, and Lamore heard the lock of a door turned sharply and the bolts thrust home. But he had little time to spare for such things. The clatter of hoofs was already loud on the cobbles.

"Halt!" The order rang out sharp and clear. Lamore smiled; his bait had caught its fish.

He slipped his sword into the leg of his right boot, and took careful aim with his pistol, resting the long barrel on his crooked left elbow. He was none too soon. A dark form, large as a calf, darkened the open doorway. For a moment Lamore saw a great hanging jaw, a pair of fierce, small eyes, and snarling teeth. His finger pressed the trigger of his pistol, and, with a howl of pain, the bloodhound sank to the ground.

One enemy—perhaps the one to be the most feared—was dead, but others followed quickly. Into the passage sprang a soldier, evidently an officer, from his uniform. He thrust savagely forward with his sword, but Lamore dodged the stroke skilfully. Two others followed this man, and Lamore found himself parrying the lunges of three men. Luckily for him the passage was narrow, and the soldiers hampered each other. Twice he managed to get strokes home; but each one only served to increase the fury of the soldiers.

A heavy blow snapped Lamore's weapon off short at the hilt, and he stood defenceless. One of the soldiers shortened his sword to strike a fatal blow; but the officer struck the weapon up.

"Hold!" he said sternly. "Alive he is worth more than dead. Mayhap it is Monmouth himself. Corporal—a light!"

Flint and steel scraped together, a feeble light flared up, and revealed Lamore's face. He passed his hand, with apparent carelessness, across his eyes, and the light fell upon Monmouth's ring.

"Monmouth!" the officer shouted gleefully.

"Ay, Colonel Norfell," Lamore answered coolly; "I believe I have had the honour of meeting ye before, have I not? How is the wounded arm?"

"Stap me, ye have little cause to jest!" Norfell answered savagely. "Bind him, two of ye!"

This order was very quickly carried out, and Colonel Norfell beckoned a corporal to him.

"To horse, Saunders!" he ordered. "Ride ye straight back to Taunton. Churchill will be there by then. Tell him that Colonel Norfell hath the rebel Monmouth safe, and awaiteth instructions from him."

Lamore saw a great, hanging jaw, a pair of fierce, small eyes, and snarling teeth. His fingers pressed the trigger of his pistol, and, with a howl of pain, the bloodhound sank to the ground. (*See page* 188.)

THE TENTH CHAPTER.

As Sir Stephen had reckoned, the coast was reached by dawn, and Monmouth, still unconscious, for the blow which he had sustained was no light one, was taken safely on board. Sir Stephen went with him, but neither Ralph nor Truman; for they had no intention of leaving Lamore to his fate. If pluck and daring could save him, they meant to make him once more a free man.

"Keep all ready to sail at once, father," Ralph said, as he shook the old man's hand. "We should be with ye, if all is well, in two days. Wait three. If by then we have not joined ye, set sail."

Truman and Ralph travelled back along the road towards the village at a slow canter, for they dared not fatigue further their already tired horses. Besides, the distance was no great one to the village where they expected to find the soldiers and their prisoner.

After two hours' riding, and as dawn was paling the sky, they reached the village. In truth they had no reason to believe that it was here that the soldiers and their prisoner were quartered, yet it seemed probable. The surmise proved correct; for as they reached the end of the street they caught sight of a score of horses, with the army trappings, tethered outside the inn door.

"What now?" Truman asked.

"Nothing," Ralph answered. "We can do naught as yet. We must wait till the night. Stay ye in the fields here out of sight, and watch for what might happen. I shall ride round to the other end, and keep watch there. If naught has happened by nightfall I shall join ye here. Then we must act as it seemeth best."

Truman rode into the field bordering the road, and Ralph, skirting the village, galloped away to his post. He dismounted behind a clump of trees, and there passed the day, watching the road. A few travellers passed, but they were of no importance. It was not until Ralph was tightening his horse's girths, with the intention of riding to join Truman, that anything of interest occurred.

A solitary horseman, wearing the uniform of the dragoons, galloped along the road and entered the village. Ralph waited for no more, but, swinging into the saddle, galloped through the fields to where Truman lay hidden.

"Nothing hath happened," the latter said, stamping about to shake the cramp from his limbs. "And ye?"

"Little enough. But the time has come to act. Mount! We ride to the inn!"

As the two men drew up at the door of the inn they saw that the dragoon horses were still there. Lamore, the supposed Monmouth, had not yet been removed; so there was still the chance of saving him. The landlord came hurrying out, and shouted to a man to take the horses.

"What would ye have, gentlemen?"

Ralph's sharp eyes had caught sight of uniforms through the window of the front room of the inn.

"A private room," he said quietly, and stepped into the passage, followed by Truman. He passed an open door, and saw a couple of soldiers within, one of whom he recognised as Colonel Norfell. Past this was another door, and Ralph pushed it boldly open and entered.

"This will do, host," he said quietly. "Bring food and wine—the best ye have."

"We are in luck, Truman," he added, as soon as the landlord had left. "How thick is the dividing wall?"

"An inch of oak," Truman answered, who had been carefully sounding the panels. "Ye will hear naught through it."

"Wait," Ralph said, with a smile. "Our first point is won; now we must learn the soldiers' plans."

The landlord brought in food and wine, and departed. Ralph promptly fastened the door, then drew his sword.

"Make ye a clatter with the knives and cups," he ordered, "'twill drown any small noise I may make."

Wondering what Ralph was about to do, Truman obeyed. He was soon enlightened as he saw Ralph, with the point of his sword, set to work to bore a hole in the wall. This was a work of some little time, for the oak was tough, but at last Ralph desisted, leaving a hole but a fraction of an inch broad at the other end, opening into the next room. He placed his ear against it and listened. Luck was with him, the officers were discussing their plans.

"Ay, I shall be glad enough to part with him," Norfell said. "Faith, we have earned a snug reward, and I am willing to part with so slippery a prisoner. Let our work end, say I, and others take the risk."

"They come to-night?" the other officer queried.

"The corporal hath brought word that two officers from Churchill will be here; an escort, a hundred strong, will follow. We are to deliver Monmouth to these officers."

EASY SHADOWGRAPHS

Any boy or girl can perform these simple silhouettes with the aid of a small screen and a lighted candle.

SHEEP

SOLDIER

GOOSE

CAT

CHAMOIS DEER.

DONKEY

BIRD FLYING

RUSTIC

BEAR

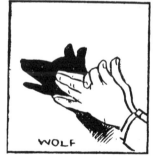

WOLF

GOAT

Ralph had heard enough. He left the wall and seated himself at the table. Hunger presses its claims at all times, and despite the danger surrounding him he made a hearty meal.

When he had finished he sat still and silent for more than an hour. At the end of that time his brow cleared, and he looked at Truman with a smile.

"To-night Lamore shall be free," he said coolly.

"And how?" Truman asked, in amazement.

Ralph told him what he had heard, but even then Truman's surprise did not vanish.

"What can we do?" he queried. "A hundred men places him beyond our reach."

"Nay, but we act when there are but two. The officers ride first; they shall never reach here, but we shall, my friend, and Lamore shall be handed over to us."

"You mean," Truman cried hoarsely, "that we waylay these officers, take their papers, and come in their place?"

"Yes. What think ye of it?"

"The only way," Truman answered excitedly. "It smacks of success."

A little later, having settled their score, Ralph and Truman rode away from the inn. The officers, drinking heavily and dicing to pass away the time, paid no heed to them. Ralph led the way straight out of the village, and pushed along down the road for a matter of three miles. Here he called a halt.

"We must take no chances," he said. "These officers might not give in to an equal number. We must have help."

"From where?"

"Give me thy hat."

Truman obeyed, and Ralph, cutting a thin branch from a tree close at hand, stuck the hat upon it. Then he drove the stick into the ground behind the hedge. In the dark the hat looked like a man peering out on to the road. He did the same with his own headpiece, and the effect was so natural that Truman could not refrain from laughing.

"Back to the hedge," Ralph ordered, "and do not move before I give the order. A slip would be fatal."

In the dark, Ralph and Truman drew their horses to opposite sides of the road, and sat ready, pistols in hand. An hour passed, and not a single traveller went by, but close upon midnight the sound of hoofs could be heard.

"Two horsemen," Ralph said, in a low voice. "Be ready."

Nearer and nearer drew the beat of the hoofs, and the hearts of the waiting men thumped painfully against their ribs. Ralph strained his eyes through the darkness, for he had no wish to stop the wrong men. He caught the glint of metal, and tightened his reins slightly.

"Now!" he cried, when the horsemen had drawn to within twenty yards.

Ralph and Truman, acting together, threw their horses across the road.

"Halt!" the former cried fiercely. "Make no attempt to resist, or ye are dead men. See, we outnumber ye." He waved his pistol towards the headpieces just showing above the hedges. "One movement towards your arms, and we shoot."

The officers had thrown their horses back on to their haunches, and now sat staring in dumb surprise at the men who had stopped them.

"What meaneth this?" one of them cried fiercely, finding his tongue at last.

"You will know soon enough," Ralph answered. "For the present it doth not concern ye. Ye have but to obey my orders."

"Thy orders?" the officer roared. "Mark ye, we are officers of the king, and ye are liable to death for this outrage."

"And ye are liable to death if ye do not curb that tongue of thine," Ralph answered sharply. "As ye see, we are two to one; resistance is useless. If ye value your lives, obey."

"What shall we do?" the other officer asked, in a slightly quieter tone than that of his companion.

"Remove your uniforms."

"Remove our—— Ye jest, sir?"

"Nay, I am quite serious. Men"—Ralph turned towards the hedge—"shoot if I am disobeyed."

The officers looked at each other, then very reluctantly clambered down from their horses and set to work to unbuckle their harness. When this was done they stopped.

Of a sudden, with a force that nearly brought him to the ground, Ralph reined in his horse, throwing him back upon his haunches. (*See page* 177.)

"Off with your clothes," Ralph ordered sternly, "and lose no time."

There was a short hesitation; but, unarmed now, the officers could do nothing but obey. The elder made a move to hide a paper behind him, but Ralph saw the action.

"Throw it to me."

The paper fell at Ralph's feet, and he picked it up with the point of his sword. It was the order to hand over Monmouth, signed by Churchill, the second in command of King James's troops.

"Get into the harness," Ralph whispered in a low voice to Truman, "and be quick."

While the officers stood shivering in distinctly scanty attire, Truman donned one of the uniforms and mounted a captured horse.

"Guard while I change," Ralph whispered.

Ten minutes later both Ralph and Truman were fully dressed as dragoon officers and mounted on the army horses.

"When we are gone ye may dress," Ralph said, turning to the shivering men.

At the same moment he struck his own horse, which he had discarded for the officer's, on the flank with the flat of his sword, and it bounded off down the road, making away from the village. The bridle of the other Ralph slipped over his arm.

"Now!" he cried.

Before the officers could guess what was happening Ralph and Truman had set spurs to their horses and were galloping back to the village, taking the spare horse with them. A volley of oaths followed them.

"Pull thy cloak up over thy face," Ralph said, as he and his companion galloped furiously along. "Ye will wait without the inn while I enter. Stay there unless I cry for help."

THE ELEVENTH CHAPTER.

RALPH and Truman pulled up at the door of the inn, from the windows of which lights glowed, snowing that the officers were still carousing. Ralph entered boldly, and clanked into the room in which the two officers sat. They rose unsteadily to their feet as he entered, his cloak drawn well up over the lower half of his face.

"Colonel Norfell?" he queried.

"I am he. What want ye?"

Without a word Ralph handed over the paper which he had taken from the officer. Norfell tore it open, read it hastily, and bowed to Ralph.

" Be seated, sir," he said. " I can offer ye a fair wine for such a village. Will ye honour us by joining us until the escort arrives ? "

" The offer is tempting, sir," Ralph answered coolly, " but my orders are explicit. My companion awaits me without. We must take the rebel Monmouth now and ride back to meet the escort."

" 'Tis hardly safe," Norfell ventured.

" The order is exact," Ralph persisted. " Would ye, as a loyal and brave officer, have me disobey ? I will but ask ye to see the rebel bound safely to the horse I have brought for him. We shall meet the escort within the hour."

" As ye will, sir."

Norfell left the room, and could soon be heard shouting orders. Within a couple of minutes Lamore, perfectly cool and composed, was led into the room. His eyes fell upon Ralph, and he started slightly, but the next moment his face was as indifferent as ever.

" A pretty king, by my faith," Ralph said, with a well-feigned sneer. " See to his binding, colonel ; we must not lose so fine a bird."

Lamore was led out between two soldiers, and Ralph was about to follow, when Norfell laid a hand upon his arm.

" Nay, sir," he said, " a cup of sack will serve to keep out the cold."

Ralph took the proffered wine, and raised it to his lips. As he did so a sudden commotion broke out just before the window of the room. He set the cup down sharply, and sprang to the door, none too soon.

The two officers, who had evidently made a run for the village, but half dressed in the garments that had been left for them, were attacking Truman, while half a score of troopers looked on, not knowing what to do. Ralph sprang sharply at the nearest of the two men, and with a blow from his fist felled him to the ground.

" Bind and gag these fellows ! " he cried sternly ; " they are rebels. Once this night already have they set upon us, mayhap knowing our mission."

Willing enough to join in any row, the troopers threw themselves upon the two men, and they were quickly gagged and bound. Ralph breathed a sigh of relief, and turned to Norfell, who had just hurried out.

" Guard these men well, colonel," he ordered ; " they are rebels. Ye have safely secured the rebel Monmouth ? Good ! Then we must ride."

Lamore's feet had been tied beneath the horse, and now Truman and Ralph mounted, riding on either side of him.

" Farewell ! " Ralph cried, as he urged his horse forward. " Take care of the reward, colonel ! "

The village was left behind, and Lamore opened his mouth to speak as Ralph slashed through his bonds.

" Not yet," the latter said sharply. " It's ride for our lives now. At any moment the truth may be discovered. We must be aboard the lugger within the hour."

Wheeling round, the three men galloped back through the fields, skirting the village, and not taking to the road until they had covered a clear three miles. Within the hour the coast was reached, and Ralph, drawing a pistol, discharged it into the air. The creak of rowlocks answered this signal, after the lapse of a few minutes, and before long the little band, leaving their horses to take care of themselves, had been pulled safely to the lugger, where they were met by Sir Stephen with open arms.

" All is well with Monmouth ? " Ralph asked.

" He hath kept his cabin, Ralph," the old man answered. " He came to shortly after ye left, and asked for ye. I told him what had happened. He bade me leave him in his cabin and not disturb him."

A short, squat man rolled up.

" The wind's i' the right quarter, sirs," he growled.

" Then up with the anchor and clap on all sail, captain," Ralph answered. " Good-bye to England ! "

Hoarse orders rang out, the anchor chain rattled through the hawse-hole, sails were shaken out, the wind stiffening them to the firmness of steel, and the lugger, with her captain at the helm, stole away from the dim, dark shore.

Ralph, Lamore, and Truman were ready enough to turn in, and it was broad daylight before they awoke on the following day. They went up on deck, and saw that on all sides there was nothing but the gently rolling sea, for the wind had held steady, and the lugger had drawn well out into mid-Channel. Monmouth neither appeared on deck nor at the first meal of the day.

" I shall go to him, father," Ralph said, as noon passed and still he had not appeared.

" He asked not to be disturbed, Ralph," the old man protested.

" I know ; but ye know not what may be wrong. His wound may have caused him fresh trouble."

Without waiting to argue further, Ralph went below, and strode to the little cabin which had been prepared for Monmouth. He knocked at the door, but received no answer. Three times he knocked, but always with the same result. Fearing that something was amiss, he thrust open the door, which was not locked, and entered the little cabin.

It was empty !

There could be no doubt about it. Ralph looked round sharply, hardly able to believe his eyes, and his glance fell upon a sheet of paper fastened against the bulkhead. He crossed over to it, knowing before he could see to read the writing upon it that it concerned the missing man.

" My good friends "—the letter ran—" I know not who will read this, but I trust that it may be ye, Ralph Truman, and Lamore, for I owe ye more than I can ever repay. I have but just heard of Lamore's sacrifice, and I cannot permit it. May he escape. I am bound to leave the ship secretly, to wander, a hunted fugitive, for I will not bring more evils upon ye. May the day soon come when ye will be free men once more.

" I thank ye, more than I can write in mere feeble words, for your allegiance to my cause, and ask ye to think kindly of him who, had the fates been more propitious, might have been your king, as he has ever wished to be your friend.   MONMOUTH."

With this paper in his hand Ralph rushed

No. 7 : Percy Bolsover

Whose voice is like the boom of guns ?
Whose boots are elephantine ones ?
And who descended from the Huns ?
> Bolsover !

Who punches tiny fags on sight ?
Who always holds that Might is Right ?
Who never fails to bark and bite ?
> Bolsover !

Who stalks about as if he meant
To boss the merry firmament ?
Who often loiters, " with intent " ?
> Bolsover !

Who throws his weight about so much
That small fags scurry from his clutch
(Or else they'd have to buy a crutch !) ?
> Bolsover !

Who, though a mighty man of muscle,
Was once defeated in a tussle
With that fine boxing star, Dick Russell ?
> Bolsover !

Who (if I don't mistake the signs),
Will carry out his base designs
Upon the writer of these lines ?
> Bolsover !

up to the deck. Sir Stephen took it from him, and his old eyes dimmed as he learnt the dread tidings. It was passed from him to Lamore and Truman, and all knew the worst.

Ralph glanced at his friends, then back at the trail of foam stretching out behind the lugger as far as the eye could see, forming a path back to the shores of old England. He touched Lamore on the arm, and pointed back along the wake.

"Shall that be our path, Lamore?" he asked, in a tense voice.

"Ye mean——"

"Ay; shall we travel back the way we have come, to make one more effort to save Monmouth?"

"That we will!" Truman, who had caught the words, broke in eagerly. "Live or die, say I, with Monmouth!" The yeoman turned, and was about to hail the captain, when Ralph stopped him.

"Not yet," he said quietly; "there are others who needs must be asked. "Father" —turning to Sir Stephen—"what say ye? Shall we go back?"

"Let youth decide, Ralph," the old man answered quietly. "My sands o' life have neared their end; the dregs can be had for the asking."

"Then we go!" Ralph cried.

"Back to Monmouth!" Truman yelled, waving his sword above his head.

"Captain, ye knave!" Lamore cried, waving his delicate hand to the seaman in charge of the lugger, "back to England! Spit me if I know the order, or I'd give it myself! Bring her round!"

Orders rang out hoarsely, men sprang to the ropes, the great mainsail swung round, and the lugger turned on her heels like a rearing horse.

Back to England!

THE TWELFTH CHAPTER.

IT was noon by the time that the lugger came in sight of England, but Ralph did not hesitate. He ordered the vessel to be run in as close to the shore as possible, and went ashore in company with Lamore, Truman, and his father. The last-named was to return to the lugger, but he could not resist the tempt-ation to once more place foot upon the land of his birth.

"Mark well what I tell ye," Sir Stephen said, as the little band stood on the beach. "Monmouth will have kept to the coast, and is probably no great distance from here, possibly hiding in the fields or harboured by some friendly peasant or farmer. If you are to succeed in your quest ye will do so within three days. At the end of that time, successful or unsuccessful, ye must join me on the lugger."

"Where?" Ralph asked.

"To-night we will drop ten miles to the westward, and anchor near the land. Should ye have found Monmouth, light a fire on the cliffs. We shall answer with a blue light, and send a boat ashore. May my old eyes see the beacon to-night!"

A hearty grip of the hand all round, and Sir Stephen reluctantly entered the boat and was pulled back to the lugger. Ralph and his two friends, who were armed only with their swords, but had their breast and back plates under their clothes, set off on foot up the beach, scaled the low cliff, and stood with a great expanse of bare turf, broken here and there by cultivated land, before them. This was practically the same spot at which the lugger had picked them up, and from which Monmouth had set out alone.

"Which way hath he gone, think ye?" Ralph queried.

"To the west," Truman answered readily. "The whole countryside there is in favour o' Monmouth, an' many a yeoman would hide him if it cost him his life."

"What think ye, Lamore?" Ralph asked.

"Faith, I side with Truman," the Cavalier answered, "though, spit me, if this isn't like hunting for a needle in a haystack."

"Nay, 'tis not so bad as ye may think," Ralph said, with a smile. "I am known in these parts. Monmouth must have begged food somewhere, and if he hath travelled this way we shall soon be on his track."

Without further argument the three men set out across the fields, keeping about half a mile from the shore. They felt certain that Monmouth would not have remained very near to the spot at which he had landed, and therefore made no inquiries at the first three homesteads which they passed. The whole country seemed deserted, and there were not even labourers in the fields. At such a time, when any man might be arrested as a rebel, innocent or guilty, farmer and labourer deemed it best to remain within the shelter of their homes.

As day was drawing into dusk Ralph sighted a larger farm than any that they had previously passed, and turned in its direction. This place was about half a mile further inland, and so planted round with trees that had it not been for the smoke from its chimneys the traveller would have passed it by without guessing its existence. Ralph knew the owner of this place, one Owen Winter, an old man who had fought stoutly for the Roundheads, and whom nothing but years had kept from joining the standard of the ill-fated Monmouth.

"There is a chance that Master Winter hath heard o' Monmouth," Ralph remarked, " for Monmouth hath heard of him."

"We'll draw the covert," Lamore said quickly ; " an' who knows but we may get the scent."

By the time the trees round the farmhouse were reached night had fallen, but not a light appeared in the windows of the house.

" A right good retreat," Truman remarked, as he loosened his sword in the scabbard. " I like not the want of lights."

" Faith, but I do," Lamore put in quickly ; " it smelleth of hidden men, and o' treason to the usurper. Methinks Ralph's instinct hath led us aright."

Passing up a narrow path, bordered thickly on both sides by trees, the trunks of which were so close together that they fell little short of a wall, the three men reached the door of the farmhouse, and Ralph struck the stout, hard door with the hilt of his sword.

There was no answer, nothing save the echo of the knock through the house. Ralph struck again, with a force that made the door, strong though it was, shake.

" He is here," Truman whispered excitedly, " or why this strange reception ? "

Three times Ralph beat upon the door, and was about to strike for the fourth time, when the sound of shuffling feet arrested his arm.

Someone was approaching the door, under which a streak of light now gleamed.

" What want ye ? " an old but firm voice demanded, the words coming only faintly through the door. " Who are ye that wake peaceful farmers from their beds ? Begone ! "

" Nay, but I had not expected such a sorry welcome, Master Winter ! " Ralph cried.

" Who are ye ? " the voice answered.

" Ralph Athelney."

A creaking of bars and bolts followed this statement, and the door opened, revealing the figure of an old man, who held a rushlight in his left hand and a long sword in his right. He thrust the light forward, scanning Ralph's face closely with dim eyes, for he was a very old man.

" Enter," he said, " and mark me well. I have near a score of stout fellows within. At such times as these be I trust no man, so beware. I have but to give the signal an' ye will not leave the place alive."

" Stap me," Lamore said, with a smile : " but for one of thy years, Master Owen Winter, thou art over warlike."

" No man is too old to give a signal," Winter answered sharply.

He led the way down the passage, after he had locked and bolted the door securely, and entered a spacious room. The rushlight's feeble flame only served to heighten the shadows in the corners, make the oak rafters and panelling still blacker, and draw a glint from the barrels of sundry fowling-pieces which adorned the walls.

" Be seated."

The three men threw themselves into chairs, and the old man stood close by the door, his long sword still in his hand. The rushlight he had placed on a small shelf, evidently designed for that purpose.

" Thy business, Master Athelney ? " he demanded sternly.

" News of Monmouth," Ralph answered coolly.

Owen Winter started sharply, and stared Ralph in the face.

" What mean ye, Master Athelney ? " he demanded hoarsely.

" Simply this. Monmouth is somewhere in this part of the country, and we are his friends. We have a vessel waiting off the coast to bear him safely abroad."

"And why came ye to me?"

"Because we knew ye to be a loyal gentleman, and so did Monmouth. But waste no time. Hath Monmouth been here?"

"More than that," Master Winter answered, after a long pause, "he is here now."

"Here?"

Ralph leapt to his feet in excitement.

"Ay," the old man answered coolly, "and ye shall see him. But beware! If ye are friends, all is well; if not—if ye be traitors —it shall mean death to ye, despite your swords."

He clapped his hands sharply, and a few seconds later a score of men, mostly of the labourer class, but all well armed, filed quietly into the room and ranged themselves round it.

"Watch these strangers, lads," Master Winter commanded; "if they attempt to leave strike and spare not."

The old man hastened out of the room, leaving Ralph and his friends to stare in amazement at the score of stern, determined faces around them.

"Good as a play," Lamore remarked coolly. "The old boy ought—— The King!"

Monmouth, his handsome face slightly flushed, stood in the doorway, Master Winter just behind him. He peered through the dim light, and his eyes fell upon the faces of his friends.

"Ralph!" he cried, in a voice shaking with emotion, springing forward and gripping Athelney by the hand. "And Lamore— safe, thank Heaven—and our good friend Truman."

"Safe, every one of us, sire," Ralph answered, "and ready to take ye to safety, too."

"What mean ye?" Monmouth asked, hardly yet certain that his eyes had not deceived him.

"That the ship awaits us—she should be anchored near to here. We have but to give a signal, then all sail for France. We must lose no time. Are ye ready to come now, sire?"

"Ay," Monmouth answered, in a shaking voice, passing a hand across his eyes. "Had mortal man ever such faithful friends before?"

"My men shall go with ye," Master Owen Winter broke in. "There's a party o' cutthroat dragoons in the neighbourhood, an' should ye come across them my men will hold 'em back while ye escape."

No time was lost.

Ralph, Monmouth, their two friends, and the score of stout yokels, under the command of Master Winter himself, left the farmhouse and marched rapidly for the shore, which lay about a mile distant.

This was reached in safety, and from the edge of the cliffs Ralph looked down upon the sloping beach. He could just make out the gleam of water a few yards distant.

"Some of ye gather sticks for a beacon," he ordered, turning to the men. "Methinks I catch the gleam of a light from time to time about a mile from the shore. It may be the ship."

The sticks were soon gathered, flint and steel were used by a dozen hands, and a tongue of flame leapt up. Ralph stood at the edge of the cliff, staring anxiously out to sea. A cry of joy broke from him as a blue light shone out across the water, not half a mile distant, revealing dimly the spars of the Revenge.

"Hark!" Lamore said sharply. "Our fire hath brought the enemy upon us."

It was true enough. From not far away came the beat of horses' hoofs. Evidently the cavalry had been passing close at hand, and, catching sight of the beacon, had decided to investigate the matter.

"Put the fire out," Ralph ordered sharply, "and scatter the ashes."

This order was obeyed promptly, and all was dark.

"Lead the way to the shore," Ralph said quietly, turning to Master Winter.

Without the slightest hesitation the old man led the way along the cliff to where a kind of natural steps led down to the shore. Down this the whole party passed in single file, reaching the shore in safety. By that time the creak of rowlocks could be distinctly heard, and later a boat grated sharply on the shore.

A cry of joy broke from Ralph as a blue light shone out across the water, not above half a mile distant, revealing dimly the spars of the Revenge. (*See page* 198.)

"'Tis ye, Ralph?" the voice of Sir Stephen asked, out of the darkness.

"Ay, and Monmouth!"

"Quick, then," the old man answered; "come aboard! Methought I heard the jingle of cavalry on the cliffs."

"Ye did, Sir Stephen," Winter answered coolly, "but ye need have no fear. They'll not find the way down, an' if they do ye'll be safe aboard by then and we'll be back at the farm!"

In the dark Monmouth and his friends clambered into the boat, after shaking old Winter warmly by the hand. Half a score of the yokels ran her out into deep water, her head was pulled round, and she cut away for the Revenge. Ralph, sitting in the stern, Monmouth beside him, listened anxiously for sounds of strife, but none had come by the time that the black side of the Revenge had been reached. Master Winter had spoken the truth, and by now was well back towards the farm with his men.

And Monmouth was safe.

THE THIRTEENTH CHAPTER.

No sooner were Monmouth and his friends aboard than the anchor chain creaked, all hands sprung to make sail, and the Revenge bore away from the shore, for the second time making her bid for the liberty of those aboard of her.

The night was cold, and the wind was on the increase. Ralph led the way below, and ten minutes later the whole of the party were busy with a rough, but to them very welcome, meal.

Hardly had this been finished before the captain of the vessel, his face wrinkled up anxiously, looked in at the door.

"There's a ship's lights to windward o' us, sirs," he said in his hoarse voice; "but we ha' the heels o' her, I'm thinkin'."

"What kind of a vessel do you take her to be?" Ralph asked quickly.

"Like as not a king's ship—frigate, from the lights."

This was bad news, and Monmouth and the others hurried up on deck. Sure enough the lights showed not more than a mile away, but even as they gazed at them they vanished.

"She's got the scent o' us, I fear," Ralph said between his teeth.

"Naught to fear from that," the captain growled, "unless a gale springs up. She'd stand to that better'n our craft."

No man thought of sleep now. Monmouth, a long cloak pulled round him, paced the heaving deck, Ralph beside him, not a word passing between them. The others stood by the bulwarks, trying to pierce the dense darkness with their eyes, and waiting for the dawn, which would tell them the best or worst. Every moment the wind increased, and sail was shortened from time to time. Even then the ship lay over before it until her bulwarks were awash, and the men on the deck had to hang on grimly to the ropes.

Daybreak. Slowly, almost imperceptibly, the sky changed from dark blue to pearly grey, a light pink showed in streaks here and there; then, with a suddenness that was almost startling, it was day.

A cry of alarm broke from Ralph. Not a mile astern, and coming on under a press of canvas, was a large ship, flying the king's colours. Hardly had Ralph sighted her before a flash of flame sprang from her bows, and a ball passed wide of the Revenge.

The captain hurried up for orders, working his way along the bulwarks, over which the spray flew in clouds.

"Orders," he said shortly.

"We keep on!" Ralph answered grimly. "Have we the heels of the frigate now, think ye?"

"No," the seaman answered, with a conviction that there was no gainsaying; "but the wind's droppin'. Give us time an' a lighter wind, an' we'll shake her off!"

"Unless we're sunk first, my friend," Lamore remarked coolly, as the frigate brought her whole broadside to bear.

"Not in this sea," the sailor answered, shading his eyes with his hand. "She's clean off the mark. Let her do that as oft as she will; each time'll give us a lead."

The wind was already dropping, and as the captain of the Revenge shouted for more sail, the rigging of the frigate grew black with men. Studding sails bellowed out, and she tore on before the wind. But now even a landsman could see that she was not gaining, and but barely held her distance.

Monmouth, his face flushed with excitement, held to the halliard, watching the king's ship. The sea ran high, causing the vessel's guns at one moment to be aiming at the sea and the next at the air. She had given up firing now, realising, as the captain of the lugger had already seen, that every time she tacked to deliver her broadside she lost ground. She was now endeavouring to outsail the smaller craft.

"We do 'em!" Lamore cried exultantly, losing his habitual indifference for a moment. "As our nautical friend there says, we have the heels of her!"

But he spoke too soon. The wind, which had dropped, sprang up again, beating the Revenge down dangerously, until sail had once more to be shortened. The frigate came plunging along a trifle faster; but she gained so slowly that the lessening of the distance between the two vessels was imperceptible except to the eye of a sailor.

The captain of the Revenge, who held the tiller, from time to time cast quick glances over his shoulder. His mouth was set hard, the lips pressed into a thin line. Once or

THE ROOKWOOD FELLOWS WAITED IN BREATHLESS EXPECTATION FOR THE SWELL OF ST. JIM'S TO SIT DOWN. *(See page 134.)*

" Not a mile astern, and coming on under a press of canvas, was a large ship, flying the King's colours ! "

The Tuckshop Tragedy.

By DICK PENFOLD.

(With apologies to
"Excelsior.")

The shades of night were falling fast
As into Mrs. Mimble's passed
A boy with much more flesh than bones
Who cried, in faint and famished tones,
　　　"Ten Doughnuts!"

His brow was sad, and moist his eye;
He drew a deep, despairing sigh;
And as he staggered to a seat
They heard his feeble voice repeat:
　　　"Ten Doughnuts!"

Said Mrs. Mimble in despair:
"You must be mad, I do declare!
I've kept this shop for many a year,
But never known a boy to clear
　　　Ten Doughnuts!"

"Rats!" cried the youth. "I'll have some ham,
Some pickles, and a jar of jam.
Those mutton patties look all right,
And, quick! don't keep me here all night—
　　　Ten Doughnuts!"

"Try not the tarts," his schoolmates said,
"Already you have overfed,
And no more room remains inside."
But loud that clarion voice replied:
　　　"Ten Doughnuts!"

When all his dainties hove in sight,
He danced the Tango with delight;
With waistcoat buttons all undone,
He then demolished, one by one,
　　　Ten Doughnuts!

Alas! his inner man was packed,
The vital organs failed to act,
And with a wild and startled cry
He sank, weighed down in anguish by
　　　Ten Doughnuts!

There, in the tuckshop, on the mat,
Writhing in agony, he sat,
And ere his eyelids closed in death,
He murmured, with his latest breath:
　　　"Ten Doughnuts!"
(William George Bunter, take warning!—ED.)

twice he glanced aloft, as if about to order more sail; but the heeling of his craft told him that it was impossible.

If only the wind would lighten!

An hour passed, and in that time the king's ship had drawn to within three-quarters of a mile. Her deck was crowded with men, and Ralph and the others could see black forms standing ready at the guns. If matters continued much longer in this way the end would come very soon.

Ralph, from his post from the bulwarks, looked round the Revenge's decks, counting the men. In all there were two dozen seamen. He clawed his way to where the captain hung on to the straining tiller, and lent a hand.

"If she comes up with us, captain," he said sharply, "will the men fight?"

"Ay," the sailor answered, a fierce light in his eyes. "They'll sink or swim with Monmouth!"

"Then give the order. Let every man be armed, and do ye bid them fight till the last drops. There shall be no surrender. I will take the tiller."

The captain clawed his way along the bulwarks to where a group of his men were hanging on, leaving Ralph in charge of the tiller. He was well equal to this task, for he was no mere landsman, who did not know a block from the capstan.

A wild hurrah broke from the crew as their captain reached them; and three of the sailors, taking their chance, made a dash for the hatchway. A little later they reappeared on deck, bearing with them cutlasses and pistols. These were served out with some difficulty; but at last it was done. The frigate carried probably more than two hundred men, but Monmouth, his friends, and the two dozen seamen had no intention of being taken without a struggle.

As soon as the arming of the crew had been accomplished, the captain made his way back to the tiller. He glanced behind him, then up at the sails. A hoarse order broke from him, and eight men leapt into the rigging.

The wind was dropping away again, and more sail could be set. There was a chance of out-sailing the enemy yet.

With a suddenness that took all aboard the Revenge by surprise, the wind veered clean round. The vessel shuddered under the shock, and her great sails bellied out with a crash. There was a cry of dismay, wild and piercing; but for the moment none heeded it, for the ship lay over to such a degree that it seemed as if she could never right herself again.

Slowly the angle of her deck lessened, and the danger was passed. Then Ralph learnt the reason for the wild cry of dismay. Monmouth no longer stood by the bulwarks.

Ralph, his heart beating wildly, looked astern, and his worst fears were realised. A dark head showed above the waves, midway between the Revenge and the frigate. It was Monmouth, who had been swept overboard.

" Bring her round ! " Ralph cried hoarsely. " We must pick him up ! " He leapt to the helm, but Lamore, throwing his arms round him, held him back.

" It is useless," he said in a hoarse voice. " Look—they have him now ! "

It was the truth. As Ralph looked back at the frigate, he saw with dismay Monmouth hauled aboard. All was over. All the efforts that had been made were useless. Monmouth was a prisoner aboard the king's ship !

Then, as if to make things worse, the wind lightened, and the Revenge began to draw away from the frigate. The latter swung round, a hail of shot passed close to the Revenge, and the chase was over. Over, yes ; but how dismally !

With an aching heart, Ralph clawed his way to the hatch and went below, realising that nothing could now save Monmouth, the man for whom he had fought so staunchly, and for whom he would willingly have died.

. . . . . .

What more is there to relate, my friends ? Little, I assure you. This story has dealt with the deeds of brave men, and we would feign close its pages with but slight reference to the time which elapsed between that period and the day when they were free once more to return to England, upon the throne of which King James II. no longer weakly sat. Let it suffice that, in good time, after those who had fought in Monmouth's cause had met with many an adventure in foreign parts, they returned to England to take up their old life. Sir Stephen, Ralph, and Truman— the last to act as steward of the estate— returned to Athelney Castle ; while Lamore, who had succeeded to a large inheritance and a castle not far distant, lived at their home almost as much as his own.

Of Monmouth little need be said. It is kinder, perhaps, to draw a veil over the sufferings through which he passed before meeting his end, in a truly kingly spirit, by the axe on Tower Hill.

Here we must end our story, and close this account of the exploits and plucky adventures of our heroes who fought " In Monmouth's Cause ! "

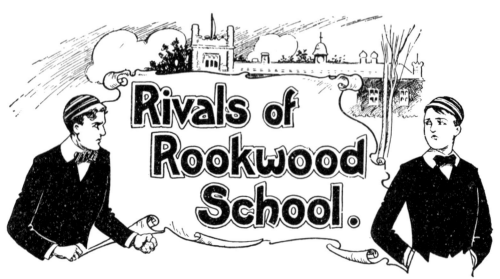

Rivals of Rookwood School.

A Complete Story of School Life and Adventure

By OWEN CONQUEST

✿ ✿ ✿ ✿ ✿ ✿ ✿

THE FIRST CHAPTER.

Lovell's Idea !

"I've got an idea ! "

Arthur Edward Lovell, of the Classical Fourth at Rookwood, made that announcement impressively.

Lovell had been silent for some minutes, while Jimmy Silver, Raby, and Newcome were deep in discussion. Lovell had evidently been thinking while the other fellows were talking.

It was a matter of some importance that the Fistical Four of Rookwood were considering, nothing less than what was to be done with the afternoon. It was a half-holiday at Rookwood—a sunny summer's afternoon. The Fourth Form were playing the Third at cricket ; but such a match did not require the services of the mighty men of the junior eleven. Jimmy Silver and Co. had willingly left the " fag " match to the lesser lights of the Fourth. And the four chums had met in the end study after dinner to discuss ginger-pop and the programme for the afternoon.

Jimmy Silver favoured a long bike spin ; Raby suggested the river ; Newcome was rather in favour of a visit to Latcham to see the " pictures." Each of the three argued the merits of his own scheme—at the same time—while Arthur Edward Lovell wrinkled his youthful brows in thought, and finally announced that he had an idea.

"You agree with me ? " asked Jimmy Silver. " That's two votes for the bikes, you fellows."

" Eh ? I didn't hear what you were saying, Jimmy—but I don't agree with you, anyhow."

" Ass ! " remarked Jimmy. " You said you had an idea. I might have guessed that you hadn't ! "

" The river's ripping," observed Raby. " We can get out a four-oar, and take Tubby Muffin to steer, if you like."

" They've got a new lot of pictures at Latcham," remarked Newcome.

" Oh, bother the pictures ! " said Lovell. " We don't want to sit indoors on an afternoon like this ! "

"The river——"

"Bless the river! Haven't I said I've got an idea?"

"You've said so!" answered Raby in a sarcastic tone, apparently hinting that in his opinion Arthur Edward Lovell was overestimating his mental powers.

"Look here, you ass——"

"Well, you look here, fathead!"

"Peace, my infants peace!" said Jimmy Silver soothingly. "If Lovell's got an idea, let's hear it. It's his first——"

"Are you going to dry up while I tell you my idea?" demanded Lovell warmly.

"Go ahead, old chap. We're all ears."

"Hold on a minute," said Raby, interrupting. "Don't say it's a stunt against the Moderns. It's too warm for ragging the Moderns. Besides, Tommy Dodd and his crowd are playing cricket."

"I'm not thinking of Tommy Dodd. Bother Tommy Dodd!"

"Oh, all right. Get on with the washing then!"

Lovell gave a grunt.

Considering that he had spent quite a considerable time thinking out his idea, there was a plentiful lack of appreciation in the end study. Somehow, the Co. did not seem duly impressed by the announcement that Lovell had an idea.

"Well," said Lovell, "there's a new kid coming to Rookwood to-day."

"Is there?" yawned Raby.

"Yes; a new kid for the Fourth Form—Modern side. A relation of Tommy Dodd, I believe."

"Didn't you say something about an idea?" asked Newcome politely.

"I'm coming to that."

"Oh, I see. When do you think you will get to it?" asked Newcome, in a tone of polite and patient inquiry.

"Are you going to listen to me?" roared Lovell.

"We've been listening for a quarter of an hour already, old scout!" Which certainly was an exaggeration on Newcome's part.

"Go it, Lovell, old top!" murmured Jimmy Silver. "Shut up, Newcome. Give Lovell a chance!"

"This new kid——" recommenced Lovell

"Leave him out, and get to the idea!"

"It's about the new kid."

"Oh!"

"He's landing along by the three train at Coombe. Tommy Dodd was going to meet him at the station, but Jimmy asked him to captain the team in the fag match, so he can't go. The new kid will be left to crawl into Rookwood on his own."

"Let him!"

"He's a Modern kid——"

"We've had that," murmured Newcome.

"My idea is——"

"You're getting to the idea?"

"Yes!" roared Lovell.

"Hurray! Go it!"

"My idea," said Lovell, breathing hard, "is this. Suppose we meet young Loring—his name's Loring—at the station——"

"Eh?"

"Suppose we meet him at the station——"

"My only hat!"

"Great Jupiter!"

"You ass!"

The ejaculations of Lovell's chums certainly seemed to hint that they were not greatly taken with Lovell's idea.

"Meet him at the station?" said Jimmy Silver, in a tone more of sorrow than of anger. "Spend a half-holiday—and a ripping afternoon—meeting a new kid at the station—and a blessed Modern kid at that! Is your mind wandering, Lovell?"

"Has he a mind to wander?" murmured Raby.

"I haven't finished yet!" roared Lovell.

"Oh, my only uncle! He hasn't finished yet! I can see how we're going to spend this afternoon," said Newcome, in a tone of resignation. "We're going to sit in this study while Lovell exercises his chin. Is there any more ginger-pop?"

Lovell jumped up.

"You silly asses, I won't tell you, then! I'll ask Mornington to go with me."

"Morny's playing cricket," said Jimmy Silver.

"Conroy, then, or Van Ryn——"

"They're playing cricket, too," grinned Jimmy. "Sit down, old top, and expound.

"Look here——!" bawled Higgs of the Fourth, flinging the study door open. Then three pretty faces dawned on Higgs, and he stuttered and vanished. Higgs, apparently, was the owner of some of the "borrowed" crockery. (See page 249.)

Your old pals are entitled to the refusal of the idea—if any! Get on with the washing."

"Well, then, my idea is to meet young Loring at the station," said Lovell. "As a new kid, I don't suppose he knows much about Rookwood—about the rows between Classicals and Moderns, and all that. We'll guy him."

"Oh! You're not proposing to take him under our wing?"

"No, ass. We'll guy him—it will be one up against the Moderns," said Lovell. "Of course, I don't mean to hurt the duffer. Just guy him, because he's a blessed Modern. As he's a relation, or something, of Tommy Dodd, it will make Tommy Dodd sit up. It's time we gave the Moderns another lesson, or they'll be forgetting that we're top side at Rookwood."

"Ahem!"

"Blessed if I see——!" began Raby.

"I haven't finished yet."

"Great Christopher Columbus! Not yet?"

"No!" howled Lovell.

"Wake me up when you have."

"My idea," said Lovell, with a glare at Raby, "is to pull his leg. We'll hire a trap in Coombe, and take him in. He'll think we're nice chaps looking after him, and all that. And we'll drive him to Bagshot School——"

"What on earth for?"

"And land him there," said Lovell. "He'll think it's Rookwood—being a silly new kid. See?"

"My hat!"

"Just picture him," chuckled Lovell. "Marching into Bagshot—presenting himself there as a new chap—when he ought to be coming to Rookwood all the time! Isn't that a ripping stunt? Just think of it! Ha, ha, ha!"

And Lovell, evidently immensely tickled with his extraordinary idea, roared.

THE SECOND CHAPTER.

A Rift in the Lute.

"HA, ha, ha!"
Arthur Edward Lovell was so taken with his idea that he roared in great merriment; and did not observe, for a moment

or two, that his three comrades had faces that displayed the solemnity of owls.

When he did observe it, his laughter died away quite suddenly.

He glared at the three.

"Well?" he demanded warmly. "Don't you think it's a ripping idea?"

"Oh, tip-top!" said Jimmy Silver, slowly.

"Gorgeous!" said Raby. "But——"

"Ripping!" said Newcome. "B-b—but—"

"Well, but what? It's the stunt of the season—the first really good idea that's ever been heard of in this study."

"Ahem! Suppose the new kid isn't so soft as you suppose——"

"Well, he's a silly Modern."

"Hum! But suppose he isn't taken in——"

"He will be."

"Suppose he don't go to Bagshot—and suppose we have all our trouble for nothing—as well as paying for the trap!"

"Oh, rot!"

"And suppose——"

"Are we going to spend the afternoon supposing, Jimmy Silver?"

"Well, suppose——"

"Oh, rot!"

"Besides, it's rather rough on the new kid," said Raby, judicially. "Of course, he's only a Modern, and we're up against the Moderns. But after all, he's a silly new kid, and doesn't know his way about, and it's rather rough——"

"What rot!"

"In fact, rather outside the limit, old chap," said Newcome, shaking his head. "Let's go to the pictures——"

Lovell rose to his feet again, with an expression of dogged determination on his face. It was not often that Arthur Edward Lovell propounded an idea—ideas not being much in his line. But when he did, he expected respectful attention. He was not receiving it.

"You don't like the idea, Jimmy Silver?"

"Well, you see——" hesitated the captain of the Fourth.

"Do you like it, Raby?"

"Not much!"

"And you, Newcome?"

"Precious little."

"Well, you can go on the river, or to the

pictures, or you can go and eat coke!" said Lovell. "I'm going to the station to meet Loring."

And he tramped to the door.

"Hold on, Lovell——"

"Well?" grunted Arthur Edward, turning his head.

"It's really rather rough on a new kid, old chap," urged Jimmy Silver. "Of course, it's a good idea—really ripping—but if it was played on us when we were new kids, we should have thought it was—was—rather—rather——"

"Rather what?" asked Lovell, with a gleam in his eyes.

"Well, rather inconsiderate, don't you think?"

"No, I don't."

"Ahem!"

"So I'm inconsiderate, am I?" demanded Lovell.

"Well, you see——"

"Oh, say what you think!" growled Lovell. "I do. For instance, I think you're a cheeky ass, Jimmy Silver, and I don't make any bones about telling you so!"

"Well, then, I do think that it's inconsiderate," exclaimed Jimmy, rather warmly. "I think it's unfeeling, if you want the exact truth."

"So I'm unfeeling?" growled Lovell.

"In this instance——"

"That's enough!"

Lovell strode to the door and dragged it open.

"Lovell, old chap——" began Jimmy.

Slam!

Arthur Edward Lovell was gone.

Jimmy Silver and Co. looked at one another. It was a storm in a teacup, so to speak, such as had sometimes happened in the end study before. Even the Fistical Four of the Fourth did not always see eye to eye with one another, though they generally managed to pull together with exemplary harmony.

"Oh, dear!" murmured Jimmy.

"It's rather a shame to pull old Lovell's leg," said Newcome, repentantly. "He can't help being a bit of an ass."

"But he oughtn't to spring ideas on the study," said Raby. "Ideas ain't in his line."

Still, we can't have old Lovell going off on his own like this. I suppose we'd better back him up in his silly stunt. After all, I'm not set on going on the river."

"And the pictures can wait!" said Newcome.

Jimmy Silver smiled.

"Come on, then," he said.

The Co. left the end study to rejoin Lovell. But Arthur Edward was not to be seen in the Fourth Form passage. Mornington and Erroll were coming out of their study, with their bats; they were figuring in the "fag" match that afternoon.

"Seen Lovell?" asked Jimmy.

"He's just gone downstairs," answered Mornington. "He was looking wrathy. I asked him what was up as he went up, and he told me to go and eat coke."

"Oh!"

Jimmy Silver and his comrades hurried on to the stairs. The junior cricketers were heading for Little Side. Wegg of the Third was carrying his bat along with an air of great importance. Wegg and Algy Silver and Grant, and other heroes of the Third, were in hopes of beating the Fourth that afternoon—especially as Jimmy Silver and Co. were standing out of the junior team.

"Hallo, Jimmy!" called out Algy Silver. "What's the matter with Lovell?"

"Have you seen him, Algy?"

Jimmy's cousin grinned.

"Yes, rather! He's gone into the quad—scowling like a demon in a panto. Looked in no end of a bate."

Jimmy and Raby and Newcome went into the quadrangle to look for Lovell. Arthur Edward was sighted at last, striding along with his hands driven deep into his pockets, with a deep line in his brows. Algy Silver's description was exaggerated; Lovell was not scowling like a demon in a pantomime. But he certainly looked disturbed and wrathy.

"Lovell!" murmured Jimmy, as the Co. joined Arthur Edward.

Lovell stared at them.

"Well?" he snapped.

"We—we—we're coming——"

"Where?"

"To the station, you know, to—to carry out that ripping idea," said Jimmy Silver.

THE
GREYFRIARS GALLERY
IN VERSE

By Dick Penfold

No. 8: Alonzo Todd

Who shines above us like a star,
And wags his finger from afar
To warn us what base wrecks we are?
                    ALONZO!

Who swallows books of fearful size?
Who laps up wisdom from the wise,
And chants their praises to the skies?
                    ALONZO!

Who once was victimised by Skinner,
And bolted Dr. Locke's own dinner,
Then found he hadn't backed a winner?
                    ALONZO!

Who hero-worships Uncle Ben,
And clucks just like a broody hen
On reading letters from his pen?
                    ALONZO!

Who uses words so long and quaint
That when he speaks without restraint
His hearers fall down in a faint?
                    ALONZO!

But who, although we take him off,
And sometimes feel inclined to scoff,
Is really every inch a toff?
                    ALONZO!

The captain of the Fourth spoke in honeyed tones, giving the soft answer which is popularly supposed to turn away wrath. In this instance it failed of its effect.

"Are you?" said Lovell grimly.

"Certainly, old chap."

"So you're going to be inconsiderate?"

"Eh?"

"And unfeeling?"

"Ahem!"

"I won't put your consciences to such a strain," said Lovell, with deep sarcasm. "You'd never sleep o' nights if you'd been inconsiderate and unfeeling, you know. I can do without you."

"Look here, Lovell——"

"Oh, give a chap a rest."

"But—I say!" began Newcome.

"Go and see your blessed pictures," said Lovell. "You don't want to be rough on a new kid. New kids are such important persons. It's better to rag your own pal than to be rough on a new kid, isn't it?"

"Look here——!"

"Oh, rats!"

Lovell, evidently in a mood to let the sun go down on his wrath, turned his back on his chums, and strode away.

"Oh, bother!" said Raby. "Lovell's got his back up—and I'm fed up, for one. He'll come round by tea-time. Let's get off somewhere. They're beginning the cricket already."

Jimmy Silver looked rather worried.

The tiff with Lovell cast rather a shadow over the bright afternoon.

Tommy Dodd, Tommy Cook, and Tommy Doyle, of the Modern Fourth, came along on their way to Little Side. The three Tommies were playing that afternoon in the Fourth-Form team.

"There's those blessed Moderns!" growled Jimmy. "Bump 'em!"

"Good egg!"

The three Moderns were certainly quite innocent, so far as the tiff with Lovell was concerned; but they were Moderns, and the three Classicals felt the need of expending their exasperation upon somebody. Tommy Dodd and Co. had come along in the nick of time, as it were. The Co. rushed upon them,

Arthur Edward Lovell went along the dusty road, experiencing the joys—or otherwise—of the frog's march. For a hundred yards along the road he went, and there the Bagshot trio left him sitting in the dust. (*See page* 218.)

and collared them, to the great wrath and indignation of the three Tommies.

"Here, wharrer you at?" roared Tommy Dodd. "I'll bat you—I'll—oh, my hat—yaroooooh!"

"Bump them!"

"Ha, ha, ha!"

The three Moderns were strewn in the quadrangle.

There was a volcanic eruption of howls and roars, as they sorted themselves out.

Jimmy Silver and Co. scudded away, chortling, leaving them to sort themselves out at their leisure, and feeling somewhat solaced. Tommy Dodd grasped his bat when he found himself on his feet again.

"After them!" he gasped. "I'll—I'll ——"

"You fellows coming?" shouted Mornington, from the direction of the cricket field. "You're late already."

"Oh, we're coming," grunted Dodd.

And the Modern juniors went on to the cricket field, postponing vengeance on the Classical trio for the present.

THE THIRD CHAPTER.

On His Own.

"OH, rotten!" growled Lovell.

Arthur Edward was dissatisfied.

Having rejected the advances of the Co., he was, naturally, left "on his own"; but somehow he did not find that satisfactory. Jimmy Silver and Raby and Newcome disappeared out of the gates, after their little scrap with the Moderns, and were lost to sight. Lovell, with his hands deep in his pockets and a frown on his brow, looked about him glumly.

He was determined to carry out that idea—if only to show the end study that he could do as he liked. That, certainly, was not a very noble spirit in which to make up his mind; but Lovell was irritated, and in an obstinate mood. He was wounded at the charge of want of feeling, too; for Lovell was the best-natured of fellows, and detested ill-nature—which made him all the more determined not to see that his proposed rag on the new " kid " was a little wanting in consideration.

But he did not want to go alone—half the fun would be lost without a comrade or two. His own chums having failed him, he looked round for support, as it were. The quad. was nearly deserted; most of the fellows were on the cricket field, or out of gates. Lovell walked down to Little Side in the hope of picking up a recruit there.

The junior match was beginning. Wegg and Algy Silver were batting for the Third, and the Fourth-Formers were in the field. Mornington was captaining the Fourth, and Conroy, Van Ryn, Pons, Oswald, Flynn, Grace, were all in the team, as well as the three Tommies and Towle of the Modern side.

Townsend and Topham, the dandies of the Fourth, were lounging on the field; but Lovell did not want them. They were too slack even for a rag. Lattrey, Peele, and Gower were in a little group, talking " geegees " —but Lovell did not want to talk geegees. Leggett, the Modern, gave him a nod; but Lovell did not return the nod—he couldn't stand Leggett.

After a look round the field, he tramped away again, with a darker shade than before upon his brow. On Big Side there was a senior match in progress; Bulkeley and Neville and Knowles, and other great men of the Sixth, were playing a visiting team. Lovell paused to look on for a few minutes, and he joined in the cheering of a mighty hit by Bulkeley, the captain of Rookwood. Then he strolled on.

In the quad. again, he found Smythe, of the Shell, chatting with Howard and Tracy major. He hesitated, and then came up to them. The Fistical Four were not on the best of terms with Adolphus Smythe and his nutty pals; but Lovell was feeling the need of somebody to accompany him in his expedition, and the time was getting close now.

" You fellows got anything on this afternoon ? " he asked, as agreeably as he could in his present humour.

Adolphus Smythe glanced at him

His glance was lofty. A series of raggings and bumpings had never convinced the great Adolphus that he was only a common mortal, and not in the least entitled to put on airs.

" Nothin' special," answered Smythe. " Life's a bore, my dear fellow. I'm fed up with everythin'."

Lovell suppressed a snort. The lackadaisical Adolphus always roused his ire, but this was not an appropriate moment for telling Adolphus what he thought of him.

" Like to take a hand in a rag ? " he asked genially.

" A rag ? " repeated Adolphus.

" Yes—a rag on the Moderns."

" Oh, gad ! "

" My dear man," said Tracy major. " We're not interested in your fag rags. Don't be funny."

" Yaas; you make me rather tired, Lovell," remarked Adolphus. " Thankin' you all the same, we won't take a hand in your faggy raggin'."

" You silly ass ! " snorted Lovell.

There was no longer any need to suppress his snort; evidently he wasn't going to pick up recruits among the nuts of the Shell.

" My dear man," said Adolphus, with a wave of his hand, " wander away ! Vanish ! Give us a rest ! Yarooooh ! " Adolphus wound up suddenly, as Lovell took him by the collar: " Yow-ow ! Leggo, you beast ! "

Shake ! Shake !

" Oh, gad ! Yoop ! Leggo ! " wailed Adolphus. " You're muckin' up my collar ! Oh, goodness ! "

Shake !

After another powerful shake, Lovell sat the great Adolphus down in the quad. with a bump, and walked away.

" Wow-wow-wow ! " said Adolphus.

Tracy major and Howard helped him up. It did not seem to occur to them to intervene while Lovell was shaking him.

" Ow ! The frightful ruffian ! " gasped Smythe. " I've a jolly good—ow !—mind to go after him—wow !—and thrash him—

groogh! But it's a bit beneath a chap's dignity to get into fag fights! Ow!"

And Adolphus—perhaps from considerations of his dignity—did not go after Lovell and thrash him—which was probably very fortunate for Adolphus.

Arthur Edward Lovell tramped on towards the gates. He had made up his mind to go alone now.

"He, he, he!"

Lovell glanced round as he heard that not very musical cachinnation. Tubby Muffin, of the Fourth, grinned at him.

"He, he, he!" he repeated. "I'm jolly glad you bumped Smythey, Lovell—the beast knocked my cap off to-day. I say, Lovell, old chap, can you do me a little favour?"

"What is it?" grunted Lovell.

"Lend me a bob!"

"Oh, rats!"

"I mean threepence," said the fat Classical. "Three D., you know, till——"

"Till the Greek Kalends?" asked Lovell sarcastically.

"He, he, he!" cackled Tubby, perhaps thinking that if he was entertained by that little joke, the three D. would be forthcoming.

But it wasn't.

Lovell turned towards the gates again; and then he turned back as a thought came into his mind. He disliked going out alone, and even Tubby Muffin's company was better than none. The fat Classical's society was not generally sought after, but it was a case of any port in a storm.

"Like to come along and see a rag, Tubby?" asked Lovell.

"Yes, old chap," answered Muffin. "Anything you like. Where are you going?"

"To Coombe."

"Might call in at the tuck-shop there."

Lovell did not seem to hear that suggestion. He walked out at the gates, Tubby Muffin trotting by his side to keep pace.

It was a sunny afternoon, and, as he walked along the leafy lane, Lovell felt his good-humour return. He explained to Tubby Muffin the nature of the "rag," and was solaced by Tubby's unqualified admiration. Indeed, it seemed to be Tubby's fat opinion that such a glorious stunt had never been

mooted before in the history of Rookwood. Admiration is always pleasing, and Lovell was pleased—especially after the reception his idea had received in the end study—and he began to think that Tubby was not such a fat duffer as was generally supposed.

Tubby slowed down as they were passing Mrs. Wicks's little shop in the High Street of Coombe.

"By the way, did you know Mrs. Wicks had a new lot of tarts in, Lovell?" he inquired.

"No," answered Lovell, without stopping.

"Her ginger-pop's jolly good, too!" murmured Tubby.

"I dare say."

"I—I say, Lovell——"

"Come on, Muffin; we don't want to be late at the station."

Tubby Muffin glanced into the tuck-shop and glanced at Lovell. That youth showed no sign of coming to a halt. With a deep sigh, Tubby Muffin trotted along on his track.

But his hearty admiration of Lovell's "stunt" seemed to have vanished now; his enthusiasm had died away. He hardly answered Lovell's remarks as they went up the village street; and by the time they reached the railway station Tubby Muffin was silent, and seemed quite gloomy.

THE FOURTH CHAPTER.

Taking the Stranger In.

"COOMBE!"

The train stopped.

A rather good-looking lad of about fifteen, with fair hair under his straw hat, glanced from a window in the train, and rose as the old porter shouted.

He stepped from the carriage, with a bag in one hand, and a rug over the other arm.

"That's the merchant!" murmured Arthur Edward Lovell.

Lovell was leaning on an automatic machine on the platform. Tubby Muffin was asking him whether he had an odd penny about him, but Lovell was not listening. He was watching the passengers alighting from the train—on the look-out for the new "kid."

There were few passengers; Coombe was not a station with much traffic. Among the

POPULAR FAVOURITES AT ROOKWOOD

Reading from left to right: George Bulkeley, Oliver Loring, Jimmy Silver, Arthur Edward Lovell, Algy Silver, Tubby Muffin, Adolphus Smythe, Teddy Grace, Tommy Dodd, Val. Mornington.

(212)

half-dozen who alighted from the train, there was only one who could possibly have been the new boy for Rookwood School, and that was the fair-haired youth with the bag and the rug.

Lovell watched him as he spoke to the porter, apparently giving directions about a box. The new fellow then stood on the platform, as the other passengers cleared off, looking about him. Possibly he expected to be met at the station; as he would have been had not Tommy Dodd, of the Modern Fourth, not been otherwise engaged on business of importance.

Lovell detached himself from the automatic machine, and approached the new junior, with Tubby at his heels.

"Excuse me," he said, with elaborate politeness, "may I ask if you are the new chap for Rookwood?"

The youth looked at him.

"That's right," he answered, in a rather pleasant voice.

"Oliver Loring?" asked Lovell.

"Yes."

"I'm Lovell of the Fourth. I've come to meet you."

"You're very kind," said Loring. "I thought perhaps Tommy Dodd would come along——"

"He's playing cricket this afternoon," explained Lovell. "As some of the fellows who usually play with the Form team are standing out, he couldn't very well get away."

"I see."

"I've come instead—and Muffin. This is Muffin."

Oliver Loring gave Tubby a pleasant nod, to which the fat Classical responded with a grin.

Tubby was wondering whether it would be possible to inveigle the new junior, who looked a very agreeable fellow, into Mrs. Wicks's shop, and "stick" him for refreshments.

"This way, Loring," said Lovell. "I've ordered a trap at the Coombe Arms to take you to the school."

"Have you really?" exclaimed Loring, in surprise.

"Oh, yes."

"That's awfully good of you."

"Not at all. Of course, I'm standing the trap," added Lovell hastily. "You see, as you're a relation of Tommy Dodd—you are his relation, I think?"

"Yes, a distant relation."

"Well, as you're Tommy's relation, we want to make you welcome," said Lovell solemnly. "We think no end of Tommy at Rookwood, you know."

"He, he, he!" came from Tubby Muffin.

Lovell gave him a look; and Tubby's chortle died away in a cough. The new boy glanced at him for a moment.

"You're a Modern, I suppose?" asked Loring.

Lovell was a little taken aback by that question. He had taken it for granted that Loring, as a new boy, would not be well "posted" in the politics of Rookwood.

"A—a Modern!" he repeated.

"I'm entered on the Modern side," said Loring, looking at him. "As you're a friend of Tommy Dodd's, I suppose you're a Modern?"

"I see you know all about Rookwood."

"Tommy's told me a lot about the school," said Loring, with a smile. "It seems that there are no end of rows between the Moderns and the Classicals. Modern side is top side in cricket and footer——"

"What rot!"

"Eh?"

"I—I mean——"

"I only know what Dodd's told me, of course," said Loring, looking at him. "He's told me that the Moderns are always ragging the Classicals. The Classicals try to keep their end up, but they haven't any earthly."

"The silly ass!"

"Oh, you're not a Modern, then?"

"I—I—I——" Lovell stammered a little. He had not intended to reveal the fact that he belonged to the Classical side; but his unguarded remarks had revealed it pretty effectually. "You—you see—well, the fact is, I'm a Classical." It had to come out, and Lovell looked rather confused as it came, "But—but I'm quite friendly with Dodd, you know. Our little rows don't make any difference to that."

" Oh, yes, I understand. Dodd's told me about it."

" That's all right, then," said Lovell.

" Good friends, and all that, but you rag the Moderns, and so on," said Loring, with another of his rather keen looks at Lovell. " You jape them, as Tommy calls it, and that kind of thing.

" Ye—e—es.

" I see ! "

" This way," said Lovell hastily. " Carry Loring's rug, Tubby."

" Oh, certainly," said Tubby Muffin. " I say, Loring, would you care to step in at Mrs. Wicks's shop ? New fellows generally like to see the place——"

" Shut up, Tubby ! This way."

" But I say, Lovell, Loring would like——"

" Shut up ! " roared Lovell.

Tubby grunted, and let the subject drop— for the present. Outside the Coombe Arms, the trap was waiting for Lovell, a stableman holding the horse. Loring's bag and rug were deposited in the trap, and the new boy followed them, and Tubby Muffin clambered in after him.

Lovell jumped in, and took the reins from the ostler.

" I say, Lovell," began Tubby Muffin, " stop at Mrs. Wicks's, will you ? Loring would like to see——"

" We're not going that way ! " snapped Lovell.

" We pass Mrs. Wicks's shop going to Rookwood ! " said Tubby, forgetting for a moment the " rag," and the fact that Rookwood was not the present destination of the party.

Lovell gave him a hunnish look.

" Oh ! I—I mean——! " stammered Tubby.

" Shut up ! "

Lovell gathered up the reins, and set the horse in motion. The trap bowled away, taking a short cut from the station into Bagshot Lane. Lovell handled the horse well, and the trap bowled along at a good speed.

An expression of deep gloom overspread Reginald Muffin's fat face. The " rag " looked like being a success ; but Tubby's thoughts were dwelling more upon the tuck-shop than the " rag." Probably the new junior, unsuspecting, would be landed at Bagshot, and left there when the trap drove off—quite a success from Lovell's point of view. But Tubby Muffin was thinking of other things, and he was not comforted.

" Much distance to Rookwood ? " asked Loring.

" Oh, not very far, at this rate," answered Lovell.

" I thought you went through the village. Dodd's told me——"

" This is a longer way round ; but it's very pleasant in the lanes, on an afternoon like this," said Lovell.

" Oh, yes. That's so."

" He, he, he ! "

Tubby Muffin suppressed his ill-timed mirth, as the new junior glanced at him rather curiously.

Loring was looking decidedly curious by this time.

Contrary to Lovell's expectations, he knew all about the rivalry at Rookwood School, having heard a great deal about it from his relation, Tommy Dodd. Indeed, he had probably heard very adorned accounts of the doings of the Rookwood juniors. And probably it struck him as odd—considering what he knew of affairs at Rookwood—that a Classical junior should take all this trouble on account of a Modern—a new fellow he had never seen before, and was not likely to have much to do with at the school.

" One mile to Bagshot ! " said Loring," reading from a finger-post as the trap was bowling along. " We're going Bagshot way, are we, Lovell ? "

" You've heard of Bagshot ? " asked Lovell, starting.

" Oh, yes—Dodd's told me——"

" Blow Dodd ! "

" Eh, what ? "

" N-n-nothing ! Lovely scenery, isn't it ? "

" Yes, lovely. Dodd's told me about Bagshot school—you play the fellows at cricket and footer, and rag them sometimes," said Loring. " Shall we pass Bagshot School ? "

" He, he, he ! "

" What are you cackling at, Muffin ? " roared Lovell, rather regretting that he had brought this exceedingly inefficient assistant with him.

ROOKWOOD SCHOOL, HAMPSHIRE.

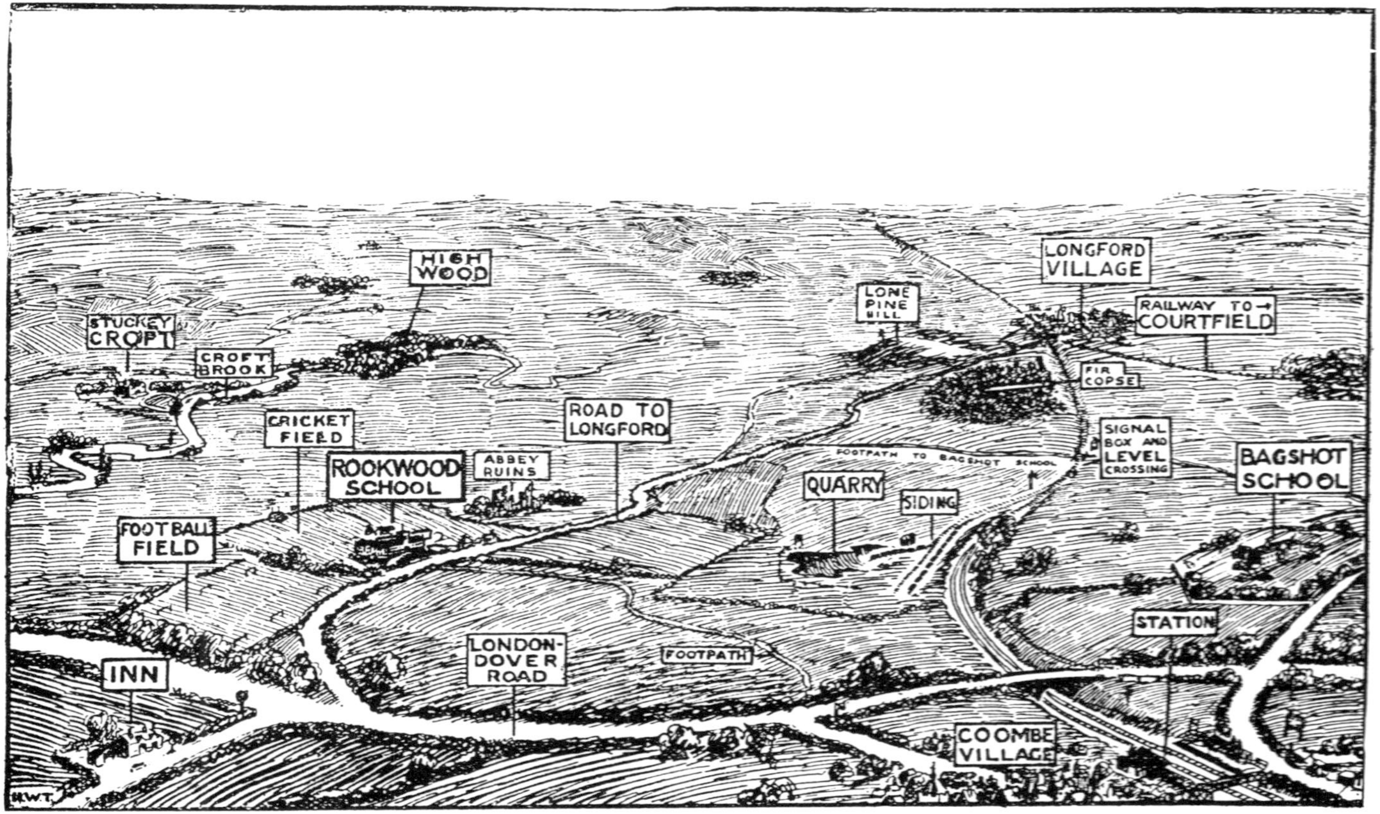

A GENERAL VIEW OF THE SURROUNDING DISTRICT.

BAGSHOT SCHOOL

LONGFORD VILLAGE

RAILWAY TO COURTFIELD

FIR COPSE

SIGNAL BOX AND LEVEL CROSSING

STATION

COOMBE VILLAGE

LONE PINE HILL

FOOTPATH TO BAGSHOT SCHOOL

SIDING

QUARRY

ROAD TO LONGFORD

FOOTPATH

LONDON-DOVER ROAD

HIGH WOOD

ABBEY RUINS

ROOKWOOD SCHOOL

CRICKET FIELD

STUCKEY CROFT

CROFT BROOK

FOOTBALL FIELD

INN

"N-n-nothing, old chap."

"Then shut up," growled Lovell.

Arthur Edward gave his attention to the horse, and did not answer Loring's question, and the new junior did not repeat it. His face wore a very thoughtful expression, however, and there was a glimmer in his eyes. Tubby Muffin, watching him, wondered whether he had "tumbled" to the fact that he was the victim of a "rag."

A big red-brick building dawned into view over the trees. Loring glanced at it.

"That's the school!" said Lovell, pointing with his whip.

"Rookwood?" asked Loring, in surprise.

Lovell cracked his whip, and did not seem to hear.

Tubby Muffin smothered a chuckle just in time.

"Not much like Dodd's description of Rookwood," said Loring.

"Isn't it?"

"Not a bit."

"Dodd isn't much of a hand at describing things," remarked Lovell casually.

"He can't be," said Loring. "I gathered from him that Rookwood was an old place—mossy stone and ivied tower, and that kind of thing."

"Did you really?" said Lovell.

"I certainly did. That show looks as if it hasn't been built twenty years," said Loring, looking at the red-brick building through the trees.

"Oh, it's older than that, you know."

"Not what I fancied Rookwood to be."

"You'll like it all right—places often disappoint a chap at first glance, you know," said Lovell.

And he avoided further discussion by dashing up to the gates of Bagshot with a flourish and a clatter.

THE FIFTH CHAPTER.

Lovell's Luck.

CLATTER!

The horse's hoofs rang on the road outside the school gates.

The big iron gates were open, and fellows could be seen within, and a glimpse of red-brick buildings and a fountain. Three juniors—well known to Lovell and Tubby Muffin—came towards the gates as the trap halted. They were Pankley, Poole, and Putter, of the Bagshot Fourth.

"Jump down!" said Lovell hastily.

He was anxious to get his passenger landed before the Bagshot fellows came on the scene. Enlightenment for the new junior would have come at an awkward moment, just then, for Lovell's scheme.

"I get down here?" asked Loring.

"Yes, certainly."

"He, he, he!"

"Here's your bag—here's your rug——"

"Aren't you getting down?" asked Loring.

"I—I—oh, yes," gasped Lovell.

He did not need telling, now, that the new boy was suspicious. And certainly it would have strengthened his suspicions if Lovell had remained in the trap, after reaching the school—supposed to be Rookwood!

Lovell jumped down.

"Hand me your bag," he said.

"Aren't you getting down, Muffin?"

"Nothing for me to get down for," answered Tubby. "I—I mean——" he stuttered, as he caught Lovell's look. "I—I mean—yes, oh, certainly."

And he got down.

Pankley and Co had arrived at the gate by that time, and they were looking curiously on.

"What's this—a visit in state?" asked Pankley.

Lovell breathed hard. The new boy was still delaying in the trap—and delay was threatening Lovell's little scheme with disaster.

"It's a new fellow for the school," explained Lovell, not specifying which school; "I've brought him along from the station."

"That's jolly good of you," said Pankley, in surprise. "Quite a good turn from the enemy."

"Oh, I wanted a drive, anyway," said Lovell carelessly. "Get a move on, Loring. What are you waiting there for?"

"Admiring the scenery," answered Loring coolly.

"Oh, get down!"

"I didn't know there was a new fellow expected," remarked Poole.

"Get down, Loring!"

Oliver Loring looked down at Lovell, with a rather whimsical smile. Then he looked at the three juniors in the gateway.

"Is Tommy Dodd at home?" he asked.

Pankley stared at him.

"Tommy Dodd! Dodd of Rookwood, do you mean?"

"Yes"

"How the thump should I know whether he's at home? Better ask at Rookwood, I should think."

"Oh!" gasped Lovell.

He stood rooted to the ground for a moment.

What happened next passed like a flash. Loring caught up the reins, cracked the whip, and the trap bowled away down the road. Lovell sat in the dust, and blinked after it dizzily. (*See page 218.*)

(217)

All had been going well—even the Bagshot fellows could not have betrayed the scheme, not knowing anything about it, but the keenness of the new junior had spoiled everything. Evidently he had been suspicious—and his suspicions had strengthened — and he had asked that question about Tommy Dodd simply to put the matter to the test.

And now he knew !

He dropped into the seat Lovell had vacated, smiling.

"What a merry joke !" he remarked. "A Classical rag, what ? Just the kind of stunt I've heard about from Tommy Dodd !"

"I—I——" stammered Lovell.

"You were going to land me at Bagshot—ha, ha ! What a screaming joke ! But the yarn won't be so funny when you tell it now, will it ?" grinned Loring.

"Get down !" roared Lovell.

"No fear !"

"If you don't get down, I'll jolly well mop you out of that trap !" shouted Lovell, quite losing his temper. The utter failure of his scheme was too much for him.

Loring looked down at him coolly.

Lovell's wrath apparently did not make him nervous. He laughed.

"You hear me ?" shouted Lovell.

"I'm not deaf."

"Will you get out ?"

"Oh, no."

"Then I'll make you."

Lovell put his foot on the step, to clamber in, Pankley and Co. watching the scene in astonishment.

Oliver Loring reached out and gave the Rookwooder a gentle shove on the chest.

"Ow !" roared Lovell, as he sat in the dust with a bump.

What happened next passed like a flash.

Loring caught up the reins, cracked the whip, and the trap bowled away down the road.

Lovell sat in the dust and blinked after it dizzily.

"Oh, my hat !" exclaimed Pankley. "What's this game ?"

"Come back !" shrieked Tubby Muffin.

"Oh, you rotter ! I can't walk to Rookwood. C-c-come back !"

Loring did not come back.

He did not even turn his head.

He was driving away cheerily : and the trap rattled on at a good speed. Arthur Edward Lovell scrambled to his feet, and roared.

"Loring ! Come back ! I'll smash you ! Come back ! I'll pulverise you—you rotter ! Oh, you Modern cad !"

The trap turned a corner and vanished from sight.

"Ow !" gasped Tubby Muffin. "We—we—we've got to walk home to Rookwood ! Oh, you silly ass, Lovell—you thumping ass—oh, dear !"

"Well, my word !" said Cecil Pankley. "Lovell, old scout, you seem to have had a jape on—if you call it a jape—and you seem to have slipped up on it ! And it seems that you've got to walk home to Rookwood—and it would be only a kindness to help you on your way. You fellows, lend Lovell a hand."

"What-ho !" chuckled Poole and Putter.

Tubby Muffin took to his heels as the three Bagshot fellows rushed out of the gateway. But Pankley and Co. did not trouble about Tubby. They collared Arthur Edward Lovell.

"Let go !" roared Lovell savagely.

"My dear chap—Yarooh !" howled Pankley, as he received Arthur Edward's knuckles forcibly on his nose.

Lovell was hitting out furiously.

But hitting out was not of much use against three. In a few moments Arthur Edward was helpless in the grasp of the old rivals of Rookwood. And he was bumped as a warning.

"Now, then," gasped Pankley ; "frog's march !"

"Go it !"

"Yow-ow ! Leggo ! Oh !"

Arthur Edward Lovell went along the dusty road, experiencing the joys—or otherwise—of the frog's march. For a hundred yards along the road he went, and there the Bagshot trio left him sitting in the dust, struggling to get his second wind.

They walked back cheerily to the school,

waving their hands to Lovell as they went; and leaving him sitting in the dust—of the dust dusty, so to speak—and with feelings that could not have been expressed in any known language.

THE SIXTH CHAPTER.

Not a Success !

"THIS right for Rookwood School ?"

Jimmy Silver, Raby, and Newcome were sauntering along the leafy lane, when a trap slackened down in the road, and the driver—a youth in Etons—called to them.

Jimmy Silver glanced up.

He recognised the trap belonging to the Coomb Arms, but its occupant was a stranger to him.

"First to the right, and second to the left," he said. "That takes you into Coombe Lane, and then it's straight on to Rookwood."

"Thanks."

"Hold on a minute, will you ?" exclaimed Jimmy. "Are you the new kid for Rookwood, by any chance ? We belong to Rookwood, you know."

"Yes, my name's Loring."

"Oh, my only aunt ! Weren't you met at the station ?" asked Jimmy.

Loring smiled.

"Yes ; a Rookwood chap met me there."

"Lovell ?" exclaimed Raby.

"He told me his name was Lovell, and another chap named Muffin. This is their trap !" said Loring cheerfully.

"Where are they, then ?" asked Newcome, with a stare.

"I left them at Bagshot School. "

"Oh, my hat !"

"They were going to leave me there—a joke, I suppose, on a new fellow," explained Loring. "So I left them there ! Rather funny, what ?"

And he drove on cheerily.

Jimmy Silver and Co. looked at one another, as the trap bowled away. Then they stared after Loring. Then they looked at one another again.

"Well, my hat !" said Jimmy Silver, at last.

Raby chuckled.

"Lovell seems to have made rather a mess of his game with the new kid," he remarked. "Landed at Bagshot. My hat ! I wonder what the Bagshot fellows will do to him ?"

"We'd better get along there," said Jimmy Silver. "Poor old Lovell will be feeling rather rotten—especially if Pankley and Co. get hold of him. We shall have to miss those blessed pictures after all, Newcome."

"Oh, all right," said Newcome

The chums of Rookwood turned in the direction of Bagshot, walking quickly. They could not help being tickled by that complete reversal of Lovell's little scheme ; but they were rather anxious about Arthur Edward, too. The discussion as to the programme for the afternoon had ended in a compromise ; the three chums were going to walk along the river to Latcham, and see the pictures there—so far as time allowed. But that programme was abandoned now. It was the duty of the loyal Co. to rally round the member of their honourable society who had fallen into disaster—even if it was his own fault.

"Hallo ! Here's Muffin !" exclaimed Newcome suddenly, as they turned into Bagshot Lane.

Tubby Muffin was pounding along in a cloud of dust, with perspiration rolling down his fat face.

"Yarooh ! Keep off !" he howled, as the three Rookwooders dawned upon him.

"Tubby, you ass !"

"Oh ! It's you, Jimmy !" gasped Reginald Muffin. "I—I thought it was those Bagshot beasts for a minute. Oh, dear !"

"What are you rolling along at that rate for ?" demanded Jimmy Silver.

"They're after me."

"Eh ! Who are ?"

"The Bagshot beasts. Ow !"

"You fat duffer ! There's nobody after you !" growled Raby.

Tubby Muffin blinked round at the open road behind him, and gasped with relief. His terrors had peopled the road with Bagshot fellows, all thirsting for his gore, so to speak.

"Oh, dear !" he gasped. "I—I thought——I—I mean don't you fellows think I was running away from the Bagshot bounders, you know. Nothing of the sort, of course."

"What were you doing, then?"

"I—I was coming for—for help for—for Lovell, you know. They've got Lovell," stammered Tubby. "I—I fought till—till I got away. I felled several of them——"

"Bow—wow!"

"I fought like a lion, you know!" gasped Tubby. "You fellows know what I'm like when I'm roused. I felled them, right and left——"

"Chuck it, Tubby! What was happening when you scooted?"

"I didn't stop to see. I—I mean, the road was fairly strewn with them. A dozen at least, felled by my terrible blows. Then I thought I'd go for help to rescue Lovell, you know."

"Oh, rats!"

Jimmy Silver and Co. did not wait for the rest of Tubby's stirring story of heroism. They were anxious about Lovell, and they proceeded at a run towards Bagshot School. The big, red-brick building was in sight in the distance, when they came on Arthur Edward at last.

He was limping along the road towards them, dishevelled and dusty, and alone. There was no sign of the Bagshot enemy.

"Hallo, Lovell!"

"Oh, you!" grunted Lovell.

He tramped on, his chums turning and walking with him. Lovell was evidently in a bad temper.

"Had bad luck?" asked Jimmy sympathetically.

"I've been frog's marched."

"I wish we'd been there, old chap."

"You ought to have been there. You would have been there if you'd backed me up as I asked you."

"Ahem! The—the new kid—we passed him on the road—he was driving a trap," said Jimmy. "We came to lend you a hand, if you wanted it, old scout."

"And you came too late!" grunted Lovell.

"Well, that couldn't be helped. Let's drop in at Coombe, shall we? You want a bit of a brush down."

"I'm going to Rookwood."

"Oh, all right, we'll go on to Rookwood, then."

"No need for you fellows to come."

"Look here," began Raby testily. But he stopped, as Jimmy gave him a warning glance.

Jimmy could feel for his chum, whose little plans had ended in such utter disaster; and he made allowances for Lovell's wrath.

"It's about time we got in for tea," remarked Jimmy.

"It's not tea-time!" grunted Lovell.

"We'll have an early tea, and then a trot out, shall we?"

"I'm not going out."

"Oh!"

"I'm going to look for that Modern cad and smash him," said Lovell, between his teeth.

"Do you mean Loring?"

"Yes; that's the cad's name."

"Is he a cad?" asked Jimmy Silver, mildly.

"Yes, he is."

"He looked a pretty decent chap for a Modern," said Newcome.

"I say he's a cad!"

"Oh, all right; he's a cad then," murmured Newcome, amicably. "I daresay he is—the Moderns are all cads, anyway."

"But—but what happened?" murmured Raby.

Lovell breathed hard.

"I met him at the station, as I said, and got him as far as Bagshot. Then he tumbled to the game—through that fool Muffin talking too much, and sniggling, I suppose. I was an idiot to bring Muffin. I shouldn't have, if my own pals had come."

"Ahem!"

"But, of course, they wouldn't have a hand in anything that was unfeeling—Modern kids are such important persons," growled Lovell.

"But—but what——"

"He knocked me over when I was going to pitch him out of the trap, the cheeky cad!"

"Well, if you were going to pitch him out, old chap——"

"And he bolted with the trap—my trap— and left me stranded. And the Bagshot rotters collared me and gave me the frog's march."

"No, I won't go!" rapped out Jimmy Silver, sharply. "You ought not to want to fight this new fellow, and I won't have a hand in any such rot!" (*See page* 224.)

"Cheeky rotters!"

"Oh, I wonder you don't say they were quite right—everybody seems to be in the right but me!" snorted Lovell. "So that is what has happened. I'm stuck for seven and six for the trap, and that cad's got it—he's driving to Rookwood, and I'm walking — and I'm dusty, and I've got bumps——"

"Ha, ha, ha!"

"Why, you rotters, what are you howling at?" roared Lovell, greatly incensed by that involuntary outbreak on the part of his comrades.

"Well, old son, it's rather funny," said Jimmy, repressing his merriment. "You do seem to have gone for wool, and returned shorn. Never mind; it's all in the day's work. We'll mop up the Moderns another time. Keep smiling."

"I'm going to smash that cad Loring!"

"What for?"

"Because I choose!"

"Oh!"

After that reply from Arthur Edward, there really seemed nothing more to be said. The Fistical Four walked on to Rookwood in silence.

THE SEVENTH CHAPTER.

Jimmy Silver Says "No"!

OLD Mack, the porter, came up to the Fistical Four as they entered the school gateway.

"It's 'ere, Master Lovell," he said.

Lovell stared at him.

"What's here?" he snapped.

"The trap," answered old Mack. "And what I want to know is this 'ere—wot's to be done with it? I can't 'ave a 'orse and trap 'anging round my lodge all day."

The juniors glanced at the trap waiting on the drive.

"So—so it was left with you, Mack?" murmured Jimmy Silver.

"Yes, sir. Noo young gentleman—Master Loring, of Mr. Manders' House, sir, came driving it. He said it belonged to Master Lovell, and was to be left 'ere for 'im. And 'ere it is," added Mack. "Wot's to be done with it, sir?"

"I don't know and don't care!" snapped Lovell.

"Wot?"

"Hang the trap!"

With that reply, which could not be called polite, Arthur Edward Lovell swung on into the quadrangle. Old Mack stared after him, and rubbed his chin, and stared at Lovell's friends.

"Wot's this 'ere mean?" he asked, gruffly. "If the trap ain't Master Lovell's, what's it 'ere for? I s'pose I'd better speak to the 'Ead——"

"Not a bit of it," said Jimmy Silver. "It's all right, Mack. The trap's got to be sent back to the Coombe Arms, where it was hired. Know anybody who'd drive it back for a couple of bob, Mack?"

"I dessay I could find somebody, sir," answered old Mack, quite genially. "Leave it in my 'ands, and I'll see to it."

The matter was left in Mack's hands—as was a two-shilling piece—and the juniors followed Lovell, who was crossing the quad. with great strides, looking neither to the right nor to the left. He attracted a good many curious glances as he went; it was not usual for a fellow to appear in the open quad. at

Rookwood in such a dusty state. Smythe and Co. burst into a chortle as they sighted him, and Lovell's ears tingled as he heard it. But he strode on unregarding.

In the doorway of the schoolhouse, however, he was met by Mr. Bootles, the master of the Fourth. Mr. Bootles raised a commanding hand, and Lovell stopped.

"Lovell!" said Mr. Bootles, with a severe blink over his glasses. "Boy! What does this mean?"

Lovell's grubby face flushed.

"Is this," continued Mr. Bootles, with greater severity, "is this the state, Lovell, in which a Rookwood boy should appear in public? Your face, Lovell, is dirty—actually dirty!"

"I—I——" stammered Lovell.

"Your collar is torn, Lovell—your trousers are rumpled and covered with dust—you are dusty from head to foot, Lovell. You are not clean. I am shocked at you, Lovell."

Lovell gritted his teeth.

"I—I couldn't help——," he began.

"Have you had an accident?" demanded Mr. Bootles.

"I—I've had a—a scrap with some fellows ——"

"That is no excuse. You should not have done so. You should endeavour, Lovell, to pass a half-holiday in quiet repose, or in some harmless game, such as cricket or—or pegtop," said Mr. Bootles.

"Cricket or—or pegtop!" murmured Lovell, almost overcome.

"You will take a hundred lines, Lovell. Now go and clean yourself immediately—immediately!" said Mr. Bootles.

Lovell was glad enough to go. The form-master's severe glance followed him, disapprovingly, as he tramped up the stairs.

Jimmy Silver and his companions had stopped in the quad. The cricketers were coming off Little Side; though on Big Side the senior game was still in progress. Mornington and Erroll joined the trio, smiling.

"No; finished already?" asked Jimmy Silver.

Mornington chuckled.

"You be!" he answered. "The Merry Third did not turn out such paladins as they expected. We declared for fifty, and made them follow on."

" And their two innings gave them thirty ! ' said Erroll, with a smile.

" Ha, ha, ha ! "

" And we're winners by an innings and uncounted wickets ! " yawned Mornington. " Next time we play the Third, you needn't ask me to captain the side—you can ask Tubby Muffin."

" Tommy Dodd might as well have gone and met his blessed relation after all ! " remarked Raby.

" Just as well—or better," grunted Jimmy Silver. " Have you fellows seen anything of a new chap—Loring, of Manders' House ? "

" There's a chap on the cricket ground now, talkin' to Tommy Dodd," answered Mornington.

Jimmy Silver glanced towards the cricket field, and discerned Oliver Loring, coming along with the three Tommies of the Modern Fourth. The Tommies were chuckling in chorus, and it was easy to guess that the new fellow was relating how Lovell, the Classical, had been dished.

" Hallo, Silver ! " called out Tommy Dodd, cheerily. " Where's Lovell ? Has he crawled in yet ? "

" He came in with us," answered Jimmy, rather gruffly.

" What did the Bagshot bounders do to him ? "

" Oh, rats ! "

" You ought to kape him on a chain intirely ! " roared Tommy Doyle. " Lovell isn't to be trusted out alone. Has he paid for the trap ? "

" Ha, ha, ha ! " roared the Moderns.

And the four walked on towards Mr. Manders' house in great spirits. Jimmy Silver and Co. looked rather grim. They could see the humorous side of the affair themselves ; but it was not exactly gratifying to see the Moderns chortling over it like this. It was " one up " against the Classical side.

" What's the merry joke ? " asked Mornington.

Jimmy explained rather briefly, and Mornington roared, and Erroll smiled.

" Poor old Lovell ! " said Morny. " I

suppose he's rather ratty now. You will have to smoothe his ruffled plumes with a tactful hand."

" And we'd better go and do it," murmured Newcome.

Jimmy nodded, and the three chums went into the house. They did not find Lovell in the end study. He was in the dormitory, putting himself to rights.

" Shall we go up ? " asked Newcome.

" Better give him time to calm down," answered Jimmy, judiciously. " It's no wonder he's a bit ratty, considering. I wish he'd never thought of the stunt at all. Poor old Lovell ! "

" What about tea ? "

" We'll get rather a spread, and soothe him with it," said Jimmy. " Music hath charms to soothe the savage breast, and tuck is still more efficacious, I believe. Let's have tea ready when he comes down."

" Right-ho ! "

Fortunately funds were not short in the end study. Newcome ran down to the school shop for supplies, while Raby lighted the fire, and Jimmy Silver laid the table.

In ten minutes there was a fragrant odour of coffee and sausages and chips in the end study—calculated to soothe any savage breast, even that of a Hun.

Then Jimmy Silver and Co. waited for Lovell.

In a few minutes more Arthur Edward appeared. He came into the end study washed and brushed — new y swept and garnished, as it were. But his face, though clean, was no more amiable in expression. His brows were knitted, and his eyes had a gleam in them.

" Tea's ready ! " announced Jimmy Silver, with determined cheerfulness.

" It's not tea-time yet."

" Well, we've been out, you know, and I'm rather peckish——"

" I'm not."

" Ahem ! These sosses are rather nice," said Jimmy. " Pour out the coffee, Raby. There's your chair, Lovell."

" I'm not going to have tea now."

" Oh ! "

" I've got something to do before tea."

" Ah ! "

" Bootles gave me a hundred lines for coming in dusty—dirty, he called it," said Lovell.

" You needn't do them before tea."

" I'm not going to. Hang the lines, and hang Bootles ! I want one of you to go over to Manders' House for me."

" What for ? "

" To take my challenge to that Modern cad, Loring."

" You want to fight him, do you mean ? "

" Of course."

" What about ? "

" You know what about. No need to jaw all that over again," growled Lovell. " Will you go ? "

Jimmy Silver looked steadily at his chum. He had never seen Lovell quite in this humour before ; and his own patience—extensive as it was—was beginning to wear thin.

" Will you go ? " repeated Lovell irritably.

" Look here, old fellow," said Jimmy at last, " there's nothing to fight the new fellow about. You tried to play a trick on him and he turned the tables on you. Take it good-temperedly. We can't expect always to score off the Moderns. No need to lose one's temper over it when it goes the other way."

" Who's lost his temper ? "

" You seem to have. Anyhow, let's have tea now, and talk it over after tea."

Jimmy Silver had a well-founded hope that after tea Lovell would be in a better humour. A comfortable meal always had a mollifying effect. But Arthur Edward Lovell was not to be mollified.

" I don't want tea now," he answered. " I've told you I'm going to settle with that Modern cad first. Will you go as my second ? "

" What the dickens am I to say to him—and to the rest ? " exclaimed Jimmy impatiently. " Am I to say that you want to fight the chap because he got the better of a jape, and you can't take it like a sportsman ? "

" Will you go ? "

" No, I won't ! " rapped out Jimmy sharply. " You ought not to want to fight him, and I won't have a hand in any such rot ! "

" I'll ask somebody else, then."

" Look here, Lovell———"

Slam !

The door closed behind Arthur Edward Lovell, with a concussion that rang the length of the passage. His heavy footsteps died away towards the stairs.

" Oh ! " murmured Newcome.

Jimmy Silver compressed his lips.

" I'm getting fed up with this," he said. " If Lovell chooses to play the goat, let him. Let's have tea."

And the three chums sat down to tea—not in the cheerfullest mood.

THE EIGHTH CHAPTER.

Wanted—a Second.

" Morny ! "

" Hallo, old top ! "

Mornington and Erroll were in the quad. when Lovell joined them, with a black brow. They smiled as he came up. As a matter of fact, they had been talking of his misadventure, but his look warned them not to make any reference to it.

" I'm looking for a second," explained Lovell.

" Fight on ? " asked Mornington, with interest.

" Yes."

" Who's the happy victim ? "

" A new Modern cad—Loring."

" Oh ! You're fightin' him ? "

" Yes ; and I want a second. Will you stand by me, and take my challenge to the cad ? "

Mornington glanced at Erroll, who compressed his lips a little. It was easy to see that Erroll disapproved of Lovell's bitterness. Mornington generally took his cue from his chum.

" Hadn't you better think about it first, old scout ? " he asked. " It's rather sudden, isn't it, to drop on a new kid before he's been a couple of hours in the school———"

" I'm not asking you for advice ; I'm asking you to act as my second."

" Oh," said Morny, nettled at Lovell's tone. " In that case, you can ask somebody else."

" That will do."

"Perhaps that will wake you up," exclaimed Lovell. He reached out suddenly, and his finger and thumb closed sharply on the new boy's nose. There was a buzz of excitement from the Fourth. (See page 233.)

Lovell walked away.

"His lordship is wrathy!" grinned Mornington. "I suppose it's time for common mortals to tremble and bow the knee! By gad!" And Mornington shrugged his shoulders.

Lovell's eyes gleamed under his knitted brows as he strode away. His own chums considered him in the wrong, and their opinion was evidently shared by Mornington and Erroll. At any other time that might have had some effect on Lovell, who was really at bottom a good-natured and easy-going fellow. But all the events of the afternoon had combined to sour him, and he was now in a bitter and obstinate temper, and not at all inclined to listen to the gentle voice of reason.

Conroy and Van Ryn and Pons were coming away from the school shop with supplies for tea, and Lovell bore down on them. The three Colonials had not yet heard of his adventure, and were not even aware of the existence of Oliver Loring, the new boy on the Modern side.

" Will one of you fellows second me ? " asked Lovell. " I've got a fight on with a Modern chap."

" Like a bird," answered Conroy at once. " I'm your man ! "

" Thanks."

" Not at all—it's a pleasure," said the Australian junior, laughing. " Who's the man—Dodd, or Cook, or Doyle, or Towle, or the merry Leggett ? "

" A relation of Dodd, I think ; a chap named Loring. He's in the Fourth, in Manders' house."

" Fighting a new chap ? " said Van Ryn, curiously.

" Yes ; a sneaking worm of a Modern ! "

" Well, I'm your man," said Conroy. " I suppose you don't want to fight him before tea ? "

" I want to get it arranged for to-day. Will you cut over and see him ? You'll find him in Manders' house."

" Right you are."

Conroy handed his parcel to Pons.

" I'll wait for you in your study," said Lovell.

" Right."

Conroy started at once for Mr. Manders' house, and Lovell went into the schoolhouse with Van Ryn and Pons, and up to No. 3 study. Both the Colonials were looking rather curious, wondering why Lovell did not call on one of his own study-mates to back him up. However, that was not their business, and they did not remark upon it.

Lovell threw himself into the study arm-chair, while Pons and Van Ryn were getting tea, to wait for Conroy's return.

A fat face looked into the doorway.

Tubby Muffin rolled into the study, and blinked in a very friendly way at the two Colonials. He did not observe Lovell in the armchair for the moment.

" I've dropped in to lend you fellows a hand," he remarked.

" Drop out again," suggested Pons.

" Ahem ! If you're going to cook those sosses, you'd better leave 'em to me. I'm an old hand at frying sosses. I say, I've had an awful time this afternoon," said Tubby Muffin pathetically, " simply awful ! I've been landed in a fearful fight with a crowd of Bagshot bounders. It's exhausted me, and I'm awfully hungry."

" Oh, go ahead," said Pons, relinquishing the frying-pan to the fat Classical. " If you are going to stay to tea, you may as well lend a hand."

" As you're so pressing, old fellow, I will stay to tea," said Tubby Muffin affably. " Leave the sosses to me ; they'll be a dream when I've done 'em. I say, I'm covered with bruises. Fancy me, you know, standing up to Pankley and Poole and Putter, and several other fellows, all at once——"

" It wants some fancying ! " grinned Pons.

" It's true, you know. It was all through Lovell, and his potty idea of taking the new kid to Bagshot and japing him."

" Eh ? "

Tubby Muffin, frying-pan in hand, had his back to the armchair, and was not yet aware that Lovell was seated in the shady corner of the study. Lovell's eyes were beginning to gleam, but he did not speak.

" Loring turned the tables on Lovell," rattled on the fat Classical. " Instead of being planted at Bagshot, you know, he stranded Lovell and me there, and drove off with the trap. Lovell's got to pay for the trap. He, he, he ! "

" Oh ! "

" Lovell's no end waxy," chuckled Tubby

Muffin. "The Bagshot bounders gave him the frog's march. Serve him right! He, he, he! I put up a terrific fight, and got away, leaving the road fairly strewn with them. My knuckles are quite sore with knocking down Bagshot fellows! Fancy that!"

"Ha, ha, ha!"

"I don't see the joke. What are you cackling at?"

"You're the joke, old top," said Van Ryn, laughing. "Keep it up. How many did you leave for dead?"

"Well, I didn't exactly leave 'em for dead," said Tubby cautiously. "They were fairly knocked out, though. If Lovell had put up a fight like me, he'd have got away all right. He hadn't it in him, you know. Lovell's not much of a fighting man. Not like me!"

"You fat idiot!" came a roar from the shady corner.

"Ha, ha, ha!"

Tubby Muffin jumped.

"Wha-a-at—who—oh! is that you, Lovell, old chap? So glad you got away, dear boy. I say, that was a splendid stunt of yours, planting the new kid at Bagshot, wasn't it?"

"Br-r r-r-r!"

"You needn't be waxy with me," said Muffin. "I didn't give you the frog's march, Lovell. And I've had to walk all the way home from Bagshot, same as you did. I've a jolly good mind to thrash that Modern chap. I would only I'm rather tired with knocking down Bagshot fellows. My poor knuckles——"

"You podgy worm!" growled Lovell. "You bolted before they could get near you."

"Look here, Lovell——"

"Oh, shut up!"

"I'll shut up when I please," answered Tubby Muffin independently. "This isn't your study, Lovell. I say, Pong, is this all the sosses?"

"That's the lot."

"What are you fellows going to have, then?"

The study door opened before the chums of No. 3 could reply to that interesting question.

THE NINTH CHAPTER.

Declined With Thanks.

CONROY of the Fourth sauntered into Mr. Manders' house, and made his way to the Fourth-Form quarters. There was a sound of merry voices and laughter from Tommy Dodd's study as the Australian junior tapped at the door.

"Come in!" sang out Tommy Dodd.

Conroy entered.

The three Tommies were at tea—cricket had given them a good appetite, and there was a handsome spread on the table—partly on account of the good appetite and partly in honour of a guest in the study. The guest was Oliver Loring, the new junior.

"Hallo, old bean!" said Tommy Dodd, as the Australian junior came in. "Looking for a tea? If so, you've come to the right shop."

"No; not exactly. I've brought over a challenge."

"Some of your Classical duffers want me to slaughter them?" yawned Tommy. "I'm the man to do it! Who is it wants to be put on the casualty list?"

"You're not the man, Dodd. I'm looking for a new chap, named Loring——"

"Little me?" said the new junior.

Tommy Dodd waved his hand towards the guest.

"That's Loring," he said.

Conroy looked at the new junior. He rather liked Oliver Loring's looks; but he was there on business, and he proceeded with it.

"You know Lovell, of our side, I suppose?" he said.

"I've met him," answered Loring, with a smile; and there was a loud chortle from the three Tommies.

Well, I suppose you've met him, as he's sent you a challenge. I'm his second, and I've come over to make arrangements."

"Does Lovell want to fight me, then?" asked Loring, raising his eyebrows.

"Looks like it, as he's challenged you."

"I don't quite see why. I certainly don't want to fight him."

"Am I to tell him that?" asked Conroy, rather dryly.

The new junior knitted his brows thoughtfully.

"Yes, you can tell him that," he said at last, after a long pause. "I don't see anything to fight about. He tried to jape me, and I turned the joke on him. He ought to take it like a sportsman."

"Certainly he ought!" said Tommy Dodd, warmly. "I'm surprised at Lovell—and at you, too, Conroy, for backing him up in playing the goat like this."

"I don't know what the row's about. Lovell asked me to be his second—that's all I know."

"Then I'll tell you."

And Tommy Dodd explained.

Conroy grinned as he listened.

"Poor old Lovell!" he said. "It was a mess-up, and no mistake. It's no wonder he's waxy, but—but there's nothing for a real fight about. If I'd known——" He paused. "Well, what am I to say to Lovell? He seems bent on a scrap."

"Tell him to think it over, and leave it till he's cooler," said Loring. "If there's an injured party in the case, I'm the man, not Lovell; but I haven't come over to the Classical side breathing fire and slaughter. If he's worried about paying for the trap, I don't mind paying for it, as I had it. But I'm not going to fight him."

"Chaps generally fight when they're asked."

Loring coloured a little.

"I'm not afraid of him, if that's what you mean," he exclaimed. "If he's in the same frame of mind to-morrow, I'll do as he wishes, but I won't fight him to-day, and that settles it. He ought to have more sense."

"Well, I'll tell him that," said Conroy, and he turned to the door.

"And you can tell him from me that he's a silly ass!" exclaimed Tommy Dodd wrathfully, "and you can tell him, too, that if he's spoiling for a fight, I'm his man, if he likes, to-day or to-morrow or any day."

"My dear man, you can tell him all that yourself," said Conroy. "One row is enough at a time. Ta-ta."

And the Australian junior left the study, leaving the Modern juniors looking rather grim.

Oliver Loring glanced at his companions, his colour deepening.

"You fellows——" he began; and stopped.

"Ahem! Another cup of tea?" asked Tommy Dodd.

"Never mind the tea now. Do you fellows think I ought to have taken up that silly ass's challenge?"

"H'm!"

"There's nothing to fight about. By to-morrow the chap will most likely have got over his wax, and will be laughing over the affair himself."

"H'm!"

Silence fell upon the three Tommies.

"If you think I've shown the white feather——" began Loring hotly.

"I—I don't think so," murmured Tommy Dodd. "But I'm pretty certain that every fellow on the Classical side will think so, as soon as they hear of this."

"There's nothing to fight about."

"Oh, I know—but there generally is nothing to fight about. But fellows do fight, all the same."

"The fact is, I don't dislike Lovell," said Loring uncomfortably. "He's a bit of an ass, and seems to have an uncertain temper; but the fact is, I like him rather than otherwise. I don't see why I should hammer him for nothing."

"He's asked you to."

"He will change his mind by to-morrow, most likely."

"And if he doesn't?"

"If he doesn't, he can go ahead, of course. I sha'n't refuse his challenge a second time."

"That's all right, then," said Tommy Dodd placably. "After all, you're not called on to fight your first day here, after a long train journey. You must be a bit tired."

"That wasn't my reason."

"Your reason, old top, is that you're a bit of an ass, and don't know Rookwood manners and customs yet. Never mind; to-morrow will do."

"You think Lovell will want to fight me to-morrow?"

"I know he will."

"Well, if he wants to, let him. Pass the jam."

"My dear man," said Adolphus, with a wave of the hand. "Wander away! Vanish! Give us a rest!" (*See page* 210.)

And the subject was dropped in Tommy Dodd's study; though the three Tommies gave Loring rather curious looks from time to time.

THE TENTH CHAPTER.

Baffled.

Arthur Edward Lovell rose from the armchair as Conroy came into No. 3 on the Classical side.

"Is it fixed?" he asked.

"Not quite."

"I suppose the cad is going to meet me, isn't he?" exclaimed Lovell.

"He doesn't seem very keen on it," answered Conroy. "The fact is, he's declined the challenge, Lovell."

Lovell set his teeth.

"Then he's a coward as well as a rotter!" he said.

"I don't know whether he's suffering from cold feet or not; but I don't see that he's a rotter, Lovell," said the Australian junior. "From what I hear, you were trying to fool him, and he got the best of the bargain. Nothing rotten in that."

Lovell grunted.

"Why not let the matter drop?" suggested Conroy. "There really doesn't seem much reason for two chaps to hammer one another in earnest over a trifling affair like that."

"Rubbish!"

"Well, I think you're playing the goat," said Conroy sharply. "It's not sporting to show so much temper over getting the worst of a joke."

"Oh, rot! I suppose I can lick a Modern cad if I like. And if he won't take my challenge and meet me in the gym., I'll go over and look for him. That will bring him up to the scratch, I think."

And Lovell tramped out of the study.

"Silly ass!" commented Conroy. And the three Colonials sat down to tea—with Tubby Muffin.

Lovell went down the stairs with a black brow, and tramped across the quadrangle to Mr. Manders' house. His wilful mind was made up; the refusal of the new junior to meet him only added fuel to his anger and bitterness.

He did not believe that Loring was "funky," and the refusal seemed to him scornful and contemptuous, as if he were being treated like a fractious child that could be disregarded. He was bitterly determined to show the new junior that he could not be disregarded.

Several Modern juniors were in the hall in Mr. Manders' house when Lovell came in. Lovell's black look was not at all propitiatory, and it drew hostile glances on him at once. Moderns and Classicals were generally ready for a "row," and Towle and Lacy, and McCarthy and the other Modern fellows were justly incensed at a Classical junior stalking into the house as if it belonged to him. There was a howl at once.

"Classical cad!"

"Where did you dig up that face, Lovell?"

"Travel off!"

Lovell gave a glare round.

"I'm looking for a Modern funk!" he retorted.

"No funks on this side—all on the Classical side!" answered Towle.

"Cheeky cad!" roared Lacy. "Kick him out!"

Five or six Modern juniors gathered round Lovell. He backed away a little, clenching his fists.

"Look here——" he began.

"Outside!"

"I'm after a funk——"

"Kick him out!"

"Bump him!"

There was a rush at Lovell, and the Classical junior went spinning through the doorway.

The Moderns roared as he rolled down the steps.

"Ha, ha, ha!"

"Hallo, he's coming back!" yelled Towle. "Look out!"

Lovell, with a flaming face, came charging back furiously. He was too enraged to care for the odds.

But the odds were rather too much for him, all the same. He was collared and whirled back to the door, and hurled out again, amid peals of laughter.

This time he came into collision with a couple of seniors who were coming into the house—Knowles and Catesby of the Sixth.

"What the thump——" gasped Knowles, as the Classical junior crashed into him. "Why —what—what——"

"Yarooh!" howled Lovell.

"Prefect!" piped Towle; and the Modern juniors vanished from the scene as if by magic.

But Lovell, with Knowles' grip on his collar, could not vanish. He wriggled in the grasp of the angry Modern prefect.

"What does this mean, you young hooligan?" exclaimed Knowles, shaking him.

"Let me go, you bully!" growled Lovell.

Knowles let him go, after administering a severe shaking and a cuff or two. Lovell staggered out into the quadrangle rather dizzily.

He made a step towards Mr. Manders' house again, but stopped. It was evidently useless to seek to track out his enemy in the enemy's quarters just then.

With a grim brow he tramped back to the Classical side.

He went into the Hall to tea, not caring to seek the society of his chums at that juncture.

After tea, however, he had to turn up in the end study for prep.

He was not looking amiable when he came in.

"Hallo! Where have you been all this time?" said Jimmy Silver, with forced cheerfulness. Lovell's persistent bad temper was beginning to get on the nerves of the end study.

Lovell gave him a sulky look.

"That cad's refused my challenge," he said.

"Shows his sense," growled Raby.

"Shows he's a funk, you mean."

"Oh, I mean anything you like," said Raby resignedly. "Anything for a quiet life."

"I went over for him, and they chucked me out," said Lovell, glowering. "He's hiding somewhere behind the rest."

"Let him hide, and be bothered to him!" said Newcome.

"For goodness' sake, Lovell, be sensible, and let the matter drop!" exclaimed Jimmy Silver. "This is really getting too much of a good thing. What's the chap done, after all?"

"Of course, I expected you to be down on me," said Lovell savagely. "That won't make any difference, though. The cad will have to turn up to classes to-morrow, and I shall nail him then."

"Are you going to fight him in the form-room, under Bootles' nose?" asked Raby, sarcastically.

"I shall find a chance of cornering the cad where he can't dodge, and can't hide behind a gang of Moderns."

"Br-r-r-r-r!"

Prep. in the end study that evening was not cheerful.

When work was done the Co. were glad to escape downstairs, and leave Arthur Edward Lovell alone with his bad temper.

Lovell ground through his lines for Mr. Bootles after prep. with a dark brow. He scribbled the lines hurriedly and carelessly, and it was not surprising that when he took them to his form-master's study Mr. Bootles gave him a lecture upon slovenliness, and ordered him to write out the imposition over again.

Arthur Edward returned to the end study in a savage mood, choked with wrath. Somewhat unreasonably, he put it all down to the account of the new junior. Oliver Loring was to pay for it all on the morrow, if Lovell had his way.

The repetition of the lines occupied him till bed-time. When the Classical Fourth went to their dormitory Lovell's brow was black and sullen, and it drew smiling glances from the other fellows.

So far as the Classical fellows could see,

Lovell was sulking because he had got the worst of a jape on the Moderns, and they did not conceal their opinion that he was making a fool of himself.

Perhaps, deep down in his heart, Lovell realised that they were right; and that he was, in point of fact, making a fool of himself. But if he realised that, it did not change his humour or lessen the bitterness that rankled in his breast.

He turned in, without answering his chums' cheery "good-night." He was the last in the Classical Fourth dormitory to fall asleep; and when he slept he dreamed of punching Oliver Loring's good-looking face, and rendering it anything but good looking. Arthur Edward Lovell had let the sun go down upon his wrath.

THE ELEVENTH CHAPTER.

Wanted—A Second.

JIMMY SILVER gave his chum a rather anxious glance in the morning when the Classical Fourth turned out at the clang of the rising-bell. Sunshine streamed in at the high windows of the dormitory, and on that sunny morning the Rookwood fellows turned out in cheery spirits. Lovell met Jimmy Silver's eyes, and coloured a little.

Like the prophet of old, Arthur Edward Lovell had said to himself that he did well to be angry; but in spite of himself, as it were, a great deal of his sullen anger had evaporated during the night.

He gave Jimmy Silver a nod and a rather forced grin.

Jimmy smiled.

"Lovely morning!" he remarked. "We can get a run in the quad. before brekker. Pull up your socks!"

"Right-o!" said Lovell.

The Fistical Four were first out of the dormitory, and they came out quite cheerily into the quadrangle. In the distance, the three Tommies could be seen sniffing the morning air; but Jimmy was relieved to note that the new junior was not with them.

Jimmy led the way, and the Fistical Four took their trot round the playing-fields before breakfast. They came in when the bell rang,

THE
GREYFRIARS GALLERY
IN VERSE

By Dick Penfold

No. 9 : Herbert Vernon-Smith

Who, when he came to Greyfriars School,
Refused to knuckle to its rule ?
Who went astray, and played the fool ?
                    THE BOUNDER !

Who sought to settle Wharton's hash,
And made a bold and daring dash
For his position—then went smash ?
                    THE BOUNDER !

Who gambled, smoked, and stayed out late ?
And sowed wild oats at such a rate
We thought " the sack " would be his fate ?
                    THE BOUNDER !

Who, though he fairly went the pace,
Could hold his own in sport or race,
And of his revels showed no trace ?
                    THE BOUNDER !

Who, after many terms, became
Acutely conscious of his shame,
And henceforth strove to play the game ?
                    THE BOUNDER !

Who, former failings swept aside,
Has won such high renown and pride
That seldom is the name applied --
                    THE BOUNDER !

and caught sight of Loring, in company with
Tommy Dodd and Co. now, heading for Mr.
Manders' house. Lovell's eyes glinted at the
sight of him, and he half-stopped ; but Jimmy
drew him on towards the school-house.

" Brekker ! " he said.

And they went in.

Lovell's chums hoped that now he had had
time to calm down, his irritation would disappear, and that the whole affair would drop.
For that reason they wanted to keep him
from coming into contact with Loring. But
when the Fourth Form turned up for morning
lessons there was no choice about the matter.

Oliver Loring came into the form-room
with the rest of the Modern Fourth, looking
fresh and smiling and good-humoured—his
face a contrast to Lovell's clouded looks. His
eyes fell on Lovell, who was already in the
form-room, and was eyeing him grimly. Mr.
Bootles had not yet arrived.

Loring paused a moment, and then, as if
suddenly making up his mind, came over to
the Fistical Four, who were lounging about
their desks till the Form-master came in.

Lovell breathed hard, and his eyes flashed.
For a moment he supposed that the new
junior was approaching him with hostile intent,
and his fists clenched instinctively.

But Loring soon showed that his intention
was not hostile.

" I seem to have annoyed you a good deal
yesterday, Lovell, without intending it," he
said, with a frankness of manner that con-
ciliated three of the four at once. " I'm sorry
if you feel yourself injured in any way. As
you were trying to pull my leg, I thought it
fair play to turn the tables on you if I could.
It was simply a joke."

Lovell eyed him, too surprised to speak.

" If you'd landed me at Bagshot in an
absurd position, it would have been rather
rotten for me," said Loring. " But I hope I
should have taken it as a joke. I don't see
any need for ill-feeling. What do you say to
forgetting about the whole matter, and saying
nothing more about it ? "

Had Lovell's better nature been uppermost
he would certainly have responded to that
appeal ; but the sulky bitterness of the
previous day was not quite ! anished yet.

" You don't want to have the gloves on, what ? " he asked, with a curl of the lip.

" I didn't mean that."

" Oh, I thought you did ! "

" Lovell ! " murmured Jimmy Silver.

Lovell gave him a steely look.

" You needn't chip in, Jimmy. I suppose Loring knows best whether he's afraid."

Loring crimsoned.

" Afraid ! " he exclaimed.

" When a fellow dodges an invitation to the gym., it's generally taken that he's got the wind up," answered Lovell, mockingly.

" He, he, he ! " came from Tubby Muffin.

" You cheeky ass, Lovell ! " shouted Tommy Dodd.

Lovell looked across at him.

" What have you got to say ? " he inquired.

" This much—if you want the gloves on, I'm your man as soon as lessons are over ! " exclaimed Tommy, hotly.

" Is Loring hiding behind you, as he was behind a gang of Modern cads yesterday ? " sneered Lovell.

Loring's eyes flashed.

" I'm not hiding behind anyone ! " he exclaimed. " You seem to misunderstand me, Lovell. I spoke to you as a decent chap ; you've answered me like a cad."

" Hear, hear ! " from Tommy Dodd.

Lovell smiled, a rather evil smile.

" So you're screwing up your courage at last, are you ? " he said. " You're not a funk after all, what ? "

" Shut up, Lovell ! " growled Jimmy Silver, quite ashamed of his chum at that moment.

" Why ? " jeered Lovell. " If the fellow's not a funk, he will put his hands up. A chap on the Classical side doesn't need asking twice. Loring seems to need asking a dozen times, and then he doesn't come up to the scratch."

" Punch his nose, bedad ! " ejaculated Tommy Doyle fiercely. " Sure, if ye don't punch his nose, Loring, I'll punch yours myself."

" Oh, he couldn't punch a rabbit's nose," said Lovell. " There, you cad ! Perhaps that will wake you up ! "

Lovell reached out suddenly, and his finger and thumb closed sharply on the new boy's nose. It was only for an instant. The Classical junior intended to tweak Loring's nose ; but the tweak never came off. Loring's right shot out as if it were suddenly electrified, and Lovell caught it with his chin. He gave a gasp and tumbled over backwards, sprawling at full length on the floor of the form-room.

There was a buzz of excitement from the Fourth.

" Well hit ! " roared Tommy Dodd, in great delight.

" Oh ! " gasped Lovell.

" Ha, ha, ha ! "

Arthur Edward Lovell scrambled to his feet, and in a moment more he would have been upon his enemy. But at that moment Mr. Bootles walked into the form-room.

" Cave ! " muttered Rawson.

Lovell dropped his hands, breathing hard, his eyes burning at the new junior. Mr. Bootles blinked round at the excited Fourth.

" What ?—what ? Why are you not in your places, boys ? Take your seats at once ! What ?—what ? "

" After lessons ! " muttered Lovell, in a choked voice.

Oliver Loring nodded.

The Fourth Form went to their desks.

THE TWELFTH CHAPTER.
Great News !

" LETTER for you, Jimmy ! "

Tubby Muffin came up to the Fistical Four in the quadrangle after dinner. Jimmy Silver and Raby and Newcombe were arguing with Lovell. The latter was unwilling to postpone the combat with Oliver Loring till after the day's lessons ; he said savagely that there was plenty of time before afternoon school. But his three chums put the veto on that.

" You're not going into the form-room with a prize nose and a fancy eye ! " Jimmy Silver declared. " Leave it till after lessons. You'll be able to keep your beauty marks out of sight till the morning, then."

" Do you think that funky cad can hurt me ? " snorted Lovell, contemptuously.

"He doesn't seem funky, and I don't see that he's a cad," answered Jimmy Silver.

"Are you backing that Modern cad up against me?" roared Lovell.

"Not a whit. We're backing you up, though you don't deserve it, as you're acting like a silly, hot-headed chump!" retorted Jimmy Silver. "And you won't lick Loring so easily as you think. I've got an eye for a fellow's form, and I think he looks pretty hefty."

"Oh, you're a dummy!"

"Well, suppose you do wallop him," said Raby. "You don't want him to take a black eye to show Manders in class this afternoon. Whichever way it works out, it's better to leave it till after classes."

Lovell growled.

"Letter for you, Jimmy."

"Oh, bother!" said Jimmy, ungratefully. "Roll away, Tubby."

"But there might be a remittance in it, you know," said Tubby Muffin.

"Bother!"

"If that's how you thank a chap, Jimmy, for bringing you a letter——" said the fat Classical, in an aggrieved tone.

"Oh, if you've brought it, hand it over," said Jimmy.

Tubby Muffin extracted a letter from his pocket, and handed it over, watching the captain of the Fourth eagerly. If there was a remittance in that letter, Tubby intended to be early with a demand for a loan.

Jimmy's face brightened as he glanced at the letter.

"Oh, good!" he exclaimed, as he opened the envelope.

"How much?" gasped Tubby Muffin, breathlessly.

"Eh! It's not a remittance, fathead."

"Why, you said it was good——"

"Ass! It's from my Cousin Phyllis."

"Your Cousin Phyllis!" repeated Tubby Muffin, with indignant scorn. "Bless your Cousin Phyllis! Bother your Cousin Phyllis! If I'd known it was only from a girl, I'd have left it in the rack till it was mouldy. Bother—yarooh—yoop—leave off kicking me, Lovell, you beast."

Tubby Muffin fled.

"What's Phyllis got to say, Jimmy?" asked Lovell, quite amiably.

Jimmy grinned.

Arthur Edward Lovell thought a very great deal of Jimmy's Cousin Phyllis, as did Jimmy himself—and with reason, for Phyllis certainly was a very charming young lady. For the moment, Lovell had forgotten even Oliver Loring and his enmity towards that harmless youth.

"Is she coming?" asked Raby, almost equally interested.

"Saturday?" inquired Newcome.

"Yes."

"Hurray!"

The Fistical Four were evidently pleased. For a whole term it had been arranged that Cousin Phyllis should pay a visit to Rookwood, and that the end study should "spread" itself on that great occasion. There was going to be tea in the study, and a great celebration generally, and canoeing on the river if the weather was fine. And the weather looked like being fine.

"Fixed for Saturday?" asked Lovell, quite cheerily.

"Yes, I asked Phil to make it Saturday, if she could, and she's made it Saturday. She's bringing a couple of friends with her—two school kids she knows at Cliff House, the girls' school near Greyfriars, you remember. You fellows know them, Marjorie Hazeldene and Clara Trevlyn. So it will be quite a merry party."

"Good egg!" said Raby, heartily.

"Phyllis is going to try my canoe," said Lovell. "I hope the weather won't change for the worse."

"And I hope your features will be normal again by Saturday," said Jimmy Silver grimly.

"Eh? Nothing's the matter with my features now, fathead."

"You haven't had your fight with Loring yet."

"Oh!" exclaimed Lovell.

"I'll tell you what," suggested Raby, with a grin. "Make it up with him."

"After he's knocked me down in the form-room!" exclaimed Lovell angrily.

"Well, you were pulling his boko, and that

The gleeful Modern juniors did not have to wait long for the coup-de-grace. Lovell was on his back in a few seconds, laid there by a terrific drive straight from the shoulder. Mornington began to count.
(See page 240.)

makes it even. Besides, you were in the wrong."

"Oh, talk sense!" growled Lovell.

"Look here——"

"I shall lick that Modern cad easily enough. I don't suppose for a moment that he'll leave a mark on me," said Lovell. "Perhaps we'd better have the gloves on, come to think of it."

"You'll certainly have the gloves on," grunted Jimmy Silver.

"I was thinking of the knuckles——"

"Time you thought again, then."

"Well, I agree to having the gloves on," snapped Lovell. "And the sooner it's over the better, I think——"

"Blessed if I believe you can think at all," said Jimmy. "We'd better see Jane, and tip her to give the study an extra rub or two. It can do with it. And we shall want some flowers—the Head's gardener will work that, for a half-crown or so. What shall we put the flowers in on Saturday?"

"We've got the jam-pots," said Raby.

Jimmy sniffed.

"Jam-pots won't do with distinguished visitors," he said. "We had an art pot, only that ass Lovell knocked it over. Bulkeley's got a couple of rather decent vases in his study——"

"He won't lend them to us."

"He might. He may be going out on Saturday, and in that case he can lend them to us after he's gone."

"Ha, ha, ha!"

"Of course, it will have to be understood that Lovell doesn't knock them over——"

Snort from Lovell.

"And we can have Townsend's new square of carpet to put down for the occasion," said Jimmy Silver. "Towny will lend it to us.——"

"More likely he won't."

"He will if we hold his head under the tap till he does."

"Oh! Yes! Quite so."

"We've got to make the place decent, with lady visitors coming; we don't have lady visitors every day. I only hope Lovell won't have a black eye to show them. How the thump shall we explain it, if he does?"

"Accident with a punch-ball is the usual thing."

"You silly chumps!" roared Lovell. "Do you think that Modern worm can give me a black eye?"

"Well, let's hope not. If you only have a swollen nose——"

"I sha'n't have a swollen nose——"

"You can explain that you ran it against something hard, without mentioning that it was Loring's fist. But——"

"Oh, rats!"

Arthur Edward Lovell stalked away in great dudgeon, leaving his chums to discuss the distinguished visit—to which, truth to tell, they gave more thought than to Lovell's forthcoming scrap with Loring of the Modern Fourth.

THE THIRTEENTH CHAPTER.

The Fight.

JIMMY SILVER and Co. did not see Oliver Loring during afternoon lessons, the Moderns being engaged on their own side with Mr. Manders. Jimmy and Raby and Newcome were not, in point of fact, wasting much thought upon him—and Lovell noted it with resentment. His quarrel was not, in his own eyes, the trifling matter his chums seemed to consider it.

After lessons Lovell's brow was clouded as he joined his chums in the corridor.

"You're going to see about it before tea, I suppose?" he said abruptly.

"After tea will do," answered Jimmy. "There's lots of time before Saturday."

"I mean about my fight with Loring."

"Oh! I—I thought you meant about furbishing up the study. All right—I'll cut over and see Loring before tea."

"I'll wait for you," grunted Lovell.

Lovell waited in the doorway of the school-house while Jimmy Silver went to the Modern side. Jimmy came back in a few minutes.

"Six o'clock, in the gym.," he said.

"Somewhere quieter would have been better," growled Lovell. "Some dashed prefect may take it on himself to interfere, if there's some real thumping."

"My dear man, I should take it upon myself to interfere, without waiting for a prefect, if there was anything too strong," answered Jimmy Silver.

"Oh, you're a silly ass!"

"Fathead!"

With that exchange of compliments, the chums parted for the time, and did not meet again till tea-time in the end study. Jimmy spent the interval in giving that celebrated apartment a few artistic touches. It was astonishing the number of things that required putting away, in readiness for the clean sweep that the boys' maid was to be induced to make—for a financial consideration—before Saturday. It was generally agreed that the end study was to be as spick and span as a new pin—chiefly for Cousin Phyllis's sake, but also to show Marjorie and Clara that boys' studies were quite as neat and tidy as the girls' studies at Cliff House.

After that useful personage, the boys' maid, had done her best, and the Fistical Four had done their best, and Bulkeley's vases had been borrowed for flowers, and Towny's new carpet for the floor, Jimmy considered that the end study would equal anything at Cliff House School. And there would be no need to mention that the study wasn't always in that glorious state.

After tea there was a general adjournment to the gym.

The Fistical Four turned up there in good time—and most of the Classical Fourth followed them. Lovell's quarrel with Oliver Loring was not taken very seriously by anybody but Lovell himself, but everyone was interested in a fight, which promised to be unusually tough. Lovell was well known as a fighting-man, and the general opinion of Loring was that he was "hefty." As Loring was a Modern, all the Classicals bestowed their very best wishes upon Arthur Edward Lovell; but Oliver Loring had an equally hearty backing on the other side of Rookwood.

Lovell's "row" with Loring, and the fight on his second day at Rookwood, had brought the new fellow into a prominence not usual at all for new fellows. He might have gone a term with half the fellows hardly knowing his name. Now he was quite well known to all the lower school, and he owed his celebrity to Lovell.

Nearly all the Fourth, Classical and Modern, turned up in the gym., with a contingent of the Third and the Second. Adolphus Smythe and Co., of the Shell, came loftily along, to look on, and to make bets among their nutty selves on the result.

"They've brought him up to the scratch," remarked Lovell, with a sneer, as Oliver Loring came in with the three Tommies.

"Rot!" said Raby. "The chap's got pluck enough, from his looks."

"He's acted like a funk!"

"Bosh!"

"Look here, Raby——"

"Keep your wool on," said Raby. "You're not going to fight me, old scout. Keep it for Loring. He looks as if he can do with all you can give give him."

"I expect I shall smash him up in a couple of rounds."

"Blessed are those that don't expect—they don't get disappointed," grinned Raby.

"Ready!" called out Tommy Dodd.

"Ready and waiting," growled Lovell.

"We won't keep you waiting any longer," said Tommy, tartly. "Off with your jacket, Oliver."

Jimmy Silver helped Lovell off with his jacket, and on with the gloves, while the Tommies were attending to their champion. Lovell was angry and restless, and eager to begin. Loring was quite calm and cool, but he had a determined look.

"Keep cool, old scout," murmured Jimmy to his principal.

"Who's not cool?" snapped Lovell.

"I mean, if you lose your temper, you're giving away chances."

"Who's losing his temper?"

Jimmy compressed his lips, and did not answer. He was feeling exasperated, but it was not a time to irritate Lovell. He was only too likely to lose his temper as it was; and that might easily spell defeat for him.

"Morny will keep time," said Tommy Dodd. "Trot out your ticker, Morny."

"I'm your pippin!" answered Mornington.

He took out his handsome watch, as the crowd of juniors cleared back, leaving a ring for the champions.

" Ready ? "

" Quite ! " said Loring quietly.

" Of course ! " grunted Lovell.

" Seconds out of the ring. Time ! "

" Go it, ye cripples ! " said Conroy.

" Go it, Lovell ! "

" Pile in, Loring ! "

The two combatants were already going it, without waiting for the encouraging shouts from the rival juniors of Rookwood.

Fifty fellows, at least, were crowded round them, watching eagerly, both Classicals and Moderns, with a keen desire to see their representative victorious.

The thick ring of onlookers screened the antagonists from general view, and as bouts with the gloves were common enough at Rookwood, the fight attracted no special attention.

Valentine Mornington kept his eyes on his watch.

The fight was according to rules, as were most of the little affairs of the kind at Rookwood.

Lovell was attacking hotly, and most of the onlookers considered that he was having things all his own way. Loring had to give ground several times, though he was very nimble in recovering it. He seemed to be contenting himself with defence—which gave an impression that he was not " up " to attack. But Tommy Dodd shook his head sagely.

" Oliver's taking his measure," he murmured to Cook and Doyle. " Oliver will wake up presently."

" Time ! "

First round was over, and nobody a penny the worse, as Raby remarked. But in the second round matters were enlivened a little.

Lovell's face was growing darker and darker, and his eyes had an angry gleam. He forced the fighting recklessly, and several heavy blows came home on the Modern champion's face. But as Lovell, spent by a furious attack, hung fire, so to speak, Oliver Loring closed in on him with right and left, and the Classical junior went spinning.

Crash !

" Time ! "

The call of time came fortunately for Lovell ; for he could never have recovered in time to avoid being counted out.

He was looking heavy and groggy as Jimmy Silver helped him to a seat and sponged his heated face.

He gasped for breath, blinking dizzily.

The Modern juniors were grinning now with delightful anticipation. They had hoped, but hardly ventured to believe, that a new fellow would succeed in getting the upper hand of so well-known a fighting-man as Lovell. But their hopes were rising now ; indeed, Leggett remarked that it looked like a " dead cert."

Jimmy Silver attended to his principal, but forbore from uttering the words that were upon his lips. It was not much use warning Lovell to keep his temper, and give himself a chance. Lovell seemed bent on losing his temper and losing the fight ; and any word of advice in his present mood would only have rendered that result more certain.

" Time ! "

Lovell stepped up at the call of time with alacrity enough. But his seeming advantage in the earlier rounds had vanished now. Oliver Loring had taken his measure, as Tommy Dodd described it. The two juniors were, as a matter of fact, about equal in strength and science, and certainly equal in pluck ; and had Lovell been in his usual mood, it might have been " anybody's " fight. But with Lovell in a hasty, savage, passionate temper, the result was hardly doubtful. It gave Loring an advantage he could not fail to make the most of.

The Classical junior forced the fighting again, though every fellow present knew that he ought to have stalled off his opponent and given himself time to recover. Close on the finish of the round, the unlucky Lovell had pumped himself out, and the Modern junior pushed the fighting home. Jimmy Silver set his lips as he looked on.

Lovell was in the wrong—wilfully unreasonable—and Jimmy knew it. But Lovell was his chum ; and it was bitter for Jimmy to see him knocked right and left like this. It was through his own folly, too ; he would have

Jimmy Silver and Raby linked hands to make a " carriage," and Phyllis was rushed away towards the school. (See *page* 251.)

had at least an equal chance if he had kept cool. Jimmy's face grew darker as he watched.

Crash !

Arthur Edward Lovell was down again, and again the call of time came luckily to save him from being counted out. Jimmy Silver raised him, and made a knee for him in grim silence.

THE FOURTEENTH CHAPTER.

Down and Out.

"LOOKS like a win for us, what?" smiled Tommy Dodd to his comrades.

"It does!" grinned Cook.

"Bedad, and it does intirely!" chuckled Tommy Doyle. "Hurray for us!"

"Modern side wins!" howled Leggett.

Lovell's eyes blazed.

"They've not won yet, Jimmy!" he muttered. "I'm good for licking that cad, anyhow. Hang him!"

Jimmy was silent.

"They're counting on a win already," said Lovell, bitterly. "Let 'em wait a bit! I'll knock that rotter out, or——" He gasped and broke off.

"Go in and win, old fellow," said Jimmy.

It was all he could say.

"Time!"

In the fourth round it was clear enough to all that Lovell was getting the worst of it. He had realised his mistake now, and was trying to keep cool; but it was too late. He was dizzy with the punishment he had already received, and he seemed in trouble for breath.

In spite of the gloves, considerable damage had been done. Lovell's nose was swelling already, and was pretty certain to swell a good deal more. Loring had not escaped scatheless, either.

"Fourth round!" smiled Tommy Dodd. "What's the betting that it's the last?"

"Last but one!" opined Tommy Cook.

"And our man's winning!"

"You bet!"

"Go it, Modern!" roared a score of voices.

Loring was attacking all the time now, and Lovell stood up gallantly to the punishment he was getting. It seemed to Jimmy Silver, looking on, that the Modern junior was not hitting as hard as he might have done. It was odd enough that he should be sparing his adversary; but it certainly seemed to the captain of the Fourth that he was doing so.

Once or twice, when there was an opening for a drive that would have sent Lovell crashing, Loring did not put it in—and certainly he was wide-awake enough. When Mornington called "Time!" again, Loring dropped his hands at once and stepped back.

Lovell staggered almost blindly.

"Better call it off, old chap," Raby whispered.

Lovell gave him a bitter look.

"Do you think I'm beaten?" he almost hissed.

"Well, you see——"

"You're a fool, Raby!"

"Well, if you come to that, you are beaten, and everybody in the gym. can see it," said Raby tartly. "What's the good of playing the goat?"

"I'll jolly well show you."

"Hallo, here comes that chap. It's not time yet," said Newcome.

Oliver Loring was stepping across towards them, with a slight flush on his face. Lovell stared at him.

"I've had enough of this, if you have, Lovell," said Loring. "What's the good of going on? It's about nothing. Let's call it a draw and shake hands over it."

"I'll shake hands with you when I've licked you, if you like."

"You refuse, then?"

"Yes, you cad!"

"It's as you like, of course."

Loring stepped back to his own side.

"You see that!" muttered Lovell. "He knows I'm going to lick him, and he wants to crawl out of it."

"He knows he's going to lick you, you ass!" exclaimed Jimmy Silver, out of all patience. "He wanted to let you down lightly."

"Oh, you're a silly fool!"

"Time!" came from Valentine Mornington.

Lovell almost staggered as he toed the line again. It was clear to everyone but himself that he was "done." It was, in point of fact, clear enough to himself, but he was determined not to admit it.

"Now for the coup-de-grace!" murmured Tommy Dodd.

The gleeful Modern juniors did not have to wait long for it. Lovell was on his back in a few seconds, laid there by a terrific drive straight from the shoulder.

Mornington began to count.

ALMOST IN THE TWINKLING OF AN EYE THE CANOE WAS CAPSIZED!

It seemed impossible that the canoe could live through such a plunge as that which lay before it!

Once, twice, Lovell made an effort to rise, but he sank back again. All eyes were upon him.

"Eight—nine——"

Lovell struggled, and half rose, sinking back from the weakness of utter exhaustion.

"Out!"

"Modern side wins!" yelled Towle.

"Hurray!"

"Bravo, Loring!"

There was a rush of the Moderns to surround the victor, to clap him on the back and congratulate him. Jimmy and Raby and Newcome helped Lovell to his feet. He hung upon them helplessly. He had gone beyond his strength, and he was utterly spent.

"This way, old chap," said Jimmy. "Sit down! That's better."

"I—I'm not licked."

"You're counted out, old fellow. Don't worry about that."

"I should have been up in another second," gasped Lovell, desperately. "I could go on now. I'm feeling all right now."

It was so evident that Lovell, far from feeling all right, was utterly at the end of his tether, that his chums could only look at him in silence. Oliver Loring came towards them.

"Well, it's all over," he said cheerily. "Give us your fist, Lovell. No malice on either side, what?"

Had there been a sign of crowing in the new junior's manner, Jimmy Silver would have hated him at that moment. But there was nothing of the kind. He was simply frank and kind, though his face was showing heavy marks of the blows that had fallen on it.

Lovell did not move.

Loring was holding out his hand; the Classical junior did not seem to see it.

"Lovell!" whispered Newcome.

Lovell raised his hand. Instead of shaking hands with Loring, however, he clenched his fist, and knocked the extended hand aside.

"Oh!" ejaculated Loring.

"That for you," said Lovell. "You've got the best of me this time. I'll lick you another time, you cad!"

Loring looked at him steadily.

"You won't!" he said quietly. "I shall not fight you again, Lovell.. I've come to Rookwood to work, not to fight every day with a hot-headed fellow about nothing. I'm willing to be friends if you are; if you're not, keep your distance, and let me alone. That's all."

And Oliver Loring walked away, rejoining the three Tommies, and leaving the gym. with them.

Lovell gritted his teeth.

"Come away," said Jimmy Silver, shortly.

The defeated champion left the gym., leaning heavily on Jimmy's arm.

Lovell did not appear in the common-room that evening.

He remained in the end study, with a brooding bitterness in his heart that was worse than the aches and pains that were the result of the conflict. He had not only been surpassed in prowess, but in generosity and good feeling; and he knew it, and he knew that his chums knew it. It was a bitter evening for the junior who was "down and out."

THE FIFTEENTH CHAPTER.

Bitter Blood.

Mr. Bootles fixed his eyes upon Arthur Edward Lovell in the form-room the following morning with a very stern glance. Lovell had contrived to avoid the form-master's eyes till then, but there was no avoiding them any longer. The "beauty marks" on Arthur Edward's face were very conspicuous, and Mr. Bootles, short-sighted as he was, could not miss them.

"Lovell," said Mr. Bootles severely.

"Yes, sir," grunted Lovell.

"You have been fighting again."

"Yes."

"On Wednesday," said Mr. Bootles in his most magisterial manner, "I gave you an imposition, Lovell, for coming into school in a disgraceful state of untidiness, following a fight. To-day you again show the signs of personal conflict, Lovell. I am afraid that you are a very quarrelsome boy."

Silence.

"This time, Lovell, I feel compelled to

cane you. You will stand out before the form," said Mr. Bootles, taking his cane from his desk.

Lovell tramped out sullenly.

Up jumped Oliver Loring in his place.

"If you please, Mr. Bootles—sir——"

"What have you to say, Loring?"

"It was I who was fighting with Lovell, sir."

"Good man!" murmured Jimmy Silver, approvingly.

Lovell gave the Modern junior a dark glance. Loring had owned up in the frankest way to take his share of the blame; but possibly Lovell would have been better pleased if the Modern had sat silent and allowed him to face the music alone. It would have helped to justify him in his bitter dislike of the new fellow.

"Dear me," said Mr. Bootles, blinking at Oliver Loring over his spectacles. "Is that the case, Loring? I did not observe—yes, I can see now that you have been fighting. You may step out before the class."

Oliver Loring joined Lovell at the form-master's desk.

Swish! Swish!

Two light swishes met the case; Mr. Bootles did not want to be hard on a new boy; and so Lovell got off more lightly in consequence. The juniors returned to their seats—one of them smiling, and the other scowling.

The Moderns were only with Mr. Bootles for first lesson that morning, after which they marched off to Mr. Manders' house. Lovell's eye lingered on the new junior as he went with the rest; Loring walked out cheerfully, evidently not feeling much the effects of the previous day's "scrap." That observation added to Lovell's bitterness, for he was feeing the effects very much indeed. His head ached, his swollen nose was very painful, and he had a weariness in his limbs that was new to him, and very depressing.

Lovell was in hot water several times that morning. His prep. had been carelessly scamped in the evening before, as was natural, considering how he had been feeling at the time. But Mr. Bootles, as was also natural, expected a junior to get his work done

whether he was bent on a "scrap" or not; and he was very severe with Lovell, who blundered through his construe in a way that made even Tubby Muffin grin.

When morning classes were dismissed, the Fistical Four came out into the sunny quad, not quite in their usual cheery spirits.

Lovell's chums were concerned for him; and his tart temper made it necessary to be very diplomatic with him. He seemed ready to quarrel with his best pals at a word.

He "mooched" away by himself after a time, and Jimmy and Raby and Newcome put in the interval before dinner at garnishing the end study for the great celebration on Saturday.

Lovell's gloomy face at the dinner-table drew Mr. Bootles' attention again. The form-master gave him a very disapproving look.

"Lovell," he said, "you are looking very sullen."

Lovell gave him a look that was something more than sullen.

"This is not right, my boy," said Mr. Bootles, in his kind but ponderous way, "I had occasion to punish you this morning, Lovell; but you should not be sullen. Sullenness is unmanly. Kindly do not look sullen, Lovell."

Some of the Classical Fourth grinned.

Lovell's face crimsoned, but it was quite out of his power to look less sullen. He looked rather more so than less, after Mr. Bootles' remarks. He was, in fact, feeling thoroughly out of sorts, and "up against" everything in general. If he had beaten the Modern junior in the fight in the gym., his ill-humour would probably have evaporated on the spot; but his defeat rankled deeply and bitterly.

After dinner Newcome and Raby went back to decorative work in the end study. Jimmy Silver would gladly have gone with them, but he felt impelled to bestow his company on Lovell in the quad.

Arthur Edward was not a cheerful companion just then. He tramped in silence under the beeches for quite a long time.

When he spoke at last to his patient companion, it was in a bitter tone.

"I'm feeling rotten, Jimmy."

Fifty fellows, at least, were crowded in the gym, watching eagerly, both Classicals and Moderns, with a keen desire to see their representative victorious. (*See page* 238.)

"I know, old chap," answered Jimmy, softly. "It will wear off, though."

"I should have licked that Modern cad if I'd been more careful."

Reading from left to right : Top row—A. E. Lovell ; G. Raby ; Tommy Dodd ; Kit Erroll ; Conroy ; Val Mornington. (Sitting—Tommy Cook ; Teddy Grace ; Jimmy Silver, captain ; Selwyn ; Tommy Doyle.

"No reason why you shouldn't have. But, after all, you put up a good fight."

"I'm going to lick him next time."

Jimmy did not answer that.

"He says he won't fi ht me again," said Lovell savagely. "I'll jolly well make him. I shall feel more fit to-morrow——"

"Phyllis will be here to-morrow."

"Oh! I'd—I'd forgotten." Lovell coloured "I'll leave the cad till next week then."

"I wish you'd get this out of your mind, old chap," said Jimmy. "I'm blessed if I can see what the fellow's done. It's not like you to e down on a chap like this for nothing, or next to nothing."

"It's because I'm inconsiderate," said Lovell, bitterly. "Because I'm unfeeling, you know."

Jimmy compressed his lips, and did not reply.

He was beginning to wonder how long he would be able to stand this new temper of Lovell's withou a "row."

The captain of the Fourth was glad when the bell rang for classes that afternoon. Lovell was heavy and despondent during classes, and came in for some more sharp words from Mr. Bootles. He listened to them with the sulkiness that seemed now to have become part of his nature.

But by tea-time Lovell seemed a good deal more like his old self. His nose was still a prominent feature ; but he was recovering from the effects of the milling in the gym. During tea he was silent and thoughtful, and he spoke abruptly when the meal was over.

"Jimmy!"

"Hallo, old scout."

"I've got over that mauling now."

"Glad to hear it."

"I played the fool yesterday," said Lovell. "I lost my temper. If I'd kept cool, I could have made rings round that cad Loring. He's not much of a boxer, that I can see."

"He seemed fairly good to me," remarked Raby, with a touch of sarcasm.

"He didn't to me. I don't think he's got over much pluck, either."

"Rot!" was Raby's rejoinder to that.

"Well, that's my opinion," said Lovell, savagely, "and I'm going to put it to the test. I'm going to tackle him again to-day. No need to wait till next week."

"You want an eye to match that nose, for Phyllis to see to-morrow!" exclaimed Newcome.

"Look here, Lovell, there's been enough of this rot," said Jimmy Silver impatiently. "Loring won't fight you again to-day. Why should he? He's got other things to do. He didn't come to Rookwood to have a fight on his hands every day. Let the fellow alone."

"I'm going to make him."

"Then you can play the goat on your own," exclaimed Jimmy wrathfully. "We sha'n't have a hand in it."

"Please yourself."

Lovell left the study. He tramped away to Mr. Manders' house, and came upon the three Tommies and Oliver Loring in the quadrangle. He stopped.

"I'm looking for you, Loring," he said grimly, without a glance at the new junior's companions.

"Well, here I am," answered Loring, good-humouredly.

"I want you to meet me in the gym. this evening."

Loring eyed him.

"Another fight, do you mean?" he asked.

"Yes."

"Then I'm not coming," aid Loring decidedly. "I've had enough of that; and you ought to have had enough, too."

"Are you afraid?"

Loring shrugged his shoulders.

"I've fought you once," he said. "The

fellows can judge whether I'm afraid or not. I won't fight you again, and that's flat. I'm fed up."

Lovell's eyes glittered.

"If you don't come I'll brand you as a coward up and down Rookwood," he said, between his teeth.

"Go ahead, then. I don't think Rookwood will believe you," said Loring. "I'll chance it, anyway."

The Classical junior clenched his fists. He seemed inclined to make an attack on the Modern fellow there and then. Tommy Dodd interposed.

"You're playing the goat, Lovell," he said. "Why can't you take a licking like any other fellow? What do you want another for? Look here, you'd better keep on your own side of the quad. If you come over here looking for trouble, you'll get bumped."

"Funk!" said Lovell, with an aggressive glare at Oliver Loring.

"Rats!" answered Loring, unmoved.

Lovell, with a black brow, tramped back to the schoolhouse, followed by a curious, half compassionate look from Oliver Loring, and a chortle from the three Tommies.

THE SIXTEENTH CHAPTER.

The Distinguished Visitors.

"GLORIOUS weather!" said Jimmy Silver, with great satisfaction.

It was Saturday morning.

Bright sunshine streamed down on the green old quadrangle of Rookwood School, and glimmered on dusky ivy and grey old stone. Jimmy Silver and Raby and Newcome walked in the quad after breakfast, in cheery humour. Lovell had not joined them as usual. He had not spoken to his chums since tea-time the previous evening.

"What time will Phyllis and Marjorie and Clara be here?" asked Newcome.

"Two-thirty train. We're bagging a trap to fetch them from the station," said Jimmy cheerfully. "We're going to have a jolly good afternoon. I've heard from Tubby that Bulkeley is going over to Latcham with Neville, so there'll be no difficulty about borrowing those vases."

" Good ! "

" Towny has agreed to let us have the carpet. The study will look ripping."

" All except Lovell's nose."

" Well, his nose is getting better—it's not quite so impressionist this morning. I hope his temper will get better, too. But Phyllis will soon put him in a good temper," said Jimmy. " That will be all right. It's rather rotten his being on such terms with Loring, though. Tommy Dodd will want to speak to Phyllis, and Loring chums with him, and they're bound to be together. Still, I suppose Lovell will behave himself."

" Let's hope so ! " grunted Raby.

There were strained relations in the end study now. Lovell did not speak to his chums before lessons that morning ; and in the form-room he avoided looking at them.

It looked as if the Co. were now among the fellows against whom he was nursing a sense of injury—and the Co. were growing rather restive under it. They could not quite understand Lovell of late. It was quite unlike him to nourish malice against anyone, and now he seemed to be feeling little else but malice.

At dinner the same state of affairs subsisted. After dinner, Arthur Edward Lovell was leaving the schoolhouse by himself, with a gloomy brow, when Jimmy Silver made up his mind to break the ice. He caught his old chum by the arm, as cheerily as if there had been no unpleasantness.

" You coming to the station ? " he asked.

Lovell started and coloured.

" I——" he stammered.

" You see, only two can go, or there won't be room in the trap for the distinguished visitors," explained Jimmy. " Newcome's going to fix up the flowers in the study, and Raby's agreed to manage the carpet. So I want you to come to the station."

Arthur Edward Lovell gulped something down.

" I—I'll come ! " he gasped.

" Right-o ! "

It was old Mack's trap that was destined to have the honour of conveying the distinguished visitors from Coombe Station. Old Mack at first would not hear of it—owing to the impossibility of trusting the horse in the hands of Fourth-Form juniors. After certain coin of the realm, however, had passed from Jimmy Silver's possession into old Mack's, it appeared that the horse could be trusted to the juniors, if they were very careful. Jimmy Silver solemnly undertook to be very careful indeed ; and he drove away with Lovell in the trap, in great spirits.

" Like to drive, Lovell ? " asked Jimmy, generously, as they bowled down the lane.

" Take it in turns," said Lovell, " I'll drive back."

" Oh ! "

" You see, we shall have to be careful, with the girls in the trap," explained Lovell.

Jimmy Silver looked at him. Apparently Lovell considered that the girls would be safer with the ribbons in his hands — which was not in the least the opinion of Jimmy Silver.

But Jimmy acquiesced. Lovell was to be " given his head " that day, in the hope of restoring his customary good temper during the distinguished visit.

On the way to the station, Arthur Edward gave his nose several dabs, as if to feel how it was getting on.

" How does it look, Jimmy ? " he inquired, as they drove into the village.

" Eh ! How does what look ? Coombe ? "

" No, you ass—my nose ! "

" Oh, your nose ! First chop."

" Is it very red ? "

" A pretty pink," answered Jimmy.

" Does it look as if it's been punched ? " demanded Lovell.

" Well, as if it's been—ahem—tapped," said Jimmy.

Lovell grunted.

Jimmy Silver brought the trap to a halt at the station with a clatter and a flourish. They were in ample time for the train ; Jimmy had taken care of that.

They waited ten minutes on the platform ; an interval chiefly spent by Arthur Edward Lovell in squinting into the cracked mirror on the automatic machine there, getting views of his nose from all sides.

" Here it comes ! " exclaimed Jimmy Silver, at last.

The train stopped.

Three charming faces, surmounted by three

" Hallo, Phil, old girl ! " cried Jimmy Silver, opening the carriage door. " How do you do, Marjorie—and you, Clara ? Ripping afternoon, isn't it ? Give me your bag—and your sunshade—Lovell, will you take Phyllis's sunshade——" Would he ? (*See this page.*)

charming hats, looked out of a carriage window.

Jimmy Silver cut across the platform, and had the carriage door open in a twinkling.

Lovell, with a face as red as his unhappy nose, followed him more slowly.

" Hallo, Phil, old girl ! How do you do, Marjorie—and you, Clara ? Ripping afternoon, isn't it ? Give me your bag—and your sunshade—Lovell, will you take Phyllis's sunshade ? "

Would he ?

Arthur Edward Lovell grinned with delight as he took Cousin Phyllis's sunshade, forgetful at that moment of even his haunting nose.

If Phyllis and Marjorie and Clara noticed that Lovell's nose presented an unusual aspect of rich colouring, they did not allow the fact to appear. So far as the three girls were concerned, Lovell might as well not have had a nose at all.

"Trap outside, Phil," said Jimmy Silver, rather loftily, "just room for five in it."

"How very nice!" said Cousin Phyllis.

"You kids are insured, I hope?"

"Insured?" exclaimed Marjorie and Clara.

"Yes; Lovell's going to drive."

"Ha, ha, ha!"

"You—you frabjous ass, Jimmy!" exclaimed Lovell, "I—I—I mean—ha, ha, ha!"

"This way," said Jimmy Silver.

Quite a merry party marched off the platform, Jimmy taking charge of Marjorie and Clara, and leaving Phyllis to the escort of Arthur Edward. Lovell stole a sidelong glance at Phyllis's pretty face. He was silent, thinking hard, as they came off the platform, and left the station; but in the street outside he found his voice.

"I—I——" he began.

Cousin Phyllis looked at him.

"Here's the trap!" said Jimmy Silver.

"I—I knocked it!" gasped Lovell.

"You knocked the trap!" exclaimed Phyllis, in surprise.

"Nunno! My—my nose—I knocked my n-n-nose——"

"Goodness gracious! You knocked your nose on the trap?" asked Phyllis. "I hope it was not hurt much."

"N-n-not on the trap! I—I just knocked it," said Lovell, "against something hard, you know."

"I'm so sorry!" murmured Phyllis.

"Against — against — against something hard," gasped Lovell, "I—I knocked it You—you see, I—I——"

"All aboard!" sang out Jimmy Silver.

Phyllis was smiling as Arthur Edward assisted her into the trap. Perhaps she guessed the nature of the "something hard" against which Lovell had knocked his nose. But Arthur Edward, feeling that the matter was

now satisfactorily explained, was greatly relieved, as the trap bowled away down the leafy lane to Rookwood School.

THE SEVENTEENTH CHAPTER.

Adolphus's Fault.

RABY and Newcome had not quite finished giving finishing touches to the end study when the distinguished visitors arrived. It was probable that if the arrival had been delayed another hour or two, they would not quite have finished. Raby had a duster in his hand, and a considerable amount of dust on his person, and Newcome was giving a final rub to the kettle with an oily bike rag, when there were footsteps and merry voices in the passage. Phyllis and Marjorie and Clara dawned on Raby and Newcome — who reddened through dust and smudges as they greeted them.

They greeted them rather incoherently, and escaped to get cleaned. Lovell lighted sticks in the grate to boil the kettle, being firmly under the impression that what lady visitors always wanted, first of all, was a cup of tea. Phyllis and Co. were greatly interested in the study. They admired, especially, the handsome vases of flowers, and the bright new carpet. Marjorie thought it was really creditable to the juniors that they kept those handsome vases in the study without breaking them—and Clara was astonished that the carpet stood the strain without showing more signs of trouble. Jimmy Silver devoutly hoped that Bulkeley of the Sixth would not come in before the visitors departed. It would have been very awkward if he had come along inquiring for his vases.

Arthur Edward Lovell was in great spirits now. His recent sulkiness had rolled off like a cloud before the sunshine.

He quite distinguished himself with the tea. Owing to a slight oversight, he made it without putting any tea into the pot, and it came out colourless—much to Lovell's surprise, and to the amusement of the girls. He made it a second time with more success. It was doubtless some confusion of mind that caused him to put in salt instead of sugar. But the third time the tea was made it was a triumphant success, and Phyllis and Co. declared that they had never tasted nicer tea—much to Arthur Edward's gratification.

Raby and Newcome turned up, spotless and smiling, in time for the tea—owing to the number of times it had been made. There was a slight difficulty about crockery, but that was overcome, Jimmy Silver slipping out quietly and returning with a bunch of saucers in one hand and a string of cups on the fingers of the other. Heavy footsteps followed him to the end study, and the wrathful face of Higgs of the Fourth looked in.

"Look here——!" bawled Higgs.

Then three pretty faces dawned on Higgs, and he stuttered and vanished.

Higgs, apparently, was the owner of some of the crockery.

After the tea had been disposed of, four cheery juniors and three smiling girls walked out of the end study in a merry company. Tubby Muffin joined them in the passage—Tubby having plenty of nerve—and other fellows eyed them enviously.

Envious glances, too, fell upon them in the quadrangle. Miss Dolly, the Headmaster's daughter, rushed up to greet Phyllis, and remained with her—giving Tubby Muffin a decidedly "marble" eye when that fat youth proffered himself as attendant cavalier.

Tommy Dodd was in the quadrangle with Oliver Loring, and he came up to speak to Phyllis. Loring followed him a step, and then stopped and raised his hat to the girls from a distance. Arthur Edward Lovell's brow darkened at the sight of the new junior.

Phyllis Silver glanced at him.

Perhaps she wondered, for a moment, why Tommy Dodd's friend did not come up with him. Loring had excellent reasons, which Phyllis was not likely to guess. He sauntered away while Tommy was chatting with the girls and the Classical juniors, and disappeared out of the gates.

Loring's good-looking face was a little dissatisfied, for once, as he went.

He would have liked very much to be presented to the three girls, and Tommy Dodd would have introduced him, as a matter of course, but for Lovell's unreasonable enmity, which kept Oliver at a distance.

Indeed, Tommy would have done so, anyway, forgetful of Lovell and his feud, had not Loring wisely walked on.

"Now for the river," said Jimmy Silver cheerily.

"You'll like my canoe, Phyllis," said Lovell eagerly, as they walked towards the gates.

Phyllis smiled and nodded.

"I'm sure I shall," she assented.

"It's really a little corker, you know——"

"I'd better come in the canoe, I think, Lovell!" remarked Tubby Muffin.

Lovell gave the fat Classical a glare.

"It's not an Atlantic liner," he answered. "It wouldn't stand your weight."

And Lovell quickened his pace, hoping to leave the fat Classical behind. But Tubby was not to be left. He was rolling cheerfully after the Co. when they arrived at the river.

"How beautiful!" exclaimed Phyllis, as they came through the trees, and the shining waters burst upon their view.

"Topping, isn't it?" said Miss Clara.

"Hallo, there's Smythey out," remarked Raby.

There was a boat on the river, with Smythe of the Shell, and Howard and Tracy, in it. Howard and Tracy were rowing in a leisurely way, and the lofty Adolphus was reclining in the stern.

Adolphus put his eyeglass to his eye, and surveyed the merry party on the bank.

"Jimmy Silver's cousin, begad!" yawned Adolphus. "Cheeky young cad, Silver. He knows perfectly well that I'd like to talk to his cousin, and he plants her with that heavy lout, Lovell, instead. Hard cheese on the poor gal."

"Awf'ly hard!" grinned Tracy, with a wink at Howard.

"They're lookin' at us," said Smythe, with a satisfied smile. "A well-dressed chap always attracts a gal's eye. I really wonder how they can stand those young Fourth-Form ruffians, by gad. Put in, you chaps, an' we'll ask 'em into the boat—what!"

"They won't leave Silver's gang," said Tracy.

"My dear chap," said Adolphus, with a superior smile, "you leave it to me. Two to one in half-sovs. that I bag one of them."

" Done ! "

The boat pulled in a little. Lovell had taken his canoe from the boat-house and run it out. Phyllis stepped lightly into the little craft, and Lovell followed.

Jimmy Silver and Co. walked on by the path along the river. They were at a little distance by the time the Shell boat came up.

Adolphus rose, and lifted his straw very gracefully to Phyllis. The other girls were out of reach, as it were, and it was clear that if Adolphus was to win his half-sov. by " bagging " one of them, the one would have to be Phyllis. But Adolphus was not troubled with doubts. He had full faith in his own fascinating personality.

" Good-afternoon, Miss Silver," he chirruped. " How delightful to see you at Rookwood again. How well you are lookin'."

Phyllis nodded rather curtly.

It would have astonished Adolphus to learn with what complete indifference he was regarded by Jimmy Silver's cousin.

" Keep clear ! " grunted Lovell.

" Did you speak, dear boy ? " asked Smythe, with elaborate politeness.

" I told you to keep clear," answered Lovell gruffly. " Don't bring that tub too close to my canoe. It's not safe."

" I rather think it's not very safe, anyway," remarked Smythe. " Miss Silver would be safer in the boat, I think. Perhaps you will honour us, Miss Silver. It would be such an honour and a pleasure——"

" Thank you, no," answered Phyllis.

" But really, Miss Phyllis, it would be a delightful pleasure to us," urged Adolphus, quite taken aback.

" Oh, sheer off ! " interposed Lovell.

" Keep steady, dear boys," said Adolphus to his comrades. " Keep close. Miss Silver is goin' to step in——"

" I am going to do nothing of the sort ! " said Phyllis coldly. " Will you please keep your boat at a safer distance ? "

" Oh, gad ! " ejaculated Smythe.

His companions chuckled. This was a facer for the lofty Adolphus ; he was not left in any doubt as to whose company Miss Silver preferred. A grin dawned on Lovell's face.

" Keep clear ! " he rapped out again.

Adolphus's eyes gleamed. The irrepressible chortle from his comrades irritated him, as well as the rebuff he had received.

" Pull, you duffers ! " he growled.

Howard and Tracy pulled, and at the same time Adolphus pulled the line, and the boat swung right on to the canoe.

Crash !

There was a yell from Lovell, and a cry from Phyllis.

Adolphus, in his obtuse annoyance, had only intended to give the canoe a bump, and perhaps splash the occupants with water. But the little craft was not designed to meet such a shock. Almost in the twinkling of an eye the little canoe capsized, and its occupants were hurled into the water.

Crash !

Splash !

" Oh, gad ! " gasped Adolphus, utterly terrified at what he had done. " Oh, gad ! Help ! Help ! Oh, gad ! "

" Help ! "

THE EIGHTEENTH CHAPTER.

By Luck and Pluck.

" HELP ! "

The cry came faintly from Phyllis Silver.

A swirl of the water swept the girl away from the capsized canoe, and her face showed white and terrified above the ripples.

Lovell gave a panting cry. He was caught in the sail as it swamped over, and was struggling frantically to free himself. Long before he could do so Phyllis was swept far from his reach.

Far away on the bank, Jimmy Silver and Co., who had seen the disaster, were running towards the river.

But the girl's cry had been heard ; and from the shade of the trees on the river-side a Rookwood junior ran, dropping a book, and then throwing off his jacket as he raced towards the water.

It was Loring of the Fourth.

He threw his hands together and plunged in, cleaving the water like an arrow.

A despairing hand was thrown up as Phyllis

sank under, but the hand was caught in a strong grasp.

Too dazed to realise what was happening, Phyllis came up, her face white, and half-conscious, her loosened hair in a cloud about her shoulders.

"Hold to me!" said Oliver Loring.

"Help!"

"Safe now."

Loring was swimming strongly. They were in deep water—deep and dangerous. But the new junior at Rookwood was as cool and collected as if he were at school "ducker."

He swam strongly and steadily, and his steady grasp kept the girl's head well above the surface of the shining water.

"Loring!" panted Jimmy Silver. "Oh, good man! Good man!"

Oliver Loring glanced towards the bank.

"All serene!" he called out. "Tell those fools in the boat to pull this way."

"Howard! Tracy!" Tommy Dodd roared.

"We're coming!"

The sudden catastrophe had utterly unnerved Smythe and Co., but they were pulling for the swimmer now. Lovell, disentangled from the swamping sail at last, hung on to the canoe and looked round him. Phyllis was at a good distance from him, but safe now. But for all the help Lovell could have given her in time she would have been at the bottom of the river, and he knew it.

"Phyllis!" gasped Lovell.

She was too far to hear him. The boat swept by him, and closed in on the swimmer. Loring caught the gunwale with one hand.

"Don't brain me, Tracy," he said coolly. "Shove that oar somewhere else, will you, not down my neck."

"Oh!" gasped Tracy.

"Oh, gad!" babbled Adolphus. "I—I—I—oh, gad!"

Phyllis was helped into the boat, and Loring followed. The girl sank into a seat, utterly exhausted, and drenched and dripping. Loring supported her with his arm.

"Pull ashore!" he rapped out. "Lovell's all right. Pull in!"

The boat shot towards the bank.

Many willing hands were there to help poor Phyllis ashore. Marjorie and Clara and Dolly

caught her and helped her out. She leaned heavily on Marjorie Hazeldene.

"Better get her to the school as quickly as possible," said Loring.

"Oh!" gasped Jimmy Silver. "Phil, old girl——" His voice broke.

Phyllis tried to smile.

"I—I am not hurt," she whispered. "I—I was frightened, I—I think——"

"Come on," said Jimmy. "Can you walk?"

"I—I think——"

"We'll carry you."

Jimmy and Raby linked hands to make a "carriage," and Phyllis was rushed away towards the school. Marjorie and Clara and Dolly hurried with her, and most of the juniors followed.

Lovell was wading out now.

He looked at Loring.

"You!" he muttered. "It—it was you ——"

"How lucky I happened to be reading my book under the trees here," said Loring.

"I—I couldn't help. I—I was tangled in that rotten sail," muttered Lovell. "I—I thought—oh, I thought——" His voice trembled, and there was a rush of tears in his eyes.

Loring looked at him curiously.

"If—if you hadn't——" stammered Lovell,

He did not speak again for a minute; he could not. He came nearer to the Modern junior, suddenly, and held out a wet hand.

"I—I'm a silly fool, Loring," he said. "I —I'm sorry! I—you offered to shake hands with me the other day, and I wouldn't! Now ——"

"Now you will," said Loring with a smile. "All serene—there's my fist. I don't quite see what you've been down on me so much for, Lovell. I'm not really a bad chap when you know me."

"Oh, I was a silly fool— n obstinate, silly ass!" said Lovell, repentantly. "I—I called you a funk, and now—now you—I'm sorry, Loring. I—I—I'd like to be friends, if you'd care to be friends with such a silly, waxy ass——"

"Nothing I'd like better, old scout. It's a go."

"Let's get in," said Lovell, abruptly.

Two drenched and dripping juniors ran for the school.

• • • •

Phyllis was a little pale, but otherwise quite her cheery self, when she came into the end study with Marjorie and Clara to tea. The Fistical Four were there, with their best bibs and tuckers on, so to speak, and a glorious spread on the table. And there was another guest in the famous study. It was not Tubby Muffin—Tubby had been forcibly persuaded to depart before the arrival of the ladies. It was Oliver Loring, cheerful and smiling—and on the best of terms with Arthur Edward Lovell, his old enemy.

Jimmy Silver and Co. had blinked when Lovell suggested asking Loring of the Modern Fourth to tea. But they assented at once, quite pleased by this change of front. It was clear that the feud was " off "—very much off.

Phyllis thanked Loring very gratefully for what he had done, and it was useless for Oliver to declare that he had simply had a swim. The three girls were convinced that he had risked his life to save Phyllis's—all the more because he was so modest about his performance. And Lovell took the same view, emphatically.

It was a merry celebration, after all, in the end study. The afternoon had very nearly been clouded with tragedy ; but now all was merry and bright.

After tea, it was time for Phyllis and Co. to catch their train ; and old Mack's trap was requisitioned once more. To Raby and Newcome fell the duty of seeing that Bulkeley's vases were taken back to his study, as soon as the visitors were gone—a duty which they luckily succeeded in carrying out just before the captain of Rookwood came home.

Quite a little army of juniors gathered to see the trap off. Lovell was going with Jimmy Silver and the visitors to the station—there was no room for more. But Lovell paused, as he was about to climb in, and came back to speak to Loring.

"I—I say, Loring," he muttered.

"Yes ? "

"You—you can go, if you like."

Oliver Loring stared for a moment, and then smiled.

"My dear chap, not at all. Jump in ! "

And Lovell jumped in, quite relieved that his heroic sacrifice was not accepted.

In the end study, that evening, Arthur Edward Lovell was in a very thoughtful mood. He looked up out of deep reflection at last, to find three grinning glances turned upon him.

Arthur Edward coloured a little.

"That fellow Loring is a splendid chap. I —I'm afraid I've been a bit of an ass," said Lovell. "That—that's all."

"My dear man, that was nothing new for you," said Jimmy, comfortingly. "We all agree—you've been a silly ass ! Don't we, you chaps ? "

"We do ! " said Raby.

"We does ! " grinned Newcome.

It was passed unanimously. And Arthur Edward Lovell laughed—his old, good-tempered laugh that his chums were glad to hear.

The End.

PUZZLE PICTURES

For Clever Boys and Girls.

Find the Farm boy's lost pig.

Find the Miller's son.

Find the Hunter and his two dogs.

Find the Landlord and his little girl.

THE FUNNY ADVENTURES OF BUBBLE AND SQUEAK, THE TERRIBLE TWINS

In a mighty procession the errand-boys came ;
They brought the Head melons, and apples and game.
" My word ! " cried Squeak. " What a topping repast !
The dear old man's birthday has come round at last ! "

Then the Head said to Squeak : " I've got a job for you, boy.
Just clear up this place, and a feed you'll enjoy.
When you've tidied my garden, pray come in to me,
And I will arrange for your luncheon, you see."

So Squeak got to work, and the turf fairly flew,
While Bubble looked on, feeling dismal and blue.
" How ripping ! " Squeak chuckled. " I've now backed a winner !
The Head's going to give me his very own dinner ! "

Then Bubble, who didn't like being left out,
Came into the garden.   Squeak put him to rout.
" Clear off ! " he exclaimed. " I am doing this job ! "
And Bubble retired with a sigh and a sob.

Then Squeak, when his task was successfully ended,
Marched into the Head, who said : " Splendid, boy, splendid !
Your labours have not been accomplished in vain.
You may now eat your dinner, but don't get a pain ! "

Then the covers were lifted, and Squeak staggered back
As he saw that there wasn't enough for a snack.
" Pray eat these nice tabloids, my boy, for your trouble."
" Ha, ha !   Did you ever get left ? " chortled Bubble.

If I were the Head

BY BOB CHERRY

F I were Headmaster of Greyfrairs, the first thing I should do would be to revise the Rules of the School as follows :

1. The rising-bell will rise—in other words, fall on our ears—at 11 a.m.

N.B.—This will not prevent any boy staying in bed for a few more hours, if he feels so disposed.

2. Breakfast will be served in bed, and will consist of fifteen courses. An electric bell will be installed beside each bed. When feeling hungry, please ring.

3. All lessons are optional ; but the boys are expected to turn up in class at least once a week for the purpose of pelting the Formmaster with paper pellets.

4. Prep. will be abolished, and on alternate evenings smoking concerts and fancy-dress balls will be held.

Breakfast will be served in bed.

5. Dinner in Hall may be obtained at any old time. There will be a varied and extensive menu ; but no one will be permitted to have more than six helpings of chicken. All refuse will be collected and handed to Billy Bunter, who will consume it on the mat.

6. There will be a half-holiday every day, with the exception of Saturdays, Sundays, Mondays, Tuesdays, Wednesdays, and Thursdays, which will be whole ones.

7. The Summer Vacation will be from May to September inclusive, and the Christmas Vacation from November to March inclusive.

8. Boys requiring late passes out of gates will obtain same from the captain of Greyfriars. Should the latter not be in, they may clear off without waiting.

9. Every boy is expected to be in bed by 2 a.m. A motor-'bus service will run during the evening to and from the Cinema.

10. Literature of all kinds will be permitted. Preference will be given to stories of imagination and mystery.

11. The studies in the Remove passage will be exquisitely and tastefully furnished, the Governors subscribing £200,000 for this purpose.

12. The Remove are entitled to fag Fifth-formers, and to keep them up to the mark should they show signs of slacking. Stout ash-plants will be provided for this purpose.

13. It is proposed by Robert Cherry, seconded by Robert Cherry, and carried unanimously by Robert Cherry, that the aforesaid Robert Cherry shall be the supreme boss of everything and everybody.

14. William George Bunter is appointed Master of the Rolls (sausage). He will also be granted the O.B.E. (Order of the Boot Everywhere.)

15. The Headmaster reserves the right to close down the school should he wish to take a trip round the world on the receipt of his first year's salary.

The Remove are entitled to fag Fifth Formers, and to keep them up to the mark should they show signs of slacking.

JIMMY SILVER

A Verse of Praise

By

The Rookwood Rhymester

Hats off to the immortal James !
  The loyal Classic leader,
Whose boyish japes, and skill at games,
  Delight each ardent reader.
He plays all those amusing pranks
  That heroes in a book would ;
Both now and evermore he ranks
  The chosen son of Rookwood.

Though Harry Wharton fills the bill,
  And likewise good Tom Merry ;
And hosts of loyal readers still
  Bow to the charms of Cherry,
It cannot be denied that when
  One's spirits are at zero,
They very soon revive again,
  Thanks to this Rookwood hero !

The daring japes of Tommy Dodd
  Compel our admiration ;
He figures as a young tin god
  In some chaps' estimation.
But even Tommy Dodd is done
  When Silver takes the platform ;
The Fourth Form Classics are A1.
  There's nothing wrong with that Form !

And yet, despite their feuds and scrapes,
  Their fierce and breathless tussles,
And all the merry fistic japes
  That exercise their muscles,
The Classic chums are staunch and true,
  Not merely gay and skittish ;
And we're convinced they'd never do
  A thing that wasn't British !

Then here's to Silver ! May he rule
  Within our hearts for ever !
Supreme alike in sport and school,
  Courageous, swift, and clever !
And British boys are all agreed
  They'd have to make a long quest,
To find such ripping yarns to read
  As those of Owen Conquest !

THE SONG OF THE TUCK !

By Dick Penfold

With fingers sticky and plump,
  With gleaming and bulging eyes,
A junior sat in Dame Mimble's shop,
  Scoffing her tarts and pies.

Champ, champ, champ !
  "I'll sample another for luck !"
And still in a voice all muffled
    and queer,
  He sang the Song of the Tuck !

"I'll tackle that currant cake,
  And a couple of seed-cakes too !
I'll scoff in a trice that strawberry ice,
  Buzz round, Mrs. Mimble, do !"

Champ, champ, champ !
  It's a wonder his jaws never stuck !
And still in a voice all muffled and
    queer,
  He sang the Song of the Tuck !

"Master Bunter, your credit's ex-
    pired !"
  The Owl was expiring, too !
He slipped from his seat with a face
    like a sheet,
  And murmured his last adieu !

Groan, groan, groan !
  He writhed on the mat and was
    stuck !
But before he burst he sadly re-
    hearsed,
  The sorrowful Song of the Tuck !

Hints to young Cricketers

By Bolsover Major, of the Remove

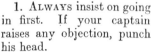

1. ALWAYS insist on going in first. If your captain raises any objection, punch his head.

2. On your way to the wickets give the bowler a ferocious glare. It will frighten the life out of him, and he will send down awfully weak stuff.

3. If the wicket-keeper gets up too close, brain him with the business-end of your bat. (A few casualties are bound to happen in cricket, and one or two more or less won't make any difference.)

4. When the first ball comes down, shut your eyes and slog hard. That is the secret of success.

5. If you happen to hit the ball, run—run for your life! You can bet you've murdered a prize cow half a mile away. And a farmer with a pitchfork is little better than a Hun.

6. If, on the other hand, you miss the ball, and your stumps start doing revolutions, and the umpire yells " Out ! " turn to him in deep disgust and say, " Why, you duffer, that was a trial ball ! "

7. Should the umpire still persist in yelling " Out ! " deal with him in the same manner as you dealt with the wicket-keeper. (Umpires are much better out of the way, they only keep interrupting the game.)

8. Of course, you will make arrangements beforehand with the scorer to credit you with two runs every time you score one. Should you smash the pavilion clock, he must credit you with twelve, otherwise he will share the same fate as the clock.

9. If the pace gets too hot, demand an interval for light refreshments. If these are served in a marquee, you will naturally get there first, and keep everybody else at bay until your inner man is satisfied.

Demand an interval for light refreshments.

10. If you succeed in making a century, throw yourself full-length in the grass, as a hint to the spectators that you wish to be carried off.

11. Should the Headmaster approach you with the remark, " Well played, my boy ! " tell him to let you off those lines he gave you.

12. Several fags will probably ask for your autograph. If they do, wring their necks.

13. Most bowlers make the wicket their objective. This is all wrong. You should take careful aim at the batsman's shins, and every time you hit him your money will be returned on the principle of cocoanut shies

Take careful aim at the batsman's shins!

A few casualties are bound to happen in cricket

IN THE EDITOR'S DEN

By MONTY LOWTHER

MIGHTY mass of MSS.,
All the study in a mess.
Ink and glue on floor and ceiling,
And that frightful fed-up feeling.
Contributions by the score.
Slumbering softly on the floor.
Manners writing " Hints on Chess,"
Gussy scribbling " How to Dress ";
Blake (on paper) getting runs ;
This child cracking charming puns.
Merry writing yards of drivel
Fit to make old Towser snivel !
Would-be authors bring their wares
Queue extends right down the stairs !
Skimpole staggers in with verses,
Strikes a pose, and then rehearses,
Till his hearers get the hump,
Exit Skimmy with a bump !
Grundy brings a redskin story,
Wild and gruesome, grim and gory.
No, it doesn't go down well ;
Grundy does, though, with a yell !
Herries brings a page of music

Which would make both me and you sick.
Then old Figgins barges in,
Followed close by Fatty Wynn.
Figgy's yarn is called " Dear heart ! "
Wynn's " The Mystery of the Tart ! "
Both, with imprecations hollow,
Are pitched out ; the authors follow !
So the merry game continues
Till, with aching limbs and sinews,
We collapse upon the floor,
Too fed-up to tackle more.
All is chaos and confusion ;
It's a snare and a delusion,
Not to say a beastly fag,
Getting out a weekly " rag."
" Time for prep ! " Tom Merry cries.
" Now, you lazy dogs, arise !
Listen to my solemn warning—
Linton's waxy in the morning."
" Bust old Linton ! " So say I,
" Bother Linton ! " rings the cry.
Let us, then, be up and doing
Nothing ! Blow the storm that's brewing !

COUNTY CRESTS

No. 2.

Is your County represented on this page?

CAMBRIDGESHIRE

SUSSEX

LEICESTERSHIRE

DEVONSHIRE

NORTHUMBERLAND

WORCESTERSHIRE

LINCOLNSHIRE

WESTMORELAND

SUFFOLK

HERTFORDSHIRE

GLOUCESTERSHIRE

THE FORTUNE TELLER

A Splendid Play in Verse for Amateur Actors

Introducing
HARRY WHARTON & Cº of GREYFRIARS.

How to Make up

Wharton (Dark Hair) **Nugent**

Cherry Curly Hair. Always smiling. **Bull**

Hurree Singh   Bunter

NOTE.—This play is copyright, but it may be performed by readers of "The Holiday Annual," without fee, on condition that the words, "By permission of the Editor of 'The Holiday Annual'" appear on the front of all programmes.

Characters:

HARRY WHARTON	The Famous
FRANK NUGENT	Five of the
BOB CHERRY	Remove.
JOHNNY BULL	
HURREE SINGH	
BILLY BUNTER	The Owl of the Remove.
COKER	The leading
POTTER	lights of the
GREENE	Fifth.
Mr. PAUL PROUT	Master of the Fifth.
GERALD LODER	The Objectionable Prefect.
WILLIAM WIBLEY	Disguised as a Palmist.

How to Make up.

Coker   **Potter**

Greene   **Loder**

Mʳ Prout   Wibley.

SCENE.—No. 1 *Study in the Remove passage.*
(*The Famous Five are present, busily engaged in clearing up the study.*)

WHARTON :
> The fortune-teller will arrive,
> If all goes well, at half-past five.
> He'll sit in this armchair in state,
> And tell our fortunes while we wait.

CHERRY : My hat ! It ought to be great fun—

NUGENT : Not if your past's a shady one !

BULL :
> The moment that he sees my hand,
> He'll tell me I'm a sportsman grand.
> A mighty man, of skill and vim,
> In class, and playing-field, and gym !

ALL : Rats !

HURREE SINGH :
> Our fortune-telling friend will be,
> A source of much delightfulness ;
> But if he treats us fraudfully,
> We will impart the smitefulness !

ALL : Hear, hear !

WHARTON (*thoughtfully*) :
> We ought to charge a certain sum,
> To fellows for admission ;

NUGENT :
> Not good enough ! They wouldn't come.
> They'd treat us with suspicion.

WHARTON :
> All right ; the chaps may come in free—

BULL :
> Provided they don't stop to tea !

(*The study door opens. Enter* WIBLEY, *clad in long, flowing robes, and with a d sky face and a dark moustache. He is also wearing a turban. The Famous Five do not know he is Wibley.*)

WIBLEY :
> I give you my salaams, young friends,
> Embracing you with kisses ;

WHARTON (*jumping back*) :
> No, no ! Reserve such odds and ends
> For your devoted missis !

WIBLEY (*seating himself in the armchair*) :
> I've travelled many a weary mile,
> My thirst is most alarming.
> Bring forth some tea ; yes, that's the style !
> Those cakes look really charming !

(*The Famous Five bustle around and provide their guest with light refreshment.*)

HURREE SINGH :
> What is your name, most honoured sir ?
> And do you come from Bhanipur ?

WIBLEY :
> Nay, not from India's coral strand,
> But from a less inviting land,
> Which is not fit for man nor beast—
> A dreary desert in the East !

ALL : My hat !

WIBLEY :
> My name is Moonshee Wotta Spoof,
> Of my great powers I'll give you proof.
> In England and in foreign lands,
> I've read Crowned Heads—I mean
>   Crowned hands !

CHERRY (*holding out his hand*) :
> You may be simply great, Moonshee !
> Please read my merry lines for me.

WIBLEY :
> Silence, ye dog ! Go hence, and quake !
> Wait till I've tackled one more cake !

(BOB CHERRY *jumps back, startled.*)
(WIBLEY *finishes his tea, and while he is doing so the door opens.*)
(*Enter* COKER, POTTER, *and* GREENE, *of the Fifth.*)

COKER :
> I hear you've got a palmist here,
> A fortune-telling fellow.

BULL :
> Look here, old son, you'd better clear,
> If you are going to bellow !

COKER : Dry up, young Bull——

BULL : You priceless fool !

COKER : My hat ! I—I'll——

BULL : You make me smile !

WIBLEY :
> Silence, ye knaves ! Or I will go
> And cancel all the merry show !

WHARTON :
> Most honoured Moonshee, we regret
>   That this should come to pass.
> But be a sport—don't leave us yet !
>   Coker's a silly ass !

WIBLEY :
> You need not emphasise the fact ;
> I saw at once that he was ' cracked ' !

COKER : Why, you beastly nigger——

WIBLEY : Stay ! Whence this fat figure ?

(*Enter* BILLY BUNTER.)

BUNTER :
    I say, you fellows,
    I happened to hear
    A rumour most startling,
    Surprising and queer !
CHERRY :
    Your bootlace happened to come undone,
    Outside the keyhole of Study One ?
BUNTER : Oh, really, Cherry——
NUGENT : It's likely, very !
BUNTER :
    My information came to me,
    From Peter Todd and Dutton—see ?
    They said a palmist would arrive,
    From Courtfield, shortly after five.
(BUNTER, *being short-sighted, has not yet seen*
WIBLEY ; *he now observes him for the first time.*)
BUNTER :
    My hat ! He's been here all the time !
    Tell me my fortune, quick, in rhyme !
(*Bunter holds out his hand.* WIBLEY *examines it.*)
WIBLEY :
    You're fat and flabby, have no pluck,
    You pilfer other fellows' tuck.
    The time you do not spend in spying,
    Is taken up with fraud and lying !
BUNTER : Why, you rotter——
WHARTON : Proceed, O Moonshee ! This is fine !
CHERRY : It's true, too—all along the line !
WIBLEY (*still holding* BUNTER'S *hand*) :
    Your father keeps the " Bunter Arms,"
    And samples much strong liquor ;
    Your maiden aunt has certain charms—
    Your uncle is a vicar.
BUNTER :
    My uncle's not !
    It's tommy-rot !
WIBLEY :
    You follow on the new boy's trail,
    As grimly as a warder ;
    And always you unfold a tale
    About a postal-order.
COKER :
    I say, you chaps, there's something in it !
    I'll hold *my* hand out, in a minute !
(WIBLEY *continues.*)
    You always boast that every post
    Will bring along a fiver,
    From so-called titled relatives,
    Who haven't got a stiver !

BUNTER : It's utter rot !
CHERRY : Dry up ! It's not !
WIBLEY (*dreamily*) :
    I see the future ! Prison bars
    Will, in the end, surround you ;
    Your friends will fret, and much regret
    That no one ever drowned you !
BUNTER :
    I'm off, you chaps ! I've had enough.
    I never heard such piffling stuff !
(*Exit* BUNTER.)
COKER : Now tell me mine, you funny freak—
WIBLEY : Ha, ha ! I hear a jackass speak !
COKER : Why, you—you—you——
WIBLEY : A jackass from the Zoo !
COKER (*threateningly*) :
    You cheeky nigger ! I shall bump you !
THE FAMOUS FIVE (*intervening*) :
    Hands off, you idiot, or we'll thump you !
(COKER *simmers down.*)
WIBLEY :
    My boot-faced friend, may I continue
    To tell the good and bad that's in you ?
COKER :
    All right, you beauty ! Go ahead !
    But tell the truth for once, instead !
WIBLEY :
    You are the blockhead of your Form ;
POTTER (*to* COKER) :
    My hat, old man, that's rather warm !
WIBLEY :
    Among the dunces you are reckoned ;
    Your place is really in the Second !
COKER (*excitedly*) : What ?
WIBLEY :
    You play at footer, with much pride,
    And kick goals—for the other side !
WHARTON :
    Right on the wicket, every time !
    Go on, Moonshee ! It's simply prime !
WIBLEY :
    You always try to boss the show,
    You cherish great ambitions ;
    You try to rule the blessed school,
    You jump at high positions.
    Then angry schoolmates jump at *you !*
    You see bright stars—and comets, too !
COKER :
    This really is a bit too thick ;
    Come on, you chaps, he makes me sick !
(*Exit* COKER, POTTER, *and* GREENE.)

HOW THE STAGE SHOULD BE ARRANGED.

No elaborate or expensive scenery is required to stage " The Fortune Teller." If it is not possible to arrange the Study door at the back of the stage as shown, it can be omitted altogether, and the various characters can enter from the side. It will be noted that one chair has only three legs. A broken chair like this may be useful for a little knockabout fun. The concert party should arrange to have a stage manager, and it should be left to him to add anything to improve the scenic effect.

CHERRY :
    Your fortune-telling, Wotta Spoof,
    Fairly brings down the giddy roof !
ALL : Yes, rather !
CHERRY :
    Well, here's my fist. Tell me at once
    If I am clever, or a dunce !
WIBLEY :
    The line of life is very full,
    You use much energy at school ;
    Not in the Form-room, sad to say,
    But in the Close, where infants play.
CHERRY : My only aunt !
WIBLEY :
    But when the world seems upside down,
    You never lose your wool, or frown ;
    You're always hoping for the best,
    And meet misfortunes with a jest.

ALL : Hear, hear !
    (*Enter* LODER.)
WIBLEY :
    Who enters this most sacred place ?
    Come, answer me, old hatchet-face !
LODER : I will not stand——
WIBLEY : Hold out your hand !
    (LODER *reluctantly obeys.*)
WIBLEY :
    The line of hate is very firm,
    You love to see your victims squirm ;
    You're full of boast and bounce and brag :
    You chastise many a harmless fag !
LODER : Of all the cheek——
WIBLEY : Be silent, freak !
LODER : I will report——
THE FAMOUS FIVE : Shut up, old sport !

WIBLEY :
    You live a life so mean and base
    That you'd be banished from the place
    If your headmaster knew that you
    Retired to rest at half-past two !
CHERRY : Good old night-bird !
WIBLEY :
    The line of caddishness is here ;
    You gamble, and it costs you dear.
    You're always getting in bad odour ;
    Your name, of course, is Gerald Loder !
LODER (*clenching his fists*) :
    Your palmistry is utter rot,
    And now you're going to catch it hot !
(LODER *is about to rush at* WIBLEY, *when*
  MR. PROUT *enters.*)
MR. PROUT :
    Dear me ! What's going on in here ?
    A most disgraceful scene, I fear !
THE FAMOUS FIVE :
    Oh, no, sir !
    It's a ripping show, sir !
MR. PROUT :
    Who is this man of dark complexion ?
LODER :
    A rogue, sir. Order his ejection !
WHARTON :
    He'll tell your fortune, sir, if you
    Will hold your left hand out to view !
MR. PROUT :
    The man knows nothing of my history ;
    To him, my past is all a mystery !
WIBLEY :
    Hold out your hand, sir, and you'll see
    Your life's an open book to me !
(MR. PROUT *holds out his hand.*)
WIBLEY :
    You're a marksman of repute ;
    When three years old you learned to
      shoot ;
    And never have you been at fault
    With pop-gun or with catapult.
MR. PROUT : Bless my soul !

WIBLEY :
    High in the Rockies, far away,
    You slew big game, sir, in your day.
    But now, alas !—how times do change !—
    You'd miss a house at two yards' range !
MR. PROUT : You insolent knave——
WIBLEY : Behave ! Behave !
MR. PROUT : Go right away !
THE FAMOUS FIVE :
    Oh, let him stay !
WIBLEY :
    You have a motor-bike, O king,
    A fearful and a hideous thing.
    You are a road-hog to the core,
    You've murdered chickens by the score !
MR. PROUT :
    Fool ! Dunderhead ! How dare you scoff ?
    But stay ! *Your eyebrow's coming off !*
(WIBLEY *clutches frantically at his eyebrow. At*
the same instant LODER *strides forward and jerks*
away the moustache and eyebrows and turban.
WIBLEY *of the Remove stands revealed.*)
THE FAMOUS FIVE : WIBLEY !
MR. PROUT :
    Ha, ha ! So I have caught you out ?
    I—even I—the great Paul Prout !
WIBLEY :
    Oh, dear ! Oh, crumbs ! Oh, help ! I'm
      done !
    I only did it, sir, for fun !
MR. PROUT :
    Cease fooling, sir, and come with me,
    You think you're very clever ;
    But I will show you that my aim
    Is just as good as ever !
WIBLEY :
    I've done it now !
MR. PROUT :
    You, Loder, will come with us, please,
    And hold him while he's yelling ;
    He'll feel so sore that never more
    He'll take to fortune-telling !
(*Exit* MR. PROUT, LODER, *and* WIBLEY.)

CURTAIN

NOW ON SALE AT THE FISHER T. FISH BARGAIN BASEMENT.

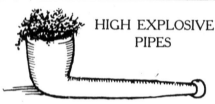

HIGH EXPLOSIVE PIPES

These pipes contain a small charge of gunpowder half-way down the stem, and a terrific explosion occurs when the pipe is lit.

Try one on your Form Master !

Price - - One Shilling

SKEATING'S POWDER

Price (per barrel) Two Shillings

Kills moths, beetles, influenza germs, and objectionable prefects.

Sprinkle some in the Sixth Form passage !

SHOCK CAKES

These are intended for use against study raiders. They look like innocent rock-cakes, but contain a powerful charge of electricity, and the victim receives a severe shock simultaneously with the first bite.

No study should be without them !

Price (per dozen) - One Shilling

Customers are requested to bring their own paper bags.

THE "PERFECT" PALM PROTECTOR !

Sold in bottles, and consists of a resinous substance which, when rubbed on the palm, renders all lickings painless.

No schoolboy should be without a bottle.

Rub it well in, and defy your Form master !

Price (per bottle) - Threepence

LATEST GINGER-BEER NOVELTY !

Give a bottle to your sworn enemy !

After the first few gurgles, he will go off pop !

The secret of this valuable preparation is known only to the inventor—Fisher T. Fish.

Price (per bottle) - One Shilling

Wonderful Toy Airship

Price (inclusive of dummy pilot) 20s.

Carries small but very powerful bombs on board.

Float it in your Form-room !

Bombs are discharged at the rate of 200 per second.

Greatest casulty-producer on record !

HOW A MOTOR-CYCLE ENGINE WORKS

An Instructive Article Written by a Well-known Motor-Cycle Racing Expert

PETROL motors of many types are now in such common use in our daily life that every boy will want to know how they work. Most boys know that petrol "makes the engine go," but exactly how it comes about that this liquid causes the engine to run, "of its own accord," as it were, they are not quite clear. I will try and explain.

The commonest form of petrol engine is what is known as the four-cycle engine, that is, one in which the piston-stroke performs four distinct operations. We will take for our illustration, therefore, the ordinary type of one-cylinder, four-cycle engine such as is fitted, for instance, to the majority of motor-cycles.

Now let us follow the petrol which "makes the engine go" from the time it is poured into the tank, and see what happens to it. When the tap is turned on it runs from a tank down a pipe into a sort of metal cup (called the carburetter) whence it is drawn by the suction of the engine through

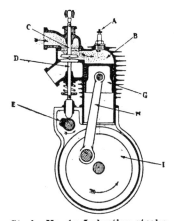

Stroke No. 1: Induction stroke

A is the sparking-plug; *B* the combustion chamber in the cylinder; *C* the inlet valve, through which the gas flows; *D* the exhaust valve; *E* is the cam which opens and closes valve D; *G* is the piston; *H* the connecting-rod; *I* is the fly wheel.

a fine nozzle in the form of spray. It then turns itself into gas—petrol turns into gas of its own accord, you know, when it is exposed to the air. The petrol gas, then, mixed with some air —this mixture being explosive now—flows along a pipe (called the inlet pipe) until it comes to a valve—the inlet valve. At certain intervals this valve is opened by means of special mechanism, and the mixture enters the cylinder-head. Now, to follow the series of operations which take place next, let us refer to our first diagram. This shows the engine with all the working parts lettered.

The piston is here seen starting on its first downward stroke, called the induction stroke. The inlet valve C is open, and the gas is being drawn through it into the combustion chamber B.

Now look at the second diagram.

The piston has got to the bottom of the induction stroke and is now beginning the first upward, or compression stroke. Note that both inlet valve C and exhaust valve D are closed. As the piston moves upwards

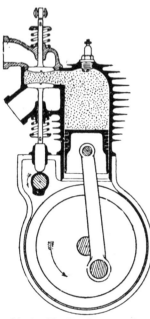

Stroke No. 2: Compression stroke

it compresses the charge of gas in the chamber B.

Now turn to the third figure.

An electric spark is now produced at the points of the sparking plug A. This spark is generated by a special piece of electrical mechanism called a magneto. The spark explodes the compressed gas in the chamber B, and the explosion forces the piston down again.

During this stroke, of course, the inlet valve C and exhaust valve D are both closed, to prevent the escape of the gas.

Now, turning to our fourth illustration, we see the piston beginning to travel upwards again, driven by the momentum of the fly wheel I.

You will notice that the exhaust valve D is now open, allowing the burnt gas to be driven out of the chamber B by the ascending piston. This gas escapes down the exhaust pipe and out into the air by way of the silencer—making the pop-popping noise which usually heralds the approach of a motor-cycle.

As soon as the piston gets to the top of this its fourth stroke, the exhaust valve closes, the inlet valve opens, and off it starts again on

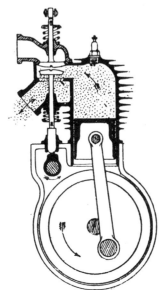

Stroke No. 4: Exhaust stroke

No. 1 cycle —the induction stroke. And so it goes on endlessly, each operation following on in its turn with unfailing regularity, the valves, actuated by a clever arrangement of cams on a shaft, being timed to open at exactly the right instant, to a nicety.

The four cycles of the petrol engine, then, shown by our diagrams are :

(1) Suction or induction, in which the gas is sucked into the cylinder.

(2) Compression, in which the gas is compressed in the combustion chamber.

(3) Explosion, or working stroke.

(4) Expulsion or exhaust, in which the cylinder is cleared of burnt gas, ready for the next induction stroke.

A FEW TIPS FOR THE NOVICE.

It is necessary for every boy to have a clear grasp of the principles on which the four-cycle engine operates, as explained above in simple language, before he can hope to manage and look after such an engine himself. The diagrams will be found especially

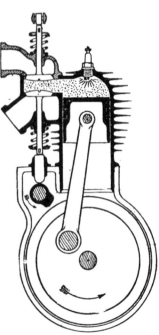

Stroke No. 3: Explosion stroke

useful, after a few minutes' study, in impressing the cycle of operations on the mind. Once this is grasped, the running of an ordinary four - stroke, single - cylinder motor - cycle becomes quite a simple matter. It will not appear so at first, because all sorts of complications will present themselves on the motor-cycle, which do not appear in the diagrams above. But once the main principles are clearly understood—the simple knowledge of "how the engine works"—everything else will come from the one other thing that is needful—experience. In motorcycling it may be truly said that the best motor-cyclist is the most experienced motorcyclist. The very best way of learning how to run a motor-cycle is to try it—actually to run one—even if you don't know all about it at first. You soon will, even if you are by no means a mechanical genius. The great majority of motor-cyclists start off on their first ride with but the haziest idea of "how the thing works." They just know the controls, where the brake is, and how to stop and start.

They hope fervently that the machine won't stop of its own accord, as they are convinced that they will never be able to discover what ails it. But they always get on all right, as a matter of fact. In many cases their machine brings them home again, in spite of somewhat unskilful driving, without any trouble at all. Or suppose the engine does stop, and obstinately refuses to start again? The novice looks at the motionless machine, feeling helpless. But perhaps, if he looks carefully enough, he will find that the petrol tap has somehow become turned off, or that the insulated cable has jumped off the sparking-plug. Perhaps a passing rider will come to the rescue, make some simple adjustment, and send the beginner off rejoicing.

In any case it will be experience, and experience teaches, especially in motorcycling, better than anything else. Any boy or girl over the age of 1¼ can become the possessor, for five shillings, of a licence to drive a motor-cycle. And I say, without hesitation, that any average boy or girl of that age is perfectly capable of using and looking after a motor-cycle.

THE LAY OF THE LAZY LORD !

By

HERBERT MAULEVERER

Some chaps in footer take delight,
  An' do their best a goal to bag ;
I find it interestin', quite,
  But too much fag !

Others, less decently inclined,
  Put money on the nimble nag ;
A pursuit which I always find
  Is too much fag !

And other fellows I could name
  Are full of bluster, bounce, and brag ;
Don't ask me why I'm not the same—
  It's too much fag !

That fellow Wharton's sloggin' still,
  An' Cherry is a lively wag ;
But their amusements make me ill—
  Groo ! Too much fag !

An' really, I must now conclude
  This verse I'm writin' for the rag ;
I can't go on—don't think me rude,
  It's too much fag !

STRAIGHT PINE'S SACRIFICE

*An Exciting Complete Story Dealing with the Adventures of
a British Boy Amongst Redskins*

THE FIRST CHAPTER.

**The Delaware Chief—
Straight Pine — The
Guarded Fire—Nat
Wild—The Feud
—Dick Wild.**

UP on the branch of
a pine a squirrel
was calling;
through the tops
of the tall trees a restless
wind rustled ; down by the
shingle of the lake the water
rippled faintly like the falling of seeds ; but the Delaware Whatawa, seated by
his little fire of dry twigs,
made no sound at all. Be-
side him lay his rifle, before
him was the fire of dry
wood—he had taken care
that it should be dry, so
that no tell-tale smoke
should arise from it—and
round both himself and
the fire had been stretched
two blankets.

Whatawa, or Straight Pine, to give him
the name by which he was usually known,
sat and stared moodily into the fire, a rather
sad look in his fine eyes. He was a handsome
man, judged by the Red Indian standard.
His brow was high and slanting, the eyes
rather near together and very bright, the
nose aquiline, the mouth thin-lipped and

Straight Pine

determined. Only the lines
and curves of paint on the
face gave it the rather re-
pellent look which it wore
just now.

Ay, the paint showed
plainly to those who knew
the Indians that the Delaware was on the warpath.

Yet why was he alone
in this great forest bordering the edge of that great
sheet of water known to
the Indians as Sheet of
Sun—to the whites as Lake
Quesna ? He was a Dela-
ware, and the tracts of this
forest were given over to
game and the ferocious
Mingoes. If it was that
he was seeking game,
surely he could have chosen
a safer hunting-ground.
If he sought the scalps of
Mingoes, the deadly ene-
mies of the Delawares,
would he have come on
such an errand alone ?

Whatawa stirred the embers of the fire
with a moccasined foot, and drew the blankets
closer together. The night was chilly, but
even then he would not have lit a fire had
he thought that enemies were near. Now
and again he rose, placed his body between
the flames and the blanket, and stepped into
the darkness without. On each occasion,

however, with a satisfied " Ugh ! " he had returned to the fire.

After a final look round outside, Whatawa scattered the embers with his tomahawk, raked earth over them, and lay down on the hard ground. The state of his moccasins showed that he had travelled far, and the fact that he was almost at once asleep suggested that his mission was one which was giving him little rest.

By some chance Whatawa had not entirely extinguished the fire, and one twig of dry wood still smouldered. The flame travelled along it, eating it up hungrily, reached other twigs, which had been placed ready to re-plenish the fire, and caught them. A little flame shot up, throwing a fitful light over the enclosure and the prostrate form of the Indian chief.

Whatawa stirred uneasily, then, without a sound, without any jerky motion, but with that strangely silent action curiously Indian-like, sat up. His left hand dropped to where his rifle lay, but stopped half-way.

" Ugh ! " he grunted, with his eyes staring straight before him.

" I guess ye're right," a deep voice observed. " I got the bead first."

Through a small opening, caused by one of the blankets being pulled aside, was thrust the barrel of a rifle. It was upon this that the Delaware's eyes, betraying no sign of emotion, dwelt. He had heard the approach of the man with the rifle too late, and had been covered before he could grasp his own weapon.

" My white brother should enter," Whatawa said calmly, in a deep, singularly mellow voice. " Without in the forest the winds are cold, but here there is warmth, and—a friend."

The blanket was drawn further aside, and a tall man, his rifle ready in his hands, though the butt was no longer pressed against his shoulder, entered the little enclosure. The faintest possible gleam of admiration showed in the eyes of the Indian as they rested upon the man.

He was certainly a fine specimen of man-hood—in height a trifle over six feet in his moccasined feet, proportionately broad of shoulder, and carrying himself with the air of one who fears neither man nor beast. His bearded face was tanned to almost as dark a hue as the Indian's through long exposure, and his dress showed that he was one of those hardy pioneers who forced their living, against considerable odds, from the forests and the plains of North America. His dress was of the skin of the buck, and slung across it by narrow thongs were his shot and powder flasks. In his belt was a bone-handled knife.

This man calmly seated himself on the ground opposite the Indian. There was a hard look in his eyes, and the set of his mouth was grim and forbidding. By reach-ing out a foot he was able to draw the other's rifle towards him. Even while doing that his eyes never left the Indian's face.

" It's war, Delaware ? " he asked, in his deep voice. " I tho't your tribe had buried the hatchet an' taken to huntin' an' trappin'."

" My white brother has the eyes of the hawk," Whatawa answered in very good English, and with something of a sneer in his voice. " Surely he must have been many moons in the great forests, that he can tell the war-paint of the Delaware ? "

" Your name ? " the trapper growled.

" Whatawa," the Indian answered coolly, though he knew well enough that this inter-view was like enough to end in his death. The blood-feud between the whites and the reds was strong. The Government were always ready to pay a price for an Indian scalp, and this trapper was therefore not likely to let this opportunity of bloodshed pass without taking advantage of it. " Other chiefs know me as Straight Pine. My speech is straight as the upright tree of the forest, and my voice has been heard much in council by the camp-fire.

" What do they call my white brother ? "

The white man snatched off his felt hat with a rather angry gesture, and bent his head just sufficiently for the light of the fire, which was burning up now, to shine upon the crown of it. The light revealed a curious thing. The man's head was covered by short, strong, curly hair, save on the crown. There, for the space of a circle some inches in circumference, was a bald spot. A look of understanding showed in the Indian's eyes, otherwise his face betrayed no sign of emotion.

"My brother is the great trapper No Scalp," he murmured.

"Ay, No Scalp it is," the trapper growled. And his fingers gripped harder on his rifle. "And so it's bin ever since a thievish Mingoe lifted it an' left me for dead. But I had his'n," Nat Wild continued, for such was his name; "jest because he had mine. Fair deal, Straight Pine?"

"My white brother is just."

Whatawa moved a hand cautiously towards his tomahawk, but the action was detected, and the trapper's rifle went up to his shoulder immediately.

"See here, Straight Pine," he growled, "I'm not wantin' ter finish this little discussion jest yet, so jest keep your hands away from the tomahawk. Guess I'll feel easier in my mind."

The Indian gave an almost imperceptible shrug of the shoulders, and stared moodily into the fire.

"What would No Scalp do?" he asked.

"Larn the reason fer that paint, chief," the trapper answered readily. "Ain't there peace with all the tribes jest now—not as you can trust 'em if there's a chance of an easy scalp about—ain't there?"

Straight Pine raised his sinewy arms, and motioned with his hands towards the surrounding woods. One had stopped and pointed away to the north.

"The Mingoes?" Nat Wild asked sharply.

"My brother has a very grey head of wisdom beneath his dark hair," Whatawa answered. "The Mingoes have dug up the hatchet against the palefaces."

"An' your tribe, the Delawares?" Nat Wild asked, cocking his rifle.

Now he knew that the reds were going to give trouble again, he deemed it his duty to put this man out of the way. It was brutal, but nothing more than the wild teaching of the woods.

"We are at peace."

The trapper laughed, and raised his rifle to his shoulder. The Indian did not flinch as it covered him, and his placid face showed no sign of anything but indifference.

"The war-paint?" Nat Wild demanded.

"I go to warn the palefaces at Fort Larabee," Whatawa answered coolly.

"You lie, you dog!" the trapper thundered, for he knew the artifices of these redskins. "Mebbe the woods round here are full of vermin like you. Guess I'll finish you, and——"

"And bring the Delaware's friends here," Whatawa sneered, "if, as the wise paleface says, the woods are full of them."

This was too much for Nat Wild, who, obviously, was not the best-tempered of men. His fingers gripped the rifle a trifle harder. The barrel became steady as the branch of a tree that has no breeze to sway it. Yet Whatawa looked down the muzzle without a sign that he knew death to be hovering near, waiting for the signal of the finger upon the trigger.

"Nat!" a voice protested sharply.

Startled for a moment, put off his guard, despite his long experience of the woods, Nat Wild turned his head in the direction of the voice, which had proceeded from a well-set-up lad of fifteen or sixteen, dressed as the trapper was, who, holding aside the blanket, was staring in, horror writ large upon his face.

Only for a moment did Nat Wild turn, but that was long enough for Whatawa. His hand shot out, the rifle was forced upwards, the jerk discharging it, and the bullet whizzed up among the branches overhead. At the same moment the Indian had regained his own rifle, and when the trapper, springing to his feet, swung his discharged weapon up, he stopped with it in mid-air.

Straight Pine still sat by the fire, but the butt of his rifle rested in the palm of his hand now. There was no trace of a look of triumph in his face.

"No Scalp will talk further with Straight Pine," he said; "and even the young paleface warrior shall have his seat by the fire."

Nat Wild's jaw dropped. All his life he had lived in the woods among the Indians, and he knew just what to expect now. He had attempted to take the Delaware's life, and it would be no more than an act of justice if the Indian, now that he was top dog, reversed the tables. Just for a second the trapper's jaw was unsteady ; then it set hard, and a calm look, with something of the Indian repose about it, took possession of his gnarled face.

" I guess you shoot," he drawled coolly.

" It is no time for the Delawares to turn against the palefaces," Whatawa answered quietly. " They will have enough fighting if they are to keep their scalps from the lodges of the Mingoes."

That the Indian really meant to spare his life, Nat Wild did not believe. He glanced sharply at Straight Pine, trying to read his thoughts ; but the calm, impassive face told him nothing.

" Savin' me for torture, Straight Pine ? " the trapper drawled, as if anything in the nature of torture was quite ordinary and commonplace, and not to be troubled about.

Whatawa stirred the embers of the fire with his feet.

" No Scalp will listen as the brave harkens for the footfall of the enemy," he said, " for Straight Pine's words are no idle ones. Let Young Horse "—the chief had already found a name for Dick Wild, the trapper's young brother—" listen, too ! He is fresh to the forest and the war-path, and it is well that he should learn soon."

Wild glanced at the Indian again, and motioned Dick, who was standing by, a look of determination on his youthful face, to keep near.

" I'm listenin', chief," he growled.

THE SECOND CHAPTER.

Straight Pine's Mission—Nat Wild Amazed —The Token of War—The Tree Fort.

STRAIGHT PINE, still with the butt of his rifle resting in the hollow of his right hand, smiled slightly at the youth whom he had named " Young Horse."

" Before another moon, Young Horse will have trod the war-trail," he said.

" You're sure ? " Dick cried eagerly, evidently not at all alarmed by the prospect.

" The very shadows of the trees are blacker, that the Mingoes and Hurons may be hidden by them," Whatawa answered.

Nat Wild, who had recovered a good deal of his self-possession by now, though he could not understand the actions of the chief, shrugged his great shoulders and laughed loudly. Straight Pine's eyes moved quickly to where the blankets did not quite meet, and he stared through the slit into the dark forest. The rifle moved slightly in his hands.

" No Scalp has the laughter of the fool," he said.

With an oath, Nat Wild took an angry step forward ; then he met the calm, unflinching eyes of the Indian, and saw that the rifle still covered him, and he stopped.

" My paleface brother will be seated ; and Young Horse will rest, too," Whatawa said ; " for with the rising of the sun they will start on the long trail to Fort Larabee."

" Guess not," Nat Wild muttered, as he threw himself to the ground, lying close to the fire. Dick seated himself close to him. It was the first time that his brother had really allowed him to come out into the great forests after buck, and he hoped that it was true that the Hurons and Mingoes were——

" See here," Nat Wild said sharply, " What's all this talk, chief, about the Mingoes ? "

Straight Pine moved his rifle a trifle, as if to place it beside him.

" Have I the white chief's word that it is peace ? " he asked.

" Ay, that you have," Nat Wild agreed quickly, with a slightly eager look in his eyes.

Whatawa laid his rifle beside him, and even as he did so the trapper snatched his own up and covered the chief. There was a ferocious look in his eyes.

" Well, Delaware," he sneered, " where's yer friends now ? "

With a slight cry, though certainly not one of alarm or fear, Dick threw himself between the Indian and his brother.

" Nat," he protested indignantly, " you promised ! "

Covered as he was by the body of the gallant boy, Straight Pine could easily have plucked his rifle up again, but he did not make the slightest attempt to do so.

" Stand clear, you young fool ! " the trapper snarled. " If it's the war-trail them reds are on, I'll send one of 'em to

the happy huntin'-grounds right now! **Stand clear!**"

"No!" Dick answered quietly. "The chief spared your life when he held it at his mercy, an' you gave your word that it was peace."

Still Straight Pine sat unmoved, his fine eyes staring into the fire. Apparently the conversation had no interest whatever for him.

With the quick action bred of a life among the dangers of the great forest, Nat Wild lowered his rifle, gripped Dick, swung him out of the way, and raised the weapon again. Straight Pine looked up, but did not flinch when he saw that the rifle was covering him.

"No Scalp should save his powder **for his**

Straight Pine slipped off his light robe, and, almost without rocking the frail canoe, plunged over into the lake. (*See page* 286.)

A JONES

enemies," Whatawa said, " who lurk already in the woods, and whose eyes and feet are turned to Fort Larabee."

There was something in the chief's voice which began to impress the trapper, and he lowered his rifle, though still holding it ready for emergencies.

" Guess we might hear some more about this, chief," he said ; then, reaching a hand behind him, touched Dick. That he was more than usually fond of the lad could be easily seen.

" Sit thee down, Dick," he said quickly. " I'm rough ; but it's the woods does it. You won't be believin' all a chief tells you when you've lived long as I have wi' the muzzle o' my gun always turned towards 'em "

" Now then, Straight Pine, what's the trouble ? "

Whatawa spread his thin hands towards the fire, and a flicker of a smile showed on his thin-lipped mouth.

" Is the paleface chief deaf ? " he murmured, " that he cannot understand Straight Pine's words ? Has he not already heard that the Hurons and Mingoes have dug up the hatchet and are on the war-path ? Many have risen ; the lodges are filled only by the children, the squaws, and the old men."

" A big fight ? " Nat Wild muttered sharply.

" Black Hawk, the Mingoe, has sworn to capture Fort Larabee," Straight Pine answered. " Also has he sworn to add the scalp of every paleface in the woods to those already hanging dry from his tent-poles."

Dick had been listening more than a little eagerly. He had had some trouble in getting his brother to allow him to come from the settlements to hunt, and the prospect of a brush with redskins was almost too good to be true.

" Will there be a fight, chief ? " he asked eagerly.

" Hist ! " Straight Pine said sharply, and dropped forward across the fire, scattering the embers. He must have burnt himself more than a little, but he gave no sign. " Follow," he whispered.

There was a dead silence ; then, from not far away, came the cracking of a twig. Nat

Wild instantly swung his rifle round in that direction, but Straight Pine touched him on the arm.

" Follow," he commanded again.

Lifting an end of the blanket, the chief crawled beneath it into the open. Dick came next, and Nat Wild last—all three with their guns cocked and ready. At this crawl, Straight Pine advanced a few yards, then rose and touched Dick on the arm.

" Up ! " he whispered, pointing to a great tree by which he stood ; and the lad, even in the darkness, could see that notches had been cut in the trunk, at equal distances, with a tomahawk.

Without hesitation, guessing correctly what was required of him, Dick started to climb the tree, and behind him followed the chief and Nat Wild. There was no question of enmity between the last two now.

Thirty or forty feet the three mounted, and, reaching a part of the trunk where broad branches spread out from it, each lay down on a branch, Whatawa showing Dick the one which he was to occupy.

Up in the tree there was absolutely no light, and the two men and a boy, although they lay within a few feet of each other, were completely hidden one from the other. Not that they troubled about that ; there were other things to think about. Straight Pine, lying like a part of the branch on which he was stretched, stared down in the direction of the little enclosure of blankets, and Nat Wild, on a branch near to him, looked in the same direction.

Once more a twig cracked, and the noise was followed by the click of the hammer of the chief's rifle. He had uncocked it while climbing the tree, but now he set it at full cock again. Nat Wild followed his example.

For the third time there came the noise of a twig snapping, and on this occasion it was much nearer. Almost as it snapped the rifle of Straight Pine altered its angle. There was a pause of a second, then the barrel belched its tongue of flame into the darkness of the night.

Up through the smoke, following close upon the heels of the report, came a wild shriek of pain.

The Tragedy of the Topper

By JACK BLAKE

1

Take it up tenderly,
Lift it with care;
Fashioned so slenderly,
Dainty and rare!
Spread it out decently
On the hall mat;
It arrived recently—
Gussy's new hat!

2

Had it a sister?
Had it a brother?
Did someone twist her?
Ask me another!
Had it a brim with it?
What silly lout
Played in the gym with it,
Knocked it about?

3

Who had a kick at it
When it first came?
Who shied a brick at it,
Skilful of aim?
Who tried to gratify
Hooligan whims?
I'll find out that if I
Search all St. Jim's!

4

This sight will terrify
Gussy, poor lad!
I do not err if I
Say he'll be mad!
He will look sinister
When this is found;
And he'll administer
Lickings all round!

5

P'raps some one mangled it
When it turned up;
P'raps Towser strangled it,
Savage bull pup!
Smothered with jam it is,
Rent and forlorn;
Crowned with calamities,
Rumpled and torn!

6

Stifle your merriment,
Gussy draws near!
As an experiment
We'd better clear!
Nothing can justify
This sorry biz:
But I shall bust if I
See Gussy's phiz!

"Ugh!" the Indian grunted softly, and, despite the awkwardness of his position, commenced to recharge his piece.

"You killed," Nat Wild whispered with evident satisfaction.

"The wounded cries loudest," Straight Pine answered. "The Mingoe dog hath life enough left to carry his scalp away on his head."

"But you wouldn't have scalped him, chief?" Dick protested hurriedly.

"Of what use is the scalp to a dead man?" Straight Pine answered calmly. "Without it the victory is not complete, and the brave shall receive no honour for it when he returns empty-handed to the wigwams of his tribe."

Dick would have said more in protest against the old Indian custom, for he had not been long enough in the woods to understand that there were two laws governing the conduct of men, one for the red and another for the white, but Straight Pine reached back and touched him warningly, at the same time crouching closer to the branch on which he lay.

That there was reason for this caution the lad felt sure, though he could not understand it. It seemed to him that, lying on these branches, he and his companions were just about as safe as they could very well be. He was soon to learn something of the cunning of the foes against whom he was fighting for the first time.

Of a sudden Nat Wild raised himself a trifle on his broad branch, and his rifle spoke sharply. No cry followed the shot, which had been aimed at an upward angle, but something large and heavy came crashing down through the smaller branches of a neighbouring tree, to land with a thud in the heavy undergrowth.

"If it hadn't bin for the white streak o' paint between his eyes," Nat Wild remarked coolly, as he reloaded his piece, "one o' us might ha' bin lying down there 'stead o' him now."

"No Scalp is right," Straight Pine assented. "The rest of the night will pass in peace, and my paleface brothers may sleep as safely as if they were in the fort."

Straight Pine proved to be correct. Throughout the night the two men and the boy lay up in the branches of the great tree, their ears strained to catch the slightest sound, but none came. With the dawn, too, there was no sign of the enemy, save the body that lay still, the light showing the paint marks of the Mingoes, in the undergrowth beneath the trees.

THE THIRD CHAPTER.

To Fort Larabee—Nat Wild Suspicious —The Herd of Moose—Straight Pine in Time—Under Cover.

NAT WILD climbed down rather stiffly from the tree, and the others followed. Dick shuddered slightly as his eyes fell upon the body of the Indian, but it was not with fear. Never before had he seen blood shed in anger, though it was a common enough thing, even close to the forts and settlements, and the sight of it stirred him. He was glad that it was not the bullet from his rifle that had pierced the redskin.

"It was well, Young Horse—the will of Manitou," Straight Pine said softly, reading the lad's thoughts as easily as if he had put them into words, and then he hurried off amongst the trees.

Just for a second the trapper raised his rifle, covering the retreating form, then hesitated and lowered it. Dick stared at his brother in amazement.

"What made you do that, Nat?" he asked.

"When you've bin in the woods as long as I have, lad," Wild answered, "ye'll learn mistrust."

Nat Wild peered among the trees in the direction that the chief had taken, but could see nothing of him. The birds were beginning to sing now, as the sun rose, and the air struck rather chill.

"Well, I'd trust the chief," Dick persisted, with something of the dogged look of his elder brother coming into his face.

From the left came the swish of a branch swinging back after it had been brushed aside. As the sound reached him, Nat caught his brother by the arm, forced him behind the trunk of a tree, and stationed himself behind another. Both looked to the priming of their guns. The chirp of a bird sounded, and Nat lowered his weapon, though without moving from the cover afforded by the trunk of the tree.

" 'Tis the Delaware," he muttered.

From among the trees, and into the little natural clearing in which Nat and Dick Wild stood, stepped Straight Pine. His face was calm as ever, betraying no emotion or feeling of any kind. He looked round sharply, and a slight smile crossed his lips.

"The Young Horse is showing his head," he said. "It would be a mark for a Mingoe bullet."

Nat Wild stepped from behind the tree, and Dick, feeling rather disgusted that he had been spotted so quickly, followed.

"Well?" the trapper growled. "Found anything, chief?"

"Much and little," Straight Pine answered. "I have found the trail of the wounded Mingoe, who travels back towards the lodges of his people."

Nat Wild laughed, and looked triumphant.

"There you are, chief," he cried. "What did I tell you? It's jest one or two o' the young braves out huntin', tryin' to get a scalp. Thar's no digging up o' the hatchet by the hull tribe."

Straight Pine looked to his rifle, and freshened up the priming in the pan.

"Yet birds that are not birds call to each other among the trees," the chief said quietly.

"Meanin' them Mingoe hounds?" the trapper demanded.

"No Scalp speaks the words of wisdom. Truly he must be great among his own people," Straight Pine agreed. "We must journey to Fort Larabee before the bird-calls change to yells of triumph, I to take warning, and you that the Young Horse and No Scalp shall be safe."

"You reckon ter tote along with us, chief?" Nat Wild asked.

Straight Pine glanced uneasily at the shadows amongst the trees, as if, even now, there might be danger lurking there.

"Without Straight Pine," he said quietly, and there was nothing of the boaster in his manner, "my paleface brothers would never reach the fort. I would not have their scalps at the belts of the Mingoes."

Nat Wild laughed angrily. He was no more than thirty years of age, but during the whole of that time he had practically lived in the forests, and flattered himself that he knew them as well as the redskins themselves. Therefore he was angry at the remark of the chief, which seemed to suggest that he had not the skill to escape the dangers which were supposed to be lurking near.

"Thar I'll prove you wrong, chief," he growled. "You go your way, we'll go ours—me an' Dick—an' I'll bet a pack o' beaver-skins that we're at the fort afore you."

Straight Pine turned quietly away, and, with his rifle at the trail, moved off towards the trees, going north, in the direction whence Fort Larabee lay. Before he had gone half a dozen steps, however, Dick hurried after him.

"Good-bye, chief," he said quietly, holding out his hand.

Straight Pine took the proffered hand, and looked down earnestly into the boy's face.

"Whatawa's scalp shall hang from the tent-pole if harm comes to the Young Horse," he said.

And disappeared amongst the trees.

Nat Wild had recovered from his outburst of temper now, and he smiled as he looked at Dick. He was very fond of the boy, and would have laid down his life for him.

"You shouldn't ha' done thet, lad," he said.

"But he's a friend, Nat," Dick protested.

"Thar ain't such a thing as friendship atween red and white," Nat continued doggedly. "An' Straight Pine's no more a friend, 'cept that he's warned us thet the Mingoes mean trouble."

"You do believe that?" the boy asked eagerly, his eyes glistening at the idea of fights in the future.

"Ay, I believe it," Nat answered. And it might have been seen that he, too, glanced round from time to time at the trees. "An' I'm gettin' you back to Fort Larabee as quick as we kin make the trail."

And the two started off through the wood

It was plain enough now that the big trapper had taken the Delaware's warning to heart, for though he moved fast, each step was taken with care, and scarcely a sound marked his progress. Dick, following close behind him, moved in his brother's footsteps, and so they stole away through the forest, some parts of which, owing to the thickness of the leaves overhead, were quite dark, making in the direction of Fort Larabee, which, with luck, they should reach in three days.

Throughout the morning the two travelled on without discovering the slightest sign of danger, until Nat, with a recklessness which was part of his nature, ceased to be so cautious in his movements, and strode on rapidly, brushing branches aside and letting dry twigs crack loudly beneath his moccasined feet.

It was shortly after noon that the man and the boy found the forest growing thinner, and presently they halted on the edge of a rolling prairie. Away to both right and left stretched the forest, to which they would keep if they wanted to make the fort, knowing that the open prairie before them would give them no chance in a brush with the Mingoes.

"Look—moose!" Dick cried excitedly.

Nat shaded his eyes with a great hand, and looked away to the right, the direction in which the boy was pointing. There, sure enough, but fully five hundred yards away still, were six large animals, undoubtedly possessing the curiously-rounded snouts and long antlers of the American moose.

"Ay, it's luck for ye, lad!" Nat said, almost as excited as his younger brother. "Ye'll be able ter see what ye can do with the rifle now."

An idea occurred to Dick, and he looked rather dejected.

"It won't be safe to fire, will it?" he asked. "There may be Injuns——"

"We've left 'em long since," Nat Wild answered, with his usual recklessness. "Come on, lad, an' we'll git ter windward, an' see what we kin do."

Moving back among the trees, Nat led the way to the right, meaning in this way to get to windward of the moose, which would then be about a couple of hundred yards distant.

From tree to tree went the two, Dick excited at the prospect of being able to test his skill with the rifle, Nat almost equally pleased at the chance offered. Nearer and nearer they drew, until the trapper, seeing one of the animals throw its head up, as if scenting danger, stopped short and raised his rifle to his shoulder.

"Now, Dick," he said sharply.

Up went the boy's rifle, butt to shoulder; but before he could even take aim a sinewy hand, darting from behind the trunk of a tree, gripped him, and heaved him into cover.

Nat turned sharply to see what had happened, and was amazed to see Straight Pine looking out at him from behind the tree.

"Mingoes," the chief whispered.

And, quick to act on such warnings, Nat leapt behind the tree, too.

"Where?" he demanded, peering round quickly, and seeing nothing.

"The moose," Straight Pine said coolly.

Nat Wild broke into a laugh, then checked himself, and looked savage.

"See here, chief," he growled. "I didn't reckon to hev you round again, an' I don't want you. Guess I know moose when I see 'em, an' those ain't no Mingoe hounds playin' the game as animals."

"Ugh!" Straight Pine grunted, and dropped full length to the ground.

Pressing his rifle forward, and resting the barrel on the trunk of a small fallen tree, Straight Pine took aim and fired. A little cloud of smoke rose between the two men and the boy and the moose, but it quickly lifted, and a sharp cry broke from Nat Wild.

The place where the supposed moose had been was empty, save for some dark skins lying on the ground, and six Indians, in full feather, were bolting for the shelter of the nearest trees.

"Will No Scalp hunt now?" Straight Pine queried calmly.

Nat Wild turned as the chief rose, and gripped him by the hand.

"Guess you've got us out of an awkward fix, chief," he said. "Not thet I'd keer for myself, it's Dick."

Straight Pine turned and smiled at the boy.

"Straight Pine the Young Horse's friend," he said quietly. "Not let scalp dry at the belt of the Mingoe dog."

THE FOURTH CHAPTER.

Teachings of the Woods—The Canoe in the Hollow Tree—The Wisp of Smoke —Down the Quesna Lake.

"BUT how did ye get here, chief?" Nat Wild asked curiously.

"Follow—plenty plain trail," the Delaware answered. "Palefaces move as if all Indians had gone to happy hunting-grounds."

"Ye're right, chief," the trapper admitted, rather shamefacedly. "Guess you made me wild, sayin' I couldn't git the boy through ter the fort, an' I didn't keer much."

He glanced towards Dick, who did not appear to be in the least bothered by the position in which he found himself.

"That why Straight Pine come back," the Delaware said quietly. "Know better way to the fort than through forest. Every tree hide brave and gun.

Straight Pine took the proffered hand, and looked down earnestly into the boy's face.
"Whatawa's scalp shall hang from the tent-pole if harm comes to the Young Horse," he said. *(See page 277.)*

No able to see them. The great lake lies smooth and still as the face of a young squaw, and across it we could hear the dip of the paddles, or the splash of the swimmer. No fight from trees there."

Nat Wild turned in amazement and said :

"But, say, chief, ain't we miles from the Quesna Lake?"

Whatawa raised a hand towards the heavens, pointing at the sun, then moved his arm round, with fine dignity, to a point further to the westward.

"By then, No Scalp," he said, "we should be at the lake."

"Reckon you know this part, then, chief?" Nat said.

The Delaware smiled, and without further argument or talk the three set off through the woods. Straight Pine led the way, moving with all the caution natural to men of his colour, especially when they have enemies upon the war-path; next came Dick, imitating the movements of the chief as nearly as he could; while the big trapper brought up the rear.

For rather more than an hour the three journeyed on. Once the Delaware stopped, dropped to his hands and knees, and drew a damp and soiled moccasin from the thick undergrowth. He grunted and handed it to Nat Wild. The latter turned it over a few times, looked puzzled, and returned it to the chief.

"Don't tell me much, Straight Pine," he said. "What do you know?"

" Yes, what does it tell you, chief ? " Dick asked eagerly, ready to learn all he could of woodcraft from so able a teacher as the Delaware.

Straight Pine turned the moccasin over, and a sharp grunt, practically the only sign of emotion that he ever allowed himself, broke from him.

Nat Wild guessed that the Delaware had discovered something important.

" What d'you know, Straight Pine ? " he demanded.

" Moccasin belong Lame Bear, the Huron chief," the Indian answered. " See, hide worn in one place only, where chief walk heavy. Only one chief among Huron do that—Lame Bear."

" Then things is bad," Nat Wild muttered, his brows knit ; " and it ain't no risin' o' jest a few rascally Mingoes. What say you, chief ? "

" All big fight," the Delaware agreed, dropping the moccasin back into the undergrowth. " Lame Bear only fight big fights. Make all speed to lake ! "

Using more precautions than ever now, the three hurried forward, and less than two hours later, bursting from the trees, they emerged on to a shingly beach or clearing. Twenty yards or so ahead lay the waters of the great lake, the opposite shore only just visible, even under the fierce rays of the afternoon sun, and on both sides of the strip of beach, which was no more than a hundred yards from end to end, the trees closed it in, growing so close to the water that their branches dipped down until the leaves touched the glimmering surface. Here and there a tree, its roots undermined by the waters of the lake, lay out into the water, some of the branches above, others below, the still surface.

A buck, drinking just in the shade of the trees, lifted his head sharply, swung round, and galloped off, alarmed at the presence of man. The Delaware grunted with satisfaction.

" No Mingoes near," he said, " or buck not drink."

" Good for you ! " Nat Wild answered, with a sigh of relief. " Reckon I'll feel easier in me mind when we're out on the lake. S'pose we'll hev to make a canoe ? "

The Delaware touched Dick on the arm, and waved a hand towards every corner of the clearing.

" Young Horse see canoe ? " he queried.

Dick looked round carefully, but certainly could see no trace of a craft of any kind.

" No, there isn't such a thing about, chief," he said, with assurance.

With a smile on his lips, Straight Pine led the way to where the trees hung down towards the water. By the edge of the lake lay a great oak, its roots out of the ground. The Indian touched these roots, and a part of them came away in his hands. A minute later he had carefully lifted out a fair-sized canoe, which was fitted with paddles and everything complete.

" But how did you see it, chief ? " Dick cried, in amazement. Then an idea occurred to him. " You've been here before, and it's yours."

Straight Pine shook his head solemnly, and helped Nat Wild to carry the canoe down to the water.

" Delaware never been here before," he said.

" Then it beats me how you found it ! " Nat Wild said.

" Mingoes all like papoose, no sense," the Delaware answered, with a contemptuous gesture back towards the forest where the Mingoes lay. " One hide canoe in tree—all hide in tree. Straight Pine's eyes see roots been disturbed—know find canoe there."

Dick sighed, and looked rather dejected.

" I thought I was going to learn everything about woodcraft this trip, chief," he said ; " but I see I'll never learn it all."

" Yengeese take longer," Straight Pine answered kindly, using the Indian term for white man ; " but Delaware teach, learn all in time. Young Horse soon be great brave— change name to Eagle Eye ! "

" Really, chief ? " the boy said eagerly.

" Straight Pine has spoken, and Young Horse has heard," the Delaware answered with dignity.

The canoe proved to be in very good condition when launched, and the three stepped into it. Dick was placed in the middle, while Straight Pine stood in the bows, paddle in hand, with Nat Wild in the stern. In this way the frail craft shot swiftly out towards the middle of the lake, for both the trapper and the Delaware were skilful with the paddle. Their rifles lay near to their hands, for there was no telling how soon shots might come whistling after them from among the trees. As they moved across the lake, the only dark object, apparently, on its polished surface, they made a splendid mark for any of the Mingoes who might be lying concealed in the forest.

When the canoe had reached a spot about two hundred yards from the shore, which was fairly well out of the range of the guns of the redskins, Straight Pine ceased paddling, and Nat Wild followed his example.

Dick stared away at the great stretches of forest, which seemed to be formed on the same great scale as the Quesna Lake. Right along the bank, save for a few little stretches of beach, stretched the magnificent trees, growing so close together that at a short distance the trunks looked like a solid wall of timber, and it seemed impossible that even a slippery Mingoe would be able to find a path among them. The ground sloped upwards from the lake, making the tops of the trees look like a sloping green field on which shrubs—the topmost tufts of taller trees—were growing sparsely.

In the canoe lay several stout fishing-lines, evidently of Indian workmanship, with hooks ready fixed. Dick, noticing these, took one up to examine it.

"Good!" Straight Pine said. "May be on lake one day, may be"—he held up one hand with all the fingers spread out—" more. The Young Horse fish, that we may have food."

" But the lad's got no bait, chief!" Nat protested.

With neat fingers the Delaware removed a bright red bead, a rather large one, from his scanty attire, and fastened it to the hook.

"Lake fish great fool," he said, " catch with bead."

Just for once, however, Straight Pine appeared to be mistaken, for though Dick hung the line over the side of the canoe, and waited patiently for a bite, not a solitary one came. There was not even a nibble to cheer him up,

and he began to think that the bead could not be the best bait after all. This want of success did not, apparently, trouble either Nat Wild or the Delaware. The former smoked pipe after pipe, his eyes closed, half dozing; while the latter squatted still as a carven image in the bows, not moving a muscle. Only his eyes, which were particularly fine and bright, continually swept the edge of the lake. All through the afternoon, while Dick fished with diminishing patience, the chief sat in this attitude. A haze was already beginning to settle over the water before anything rewarded his watchfulness.

"Camp in forest," he said, turning his head for a moment towards Nat Wild.

Shading his eyes with his hand, the trapper stared hard in the direction indicated by Straight Pine. Half a mile or so inland a faint line of smoke, almost white, was rising over the tops of the trees. Already it was nearly invisible in the darkness.

"Scarce like a Mingoe to show as plain a trail as thet, chief," said Nat Wild.

"Mingoe on war-path, but not near fort yet," Straight Pine answered readily. " Young braves at fire sure scalp us, not trouble about damp wood like wise brave."

"Perhaps you're right," Nat agreed, as the darkness hid the smoke from his eyes. " Reckon I'll be glad when it's dark eno' ter strike down the lake. Never knew the fort seem sich a long way off as it does now."

Night fell rapidly; and as soon as the shores were quite invisible Straight Pine rose to his feet, paddle in hand. Nat followed his example, and the canoe began to glide swiftly across the water. What little current there was was in their favour, so that there was nothing to hinder them making rapid progress.

Mile after mile was covered in this fashion, the chief glancing round continually, as if even in the darkness he could see; though Dick, strain his eyes though he would, could not pierce the blackness for more than a few feet in any direction.

Midnight passed, but even then the Delaware called no halt, and for a couple of hours more he paddled on, showing no signs whatever that the exertion was telling upon him.

Yet Nat Wild, enormously powerful though he was, was fairly dripping with perspiration, though he said no word, either of complaint or suggestive of weariness. He knew well enough that if Fort Larabee was to be reached, it would be by the aid of Straight Pine. Unless——

Once again suspicious thoughts entered the trapper's head. All his life he had spent in the woods, and he knew the craftiness of the redskin. It was possible, even now, that the Delaware, although he had served them, was only awaiting his opportunity to take their scalps, their rifles, and any other trifles of value that they might possess. Nat remembered how easily the chief had found the canoe, as easily as if he had himself hidden it, and he stared suspiciously at the naked, sinewy back of the chief, as if expecting that it would tell him the truth.

Straight Pine turned his head a trifle and swung his paddle outwards, bringing the canoe half round, and almost stopping its motion.

"Good place for halt!" he whispered.

Then for the first time Nat Wild saw that the chief had guided the canoe to a spot where several flat rocks rose above the water, two or three to a height of about two feet. Many such rocks existed in the lake, most of them within a hundred yards or so of the shore.

THE FIFTH CHAPTER.

The Paddleless Canoe—The Drifting Bushes.

" LAND here," the chief whispered quietly, holding the canoe steady by keeping a hand on the rock.

Without the slightest hesitation—for he wished to show that he, at least, did not suspect the redskin—Dick landed, taking his rifle with him; but Nat Wild hesitated.

"What for, Delaware?" he demanded.

"Safe there, fight many braves," Straight Pine answered. "Straight Pine go scout in canoe, see no Mingoe fish about!"

That there was wisdom in this suggestion the trapper could not help realising, and he landed on the rock. As soon as he was there the Delaware pushed the canoe off, took up a paddle and, standing in the stern of the frail craft, disappeared into the darkness. He moved against the slight current, knowing that swimmers would most likely come down with it rather than force a passage against it.

Squatting on the rock, his rifle across his knees, Dick close beside him, Nat Wild stared moodily across the water, his ears strained to catch the slightest sound. The faint noise of the dipping paddle had already been swallowed up by distance, and not a sound broke the rather fearsome stillness of the night.

"Go to sleep, Dick," he said, a trifle gruffly, without looking towards the boy. "You'll be fresher on the morrow."

Dick laid his rifle down carefully, stretched himself on the rock, and was soon fast asleep.

It was not until the dawn that Dick awoke, stretched himself, and sat up hastily. Nat still squatted in the same position, his rifle ready across his knees, his eyes, rather red with their long vigil, roving round the surface of the lake.

"Keep down, lad," he said sharply, "or you may be seen from the shore. If the Mingoes know we're right here, you'd git a dozen bullets when you showed your scalp!"

That Straight Pine had not returned Dick could see, and he looked round anxiously, searching the lake for the canoe. A sigh of relief escaped him as he caught sight of it, not more than half a mile away. Then the sigh changed to a gasp.

There was the canoe sure enough, drifting down with the current, but to all appearances she was empty.

"He has been captured!" Dick cried.

"Not he!" Nat growled. "Trust a Delaware for bein' too cunnin' fer that! Whar's yer eyes, boy? Look to the side o' the canoe farthest from the shore."

Dick looked, and saw something had escaped him at the first glance. A dark arm was thrust over the side, and a hand was beating the water like a paddle. The speed obtained in this way was not great, the canoe simply looking as if carried along by a rather strong current; but it was quite enough to bring it perceptibly closer to the rocks, even as the boy watched it.

"But suppose it isn't Straight Pine?" he said suddenly. "He might have been captured, the canoe taken, and the man paddling it may be a Mingoe."

"Good for you, Dick!" the trapper answered, with a glance of pride at his young brother. "It's mebbe that, but it ain't likely. No more'n three o' the hounds could git into thet canoe, an' they wouldn't attack if thar wasn't a clear dozen of them."

By now the canoe had drawn quite near, and the hand over the side, working more skilfully, steered the fragile craft to the rocks. Nat, holding his rifle ready, moved nearer to the edge of the rock to meet it.

The grave face of the Delaware chief was raised, and the Indian clambered out on to the rock.

"Ugh!" he said, with a slight smile at Dick, giving the customary Indian greeting.

"What news, chief?" the trapper asked.

"Fort too far away, No Scalp," the Delaware answered meaningly.

Nat Wild understood the Indian's words, and looked more than usually grave.

"The hounds mean business, then?"

"The Mingoe braves yearn for scalps as a young squaw yearns over her husband," Straight Pine answered. "Many of them are there in the woods, silent as the snakes lying among the grasses, and their paint is fresh as the scalps that will hang from their belts before they return to their lodges across the hills."

"Humph! Cheerful!" the trapper muttered, for he knew that the Delaware meant that the situation was more than usually grave.

He looked round, and was relieved to see how isolated the rocks were. They stretched away for fully twenty to thirty yards towards the shore, but a clear space of two hundred yards of water lay between the nearest rock and the land.

"Well, they can't attack by daylight, anyway," Nat Wild said, with confidence, "thet's one comfort, for we'll be able to git further out into the lake when it's dark, an' run nearer down towards the fort."

Straight Pine turned towards the trapper and eyed him solemnly.

"Many years has No Scalp lived in the woods," he said, "but he has yet much to learn. Can he not see that the attack of the Mingoes will be soon?"

"I'll be hanged if he can!" Nat growled. "An' I don't believe you can, either, chief."

"Straight Pine will prove his words," the Delaware said composedly, with the air of a man who has no fear of being proved wrong.

The redskin looked to his gun and freshened up the priming, an operation over which he exercised care, but in this case he appeared to use even more than usual, and the trapper, noticing this, looked to his own weapon. Dick, always ready to follow the lead of the chief, was already doing the same. All three weapons were ready in the hands of their owners for anything that might happen.

Close to the edge of the rock sat the Delaware, his eyes fixed on a part of the shore, fully four hundred yards away, that he could see round the corner of the stone. His face was absolutely devoid of expression, and even his eyes, expressive though they were, told nothing.

"The Young Horse sees something on the lake?" he queried presently, turning to Dick.

The boy shaded his eyes from the glare, for the sun was getting up now, and looked hard in the direction indicated by the Delaware.

"Looks like bushes floating with the current," he said, catching sight of eight or nine dark objects fifty or sixty yards from the shore, which were floating towards the rocks, moving as leisurely as the current which bore them along.

"Young Horse's eyes are good," the Delaware murmured. "Does No Scalp see them?"

"Ain't blind!" the trapper growled. "Guess I know a bush when I see it."

Straight Pine bent his head with a stately gesture.

"Truly the paleface speaks wisdom!" he murmured.

And though the trapper glanced at the chief sharply, he could not detect anything suggestive of a sneer on the painted face.

Very slowly the bushes drew nearer, moving as surely towards the farther end of the rocks as if they were being pulled in that direction by a line; but it was not until they were within a hundred yards that Straight Pine appeared to take any more notice of them. Then he turned to Dick.

"The Young Horse shall try his aim with the rifle," he said quietly. "Let him get behind that rock"—he indicated a fair-sized stone close at hand—"and see if he can hit the nearest of the bushes."

"Waste o' powder an' ball," Nat growled.

"Not so, No Scalp!" the Delaware continued. "The test of a hawk's eye should be sure, so that he may know its power against his enemies."

Nothing loth to try his skill with the rifle, Dick crawled to the rock indicated, rested the barrel of his rifle upon it, and took a careful aim at the nearest of the bushes. Straight Pine watched the bushes, and not the marksman.

"The Young Horse should fire low," he said. "Rather hit the body of a foe and wound it than miss putting a hole through the brain."

Dick slightly shifted his aim, and his finger pulled steadily at the trigger. The rifle cracked, and the bush at which it had been aimed moved as sharply as if a cannon-ball had brushed it. Not only did it move, too, for suddenly it disappeared beneath the water, and a muffled yell reached the ears of those on the rocks.

Then Nat saw how he had been deceived, and, dropping to full length on the rock, he aimed at the bushes. His rifle cracked the moment the sight was taken, and a shriek of pain followed close upon the heels of the report.

"Is it a waste of powder, No Scalp?" the Delaware asked coolly.

Nat looked up sharply from the reloading of his rifle.

"Why couldn't ye tell me it was them skunks o' Mingoes wi' bushes tied to their heads?" he demanded, eyeing the remaining bushes, which were now moving rapidly towards the shore.

"No Scalp has eyes," Straight Pine answered unconcernedly.

For a moment the big trapper looked wild, then he laughed heartily, and held out his hand to the chief. Once more it was not taken.

"Straight Pine has not proved his friendship yet, No Scalp," he said proudly.

Down the Lake Again—Anchored for the Night—The Floating Log—Dick Wild Captured.

"WHAT next, chief?" Nat asked, glancing round the lake, as if fearing that the Mingoes were likely to attack again, though it was not likely, as they had had two of their braves injured while trying to reach the rocks under cover of the bushes.

"It is no longer well to stay here," the Delaware answered. "We must push down the lake, and trust to finding the Mingoes asleep long enough for us to land. Only a turn of the sun will be between us and the fort then."

"True, chief," Nat Wild agreed, "thar don't seem any other way."

In a very few minutes the canoe was freed and the two men and the boy stepped warily into her. Straight Pine and the trapper took the paddles, and under their vigorous strokes she shot out from the shelter of the rocks into the lake. To take her out of sight of the keen eyes watching from the forest was impossible, as the Delaware knew, so he was content to travel along at a distance of some two hundred yards from the shore, which was well out of reach of the rifle of the average Mingoe, most of which were not to be relied upon at any distance over a hundred yards.

Working easily, so as not to fatigue themselves early, yet sending the canoe along rapidly, the two men worked as steadily and evenly as machines. Dick, his eyes always turned towards the forest-bordered bank, found it difficult to realise that there really could be bloodthirsty savages lurking there. Nowhere was there a sign of life, yet he knew, as well as his brother or the Delaware, that swift-footed Indians, forcing their way through the forest, were keeping pace with the canoe.

Right through the day the canoe was kept moving, save for one or two brief halts for rest. Dick took a turn at the paddle, too, only to find that his want of skill made the progress of the canoe much slower than it was under the hands of Straight Pine and his brother. And, curiously enough, as it seemed to Dick, never a Mingoe showed for an instant among the trees,

There was the canoe sure enough, drifting down with the current, but to all appearances she was empty. "Straight Pine has been captured!" Dick cried. "Not he!" Nat growled. "Whar's yer eyes, boy? Look to the side o' the canoe farthest from the shore." (*See page* 282.)

and the shore looked as deserted as if nothing but the animals of the forest came there to drink.

"I suppose they are following," Dick muttered, giving voice to his thoughts.

"Does the she-bear forsake her young," the Delaware answered, "more than the Mingoe brave hankers for scalps?"

Nat paused in his paddling, wiped the sweat from his brow with his hand, and stared away at the trees.

"If we was ter run a hundred yards closer in,

(285)

lad," he said, " ye'd soon learn thet the hounds is thar. It ain't safe ter think o' them trees 'cept that each hides a redskin."

Once more the canoe moved on, and Dick, trailing a line overboard, for there was no chance of landing a Mingoe instead of a fish in broad daylight, caught three fair-sized fish, much to the satisfaction of the big trapper, whose huge form required a large amount of nourishment, though he could do without it when occasion demanded the sacrifice.

And so hour after hour passed, the forest slipping monotonously by, indented here and there by a strip of shingly beach, until day changed to dusk, and dusk to night. Before this hour had come, however, the shores of the lake had narrowed considerably, until they were little more than three hundred yards apart, and it was only by keeping right to the centre of the water that those in the canoe could keep out of range of Mingoe or Huron bullets. It was lucky for them that the redskins were unlikely to try shooting at a range greater than a hundred yards.

Under cover of the darkness the canoe still kept on, the two men paddling more carefully than ever, rising and dipping noiselessly, save for the occasional drip of the water from the paddles finding its way back into the lake.

Straight Pine swung his paddle in a wide semicircle, altering the course of the canoe, and was only just in time to avoid running into a heavy log, a collision with which might have sunk the frail bark canoe.

" Ugh ! " he grunted softly, paddling on again, and making a sign to Nat Wild, who had opened his lips to speak, to remain silent.

The canoe still kept on, the water rippling back from her bows. The Delaware had changed his standing position to a kneeling one, and his head and shoulders were thrust forward, his luminous eyes peering sharply into the blackness ahead. From time to time he would cease paddling, the trapper always following his example without spoken order, and listen intently. Once he picked up his rifle and looked to the priming.

For the second time Straight Pine swung the canoe out of the way of a floating log, which showed suddenly in the darkness. He stopped paddling, and crouched low down,

his left hand resting on his rifle. Dick felt a hand on his shoulder, and his brother, clambering over him as surely as if he had been in a heavy boat, knelt behind Straight Pine. The boy promptly shifted back, so as to make the weight in the canoe more evenly distributed.

" Many logs about, No Scalp," the Delaware whispered, a curious note in his voice.

" Ay, I've noticed 'em," Nat Wild answered. " Question is, chief, air they jest logs washed from the shore, or air they some devilish work o' them Mingoe hounds ? "

" Straight Pine will know if the logs drift," said the chief quietly.

At war-time the redskins are not given to the wearing of many garments, and Straight Pine was no exception to the rule. He now slipped off his light robe, and, almost without rocking the frail canoe, plunged over into the lake. He was quickly on the surface again, and resting one hand on the gunwale of the canoe.

" No Scalp will wait," he said, " and guard the Young Horse. Let him fire at anyone who approaches unless he give the call of the wren."

" I understand ye, chief," the trapper answered. " But aren't ye runnin' a mighty lot o' risk if them logs is——"

" The Young Horse must be saved," Straight Pine interrupted, glancing towards the boy, and, before further protest could be made, he had released his hold of the canoe and swum gently off into the darkness, his limbs working so smoothly that not a sound was made.

Dick, sitting in the stern of the canoe, watched the chief's head until it was swallowed up completely by the darkness, then he turned to his brother.

" Wish he hadn't gone, Nat," he whispered.

" Ay, ye're right in a way," the big trapper answered, " though I reckon I'd rather see Straight Pine lose his scalp than you. Redskins air built that way, and it's the usual manner fer them to take leave o' this world."

" He's a fine man, anyway," Dick continued enthusiastically. " Why should he trouble about us ? "

Nat grunted doubtingly, then laughed.

"Guess you're right again," he muttered. "I mistrusted the chief—his colour's agin him—but I reckon he's provin' himself white-hearted."

The end of a log bumped the canoe, causing the frail craft to rock badly. Dick leant over the side to push it away, for fear that it might pierce the bark, and a cry of surprise broke from his lips.

Along the log, lying so close to it that he looked almost like a part of the timber, lay a Mingoe, his face hideous with the war-paint of his tribe.

As Dick cried out Nat turned sharply, but, quick though he was, the Mingoe was quicker. He rose on the log as surely as if he had been on firm ground, seized the surprised boy by the collar, and jerked him clean from the canoe into the water, into which they both fell struggling.

With a fierce cry of rage, Nat snatched up his rifle, meaning to aim at the bobbing head of the Indian as soon as he could be sure of not hitting Dick, but before he could do so he had other matters to occupy his attention.

Nine or ten more logs came gliding to the canoe, and tomahawks and knives glittered as the Hurons and Mingoes on them prepared for battle. Their awe-inspiring war-cry echoed across the lake, and, for the moment at least, the big trapper forgot about Dick's peril; not that he could have done much in any case.

Nat's rifle cracked, and a yell, rising even above the war-cry, showed that he had not wasted powder and shot.

"Thet's one varmint!" he growled, and swung his rifle by its long barrel as the nearest of the Indians aimed a quick blow at him with a tomahawk.

The butt of the rifle fell, true as a sledge-hammer wielded by a sure hand, and the tomahawk fell into the water, the Huron's wrist snapped like a pipe-stem.

"Two!" the big trapper snarled, and ducked as a hatchet came whirling through the air. Quick though he was, it carried away his hat.

Keeping to his knees, so as not to risk the upsetting of the canoe, Nat swung the rifle like a flail. Once he reached a Mingoe, the butt catching him on the side of the neck and flinging him into the water, then the rest, leaving their logs, swam away into the darkness. They were not the men to risk more casualties, but were quite ready to wait a chance to win without danger to their precious bodies.

With the instinct of the pioneer, Nat methodically reloaded his rifle, then searched the water with his eyes. His jaw was set grimly and his brows knit hard. A little pulse seemed to be beating furiously at the top of his head.

"Dick!" he cried hoarsely. "Dick!"

There was no answer.

"Dick!" the trapper cried again, his voice hoarse with emotion, but still there was no answer.

From the left shore of the lake came a wild yell, and Nat Wild knew what it meant : that Dick or his scalp had been landed. A shudder ran through him as he thought the lad might be already dead, and therefore past aid.

Past aid—yes, but not beyond vengeance. Nat's jaw set harder than ever, and, dropping his rifle, he seized a paddle. He would land, and force his way into the very camp of the savages. He would at least die as Dick had died.

The call of a wren came softly across the water, and the trapper, hearing it, paused with the paddle already in the water. It was a strange hour for the bird to be calling to its mate, and might mean——

Nat remembered that it was the signal arranged by Straight Pine, and remained still in the canoe, searching the water with his eyes in the direction from whence the call had come. Soon he caught sight of the head of the Delaware, then a hand gripped the canoe, and, with an agility that no white man could have equalled, he managed to enter the frail craft.

"Ugh!" he grunted dismally, as he sat down and panted for breath.

"Dick's gone!" the trapper cried wildly. "Scalped by them——"

"The Young Horse still lives," the Delaware interrupted.

A gasp of relief broke from Nat, and he bent forward eagerly.

"How d'ye know, chief?" he demanded.

"Straight Pine swim in the lake," the Delaware answered, "his eyes see the fight and the fall of Young Horse. Straight Pine fought with Mingoe. Other Mingoe hounds come, make Young Horse prisoner; Straight Pine swim away that he may save to-morrow."

THE SEVENTH CHAPTER.

On Parole—The Mingoes' Terms— Straight Pine's Sacrifice.

THE night passed very slowly to the two men, Nat showing it in his impatient, restless movements; the Delaware in the occasional discontented "Ugh!" which issued from his lips.

Dawn at last!

With the first flash of light Straight Pine looked sharply round, saw that the canoe had drifted to within eighty or ninety yards of the shore where he knew that the Mingoes and Hurons were encamped with their prisoner, and, taking up a paddle, he forced the canoe out into the centre of the water again. Running unnecessary risks would do Dick no good.

"What now, chief?" the trapper asked hoarsely as the Delaware laid down his paddle.

Nat Wild's face showed the strain that was upon him. It looked thinner, the eyes had a haggard look about them, and the lips were twisted grimly downwards. It was going to be hard for the Mingoe who came within reach of the big trapper.

Straight Pine's eyes were upon the forest, and he nodded to where a line of smoke was rising up among the trees.

"Great fire for braves on war-path," he said. "Chiefs holding council by the fire. Young Horse safe as yet."

Nat Wild picked up his rifle and renewed the priming. He stared hard at the smoke rising above the tops of the tall trees.

"See here, chief!" he said sharply. "We could land now, runnin' the canoe on ter the beach thar; an' I reckon we'd settle a few o' them hounds afore they got our scalps!"

"And Young Horse?" Straight Pine asked quietly.

The trapper groaned, realising what the Delaware meant. Any attack upon the camp would only too surely hasten the end of the boy.

"Can't we do anythin'?" he muttered. "I'd rather they had me ter torture than Dick."

"Also shall they have Straight Pine," the Delaware said, "if that would save the Young Horse. Wait for the fire to——"

"Look!" the trapper gasped in amazement, reaching out for his rifle. "Reckon I never knew a Mingoe risk his hide like that before!"

From out of the trees had stepped a solitary figure, carrying a small canoe on his head. He was moving straight down towards the edge of the lake.

"Thet'll be one of 'em less!" Nat Wild growled.

And the butt of his rifle pressed against his shoulder. His eye glinted along the sights, his finger already bearing upon the trigger, but before he could fire the barrel had been forced up by the Delaware.

"Young Horse," he announced calmly, as if the words conveyed nothing out of the ordinary.

The man carrying the canoe lifted it from his head and lowered it into the water.

"Dick!" Nat Wild gasped, then turned in amazement to the Delaware. "They carn't ha' freed him!" he said. "An' he's not movin' slick enough fer a man escapin'. What's it mean?"

"The Young Horse paddles to us, No Scalp," Straight Pine answered coolly. "We shall learn."

The trapper would have seized a paddle and gone to meet his brother, but the Delaware restrained him.

"The Mingoes watch from the forest," he said warningly.

The other canoe, paddled swiftly by Dick, drew nearer, until Nat was able to see the boy's face. It wore a gloomy expression, and not one indicative of joy at being free.

"Safe, Dick!" Nat cried gleefully, caring about nothing more than that the lad, apparently unharmed, was coming across the lake to him.

The two canoes came together, and Dick was almost lifted by Nat into the larger craft.

"But how did ye get away, boy?" the trapper asked excitedly.

"I didn't," Dick answered; "they let me come."

"They let——"

"On parole," Dick added quietly.

"Ugh!" Straight Pine grunted, to show that he understood.

Nat turned towards him.

"What's it mean, chief?" he asked. "Never heard o' sich things bein' done afore by the Mingoes."

"It means," Straight Pine answered, "that Young Horse has won the trust of the Mingoe and Huron chiefs, and that he has been released for some hours to come out to us. At the end of that time he has given his word that he will return."

"Is that so?" Nat demanded, turning to his brother.

"That's it, Nat," Dick agreed. "I am free until sunset. As soon as the sun begins to sink I must go back to the camp."

The boy shuddered a trifle, but showed no other sign of emotion or fear.

"Will ye?" the big trapper snarled, glaring in the direction of the camp.

"Young Horse has given his word," the Delaware murmured. "But why did the chiefs let him come?"

Dick started, and did not meet the eyes of Straight Pine.

"Oh, just to say good-bye," he answered, with a catch in his voice.

Straight Pine bent forward and touched the boy on the arm.

"Young Horse cannot lie like a Huron," he said quietly; "the look of his eye betrays him. Why has he been sent to his friends?"

Dick hesitated, and his face flushed angrily.

"I was told to give a message," he said slowly.

"What is it, lad?" Nat asked sharply.

"I would rather not give it," Dick answered.

"The words of Young Horse can do no harm," the Delaware said. "Let him not fear to let the ears of his friends receive them."

But still Dick hesitated. His face looked older than it had only a few hours back, and the mouth was as hard set as that of a man who has lived in the face of danger, and who is ready to die with a stiff upper-lip when the time comes.

"The Mingoe and Huron chiefs say this," he said hesitatingly: "Young Horse is in their hands, and though the torture-fires burn low, the squaws already gather fresh fuel. But he is young, and has not been on the war-trail. On the lake is Straight Pine, a chief who has many scalps on the poles of his wigwams, and——"

The boy stopped, his teeth clenched.

"And Young Horse will be freed if Straight Pine will take his place," the Delaware finished quietly. "Are the words truth?"

Dick nodded his head silently, then looked up proudly into the chief's face.

"You would have the message, chief," he said, "or I shouldn't have given it. Neither would I have brought it, only that it gave me the chance of seeing you both again."

"Ay, an' stayin' with us, too!" Nat Wild growled determinedly.

"I have given my word to return, Nat," Dick said sharply.

And the big trapper flushed under the note of indignation in the boy's voice.

"Ay, but what is a word given to a Mingoe?" Nat persisted. "It ain't——"

"I shall keep mine, Nat."

"Young Horse speaks the words of the true brave," Straight Pine said. "But he shall not suffer torture at the hands of his enemies."

Nat wheeled round upon the chief, an eager look in his eyes.

"Ye don't mean to say as you'll take his place, chief?" he gasped.

"I have spoken," the Delaware murmured proudly.

"But you sha'n't!" Dick cried. "Why should you sacrifice yourself? You have only known me a short time, and——"

"The eye of Straight Pine is quick to see," the Delaware interrupted, "and he sees in Young Horse a great chief. He is too young to die; his hand has not yet done its work. The happy hunting-ground shall not be roamed before these forests have given their all to him." The chief waved a hand with dignity towards the forests. "Straight Pine has been a warrior many years, and his name causes Mingoe and Huron dogs to tremble, even when they hear it whispered in their lodges. He has done his work; it is nothing to him that he should die."

Nat stretched out his hand, and this time the Indian took it without hesitation.

"I've wronged ye more than once in the past, chief," the big trapper said hoarsely; "but I won't hev ye do this now. It's my place ter go instead o' the lad, an' ye kin take him safe through ter the fort, an' mebbe keep an eye on him in the future."

"No Scalp is great warrior," the Delaware objected, with a shake of his head, "but more scalps hang at the belt of Straight Pine, and the Mingoes long to see him at the torture."

Dick Wild, as he had truly said, had only consented to bring the message in order that he might see his brother and the Delaware again, and he had no intention of allowing Straight Pine to make such a sacrifice for him. That the Indian was really prepared to do it he could see, but that did not influence him.

"The Mingoes shall pay more than the scalp of Young Horse for the life of Straight Pine," the Delaware continued quietly. "It shall take my paleface brother in safety to the fort."

"You will bargain with them that they let us go through free?" Nat asked quickly.

"I have spoken," Straight Pine murmured.

Dick turned upon his brother, a look of amazement in his eyes.

"You won't let the chief do this?" he cried.

"Mebbe I don't want to, boy," Nat answered huskily. "Heaven knows I'd take his place if them hounds would let me; but, as the chief says, I'm not big eno' game for 'em! I can't let you go, lad; and if the chief means this I kin only let him go. Sooner him than you."

"Ugh!" the Delaware grunted, with obvious satisfaction, for the knowledge of the tortures to which he was voluntarily going did not seem to worry him in the least, though he, as an Indian chief, knew quite well enough how awful they would be.

Straight Pine turned to Dick now, and laid a hand on his shoulder.

"The Young Horse will go back now," he said firmly, "and say that Straight Pine would talk with a chief." He took off his belt of wampum and gave it to the boy. "That will hold the chief's life safe when he comes to meet me."

Dick shook his head, but Nat, picking him up by sheer strength, dropped him back into the other canoe.

"It's the only way, boy," he said sternly. "You carries thet message, an' comes back wi' the chief, or I land now an' ha' a shot at them hounds afore they kill me."

Still Dick hesitated, but, boy though he was, he realised that it would be better for one life than three to be sacrificed. He would have been willing to let the one be his. He took up the paddle gloomily, and paddled back slowly towards the shore. More than once he hesitated, half bringing the nose of the canoe round again; but at last he reached the shore, beached his craft, and disappeared among the trees.

As the boy vanished from sight Nat turned to Straight Pine and once more took his hand.

"Chief," he said earnestly, "I've knowed many redskins since I first came to the woods, but never a lion-heart like ye."

"The words of No Scalp cheer the heart of Straight Pine," the Delaware answered quietly, "and the sacrifice is but the snapping of a dry and withered branch."

No more was said, both men sitting silently in the canoe, their eyes upon the forest. The big trapper could think of no more to say; the Delaware had stated his intention—that was enough for him.

From out of the forest, only a few minutes after Dick had gone into it, came the boy and a tall Indian, both of whom embarked in the canoe.

"Ugh!" Straight Pine grunted, a look of satisfaction on his face. "It is Flying Deer who answers the message of the wampum."

With Dick working the paddle, and the chief of the Hurons standing stiffly in the canoe, as motionless as a carven image, the craft drew near, the Huron motioning Dick to cease paddling when only a matter of twenty yards of water separated the canoes.

The call of the wren sounded softly, for the big trapper was as expert in such things as any redskin, and Nat, peering round the trunk of a tree, entirely hidden by the shadows, looked to see if his signal would be answered. (*See page* 297.)

"Greeting!" the Huron cried. "Flying Deer would speak with the Straight Pine."

"Is there anything to stop him?" the Delaware answered with the suggestion of a sneer in his voice, for he had no love for the Hurons or their chiefs.

"To-day the Young Horse is a prisoner in our camp," Flying Deer continued in his level voice; "but we would part with him,

knowing that No Scalp craves for him, if Straight Pine will take his place at the torture-stake."

"Flying Deer talks like a young brave who is not called to the council fire," the Delaware answered. "Straight Pine has a hundred dry scalps at the poles of his wigwams, the Young Horse has none. Is it a fair exchange?"

The Huron shrugged his shoulders, otherwise he showed no sign of emotion.

"It hath been decided that one must die," he said.

"It is but war," Straight Pine murmured.

"Yet is the Huron as merciful as Manitou," Flying Deer continued quickly; "for will he not set free the beloved of the paleface warrior and take in exchange the Delaware chief?"

"Flying Deer wastes breath," Straight Pine remarked. "Are his ears closed, that he has not heard? More than the paleface boy will be asked for Straight Pine."

Flying Deer's eyes glanced sharply into the other Indian's face, but he could read nothing there.

"Let Straight Pine speak," he said.

Straight Pine drew himself up to his full height.

"For this will I give myself up," he said. "The Young Horse shall be set free to join No Scalp on the lake. Also shall they be permitted to journey unmolested to Fort Larabee. I have spoken."

"And the words are but sounds," the Huron sneered. "Are we squaws, that we cannot come out on to the lake and take our enemies alive for the torture?"

"Where are the scalps of the braves who have tried?" Straight Pine demanded, touching his waist, where the ghastly trophies hung.

"They were but young," Flying Deer answered hastily; "but when Flying Deer and his braves come out, then shall there be three more scalps in the wigwams of the Hurons."

"Guess not," Nat muttered, smiling grimly, as he touched the bald spot on his head.

The two chiefs stood facing each other, neither showing any outward sign of emotion.

"The other chiefs shall hear," the Huron said at last, when it was plain to him that the Delaware did not mean to speak. "At sunset will he bring the word to Straight Pine and No Scalp."

Flying Deer spoke to Dick, and the boy, after waving his hand to his friends, dipped his paddle, swung the canoe round, and sent the light craft dancing back towards the shore.

Straight Pine stood watching it, only turning his eyes away when the man and the boy had disappeared among the trees.

"To-night Straight Pine will take the Young Horse's place," he said composedly, squatting down in the canoe.

"You think they'll do it then, chief?" the big trapper answered eagerly.

"Straight Pine great warrior," the Delaware answered coolly, without the slightest suggestion of boasting; "his scalp worth those of two palefaces to the Huron chiefs."

THE EIGHTH CHAPTER.

Given Up—Nat Goes Back to the Camp— News of Lame Bear—The Sentry Silenced.

"THE Young Horse comes," the Delaware announced quietly hours later, as the dusk grew deeper, and only the keenest of eyes could have seen the canoe creeping out from the bank.

Straight Pine divested himself of his robe, touched his rifle as if saying farewell to it, and held out his hand to the trapper.

"Rear the Young Horse well, my brother," he said gravely. "Farewell! I go now, that he may not grieve over my departure."

Before Nat could answer a word, Straight Pine had slipped out of the canoe into the water, and was swimming with strong strokes towards the shore, travelling at a slant, so that he might avoid Dick's canoe, which was coming along rapidly.

"Where's Straight Pine?" the boy asked eagerly, as he came alongside. "I've come to tell him that I will not accept his sacrifice."

"Thou art too late, boy," Nat answered huskily, pointing towards the shore, which was still faintly visible. "Look!"

The boy turned, and his keen eyes just made out a solitary figure marching with great dignity towards the trees, to disappear in their shadows.

A yell of triumph, repeated again and again, came from the shore, and Dick knew that it really was too late. Already the Hurons and Mingoes were rejoicing over the capture of their great enemy, Straight Pine the Delaware. The boy's face turned hard, and lost much of its usually youthful look.

"Nat," he said quietly, "I must go back; I can't let the chief suffer for me!"

That the boy meant to do as he said there could be no doubt, and the trapper was only just in time to grip him as he swung the nose of the canoe back towards the shore.

"Don't be a fool, lad!" he said sternly. "'Tis no good both dyin', an' ye needn't think as them hounds would give Straight Pine up if they got you again. Compared with him you ain't so much as a twig. It goes against the grain I allow, but ye can't do no good by goin' back."

Once more the wild, triumphant yells of the Mingoe and Huron savages came from the bank, which was now no longer even faintly visible. Dick dashed his paddle into the water as they reached his ears, but Nat had him hard by the sleeve, and he could not move.

"Let me go, Nat!" he cried. "Surely you wouldn't have a brother of yours stay here at such a time?"

"I would hev him live," the trapper said huskily, then a gleam came into his eyes. "Come into the canoe, lad, an' we'll hev a fling at savin' the chief yet."

There was no mistaking the earnestness of Nat Wild's tones, and, without hesitation, the boy stepped into the larger canoe. The small craft was abandoned, man and boy took up the paddles, and the canoe stole away across the surface of the lake. Before them lay the waters that would lead them to within ten miles of Fort Larabee, which there now seemed to be every chance that they would reach in safety. The savages had promised not to molest them, and, strange though it may seem, such promises were sometimes kept. The great danger would be when the two landed to cover the last ten miles on foot, for there were sure to be small parties of braves roaming about, many of whom would not own allegiance to those who had made the promise to the palefaces.

But of none of this did Nat and Dick Wild think just at present, for their brains had only room for one thought—the saving of Straight Pine.

It was the trapper who guided the canoe, and he slanted away towards the shore, guiding himself by the stars, for even the dense

No. 10 : Harold Skinner

Who plays the game with might and main?
(The game of "nap," to be quite plain.)
Who hunts for pleasure, then finds pain?
   Why, Skinner!

Who, if he were a moneyed "star."
Would swagger in a handsome car,
And proudly puff a fat cigar?
   Why, Skinner!

Who bets on gee-gees (when he can!)
And thinks himself a "sporty" man,
Then finds his horse is "also ran"?
   Why, Skinner!

Who gets up japes, but seldom scores?
Who sits and smokes behind locked doors?
Who's always getting in the wars?
   Why, Skinner!

Who's always full of bounce and brag?
Who thinks himself a witty wag?
Who makes us use the verb, "to scrag!"?
   Why, Skinner!

Who, if he lives (no doubt he will!)
Will end his labours, "lying" still,
Within the walls of Pentonville?
   Why, Skinner!

A SPORTS TRAGEDY

INTRODUCING SOME WELL-KNOWN NAMES AT GREYFRIARS AND ST. JIM'S

By DICK PENFOLD

"Although I've only got WUN LUNG,
   I'm sure I can HOP HI;
I'll POTTER home, too, in the
   mile,
   And beat the smaller FRY."

So spake young BROWN, a NOBLE
   youth,
   Whose heart was light and GAY;
He meant to stand the CUTTS and
   KNOX
   That chanced to come his way.

Just then a BULSTRODE on the
   GREENE,
   BROWN promptly seized a RAKE;
And said, "Great SCOTT! I'm feeling
   hot!
   My MERRY life's at stake!"

His TEMPLE throbbed; his head did
   SINGH,
   He floundered like a FISH;
Said he, "I'll TODD-le right away
   From this absurd posish!

But then the BULL, in fierce dis-DANE,
   Came forward with a roar;
And BROWN could never REILLY WYNN
   The monster had his GORE!

GREYHOUND.

EASY SHADOWGRAPHS

Any boy or girl can perform these simple silhouettes with the aid of a small screen and a lighted candle.

MAN SMOKING

SWAN

CAMEL

DOG

mass of trees could not be seen. It was a night for such a venture—for sudden death and snatching away from death—a night when a nervous man in the woods would have started and shivered at the cracking of a twig beneath his heel.

With a gentle, grating sound the canoe touched the slanting beach, and Nat, taking his rifle with him, stepped out into the shallow water. Dick would have followed, but his brother pushed him back into his seat, and whispered to him, his lips close against the boy's ear. There was no telling how near an enemy might be.

" Keep the canoe from the shore, lad," he whispered, " an' try an' make for the fort if I'm not back within the hour."

Softly as a panther, despite his bulk, Nat slipped among the trees, and stole along in the direction of the spot where the camp of the Mingoes lay. That he was taking his life in his hands he knew perfectly well, just as he knew that somewhere among the trees there were sure to be sentries, unless the savages, deeming themselves safe from attack in the woods, had not troubled to throw any out. It was unlikely that they had left the camp so unguarded.

Moving with the utmost caution, for the snap of a twig beneath his moccasined feet might have heralded death, Nat moved steadily forward, shifting from tree to tree, keeping behind cover as much as possible, and with his rifle ever ready to return the fire of an enemy. That was the last thing that he wanted, however, for even if he escaped, it would mean the finish and failure of the attempt to rescue Straight Pine.

Something rustled in the undergrowth away to the big trapper's left, and he stopped, stiff and still as a statue, the butt of his gun resting in the palm of his hand, his ears pricked to catch a repetition of the sound. It did not come again, and he once more moved softly forward.

Ahead, through the trees, a fitful flame glimmered, now coming, now going, as trunks of trees or little open spaces revealed or hid it from the trapper's eyes. Now he moved even more cautiously, if that were possible, and, reaching a kind of natural track, dropped full length to the ground and wriggled along it like a serpent, forcing his rifle ahead of him.

In this way, making slow but sure progress, Nat Wild approached the camp of the Hurons and Mingoes. At any moment he expected to feel the dull thud of a bullet against his head, but that did not deter him. Only once did he hesitate, and that was when he thought of Dick trying to get to Fort Larabee alone. He put the thought from him, however, remembering that the lad would most probably have been dead by now if it had not been for the Delaware, and crawled on.

The light from the fire soon showed more plainly, and Nat, turning off among the trees again, rose to his feet and crept forward to the edge of the small natural clearing in which the camp had been pitched. He reached it without interference, and stood, half behind a tree and half in the shadow cast by it, within eight or nine yards of the braves squatting round the camp-fire.

It was not a large camp, and the rough lodges, that had been built of thin boughs, showed that the savages had no intention of remaining long. Probably they were awaiting reinforcements before pushing on to attack Fort Larabee, which Straight Pine the Delaware had said was their intention.

Round the fire, or lounging near the lodges, were about a score of savages of the Mingoe and Huron tribes, each with his rifle close to his hand and his tomahawk at his belt. Over all these Nat just cast his eyes, which stopped attentively on one man, who sat, rather by himself, before the fire. All around him were painted men, who sat quite close to each other, yet on both sides of him there was a distinct gap. It was Straight Pine the Delaware, his fine eyes staring moodily and unconcernedly into the fire. His limbs were not bound, but he was as much a prisoner as if he had been loaded down by irons. One sharp movement would be enough to lodge a bullet in his brain. A white man in the same position would probably have contemplated a dash for freedom, but the chief knew that such a move could end in nothing but death. Still, a bullet in the brain would have been preferable to the tortures which were undoubtedly in store for him.

FAMOUS COUNTY CRICKETERS & THEIR AUTOGRAPHS

Only a foot at a time, for the slightest slip would have had disastrous consequences, Nat moved round the clearing, keeping well back among the trees, until he had reached a spot exactly behind where Straight Pine sat by the fire.

His chief reason for doing this was that the trees ran to within a few feet of the fire here, and that the Delaware would be able to hear anything happening behind him in the wood. The riskiest part of the trapper's mission had now arrived. He had got to attract Straight Pine's attention.

How was he to attract the Delaware's attention? The braves round the fire sat in solemn silence, some smoking, most merely staring into the flames. The slightest suspicious sound would be heard by them.

Nat thought of the call of the wren, which the chief had previously used as a signal, and, knowing that the quick mind of the Delaware would probably at once grasp the significance of such a call, he decided to use it now, though what he was going to do even after the chief knew that he was among the trees he had not the faintest idea.

The call of the wren sounded softly, for the big trapper was as expert in such things as any redskin, and Nat, peering round the trunk of a tree, entirely hidden by the shadows, looked to see if his signal would be answered.

Straight Pine, sitting by the fire, his blanket round his shoulders, made not the slightest sign, nor did any of the other braves seem to attach any significance to the chirping of a bird.

For the second time the faint call came from among the trees, but still the chief gave no sign, and, almost in despair, Nat chirped for the third time.

Very gently, so slowly, indeed, that the trapper did not at first notice it, one of Straight Pine's hands stole out behind him. Only for a second or two did it remain there, before being withdrawn once more to his side. It was enough for the trapper, however, who knew that his signal had been understood.

What would Straight Pine do, that was the question? Nat felt sure that he would try to communicate with him, yet he could not see how he would do it. Knowing the Indian cunning, and especially the craftiness of the Delaware, he waited quietly among the trees.

Five minutes later, when the calling of the wren had been forgotten, if it had ever been noticed by the Mingoes and Hurons, Straight Pine shifted slightly, and spoke, with his eyes still on the fire, in his curiously deep, mellow voice.

" Flying Deer rests long," he said, " as the bear sleeping through the winter. Is it that he fears the palefaces at the fort, and waits until his braves are many as the trees in the forest ? Does he fear that the Delaware will escape under the torture, that he does not order his young braves to gather wood for the fire ? "

Flying Deer, who was seated at the other side of the fire, answered without raising his head.

" The words of the Delaware are but the senseless falling of waters," he said. " The scalps of the palefaces at the fort await the knives of the Mingoes. As for the torture, the fire burns low until Lame Bear shall have come into the forest. To-morrow night Straight Pine shall bend and crack like the old tree."

Nat had not been wrong in believing that the chief would manage to convey a message to him, for he had already done so. The trapper now knew that Straight Pine was not to be tortured until the morrow, so that there were now some hours in which to try to rescue him.

But how was it to be done ?

The first thing, Nat decided, was to get back to the canoe, for otherwise he might be discovered among the trees, and that would mean the end of all plans for both himself and the chief.

Very softly Nat drew away from the clearing, moving as stealthily as any Indian, and it was not long before he had put a hundred yards between himself and the fire. A little later he reached the beach, the canoe ran silently forward across the water to meet him, and, clambering aboard and taking a paddle, Nat urged the frail craft out until she lay more than a hundred yards from the edge of the forest.

THE NINTH CHAPTER.

A Dash for the Fort—Over the Rapids— Claiming Help—To Save Straight Pine.

"WHAT have you done, Nat?" Dick asked eagerly, as soon as his brother stopped paddling.

"Nothing, boy," the trapper answered moodily, "save learnt that the chief is not to be tortured until to-morrow night."

"And why are they waiting?"

"For the arrival of Lame Bear," Nat explained gruffly. "If I thought it could do good, I'd wait for Lame Bear, an' see as how he never reached the camp."

Dick touched his brother sharply on the arm.

"We've still got time to save the chief, Nat," he said eagerly.

"Ye're right, Dick," he said sharply; "an' we'll try. Thar's a way by which we, kin reach the fort by water, though it means riskin' our necks over the rapids. Air ye ready to try? If we git through we'll be at the fort by dawn. None too soon, either, for those soldiers'll need all the blessed day ter git up through the woods."

"I'll risk anything if there's a chance of saving the chief, Nat," Dick answered quietly. "He saved me, you know."

"Then to the fort!" Nat said, between his teeth; and his paddle dipped into the water, throwing the canoe round until her nose pointed down-stream.

That there was no time to lose Nat knew well enough, or he would never have suggested the shooting of the rapids. Most parties bound for the fort left the water ten miles from that place, just above the rapids. Only a few of the hardiest men had been known to shoot the rapids successfully, and there was a long list of the foolhardy who had tried and failed and met their deaths among the rocks and the broken water.

With the paddles working steadily and evenly, Dick finding extra strength in the knowledge of the mission upon which he was bound, the light bark canoe swept swiftly along the water, aided by the current, which was now fairly powerful as it reached the outlet of the lake, to dash on down the fast-running stream and over the tumbling rapids, until it reached another lake.

Few men knew the waters of the Quesna Lake better than the big trapper, and he steered the canoe now as surely as if it had been broad daylight, swinging her round bends, and missing headlands that jutted out into the narrow water with a skill that was little short of miraculous. His blood was fired by his mission, and he would have faced more than the chance of death in the rapids to save Straight Pine.

And Dick, working like a man in the stern, had inspired him to it. Nat was a man of fine courage, yet if it had not been for the boy he would have given the Delaware chief up as lost. He knew it, and felt prouder of the lad than he had even been before.

Still, too, was there the chance that the Mingoes were waiting on the shores to take the scalps of the two palefaces. Many of the savage tribes were to be depended upon once they had given their word; but Nat knew that the Mingoes and Hurons were not of those tribes. Never once did he glance to the right or the left, yet at any moment he expected to hear the crack of the rifles and to feel the zip of the bullets through the air. Mile after mile was covered, and the trapper began to feel more confident. Most probably, he decided, the savages were waiting in the woods below the spot where travellers to the fort usually landed. Well, by sticking to the stream, the intrepid man and boy would pass them as easily as if borne on the wings of the wind.

Every mile, every yard almost, in fact, the current whirled the canoe on faster, until Nat's efforts with the paddle were chiefly confined to keeping the head of the canoe straight. Already the waters were eddying and whirling in places, showing that the rapids were very near. The lake had turned into nothing more than a broad stream now, so narrow that men on either bank, even in the darkness, would have found the canoe a pretty easy mark. Thinking of this, Nat dropped his paddle for a brief second while he examined his rifle. Then to the paddle again, and the guiding of the racing canoe down the turbulent stream.

With a cry almost as savage as that of a Huron, Nat leapt into the open, and Dick followed.

(*See page* 301.)

ahead now, his eyes always on the waters.

The canoe, seemingly at the mercy of the current now, raced on towards the rapids and falls, until the beating of the falling waters was loud in the ears of the man and boy. Dawn was just beginning to break, and Nat looked up eagerly at the sky, hoping that there would be enough light for him to see his way between the rocks.

Five minutes passed, and the thunder of the waters was so loud that it seemed to Dick impossible that the canoe could live through such a plunge as that which lay before it. He stared forward, able to see a few feet ahead now.

"Crouch down in the bows!" Nat cried, shouting to make his voice heard above the

"We're past the spots where the varmints was likely to hev an ambush, Dick," Nat said at last; but his voice betrayed no note of exultation.

"Then we'll reach the fort all right, Nat," the boy answered gleefully.

"'Tis more in the hands of Providence than ours, lad," the trapper said. He stared hard roar ; and at the same moment, with a lightness which was remarkable in a man of his build, he moved further back into the stern.

Like a bubble on the water the canoe raced on, and Dick caught a glimpse of a ragged rock right ahead. He was about to call out, but before he could do so the canoe's course had been shifted, and the rock flashed by, so close that it looked as if the bark of the canoe touched it.

The next few seconds held nothing clear for Dick. All around him the water roared and eddied. He caught glimpses of dark rocks, which the canoe appeared to dodge in miraculous fashion ; then she lifted bodily, a spray of cold water swept into Dick's face, and the canoe was riding in comparatively smooth water.

A wild cheer broke from Nat, and Dick, realising that the danger of the waters was passed, echoed it heartily.

" An' thar's the fort ! " the trapper cried, pointing to the right bank, where, through the growing light, could be seen a large palisade inside which rose several wooden roofs.

Straight to the shore Nat drove the canoe, and leapt on to dry land, followed by Dick. From the palisade a soldier, in red coat and leather stock, came running, his rifle at the slope.

" Halt ! " he commanded.

" Is Captain Waring about yet ? " the trapper answered sharply, advancing to meet the man.

" Nay, an' not likely ter be for a couple of hours," the soldier answered.

" There ye're mistaken, my lad," Nat Wild said coolly ; " fer the Mingoes an' Hurons air out again, an' ye've got ter send me right through ter the cap'n now. He knows me, so send word to him."

The soldier led the way to the palisade, and Dick was able to see the wooden houses of the soldiers within, also the few huts built near to the fort, so that their inhabitants could take refuge with the soldiers once an alarm was raised. The message was sent to Captain Waring by another soldier, and inside five minutes Nat and Dick were sent through to the presence of the officer commanding the fort.

They found him already half-dressed, while a soldier was busy sharpening his sword.

" So they're up again, Nat ? " Captain Waring said, for he had met the trapper before ; " an' there's a chance of death or glory for some of us ? "

" It's dead right, cap'n," the trapper answered ; " an' you an' your men 'll hev ter look sharp if they're ter save the life of the man who was comin' here to warn you."

" Who's that ? " the officer asked sharply.

" Straight Pine, the Delaware chief."

" A redskin ! " Captain Waring said indifferently.

" Ay, a redskin, cap'n," the trapper repeated earnestly, " with as white a heart as your own."

In as few words as possible Nat Wild told the story of the last few days, and of the Delaware's sacrifice. At the end the eyes of the officer were glowing, and he turned impatiently to the man who was putting the finishing touches to the edge of his sword.

" Haste ye, Saunders," he commanded. " Such a man must not be let die, whatever his colour."

THE TENTH CHAPTER.

Back Through the Woods—Nat and Dick Ahead—Awaiting Torture—The Wounded Mingoe — A Desperate Fight — The British in Time.

ALREADY the sun had long passed the spot in the heavens which showed that it was noon, hours since the soldiers, two score in number, had halted among the trees and made their midday meal as coolly as if they had been within the palisade of Fort Larabee : yet the camp of the Hurons and Mingoes still lay a full ten miles ahead. The soldiers were not used to this kind of warfare, despite the fact that some had been at the frontier fort for years, and they made but slow progress.

They just marched on, stolidly and silently, yet making enough noise to have reached the sharp ears of a savage a full half mile away. But then, they held the redskins in contempt as mere savages, despite the fact that most of them had known men whose scalps were now drying on the lodge poles of the Hurons and Mingoes.

Striding ahead to show the way, Dick trudging manfully beside him, was Nat Wild. Despite all that the two had been through, they still walked faster than the soldiers—having, indeed, to halt from time to time to allow them to come up.

"Why not push on ahead, Nat?" Dick suggested. "We might be able to do some good if the worst came to the worst."

Captain Waring made no objection, and the trapper and Dick, quickening their pace, yet moving noiselessly, as do all men long-trained to the ways of the woods, forged ahead, until within a pretty short time they could not even hear the advance of the soldiers, despite the noise that they were making.

It still wanted two hours to sunset, but that was none too long in which to reach the redskin camp, and Nat made the pace warm, so warm, in fact, that Dick more than once had to trot behind him. Still, the boy cared nothing so long as the Delaware was saved.

Nearly the whole of the two hours passed before Nat began to advance more cautiously, and the last mile towards the camp took close upon an hour to cover. It was dark as pitch when the man and the boy halted, hidden by the trees, at the edge of the clearing. That they were none too soon they could plainly see. A great fire was already burning in the centre of the clearing, and close to it a pile had been driven into the ground. To this the prisoner would be lashed, then the fire would be raked towards him.

For the present Straight Pine had not been subjected to the torture. He lay by the fire, bound now, and round him squatted a score or so of braves, their weapons handy.

"May the redcoats come soon, boy!" Nat whispered.

"They can't be long," Dick whispered back. "They must have gained on us in the the last hour, so that——"

A wild yell broke in upon the boy's speech, and Nat half raised his rifle, thinking that they had been discovered. Then he saw his mistake, and lowered it. Into the circle of light thrown from the fire a young brave, bleeding badly from a cut on the temple, had staggered.

"Paleface soldiers!" he panted, waving his arms towards the woods.

The alarm was thorough, and the redskins snatched up their arms, and would have fled to the shelter of the trees had not an order from Flying Deer stayed them.

"Let not Straight Pine escape!" he cried. "To the fire!"

Four men leapt upon the Delaware, and snatching him up, bore him towards the fire. A rifle cracked crisply, and one of the bearers fell to the ground.

With a yell almost as savage as that of a Huron, Nat leapt into the open, and Dick followed.

Under the swinging blows of Nat's clubbed rifle two more of the Indians fell, while Dick accounted for a third. The suddenness of the onslaught, too, was in favour of the attackers, for the redskins, thinking that the soldiers had come, turned and bolted for the trees.

Kneeling down, and drawing out his knife, Nat quickly freed the Delaware, who, leaping to his feet, and snatching up a rifle that had fallen from the hands of a Mingoe, was ready to join in the fight, too. The terrible war-cry of his tribe broke from his lips, and went echoing after the flying enemy. As it died away, Captain Waring and his men came dashing into the clearing.

"Where have the fiends gone?" he cried.

"The hounds run for their lodges," Straight Pine answered, pointing away into the forest.

And the soldiers, led by the captain, at once started off in that direction, but neither Nat nor Dick nor the chief attempted to follow.

It was the last named who spoke now, a smile on his lips, his eyes upon Dick Wild.

"The heart of Straight Pine is glad," he said, in his full voice, "for the Young Horse did not forsake him in his hour of peril."

"Isn't likely, is it, chief?" the boy protested, "seeing that you gave yourself up for me."

Straight Pine smiled again, and laid a hand on the boy's shoulder.

"Many are the palefaces who speak great words," he said, "that are but as empty of meaning as the wind that blows them from the lips. To them a promise means no more than the crack of a rifle to a buck who has long roamed distant from the grounds of the hunter. But Young Horse's words are those of the great brave, and Straight Pine holds him as a brother."

"That'll make two he's got, chief," Nat said, with a grin, squatting on the ground as coolly as if anything in the shape of Indians was certainly miles away.

"And his brothers shall teach him many things," the Delaware continued. "The best places for the buck, the following of the trail, the very call of the birds, until no such paleface brave shall there have been before."

"You will really teach me, chief!" Dick cried eagerly.

The Delaware laid a hand on the boy's shoulder again.

"I have spoken," he said.

THE END.

The King's Royal Rifles.　　The Royal Horse Guards.　　The Welsh Fusiliers.

TYPES OF THE BRITISH ARMY

Fighting for His Honour!

A Complete Story of School Life and Adventure

By FRANK RICHARDS.

THE FIRST CHAPTER.

The New Boy.

BOB CHERRY paused on the School House steps, and looked across the green, sunny Close. Bob had a cricket-bat under his arm, and his cap at the back of his head. It was quite impossible for Bob Cherry ever to keep his cap on straight, and he had long ago given up trying. Bob had just finished writing out an impot, and he was hurrying out to join the cricketers on the junior ground, when the sight of a youth coming towards the house arrested him.

"Hallo, hallo, hallo!" Bob ejaculated.

The youth coming towards him looked up. He was a lad about Bob's own age—and a stranger at Greyfriars. He was not a nice-looking fellow. He had thin lips, which seemed to be drawn tightly across his teeth, and light brown eyes with a peculiar glitter in them, as if he were continually on the watch. He carried a bag in his hand and a rain-coat on his arm, and had evidently just arrived at Greyfriars.

"You're the new chap?" asked Bob Cherry.

The other nodded.

"I'm the new chap," he said. "At all events, I'm a new chap. I've only just got here."

"Your name's Heath?"

"Yes." The new boy looked Bob Cherry up and down. "Any more questions?"

Bob flushed.

"I'm not asking you out of curiosity," he said. "My Form-master told me that a new boy was coming into the Remove, and that he was to be put into my study. I thought I would keep an eye open and speak to you when you came."

"Oh, I see. Kind of you!"

"My study's No. 13 in the Remove passage," said Bob Cherry. "Anybody will tell you where the Remove passage is. I can't stop now as I've got to get down to cricket."

"Don't let me detain you."

Bob Cherry gave him a look. There was little in the words, but there was a great deal in the way they were uttered. There was something strikingly unpleasant about this new boy—a deliberate ungraciousness of manner that jarred on Bob Cherry. Bob was always thoughtlessly open and hearty, and he expected as much of others.

"Oh, very well!" he said. "I shall be

coming in to tea, and then I can look after you a bit, if you like."

"Thanks! I daresay I can look after myself!"

Bob Cherry restrained his desire to wipe the steps down with the new boy, and walked off to the cricket-field. He wondered why some fellows went out of their way to make themselves disagreeable. The new boy glanced after him carelessly, and went into the house.

Bob Cherry joined the cricketers.

"Nothing wrong?" asked Harry Wharton, noting the flush in Bob Cherry's cheeks, and the expression upon his rugged face of less than his usual pleasant cheerfulness.

"Well, no," said Bob. "I've just been talking to a chap who gets on my nerves, that's all."

"Billy Bunter?"

Bob laughed.

"No; the new chap. You remember Quelch told us there was a new chap coming to-day, and he was to be put into No. 13 Study, as there are only two of us there—Linley and myself?"

"Yes. Has he come?"

"He has. I'd forgotten about him, as a matter of fact, but as I came out of the house I met him," said Bob. "I wanted to make myself agreeable, but—well, the chap is a disagreeable bounder, that's all! It will be rotten having him in the study, but I suppose it can't be helped."

Harry Wharton laughed.

"He may be decent, all the same," he said. "Give the chap a chance, you know."

"Well, yes; but I know he's a beast!" said Bob.

"If you make up your mind that he's a beast now, you're not likely to see any good in him," Frank Nugent remarked.

"Yes, you're right; but—well, I'll try to be fair to him," said Bob. "But sometimes, you know, you dislike a chap instinctively. You feel that he's horrid mean. That's the sort of chap this is. But I'm going to be fair to him. I'm going to keep the peace in the study if I can."

"That's right," said Harry. "Look after him a little, as he's a new chap, and make him comfy. Take in some grub for tea, and feed him. That's the way to bring out his good qualities if he's got any."

Bob Cherry grinned.

"Well, I'll try it," he said.

Bob Cherry stopped at the school tuck-shop to carry out Harry Wharton's advice. The others went on their way. Bob expended the sum of two shillings—not an inconsiderable sum to a junior in the Lower Fourth—upon good things for the tea-table, and carried them into the house with him.

The new boy should have no cause to complain of the hospitality of No. 13 Study in the Remove!

With a parcel under one arm and a paper bag of eggs in the other hand, Bob Cherry went upstairs, and tramped along the Remove passage. No. 13 was almost at the end of the passage. Bob wondered whether he would find the new boy there.

Mark Linley, he knew, was gone down to the village with John Bull and Fisher T. Fish, so if the new boy was in No. 13, he was alone there.

That somebody was in the study was quite clear as Bob Cherry came along the passage. From the closed door came a sound that made Bob start in surprise. It was a loud and painful mew of a cat!

"Miau-miau-ou!"

"My hat!" Bob Cherry ejaculated. "That must be Mrs. Kebble's cat. But what on earth is it doing in my study? I suppose the poor thing has got shut in and can't get out!"

"Miau-miau-ou!"

Bob Cherry's brows darkened as he quickened his pace. The mewing of the cat might have been caused by the animal being shut up in the study, and trying to attract attention to get the door opened. But it sounded as if it were in pain. What was happening in No. 13 study?

Bob ran on and threw the door wide open. There was a startled exclamation within.

"What—I——"

Bob Cherry burst into a roar of rage.

"You hound!"

THE SECOND CHAPTER.

A Rascal Well Licked.

THE new boy was in the study. He was evidently amusing himself. His idea of amusement was a peculiar one—though it might have been guessed from the spiteful curve of his lips, and the shifty, unpleasant glitter in his eyes.

The cat was tied up by the leg to a chair in the corner of the room. The new boy had a catapult in his hand, and he was evidently practising his shooting upon the unfortunate cat at close range. He could have practised just as easily at a mark on the wall. But that would not have inflicted pain, and, therefore, would have been useless to a boy of Heath's peculiar disposition. At such close range every pellet that struck the unlucky cat elicited a howl of pain from the animal, and it was springing and clawing wildly in its endeavours to escape. And Heath seemed to be a good shot. He was exactly the kind of boy to be expert with the catapult, and to be ever ready to display his skill upon some unfortunate bird or beast.

Bob Cherry was not in the least "soft" or goody-goody, and he was not given to criticising others, but to see a fellow torturing an animal was a little more than he could stand. And it was in his study, too!

"If you won't fight, you can take your licking like a kid in the First Form," said Bob Cherry. "So here goes!" (*See page* 307.)

Bob Cherry's hands trembled with rage as he laid his parcels on the table. The new boy looked at him with a sour grin.

"Like to have a shot?" he asked.

"What?" roared Bob.

"It's fun to see the beast hop!" said Heath. "I'm trying to get a shot at his eye, but he won't keep his head still."

Bob Cherry breathed hard with a loud noise. He felt that he was choking. He turned on the new boy with flaming face.

"Put that catapult down!" he said.

"What?"

"Put it down!" roared Bob.

Heath looked at him doubtfully for a second, and then threw the catapult on the table. Bob did not look like a fellow to be trifled with at that moment.

Bob took the catapult, and smashed it to pieces under his heavy boot. Heath gave a yell.

"What are you doing? That's mine."

"It's not much use to you now," said Bob savagely. "You cad! You coward! How dare you torture a cat—and in my study? You—you unspeakable beast!"

Heath sneered.

"I suppose you never do anything of that sort?"

"No, I don't!" roared Bob. "Only a dirty, low, mean, crawling viper would torment an animal—only a fellow like you."

Heath whistled.

"Thanks for your good opinion," he said.

"I suppose you're going to be a vivisectionist when you grow up?" said Bob. "It's the sort of job that would suit you."

Heath grinned.

"I shouldn't wonder," he said. "I should like it, I think. It would be amusing to see the beggars wriggle, wouldn't it?"

Bob Cherry snorted.

"Well, I'm going to see you wriggle a bit now, and you can see if that's just as amusing," he said. "Put up your hands."

"What!"

"Put up your hands."

Heath backed away.

"Look here, I don't want to fight you," he exclaimed. "I'm not going to fight you. I don't like fighting."

"I dare say you'd fight a very small boy fast enough," said Bob. "Chaps who torture animals are that sort. But, you're going to fight me now. You're bigger than I am, and you've got to put up your hands."

"I—I won't."

"Then you'll take the licking with your hands down—for you're going to be licked in any case, you worm!"

"Look here, I've got no quarrel with you," said Heath, backing away round the table. "It was only my fun with the blessed old cat——"

"This is only my fun, too," said Bob.

"I'll let the beast go. Look here, I'm not going to fight you. I don't like fighting, and I won't! I'll complain to the head-master if you touch me."

"You dirty sneak!"

"Sneak or not, I'm not going to fight you, or anybody else," said Heath, striding towards the door.

Bob Cherry grasped him by the shoulder and swung him back.

"Stay here!"

"I—I won't!"

Bob Cherry placed himself between the new boy and the door.

"Put up your hands," he said, between his teeth.

"Hang you!"

"Take that, then!"

Smack!

Bob's open palm smote the new boy full across the face.

Heath staggered back from the smack.

"Oh!" he gasped. "Oh!"

"Now will you put your hands up?"

Heath gave him a deadly look.

"No, I won't!"

Bob could only stare at him.

"You utter coward!" he said.

"I'm not going to fight you," said Heath, with a livid face. "I won't fight you! But I'll make you sorry for this—I'll make you suffer for it."

Bob Cherry laughed scornfully. He pointed to the cat, who was still mewing faintly in the corner.

"Set that cat loose," he said. "Mind, without hurting him."

Heath sullenly obeyed. He would gladly have kicked the cat as it scuttled joyfully out of the study. But Bob Cherry's eye was gleaming upon him. Heath made an attempt to follow from the study. But Bob closed the door.

"Now," he said, "you're going to have your licking. I may explain to you that we don't torture animals at Greyfriars. If the masters knew, you would be caned or flogged —you ought to be expelled. I'm not going to tell the masters, but I'm going to lick you. Will you put up your hands?"

"No."

"You coward! You can torture a cat, but you won't fight a chap smaller than yourself," Bob said contemptuously. "But if you think you're going to get off by being a coward, you're making a big mistake."

He advanced upon Heath.

The new boy dodged round the table. His face was white now, and his eyes gleaming with fear and spite.

He made a rush across to the door, and then Bob Cherry's grasp fell upon him. The new boy collapsed at once.

"Let me alone!" he shrieked. "Help!"

"You cad!"

Bob Cherry's face was grim with determination. He sat down, and dragged Heath across his knee and caught up a slipper.

"If you won't fight, you can take your licking like a kid in the First Form," he said.

" So here goes ! "

Smack ! Smack ! Smack !

" Ow ! Ow ! Yow ! "

Smack ! Smack !

" Yarooh ! Help ! "

The slipper rose and fell with deadly persistence, and the dust came in little clouds from Heath's garments. Bob Cherry put all the strength of his strong arm into that thrashing.

It was well deserved, and it was well laid on. Heath yelled and writhed and squirmed, but the merciless slipper rose and fell till Bob's arm was tired.

He threw it aside at last.

" There ! " he gasped, pitching Heath over on the carpet. " There you are ! I hope you'll take that to heart, and drop your dirty tricks while you're at Greyfriars."

" Ow ! Ow ! Ow ! "

" Oh, don't blub ! "

Heath lay writhing and gasping and whimpering on the floor. His face was white, and twisted with spite. Bob Cherry went to the door. It was his own study, but he did not care to remain there with Heath.

Bob, with his face still rather excited, tramped down the passage, leaving Heath to his own devices. The new boy rose to his feet, and shook his fist at the closed door, his face convulsed with rage.

" Oh, you wait a bit ! " he muttered. " You wait a bit ! My turn will come—my turn will come ! And you'll be sorry for this ! "

Bob Cherry, with a clouded brow, tramped down the passage to No. 1. Harry Wharton and Frank Nugent were there, having tea. They looked up at him with genial welcome.

" Come in, Bob ! " said Wharton.

Bob Cherry walked in.

" Can I have tea with you chaps ? " he asked abruptly.

" Of course you can, old son. Shove the kettle on again, Franky. But what's the matter, Bob ? Haven't been quarrelling with Bulstrode, have you ? "

" No ! " Bob snorted. " It's that new chap ! I can't stay in the study with him— he makes me sick ! "

" Stay here, then, old son," said Harry. " You used to be here with us, you know—

and now Inky's gone there's plenty of room. But what's the new fellow been doing ? "

Bob Cherry explained.

" The cad ! " said Harry.

" The worm ! " said Nugent.

" I can't stand him ! " said Bob. " I knew I couldn't stand the unspeakable beast when I first saw him. It's simply awful to have him in the study. I shall ask Mr. Quelch to change me out—only it would be too bad to leave Marky alone with the beast ! I don't know what to do ! "

" Have tea—and some poached eggs," said Nugent. " They're prime ! "

And Bob Cherry laughed, and had tea.

THE THIRD CHAPTER.

No Success.

BILLY BUNTER looked in at the door of No. 13. Heath was sitting in the arm-chair, twisting very uncomfortably. Bob Cherry had thrashed him pretty severely, and the new boy did not like pain. He was still looking very white, and very savage and spiteful. He scowled at Billy Bunter as he came in.

Bunter blinked at him with the most agreeable expression he could muster.

" I say, you know," he began. " You're the new chap, ain't you ? "

" Yes ! " snapped Heath.

" I'm Bunter—Bunter of the Remove," the fat junior explained. " The fact is, you know, that it's a custom here for a new boy to stand a bit of a feed to the principal members of the Form," said Bunter. " I'm a principal member of the Form."

" You won't get any feed out of me ! "

" Ahem ! In this case, for the sake of—of hospitality, I'm willing to reverse the usual order of things, and stand you a feed instead," he explained.

Heath looked a little less savage.

" Now you're talking ! " he said.

" You see, I always like to do the decent thing by new boys," said Bunter. " How would you like a nice little feed in the tuck-shop—say muffins and tea, and then some cake, and some sausage-rolls and dough-nuts, and plenty of jam puffs ? "

" Good ! "

" Come on, then. Oh, by the way, I forgot one thing," said Bunter, as if struck by a sudden recollection. " I've run out of cash. I'm expecting a postal order this evening, and if you care to advance me a few shillings, I'll hand you the postal order as soon as it comes. I suppose that will be all right ? "

Heath had risen to follow Bunter. A very unpleasant expression came over his face now. Heath was far from being the kind of person to be taken in by Bunter's clumsy diplomacy.

" You fat cad ! " he said. " So I'm to pay for the feed, am I ? "

" Ahem ! Only temporarily. You see, I was expecting that postal order this afternoon. It's from a titled friend of mine, and it's certain to come. If you care to advance me the ten shillings——"

" You cheeky cad ! "

" Ahem ! If you care to advance me the ten shillings—or, say, five shillings—if you care to advance me the two-and-six, you know, you can have the postal order immediately it comes, and it will be the same thing."

" Get out ! "

" By the way, I should like you to come in my study, if you'd prefer it to this. You are just the kind of person I could chum with, and——"

" Outside, I tell you ! I've had more than enough of you ! " said Heath.

He was not afraid of the fat, short-sighted junior.

Bunter's expression changed. The agreeable grin faded away, and he looked very spiteful.

" You rotten outsider ! " he exclaimed. " Catch me being chummy with a new boy again ! You low bounder ! Ow ! "

Heath twisted the fat junior round, and planted a kick upon his fat person that sent him staggering out into the passage. Bunter collapsed upon the linoleum with a wild gasp.

" Ow ! " he gasped. " Beast ! "

Heath slammed the door.

Bunter rolled away down the passage, groaning. He blinked in at the doorway of No. 1, and groaned again. The chums of the Remove grinned at him.

" Got on all right with the new chap ? " asked Harry Wharton.

" Ow ! He's a beast ! "

" Ha, ha, ha ! "

" I was very courteous to him, and he rushed at me like a wild beast and kicked me ! " said Bunter. " Ow ! I'm seriously injured ! Ow ! I think you chaps ought to rag him ! Ow ! "

" Ha, ha, ha ! "

Bunter snorted, and rolled away. There was evidently no sympathy to be had in No. 1 Study. Bob Cherry kicked the door shut after him.

" I've got an idea," Harry Wharton remarked. " You know my aunt is coming home from Switzerland and I'm going with my uncle to meet her to-morrow. I shall be away from Greyfriars at least a week. Nugent will be alone here. Suppose you two chaps dig in this study while I'm away, and leave Heath No. 13 to himself. Before I get back, you may be able to arrange about a new study for him."

" Good egg ! " said Bob. " If Nugent doesn't mind——"

" I shall be jolly glad," said Nugent. " I don't want to dig here alone."

" What do you say, Marky ? "

" I shall be glad."

" Then it's a go ! " said Harry Wharton.

And so it was settled. On the following morning Harry Wharton was to leave Greyfriars for a time, but he little dreamed of what was to happen before he returned.

THE FOURTH CHAPTER.

On His Own.

THE next morning Harry Wharton did not take his place in the Form-room as usual. Just before first lesson the trap came round to take him to the station, and the juniors gathered to see him off. Bulstrode, the new captain of the Remove, was there, and he shook hands with Harry before the latter mounted into the trap.

" I'm sorry you're going," he said. " We haven't been very good friends, but—well, I'm sorry. Especially about the cricket. We shall miss you from the eleven."

Bob Cherry's face was dark with anger. "Who did that?" he exclaimed, in a choking voice. "Who did that?" (*See page* 322.)

" I'm sorry, too," said Harry. "I hope you'll pull it off all right with the Courtfield chaps. I shall be back in time for the next match with Highcliffe, if you want to play me."

Bulstrode grinned ruefully.

" Of course I shall want to play you ! " he said. "I know some of the fellows expected me to act the giddy ox as soon as I became captain of the Remove, but I hope I've got some sense. Come back as soon as you can."

" Right-ho ! "

" Good-bye, Wharton ! "

Wharton waved his hand to the crowd as the trap drove away. He was sorry to be going away from Greyfriars himself just then, though at the same time he was looking forward to the holiday with his uncle. But it was to be only for a week. As he glanced back from the gateway Bob Cherry waved his hand, and that was the last Harry saw of the juniors of Greyfriars just then.

The Removites turned in to go to their Form-room.

" We'll get our books and things into No. 1 after first lesson," Bob Cherry said to Nugent.

" Good ! " said Frank.

Heath was near them, and he turned quickly.

" Does that mean that you are leaving my study ? " he asked.

" Yes," said Bob Cherry.

" What for ? "

" Because I can't stand you ! "

Bob Cherry was always frank. Some of the juniors laughed, and Heath turned red.

" Very well," he said, " I shall be glad enough for you to go, that's certain. Is the other fellow going ? "

" Linley ? Yes ; he's coming with me."

" You can both go to the dickens, for all I care. I shall be glad enough to have the study to myself." said Heath.

" Well, you'll have it to yourself ; till

Wharton comes back, at any rate," said Bob. "And I'll see if I can't get changed into another study then. It would make me ill to have to dig with you."

Heath sneered, but made no reply.

The looks of the other fellows showed that they shared Bob Cherry's opinion. Heath had not made a good impression upon the Form.

During the next day or two Bob Cherry and Mark Linley settled down very comfortably in No. 1 Study, in the place of Harry Wharton and Hurree Jamset Ram Singh, both of whom were now away from Greyfriars. Heath had No. 13 to himself, and when he was there he was generally left alone. The Remove fellows did not take to him. If he made a friend at all, it was Vernon-Smith, the Bounder of Greyfriars—a fellow whose friendship was not much credit to anybody. And the Bounder only took Heath up when he had no other companion and needed one. At other times he seemed to be unconscious of Heath's existence—all of which added to the anger and spite that burned in the breast of the new junior.

He attributed it all to Bob Cherry, and in that he was very unjust. Bob certainly had not held his tongue about the incident in the study, but the fellows were willing to give Heath a chance; but the new junior seemed to have no good qualities at all. He never by any chance fell into a fight with a fellow near his own size or age, but more than once he was found bullying little fags in the First or Second Forms. His love for tormenting animals was evidently a ruling passion, and several fellows who kept pets, and found him worrying them, fell out with him on that account. Two lickings a day was Heath's average for the first three days at Greyfriars.

By that time he was generally disliked and let alone. Bob Cherry never took any notice of him. The new boy would give him spiteful looks, in class or in the Close, but Bob did not look at him. Heath might have been an insect or a microbe for all the notice Bob Cherry took of him.

Heath did not play cricket, and he did not box; he did not run, he did not swim. He seemed to have no pleasures but hanging about with his hands in his pockets, smoking cigarettes, tormenting animals, and speaking evil of other fellows behind their backs. Of all fellows, he was the least likely to get on in the Greyfriars Remove. And on the fourth day at Greyfriars his intermittent friendship with the Bounder came to a sudden termination.

Vernon-Smith came into his study with a furious face as he was at prep. that evening, and Heath jumped up in alarm at the look of him.

"Hallo!" he exclaimed. "Come in for a smoke?"

Vernon-Smith closed the door.

"No," he said, "I haven't come in for a smoke. I've come in about my canary."

Heath turned red.

"Your canary?" he stammered.

"Yes; it's dead."

"Sorry," said Heath. "I don't see what it's got to do with me. I can't bring dead canaries to life again, you know."

"You can stop catapulting live ones, though, you cad!" said the Bounder. "Tubb of the Third saw you doing it at my study window."

"I—I——"

"You've done for my canary, and now I'm going to lick you! Put up your hands, if you've got courage enough, you miserable cad!"

Heath, apparently, hadn't courage enough, for he dodged round the table, and tried to escape from the study; but the Bounder did not let him go. Vernon-Smith was in a towering rage, and one of the few soft spots in his nature had been for that canary. He piled upon the new junior furiously, pommelling him right and left; and when he left the study, five minutes later, Heath lay gasping and groaning on the floor. It was his seventh licking at Greyfriars, and the most severe of all.

THE FIFTH CHAPTER.

A Remittance from Todd!

"A LETTER for you, Nugent!"

"Chuck it over!" said Frank Nugent.

John Bull took the letter down from the

rack and tossed it over to Nugent. Frank glanced at it, expecting to see Harry Wharton's handwriting. But it was not from Wharton.

"I guess I know that fist," said Fisher T. Fish, glancing at the superscription over Frank's shoulder in his cool, American way. "I guess that's from Todd."

"Hallo! hallo! hallo! A letter from Todd!" exclaimed Bob Cherry.

"I guess so."

Nugent nodded.

"Yes, it's Todd's hand," he said. "I'm glad to hear from him. I hope he's better than when he left. You fellows want to hear from Todd?"

"Yes, rather."

"Listen, then!"

Removites gathered round on all sides. They all wanted to hear from Todd. Alonzo Todd, who had been known as the Duffer of Greyfriars, had left the old school in a very weak state of health, and was likely to stay away for a very long time. The fellows naturally wanted to know how he was getting on. Alonzo had been very, very simple in his ways, but the fellows had all liked him. Many of them missed the kind, obliging, absent-minded Duffer of Greyfriars.

Nugent opened the letter.

"Dear Nugent,—I am sure that you will be very pleased to hear that I am getting on very nicely indeed, and that my Uncle Benjamin is quite satisfied with my slow but sure progress towards convalescence. The neighbourhood in which we have fixed our rural retreat is delightfully rustic and exceedingly conducive to repose. The state of my health precludes me from inditing a lengthy epistle, but I should be extremely delighted and, indeed, very gratified to receive communications from any of you fellows. I hope you are all enjoying your normal physical health at Greyfriars, and that you sometimes allow your thoughts to turn to your absent schoolmate. My Uncle Benjamin says that absence makes the heart grow fonder, and I am sure that I reflect upon Greyfriars with a very sincere, affectionate regard. I enclose a postal-order for the sum of ten shillings in repayment of the kind loan you made me ere I quitted Greyfriars. My Uncle Benjamin has kindly provided me with the necessary financial aid for the repayment of this obligation. Kindest regards to all the fellows.—

"Always yours sincerely,
"ALONZO TODD."

The juniors grinned over the letter.

Alonzo Todd's delicate state of health had evidently made no difference to his love for long words, and had not simplified his Johnsonian phraseology at all. But it was a kind and sincere letter, and just like the Duffer of Greyfriars.

"Good old Todd!" said Tom Brown. "I shall be glad, for one, when he comes back."

"Yes, rather."

"What a giddy windfall!" said Bob Cherry, looking at the postal-order.

"Yes, rather," said Nugent. "I'd forgotten all about the ten bob. Chaps who leave school owing money don't, as a rule, send along the giddy postal-orders."

"Todd wasn't that sort."

"No; here's the cash. This will just get me my new bicycle lamp, and I sha'n't have to write to my pater," said Nugent, with much satisfaction.

"Good old Toddy!"

Heath, the new boy, was in the crowd listening to the letter. Heath did not, of course, know Todd, who had left before he arrived at Greyfriars. But there was an expression of keenest interest upon Heath's face. He was looking very thoughtful as he strolled away from the spot. Some thought was evidently working in his mind, and to judge by the gleam in his eyes, it was some thought that boded no good to someone else.

Nugent thrust the postal-order, along with the letter, carelessly into his inside pocket, and the Remove went to lessons.

After morning school. Bulstrode called the cricketers out to practice. Bulstrode was keeping the junior eleven very much up to the mark. The morrow was Saturday, when the Courtfield match was to be played again, for the third time, both sides having agreed to play and replay till the matter was decided one way or the other. And Bulstrode, feeling sorely the loss of Harry Wharton from the junior eleven, meant to make all the others toe the line.

Nugent went up to his study to change his jacket for a blazer before going out. He hung his jacket on the door, carelessly enough. He was in a tearing hurry, for Bulstrode was calling up the stairs to him.

He had quite forgotten the postal-order for the moment. But if he had thought of it, he would hardly have taken the trouble to remove it from his pocket. He would never even have thought of a possible theft. Even Billy Bunter would not go so far as to take a postal-order out of a fellow's pocket.

Heath was in the passage as Nugent came out. Nugent glanced at him, but did not speak. He ran on, with his cricket bat under his arm, and joined Bulstrode in the lower passage.

" I'm ready ! " he announced.

" Good ! Come on ! Come on, Cherry ! "

" Right-o ! " said Bob Cherry cheerfully.

The Remove cricketers went down to the juniors' ground. Vernon-Smith was in the team. The Bounder of Greyfriars, hopeless slacker as he always was, had proved on one occasion, at least, that he could play cricket with the best ; and Bulstrode asked him to rejoin the eleven ; whereat Vernon-Smith, as his nature was, swanked considerably, and consented in a very lofty way, and showed his great importance by turning up late for practice, and affecting to regard the whole matter as a bore.

Vernon-Smith lounged upon the cricket field with a cigarette between his teeth. That **was** sheer " cheek " on his part, for if a **prefect** had seen him he would certainly have been caned.

Bulstrode flushed as he saw him.

" Throw that cigarette away, Smith ! " he called out. " What are you playing the fool like that for ? "

" Oh, rats ! " said Smith.

Bob Cherry, who was near him, jerked up his hand, and jerked the cigarette from his mouth ; and with the same movement, accidentally or not, his knuckles came into hard contact with the Bounder's nose.

Vernon-Smith uttered a yell.

" Ow ! You fool ! "

" Only helping you to get rid of the cigarette," said Bob politely.

" Ha, ha, ha ! "

" Serve you jolly well right, Smith ! " said Bulstrode. " Go on and bowl, and don't play the giddy goat here ! "

Vernon-Smith sulkily caught the ball as it was tossed to him, and went to the bowler's end. Bob Cherry took the bat. There was a very spiteful expression upon the Bounder's face, and if Bob had been of a more suspicious nature he would not have stood up to the bowling at that moment.

But Bob was the last fellow in the world to suspect anybody of foul play.

Vernon-Smith set his teeth hard, and his eyes gleamed as he bowled. The ball did not go anywhere near the wicket. Perhaps Vernon-Smith's foot slipped. Perhaps it did not. Bob Cherry uttered a cry of pain, dropped the bat, and caught his ankle in both hands, hopping on one leg.

" Ow ! " he roared. " Oh, ow ! "

Bulstrode turned furiously upon the Bounder.

" What did you do that for ? " he shouted.

" Accident ! "

" You threw the ball ! Do you call that bowling ? "

" My foot slipped."

" Ow ! " groaned Bob Cherry. " You cad ! Ow ! "

" I'm sorry ! " said the Bounder. " Was that leg before wicket ? "

" You know it wasn't ! " said Nugent wrathfully. " You did it on purpose, you miserable worm ; you know you did ! "

Bob Cherry hopped off the pitch.

" I can't go on," he said. " I don't know whether Smith did that on purpose. I shouldn't wonder. If I thought he did, for certain, I'd smash him ! Ow ! "

And Bob sat on the grass to recover. There was a big bruise on his ankle. He had not been wearing pads, and the blow had been severe.

" Next man in," said Bulstrode.

Nugent shook his head.

"I'm not going to let Smith bowl at me," he said.

"Look here, Nugent——"

"One accident is enough," Frank said drily. "You can put a new bowler on, or you can drop me out. I don't want any Bounder."

The Bounder threw down the ball, which had been fielded and returned to him.

"Just as you like," he said. "I don't want to go on."

And he put his hands in his pockets, and walked away. Bulstrode looked worried. He did not want to lose a player like Vernon-Smith, but he knew it would be difficult to get the team to trust him after what had happened. The practice went on without the Bounder; and Bob Cherry, limping a great deal, went off the field.

THE SIXTH CHAPTER.

Nugent Misses His Postal Order.

"How's the ankle, Bob?"

Mark Linley asked the question, looking into No. 1 Study a quarter of an hour later. The Lancashire lad was fresh from the cricket field, and he had a glow of health and colour in his cheeks. Mark was rather given to working hard indoors, "swotting" at studies which were outside the usual curriculum at Greyfriars; and the cricket did him worlds of good. He clumped down his bat, and took Liddell and Scott off the shelf.

Bob Cherry was seated in the armchair, with his trouser leg rolled up, rubbing his ankle with Elliman's. He grunted.

"There's a beastly big bruise," he said.

"Hard cheese, old chap!"

"Yes, rather! I believe the Bounder did it on purpose."

Mark looked at the bruise.

"It's rotten," he said. "I hope you'll be all right for the match to-morrow, Bob."

"Oh, yes; it's not so bad as that. I've been rubbing it for a quarter of an hour nearly, and it's done it a lot of good."

Nugent came in, and threw off his blazer.

"How's the old leg, Bob?"

"Getting on all right."

"Feel inclined for a trot down to Friardale

THE

GREYFRIARS GALLERY
IN VERSE

By Dick Penfold

No. II: Tom Dutton

Who never hears a word that's said
Unless you seize him by the head,
And yell enough to wake the dead?
Why, Dutton!

Who makes his fed-up schoolmates groan,
And murmur, in an undertone:
"My kingdom for a megaphone!"
Why, Dutton!

Who, when you seek a loan to beg,
Imagines that you pull his leg,
And bowls you over middle peg?
Why, Dutton!

Who, when you try to be polite,
Misunderstands, shoots out his right,
And sets the atmosphere alight?
Why, Dutton!

But who, in spite of his defect,
Is really one of the elect,
When games are played, or studies wrecked?
Why, Dutton!

Perhaps I'd better end this screed;
He cannot hear—but he can read!
And I don't want my nose to bleed
Through Dutton!

after dinner ? " Nugent asked. " I've got a pass from Wingate to go down and get my new lamp."

Bob shook his head.

" No, I think not. I won't do much walking to-day, I think. I don't want to risk being crocked for the Courtfield match."

" Quite right," said Frank. " You come with me, Marky ? "

Mark smiled, and shook his head.

" I should like to," he said ; " but I've got some Greek translations to do. Mr. Quelch has promised to look over them for me, and he's setting the time aside specially."

" Oh, rats ! I'll ask Bull, then."

" Hallo ! " said the cheery voice of John Bull at the door. " Who's taking my name in vain ? " And John Bull and Fisher T. Fish looked in.

" Come down to Friardale with me ? " asked Nugent. " I'm going to the post-office to cash Todd's remittance, and blow it in a new bike lamp. There will be a tanner to spare, and we can have some ices."

" I'll come ! "

Nugent put on his jacket, and felt in the pocket for the postal-order. He took out Todd's letter, and looked into it, and then felt in the pocket again. The pocket was empty !

" That's very odd ! " he said.

" What's very odd ? "

" I'd have sworn I put the postal-order into this pocket along with the letter," said Nugent. " I suppose I shoved it into another pocket. I'm getting as absent-minded as poor old Alonzo himself."

" Well, make sure you've not lost it before we start," said John Bull, the practical. " Don't want to amble down to Friardale for nothing."

" Oh, it must be here somewhere."

Nugent felt in the other pocket.

" My hat ! "

" Got it ? "

" It's not here ! "

" Try your bags," said Bull.

Nugent felt in his trousers pockets. But the result was the same ; the postal order was not to be found. Frank looked very much puzzled.

" Blessed if I can make this out ! " he exclaimed.

" You've lost it ? " asked John Bull.

" No, I haven't lost it. I put it into my pocket, and then I hung my jacket up here when I went down to the cricket."

John Bull whistled.

" My word ! Do you mean to say that it's been taken from your pocket ? "

" What else can have happened to it ? "

" Phew ! "

" Hang it all ! " said Bob Cherry. " Hang it all, Franky ; make sure about it before you say a thing like that outside the study."

" I have made sure," said Nugent, somewhat tartly.

The juniors looked at one another very seriously. If the postal order had been removed from Nugent's pocket in that way, it meant only one thing—that there was a thief in the school.

The fact that the name of the payee was not filled in on the order made it a very easy thing to cash it if it were stolen : the thief had simply to fill in his own name. The number of the order, of course, could be ascertained by writing to Todd, and it could be traced. But——

" The curious thing is that the fellow who took it must have been awfully quick about it," said Mark Linley. " You've been here a quarter of an hour, Bob ? "

" Quite that," said Bob.

" And it's not more than twenty minutes since I hung the jacket up," Nugent said.

Bob Cherry nodded.

" That's right. I wasn't on the cricket-field more than five minutes."

" I've got it ! " said Fisher T. Fish suddenly.

They turned upon him.

" You ! You've got it ? "

" I guess so."

" Hand it over, then, you fathead ! "

" Eh ? Hand what over ? "

" The postal-order, if you've got it."

" Ha, ha, ha ! "

" Well, what are you cackling at, you silly image ? " asked Nugent, whose temper was growing a little acid.

" I guess I didn't mean I'd got the postal-order, sonny. I mean I've got it—I've got it, who it was that's taken it."

" Oh, I see."

"You've seen somebody in the study?" asked Bob.

"Oh, no; I was at the cricket all the time. But I can guess."

"And whom do you guess?"

"Bunter!"

And each of the juniors nodded. It seemed only too likely.

"Bunter!" repeated Nugent.

"Well, I guess he's more likely than anybody else," said Fisher T. Fish.

"You're right."

"We'd better question Bunter before we go further," said Mark Linley quietly.

"Good! Will you come, Bob?"

"No, I'll stay here—I don't want to limp around."

"All serene!"

And leaving Bob Cherry to continue his treatment of the bruise upon his ankle, Nugent and Linley and Bull and the American left the study in search of Bunter.

THE SEVENTH CHAPTER.

Not Bunter.

BILLY BUNTER was discovered outside Mrs. Mimble's little tuck-shop, in the corner of the Close, behind the old elms. Bunter was looking into Mrs. Mimble's window with a longing eye. He had been inside the shop, trying to persuade Mrs. Mimble that a system of credit would be of immense service to her business. Mrs. Mimble did not see it in the same light. She had been very sharp with Bunter, and the Owl of the Remove had rolled out of the shop in a disappointed frame of mind. Mrs. Mimble had a fresh array of jam tarts that day, and the sight of them made Bunter's mouth water. He was looking in at the window, and feeling in his pockets in the desperate hope that some overlooked coin might yet linger there, when the four juniors found him, and Frank Nugent clapped him heavily upon the shoulder. Bunter jumped, and blinked round at him.

"Ow! Oh, really, Nugent——"

"I want to speak to you, Bunter."

Bunter's eyes glistened behind his big spectacles.

"Good!" he said. "Come into the shop,

will you; we can talk much more comfortably there. Mrs. Mimble's got a fresh lot of tarts——"

"Never mind the tarts now——"

"They're jolly good, and quite fresh——"

"Have you been feeding?" asked John Bull, with a searching glance at the fat junior's face. As a rule, Bunter showed signs of having had a feed.

The fat junior shook his head disconsolately.

"No; Mrs. Mimble is a most unbusinesslike woman. I've explained to her that I'm expecting a postal-order this evening, and that big businesses are always built up on a system of credit. But she can't see it."

"You haven't been cashing a postal-order, by any chance?"

"I haven't had one yet," said Bunter. "I was disappointed about a postal-order this morning. I was expecting one from a titled friend of mine, and it hasn't come—there's been some delay in the post. It's rotten! I've been thinking of writing to the Postmaster-General about it. Look here, if any of you fellows would advance me the ten bob, you could have the order when it comes, and——"

"Shut up, and come in!"

Nugent grasped the fat junior by the collar, and marched him into the shop. Mrs. Mimble came out of her little parlour.

She had a frown for Bunter, and a pleasant smile for the other fellows, so the expression upon her plump face was a little mixed.

"Did Bunter get in here immediately after morning school, Mrs. Mimble?" Nugent asked, coming to the point at once.

The good dame looked surprised.

"I think so, Master Nugent," she said. "He was here very soon after half-past twelve."

"Before twenty-five minutes to one?"

"Yes, I am sure of that."

"H'm! Then he was here by the time I got to the study," said Frank. "How long did he stay, Mrs. Mimble?"

"Oh, quite a long time," said Mrs. Mimble. "He was talking a great deal of nonsense to me about a credit system. He wanted me to give him some tarts, which I knew very well he would never pay me for."

"Oh, really, Mrs. Mimble——"

"You know very well you never intended

to pay me, Master Bunter. You owe me fourteen shillings and threepence halfpenny now."

"I am expecting a postal-order——"

"Nonsense, Master Bunter!"

"How long was Bunter here?" interrupted Nugent. "As much as five minutes?"

"Oh, yes, quite—nearer ten minutes."

"You are quite sure of that, Mrs. Mimble?"

"Quite sure, Master Nugent; though I really do not see what is the importance of it," said Mrs. Mimble, in wonder.

"It is really very important. You see, we suspect Bunter of having taken something, and if he was here ten minutes, he couldn't have done it, as it was taken just at that time," Nugent explained.

"I am sure he was here seven or eight minutes at least."

"Thank you, Mrs. Mimble."

"And I've stayed outside the shop all the time since," said Billy Bunter, in an extremely injured tone. "I've been waiting to see some chap who would be decent enough to lend me a few bob in advance upon my postal-order to-night——"

"Oh, rats!"

The juniors turned towards the door. They were satisfied upon the point they had set out to ascertain. Billy Bunter was not the guilty party, and they were done with the fat junior now.

But the Owl of the Remove was not so easily got rid of. He rolled after them, and caught Nugent by the sleeve.

"I say, Nugent——"

Frank jerked his arm away.

"Look here, you know, you suspected me of boning that postal-order, you know you did," said Billy Bunter. "It was jolly mean of you."

"It was your own fault for being that kind of a worm," said John Bull, in his direct way. "We shouldn't have suspected a decent chap."

The four juniors quitted the shop, and walked slowly towards the house. The bell was sounding for dinner.

"It wasn't Bunter," said Mark Linley, breaking a long silence, as they met Bob Cherry on the steps of the house. Bob Cherry was still limping.

"Proved it?" asked Bob.

"Yes; Mrs. Mimble's proved an alibi for him. He went to the tuck-shop immediately after lessons, and stayed there nearly ten minutes."

"Then he wasn't the chap," said Bob. "Whoever took the postal-order nipped into the study and took it after you left, Frank, and before I came in—and that wasn't more than five minutes at the most."

"Just so."

"Then we've got to find out who nipped into the study between twenty-five to one and twenty minutes to," said John Bull.

"And then we find the thief," said Bob.

"Exactly!"

"As to who it is——"

"I haven't the faintest idea, for one," said Mark Linley. "It seems impossible to believe that there is a thief in the Remove."

"It's horrible!"

"Suppose we say nothing about it till we've found out more," Bob Cherry suggested.

Nugent made a grimace.

"Too late!" he said.

"How so?"

"Bunter knows."

That settled it. Whatever Bunter knew was pretty certain to be known shortly over all the Lower School. Bunter came rolling in for dinner with a smear of jam on his face; and before dinner was over all the Remove knew that a postal-order—Todd's postal-order—had been stolen from Frank Nugent's jacket pocket in his study.

And when the Form crowded out of the dining-room, the news went buzzing through the Lower School. There was a thief in the Remove, and it was no longer possible to disguise the fact or to keep it secret.

THE EIGHTH CHAPTER

Halves!

"Found your postal-order, Nugent?"

"No!"

"Found who's taken it?"

"No!"

Frank Nugent had the same answer to make every time he was asked, which was pretty frequently. The news had sent quite a thrill through the Remove, and the fact that Billy Bunter's innocence was clear made the question all the more puzzling.

"Blessed if I can make it out," Bob Cherry said, talking it over with a group of fellows just before afternoon school. "The chap, whoever he was, nipped in and did it just in time. I don't remember seeing anybody near the study when I came in."

Some of the fellows looked at Bob Cherry curiously. He did not notice it.

As a matter of fact, it had already occurred to some of the Remove that the theft might not have taken place in that special five minutes.

Bob Cherry had been alone in the study for a quarter of an hour. He had had ample opportunity to take the postal-order if he had wanted to!

True, Bob was the very last fellow in the world.

The outstretched hand of the Friardale postmistress pointed directly at Bob Cherry. "That is the boy, sir!" (*See page* 328.)

whom anyone would have suspected of anything savouring of dishonesty.

But, then, everybody else was really above suspicion too; and if suspicion was to fall upon someone, Bob could not expect to be exempt.

That thought was in several minds now, but no one had cared to give it utterance.

It did not occur to Bob himself. He went in with the rest to afternoon lessons without dreaming that the finger of suspicion might point to him.

Billy Bunter blinked at him in class several times, with a mysterious manner which caught Bob Cherry's attention at last and made him wonder. Bunter's manner seemed to hint that he knew what he knew, so to speak.

There was an under-current of whispering in the class which could not fail to draw Mr. Quelch's attention during lessons.

The Remove master was very sharp with some of the class, and at last he rapped his desk impatiently with the ruler.

"What are you whispering about, Skinner?" he exclaimed.

Skinner started.

"I, sir?"

"Yes. You were whispering to Snoop."

"If you please, sir—"

"There seems to me to be something the matter with this class this afternoon," said Mr. Quelch, frowning.

The dead silence, and significant looks, that followed this remark made the Form-master realise that he had hit the mark by chance.

"What is the matter?" he exclaimed sharply.

"N-n-nothing, sir," said Skinner.

"Nonsense! You explain, Bulstrode."

Bulstrode stood up, looking very red and awkward.

"It's a—a—a rather unfortunate matter, sir," he said. "Nugent has missed a postal-order, sir."

"What!"

"Nugent had a postal-order this morning, sir, from Todd, who owed him ten bob—shillings when he went away. Somebody's taken the postal-order out of Nugent's pocket, sir, while his jacket was hanging on the door of his study."

"Good heavens! Is this correct, Nugent?"

"Yes, sir," said Frank, reluctantly.

"You do not know who has taken it?"

"No, sir."

"You are sure you did not lose the postal-order?"

"Quite sure, sir."

"Kindly explain the full circumstances to me."

Nugent did so.

"This is a most unfortunate occurrence," said Mr. Quelch. "I prefer to think that some foolish boy has taken the postal-order for a joke. If this is the case, I call upon the boy in question to tell the truth, here and now, and I am sure Nugent will freely look over the occurrence."

"Certainly, sir," said Frank.

A silence followed.

No one was inclined to own up to having taken the postal-order, whether for a joke or not. Mr. Quelch's face seemed to grow very lined.

"I hope it is not possible that there is a thief in the Remove," he said. "It would be terrible to think so. I hope that the postal-order will be discovered. If it is not found by bedtime to-night, Nugent, kindly tell me so."

"Very well, sir."

The lesson went on.

The juniors were glad enough when classes were dismissed. The affair of the postal-order was in every mind, and weighed upon all thoughts. Billy Bunter gave Bob Cherry one of his mysterious glances as they came out of the Form-room, and touched the sturdy Removite on the arm.

Bob shook him off as if he were some troublesome insect, and the fat junior coloured angrily.

"Look here, I want to speak to you, Cherry." he said, in a shrill whisper.

"Oh, go and eat coke."

"Now, look here," said Bunter, lowering his voice cautiously, "I don't want to be hard on you."

"Eh?"

"I say I don't want to be hard on you."

"What?"

"I know how fellows come to do these things," said Bunter.

"What things?"

"Oh, you can't pull the wool over my eyes," said Bunter impatiently. "Don't play the giddy ox. I say I don't want to be hard on you. What I say is—halves!"

"Eh?"

"Halves!" said Bunter.

"Are you stark mad?" asked Bob Cherry.

"Look here, it's halves, or there will be trouble," said Bunter.

"Halves of what?"

"The ten bob."

"Ten bob?" repeated Bob Cherry, dazedly.

"Yes."

"What ten bob?"

"Oh, don't beat about the bush," said Bunter. "Ten bob is five for me and five for you; and if you don't go halves I'll tell Nugent you took it."

Bob Cherry stared at him blankly, Bunter's meaning slowly dawning upon his mind. When it had fairly dawned upon him, Bob Cherry flushed a sudden crimson, and his right hand rose and fell—and Bunter fell, too, going with a crash to the floor.

THE NINTH CHAPTER.

Under Suspicion.

BOB CHERRY stood over the Owl of the Remove, his face burning, his eyes flashing fire, his chest heaving with passionate anger. There was a rush to the spot of the fellows who had been watching the scene with great curiosity.

"What's the row?" asked Bulstrode.

"Oh!" groaned Bunter. "Ow! I'm killed—ow—I'm dying! Beast! Ow!"

"What's the trouble?" Nugent asked.

"Only this," panted Bob. "He says I took the postal-order out of your pocket, and he says he'll tell you unless I go halves."

" What ! "

" My hat ! "

Bunter sat up.

" I didn't ! " he roared. " I never said anything of the sort ! Ow ! I said I knew it was Bob Cherry, and I'd give him a chance to put the postal-order back ! Ow ! "

" What makes you think so, you crawling worm ? " asked John Bull.

" Because he was in the study, and I know he took it. Of course he did ! Nobody else had a chance to take it."

" It's all rot ! " said Nugent. " As if Bob would dream of touching money that didn't belong to him ! The only likely chap was Bunter——"

" Oh, really——"

" And as it wasn't Bunter, it's a giddy mystery. But any chap who says it might have been Bob Cherry is a fool and a dummy, and that's plain English ! " said Nugent warmly.

" Thank you, Franky," said Bob, in a low voice. " I know you're not likely to think such a thing of me, anyway."

" No fear ! "

" Of course not ! " said John Bull. " As for Bunter, if he doesn't wriggle away, I'll stamp on him, and burst him ! "

" Ow ! " gasped Bunter.

The fat junior scrambled away at top speed, leaving the fellows grinning. But the evil he had done remained behind him. The vague suspicion had been in many minds before. Now Bunter's words had crystallised it, so to speak.

Bob Cherry looked round at the faces of the juniors, and on many, many of them he saw the dark cloud of uneasiness and suspicion. There was a grin of malice on Vernon-Smith's face. He evidently enjoyed the situation. And Snoop, and Skinner, and Heath and other fellows who had never got on well with Bob Cherry, could hardly conceal their satisfaction. The Bounder did not attempt to do so.

" You fellows," said Bob Cherry, looking round, " you—you can't believe I did it ? " His voice grew hoarse and husky.

There was a grim silence.

The juniors moved away one by one. But Bob's own friends remained round him— John Bull, and Nugent, and Fisher T. Fish, and Tom Brown, and Mark Linley and Micky Desmond. They were not likely to believe a word against him.

Bob looked crushed.

To a free and frank nature like his own, a nature that was the very essence of honour and straight dealing, such an accusation was horrible. And the impossibility of proving his innocence, at all events until the actual thief could be discovered, occurred to him at once.

He ran his fingers through his thick shock of flaxen hair, a trick he had when he was worried or bewildered.

" Cheer up, Bob ! " said Frank Nugent encouragingly. " It's all rot, you know— just Bunter's rot ! And we'll have the real thief soon, anyway."

" The Remove can't believe such a thing of me," said Bob, in a broken voice. All his excitement was gone now.

" Of course not, old chap ! "

" I guess not," said Fisher T. Fish. " I guess you are straight goods, Bob, from the word go ! And we'll have the real rotter known soon, I guess ! "

" It's horribly unfortunate that you were alone in the study so long," said Frank. " I didn't look at it in that light before. You see, you really had more time than anybody else for taking the beastly thing. Any other chap had to dodge into the study in the five minutes or so that it was empty, and you were there alone for a quarter of an hour. That makes the thing look rotten. But no one in his senses would imagine for a second that you did it."

Bob Cherry nodded gloomily. He could see that a great many of the Remove imagined that he might have done it.

" But look here, we'll jolly soon clear it up," said Nugent. " I'll wire to Todd to send me the number of the order. The thief must have taken it, I suppose, to cash it. Well, we can inquire after it when we know the number, and, if it is cashed, we shall get on to the chap who did it."

" Yes, if it's cashed," said John Bull.

" The thief may keep it back," said Mark Linley.

" That's not really likely ; for a chap isn't likely to steal, and run the risk of being expelled, unless he was in pretty severe need of money," said Nugent, " and if he's hard pushed, he must use it."

" I guess that's correct."

" I suspect that it's some young ass who's in tow with Cobb and that gang at the Cross Keys," said Nugent. " Some fool who owes money on betting, or something of the sort. The postal order may have been sent to some cad at the Cross Keys already."

" Very likely."

" Buck up, Bob ! "

Bob Cherry was not listening. He nodded absently to his chums, and walked away with his hands thrust deep into his pockets, and his head drooping. The shameful accusation seemed to have knocked him quite over.

The other fellows looked very glum.

" I say, this is simply rotten ! " Nugent remarked. " It's beastly unfortunate about Bob having been in the study all the time ! "

" He's taking it very much to heart."

" And all through that fat cad Bunter ! "

" Well, I don't know about that ; some of the fellows had been thinking of it, I'm sure," said John Bull. " I've seen it in their faces, though Bob never suspected it. But buck up and get the number from Todd, Nugent ; Bob will be under a cloud until we've found out who really took the note."

" Come down to the post office, and I'll send the wire now," said Frank.

And a quarter of an hour later the wire was sent.

THE TENTH CHAPTER.

Broad Arrows.

HEATH, the new junior, looked out of his study window. Bob Cherry was crossing the Close, with his hands thrust deep into his pockets. Bob's attitude as he walked was very different from usual. He seemed like a fellow upon whom some heavy burden had suddenly fallen. To the frank, free nature, suspicion was intolerable, and Bob had all the feeling of an animal caught in a net from which escape was impossible. A cold, cruel smile crossed Heath's lips as he looked at him. From Esau Heath Bob was not likely to get much sympathy in his misfortune.

Bob tramped down to the gates, and went out. He wanted to be alone ; now that he knew that some of the Remove suspected him, the unhappy lad saw suspicion in every glance. Even his own chums, he felt, might allow cold doubt and suspicion to creep into their hearts.

Heath watched him till he was gone.

Then he turned from the window, and locked the door of his study, and opened a bag that lay upon his table.

For ten minutes or more Heath was busy in examining the contents of that bag ; and then he left the study, carrying the bag in his hand, and he also left Greyfriars.

Half an hour later Nugent and his friends came in. They had wired to Alonzo Todd to send them the number of the missing postal-order. When the number was ascertained, further inquiry could be made.

Until then, nothing could be done.

" Where's Bob, I wonder ? " Nugent said, as he glanced into No. 1 study, and found it dark and deserted.

" Bob ! Bobby ! " John Bull shouted along the passage.

" He's gone out," said Hazeldene, looking out of his study.

" Alone ? "

" Yes."

" Poor old Bob ! " said Mark Linley. " He feels this awfully ; it's too beastly of the fellows to get such an idea into their heads."

" It's rotten ! " said Hazeldene.

" No good moping alone, though," said Bull. " We'd better look after Bob, and stick to him, and keep him from thinking about it too much. I wish Wharton were here ; he might be able to help."

" I'll write to him to-night about it," said Frank.

It was some time before Bob Cherry came back. Heath had returned long before then, but no one was taking any notice of Heath's movements. Bob did not return till after the gates were locked, and he had to ring up Gosling, the porter, and was reported for missing calling-over. He had to go into Mr.

Quelch's study, and face the Form-master. The haggard expression of his face arrested Mr. Quelch's attention at once, and he laid down the cane he had picked up, and fixed his eyes upon the junior.

" Are you ill, Cherry ? " he exclaimed.

" No, sir," said Bob.

" You are looking very strange."

" I'm all right, sir."

" Come, Cherry, what is the matter ? " Mr. Quelch said kindly. " I can see that there is something wrong with you. Why did you miss calling-over ? "

" I hadn't come in, sir."

" But why had you not come in ? "

" I—I forgot about the time, sir."

" You were very busily occupied, I suppose?"

" N-n-no, sir."

" Come, my lad. You have stayed out till long after dark, a most unusual and reprehensible thing to do, unless you have a pass from a prefect. Why did you do it ? What have you been doing ? "

" Walking about, sir."

" Where ? "

" In the lanes, sir."

" Why ? "

Bob Cherry was silent.

" I think you had better explain, Cherry," said Mr. Quelch.

" I—I—I've been thinking it over, sir," said Bob miserably.

" Thinking what over ? "

" About that postal-order."

" Ah, yes ! But why should that matter weigh upon your mind, Cherry, more than upon anyone else ? " asked Mr. Quelch.

Then Bob burst out :

" They suspect me of having taken it, sir."

Mr. Quelch started.

" They suspect you, Cherry ? "

" Yes, sir," groaned Bob.

" You are surely innocent ? "

" Oh, sir ! "

" Why should they suspect you ? "

" Because I was in the study nearly all the time. Of course, I could have taken it easily if I had wanted to."

" It is ridiculous," said Mr. Quelch. " Utterly ridiculous ! I should not entertain such a suspicion for a second. It is cruel and absurd."

" Thank you, sir," said Bob gratefully. " My own friends don't think it, but—but a lot of the fellows do."

" I hope they will think better of it," said Mr. Quelch, frowning. " The postal-order has not, of course, been found ? "

" No, sir."

" I shall acquaint the Head with the matter this evening, then, and a searching inquiry will be made," said Mr. Quelch. " I do not think you need have any fear but that your innocence will be proved, Cherry."

" Thank you, sir."

" You may go."

And Bob Cherry went, unpunished.

But Bob's face was very gloomy when the Remove went up to bed. Bob's special enemies in the Form were in high feather over it. Vernon-Smith and Heath had made up their quarrel, for the special purpose of enjoying Bob's discomfiture together. They were grinning and chuckling, and Bob knew very well what they were whispering about.

There was little sleep for Bob Cherry at first, but towards midnight he fell into a deep slumber, and dreamed of postal-orders, policemen, and detectives. He did not wake again till the rising-bell was clanging through the sunny morning.

He started, and sat up in bed. Immediately upon waking the remembrance of the wretched happenings of the day before crowded into his mind. His face, usually as bright as the sunshine itself in the morning, clouded over.

He stepped out of bed, and reached for his clothes. Then a cry of rage escaped his lips. The clothes were not folded up neatly as he had left them.

Someone had disturbed them in the night. Bob Cherry caught up the jacket and trousers. He held them up, and looked at them in almost speechless rage.

Upon the dark cloth, broad arrows, in imitation of those upon a convict's garb, had been daubed in white paint.

Bob's exclamation brought all eyes in his direction.

" What on earth's that ? " Bulstrode exclaimed.

" Broad arrows ! " ejaculated Skinner. " Ha, ha, ha ! "

There was a loud laugh from Vernon-Smith and Heath and Snoop. Bob's face was dark with fury.

"Who did that?" he exclaimed in a choking voice. "Who did it?"

"Ha, ha, ha!"

"What rotten cad did that?" roared Bob. "Hasn't he pluck enough to own up to what he's done?"

There was no reply.

"Was it you, Snoop?"

"No, it wasn't," said Snoop.

"Was it you, Heath?"

"My dear chap, don't ask questions."

"Was it you, you cad?"

"Well, no, it wasn't," said Heath.

"I believe you're lying."

"Thank you."

Heath turned away to his washstand. Many of the fellows were grinning. Bob threw down the clothes.

He dressed in another suit, and left the dormitory without speaking another word, either to friend or to foe. But the expression on his face was enough to give pause to those who felt inclined to "chip" him on the subject. Heath was the last fellow to leave the dormitory, and before he went he removed a little pot of white paint and a brush that had been concealed under his mattress, and concealed them under his jacket to convey them downstairs.

THE ELEVENTH CHAPTER.

"R. Cherry."

"HERE you are, Nugent!" said Ogilvy. It was a letter for Frank, addressed in Todd's handwriting. Frank opened it in the midst of a crowd. The former Greyfriars fellow had not been long in answering. The letter ran as follows, as Frank read it out:

"My dear Nugent,—I was considerably astonished and perturbed by the receipt of your wire. I sincerely trust that by this time you have succeeded in recovering the missing postal-order. I proceeded immediately to ascertain the number of the order, paying a visit to the post-office where I purchased it for that purpose. The number is 00012468. I have requested my Uncle Benjamin to check the number, in order to obviate any possible error in so important a matter.

"With kind regards from Uncle Benjamin,
"Always yours,
"ALONZO TODD."

"P.S.—I sincerely trust that the postal-order has not been extracted from your pocket by any person of dishonest proclivities. If such should prove to be the case, I should be glad to send some excellent tracts for the perusal of the unfortunate youth who has strayed into the paths of moral turpitude."

"Good old duffer!" said Tom Brown.

"The number's 00012468," said Nugent. "That's the important point. We'll get down to the post-office as quickly as we can, and see whether it's been presented there."

"Good egg!"

"Let's ask Mr. Quelch for leave off first lesson," said John Bull. "It's a jolly important matter, and it ought to be settled at once."

"Yes, we'll ask him."

Mr. Quelch readily gave leave to Nugent and John Bull, when he was asked, to go down to the village post-office instead of attending for first lesson. The Form-master was as anxious as the juniors could be to get the matter cleared up.

"It will be all right now, Bob," Nugent said.

Bob Cherry shook his head.

"I don't suppose the order has been presented," he said.

"Why not?"

"Well, after all this talk about it, the chap would be afraid to take it to the post-office for payment, I should think."

"But he must be in need of the money, or he wouldn't have stolen it."

"Yes; but——"

"Besides," said John Bull, "he may have cashed it before he knew that such a fuss was going to be made."

"Well, we'll see, anyway," said Nugent.

And Nugent and Bull went down to the gates while the other fellows were going into the Form-room. Bob Cherry went into the Form-room with downcast eyes. Fellows in other Forms looked at him very curiously, as well as the Removites.

Nugent and Bull walked quickly down to the village. They were anxious to see the post-mistress and get the matter over. If the post-office was drawn " blank," they would have to try further ; but Nugent hoped to get a clue there.

They reached the post-office of Friardale, a small establishment that was also a grocer's shop. The post-mistress, a kind-looking, middle - aged lady in spec-tacles, peer-ed at them over the lit-tle partition.

" Y e s ? " she said.

" I f y o u p l e a s e, we w a n t t o know if a postal - order was cashed here yester-d a y," said Frank. " By one of the chaps from t h e school, I mean. A postal - order has been lost —and we're t r y i n g to trace it."

" Yes, cer-tainly," said Mrs. Brett. " A postal-order for ten shillings was cashed here last evening by a schoolboy. I was here."

Nugent and Bull exchanged glances.

" We're on the track now," Bull mur-mured.

" By a Greyfriars chap ? " asked Nugent.

" Yes ; he wore a Greyfriars cap, at all events."

" That's certain enough, then. Do you know his name, ma'am ? "

" I do not, but it is written on the order," said the postmistress. " I forget the name." She looked puzzled. " Is there anything wrong about it ? "

I'm afraid there is," said Nugent. " Is he a chap you know by sight, ma'am ? "

" Yes ; I have seen him here before, with you."

" With me ? " Nugent exclaimed in surprise.

" Y e s, Master Nu-gent."

" B - b - by Jove ! " said J o h n Bull. " This is get-ting rather thick. I ad-mit that I had a hope that it might t u r n o u t to be that new c h a p, Heath."

" It wasn't Billy Bunter, ma'am ? "

" Oh, no."

" Was the name signed ' Heath '? "

" No."

" I sup-pose you still h a v e t h e postal - order here ? " Nu-gent asked.

" I have the number of the one that is missing. Will you tell me if it is the same ? "

" Certainly."

The post-mistress opened a drawer, and took out a small bundle of postal-orders fastened in an elastic band. From the bundle she selected one.

" What is your number ? " she asked.

Nugent read it out from Todd's letter.

" What on earth are you kids doing ? " exclaimed Wingate. " Searching," said Skinner. (*See page* 348.)

"00012468."

"That is the number, Master Nugent."

"My hat!"

"It's the same," John Bull exclaimed. "It's Todd's postal-order that was cashed here last night, Franky. We've only got to find out the name of the rotter who cashed it, and all's serene."

"Good!"

"You see, ma'am," Nugent explained to the post-mistress, "I had that order by post, and the name of the payee was not filled in. Somebody boned it out of my pocket, and he must have filled in his name to cash it. Will you tell me what is the name filled in on the order?"

The post-mistress held the order up closer to her spectacles.

"R. Cherry," she said.

"What?"

"WHAT!"

Nugent staggered back.

John Bull stood petrified.

A thunderclap from the clear summer sky could not have startled them more.

"R. Cherry," said the post-mistress in surprise. "The order is filled in: 'Pay R. Cherry,' and it is signed 'R. Cherry.'"

"Good heavens!"

"Impossible!"

Nugent and Bull looked at one another in blank dismay. R. Cherry! Bob Cherry! What did it mean?

"Oh, I've got it!" John Bull exclaimed breathlessly. "I ought to have thought of it at first. Of course, the dirty thief wouldn't fill in his own name, would he? That would be giving himself away at the first shot."

"He'd have to, to cash it here," said Nugent, with a haggard face. "If any other chap came in and signed it 'R. Cherry,' it wouldn't be paid. Mrs. Brett doesn't happen to remember his name. But Mr. Brett knows him well, and so does young Sam Brett. A chap wouldn't risk coming in here and signing himself 'R. Cherry' unless——"

"Unless that was his name?"

"Yes."

"But it can't have been Bob."

Nugent did not reply. In spite of his firm and loyal faith in his friend, a horrible doubt was creeping into his mind.

"It can't—it can't have been Bob!" repeated John Bull, but a faltering tone was in his voice now.

"Will you let me see the postal-order, Mrs. Nugent. "I know R. Cherry—he's a chum of mine—I know his writing as well as my own. Let me see the postal-order, please."

"You may see it, certainly."

The post-mistress handed him the order. Nugent held it up to the light and looked at the signature.

"R. Cherry."

A wave of deadly paleness came over Nugent's face. For he knew the hand, and even in his heart there could be no further doubt. It was Bob Cherry's writing, or else the work of a skilled and cunning forger. And what skilled and cunning forger was there likely to be in a junior form at a public school? That was a wild supposition.

It was Bob Cherry's handwriting!

THE TWELFTH CHAPTER.

Fish Guesses He Knows.

NUGENT handed the postal-order back to Mrs. Brett without a word. He could not speak. He seemed stunned. Without even thanking the post-mistress, he walked out of the post-office with an unsteady step. John Bull followed him, in the same frozen silence.

Second-lesson was about to commence when they reached the school, and entered the Remove Form-room.

Mr. Quelch signed to them to come up to his desk.

"You have been to the post-office?"

"Yes, sir," said Nugent.

"What have you discovered?"

"The postal-order was cashed there last evening, sir."

"Is that certain?"

"I have the number from Todd, sir, and it's the same as that on the postal order the post-mistress paid out on."

"That is unquestionable, then. I understand that the payee's name was left blank on the order Todd sent you?"

"Yes, sir."

" Then some false name was filled in ? "

" Yes, sir."

" What was the name ? If the thief filled in his own name his discovery should be perfectly easy," said Mr. Quelch.

Nugent's lips seemed frozen.

The Form-master looked at him in irritated surprise.

" Why do you not answer me, Nugent ? You are wasting my time."

" Ye-e-es, sir."

" What was the name filled in on the postal order, then ? "

" R. Cherry, sir."

" What ? "

" R. Cherry, sir," said Nugent, in a low voice. But it was not too low for most of the class to hear. There was a buzz in the Remove.

Mr. Quelch frowned.

" Silence ! " he said.

Bob Cherry sat immovable. He heard what was said, but the words hardly conveyed their proper meaning to his brain. He doubted his own senses.

" ' R. Cherry ' was the name filled in," said Mr. Quelch. " And the order, of course, was signed ' R. Cherry ' by the person to whom the money was paid ? "

" Yes, sir."

" Cherry, stand up ! "

Bob Cherry stood up.

" Did you cash a postal-order at Friardale Post Office last evening, Cherry ? "

" No, sir."

" Did you go to the post-office at all ? "

" No, sir."

" You were not in the school when the postal-order was being cashed ? " Mr. Quelch said, with a sudden remembrance of Bob Cherry's escapade of the previous evening.

" No, sir. I've told you where I was," said Bob dully.

" Were you quite alone while you were away from the school last evening, Cherry ? "

" Yes, sir."

" Then there is no corroboration of your statement that you spent so much time in aimless wandering in the lanes ? "

" I hope my word doesn't need corroborating, sir," said Bob Cherry, with a flash of spirit. " I don't tell lies, sir."

" I am afraid that in so serious a matter as this, Cherry, proof will be required," said Mr. Quelch drily. " Did the post-mistress recognise Cherry, Nugent ? "

" She said the order was cashed by a Greyfriars chap, sir, whom she knew by sight, that's all," said Frank.

" Did you see the order, Nugent ? "

" Yes, sir."

" Did the writing look like Cherry's ? "

" It looked like it, sir."

" Would you have taken it for Cherry's signature ? "

" Yes, sir, if I'd seen it on anything else. Of course, I knew Bob wouldn't sign a postal order that didn't belong to him, so——"

" H'm ! You may go to your place, Nugent."

Nugent and Bull went to their forms.

" I shall speak to Dr. Locke about this at once," said Mr. Quelch. addressing the class. " For the present, a prefect will take charge of the Remove. The post-mistress will be sent for immediately after lessons, and requested to identify the boy who cashed the postal order. If you are innocent, Cherry, you have nothing whatever to fear—no one who is innocent need fear anything. Mrs. Brett is a sensible woman, and not in the least likely to make mistakes in so simple a matter."

Mr. Quelch quitted the Form-room.

There was a buzz of voices the moment he was gone.

" I guess I can see the how of it now," said Fisher T. Fish.

" What do you know about it, Fishy ? " demanded half-a-dozen voices.

The American grinned serenely.

" Jevver get left ? " he said. " I guess I can see as far into a millstone as anybody. Of course, the chap who cashed the order knew all about Bob being already suspected by some of you fools——"

" Oh, draw it mild ! "

" Some of you fools," went on the American imperturbably ; " and of course, as he wasn't going to sign his own name, he signed Bob's, by choice. It was just the trick a cunning hound would think of."

" Of course," said Nugent, greatly relieved at the idea.

" What about the writing being just like Cherry's ? " demanded Snoop.

" I suppose a chap could easily get hold of some of Cherry's writing to imitate ? " said Fish. " He could get an old impot of Bob's, or he could get some old letter, and after a bit of practice he could imitate the signature. I guess it would be as easy as rolling off a log."

" Too steep," said Skinner.

" Rats ! "

Wingate came into the Form-room.

" Order, here ! " he exclaimed. " This isn't a conversazione."

And the juniors resumed work under the charge of the captain of Greyfriars. But all their thoughts were in the mystery of the postal-order. Bob Cherry gave his lessons no attention, but Wingate carefully passed him over. The Greyfriars captain knew of what the lad was suspected, and he knew what his state of mind must be, especially if he was innocent. Was he innocent ?

It was a question that even his own friends were beginning to ask themselves now.

THE THIRTEENTH CHAPTER.

Identified!

AFTER lessons that day the Removites had expected to be thinking of nothing but the Courtfield match, arranged for the afternoon. But as it happened, hardly a thought was given to the Courtfield match now.

The question of Bob Cherry's guilt or innocence occupied every mind to the exclusion even of cricket.

Bulstrode, as cricket captain, was thinking about the match, but his suggestion of a little practice at the nets before dinner was disregarded.

Nobody wanted to go down to the nets.

The Remove knew that the post-mistress at Friardale had been sent for to identify the boy who had cashed the postal-order, and they wanted to be on the scene when she arrived.

Dr. Locke had sent a very polite request to Mrs. Brett to come up to the school, and had sent his own trap for her, and she was expected soon after lessons were over.

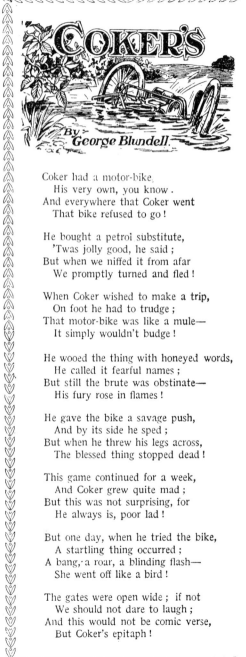

COKER'S

By George Blundell.

Coker had a motor-bike,
  His very own, you know .
And everywhere that Coker went
  That bike refused to go !

He bought a petrol substitute,
  'Twas jolly good, he said ;
But when we niffed it from afar
  We promptly turned and fled !

When Coker wished to make a trip,
  On foot he had to trudge ;
That motor-bike was like a mule—
  It simply wouldn't budge !

He wooed the thing with honeyed words,
  He called it fearful names ;
But still the brute was obstinate—
  His fury rose in flames !

He gave the bike a savage push,
  And by its side he sped ;
But when he threw his legs across,
  The blessed thing stopped dead !

This game continued for a week,
  And Coker grew quite mad ;
But this was not surprising, for
  He always is, poor lad !

But one day, when he tried the bike,
  A startling thing occurred ;
A bang, a roar, a blinding flash—
  She went off like a bird !

The gates were open wide ; if not
  We should not dare to laugh ;
And this would not be comic verse,
  But Coker's epitaph !

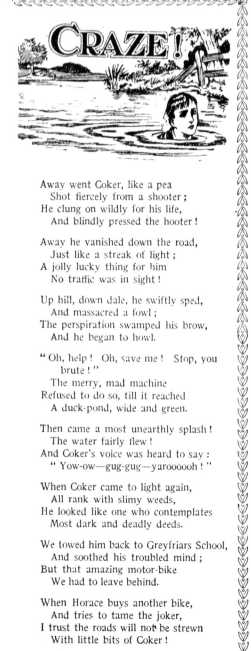

Away went Coker, like a pea
  Shot fiercely from a shooter ;
He clung on wildly for his life,
  And blindly pressed the hooter !

Away he vanished down the road,
  Just like a streak of light ;
A jolly lucky thing for him
  No traffic was in sight !

Up hill, down dale, he swiftly sped,
  And massacred a fowl ;
The perspiration swamped his brow,
  And he began to howl.

"Oh, help ! Oh, save me ! Stop, you
    brute !"
  The merry, mad machine
Refused to do so, till it reached
  A duck-pond, wide and green.

Then came a most unearthly splash !
  The water fairly flew !
And Coker's voice was heard to say :
  "Yow-ow—gug-gug—yaroooooh !"

When Coker came to light again,
  All rank with slimy weeds,
He looked like one who contemplates
  Most dark and deadly deeds.

We towed him back to Greyfriars School,
  And soothed his troubled mind ;
But that amazing motor-bike
  We had to leave behind.

When Horace buys another bike,
  And tries to tame the joker,
I trust the roads will not be strewn
  With little bits of Coker !

Bob Cherry stood alone.

Most of the Remove had made up their minds on the subject, after the report Nugent and Bull had brought back from the post office. Even Nugent himself was sorely troubled in mind.

Everything seemed to point to Bob's guilt, every fresh discovery made the case blacker and blacker against him.

What would the post-mistress say when she came ?

Bob Cherry was to be placed in a row of boys in the Form-room, and Mrs. Brett was to be asked to pick out the junior who had been to the post office the previous evening with the stolen order.

If she identified Bob Cherry the case was complete.

"You fellows get into the Form-room," said Wingate, coming along. "All the Remove are to go in and form up."

"Righto, Wingate."

"Now we'll see what we shall see," said Heath, with a sneer.

Nugent turned on him quickly.

"What do you mean, you cad ?"

Heath shrugged his shoulders.

"I mean that the truth's coming out," he said. "If it wasn't Bob Cherry did it, I'm sure I shall be pleased."

"Liar !" said John Bull.

"But you know what my belief is," said Heath.

"Oh, hang your belief !"

"Somebody's going to be found out, at all events," Hazeldene remarked as the juniors crowded into the Form-room again. "Mrs. Brett will identify the chap, whether it's Bob Cherry or not."

"It mayn't be anybody in the Remove at all," said Ogilvy. "I fancy it is, though."

Mr. Quelch came into the Form-room. He formed up the boys in a rank along the wall, ready for the identification.

The sound of wheels could be heard outside. Mrs. Brett, the post-mistress of Friardale, had arrived in the doctor's trap. She came into the Form-room with Dr. Locke. The Head's face was severe. Mrs. Brett looked worried and ill at ease. It was not a pleasant task that was before her. But it was a duty to be done.

Dr. Locke glanced along the silent, expectant Remove.

"You know why Mrs. Brett is here, my boys," he said. "She has kindly consented to help establish the truth by identifying the boy who cashed a postal-order for ten shillings at Friardale Post-Office last evening. If Mrs. Brett succeeds in identifying the boy, all doubt upon the subject will be set at rest."

There was a murmur.

All eyes were turned upon Bob Cherry. He stood erect, his eyes fixed straight before him, and a flush in his cheeks. But he did not look afraid.

Some of the other boys looked more nervous than he. It was no pleasant task to stand there and be scanned by a short-sighted old lady who might possibly make a mistake.

"Now, madam," said the Head.

"Ye-es, sir, I am ready," said Mrs. Brett nervously.

"Please look at the boys carefully, and tell me which is the one who came to the post-office last evening."

"Certainly, sir."

Mrs. Brett passed slowly down the line, peering at the breathless, expectant boys through her spectacles.

There was a deep, tense silence in the Form-room.

The Head stood like a statue. Mr. Quelch was grimly quiet. The boys were nervous and ill at ease, some of them standing erect, some shifting their feet.

Mrs. Brett scanned each face in turn.

She stopped half-way down the line.

There was an audible murmur again. The post-mistress of Friardale had stopped directly opposite Bob Cherry!

Bob's face showed a tremor for a moment.

Then it was firm again.

His clear, steady gaze met the peering eyes of the post-mistress firmly, bravely, unfalteringly.

"Well, Mrs. Brett," said the Head's deep voice, "have you found the boy?"

"Yes, sir."

"Kindly point him out to me."

Mrs. Brett raised her hand, and pointed.

Bob Cherry grew deadly pale.

The outstretched hand of Mrs. Brett, the Friardale post-mistress, pointed directly at him.

"That is the boy, sir!"

THE FOURTEENTH CHAPTER.

Condemned!

"THAT is the boy!"

Bob Cherry stood rooted to the floor.

His startled gaze was fastened upon the post-mistress in a kind of fascinated stare.

Dr. Locke came forward.

"That is the boy?" he repeated.

"Yes, sir."

"Robert Cherry! What have you to say?"

Bob gave a hoarse cry.

"Oh, sir! I—I am innocent! There is a horrible mistake!"

The Head's face was as hard as iron. He turned to Mr. Quelch.

"I understand, Mr. Quelch, that Cherry was left alone in the study from whence the postal-order was stolen, and had more opportunity than any other boy for committing the theft?"

"Yes, sir," said the Remove master.

"The postal order was filled in with the name of R. Cherry, Mrs. Brett?"

"Certainly, sir."

"You have it with you?"

"It is here."

"Kindly let me see it."

The postal-order was handed to the Head. There was a dead silence in the room The Head's brow was lined and dark.

"The number of this postal-order is 00012468," he said. "Was that the number of the postal-order sent you by Todd, Nugent?"

"It was, sir."

"Then this is undoubtedly the same order. Mr. Quelch, will you look at that signature. Is that Robert Cherry's handwriting?"

The Remove master looked closely at the signature. He nodded his head.

"That is certainly Cherry's handwriting, sir," he said.

"Very well! You positively identify this boy, Mrs. Brett, as the boy who came to the post-office last evening?"

Nugent minor greeted the juniors with a jammy grin, and jerked his thumb in the direction of the tuck-shop. " Better go inside," he said. " It's all tree !" (*See page 346.*)

" Yes, sir," said Mrs. Brett, looking very much distressed.

" Do you deny it, Cherry ? "

" Yes," gasped Bob Cherry, in a dry, choking voice, " I—I deny it, sir. It's not true, sir. I never went near the post-office last evening."

" I cannot believe you, Cherry. I regard it as sheer impudence on your part to endeavour to cast doubt upon this good lady's word."

" I—I don't, sir ! I think Mrs. Brett has made a mistake."

" You are quite sure, Mrs. Brett ? "

" Quite sure, sir."

" You noticed the boy particularly ? "

" I can't say that, sir. But I noticed especially that he had fair hair, and a great deal of it, sir, and his straw hat on the back of his head. There is no other boy here with hair like that."

That seemed to settle it. Bob Cherry's shock of hair, that never would yield to brush or comb, was a standing joke in the Remove.

Belief in his guilt was written in every face.

What further doubt was possible ? Even Mark Linley was staggered. Nugent could doubt no more—horrible, impossible as it seemed, Bob Cherry was a thief !

Bob Cherry had stolen the postal-order, Bob Cherry had written his name upon it as the payee, and Bob Cherry had cashed it.

There was not a loophole of escape left.

Doubt seemed impossible.

Up to the last moment, Nugent had entertained a hope that Mrs. Brett would identify

(329)

somebody else as the boy who had come to the post-office, or would fail to identify any member of the Remove at all.

But she had decided upon Bob Cherry at once—and Bob was not a common type of boy; he stood out from the rest in many ways.

Bob turned a haggard glance round him.

"Oh! What can I say?" panted Bob. "It's a mistake—it's a horrible mistake! Do you fellows all believe me guilty?"

Silence.

"Nugent, you're my chum—you've always said so—Franky, old man, say you don't believe that I'm a thief!" shrieked Bob.

Nugent groaned aloud, but he spoke no word.

Bob gave a wild glance at the boys.

The passion died out of his face, leaving it white, and drawn, and haggard, and strangely old.

"And there isn't one of you to stand by a fellow when he's down?" he muttered brokenly. "Not one!"

"There is one, Bob." It was Mark Linley's voice, and the Lancashire lad came out of his place towards Bob. "I believe you, Bob; I know it's a horrible mistake—I know it must be. I know you're innocent, old chap."

The Head's voice rapped out with unusual sharpness.

"Go back to your place, Linley."

Mark stepped back obediently.

"Cherry!" Dr. Locke's voice was deep and stern. "You are guilty; in the face of such conclusive proof, I marvel at your audacity in venturing to deny your guilt. You are guilty—of theft, of lying, of such rascality as I hope is very uncommon in one so young as you are! You are a thief, and not fit to associate with the boys of this school! You will be expelled from Greyfriars to-day, Cherry, in the presence of the whole school; and until then you will stay in your room."

The Head pointed to the door.

Bob Cherry gave one wild glance round, and then staggered to the door, and disappeared.

"The school will assemble in hall at four o'clock, to witness an expulsion," said the Head quietly; and then he, too, left the Form-room.

THE FIFTEENTH CHAPTER.

Expelled!

FOUR o'clock had struck, and the great hall of Greyfriars was packed. The school had assembled, all the Forms in their places, when Dr. Locke entered.

"Cherry!"

Bob stepped forward. His chest was heaving, his eyes blazing, and his face was burning. His breath came in short gasps.

"Cherry! You are going to be expelled!"

"I am not, sir!"

"What?"

"I am innocent, sir," rang out Bob Cherry's voice. "I am innocent, and I won't be expelled!"

Dr. Locke looked at Bob Cherry. All other eyes in the great hall were fastened upon him, too.

It was a scene such as Greyfriars had never witnessed before.

It had fallen to Dr. Locke to expel fellows once or twice, though it was rare. But never had he experienced anything like this.

Rebellion and resistance in the face of the whole school—a refusal to accept the sentence of expulsion—it was incredible!

But there it was. Bob stood the embodiment of fierce and indignant resistance.

There was an indefinable murmur from the school. They believed Bob Cherry to be guilty; yet they could not fail to admire his pluck. He was putting up a good fight for his honour, at all events.

"Silence!" said Mr. Quelch.

The murmur died away.

The Head was at a loss for words for some moments. He could only look at the panting boy, nonplussed.

But his anger was rising.

"Cherry," he said at last, "this disgraceful conduct will not help you in any way."

"I don't think a chap is called upon to submit to injustice, sir."

"You have been found guilty——"

"I am not guilty!"

"Silence!"

"I am sorry, sir, but I can't allow even you to say that I am guilty when I am nothing of the sort."

There was a gasp from the school. For cool, sublime "cheek," the fellows thought they had never heard this equalled.

"Cherry, it has been proved to my satisfaction, and to the satisfaction of Greyfriars, that you are guilty. The identification by the post mistress completed the proof against you, which was already overwhelming."

"I am innocent!"

"You are adjudged guilty. You will be expelled from Greyfriars——"

"I won't go!"

"What?"

"I won't go!" said Bob undauntedly. "I'm not guilty, and I won't go as if I were guilty. I won't leave Greyfriars unless I'm chucked out by force, and then you will hear from my people about it!"

"Silence!" thundered the Head. "Silence, you insolent boy! I am amazed at your impudence in asserting your innocence in the face of such proof. You have been found guilty of theft, of lying, of acting more like a grown-up criminal than a schoolboy. Robert Cherry, you are expelled from Greyfriars. Go!"

Bob did not move.

The Doctor's hand rose majestically, and pointed to the door.

"Go!" he thundered.

"I refuse to go, sir!"

"Cherry!"

"I am innocent—and I won't go!"

The Head's face flushed.

"The prefects will remove that boy," he said.

Wingate, Courtney, and two or three other prefects made a simultaneous movement towards Bob Cherry. They were looking very angry. Believing Bob to be guilty, like all the rest, they put his conduct down to desperate hardihood, and they were naturally indignant at seeing the authority of their headmaster flouted.

"Come out, you young cad!" muttered Wingate.

Bob sprang back, his fists clenched.

"I won't go!"

"Then you'll be taken, you young fool! Collar him!"

"Hands off!"

"Collar him!"

The prefects rushed upon Bob. The junior hit out desperately, savagely. His blood was up to boiling-point now.

Wingate, the powerful athlete of the Sixth, staggered back from a furious blow, and fell. There was a gasp of amazement from the school. Wingate had been knocked down—by a junior! But the other seniors closed on Bob, and he was grasped by many hands, and whirled away off his feet towards the door.

Wingate staggered up. A struggling crowd of fellows whirled doorwards, Bob Cherry, fighting like a madman, in the midst.

Dr. Locke looked on with a stony face. The masters shouted to the boys to keep their places.

But the excitement was too great. The fellows crowded round the struggling group, exclaiming and shouting.

The hall was the scene of the wildest disorder and uproar now.

Bob Cherry was got to the door at last, and he went sweeping through, in the grasp of the prefects, and the whole bunch of them rolled over in the passage outside.

"Out with him!" gasped Courtney.

With a last big effort, Bob Cherry was whirled out of the house, into the sunshine of the Close, and sent sprawling on the gravel walk.

He lay there for some moments, half-stunned.

He staggered up at last, to see the steps and the doorway crowded with hostile faces, to see scores of fists shaken at him, to hear derisive words and shouts.

"Get out!"

"No thieves wanted!"

"Kick him out!"

Bob tried to find his voice. But only a dry, choking sound came from his throat. His voice was gone.

Twice he tried to speak, but no sound would come, and the yells of scorn and derision were growing louder.

The unhappy lad turned away, and staggered through the sunshine, with scornful shouts ringing behind him.

He was expelled!

THE SIXTEENTH CHAPTER.

Harry Wharton's Task.

HARRY WHARTON stepped out of the train at Friardale Station, and ran across the platform. He had a bag in one hand and a ticket in the other. He threw the ticket to the old porter at the barrier, and dashed out of the station, and the old Friardale porter scratched his grizzled head, and looked after him in slow amazement. Wharton rushed from the quiet little station, and shouted to the driver of the ancient, time-worn hack that stood outside.

" Hack ! Driver ! Quick ! "

The old driver slowly detached himself from a post, and took a pipe out of his mouth.

" Yes, Master Wharton ! " he said. " 'Ack, sir ? "

" Yes—quick ! "

" Werry good, sir ! "

And the old driver rolled towards his old horse, and Wharton jumped into the old hack. Horse and driver and hack seemed as if they had been outside Friardale Station from the Dark Ages, and seemed part and parcel of the slow, sleepy old place. But Wharton was wildly impatient now. The slowness seemed horrible to him. He put his head out of the hack as the driver gathered up his reins in a leisurely manner.

" Quick ! " he shouted.

" Yes, Master Harry."

" I'm in an awful hurry ! It's fearfully important ! "

" Yes, Master Harry."

" Oh, do move ! "

" Yes, Master Harry."

And the hack started at a jog-trot, but it was faster than walking, to a lad tired from a long journey. Harry Wharton had travelled fast and far that day. He threw himself back on the old smelly leather cushions, panting. The bag had dropped to the bottom of the hack. Harry Wharton drew a letter from his pocket, and looked at it. It was in Frank Nugent's hand.

" Poor old Bob ! Poor old Bob ! "

It was Nugent's letter—the letter that had told Harry of the happenings at Greyfriars School ; a letter that was full of trust in Bob Cherry. It had been written before the identification scene in the Form-room.

Of what had happened since, Harry Wharton, of course, knew nothing. But immediately he had received Nugent's letter, he had explained matters to his uncle, and had started off to return to Greyfriars. His only thought was to get back to his chum, and stand by him in this terrible hour.

Travelling, even by express trains that flashed through the shimmering landscape, seemed too slow to Harry. He was wildly impatient to reach the school. What had happened since Nugent wrote ?

Had Bob's innocence been proved, or—— Wharton hardly dared to think of the alternative Could circumstantial evidence have proved so strong that Bob had been adjudged guilty ?

It seemed impossible ; yet such things had happened. Oh, if he were only at Greyfriars to stand by old Bob and help him in this difficulty, and assure him that one chum, at least, still believed him, and would believe in him and be loyal to him to the last, whatever happened !

The hack seemed to crawl, though the old horse was going at a speed that astonished itself. Wharton looked out again.

" Hurry up ! Hurry up ! "

" Yes, Master Harry ! "

The hack rolled on. The green hedges glided by ; the grey old tower of the school rose into view among the trees.

Greyfriars at last !

Wharton leaned out of the window. He could see the tower over the trees, and now the great stone gateway, and—what was that in the road ?

A schoolboy's box, and a fellow sitting on it in an attitude of utter dejection and exhaustion. It was Bob Cherry !

Harry leaped from the hack without waiting for it to stop, and ran.

" Bob ! "

Bob Cherry looked up at the sound of the voice and at the footfalls. He started to his feet, his face flushing deep scarlet.

" Harry ! " he stammered.

" Bob, old man, what's happened ? "

" Harry ! "

Bob made a gesture towards the box.

" Can't you see ? " he said bitterly.

" Your box, Bob, and you out here ! You —you haven't left the school ? " Harry Wharton exclaimed, in dismay.

" I've had to ! "

" Not—not—not expelled ! "

" Yes."

" Oh, Bob ! "

Harry Wharton looked at his chum, the words dying on his lips. Bob Cherry expelled from the school—driven from Greyfriars ! It seemed impossible.

" How did it happen, Bob ? " he gasped, at last. " What are you so mucked up for ? Have you been licked ? "

Bob Cherry glanced down at his dusty, dis-ordered clothes.

" I didn't give in," he said. " I made them chuck me out. I was innocent, and I wouldn't stand it. That's how it was."

" And the other chaps—some of them stood by you, surely ? " Wharton exclaimed in-dignantly. " Surely the Remove stood by you, Bob ? "

" Mark Linley was the only chap who stood by me," said Bob heavily, " and he was ordered to go to his study for speaking a friendly word. They all think I'm guilty—masters and fellows —everybody but Marky. Oh ! "

" Good heavens, Bob ! "

" The evidence is strong enough," said Bob drearily. " I dare say you'll believe me guilty, too, when you've heard it."

Wharton shook his head.

" Never ! " he said.

" You haven't heard it yet ! "

" I don't care ! I shall never believe any-thing against you, Bob, while you tell me that you're innocent."

" I am innocent, Harry ! "

" I know you are ! This must be some plot. It can't be all circumstantial," said Harry. " Some cad has fixed it up for you—Vernon-Smith, perhaps, or Snoop, or that new chap, Heath. Tell me about it."

The hack was standing in the road, the driver stolidly smoking his pipe. Standing there in the sunny lane, Bob Cherry told his chum what had happened.

Wharton's face went pale as he listened.

He would not allow doubt to creep into his mind. But he could not help seeing how terribly strong was the chain of evidence that had wound itself about the unfortunate junior.

" You see," said Bob miserably, " whoever took the postal order must have nipped in in those few minutes that the study was empty, and I was there a long time. That was the first thing that made the fellows doubtful. Then it turned out that the villain had signed my name on the order, and imitated my handwriting, so that even Nugent didn't know it from the original."

" The scoundrel ! "

" Then a chap looking like me cashed the order. You see, there's no doubt that Mrs. Brett was telling the truth, so far as she knew it, when she identified me."

" And she knows you well by sight, Bob ? "

" Yes, I can't understand it," said Bob desperately. " She must have mistaken some other chap for me—and there isn't a chap in the Remove much like me—or at Greyfriars at all, for that matter. She made a special point of having noticed my hair—and that's not like any other chap's in the Remove."

And Bob ran his fingers helplessly through the shock of flaxen hair that was now untidier than ever.

Wharton's brows contracted. The whole thing seemed to him a hopeless, horrible puzzle. He had not expected anything like this when he came back to Greyfriars.

" The truth's got to be found out," said Bob. " I've been kicked out of Greyfriars, but the matter doesn't end here. My father won't let it rest. My people won't see me disgraced like this. There will be an inquiry, and the police will have to undertake it. I know my pater well enough. He won't leave a stone unturned ! "

" Quite right, too," said Wharton. " And while your pater's doing that, Bob, I'm going to work for you at Greyfriars, and see if I can't find the villain out."

Bob shook his head.

" He's covered up his tracks too well, Harry, whoever he is."

Wharton gritted his teeth.

" I am going to try," he said. " I've got a

pretty clear theory, anyway, of what was done, and the thing is to find out the chap who did it, and bring it home to him, so that he can't wriggle out of it. And you, Bob——"

Bob drew a deep breath.

"I'm going, Harry," he said. "I shall have to go now. But God bless you for what you've said, old chap. It's put new life into me!"

"Take the hack, Bob. You'd better go. But you'll come back to Greyfriars soon—come back with your name cleared—and all the fellows will tell you they're sorry they were such fools as to suspect you."

"I don't care for them," said Bob bitterly. "A chap who can't believe in me can do the other thing! I don't want to speak to any of them again. Let them go. You and Marky are the only two who've stood by me. I shall remember that!"

Wharton did not reply. Bob's bitterness was natural enough under the circumstances; but in the happy day when his innocence should be proved there was no doubt that he would forgive those who had failed him—those to whom the terrible mass of evidence had proved overwhelming.

The box was lifted upon the hack. Bob stepped into the old vehicle, and it turned round in the road. Harry Wharton shook hands with his chum at the door of the hack.

"Good-bye, Bob, old son—and keep your pecker up!" he said. "Remember you've got friends here working for you—working to clear your name."

Bob squeezed his hand.

"Thanks, Harry; thanks, old man! Good-bye!"

Wharton signed to the driver, and the hack rolled away.

Bob Cherry was gone!

Harry Wharton stood in the lane looking after the hack as it rolled slowly off, till it disappeared beyond the turn of the lane, and the sound of the slow rolling wheels died away in the distance.

Harry Wharton's face was pale, and his eyelashes were wet. Bob Cherry was gone—Bob, the frank and free-hearted, the last fellow in the world to do any mean action—

he was gone, in black disgrace, with a stain upon his name, a shadow upon his honour.

Would that shadow ever be lifted?

Harry Wharton was determined that it should. His face was set and resolute as he turned and strode towards the school gates. His holiday was over. He was going back to Greyfriars—to seek out the unknown plotter, to bring the truth to light, to fight for the honour of his chum!

THE SEVENTEENTH CHAPTER.

The Major Ramps.

DR. LOCKE was in his study.

He was expecting to receive a visit from Major Cherry, but it was not a state of happy expectation.

To meet a boy's father, and explain to him how his son had been convicted of theft, and expelled with ignominy from the school, could not have been at any time a pleasant task. It could not have been pleasant, even if the father had been convinced of the truth of the charge.

But it was doubly unpleasant in a case like this. For Major Cherry, so far from being convinced of the truth of the charge, scouted the mere idea of it. Any evidence which told against Bob was, in his eyes, no evidence at all.

It was useless to attempt to convince a man in that frame of mind. The Head looked forward to the interview with great uneasiness.

Trotter had orders to show the visitor in the moment he arrived, and the sound of wheels in the Close warned the Head that his visitor was coming.

He coughed, shifted a little in his chair, and coughed again.

The door opened.

"Major Cherry!"

The major came in. He was so stout and powerful, and red-faced, and excited, that he seemed to breathe up, as it were, all the atmosphere in the room, and leave the unfortunate doctor gasping.

Dr. Locke rose to his feet.

"Good-afternoon, major——"

The major waved his hand.

" I have not come here for polite formalities, sir," he said, in a voice that could be distinctly heard at the end of the passage ; " I have come here to speak about the flagrant wrong and injustice that has been inflicted upon my boy, sir ! "

" My dear sir——"

" And to speak in plain language, by Jove, sir ! "

" Pray be seated."

" I decline to be seated," said the major. " I have but little to say, sir, and that will soon be said. A charge has been trumped up against my son——"

" Sir ! "

But the Head's most terrifying frown had no effect whatever upon the major.

He struck the table with his fist.

" I repeat it ! " he roared. " A charge has been trumped up against my son. I demand to know the particulars of that charge, sir, so that I can dash it to pieces, sir ! "

" If you will be calm——"

" Calm ! " roared the major. " Do you expect a father to be calm, sir, when his son is branded as a thief, sir, and driven from school, sir ? Calm ! I am quite calm."

And the major made that statement in a voice that was far from being evidence of calmness.

" My dear major——"

" I demand to know the particulars of this disgraceful business, sir. By Jove, sir ! "

" I am perfectly ready to explain, Major Cherry," said the Head. " Surely you must know that this whole occurrence is as painful to me as it can be to anyone. You do not imagine that I decided lightly, and without careful consideration, that your son was guilty of the charge made against him."

" He was not guilty ! "

" The evidence was crushing."

The major snapped his fingers.

" Bah ! That for the evidence. But let me hear this precious evidence. I will dash it to pieces, by Jove, sir ! "

" Very well," said the Head, with a sigh. " In the first place, a postal-order was missing from the pocket of a jacket belonging to Nugent, of the Remove—your son's form. Your son was in the study at the time it dis-appeared—it could only have been taken at a certain period—and during that period of twenty minutes, your son was in the study for a quarter of an hour, leaving only five minutes in which a possible thief might have entered and taken the order."

" Five minutes would have been enough, sir—five seconds, by Jove, sir ! "

" Very well. The next point is, that the order was filled in to R. Cherry, the name of the payee happening to be left blank before, and was signed ' R. Cherry ' by the person who presented it for payment."

" I suppose it is not the first time that a forgery has been committed ? "

" The post-mistress at Friardale Post Office, a most respectable lady, whose statement is unimpeachable, has positively identified Robert Cherry as the boy who cashed the postal-order."

" Stuff ! "

" Cherry was placed in a row with the whole of his Form, and the post-mistress picked him out at once, without the slightest hesitation."

And the Head leaned back in his chair, as if he had thoroughly disposed of the matter now. But the veteran of Bengal was not so easily disposed of.

His white moustache curled up as he sneered.

" Do you call that evidence ? " he demanded.

" I call it complete and incontrovertible evidence," said Dr. Locke tartly. " In a law-court, no further evidence would be wanted."

" Very well, sir. I take it that the governors of Greyfriars uphold you in the action you have taken."

" Unquestionably. I consulted with the chief governor before expelling Cherry."

" Very well. They will take the consequences."

The Head looked at him.

" The consequences ? I do not understand you, sir. The matter is closed now, and ended."

" Closed ! Ended ! " The major trembled with rage. " Closed ! Ended ! And my son's career is closed and ended, I suppose ? He is to sit down quietly under the imputation of being a thief, and to have his character blackened for ever. You will shortly learn, sir, that the matter is not closed ; that it is by no means ended. My solicitors are already preparing to take action, sir."

"Your—your solicitors ? " stammered the Head.

"Yes, sir. You and the governors of this school will be called upon to face an action for libel, sir, for defamation of character."

Dr. Locke sank back into his seat.

"An action ! Libel ! "

"Yes, sir, " thundered the major. "And unless you can prove your charge against my boy, sir—prove it up to the hilt, you will have to pay damages, sir—heavy damages—and be held up to the scorn and contempt of all England, sir."

"Good heavens ! "

"That is what you have to prepare for, sir ; that is the warning I have to give you," the major roared.

And he stamped out of the room, and closed the door with a bang that rang through the school.

THE EIGHTEENTH CHAPTER

A Clue at Last.

HARRY WHARTON was in No. 1 Study doing his preparation. Frank Nugent shared that study with him. Just lately Nugent had kept out of the study a great deal ; relations had been a little strained. Nugent had his tea with John Bull as a rule, and did his prep. in Bull's study.

Harry Wharton was not alone, however. Mark Linley was with him. Linley properly belonged to Heath's study ; but he could not stand Heath, and Wharton was glad of the Lancashire lad's company.

Wharton looked up with a pleasant expression as Nugent came in. The breach had been widening between them, owing to the difference of opinion over the case of Bob Cherry, much against Harry's wish. He could not give up his own belief in Bob to please anybody ; but he could not induce Nugent to share that belief.

"Hallo, Franky ! " he exclaimed. "Coming to do your prep. ? "

Nugent shook his head.

"No. I've got news for you."

Wharton jumped up.

"About Bob ? "

"Yes."

"Have they discovered anything ? "

"No," growled Frank, "they haven't ! What is there to discover ? "

"Proof of his innocence."

"Rats ! "

"Look here, Frank——"

"Oh, don't let's argue about that ! " Nugent exclaimed impatiently. "We shall only quarrel. Let's agree to differ."

"Very well. But what's the news ? "

"Cherry's people are beginning an action against Dr. Locke and the governors of Greyfriars."

"My hat ! "

"The whole blessed case is going to be dragged through the Law Courts," said Frank. "Dr. Locke will have to appear and give evidence. They'll have the head governor up, too, and most likely I shall have to go, as it was my postal-order that was stolen. Nice, isn't it, for a decent school ? "

"It's rotten ! "

"I should think you'd drop backing up that blessed family now," said Nugent.

Wharton shook his head.

"No fear," he replied. "It's rotten, certainly ; but Major Cherry isn't to blame. If I were a father, and my son were charged as Bob has been, I'd fight tooth and nail to clear him, and carry the case on to the very end, and spend every blessed penny I'd got on it."

"That's all very well, if the chap were innocent."

"Well, his father believes he's innocent, at all events, and he's bound to act on that belief," said Mark.

Nugent sniffed.

"I'm sick of the whole bizney," he said. "It would have been much more decent of the Cherry family if they had shut up about it, and not dragged their own name, and the name of Greyfriars through the mire."

"I can't agree with you, Frank," said Harry. "Bob's good name and his whole career are at stake. After being expelled from Greyfriars on a charge like that, he wouldn't be admitted to any decent school. You can't expect his people to take it lying down. I know mine wouldn't."

"Oh, rats!"

"Now, look here," said Harry quietly. "Why won't you talk the matter over sensibly, Frank, and let's see if we can get to the truth of it?"

"We've got to the truth of it, and all the talk in the world won't make any difference," said Nugent heatedly.

"I was away from Greyfriars at the time," said Wharton. "If I had been here, I think I should have looked into it somehow, and upset it. Nobody seems to have tried to take up Bob's point of view, except Mark here."

"And I couldn't find out anything to help Bob," said the Lancashire lad.

"I stood by Bob as long as I could," said Nugent doggedly. "You can't expect a chap to stand by a proved thief."

"Look here, Frank, why should Bob have stolen your postal-order?" said Wharton earnestly. "If he'd been so badly in want of money you'd have lent it to him if he'd asked you—or even given it to him."

"He couldn't very well ask that, I suppose."

"Better than stealing it, I should think. That would be a last resource even with a dishonest chap, and you know Bob wasn't that."

"He's proved that he was."

"I think he had a right to expect more faith from you, Frank. I don't believe that he would ever have doubted you."

"He would never have had any reason to," said Frank tartly.

"I believe you could help me get at the truth, if you would," said Wharton. "So far as I can see, the case concentrates on this point. You hung your jacket up in this study at twenty-five minutes to one, and left it, and Bob came in at about twenty to one, and stayed in here. He was still here when you looked in your pocket for the postal-order and found that it was missing. But it would have been perfectly easy for anybody to nip in during the five minutes the study was empty."

"Easy—not likely, though."

"Did you see anybody hanging about the study when you left it, Frank?"

"There were several fellows in the passage."

"Where were you going at the time?"

"I was going down to the cricket."

"Then I suppose most of the fellows in the passage were going out, too?" Harry Wharton asked.

"I suppose so," said Nugent impatiently. "What the dickens are you getting at?"

"Patience, a minute. I think I am getting at something," said Wharton. "When you came into this study, and went out again in a blazer, the chaps in the passage would naturally know that you had left your jacket here."

"Yes, if they noticed me at all. I don't suppose they would."

"Most of the Remove had seen you put the postal-order in your jacket pocket along with Todd's letter?"

"Yes, most of the Form had been standing round, listening to my reading Todd's letter out," said Nugent.

"Good! Then we may take it that all the fellows in the passage knew that the postal-order was in your pocket, and that your jacket was hanging up here, with nobody in the study?"

Nugent yawned.

"Oh, I suppose so," he said.

"Most of the fellows, too, would be going down to the cricket," said Harry. "That would leave the passage empty?"

"Well?"

"Unless there was some chap who didn't go down to the cricket," said Wharton.

Nugent started a little.

"What do you mean?" he asked.

"Take the fellows who don't play cricket," went on Harry steadily. "Take, say, Bunter, and Snoop, and Heath, and Skinner. Any one of those, you will admit, was much more likely to steal the postal-order than old Bob was."

"I should have said so then, of course. I've changed my opinion since. As for Bunter, Fish suggested him first of all, and we investigated, and Mrs. Mimble proved that he had been in the tuck-shop all the time."

"Leave out Bunter, then. Did you see Snoop, or Skinner, or Heath about the passage on that occasion, or any other fellow of the same style?"

"I saw Heath."

Wharton gave a jump.

He had hoped to hear something of this sort—he had hoped for a clue. But he had not expected instant success—he had not dared to expect it.

"Heath!" he repeated.

"Yes," said Nugent irritably. "I remember Heath was in the passage. I remember seeing him there for a moment. I think he was going to his own study. But I suppose even Heath could be in the passage without intending to burgle a chap's study."

"Heath didn't go to the cricket-ground?"

"You know he doesn't play cricket."

"But did he come to look on?"

"So far as I remember, he didn't."

"Then he probably remained up here while all the other fellows were out."

Nugent seemed a little struck by this remark. He looked thoughtful.

"Well, it's quite possible," he said; "but I don't see——"

"And as the study was quite empty for five minutes before Bob Cherry came in, Heath had every opportunity, if he wanted, of nipping in and taking the postal-order?"

"I suppose he had the opportunity; so had many others, if they had chosen to take it," said Nugent.

"I'm speaking of Heath now. Heath is a cad—a rotten cad, mean enough for anything, and he had a special feud with Bob Cherry. Bob licked him for tormenting Mrs. Kebble's cat, and we all know that Heath said he would make him suffer for it."

"Oh, fellows say those things, and forget all about them."

"Heath isn't the chap to forget a grudge."

Nugent made an impatient gesture.

"It seems to me that you're willing to suspect anybody of anything rather than Bob," he said. "You can't suspect Bob of theft; but you're ready to suspect Heath of theft, forgery, and impersonation without a shred of evidence."

"He's that kind of chap."

"Oh, rot!"

Wharton flushed.

"Well, I can't say you're very civil about it," he exclaimed. "I should have thought you'd be glad of a chance of helping to clear Bob."

"You can't clear a guilty chap."

"I tell you——"

"And I tell you——"

"Look here——"

"Rats! I——"

"No good quarrelling about it," Mark Linley suggested quietly. "We shall get at the truth some time; and I'm sure that's what we all want."

"I'm not going to have Wharton saying that I've gone back on a friend, and treated him badly," said Nugent angrily. "I should have stood by Cherry if he had been innocent. Wharton's practically accusing me of slandering a chap."

"You've made a mistake."

"Yes; all the school has made a mistake and you two are in the right," said Nugent savagely. "You two know all about it; and Dr. Locke and all the masters and all the fellows have made fools of themselves!"

"I don't say that——"

"Yes, you do. And I've had enough of it! I don't want to hear Bob Cherry's name again."

And Frank Nugent flung out of the study, and slammed the door behind him, with a slam that rang the length of the Remove passage.

THE NINETEENTH CHAPTER.

Cash in Advance.

HEATH was busy in his study in the Remove passage.

Heath's occupation was a peculiar one, and would have surprised the fellows if they had seen him engaged as he was.

He stood in the study looking round him. There was not a corner of the room he had not diligently searched, and not for the first time, either. Every day, perhaps twice in a day, Heath had been searching through his study.

More than once a fellow looking in from the corridor had found him so occupied, and wondered.

Heath had snappishly explained that he had lost a letter from his father—a letter containing a remittance.

"I am innocent, sir," rang out Bob Cherry's voice. "I am innocent, and I won't be expelled!" (*See page* 331.)

If that was the case, he had certainly not found it. His long and frequent searches of the study had led to nothing.

He knew, he realised, that the searching was in vain. What he was seeking could not be in any nook or cranny of the room. Yet, in desperation, he had searched again and again. It might have been pushed into some nook—it might have been concealed by chance between the leaves of a volume; there was a chance. But every fresh search had the same result.

"Hang it! Hang it! Where can it be? I know I didn't destroy it—I'm certain not! Yet it must be in the study, if I didn't! Where can it be? Suppose somebody else got hold of it?"

He seemed to turn sick at the thought.

The door opened, and Heath turned round furiously. The fat face of Billy Bunter glim-

mered in from the passage, and Bunter blinked at the new junior through his big spectacles.

"I say, Heath——"

"Get out!" shouted Heath. "Get out, you fat cad! What are you spying here for?"

Bunter was one of the few fellows in the Remove of whom Heath was not afraid. Heath clenched his hands and advanced towards him as he spoke.

"I—I say, hold on!" said Bunter. "I only want to speak to you! What makes you think I'm spying? What is there to spy on?"

Heath checked himself. His excitement, apparently about nothing, was the best way to cause suspicion. He knew that.

"I—I—— What do you want?" he snapped.

"Have you found it yet?"

"I—I haven't been looking for anything."

Bunter grinned.

"I've been watching you through the keyhole for the last five minutes, and I heard what you said to yourself, too," he replied.

"You—you cad!"

"I've watched you half a dozen times before, if you come to that," said Bunter. "And I've heard Micky Desmond mention about hearing you rummaging over the room —his study is next, you know—and Bulstrode and Skinner have both found you turning the study out at different times."

"I've been looking for a letter from my father."

"Rats!"

Heath tried to recover his nerve. His little evil eyes gleamed very evilly at Bunter.

"What do you mean, you cad?" he asked.

"You're not looking for a letter," said Bunter coolly. "You're looking for a sheet of foolscap."

Again Heath's face grew deadly white.

"How do you know?"

"Because I've got it."

Heath sprang up.

"You've got it!" he shouted.

"Yes."

Heath did not speak again. He made a rush straight at Bunter. The fat junior skipped round the table.

"Hold on, you ass!" he roared. "I haven't got it with me! You don't think I should be idiot enough to bring it here, do you?"

"Oh!" Heath paused. "Oh! Where is it then?"

"Where you won't find it," said Bunter breathlessly. "And if you go for me again, I'll jolly well hand it over to Wingate!"

"You—you young villain!"

"I know which is the villain of us two," said Bunter, with a sneer. "I haven't sat down in my study making copies of a chap's signature——"

"Silence!"

"Well, you shut up, then," said Bunter. "Of course, I dare say you were only amusing yourself, whiling away the time, as it were, by scrawling 'R. Cherry' over a sheet of paper——"

"Hold your tongue!"

"But it would look jolly suspicious if anybody saw the paper. Don't you think so?" said Bunter, with a grin of enjoyment as he blinked at the trembling cad of the Remove.

"It—it was only a pastime," said Heath, and his voice trembled and stuttered. "I— I——. But how did you get hold of the paper?"

Bunter chuckled.

"I found it."

"You stole it, you mean," Heath hissed. "I hid it under a heap of foolscap on my table, when I was called away suddenly; and I always lock my study door and take the key out when I go."

"You see, you're not half so deep as you think," grinned Bunter. "And you're new to Greyfriars, too. These two studies—Nos. 13 and 14, are new rooms, built out of old lumber-rooms that used to be at the end of the passage. The same chap put the locks on, and he put on the same pattern locks. I was in No. 14 at one time, and I had a key. That key fits this lock as well as the lock in No. 14."

"And—and you unlocked my door while I was out?"

"You see, I wondered why you locked it," Bunter explained. "I naturally suspected that you were having feeds here on your own, and you didn't want to share out. Under the circumstances, I thought I was entitled to look in the cupboard. That's why I came in. I didn't know you were amusing yourself by practising forgery."

Heath panted.

"I—I——"

"When I found there wasn't any grub, I just investigated matters," Bunter went on. "And I found the sheet of paper. As Bob Cherry had been expelled that same day, it seemed to me very odd that there should be a sheet of paper in this study covered over with ' R. Cherry,' in handwriting very like his—like yours at the top of the page, and getting more and more like his towards the bottom."

"Oh!"

"And I shoved it in my pocket," said Bunter cheerfully. "You see, I didn't quite know what to make of it, but I thought it might be useful. Since then, I've kept my eyes open. When I found that you've been searching up and down the study ever since, again and again, it's not hard to guess what paper you're looking for."

Heath gave a groan.

" Of course that—that had nothing whatever to do with the case against Bob Cherry," he said.

" Of course not," agreed Bunter, with a malicious grin.

" Why haven't you said anything about it before ? " said Heath slowly.

" Because "—Bunter blinked at him across the table—" you're such a cunning hound. I didn't know what to make of it at first ; and when I thought it over afterwards, I was afraid to do anything. I knew you were a born criminal, and I was afraid you might be able to fix it on me if I showed it."

Heath's eyes gleamed.

" And I could—and would—and will ! " he said. " You've got no proof that you found the paper in my study. I'll swear I've never seen it. My hat ! I'll make you suffer if you don't give it up ! I'll make out that you've written it yourself to extort money from me ! "

" Just exactly what I thought," said Bunter. " I knew you'd work up something like that, and get me served in the same way as Bob Cherry. And as lots of fellows have a prejudice against me, they'd be sooner down on me than they were on Bob Cherry. Two or three fellows I've had little loans from because —because I knew little things about them, would come forward to speak against me. You rotter, I could see myself being sacked from the school ! "

" You'll see it yet, unless——"

" Hold on," said Bunter coolly. " You've forgotten that circumstances have changed now. Major Cherry is bringing an action against the governors of Greyfriars."

" What about it ? "

" I rather think his lawyers would be glad of some evidence," said Bunter. " It's all different now. If I send that paper to Messrs. Sharpe & Keene, and offer to give evidence about finding it here, I think that will settle you. You won't be able to stand up in a court of law, on your oath, and lie as you

would in the Head's study. And those lawyers are so jolly sharp, they'd bowl you out in no time, and make you give yourself away. You know you would ! You know you daren't stand up before a lawyer and a judge and commit perjury."

Heath's lips trembled.

He did know it—he knew it only too well. He could lie himself out of a scrape at Greyfriars, but the thought of the crowded court, the wigged judge, the stern-eyed, examining lawyer, made him tremble and feel sick.

" You young hound ! " he muttered. " What will you take for the paper ? "

Bunter chuckled.

" So you're coming to terms ? " he asked.

" Yes, of course. I—I was only writing that paper for fun," stammered Heath. " I—I wanted to see whether it was possible to—to copy a signature, because—because Linley was saying that that was what had been done. It was only in fun, and it was after—after what happened about the postal-order."

" You can tell that to a judge and jury if you like."

" What will you take for it ? "

" A sovereign," said Bunter.

" Bring it here, and——"

Bunter laughed.

" No fear ! Cash in advance."

" I won't ! I——"

" Very well ! Will you lend me a stamp ? "

" A stamp ! " said Heath, staring. " What for ? "

" To stamp my letter to Mr. Sharpe."

Heath caught his breath.

" Here's the sovereign," he said. " Now bring me the paper immediately, Bunter."

And Billy Bunter quitted the study with a sovereign in his waistcoat-pocket. He left Heath shaking and trembling like one with the ague. There was a smile of fat satisfaction on Bunter's face. He knew that Heath was well off, and he anticipated that the new junior would prove a regular horn of plenty for him now—at all events, so long as the case of Bob Cherry should occupy the courts. As for the utter baseness of what he was doing, Billy Bunter did not seem to realise that at all.

Bunter's idea was to avoid all trouble for

himself, and make as good a thing for himself as he could. It did not seem to occur to him that there were any other considerations in the matter at all.

In excuse for the fat junior, it must be said that he was too dense and too stupid to know really what was right and what was wrong, and that he generally preserved the highest possible opinion of himself through his shadiest adventures.

Bunter did not go to his study for the paper now. He quitted the School House, and headed for the tuck-shop.

Heath remained in his room, waiting for the return of the fat junior, but waiting in vain. Billy Bunter was far too busy to think of returning, and he had nothing to return for. For he had no more idea of really handing the incriminating paper to Heath than he had of paying his debts with the sovereign he had extracted from the cad of the Remove.

THE TWENTIETH CHAPTER.

On the Track.

HARRY WHARTON rose and put his books away, with a determined frown upon his face. He had been thinking over the mystery instead of getting his work done, but he could not help it.

The affair of Bob Cherry was in his mind all the time; he could not get rid of it. His promise to Bob to work hard to clear his name at Greyfriars was never out of his thoughts. And as yet, in spite of the time that had elapsed, he had done nothing—there seemed to be nothing to be done. Yet there must be some way of penetrating the veil of mystery that hung over the business of the stolen postal order. One clue he had obtained from Frank Nugent—extracting it from him, as it were, against his will—the fact that Esau Heath had been near Study No. 1 when the postal order was stolen. But even before that, his suspicions had turned upon Heath.

Mark Linley looked up from his Anabasis.

" Going down ? " he asked.

" Yes, and out."

" Shall I come ? "

" Yes, rather. I'm going to the post-office."

" About Bob ? "

" Yes."

Mrs. Brett greeted the juniors very civilly in the little grocery post-office of Friardale. The kind old lady regretted very much the part she had taken in the downfall of Bob Cherry, but she had been bound to speak the truth, or what appeared to her to be the truth.

" Good-afternoon, Master Wharton ! " she said.

" Good-afternoon, Mrs. Brett ! I want to speak to you about that affair," Wharton said abruptly. " Can you give me a few minutes ? "

The good lady looked distressed.

" Certainly, Master Wharton ! I'm very, very sorry about that, indeed I am, but I could only tell the headmaster what I knew, couldn't I ? "

" Of course," said Harry. " I don't blame you. But I think there must have been a mistake in the identity, Mrs. Brett."

The post-mistress shook her head.

" It was Master Cherry sure enough," she said. " I remember him specially by his hair --flaxen colour, and bunched upon his forehead. There was no other boy in all those I saw who had hair anything like it."

Harry Wharton nodded.

" Yes, I know that sounded jolly convincing at the time," he remarked, " but since then it's occurred to us, Mrs. Brett, that the chap may have been disguised."

" Disguised, Master Wharton ? "

" Yes. I believe it was in the dusk when he came in ? "

" Yes, it was getting dusky."

" The shop hadn't been lighted then ? "

" No, not for another ten minutes."

Wharton looked at Mark with satisfaction. The facts were certainly working out to fit his theory. An impersonator would certainly choose the half-light to effect his purpose, if he possibly could. Many little points that might be visible in the daylight, or in the lamplight, might escape observation in the dark.

" But it was Master Cherry," the post-mistress added.

" He was just Cherry's size ? " asked Wharton.

" I did not notice particularly, of course ; but he was a very big lad for a junior boy."

"So is Heath!" murmured Mark.

"How was he dressed?" asked Harry.

"In Etons, with a cap."

"Cap on the back of his head, I suppose, and a mop of hair sticking out under it?" Wharton asked.

The post-mistress smiled.

"Yes, Master Wharton."

"Well, that was Bob's style, at all events. Did he talk much?"

"No; he seemed to have a slight cold."

Wharton started eagerly.

"He had a cold!" he shouted.

"He did not say so, Master Wharton, but he mumbled a great deal, and spoke very little, and kept his handkerchief over his mouth."

"My hat!"

Wharton's eyes were blazing now. His theory was correct, beyond a doubt. For a flaxen wig, and a touch of charcoal on the eyebrows would be a sufficient disguise, so long as the lower part of the face was covered. Heath's thin, spiteful mouth and sharp chin did not resemble Bob Cherry's in the least, and could hardly be made to do so. But the device of affecting to have a cold had covered up all that.

"Bob never had a cold," said Mark.

"Didn't he take the handkerchief away from his face all the time, Mrs. Brett?" asked Harry.

"I think not, sir; but he was only in here a minute," said Mrs. Brett. "He seemed to be in rather a hurry to get the money, and I served him at once."

"Did you notice his necktie?" asked Harry.

Mrs. Brett made an effort to remember.

"Yes, it was a bright blue one," she said.

Wharton nodded. The impersonator had been as thorough as he could. Bob Cherry, in spite of the rule at Greyfriars that the fellows should dress very quietly, had a taste for flaming neckties, which he frequently gratified. The unruly flaxen hair and the bright blue necktie had been quite enough to identify Bob.

"Thank you very much, Mrs. Brett," said Harry. "I suppose, now, you will admit that it was possible, at least, that another chap about Cherry's size may have impersonated him."

"I—I suppose it's possible, Master Wharton. I never thought of such a thing till this minute."

"That's all right. Thank you very much!"

And the two juniors quitted the village post-office.

THE TWENTY-FIRST CHAPTER.

The Unknown.

MARK LINLEY looked inquiringly at his companion as they came out into the old High Street of Friardale, and stopped under the big elm outside the post-office.

"What's the next move?" he asked.

"This way," said Harry. They walked down the street. "Look here," Wharton went on abruptly, "suppose a chap at Greyfriars made up his mind to play this trick, what do you think would be his first move?"

"To get the disguise, I suppose."

"Exactly. A flaxen wig to look like Bob's would be easy to pick up at any costumier's, of course; but it's not the thing a fellow would have about the house ready. The rascal would have to get it—and where would he get it? We've got a lot of props. among our amateur theatrical things at Greyfriars, but not a wig of that sort. He would have to get it outside the school."

"That's so."

"It would be safest to have it from London by post, certainly; but there couldn't have been time for that. The postal-order was cashed on the evening of the day that it was stolen, I understand?"

"Yes, the same evening."

"Then the chap must have got his flaxen mop close at hand. There's a costumier's in Friardale—old Moses, who runs the second-hand clothes shop, does the costume business, too. He keeps things for the fancy-dress balls, and so on, that are given in the neighbourhood. Unless the chap got the wig there, I don't see where he could have got it. He might have gone over to Courtfield, but if we draw Moses blank, we can go over to Courtfield, too, and see."

"Good!"

"Here's Moses' place. Come on!"

A stout little gentleman of the Hebrew

THE GREYFRIARS GALLERY IN VERSE

By Dick Penfold

No. 12 : George Wingate

❦·❧·❦·❧·❦·❧·❦

Who stands for what is right and true,
A sportsman, keen to dare and do?
A chap whose actions are true blue?
Old Wingate!

Who leads his stalwarts on the field,
Resolved to fight, and not to yield?
Who ever stands our strength and shield?
Old Wingate!

Who, in the dim and distant past,
By Gerald Loder was surpassed?
A startling change—which didn't last!
Old Wingate!

Who tucks us in our little beds,
And piles up pillows round our heads,
Then softly from our presence treads?
Old Wingate!

Who keeps a nasty-looking cane,
Which gives the victim so much pain
He feels he can't sit down again?
Old Wingate!

Who, though he sometimes gives us "gyp,"
Is qualified to steer our ship?
So give three cheers—and let 'em rip
For Wingate!

persuasion, with a fat, good-natured face, greeted the juniors as they entered. When the amateur dramatic fever had been strong in the Remove at Greyfriars, Harry Wharton & Co. had been good customers of Mr. Moses, and he was glad to see them.

"Goot afternoons, shentelmens!" said Mr. Moses, rubbing his hands. "Vat can I do for you this afternoons, shents?"

"It's about that wig," said Harry.

Mark Linley glanced at him. Wharton was taking a bold line.

"That wig?" repeated Mr. Moses.

"Yes—you remember a flaxen-coloured wig you sold to a Greyfriars chap last week," said Wharton.

Mr. Moses nodded his head.

"My gootness!" he said. "Is not the young shentelman satisfied with that wig? I sell it to him at less than cost price, my gootness!"

Wharton's eyes glittered.

His shot had struck home.

A Greyfriars fellow had purchased a flaxen wig at Mr. Moses' place the previous week. Matters were going splendidly.

"I tink that wig was splendid," said Mr. Moses, "and I am sure that the young shent took enough of my time trying on every wig in the place, and complaining all the time if it was not curly enough. And he would have nozzing but that particular colour—no ozzer colour would suit him in the least. My gootness!"

"Have you any more wigs like it?" Harry asked.

"I have vun more," said Mr. Moses, "but not so good—not so curly. Here it is."

He brought out a wig on his dusty counter.

Wharton took off his cap, and put the wig on his head, and looked at it in the dusty, cracked mirror.

The resemblance it gave him to Bob Cherry was amazing.

He put up his handkerchief to his face, and covered his mouth and nose, and then only his eyes remained to show that he was Harry Wharton and not Bob Cherry.

"Good!" said Mark.

Mr. Moses watched them in some surprise.

"Is not the young shent satisfied with the

vig?" he asked. "I sell it to him very cheap, as low as cost price, to please a customer."

"Oh, that's all right!" said Harry. "The chap I'm speaking of—by the way, what was the name of your customer?"

"He gave me no name, sir."

"He was a junior?"

"About your own age, Master Wharton."

"H'm!" said Harry. "Was he a fellow you knew well— one of our set, I mean?"

Mr. Moses shook his head.

"No, sir, I had never seen him before, but I knew that he came from the school, of course. He had a Greyfriars cap."

"Had he a thin mouth, with a sort of spiteful look?"

Mr. Moses grinned.

The major struck the table with his fist. "A charge has been trumped up against my son," he said. "I demand to know the particulars of that charge, sir, so that I can dash it to pieces!" (See page 335.)

"I don't know, Master Wharton. I tink tat he had a cold, for he keep his mouth covered vith a handkerchief."

"Good!"

"You do. not vant the vig?" Mr. Moses asked, as Wharton laid it on the counter.

"Thank you, no; as a matter of fact, we want to find who it was bought that wig of you," said Harry frankly. "There's been a rotten trick played, and we want to get at the chap. Would you know him again?"

Mr. Moses hesitated.

"I tink so," he said. "Yes, perhaps, I suppose. But he keep his mouth cover all the time, you see. Perhaps he not want me to know him."

"Very likely," said Wharton drily. "What day was it?"

"Friday."

"In the afternoon or evening?"

"In the afternoon."

"How did he take the wig away—in a parcel?"

"No, in a bag," said Mr. Moses—"a bag with a lock and key, and he was very careful to lock the bag, I remember."

"Thank you very much."

"Not at all, young shents, always pleathed to see you and do bithneth," said Mr. Moses, with a wave of his hand.

The chums could not contain their satisfaction as they went into the street again. Harry Wharton had thought out the matter thoroughly, and he had decided upon this line of investigation—and it was yielding unexpected results.

"It's splendid," said Mark.

"Gorgeous," said Harry. "I wonder what the Head would say if he knew that a Greyfriars chap had bought a wig in Friardale, just like old Bob's mop, on the afternoon of the day the postal-order was cashed."

"It would make a difference."

"Yes, rather; but we've got to get the proof complete before we talk," said Harry. "I feel certain it was Heath—but whether it was Heath or not, we've got to unearth that wig. The question is, where is it? A wig isn't so jolly easy to get rid of, you know. It would make a smother burning it in his study, and there's nowhere else he could burn it, so we can take it, I think, that it isn't burnt. There's the value of it, too; and Heath, though he has plenty of money, is the meanest rotter in Greyfriars, and awfully keen after getting value for his money. I should say he's keeping the wig."

"Then if we can find it——"

"That ought to settle him. If he's keeping the wig, we'll find it; if he's hidden it, we'll rout it out. If it's destroyed, that will be a bit of a set-back; but I don't suppose it is."

Mark nodded cheerfully.

"Even then we can have Mr. Moses down to see Heath, and see if he's the chap that bought the wig," he said. "Heath can explain then what he bought it for, and what he's done with it."

Wharton laughed.

"Yes, we can have a new identification scene, with Heath in the principal part instead of Bob Cherry. Ha, ha, ha!"

In much more cheerful spirits than of late, the two juniors entered the gates of Greyfriars. There seemed to be some little excitement going on in the direction of the school shop in the corner behind the elms, and they turned in that direction. Nugent minor, of the Second Form, and Tubb, of the Third, met them, both the fags eating jam tarts from paper bags under their arms. Nugent minor greeted them with a jammy grin, and jerked his thumb in the direction of the tuck-shop.

"Better go and have your whack," he said.

"What's happening, Dicky?"

"Bunter's in funds."

"Bunter!"

"Yes. His postal order's come at last, and he's standing jam tarts to all the Remove," said Dicky Nugent.

And he marched off munching jam tarts.

THE TWENTY-SECOND CHAPTER.

Above Board.

PREP. was over, but Harry Wharton and Mark Linley were still in Study No. 1. The feeling against them in the Remove was so strong that they did not care to go down to the common-room. And Harry Wharton's plan with regard to a search for the flaxen wig remained to be carried out. Harry was very much exercised in his mind over that matter. To find the wig, if it was hidden in Heath's quarters, meant a search of Study No. 13. Heath, of course, would oppose the search, if he knew of it. Indeed, the mere suggestion of it would make him resort to any desperate measures to destroy the wig, if it was still in existence. It must be done without his knowledge—but the idea of searching through a fellow's quarters without his knowledge was utterly repugnant to both Wharton and Linley.

"It's rotten!" said Wharton restlessly. "It seems such an utterly caddish thing to do, to look through a chap's room when he's away."

Mark nodded.

"I don't like the idea any more than you do," he said. "It's horrible—it seems like spying—it's the kind of thing Heath himself does; and we despise him for it."

"The question is, whether the end justifies the means," said Wharton. "We have jolly good reason to suspect that Heath impersonated Bob——"

"True."

"If he did, the wig would be the most incriminating evidence possible, and it ought to be found."

"True again."

"And it can only be found by searching for it without Heath knowing what we're up to."

"Quite so."

"And so it comes to this, that we must sneak into a chap's room when he's not there, and look through his belongings like a pair of blessed thieves," said Harry, biting his lip. "They say that the end justifies the means—and it really seems fair to use any method of clearing Bob. But——"

"But there's a but," said Mark, with a rueful smile. "I don't feel as if we ought to do it, Wharton, and that's a fact."

"Yet for so jolly good a purpose——"

"I don't want to preach," said the Lancashire lad in his quiet way. "But we are told in the Good Book that we should not do evil that good may come of it."

"Quite right. If people generally started doing rotten things with good intentions, I suppose it wouldn't do."

"It wouldn't."

"I suppose a blessed detective would do it—but then, we're not blessed detectives," said Harry restlessly. "We can't do it."

"I'm afraid we can't."

"But we've got to find the wig. We've got to look for it. The only thing is to do it openly and above board in an honest way."

"I suppose so. That will place Heath on his guard at once."

"It can't be helped. It's no good thinking we can do mean things with good intentions," said Harry. "Better be open about it. We'll tell Heath just what we're going to do, and wring his neck if he tries to stop us."

Mark laughed.

"Very well."

"We'll jolly well have it out before all the Form, too," said Harry, his eyes flashing. "They sha'n't be able to accuse us of being underhanded."

"Good!"

They left the study. Heath's study was dark, so he was evidently not there. The chums went down into the junior common-room. It was crowded with fellows chatting before going to bed.

Most of them looked round when Wharton and Linley came in. The two were coming to be very marked personages in the Greyfriars Remove.

"Here they come, the champions of injured innocence!" sang out Skinner.

"Ha, ha, ha!"

"Look out for your pockets!" said someone.

And there was a fresh roar of laughter.

Wharton turned red, but took no notice of the taunt. He recognised Heath's voice, but it was not his cue to quarrel with the cad of Greyfriars just then.

"Keep near the door, in case he tries to bolt, Marky," he whispered. "He may dodge off to the study to get the wig, if it's there, when I begin."

"What-ho!" said Mark.

The Lancashire lad leaned on the doorpost in a careless attitude, but quite ready to dispute Heath's passage if he tried to get out. The cad of the school was not likely to be able to pass the sturdy lad from Lancashire.

Wharton looked round at the hostile, mocking faces.

"I have a theory——" he began.

"Ha, ha, ha!"

"A theory that a fellow impersonated Bob Cherry in cashing the postal order at the post office in Friardale——"

Heath burst into a scornful laugh.

"So that's it, is it?" he exclaimed. "And you're going to accuse me of having passed myself off as Bob Cherry?"

"What rot!" said Bulstrode.

"Utter rot!" said Hazeldene. "Why, Heath isn't anything at all like Bob Cherry. He's about the same size, only he's got short, dark hair, and you all remember Bob Cherry's light-coloured mop."

"Yes, rather!"

"If you haven't anything better than that to suggest, Wharton, you'd better shut up," said Vernon-Smith. "I suppose you got that idea out of some blessed newspaper serial story?"

"I thought it out," said Harry. "I knew Bob didn't cash the postal order, so I worked it out that he had been impersonated."

"Rats!"

"But Heath isn't in the least like Bob Cherry," said Bulstrode. "I really think you must be right off your rocker to suspect such a thing!"

"Not quite. He was disguised, of course."

"Oh, this is a six-shilling novel!" said Vernon-Smith. "Chaps don't disguise themselves in real life."

"Shut up a minute, please. A chap who

put a wig on his head, and kept a handkerchief over the lower half of his face, could pass himself off as Bob Cherry, in the twilight, to a short-sighted old lady."

" Ahem ! "

" It's too steep, really, you know ! "

" Oh, let him prove it ! " said Heath. " He's brought this accusation against me out of sheer spite. Let him prove it ! "

" That's right ! "

" Prove it ! "

" Prove it, Wharton ! "

" That's what I want to do," said Harry. " Is Heath willing to let a party of fellows search his belongings, to see whether there's a wig hidden away there ? "

" Phew ! "

" What do you say, Heath ? "

And all eyes were fixed upon the cad of the Remove.

THE TWENTY-THIRD CHAPTER.

The Search-Party.

HEATH did not falter for a moment. Guilty or innocent, he had his nerve in control now ; and he did not flinch before the general gaze that was turned upon him.

" Are you willing, Heath ? " asked Bulstrode.

Heath nodded carelessly.

" Quite willing," he said.

Wharton's face fell for a second. If Heath was willing for his study to be searched, it was pretty certain that the wig was not hidden there, at all events.

Heath saw his expression, and sneered.

" I'm quite willing," he repeated. " Perfectly willing. You can turn my study inside out, and upside down, if you like. You can take up the floor-boards if you like, and send a fag up the chimney."

" Ha, ha, ha ! "

" If you find any wigs, or false beards, or revolvers, or anything of that kind——"

" Ha, ha, ha ! "

" I'll undertake to eat them ! " said Heath.

" Well, that's fair enough," said Bulstrode, " and if nothing is found, I should think that Wharton would have the grace to apologise."

" Yes, rather ! "

" Let's look through the study first," said

Harry. " I could have searched it myself, without saying a word, but I wanted everything to be fair and above-board."

" I'm ready," said Heath.

" Come on, you fellows ! " said Bulstrode.

Quite a crowd of fellows accompanied Heath and Wharton upstairs. Wharton was feeling a keen sense of disappointment. He meant to go through with the search of the new boy's study ; but he had little hope now that it would yield anything.

The juniors crowded into the study.

The fun of the thing rather appealed to them—and Heath had always been so secretive, keeping his study door locked on most occasions, that many of the fellows were keen to lend a hand in turning it out.

There was no doubt that the search would be a thorough one.

Skinner started by pitching the books out of the bookcase in a heap on the floor, and Snoop dragged out the drawers of the table, letting them, with their contents, fall in a heap on the floor.

" Here, hold on ! " exclaimed Heath. " I didn't bargain for that sort of thing. You needn't wreck the place ! "

The noise of bumping furniture brought a prefect along the passage by the time the raggers had finished.

It was Wingate, the captain of Greyfriars. He looked into the disordered study in blank astonishment.

" What on earth are you kids doing ? " he exclaimed.

" Searching," said Skinner.

" What are you searching for ? "

" A wig. Wharton thinks that Heath impersonated Bob Cherry at the post-office——"

" What ? " shouted Wingate.

" And he thinks he wore a wig, and keeps it hidden here. Heath's given us permission to search his study."

" But not to upset it in this way, I should think."

" Well, the things were bound to get a little disturbed."

Wingate turned to Wharton. There was a deep frown upon his brow, and an angry light in his eyes.

" Look here, Wharton," he exclaimed,

"you're keeping up this rot too long! Bob Cherry's guilt has been proved, and you're doing no good to anyone by keeping the matter alive in this way. How dare you bring such an accusation against Heath!"

"I believe it's true."

"Have you any evidence against Heath?"

"Not very strong evidence. But——"

"I think you should be ashamed of yourself," said Wingate. "You seem to be willing to bring the wildest accusations against anybody, rather than admit the plain truth against Cherry."

"I——"

"Hear, hear!" said the juniors in chorus.

"You'd better let this matter drop, I warn you, Wharton," said Wingate. "You'll get into trouble if you don't, and that's flat."

And, with a warning frown to Wharton, Wingate strode away.

The juniors crowded out of the study. They had searched every inch of it, and certainly proved that the supposed wig was not there. And they had left it in such a state that it would take Heath hours to put it right.

Wharton and Linley went along to No. 1. They had received a check, and it was a bitter disappointment. But they were far from losing hope.

"I don't believe the wig is destroyed," Wharton said. "I believe the rascal has hidden it somewhere. When you come to think of it, Marky, he wouldn't hide it in his study. It might be found there by the maid —or Bunter might rummage about. He's put it in a safer place than that."

"But now he knows that it's being searched for, I think he is very likely to attempt to destroy it," the Lancashire lad remarked.

"Yes, very likely."

"In that case, he will have to go to its hiding-place——"

"Certainly."

"And if we watch him——"

Wharton's eyes gleamed.

"Good! We'll take it in turns to watch the cad, and never have our eyes off him—night and day. If he's got the wig hidden somewhere, he's most likely to try and get at it by night. You see, he may have hidden it immediately after using it, and not dared to go near the spot since. We'll watch the cad!"

And after that always one or other of the chums was within easy distance of Esau Heath, keeping an apparently careless eye upon him—but never allowing him to escape observation.

Wharton took off his cap, and put the wig on his head, and looked at it in the dusty, cracked mirror. The resemblance it gave him to Bob Cherry was amazing! (*See page* 344.)

THE TWENTY-FOURTH CHAPTER.

A Financial Mystery.

"IT'S a giddy miracle!" said Ogilvy. "It must be."

"I can't understand it."

"You see," Ogilvy went on, "his people are not rich. We know perfectly well that his people are jolly poor."

"Quite so."

"His yarns about receiving postal-orders are all bunkum; we know that."

"I guess so."

"Then where is he getting the money from?"

"It's a mystery."

"He can't be boning it, or someone would be complaining of losing money." Frank Nugent said thoughtfully. "But he's had three pounds in one day."

The juniors were discussing Bunter.

Billy Bunter had often surprised and exasperated the Remove. But he had never surprised them, never puzzled them, so much as now.

Bunter's stories of great wealth and titled friends were a joke in the Form. But the fat junior was really in funds at last.

"I say, you fellows——"

"We were just wanting to see you, Bunter——"

"Good! I was looking for you, too. Who says ices?"

"Ices!"

"Come on, then," said Bunter. "Mrs. Mimble's got a fresh lot of ice-cream, and it's simply ripping. I'm standing treat."

"You are?"

"Yes, rather! Come on, every one of you."

"So you've got some more money?" said Nugent.

"Yes," said Bunter, blinking at him. "I've just had a postal-order."

"You've just had a postal-order?" repeated Hazeldene. "By post?"

"Yes."

"How much?"

"A sovereign."

"You blessed fibber," said Hazeldene. "The last post isn't in yet, and your last sovereign came by the other post. The postman hasn't been since."

"My hat! So he hasn't," said Bulstrode. "Where did you get that postal-order?"

"I—I—I——"

"Let's see it," said Nugent.

"I've cashed it," said Bunter. "Here's

the pound note, if you don't believe me." He held up a Treasury note between his fat finger and thumb. There was no doubting the genuineness of the note, and the juniors could only stare at it.

"That's real enough," said Tom Brown.

"I guess so; that's the right article, sonny."

"Look here," said Bulstrode, "this is getting serious. Where did you get that quid, Bunter?"

"I've had a postal-order——."

"Don't tell crammers. The postman hasn't been."

"I—I meant to say that there were two in my last letter, and I cashed only one of them then," said Bunter. "Now I'm using the other, as I expect to have some more in the morning, you see."

"Oh!" said Bulstrode.

"Who cashed this order for you, then?" asked John Bull suspiciously. "You certainly haven't been down to the post-office."

"I—I asked a fellow to cash it for me."

"What fellow?"

"Oh, really, Bull—— I—I say, you fellows, I—I forgot, you know. I remember now. It was Heath!"

"Heath?"

"Yes."

"Will he say so himself?"

"Oh, really, of course he will! Just you ask him."

"Well, we'll give you one more chance," said Bulstrode. "We'll ask Heath. Is Heath here?"

Heath was not there. But two or three fellows volunteered to fetch him; and they went in search of him, and Billy Bunter waited, with Bulstrode's hand on his collar, for Heath to appear.

THE TWENTY-FIFTH CHAPTER.

The Upper Hand.

HEATH came in a few minutes, with Micky Desmond and Frank Nugent on either side of him. They had not told him what was wanted of him; he had merely been told that Bulstrode wanted to speak to him. Heath was naturally suspicious, and he felt uneasy;

but he had no choice about coming. His little eyes were scintillating like a rat's with anxiety as he joined the crowd of juniors in the Form-room passage.

Bulstrode beckoned to him.

"Come here, Heath," he said. "I want to ask you a question. Bunter says that you cashed a postal-order for a pound for him. Did you?"

Heath's eyes gleamed on Bunter.

"You remember, Heath," panted the fat junior. "I came to you in your study about ten minutes ago, and—and asked you to cash an order for a pound, as—as it was too late to go down to the post-office."

Heath nodded.

"Yes, I remember," he said.

Bulstrode started.

"Then it's true?" he said.

"Yes," replied Heath.

"You cashed a postal-order for Bunter—an order for a pound?"

"Yes."

Bulstrode released the fat junior.

"Well, if that's the case, it's all right," he said. "If you've really had the postal-orders, Bunter, I suppose the money belongs to you."

"Of course it does," said Bunter, in a very injured tone. "Of course it does, Bulstrode! I really think you might take a fellow's word for it—especially such an honourable chap as I am. I don't like having my word doubted, you know."

"Oh, rats!"

"Look here! The offer's still good," said Bunter. "Any of you fellows that would like to have some ices can come along——"

"What-ho!"

And the juniors thronged off towards the tuck-shop. Heath made a sign to Billy Bunter to stop.

"I want to speak to you about—about that postal-order, Bunter," he said.

"Can't stop now, Heath——"

"It's important."

"Oh, all right; I'll join you fellows in a minute," said Bunter. "Tell Mrs. Mimble to put it down to me."

"Right-ho!" said Skinner.

Harry Wharton and Mark Linley had been spectators of the scene, without taking part in it. They walked away now, as Heath's suspicious eye turned upon them. They did not desire to play the part of eavesdroppers. Heath drew Bunter into the recess of a deep window, and there, out of the general view, he grasped the fat junior by the shoulder, and shook him till he gasped.

"Ow! Oh, really, Heath!" stammered Bunter. "Leggo! Yow!"

"You fool—you fat fool!" said Heath, in low, savage tones. "You mad idiot! Can't you see that you're making this matter the talk of the Form?"

"Oh, really——"

"You've had four pounds out of me now, altogether——"

"I'm going to repay it all when my postal-orders come," said Bunter. "I'm expecting several remittances from some titled friends ——"

"Stop that rot!" said Heath savagely. "You're getting this money out of me because you've got that paper. Each time you've promised to give it up, and you haven't done it."

"I've mislaid it——"

"Liar!"

"Oh, really——"

"If you won't give me the paper," said Heath, in a choking voice, "will you be a bit more careful about keeping up appearances? It will be as bad for you as for me, if the truth comes out. You are making the whole Form excited and curious by swanking about with all that money."

"Oh, that's all right. It's supposed to come from my titled friends."

"Do you think anybody believes those rotten lies!" said Heath savagely.

"I decline to listen to language of this sort," said Bunter loftily. "And I've said before that I don't care to keep up your acquaintance in public, Heath. If I want to speak to you, I'll come to your study."

And he rolled away, leaving Heath trembling from head to foot with rage and fear.

The way of the transgressor is hard, as the schemer of the Remove was beginning to find out.

THE TWENTY-SIXTH CHAPTER.

Caught!

HARRY WHARTON and Mark Linley went upstairs. There was no light in Heath's study, as Harry Wharton glanced at the door. But there was a light under Billy Bunter's door, and Wharton started as he observed it.

He pointed to the streak of light under the door, glimmering out upon the dimly lighted passage.

"Somebody's in Bunter's study," he said.

"Heath!"

"Well, we know it isn't Bunter, as he's in the tuck-shop with the fellows, and we know Bunter has no study-mate," said Harry. "Bunter has the study to himself."

"Heath," repeated Linley.

"Suppose," said Harry, in a low voice—"suppose Bunter had found something—say the wig, for instance—that might be the reason——"

"The reason for the four pounds."

"Exactly."

"I shouldn't wonder."

Wharton paused outside the door. There was a sound within the study that was unmistakable—a sound of rummaging. Shelves and drawers were being turned out by an eager searcher, the sounds proved it clearly.

"It's Heath," said Harry, setting his lips. "He's looking for something in Bunter's study. Something that belongs to him, perhaps."

"Open the door."

"Good!"

Wharton flung open the door of the study. There was a startled cry from within.

Heath was bending over the drawer of Bunter's table, going through the contents with eager, quick fingers, when the door opened.

He started up, his face becoming chalky white, and his startled eyes gleaming upon the two juniors like a frightened cat's.

"What are you doing here?" exclaimed Harry Wharton sternly.

"Oh, I—I——"

"What are you doing?"

"Mind your own business!" cried Heath

angrily. "You can get out! This isn't your study, is it? Mind your own business."

"What are you looking for?" asked Harry.

"Nothing."

"You are turning the study out. What are you searching for?"

"Find out?"

"I am going to," said Harry quietly. "I'm going to find out how you have succeeded in blackening Bob Cherry's name, and driving him from school. You're getting to the end of your tether, Heath."

"Hang you—hang you! Leave me alone!"

"Marky," said Harry quietly, "go and tell Bunter that Heath is searching his study. I'll keep the rotter here while you're gone."

"Right-ho!" said Mark.

He ran quickly along the passage. Heath clenched his fists convulsively.

"I'm not going to stay here," he said.

"You are!"

"I won't! I—I refuse! Let me pass!" shouted Heath, coming towards the doorway.

Harry Wharton stood in the open doorway, his hands up. His eyes were fixed upon the furious, passionate Heath.

"You are not coming out," he said. "You came here of your own accord, and you are staying here till the owner of the study returns. You can explain to him."

"Let me pass!"

"You shall not pass."

Heath made a rush to force his way out. Wharton caught him by the shoulders, and, with a single swing of his strong arm, sent him spinning across the study.

Heath fell against the wall, and slid to the floor. He lay there, gasping and panting, his eyes glittering like a rat's.

"Oh, hang you!" he groaned.

"I don't want to handle you," said Wharton quietly; "but you don't leave this study. You have been searching it. You can explain to the owner what you've been searching it for."

"I—I had Bunter's permission."

"Then you can stay and see Bunter."

"I tell you, I—I won't stay! Look here!"

Wharton squared his shoulders. He stood in the doorway, truly a lion in the path.

Bob Cherry was drawn back to Greyfriars on the top of the old station "growler." Never had such a scene been witnessed before! (*See page* 358.)

Heath could no more have moved him than he could have moved the solid walls.

The cad of the Remove threw himself sullenly into a chair to wait. Bunter, apparently, was not in a hurry to come. Perhaps the tuck-shop held him with a peculiar fascination. But there was a sound of footsteps on the stairs at last.

Heath started to his feet.

"Will you let me pass?" he hissed.

"No!"

The new junior caught up the chair he had been sitting upon, swung it into the air with both hands, and rushed furiously at Wharton.

Harry started back a pace.

But he did not flinch further. As Heath brought down the chair with desperate force, the active junior dodged the sweeping blow, caught the chair by the rail, and jerked it out of the other's hand.

The chair went to the floor with a crash, and the next moment Wharton's clenched fist was planted upon Heath's jaw, and he rolled on the carpet.

"I—I say, you fellows!"

Bunter had arrived. He came running up the Remove passage with three or four other fellows. He blinked into the study through his big spectacles. His little round eyes were glimmering with rage behind his glasses.

"Heath, you worm! You've been searching my study, have you?" he exclaimed. "Has he found the paper, Wharton?"

"What paper?"

"The—the—I—I mean, I don't mean a paper!" stammered Bunter, realising that he was speaking too freely. "Has he found anything?"

"I don't know."

"I wasn't searching the study," said Heath. "I—I was looking for—for a postal-order—one you said you wanted me to cash. I've got a pound note ready to give you for it."

Bunter blinked at him.

"Hand over the quid," he said.

Heath handed it over.

"I'll look for the—the postal-order myself and let you have it," said Bunter, slipping the note into his pocket. Now get out of my study."

Heath slunk out.

The other fellows followed, and Bunter locked the door after them. In the passage, Wharton and Linley exchanged glances.

"So it's a paper," Wharton muttered.

Mark nodded.

"Yes, some paper that Bunter holds, that Heath pays him to keep quiet. What on earth can it be?"

"If it's nothing to do with Bob Cherry," said Harry, "it's no business of ours. But if it concerns this case, we're going to know all about that paper."

"Yes, rather."

"After this, I don't think Bunter will trust it in a hiding-place. He will carry it about with him," said Harry in a low tone.

"I should say so, and that——"

"That's where we come in," said Harry Wharton.

THE TWENTY-SEVENTH CHAPTER.

In the Dark Hours.

HEATH, as a rule, was able to keep a mask of indifference upon his face; but just now the anxiety he was labouring under could not be concealed. When the Remove went up to bed, Heath was pale and harassed-looking.

During the night and the day following, he had to regain possession of that paper, or else face the consequences of what he had done. He realised that very clearly.

Heath watched Bunter as he went to bed.

Bunter put his waistcoat under his mattress, so that he would be lying on it all through the night. That was enough to convince Heath that the paper was now in a pocket of the waistcoat. But there was little likelihood that he would be able to get at it during the night without waking the fat junior.

Still, Bunter was a heavy sleeper, and there was a chance; and that chance Heath meant to try as soon as the Remove were all asleep.

As a matter of fact, the Remove were not likely to be all asleep at any time that night. Wharton and Mark Linley were going to watch the cad of the Form, and they had arranged to take it in turns.

Loder, the prefect, saw lights out, and the Remove, after the usual chatter, settled down to sleep.

There was a glimmer of moonlight in at the high windows of the dormitory, and it was possible to see objects dimly. If a fellow should leave his bed, Harry Wharton knew that he would see him.

Wharton did not sleep. He was sleepy; but he was keenly alive to the necessity of keeping awake. The clearing of Bob Cherry's name might depend upon it.

An hour passed—and another.

Occasional low sounds in the dormitory warned Wharton that at least one of the Form was awake, and moving restlessly while the dull minutes crawled by; and he had little doubt that it was Heath.

Half-past eleven!

Heath sat up in bed.

"You fellows asleep?" he asked, in a low voice.

There was no reply. Wharton had been expecting it, yet it thrilled him strangely to hear the low, cautious voice in the darkness.

There came no sound but regular breathing in answer to Heath, and after a pause of a minute or more, the new boy stepped cautiously out of bed.

Wharton lay on his elbow, breathing hard.

Dimly he saw the form of the junior move towards Bunter's bed. Heath knelt down beside the bed, and a faint rustling sound showed that he was trying to insert his hand under the mattress without waking the fat junior.

Wharton rose silently to a sitting posture. He reached out towards his washstand, and grasped the sponge, and raised his hand in the air. As Heath bent towards Bunter's bed, Wharton hurled the sponge. In spite of the gloom, the aim was unerring.

The sponge struck Heath on the back of the head.

The blow was, of course, not severe; but coming suddenly and totally unexpectedly as it did, it hurled Heath forward, and he sprawled across Bunter's bed with a startled cry.

There was a yell from the fat junior.

Bunter threw out his arms, and grasped Heath as he scrambled back from the bed.

"Ow!" yelled Bunter. "Help! Burglars!"

"Let go!" muttered Heath, in a stifled voice. "It was only a lark! It's not burglars! Let go! You ass, let go!"

"Help! Help!"

Frank Nugent jumped up and lighted a candle.

Heath was striving to tear himself away from Bunter's grasp, and he was nearly dragging the fat junior out of bed in the effort.

Bunter relaxed his grasp as the light flared up.

"Help!" he gasped.

"What the dickens——"

"It's—it's only a jape!" stammered Heath. "I—I—I was going to mop Bunter with a sponge, that's all! It was only a lark."

"It's a lie!" roared Bunter. "He was going to rob me."

"Shut up!" roared a dozen voices.

And Bunter grunted, and shut up. Heath got back into bed, and he did not stir from it again that night. But there was little sleep for him through the long hours of darkness.

THE TWENTY-EIGHTH CHAPTER.

The Triumph of Truth.

HEATH was the first out of bed in the morning. The rising-bell had not yet clanged when he rose and dressed himself. Wharton watched him from his bed quietly. That Heath had intended to leave the dormitory during the night, if Bunter had not caused an alarm, Harry felt sure. And Wharton guessed

shrewdly enough that what Heath was now concerned about was the hidden wig.

The expression of the junior's face showed how worry and stress of mind were telling on him. He was feeling driven into a corner, with his cowardly plot in danger of falling about his ears at every moment.

He glanced along the line of white beds. No one was stirring. Heath left the dormitory quietly, and closed the door behind him.

Wharton leaped out of bed.

"Marky!"

Mark Linley started out of a doze.

"Yes, Harry!"

"Up you get!"

The Lancashire lad did not stop to ask questions. He rose quickly, and began to dress. Harry Wharton ran to the window, and dressed with one eye on the Close. The figure of Esau Heath appeared in sight.

He was tramping away from the house across the Close.

Wharton watched him while he dressed.

Heath disappeared at the ruined chapel— that relic of ancient times which was the pride of Greyfriars. He passed in at the little low door, and vanished. Harry Wharton's eyes gleamed. That place, of all at Greyfriars, was fullest of odd nooks and crannies where any small article might be hidden in perfect safety.

"Come on, Marky."

Bulstrode sat up in bed.

"Hallo! Where are you fellows going?"

They did not stop to reply. They left the dormitory, and ran down the passage and the stairs. An early housemaid was the only person about. Through the open doorway the keen, fresh air of morning blew in from the Close.

Wharton and Linley ran across to the ruined chapel. They reached it in a minute or less. The stone stairs that led down to the crypt were before them. The opening had been covered by a modern wooden trapdoor for safety's sake. The trapdoor was raised now, and from below came a glimmer of light.

Someone was down there with a candle or a lantern. The juniors did not need telling whom it was.

Even as they looked down the stairs, Esau Heath came into sight. He was carrying a bicycle lantern in one hand, and in the other he had a parcel wrapped in brown paper.

The two juniors stepped back quickly.

Heath was coming up the stairs from the crypt, and he had not seen them. They drew back into the cover of the shattered masonry, and waited for the new boy to emerge from the crypt.

Heath came up, extinguished the lantern, and concealed it in a crevice in the stone-work.

Then he turned to the door of the chapel.

At the same moment, Wharton and Mark Linley stepped from their cover, reached him, and pinioned him by either arm.

Heath started convulsively.

"You—you——" he muttered. "Oh!"

"Caught!" said Wharton grimly. "What's in that parcel, Heath?"

"The—the parcel?"

"Yes. What's in it?"

"Some—some things belonging to me," said Heath, with white lips and stammering voice. "Nothing of any value—it's of no importance."

"Very well, come on."

"W-w-what do you mean? Why should I come with you?"

"Because you've got no choice," said Wharton grimly. "You're going to open that parcel in public, and show the contents. If they're of no importance, as you say, it won't hurt you their being shown."

"I—I——"

"Come on."

Heath resisted feebly. Wharton and Mark Linley took no notice of his resistance. They marched him on forcibly towards the School House. The rising-bell was clanging out now, and a few early risers were already up. Heath was marched by sheer force into the House, up the stairs, and to the door of Wingate's room.

Wharton knocked at the door.

"It's all right!" called out the captain of Greyfriars. "I'm up!"

"Want to speak to you, Wingate."

"Wait till I'm dressed."

"Buck up, then."

In a few minutes Wingate opened the door. He was in shirt and trousers, and he stared in blank astonishment at the juniors and their prisoner.

"What the dickens does this mean?" he exclaimed. "Is this a jape?"

"No," said Harry.

"Then what——"

"You remember I told you I suspected that Bob Cherry was impersonated at the post-office by a chap who got himself up in disguise?"

"Well?" said Wingate irritably.

"We've inquired in Friardale, and Mr. Moses is willing to give evidence that he sold a flaxen wig to a Greyfriars chap last Friday."

"Oh!" said Wingate.

"We suspected Heath, and we've watched him. He fetched this parcel out of the old chapel crypt just now. We want you to see what's in it. We suspect that it's the wig. Then we want Mr. Moses to be brought here to see if he can identify Heath as the chap who bought the wig."

Wingate looked hard at the white-faced, shivering Heath. If ever guilt was written on a fellow's face, it was written on Esau Heath's then.

"Are you willing for the parcel to be opened, Heath?" Wingate asked sternly.

"No," said Heath, gaining courage a little, "I—I refuse."

"Then," said Wingate sharply, "I shall open it by my authority as head prefect, and I'm willing to answer to the Head for what I do."

He took the parcel from Heath's nerveless hand, cut the cord, and opened the paper. A tightly-rolled wig of flaxen colour rolled out.

Wingate's eyes gleamed.

"It is a wig—a wig just the colour of Bob Cherry's hair."

"I own up to that," he said. "I—I got it for private theatricals. I—I was scared when I heard Wharton suggesting that—that a chap had worn a wig and impersonated Bob Cherry. I—I knew he would bring some accusation against me if he could. So I—I hid the wig in the crypt. That's all."

Wingate's hard glance never left his face. It was an ingenious lie, but it was evidently a lie on the face of it.

"You admit buying the wig of Mr. Moses?"

"Ye-e-es."

"On Friday, before the postal-order was cashed at Friardale post-office?"

"Ye-e-es."

"Very well. I am afraid you will find it a little difficult to convince the Head that you bought it for private theatricals," said Wingate drily. "Wharton!"

He looked round. Wharton had disappeared. Mark Linley met his glance.

"Wharton's gone for Bunter," he said.

"Bunter! What has Bunter to do with this?"

"I believe he knows a great deal."

"He—he doesn't!" Heath exclaimed, in a hoarsely shrill voice. "What could Bunter know? You know what a liar Bunter is!"

"We know that you gave Bunter four or five pounds yesterday," said Mark Linley coldly. "We know you did not do it for nothing."

Wingate gave a start.

"You gave Bunter such a sum as that, Heath?"

"I—I cashed postal-orders for him," stammered Heath.

"Oh! You are asking me to believe that Bunter had postal-orders for four or five pounds in a single day?" said Wingate drily. "Well, if Bunter can give me the names of the senders, and they can answer inquiries, I will believe it—not otherwise."

Heath groaned.

There was a squeaky voice heard from the passage.

"Ow! Oh, really, Wharton! I'm coming quietly—I tell you I'm coming! You might let a chap fasten his beastly braces! Ow! Leggo my ear!"

"Come on, then," said Wharton angrily.

"Oh, really—— Ow!"

Billy Bunter, with evident reluctance, was marched into Wingate's room. He stood there half-dressed, palpitating with anger and fear.

"We want you to question Bunter, Wingate," said Wharton. "It's better for you to do it; you can't be suspected of working things for Bob Cherry. We might be. Bunter has a paper about him, and Heath has been paying him pounds to keep it dark. I don't know what it is, but I feel pretty certain it bears on this case. I think you ought to make Bunter show you the paper."

"Give me the paper."

Bunter handed the paper over. Heath flung himself into a chair, and covered his face with his hands. All was over now, and he knew it. Wingate opened out the paper, and he and the juniors looked at it eagerly.

"R. Cherry!"

Bob Cherry's name was scrawled on the paper over and over again. At the top it was unmistakably in Heath's writing, but as it progressed down the page it grew more and more like Bob Cherry's, till at the bottom it was a fair imitation of Bob's own signature.

Heath had evidently been practising from a copy of Bob's signature, and he had certainly shown great aptitude for the peculiar work of a forger.

Wingate's face grew as black as thunder.

"You young hound!" he said. "You unspeakable worm! I don't think we need any further proof that Bob Cherry's name was forged, and that he was impersonated at the post-office—and that you did it! You utter cur, come with me!"

His strong hand on Heath's shoulder dragged the wretched boy to his feet. Heath looked at him with a face like death.

"I—I suppose it's all up now," he said, in a husky, broken, whispering voice. "I—I did it because—because he licked me, and I hated him! I said I'd make him suffer, and —and I did! I—I suppose I shall be expelled."

"You're not likely to be allowed to remain at Greyfriars," said Wingate drily. "If you don't go to prison, you will be lucky. Come with me—to the Head."

Heath groaned, and followed the captain of Greyfriars.

.   .   .   .   .   .

Of that interview between the Head of Greyfriars and the wretched boy whose sins had come home to him, we need not speak. Heath's grovelling terror, and his half-sincere repentance now that punishment was about to fall, did not make a pleasant spectacle. His confession, which was hardly needed now to establish the truth, was full and complete. It more than exonerated Bob Cherry. The whole wretched plot was exposed to the light of day. Greyfriars heard it and wondered.

Heath could not save himself, and he did not spare Bunter. Bunter's well-known stupidity saved him from sharing Heath's fate—expulsion from the school. The Head reasoned that the fat junior had been hardly conscious of the full wickedness of his conduct, and he was sentenced to a flogging instead. That flogging was administered severely, and Bunter did not forget it soon. For hours afterwards groans were heard proceeding from Bunter's study; but as no one took any notice of the groans, they ceased at last. Bunter seemed to be surprised when he found that no one in the Remove would speak to him afterwards. His discovery of the paper bearing the forged signatures had certainly helped to clear Bob Cherry; and the fat junior seemed to expect that a great deal of credit would be given him. He was disappointed!

And Bob Cherry?

Needless to say that, when Bunter had been flogged, and Heath expelled from Greyfriars, Bob Cherry was recalled. Dr. Locke wrote immediately to Major Cherry, explaining the matter, and asking Bob's pardon in the most sincere manner—in a way that even the fiery and exacting major could take no exception to.

Major Cherry arrived with Bob the same afternoon. And then, when nearly the whole school had been to see Bob's father off from the station later in the day, Bob Cherry was drawn back to Greyfriars on the top of the old station "growler." Never had such a scene been witnessed in Greyfriars before.

The libel action, of course, was stopped. The question of damages—and the major had, in his wrath, intended to claim enormous damages from the governors of Greyfriars—was waived. The fullest compensation was made for the expenses he had been put to, and there the matter was suffered to drop.

As for Bob, he was too happy at having his name cleared to care for anything else. He seemed to be walking on air when he came back to the school.

In his bitterness at the injustice that had been done him, Bob had thought he would never be able to forgive the friends who had failed to stand by him in his hour of need. But in this joyous hour, he could realise that they were not wholly unjustified, at all events, in being swayed by so strong a mass of evidence. And their repentance was frank and sincere.

Nugent and John Bull, and Fish and Tom Brown, and the rest, gathered round Bob as he came into the junior common-room with Wharton and Mark Linley.

"We've been a set of silly asses, Bob," said Nugent humbly. "You can kick us all if you like, and we won't say a word."

"I guess not," said Fisher T. Fish. "Kick away."

"It's all right, kids," he said. "When you come to think of it, the evidence was awfully strong, and you haven't so much sense as Wharton and Marky, so what could a fellow expect?"

"Ahem!"

"It's all over now—bygones are bygones—and I dare say we shall all get on famously now that bounder is gone."

"Hear, hear!"

Fish held out his hand. "Shake!" he said.

And Bob "shook." And with a hearty handshake all round, the past was buried. Never again were the juniors likely to waver in their faith in Bob Cherry's honour.

THE FUNNY ADVENTURES OF BUBBLE AND SQUEAK, THE TERRIBLE TWINS

While Bubble was deep in a nice little book,
The Head came along with a sweet, saucy look.
"I want you to send off this wire, please, for me.
It's very important, my boy, as you'll see."

So Bubble sped off, at a very smart pace,
As if he were running a Marathon race.
The book was forgotten ; the twin let it rip,
For he hoped to receive a substantial tip !

Then Squeak came along, and he picked up the book.
"It's a wonderful story of Charlie the Crook !
That silly ass Bubble has left it behind !
I'll sit down and read it ; I'm sure he won't mind."

The Head rustled up with a frown (and a cane !)—
"Lazy boy !" he exclaimed. "You are reading again !
I asked you to send off a telegram, Bubble !
Why have you not done so ? Now look out for trouble !"

"I'm Squeak !" wailed the twin ; but the Head heeded not.
He wielded his cane, and poor Squeak got it hot.
"Don't argue with me !" said the Head, with a frown.
And for quite a week later Squeak couldn't sit down !

Then Bubble came up to the angry old Head.
"I sent off your wire right away, sir !" he said.
"You did ? Oh, good gracious !" The Head gave a shriek,
But the mischief was done – there was no help for Squeak !

BUSY DAYS FOR THE NEWSAGENT!

New Long Complete School Stories of
JIMMY SILVER & Co.
Appear *Every Monday* in
THE BOYS' FRIEND 1½d

New Long Complete School Tales of
HARRY WHARTON & CO.
Appear *Every Monday* in
THE MAGNET LIBRARY 1½d

New Long Complete School Stories of
TOM MERRY & CO.
Appear *Every Wednesday* in
THE GEM LIBRARY 1½d

Printed and Published by the Amalgamated Press, Ltd., Fleetway House, Farringdon Street. E.C. 4.